The Mysteries of Udolpho

Ann Radcliffe

Dover Publications, Inc.
Mineola, New York

Bibliographical Note

This Dover edition, first published in 2004, is an unabridged republication of the work originally published in 1794 by G. G. and J. Robinson, London, under the title *The Mysteries of Udolpho, A Romance; Interspersed with Some Pieces of Poetry*. The Introduction to this reprint is comprised of an excerpt from a contemporaneous review of *The Mysteries of Udolpho* from *The British Critic*, 4 (1794), 110–21; the review is ascribed to Samuel Taylor Coleridge.

Library of Congress Cataloging-in-Publication Data

Radcliffe, Ann Ward, 1764–1823.
    The mysteries of Udolpho / Ann Radcliffe.
       p. cm.
   ISBN 0-486-44033-8 (pbk.)
    1. Inheritance and succession—Fiction. 2. Guardian and ward—Fiction. 3. Young women—Fiction. 4. Orphans—Fiction. 5. Castles—Fiction. 6. Italy—Fiction. I. Title.

PR5202.M8 2004
823'.6—dc22

2004041423

Manufactured in the United States of America
Dover Publications, Inc., 31 East 2nd Street, Mineola, N.Y. 11501

Introduction*

W e so very seldom find, in a work of imagination, those qualities combined, which are necessary to its successful accomplishment, that when the event does happen, we distinguish
it as a place of repose from our fevered labours, and are happy to
beguile the hours of weariness and chagrin beneath the shade which
fancy spreads around. A tale, regularly told, neither offending probability by its extravagance, nor fatiguing by its want of vivacity or incident, has ever been esteemed among those labours of the mind which
the critic cannot disdain to commend, nor genius to introduce, and
when it is further embellished by the charms of good writing, is the
vehicle of ingenuous sentiments, and inculcates the purest morality, it
eminently takes the lead in that class of writings, which is professedly
designed for entertainment.

Mrs. Radcliffe [née Ann Ward, 1764–1823] had before obtained
considerable reputation from the cultivation of this branch of literature, and we are happy that it has fallen to our province to record one
of the best and most interesting of her works. We wish to render all possible honour to her talents, and we think that this cannot be more effectually done, than by immediately placing before our readers the
outlines of the story which these volumes† communicate.

Emily St. Aubert is represented as the lovely daughter of a French
gentleman, the descendant of a younger branch of a noble family, who
preferring contented solitude to the glare of the metropolis, and stu-
dious ease to the splendour of dissipation, retires, with his wife and children, to a small paternal inheritance on the pleasant banks of the
Garonne, in the Province of Gascony. Here, having lost two sons, he
dedicates his time to the improvement of his daughter's mind, now his

---

*[This Introduction is comprised of an excerpt from a contemporaneous review of *The
Mysteries of Udolpho* from *The British Critic*, 4 (1794), 110–21; the review is ascribed
to Samuel Taylor Coleridge.—ed.]
†[*The Mysteries of Udolpho* was originally published in four volumes.—ed.]

only child. His care is attended with the greatest success, and Emily is
distinguished by every amiable virtue, and excellent accomplishment.
St. Aubert loses his wife, and perceiving his own health impaired, and,
by the failure of a merchant in whom he trusted, his fortunes diminished, he proceeds with his daughter to travel. Proceeding along the
feet of the Pyrenees towards Languedoc, accident introduces them to
Valancourt, the hero of the tale. An attachment is formed, but their different objects and pursuits oblige them to separate. In the progress of
St. Aubert's journey, his health grows worse, and the gentle Emily loses
her father. Now become an orphan, she finds herself, by her father's
will, under the guardianship of an aunt, Madame Cheron, an insolent
and vain woman, from whose indiscreet marriage with an Italian
adventurer, our heroine is involved in a series of calamities of the most
formidable and melancholy nature. Valancourt again appears, and is
received as the future husband of Emily, till the above-mentioned marriage of her aunt subjects the fortune and destiny of them both to the
will of Montoni, whose character is admirably supported. The Italian
takes the ladies first to Venice, and afterwards to his Castle of Udolpho,
the mysteries of which do indeed *harrow up the foul.*[‡] —In this Castle
the aunt dies, and Emily finally makes her escape, with the fond hopes
of returning to her country, and the arms of Valancourt. But when the
lovers parted, *Valancourt*, it seems, *had not seen Paris.* On losing his
mistress, the young man visited the metropolis; and here, from the contagion of vicious companions, became, for a while, a thoughtless and
dissipated character.—Accident places Emily under the protection of
the Count de Villefort, a worthy nobleman, whose Chateau is the
scene of almost as many *terrible* mysteries as the Castle of Udolpho. He
informs her of Valancourt's unworthiness, and the union is for a while
dissolved.—After a variety of incidents and episodes, agreeably and
skillfully interspersed, Valancourt is reformed, and becomes the husband of Emily.

Such is the outline of the story; but to render justice to the lively and
interesting descriptions of scenes and places, to the faithful consistency
with which the different characters are supported, to the pathos which
breathes in every page, to the art with which curiosity is excited, suspended, and finally satisfied, would be a task of infinite delicacy and
labour, and could lead, after all, only to that which would render it
superfluous, the perusal of the volumes themselves. . . .

---

‡[All the italics herein are the author's.—ed.]

THE MYSTERIES OF UDOLPHO
by Ann Radcliffe

A Romance

Interspersed with Some Pieces of Poetry

Fate sits on these dark battlements, and frowns,
And, as the portals open to receive me,
Her voice, in sullen echoes through the courts,
Tells of a nameless deed.

Contents

VOLUME 1

CHAPTER I

home is the resort
Of love, of joy, of peace and plenty, where,
Supporting and supported, polish'd friends
And dear relations mingle into bliss.

THOMSON

ON the pleasant banks of the Garonne, in the province of Gascony, stood, in the year 1584, the chateau of Monsieur St. Aubert. From its windows were seen the pastoral landscapes of Guienne and Gascony, stretching along the river, gay with luxuriant woods and vines, and plantations of olives. To the south, the view was bounded by the majestic Pyrenées, whose summits, veiled in clouds, or exhibiting awful forms, seen, and lost again, as the partial vapours rolled along, were sometimes barren, and gleamed through the blue tinge of air, and sometimes frowned with forests of gloomy pine, that swept downward to their base. These tremendous precipices were contrasted by the soft green of the pastures and woods that hung upon their skirts; among whose flocks, and herds, and simple cottages, the eye, after having scaled the cliffs above, delighted to repose. To the north, and to the east, the plains of Guienne and Languedoc were lost in the mist of distance; on the west, Gascony was bounded by the waters of Biscay.

M. St. Aubert loved to wander, with his wife and daughter, on the margin of the Garonne, and to listen to the music that floated on its waves. He had known life in other forms than those of pastoral simplicity, having mingled in the gay and in the busy scenes of the world; but the flattering portrait of mankind, which his heart had delineated in early youth, his experience had too sorrowfully corrected. Yet, amidst the changing visions of life, his principles remained unshaken, his benevolence unchilled; and he retired from the multitude "more in *pity* than in anger," to scenes of simple nature, to the pure delights of literature, and to the exercise of domestic virtues.

He was a descendant from the younger branch of an illustrious family, and it was designed, that the deficiency of his patrimonial wealth should be supplied either by a splendid alliance in marriage, or by success in the intrigues of public affairs. But St. Aubert had too nice a sense of honour to fulfil the latter hope, and too small a portion of ambition to sacrifice what he called happiness, to the attainment of wealth. After the death of his father he married a very amiable woman, his equal in birth, and not his superior in fortune. The late Monsieur St. Aubert's liberality, or extravagance, had so much involved his affairs, that his son found it necessary to dispose of a part of the family domain, and, some years after his marriage, he sold it to Monsieur Quesnel, the brother of his wife, and retired to a small estate in Gascony, where conjugal felicity, and parental duties, divided his attention with the treasures of knowledge and the illuminations of genius.

To this spot he had been attached from his infancy. He had often made excursions to it when a boy, and the impressions of delight given to his mind by the homely kindness of the grey-headed peasant, to whom it was intrusted, and whose fruit and cream never failed, had not been obliterated by succeeding circumstances. The green pastures along which he had so often bounded in the exultation of health, and youthful freedom—the woods, under whose refreshing shade he had first indulged that pensive melancholy, which afterwards made a strong feature of his character—the wild walks of the mountains, the river, on whose waves he had floated, and the distant plains, which seemed boundless as his early hopes—were never after remembered by St. Aubert but with enthusiasm and regret. At length he disengaged himself from the world, and retired hither, to realize the wishes of many years.

The building, as it then stood, was merely a summer cottage, rendered interesting to a stranger by its neat simplicity, or the beauty of the surrounding scene; and considerable additions were necessary to make it a comfortable family residence. St. Aubert felt a kind of affection for every part of the fabric, which he remembered in his youth, and would not suffer a stone of it to be removed, so that the new building, adapted to the style of the old one, formed with it only a simple and elegant residence. The taste of Madame St. Aubert was conspicuous in its internal finishing, where the same chaste simplicity was observable in the furniture, and in the few ornaments of the apartments, that characterised the manners of its inhabitants.

The library occupied the west side of the chateau, and was enriched by a collection of the best books in the ancient and modern languages. This room opened upon a grove, which stood on the brow of a gentle declivity, that fell towards the river, and the tall trees gave it a melancholy and pleasing shade; while from the windows the eye caught, beneath the spreading branches, the gay and luxuriant landscape stretching to the west, and overlooked on the left by the bold precipices of the Pyrenées. Adjoining the library was a green-house, stored with scarce and beautiful plants; for one of the amusements of St. Aubert was the study of botany, and among the neighbouring mountains, which afforded a luxurious feast to the mind of the naturalist, he often passed the day in the pursuit of his favourite science. He was sometimes accompanied in these little excursions by Madame St. Aubert, and frequently by his daughter; when, with a small osier basket to receive plants, and another filled with cold refreshments, such as the cabin of the shepherd did not afford, they wandered away among the most romantic and magnificent scenes, nor suffered the charms of Nature's lowly children to abstract them from the observance of her stupendous works. When weary of sauntering among cliffs that seemed scarcely accessible but to the steps of the enthusiast, and where no track appeared on the vegetation, but what the foot of the izard had left; they would seek one of those green recesses, which so beautifully adorn the bosom of these mountains, where, under the shade of the lofty larch, or cedar, they enjoyed their simple repast, made sweeter by the waters of the cool stream, that crept along the turf, and by the breath of wild flowers and aromatic plants, that fringed the rocks, and inlaid the grass.

Adjoining the eastern side of the green-house, looking towards the plains of Languedoc, was a room, which Emily called hers, and which contained her books, her drawings, her musical instruments, with some favourite birds and plants. Here she usually exercised herself in elegant arts, cultivated only because they were congenial to her taste, and in which native genius, assisted by the instructions of Monsieur and Madame St. Aubert, made her an early proficient. The windows of this room were particularly pleasant; they descended to the floor, and, opening upon the little lawn that surrounded the house, the eye was led between groves of almond, palm-trees, flowering-ash, and myrtle, to the distant landscape, where the Garonne wandered.

The peasants of this gay climate were often seen on an evening, when the day's labour was done, dancing in groups on the margin of the river. Their sprightly melodies, *debonnaire* steps, the fanciful figure of their dances, with the tasteful and capricious manner in which the girls adjusted their simple dress, gave a character to the scene entirely French.

The front of the chateau, which, having a southern aspect, opened upon the grandeur of the mountains, was occupied on the ground floor by a rustic hall, and two excellent sitting rooms. The first floor, for the cottage had no second story, was laid out in bed-chambers, except one apartment that opened to a balcony, and which was generally used for a breakfast-room.

In the surrounding ground, St. Aubert had made very tasteful improvements; yet, such was his attachment to objects he had remembered from his boyish days, that he had in some instances sacrificed taste to sentiment. There were two old larches that shaded the building, and interrupted the prospect; St. Aubert had sometimes declared that he believed he should have been weak enough to have wept at their fall. In addition to these larches he planted a little grove of beech, pine, and mountain-ash. On a lofty terrace, formed by the swelling bank of the river, rose a plantation of orange, lemon, and palm-trees, whose fruit, in the coolness of evening, breathed delicious fragrance. With these were mingled a few trees of other species. Here, under the ample shade of a plane-tree, that spread its majestic canopy towards the river, St. Aubert loved to sit in the fine evenings of summer, with his wife and children, watching, beneath its foliage, the setting-sun, the mild splendour of its light fading from the distant landscape, till the shadows of twilight melted its various features into one tint of sober grey. Here, too, he loved to read, and to converse with Madame St. Aubert; or to play with his children, resigning himself to the influence of those sweet affections, which are ever attendant on simplicity and nature. He has often said, while tears of pleasure trembled in his eyes, that these were moments infinitely more delightful than any passed amid the brilliant and tumultuous scenes that are courted by the world. His heart was occupied; it had, what can be so rarely said, no wish for a happiness beyond what it experienced. The consciousness of acting right diffused a serenity over his manners, which nothing else could impart to a man of moral perceptions like his, and which refined his sense of every surrounding blessing.

The deepest shade of twilight did not send him from his favourite plane-tree. He loved the soothing hour, when the last tints of light die away; when the stars, one by one, tremble through æther, and are reflected on the dark mirror of the waters; that hour, which, of all others, inspires the mind with pensive tenderness, and often elevates it to sublime contemplation. When the moon shed her soft rays among the foliage, he still lingered, and his pastoral supper of cream and fruits was often spread beneath it. Then, on the stillness of night, came the song of the nightingale, breathing sweetness, and awakening melancholy.

The first interruptions to the happiness he had known since his retirement, were occasioned by the death of his two sons. He lost them at that age when infantine simplicity is so fascinating; and though, in consideration of Madame St. Aubert's distress, he restrained the expression of his own, and endeavoured to bear it, as he meant, with philosophy, he had, in truth, no philosophy that could render him calm to such losses. One daughter was now his only surviving child; and, while he watched the unfolding of her infant character, with anxious fondness, he endeavoured, with unremitting effort, to counteract those traits in her disposition, which might hereafter lead her from happiness. She had discovered in her early years uncommon delicacy of mind, warm affections, and ready benevolence; but with these was observable a degree of susceptibility too exquisite to admit of lasting peace. As she advanced in youth, this sensibility gave a pensive tone to her spirits, and a softness to her manner, which added grace to beauty, and rendered her a very interesting object to persons of a congenial disposition. But St. Aubert had too much good sense to prefer a charm to a virtue; and had penetration enough to see, that this charm was too dangerous to its possessor to be allowed the character of a blessing. He endeavoured, therefore, to strengthen her mind; to enure her to habits of self-command; to teach her to reject the first impulse of her feelings, and to look, with cool examination, upon the disappointments he sometimes threw in her way. While he instructed her to resist first impressions, and to acquire that steady dignity of mind, that can alone counterbalance the passions, and bear us, as far as is compatible with our nature, above the reach of circumstances, he taught himself a lesson of fortitude; for he was often obliged to witness, with seeming indifference, the tears and struggles which his caution occasioned her.

In person, Emily resembled her mother; having the same elegant symmetry of form, the same delicacy of features, and the same blue eyes, full of tender sweetness. But, lovely as was her person, it was the varied expression of her countenance, as conversation awakened the nicer emotions of her mind, that threw such a captivating grace around her:

> Those tend'rer tints, that shun the careless eye,
> And, in the world's contagious circle, die.

St. Aubert cultivated her understanding with the most scrupulous care. He gave her a general view of the sciences, and an exact acquaintance with every part of elegant literature. He taught her Latin and English, chiefly that she might understand the sublimity of their best poets. She discovered in her early years a taste for works of genius; and it was St. Aubert's principle, as well as his inclination, to promote every innocent means of happiness. "A well-informed mind," he would say, "is the best security against the contagion of folly and of vice. The vacant mind is ever on the watch for relief, and ready to plunge into error, to escape from the languor of idleness. Store it with ideas, teach it the pleasure of thinking; and the temptations of the world without, will be counteracted by the gratifications derived from the world within. Thought, and cultivation, are necessary equally to the happiness of a country and a city life; in the first they prevent the uneasy sensations of indolence, and afford a sublime pleasure in the taste they create for the beautiful, and the grand; in the latter, they make dissipation less an object of necessity, and consequently of interest."

It was one of Emily's earliest pleasures to ramble among the scenes of nature; nor was it in the soft and glowing landscape that she most delighted; she loved more the wild wood-walks, that skirted the mountain; and still more the mountain's stupendous recesses, where the silence and grandeur of solitude impressed a sacred awe upon her heart, and lifted her thoughts to the GOD OF HEAVEN AND EARTH. In scenes like these she would often linger alone, wrapt in a melancholy charm, till the last gleam of day faded from the west; till the lonely sound of a sheep-bell, or the distant bark of a watch-dog, were all that broke on the stillness of the evening. Then, the gloom of the woods; the trembling of their leaves, at intervals, in the breeze; the bat, flitting on the twilight; the cottage-lights, now seen, and now lost—were circumstances that awakened her mind into effort, and led to enthusiasm and poetry.

Her favourite walk was to a little fishing-house, belonging to St. Aubert, in a woody glen, on the margin of a rivulet that descended from the Pyrenées, and, after foaming among their rocks, wound its silent way beneath the shades it reflected. Above the woods, that screened this glen, rose the lofty summits of the Pyrenées, which often burst boldly on the eye through the glades below. Sometimes the shattered face of a rock only was seen, crowned with wild shrubs; or a shepherd's cabin seated on a cliff, overshadowed by dark cypress, or waving ash. Emerging from the deep recesses of the woods, the glade opened to the distant landscape, where the rich pastures and vine-covered slopes of Gascony gradually declined to the plains; and there, on the winding shores of the Garonne, groves, and hamlets, and villas—their outlines softened by distance, melted from the eye into one rich harmonious tint.

This, too, was the favourite retreat of St. Aubert, to which he frequently withdrew from the fervour of noon, with his wife, his daughter, and his books; or came at the sweet evening hour to welcome the silent dusk, or to listen for the music of the nightingale. Sometimes, too, he brought music of his own, and awakened every fairy echo with the tender accents of his oboe; and often have the tones of Emily's voice drawn sweetness from the waves, over which they trembled.

It was in one of her excursions to this spot, that she observed the following lines written with a pencil on a part of the wainscot:

SONNET

Go, pencil! faithful to thy master's sighs!
Go—tell the Goddess of the fairy scene,
When next her light steps wind these wood-walks green,
Whence all his tears, his tender sorrows, rise;
Ah! paint her form, her soul-illumin'd eyes,
The sweet expression of her pensive face,
The light'ning smile, the animated grace—
The portrait well the lover's voice supplies;
Speaks all his heart must feel, his tongue would say:
Yet ah! not all his heart must sadly feel!
How oft the flow'ret's silken leaves conceal
The drug that steals the vital spark away!
And who that gazes on that angel-smile,
Would fear its charm, or think it could beguile!

These lines were not inscribed to any person; Emily therefore could not apply them to herself, though she was undoubtedly the nymph of these shades. Having glanced round the little circle of her acquaintance without being detained by a suspicion as to whom they could be addressed, she was compelled to rest in uncertainty; an uncertainty which would have been more painful to an idle mind than it was to hers. She had no leisure to suffer this circumstance, trifling at first, to swell into importance by frequent remembrance. The little vanity it had excited (for the incertitude which forbade her to presume upon having inspired the sonnet, forbade her also to disbelieve it) passed away, and the incident was dismissed from her thoughts amid her books, her studies, and the exercise of social charities.

Soon after this period, her anxiety was awakened by the indisposition of her father, who was attacked with a fever; which, though not thought to be of a dangerous kind, gave a severe shock to his constitution. Madame St. Aubert and Emily attended him with unremitting care; but his recovery was very slow, and, as he advanced towards health, Madame seemed to decline.

The first scene he visited, after he was well enough to take the air, was his favourite fishing-house. A basket of provisions was sent thither, with books, and Emily's lute; for fishing-tackle he had no use, for he never could find amusement in torturing or destroying.

After employing himself, for about an hour, in botanizing, dinner was served. It was a repast, to which gratitude, for being again permitted to visit this spot, gave sweetness; and family happiness once more smiled beneath these shades. Monsieur St. Aubert conversed with unusual cheerfulness; every object delighted his senses. The refreshing pleasure from the first view of nature, after the pain of illness, and the confinement of a sick-chamber, is above the conceptions, as well as the descriptions, of those in health. The green woods and pastures; the flowery turf; the blue concave of the heavens; the balmy air; the murmur of the limpid stream; and even the hum of every little insect of the shade, seem to revivify the soul, and make mere existence bliss.

Madame St. Aubert, reanimated by the cheerfulness and recovery of her husband, was no longer sensible of the indisposition which had lately oppressed her; and, as she sauntered along the wood-walks of this romantic glen, and conversed with him, and with her daughter, she often looked at them alternately with a degree of tenderness, that filled her eyes with tears. St. Aubert observed this more than once, and gently reproved her for the emotion; but she could only smile, clasp his hand, and that of Emily, and weep the more. He felt the tender enthusiasm stealing upon himself in a degree that became almost painful; his features assumed a serious air, and he could not forbear secretly sighing—"Perhaps I shall some time look back to these moments, as to the summit of my happiness, with hopeless regret. But let me not misuse them by useless anticipation; let me hope I shall not live to mourn the loss of those who are dearer to me than life."

To relieve, or perhaps to indulge, the pensive temper of his mind, he bade Emily fetch the lute she knew how to touch with such sweet pathos. As she drew near the fishing-house, she was surprised to hear the tones of the instrument, which were awakened by the hand of taste, and uttered a plaintive air, whose exquisite melody engaged all her attention. She listened in profound silence, afraid to move from the spot, lest the sound of her steps should occasion her to lose a note of the music, or should disturb the musician. Every thing without the building was still, and no person appeared. She continued to listen, till timidity succeeded to surprise and delight; a timidity, increased by a remembrance of the pencilled lines she had formerly seen, and she hesitated whether to proceed, or to return.

While she paused, the music ceased; and, after a momentary hesitation, she re-collected courage to advance to the fishing-house, which she entered with faltering steps, and found unoccupied! Her lute lay on the table; every thing seemed undisturbed, and she began to believe it was another instrument she had heard, till she remembered, that, when she followed M. and Madame St. Aubert from this spot, her lute was left on a window seat. She felt alarmed, yet knew not wherefore; the melancholy gloom of evening, and the profound stillness of the place, interrupted only by the light trembling of leaves, heightened her fanciful apprehensions, and she was desirous of quitting the building, but perceived herself grow faint, and sat down. As she tried to recover herself, the pencilled lines on the wainscot met her eye; she started, as if she had seen a stranger; but, endeavouring to conquer the tremor of her spirits, rose, and went to the window. To the lines before noticed she now perceived that others were added, in which her name appeared.

Though no longer suffered to doubt that they were addressed to herself, she was as ignorant, as before, by whom they could be written. While she mused, she thought she heard the sound of a step without the building, and again alarmed, she caught up her lute, and hurried away. Monsieur and Madame St. Aubert she found in a little path that wound along the sides of the glen.

Having reached a green summit, shadowed by palm-trees, and overlooking the vallies and plains of Gascony, they seated themselves on the turf; and while their eyes wandered over the glorious scene, and they inhaled the sweet breath of flowers and herbs that enriched the grass, Emily played and sung several of their favourite airs, with the delicacy of expression in which she so much excelled.

Music and conversation detained them in this enchanting spot, till the sun's last light slept upon the plains; till the white sails that glided beneath the mountains, where the Garonne wandered, became dim, and the gloom of evening stole over the landscape. It was a melancholy but not unpleasing gloom. St. Aubert and his family rose, and left the place with regret; alas! Madame St. Aubert knew not that she left it for ever.

When they reached the fishing-house she missed her bracelet, and recollected that she had taken it from her arm after dinner, and had left it on the table when she went to walk. After a long search, in which Emily was very active, she was compelled to resign herself to the loss of it. What made this bracelet valuable to her was a miniature of her daughter to which it was attached, esteemed a striking resemblance, and which had been painted only a few months before. When Emily was convinced that the bracelet was really gone, she blushed, and became thoughtful. That some stranger had been in the fishing-house, during her absence, her lute, and the additional lines of a pencil, had already informed her: from the purport of these lines it was not unreasonable to believe, that the poet, the musician, and the thief were the same person. But though the music she had heard, the written lines she had seen, and the disappearance of the picture, formed a combination of circumstances very remarkable, she was irresistibly restrained from mentioning them; secretly determining, however, never again to visit the fishing-house without Monsieur or Madame St. Aubert.

They returned pensively to the chateau, Emily musing on the incident which had just occurred; St. Aubert reflecting, with placid gratitude, on the blessings he possessed; and Madame St. Aubert somewhat disturbed, and perplexed, by the loss of her daughter's picture. As they drew near the house, they observed an unusual bustle about it; the sound of voices was distinctly heard, servants and horses were seen passing between the trees, and, at length, the wheels of a carriage rolled along. Having come within view of the front of the chateau, a landau, with smoking horses, appeared on the little lawn before it. St. Aubert perceived the liveries of his brother-in-law, and in the parlour he found Monsieur and Madame Quesnel already entered. They had left Paris some days before, and were on the way to their estate, only ten leagues distant from La Vallée, and which Monsieur Quesnel had purchased several years before of St. Aubert. This gentleman was the only brother of Madame St. Aubert; but the ties of relationship having never been strengthened by congeniality of character, the intercourse between them had not been frequent. M. Quesnel had lived altogether in the world; his aim had been consequence; splendour was the object of his taste; and his address and knowledge of character had carried him forward to the attainment of almost all that he had courted. By a man of such a disposition, it is not surprising that the virtues of St. Aubert should be overlooked; or that his pure taste, simplicity, and moderated wishes, were considered as marks of a weak intellect, and of confined views. The marriage of his sister with St. Aubert had been mortifying to his ambition, for he had designed that the matrimonial connection she formed should assist him to attain the consequence which he so much desired; and some offers were made her by persons whose rank and fortune flattered his warmest hope. But his sister, who was then addressed also by St. Aubert, perceived, or thought she perceived, that happiness and splendour were not the same, and she did not hesitate to forego the last for the attainment of the former. Whether Monsieur Quesnel thought them the same, or not, he would readily have sacrificed his sister's peace to the gratification of his own ambition; and, on her marriage with St. Aubert, expressed in private his contempt of her spiritless conduct, and of the connection which it permitted. Madame St. Aubert, though she concealed this insult from her husband, felt, perhaps, for the first time, resentment lighted in her heart; and, though a regard for her own dignity, united with considerations of prudence, restrained her expression of this resentment, there was ever after a mild reserve in her manner towards M. Quesnel, which he both understood and felt.

In his own marriage he did not follow his sister's example. His lady was an Italian, and an heiress by birth; and, by nature and education, was a vain and frivolous woman.

They now determined to pass the night with St. Aubert; and as the chateau was not large enough to accommodate their servants, the

latter were dismissed to the neighbouring village. When the first compliments were over, and the arrangements for the night made
M. Quesnel began the display of his intelligence and his connections;
while St. Aubert, who had been long enough in retirement to find
these topics recommended by their novelty, listened, with a degree of
patience and attention, which his guest mistook for the humility of
wonder. The latter, indeed, described the few festivities which the turbulence of that period permitted to the court of Henry the Third, with
a minuteness, that somewhat recompensed for his ostentation; but,
when he came to speak of the character of the Duke de Joyeuse, of a
secret treaty, which he knew to be negotiating with the Porte, and of the
light in which Henry of Navarre was received, M. St. Aubert recollected enough of his former experience to be assured, that his guest
could be only of an inferior class of politicians; and that, from the
importance of the subjects upon which he committed himself, he
could not be of the rank to which he pretended to belong. The opinions delivered by M. Quesnel, were such as St. Aubert forbore to reply
to, for he knew that his guest had neither humanity to feel, nor discernment to perceive, what is just.

Madame Quesnel, meanwhile, was expressing to Madame St.
Aubert her astonishment, that she could bear to pass her life in this
remote corner of the world, as she called it, and describing, from a
wish, probably, of exciting envy, the splendour of the balls, banquets,
and processions which had just been given by the court, in honour of
the nuptials of the Duke de Joyeuse with Margaretta of Lorrain, the sister of the Queen. She described with equal minuteness the magnificence she had seen, and that from which she had been excluded; while
Emily's vivid fancy, as she listened with the ardent curiosity of youth,
heightened the scenes she heard of; and Madame St. Aubert, looking
on her family, felt, as a tear stole to her eye, that though splendour may
grace happiness, virtue only can bestow it.

"It is now twelve years, St. Aubert," said M. Quesnel, "since I purchased your family estate."—"Somewhere thereabout," replied St.
Aubert, suppressing a sigh. "It is near five years since I have been
there," resumed Quesnel; "for Paris and its neighbourhood is the only
place in the world to live in, and I am so immersed in politics, and have
so many affairs of moment on my hands, that I find it difficult to steal
away even for a month or two." St. Aubert remaining silent, M.
Quesnel proceeded: "I have sometimes wondered how you, who have
lived in the capital, and have been accustomed to company, can exist
elsewhere;—especially in so remote a country as this, where you can
neither hear nor see any thing, and can in short be scarcely conscious
of life."

"I live for my family and myself," said St. Aubert; "I am now contented to know only happiness;—formerly I knew life."

"I mean to expend thirty or forty thousand livres on improvements," said M. Quesnel, without seeming to notice the words of St. Aubert; "for I design, next summer, to bring here my friends, the Duke de Durefort and the Marquis Ramont, to pass a month or two with me." To St. Aubert's enquiry, as to these intended improvements, he replied, that he should take down the whole east wing of the chateau, and raise upon the site a set of stables. "Then I shall build," said he, "a *salle à manger*, a *salon*, a *salle au commune*, and a number of rooms for servants; for at present there is not accommodation for a third part of my own people."

"It accommodated our father's household," said St. Aubert, grieved that the old mansion was to be thus improved, "and that was not a small one."

"Our notions are somewhat enlarged since those days," said M. Quesnel;—"what was then thought a decent style of living would not now be endured." Even the calm St. Aubert blushed at these words, but his anger soon yielded to contempt. "The ground about the chateau is encumbered with trees; I mean to cut some of them down."

"Cut down the trees too!" said St. Aubert.

"Certainly. Why should I not? they interrupt my prospects. There is a chesnut which spreads its branches before the whole south side of the chateau, and which is so ancient that they tell me the hollow of its trunk will hold a dozen men. Your enthusiasm will scarcely contend that there can be either use, or beauty, in such a sapless old tree as this."

"Good God!" exclaimed St. Aubert, "you surely will not destroy that noble chesnut, which has flourished for centuries, the glory of the estate! It was in its maturity when the present mansion was built. How often, in my youth, have I climbed among its broad branches, and sat embowered amidst a world of leaves, while the heavy shower has pattered above, and not a rain drop reached me! How often I have sat with a book in my hand, sometimes reading, and sometimes looking out between the branches upon the wide landscape, and the setting sun, till twilight came, and brought the birds home to their little nests among the leaves! How often—but pardon me," added St. Aubert, recollecting that he was speaking to a man who could neither comprehend, nor allow for his feelings, "I am talking of times and feelings as old-fashioned as the taste that would spare that venerable tree."

"It will certainly come down," said M. Quesnel; "I believe I shall plant some Lombardy poplars among the clumps of chesnut, that I shall leave of the avenue; Madame Quesnel is partial to the poplar, and tells me how much it adorns a villa of her uncle, not far from Venice."

"On the banks of the Brenta, indeed," continued St. Aubert, "where its spiry form is intermingled with the pine, and the cypress, and where it plays over light and elegant porticos and colonnades, it, unquestionably, adorns the scene; but among the giants of the forest, and near a heavy gothic mansion——"

"Well, my good sir," said M. Quesnel, "I will not dispute with you. You must return to Paris before our ideas can at all agree. But *à-propos* of Venice, I have some thoughts of going thither, next summer; events may call me to take possession of that same villa, too, which they tell me is the most charming that can be imagined. In that case I shall leave the improvements I mention to another year, and I may, perhaps, be tempted to stay some time in Italy."

Emily was somewhat surprised to hear him talk of being tempted to remain abroad, after he had mentioned his presence to be so necessary at Paris, that it was with difficulty he could steal away for a month or two; but St. Aubert understood the self-importance of the man too well to wonder at this trait; and the possibility, that these projected improvements might be deferred, gave him a hope, that they might never take place.

Before they separated for the night, M. Quesnel desired to speak with St. Aubert alone, and they retired to another room, where they remained a considerable time. The subject of this conversation was not known; but, whatever it might be, St. Aubert, when he returned to the supper-room, seemed much disturbed, and a shade of sorrow sometimes fell upon his features that alarmed Madame St. Aubert. When they were alone she was tempted to enquire the occasion of it, but the delicacy of mind, which had ever appeared in his conduct, restrained her: she considered that, if St. Aubert wished her to be acquainted with the subject of his concern, he would not wait for her enquiries.

On the following day, before M. Quesnel departed, he had a second conference with St. Aubert.

The guests, after dining at the chateau, set out in the cool of the day for Epourville, whither they gave him and Madame St. Aubert a pressing invitation, prompted rather by the vanity of displaying their splendour, than by a wish to make their friends happy.

Emily returned, with delight, to the liberty which their presence had restrained, to her books, her walks, and the rational conversation of M. and Madame St. Aubert, who seemed to rejoice, no less, that they were delivered from the shackles, which arrogance and frivolity had imposed.

Madame St. Aubert excused herself from sharing their usual evening walk, complaining that she was not quite well, and St. Aubert and Emily went out together.

They chose a walk towards the mountains, intending to visit some old pensioners of St. Aubert, which, from his very moderate income, he contrived to support, though it is probable M. Quesnel, with his very large one, could not have afforded this.

After distributing to his pensioners their weekly stipends, listening patiently to the complaints of some, redressing the grievances of others, and softening the discontents of all, by the look of sympathy, and the smile of benevolence, St. Aubert returned home through the woods,

> where
> At fall of eve the fairy-people throng,
> In various games and revelry to pass
> The summer night, as village stories tell.*

"The evening gloom of woods was always delightful to me," said St. Aubert, whose mind now experienced the sweet calm, which results from the consciousness of having done a beneficent action, and which disposes it to receive pleasure from every surrounding object. "I remember that in my youth this gloom used to call forth to my fancy a thousand fairy visions, and romantic images; and, I own, I am not yet wholly insensible of that high enthusiasm, which wakes the poet's dream: I can linger, with solemn steps, under the deep shades, send forward a transforming eye into the distant obscurity, and listen with thrilling delight to the mystic murmuring of the woods."

"O my dear father," said Emily, while a sudden tear started to her eye, "how exactly you describe what I have felt so often, and which I thought nobody had ever felt but myself! But hark! here comes the sweeping sound over the wood-tops; — now it dies away; — how solemn the stillness that succeeds! Now the breeze swells again. It is like the voice of some supernatural being—the voice of the spirit of the woods, that watches over them by night. Ah! what light is yonder? But it is gone. And now it gleams again, near the root of that large chestnut: look, sir!"

"Are you such an admirer of nature," said St. Aubert, "and so little acquainted with her appearances as not to know that for the glow-worm? But come," added he gaily, "step a little further, and we shall see fairies, perhaps; they are often companions. The glow-worm lends his light, and they in return charm him with music, and the dance. Do you see nothing tripping yonder?"

Emily laughed. "Well, my dear sir," said she, "since you allow of this alliance, I may venture to own I have anticipated you; and almost dare venture to repeat some verses I made one evening in these very woods."

"Nay," replied St. Aubert, "dismiss the *almost*, and venture quite; let

---

*THOMSON.

us hear what vagaries fancy has been playing in your mind. If she has given you one of her spells, you need not envy those of the fairies."

"If it is strong enough to enchant your judgment, sir," said Emily, "while I disclose her images, I need *not* envy them. The lines go in a sort of tripping measure, which I thought might suit the subject well enough, but I fear they are too irregular."

THE GLOW-WORM

How pleasant is the green-wood's deep-matted shade
    On a mid-summer's eve, when the fresh rain is o'er;
When the yellow beams slope, and sparkle thro' the glade,
    And swiftly in the thin air the light swallows soar!

But sweeter, sweeter still, when the sun sinks to rest,
    And twilight comes on, with the fairies so gay
Tripping through the forest-walk, where flow'rs, unprest,
    Bow not their tall heads beneath their frolic play.

To music's softest sounds they dance away the hour,
    Till moon-light steals down among the trembling leaves,
And checquers all the ground, and guides them to the bow'r,
    The long haunted bow'r, where the nightingale grieves.

Then no more they dance, till her sad song is done,
    But, silent as the night, to her mourning attend;
And often as her dying notes their pity have won,
    They vow all her sacred haunts from mortals to defend.

When, down among the mountains, sinks the ev'ning star,
    And the changing moon forsakes this shadowy sphere,
How cheerless would they be, tho' they fairies are,
    If I, with my pale light, came not near!

Yet cheerless tho' they'd be, they're ungrateful to my love!
    For, often when the traveller's benighted on his way,
And I glimmer in his path, and would guide him thro' the grove,
    They bind me in their magic spells to lead him far astray;

And in the mire to leave him, till the stars are all burnt out,
    While, in strange-looking shapes, they frisk about the ground,
And, afar in the woods, they raise a dismal shout,
    Till I shrink into my cell again for terror of the sound!

But, see where all the tiny elves come dancing in a ring,
    With the merry, merry pipe, and the tabor, and the horn,
And the timbrel so clear, and the lute with dulcet string;
    Then round about the oak they go till peeping of the morn.

Down yonder glade two lovers steal, to shun the fairy-queen,
    Who frowns upon their plighted vows, and jealous is of me,

That yester-eve I lighted them, along the dewy green,
   To seek the purple flow'r, whose juice from all her spells can free.

And now, to punish me, she keeps afar her jocund band,
   With the merry, merry pipe, and the tabor, and the lute;
If I creep near yonder oak she will wave her fairy wand,
   And to me the dance will cease, and the music all be mute.

O! had I but that purple flow'r whose leaves her charms can foil,
   And knew like fays to draw the juice, and throw it on the wind,
I'd be her slave no longer, nor the traveller beguile,
   And help all faithful lovers, nor fear the fairy kind!

But soon the *vapour of the woods* will wander afar,
   And the fickle moon will fade, and the stars disappear,
Then, cheerless will they be, tho' they fairies are,
   If I, with my pale light, come not near!

Whatever St. Aubert might think of the stanzas, he would not deny
his daughter the pleasure of believing that he approved them; and, having given his commendation, he sunk into a reverie, and they walked
on in silence.

> A faint erroneous ray
> Glanc'd from th' imperfect surfaces of things,
> Flung half an image on the straining eye;
> While waving woods, and villages, and streams,
> And rocks, and mountain-tops, that long retain
> The ascending gleam, are all one swimming scene,
> Uncertain if beheld.*

St. Aubert continued silent till he reached the chateau, where his
wife had retired to her chamber. The languor and dejection, that had
lately oppressed her, and which the exertion called forth by the arrival
of her guests had suspended, now returned with increased effect. On
the following day, symptoms of fever appeared, and St. Aubert, having
sent for medical advice, learned, that her disorder was a fever of the
same nature as that, from which he had lately recovered. She had,
indeed, taken the infection, during her attendance upon him, and, her
constitution being too weak to throw out the disease immediately, it
had lurked in her veins, and occasioned the heavy languor of which she
had complained. St. Aubert, whose anxiety for his wife overcame every
other consideration, detained the physician in his house. He remembered the feelings and the reflections that had called a momentary
gloom upon his mind, on the day when he had last visited the fishing-
house, in company with Madame St. Aubert, and he now admitted a

---

*THOMSON.

presentiment, that this illness would be a fatal one. But he effectually concealed this from her, and from his daughter, whom he endeavoured to re-animate with hopes that her constant assiduities would not be unavailing. The physician, when asked by St. Aubert for his opinion of the disorder, replied, that the event of it depended upon circumstances which he could not ascertain. Madame St. Aubert seemed to have formed a more decided one; but her eyes only gave hints of this. She frequently fixed them upon her anxious friends with an expression of pity, and of tenderness, as if she anticipated the sorrow that awaited them, and that seemed to say, it was for their sakes only, for their sufferings, that she regretted life. On the seventh day, the disorder was at its crisis. The physician assumed a graver manner, which she observed, and took occasion, when her family had once quitted the chamber, to tell him, that she perceived her death was approaching. "Do not attempt to deceive me," said she, "I feel that I cannot long survive. I am prepared for the event, I have long, I hope, been preparing for it. Since I have not long to live, do not suffer a mistaken compassion to induce you to flatter my family with false hopes. If you do, their affliction will only be the heavier when it arrives: I will endeavour to teach them resignation by my example."

The physician was affected; he promised to obey her, and told St. Aubert, somewhat abruptly, that there was nothing to expect. The latter was not philosopher enough to restrain his feelings when he received this information; but a consideration of the increased affliction which the observance of his grief would occasion his wife, enabled him, after some time, to command himself in her presence. Emily was at first overwhelmed with the intelligence; then, deluded by the strength of her wishes, a hope sprung up in her mind that her mother would yet recover, and to this she pertinaciously adhered almost to the last hour.

The progress of this disorder was marked, on the side of Madame St. Aubert, by patient suffering, and subjected wishes. The composure, with which she awaited her death, could be derived only from the retrospect of a life governed, as far as human frailty permits, by a consciousness of being always in the presence of the Deity, and by the hope of a higher world. But her piety could not entirely subdue the grief of parting from those whom she so dearly loved. During these her last hours, she conversed much with St. Aubert and Emily, on the prospect of futurity, and on other religious topics. The resignation she expressed, with the firm hope of meeting in a future world the friends she left in this, and the effort which sometimes appeared to conceal her sorrow at this temporary separation, frequently affected St. Aubert so much as to oblige him to leave the room. Having indulged his tears awhile, he would dry them and return to the chamber with a countenance composed by an endeavour which did but increase his grief.

Never had Emily felt the importance of the lessons, which had taught her to restrain her sensibility, so much as in these moments, and never had she practised them with a triumph so complete. But when the last was over, she sunk at once under the pressure of her sorrow, and then perceived that it was hope, as well as fortitude, which had hitherto supported her. St. Aubert was for a time too devoid of comfort himself to bestow any on his daughter.

CHAPTER II

I could a tale unfold, whose lightest word
Would harrow up thy soul.
                                   SHAKESPEARE

MADAME ST. AUBERT was interred in the neighbouring village church; her husband and daughter attended her to the grave, followed by a long train of the peasantry, who were sincere mourners of this excellent woman.

On his return from the funeral, St. Aubert shut himself in his chamber. When he came forth, it was with a serene countenance, though pale in sorrow. He gave orders that his family should attend him. Emily only was absent; who, overcome with the scene she had just witnessed, had retired to her closet to weep alone. St. Aubert followed her thither: he took her hand in silence, while she continued to weep; and it was some moments before he could so far command his voice as to speak. It trembled while he said, "My Emily, I am going to prayers with my family; you will join us. We must ask support from above. Where else ought we to seek it—where else can we find it?"

Emily checked her tears, and followed her father to the parlour, where, the servants being assembled, St. Aubert read, in a low and solemn voice, the evening service, and added a prayer for the soul of the departed. During this, his voice often faltered, his tears fell upon the book, and at length he paused. But the sublime emotions of pure devotion gradually elevated his views above this world, and finally brought comfort to his heart.

When the service was ended, and the servants were withdrawn, he tenderly kissed Emily, and said, "I have endeavoured to teach you, from your earliest youth, the duty of self-command; I have pointed out to you the great importance of it through life, not only as it preserves us in the various and dangerous temptations that call us from rectitude and virtue, but as it limits the indulgences which are termed virtuous, yet which, extended beyond a certain boundary, are vicious, for their consequence is evil. All excess is vicious; even that sorrow, which is amiable in its origin, becomes a selfish and unjust passion, if indulged at the expence of our duties—by our duties I mean what we owe to ourselves, as well as to others. The indulgence of excessive grief enervates the mind, and almost incapacitates it for again partaking of those various innocent enjoyments which a benevolent God designed to be the sun-shine of our lives. My dear Emily, recollect and practise the precepts I have so often given you, and which your own experience has so often shewn you to be wise.

"Your sorrow is useless. Do not receive this as merely a common-place remark, but let reason *therefore* restrain sorrow. I would not annihilate your feelings, my child, I would only teach you to command them; for whatever may be the evils resulting from a too susceptible heart, nothing can be hoped from an insensible one; that, on the other hand, is all vice—vice, of which the deformity is not softened, or the effect consoled for, by any semblance or possibility of good. You know my sufferings, and are, therefore, convinced that mine are not the light words which, on these occasions, are so often repeated to destroy even the sources of honest emotion, or which merely display the selfish ostentation of a false philosophy. I will shew my Emily, that I can practise what I advise. I have said thus much, because I cannot bear to see you wasting in useless sorrow, for want of that resistance which is due from mind; and I have not said it till now, because there is a period when all reasoning must yield to nature; that is past: and another, when excessive indulgence, having sunk into habit, weighs down the elasticity of the spirits so as to render conquest nearly impossible; this is to come. You, my Emily, will shew that you are willing to avoid it."

Emily smiled through her tears upon her father: "Dear sir," said she, and her voice trembled; she would have added, "I will shew myself worthy of being your daughter;" but a mingled emotion of gratitude, affection, and grief overcame her. St. Aubert suffered her to weep without interruption, and then began to talk on common topics.

The first person who came to condole with St. Aubert was a M. Barreaux, an austere and seemingly unfeeling man. A taste for botany had introduced them to each other, for they had frequently met in their wanderings among the mountains. M. Barreaux had retired from the world, and almost from society, to live in a pleasant chateau, on the skirts of the woods, near La Vallée. He also had been disappointed in his opinion of mankind; but he did not, like St. Aubert, pity and mourn for them; he felt more indignation at their vices, than compassion for their weaknesses.

St. Aubert was somewhat surprised to see him; for, though he had often pressed him to come to the chateau, he had never till now accepted the invitation; and now he came without ceremony or reserve, entering the parlour as an old friend. The claims of misfortune appeared to have softened down all the ruggedness and prejudices of his heart. St. Aubert unhappy, seemed to be the sole idea that occupied his mind. It was in manners, more than in words, that he appeared to sympathize with his friends: he spoke little on the subject of their grief; but the minute attention he gave them, and the modulated voice, and softened look that accompanied it, came from his heart, and spoke to theirs.

At this melancholy period, St. Aubert was likewise visited by Madame Cheron, his only surviving sister, who had been some years a widow, and now resided on her own estate near Tholouse. The intercourse between them had not been very frequent. In her condolements, words were not wanting; she understood not the magic of the look that speaks at once to the soul, or the voice that sinks like balm to the heart: but she assured St. Aubert that she sincerely sympathized with him, praised the virtues of his late wife, and then offered what she considered to be consolation. Emily wept unceasingly while she spoke; St. Aubert was tranquil, listened to what she said in silence, and then turned the discourse upon another subject.

At parting she pressed him and her niece to make her an early visit. "Change of place will amuse you," said she, "and it is wrong to give way to grief." St. Aubert acknowledged the truth of these words of course; but, at the same time, felt more reluctant than ever to quit the spot which his past happiness had consecrated. The presence of his wife had sanctified every surrounding scene, and, each day, as it gradually softened the acuteness of his suffering, assisted the tender enchantment that bound him to home.

But there were calls which must be complied with, and of this kind was the visit he paid to his brother-in-law M. Quesnel. An affair of an interesting nature made it necessary that he should delay this visit no longer, and, wishing to rouse Emily from her dejection, he took her with him to Epourville.

As the carriage entered upon the forest that adjoined his paternal domain, his eyes once more caught, between the chesnut avenue, the turreted corners of the chateau. He sighed to think of what had passed since he was last there, and that it was now the property of a man who neither revered nor valued it. At length he entered the avenue, whose lofty trees had so often delighted him when a boy, and whose melancholy shade was now so congenial with the tone of his spirits. Every feature of the edifice, distinguished by an air of heavy grandeur, appeared successively between the branches of the trees—the broad turret, the arched gate-way that led into the courts, the drawbridge, and the dry fosse which surrounded the whole.

The sound of carriage wheels brought a troop of servants to the great gate, where St. Aubert alighted, and from which he led Emily into the gothic hall, now no longer hung with the arms and ancient banners of the family. These were displaced, and the oak wainscotting, and beams that crossed the roof, were painted white. The large table, too, that used to stretch along the upper end of the hall, where the master of the mansion loved to display his hospitality, and whence the peal of laughter, and the song of conviviality, had so often resounded, was now removed; even the benches that had surrounded the hall were no longer there. The heavy walls were hung with frivolous ornaments, and every thing that appeared denoted the false taste and corrupted sentiments of the present owner.

St. Aubert followed a gay Parisian servant to a parlour, where sat Mons. and Madame Quesnel, who received him with a stately politeness, and, after a few formal words of condolement, seemed to have forgotten that they ever had a sister.

Emily felt tears swell into her eyes, and then resentment checked them. St. Aubert, calm and deliberate, preserved his dignity without assuming importance, and Quesnel was depressed by his presence without exactly knowing wherefore.

After some general conversation, St. Aubert requested to speak with him alone; and Emily, being left with Madame Quesnel, soon learned that a large party was invited to dine at the chateau, and was compelled to hear that nothing which was past and irremediable ought to prevent the festivity of the present hour.

St. Aubert, when he was told that company were expected, felt a mixed emotion of disgust and indignation against the insensibility of Quesnel, which prompted him to return home immediately. But he was informed, that Madame Cheron had been asked to meet him; and, when he looked at Emily, and considered that a time might come when the enmity of her uncle would be prejudicial to her, he determined not to incur it himself, by conduct which would be resented as indecorous, by the very persons who now showed so little sense of decorum.

Among the visitors assembled at dinner were two Italian gentlemen, of whom one was named Montoni, a distant relation of Madame Quesnel, a man about forty, of an uncommonly handsome person, with features manly and expressive, but whose countenance exhibited, upon the whole, more of the haughtiness of command, and the quickness of discernment, than of any other character.

Signor Cavigni, his friend, appeared to be about thirty—his inferior in dignity, but equal to him in penetration of countenance, and superior in insinuation of manner.

Emily was shocked by the salutation with which Madame Cheron met her father—"Dear brother," said she, "I am concerned to see you look so very ill; do, pray, have advice!" St. Aubert answered, with a melancholy smile, that he felt himself much as usual; but Emily's fears made her now fancy that her father looked worse than he really did.

Emily would have been amused by the new characters she saw, and the varied conversation that passed during dinner, which was served in a style of splendour she had seldom seen before, had her spirits been less oppressed. Of the guests, Signor Montoni was lately come from Italy, and he spoke of the commotions which at that period agitated the country; talked of party differences with warmth, and then lamented the probable consequences of the tumults. His friend spoke with equal ardour, of the politics of his country; praised the government and prosperity of Venice, and boasted of its decided superiority over all the other Italian states. He then turned to the ladies, and talked with the same eloquence, of Parisian fashions, the French opera, and French manners; and on the latter subject he did not fail to mingle what is so particularly agreeable to French taste. The flattery was not detected by those to whom it was addressed, though its effect, in producing submissive attention, did not escape his observation. When he could disengage himself from the assiduities of the other ladies, he sometimes addressed Emily: but she knew nothing of Parisian fashions, or Parisian operas; and her modesty, simplicity, and correct manners formed a decided contrast to those of her female companions.

After dinner, St. Aubert stole from the room to view once more the old chesnut which Quesnel talked of cutting down. As he stood under its shade, and looked up among its branches, still luxuriant, and saw here and there the blue sky trembling between them; the pursuits and events of his early days crowded fast to his mind, with the figures and characters of friends—long since gone from the earth; and he now felt himself to be almost an insulated being, with nobody but his Emily for his heart to turn to.

He stood lost amid the scenes of years which fancy called up, till the succession closed with the picture of his dying wife, and he started away, to forget it, if possible, at the social board.

St. Aubert ordered his carriage at an early hour, and Emily observed, that he was more than usually silent and dejected on the way home; but she considered this to be the effect of his visit to a place which spoke so eloquently of former times, nor suspected that he had a cause of grief which he concealed from her.

On entering the chateau she felt more depressed than ever, for she more than ever missed the presence of that dear parent, who, whenever she had been from home, used to welcome her return with smiles and fondness; now, all was silent and forsaken.

But what reason and effort may fail to do, time effects. Week after week passed away, and each, as it passed, stole something from the harshness of her affliction, till it was mellowed to that tenderness which the feeling heart cherishes as sacred. St. Aubert, on the contrary, visibly declined in health; though Emily, who had been so constantly with him, was almost the last person who observed it. His constitution had never recovered from the late attack of the fever, and the succeeding shock it received from Madame St. Aubert's death had produced its present infirmity. His physician now ordered him to travel; for it was perceptible that sorrow had seized upon his nerves, weakened as they had been by the preceding illness; and variety of scene, it was probable, would, by amusing his mind, restore them to their proper tone.

For some days Emily was occupied in preparations to attend him; and he, by endeavours to diminish his expences at home during the journey—a purpose which determined him at length to dismiss his domestics. Emily seldom opposed her father's wishes by questions or remonstrances, or she would now have asked why he did not take a servant, and have represented that his infirm health made one almost necessary. But when, on the eve of their departure, she found that he had dismissed Jacques, Francis, and Mary, and detained only Theresa the old housekeeper, she was extremely surprised, and ventured to ask his reason for having done so. "To save expences, my dear," he replied— "we are going on an expensive excursion."

The physician had prescribed the air of Languedoc and Provence; and St. Aubert determined, therefore, to travel leisurely along the shores of the Mediterranean, towards Provence.

They retired early to their chamber on the night before their departure; but Emily had a few books and other things to collect, and the clock had struck twelve before she had finished, or had remembered that some of her drawing instruments, which she meant to take with her, were in the parlour below. As she went to fetch these, she passed her father's room, and, perceiving the door half open, concluded that he was in his study—for, since the death of Madame St. Aubert, it had been frequently his custom to rise from his restless bed, and go thither to compose his mind. When she was below stairs she looked into this room, but without finding him; and as she returned to her chamber, she tapped at his door, and receiving no answer, stepped softly in, to be certain whether he was there.

The room was dark, but a light glimmered through some panes of glass that were placed in the upper part of a closet-door. Emily believed her father to be in the closet, and, surprised that he was up at so late an hour, apprehended he was unwell, and was going to enquire; but, considering that her sudden appearance at this hour might alarm him, she removed her light to the stair-case, and then stepped softly to the closet. On looking through the panes of glass, she saw him seated at a small table, with papers before him, some of which he was reading with deep attention and interest, during which he often wept and sobbed aloud. Emily, who had come to the door to learn whether her father was ill, was now detained there by a mixture of curiosity and tenderness. She could not witness his sorrow, without being anxious to know the subject of it; and she therefore continued to observe him in silence, concluding that those papers were letters of her late mother. Presently he knelt down, and with a look so solemn as she had seldom seen him assume, and which was mingled with a certain wild expression, that partook more of horror than of any other character, he prayed silently for a considerable time.

When he rose, a ghastly paleness was on his countenance. Emily was hastily retiring; but she saw him turn again to the papers, and she stopped. He took from among them a small case, and from thence a miniature picture. The rays of light fell strongly upon it, and she perceived it to be that of a lady, but not of her mother.

St. Aubert gazed earnestly and tenderly upon this portrait, put it to his lips, and then to his heart, and sighed with a convulsive force. Emily could scarcely believe what she saw to be real. She never knew till now that he had a picture of any other lady than her mother, much less that he had one which he evidently valued so highly; but having looked repeatedly, to be certain that it was not the resemblance of Madame St. Aubert, she became entirely convinced that it was designed for that of some other person.

At length St. Aubert returned the picture to its case; and Emily, recollecting that she was intruding upon his private sorrows, softly withdrew from the chamber.

CHAPTER III

O how canst thou renounce the boundless store
Of charms which nature to her vot'ry yields!
The warbling woodland, the resounding shore,
The pomp of groves, and garniture of fields;
All that the genial ray of morning gilds,
And all that echoes to the song of even;
All that the mountain's shelt'ring bosom shields,

And all the dread magnificence of heaven;
O how canst thou renounce, and hope to be forgiven!

*   *   *

These charms shall work thy soul's eternal health,
And love, and gentleness, and joy, impart.

THE MINSTREL

ST. AUBERT, instead of taking the more direct road, that ran along the feet of the Pyrenées to Languedoc, chose one that, winding over the heights, afforded more extensive views and greater variety of romantic scenery. He turned a little out of his way to take leave of M. Barreaux, whom he found botanizing in the wood near his chateau, and who, when he was told the purpose of St. Aubert's visit, expressed a degree of concern, such as his friend had thought it was scarcely possible for him to feel on any similar occasion. They parted with mutual regret.

"If any thing could have tempted me from my retirement," said M. Barreaux, "it would have been the pleasure of accompanying you on this little tour. I do not often offer compliments; you may, therefore, believe me, when I say, that I shall look for your return with impatience."

The travellers proceeded on their journey. As they ascended the heights, St. Aubert often looked back upon the chateau, in the plain below; tender images crowded to his mind; his melancholy imagination suggested that he should return no more; and though he checked this wandering thought, still he continued to look, till the haziness of distance blended his home with the general landscape, and St. Aubert seemed to

Drag at each remove a lengthening chain.

He and Emily continued sunk in musing silence for some leagues, from which melancholy reverie Emily first awoke, and her young fancy, struck with the grandeur of the objects around, gradually yielded to delightful impressions. The road now descended into glens, confined by stupendous walls of rock, grey and barren, except where shrubs fringed their summits, or patches of meagre vegetation tinted their recesses, in which the wild goat was frequently browsing. And now, the way led to the lofty cliffs, from whence the landscape was seen extending in all its magnificence.

Emily could not restrain her transport as she looked over the pine forests of the mountains upon the vast plains, that, enriched with woods, towns, blushing vines, and plantations of almonds, palms, and olives, stretched along, till their various colours melted in distance into one harmonious hue, that seemed to unite earth with heaven. Through the whole of this glorious scene the majestic Garonne wandered;

descending from its source among the Pyrenées, and winding its blue waves towards the Bay of Biscay.

The ruggedness of the unfrequented road often obliged the wanderers to alight from their little carriage, but they thought themselves amply repaid for this inconvenience by the grandeur of the scenes; and, while the muleteer led his animals slowly over the broken ground, the travellers had leisure to linger amid these solitudes, and to indulge the sublime reflections, which soften, while they elevate, the heart, and fill it with the certainty of a present God! Still the enjoyment of St. Aubert was touched with that pensive melancholy, which gives to every object a mellower tint, and breathes a sacred charm over all around.

They had provided against part of the evil to be encountered from a want of convenient inns, by carrying a stock of provisions in the carriage, so that they might take refreshment on any pleasant spot, in the open air, and pass the nights wherever they should happen to meet with a comfortable cottage. For the mind, also, they had provided, by a work on botany, written by M. Barreaux, and by several of the Latin and Italian poets; while Emily's pencil enabled her to preserve some of those combinations of forms, which charmed her at every step.

The loneliness of the road, where, only now and then, a peasant was seen driving his mule, or some mountaineer-children at play among the rocks, heightened the effect of the scenery. St. Aubert was so much struck with it, that he determined, if he could hear of a road, to penetrate further among the mountains, and, bending his way rather more to the south, to emerge into Rousillon, and coast the Mediterranean along part of that country to Languedoc.

Soon after mid-day, they reached the summit of one of those cliffs, which, bright with the verdure of palm trees, adorn, like gems, the tremendous walls of the rocks, and which overlooked the greater part of Gascony, and part of Languedoc. Here was shade, and the fresh water of a spring, that, gliding among the turf, under the trees, thence precipitated itself from rock to rock, till its dashing murmurs were lost in the abyss, though its white foam was long seen amid the darkness of the pines below.

This was a spot well suited for rest, and the travellers alighted to dine, while the mules were unharnessed to browse on the savoury herbs that enriched this summit.

It was some time before St. Aubert or Emily could withdraw their attention from the surrounding objects, so as to partake of their little repast. Seated in the shade of the palms, St. Aubert pointed out to her observation the course of the rivers, the situation of great towns, and the boundaries of provinces, which science, rather than the eye, enabled him to describe. Notwithstanding this occupation, when he had talked awhile he suddenly became silent, thoughtful, and tears often swelled to his eyes, which Emily observed, and the sympathy of her own heart told her their cause. The scene before them bore some resemblance, though it was on a much grander scale, to a favourite one of the late Madame St. Aubert, within view of the fishing-house. They both observed this, and thought how delighted she would have been with the present landscape, while they knew that her eyes must never, never more open upon this world. St. Aubert remembered the last time of his visiting that spot in company with her, and also the mournfully presaging thoughts which had then arisen in his mind, and were now, even thus soon, realized! The recollections subdued him, and he abruptly rose from his seat, and walked away to where no eye could observe his grief.

When he returned, his countenance had recovered its usual serenity; he took Emily's hand, pressed it affectionately, without speaking, and soon after called to the muleteer, who sat at a little distance, concerning a road among the mountains towards Rousillon. Michael said, there were several that way, but he did not know how far they extended, or even whether they were passable; and St. Aubert, who did not intend to travel after sunset, asked what village they could reach about that time. The muleteer calculated that they could easily reach Mateau, which was in their present road; but that, if they took a road that sloped more to the south, towards Rousillon, there was a hamlet, which he thought they could gain before the evening shut in.

St. Aubert, after some hesitation, determined to take the latter course, and Michael, having finished his meal, and harnessed his mules, again set forward, but soon stopped; and St. Aubert saw him doing homage to a cross, that stood on a rock impending over their way. Having concluded his devotions, he smacked his whip in the air, and, in spite of the rough road, and the pain of his poor mules, which he had been lately lamenting, rattled, in a full gallop, along the edge of a precipice, which it made the eye dizzy to look down. Emily was terrified almost to fainting; and St. Aubert, apprehending still greater danger from suddenly stopping the driver, was compelled to sit quietly, and trust his fate to the strength and discretion of the mules, who seemed to possess a greater portion of the latter quality than their master; for they carried the travellers safely into the valley, and there stopped upon the brink of the rivulet that watered it.

Leaving the splendour of extensive prospects, they now entered this narrow valley screened by

Rocks on rocks piled, as if by magic spell,
Here scorch'd by lightnings, there with ivy green.

The scene of barrenness was here and there interrupted by the spreading branches of the larch and cedar, which threw their gloom over the cliff, or athwart the torrent that rolled in the vale. No living creature appeared, except the izard, scrambling among the rocks, and often hanging upon points so dangerous, that fancy shrunk from the view of them. This was such a scene as *Salvator* would have chosen, had he then existed, for his canvas; St. Aubert, impressed by the romantic character of the place, almost expected to see banditti start from behind some projecting rock, and he kept his hand upon the arms with which he always travelled.

As they advanced, the valley opened; its savage features gradually softened, and, towards evening, they were among heathy mountains, stretched in far perspective, along which the solitary sheep-bell was heard, and the voice of the shepherd calling his wandering flocks to the nightly fold. His cabin, partly shadowed by the cork-tree and the ilex, which St. Aubert observed to flourish in higher regions of the air than any other trees, except the fir, was all the human habitation that yet appeared. Along the bottom of this valley the most vivid verdure was spread; and, in the little hollow recesses of the mountains, under the shade of the oak and chestnut, herds of cattle were grazing. Groups of them, too, were often seen reposing on the banks of the rivulet, or laving their sides in the cool stream, and sipping its wave.

The sun was now setting upon the valley; its last light gleamed upon the water, and heightened the rich yellow and purple tints of the heath and broom, that overspread the mountains. St. Aubert enquired of Michael the distance to the hamlet he had mentioned, but the man could not with certainty tell; and Emily began to fear that he had mistaken the road. Here was no human being to assist, or direct them; they had left the shepherd and his cabin far behind, and the scene became so obscured in twilight, that the eye could not follow the distant perspective of the valley in search of a cottage, or a hamlet. A glow of the horizon still marked the west, and this was of some little use to the travellers. Michael seemed endeavouring to keep up his courage by singing; his music, however, was not of a kind to disperse melancholy; he sung, in a sort of chant, one of the most dismal ditties his present auditors had ever heard, and St. Aubert at length discovered it to be a vesper-hymn to his favourite saint.

They travelled on, sunk in that thoughtful melancholy, with which twilight and solitude impress the mind. Michael had now ended his ditty, and nothing was heard but the drowsy murmur of the breeze among the woods, and its light flutter, as it blew freshly into the carriage. They were at length roused by the sound of fire-arms. St. Aubert called to the muleteer to stop, and they listened. The noise was not repeated; but presently they heard a rustling among the brakes. St. Aubert drew forth a pistol, and ordered Michael to proceed as fast as possible; who had not long obeyed, before a horn sounded, that made the mountains ring. He looked again from the window, and then saw a young man spring from the bushes into the road, followed by a couple of dogs. The stranger was in a hunter's dress. His gun was slung across his shoulders, the hunter's horn hung from his belt, and in his hand was a small pike, which, as he held it, added to the manly grace of his figure, and assisted the agility of his steps.

After a moment's hesitation, St. Aubert again stopped the carriage, and waited till he came up, that they might enquire concerning the hamlet they were in search of. The stranger informed him, that it was only half a league distant, that he was going thither himself, and would readily shew the way. St. Aubert thanked him for the offer, and, pleased with his chevalier-like air and open countenance, asked him to take a seat in the carriage; which the stranger, with an acknowledgment, declined, adding that he would keep pace with the mules. "But I fear you will be wretchedly accommodated," said he: "the inhabitants of these mountains are a simple people, who are not only without the luxuries of life, but almost destitute of what in other places are held to be its necessaries."

"I perceive you are not one of its inhabitants, sir," said St. Aubert.

"No, sir, I am only a wanderer here."

The carriage drove on, and the increasing dusk made the travellers very thankful that they had a guide; the frequent glens, too, that now opened among the mountains, would likewise have added to their perplexity. Emily, as she looked up one of these, saw something at a great distance like a bright cloud in the air. "What light is yonder, sir?" said she.

St. Aubert looked, and perceived that it was the snowy summit of a mountain, so much higher than any around it, that it still reflected the sun's rays, while those below lay in deep shade.

At length, the village lights were seen to twinkle through the dusk, and, soon after, some cottages were discovered in the valley, or rather were seen by reflection in the stream, on whose margin they stood, and which still gleamed with the evening light.

The stranger now came up, and St. Aubert, on further enquiry, found not only that there was no inn in the place, but not any sort of house of public reception. The stranger, however, offered to walk on, and enquire for a cottage to accommodate them; for which further civility St. Aubert returned his thanks, and said, that, as the village was so near, he would alight, and walk with him. Emily followed slowly in the carriage.

On the way, St. Aubert asked his companion what success he had
had in the chase. "Not much, sir," he replied, "nor do I aim at it. I am
pleased with the country, and mean to saunter away a few weeks among
its scenes. My dogs I take with me more for companionship than for
game. This dress, too, gives me an ostensible business, and procures me
that respect from the people, which would, perhaps, be refused to a
lonely stranger, who had no visible motive for coming among them."

"I admire your taste," said St. Aubert, "and, if I was a younger man,
should like to pass a few weeks in your way exceedingly. I, too, am a
wanderer, but neither my plan nor pursuits are exactly like yours—I go
in search of health, as much as of amusement." St. Aubert sighed, and
paused; and then, seeming to recollect himself, he resumed: "If I can
hear of a tolerable road, that shall afford decent accommodation, it is
my intention to pass into Rousillon, and along the sea-shore to
Languedoc. You, sir, seem to be acquainted with the country, and can,
perhaps, give me information on the subject."

The stranger said, that what information he could give was entirely
at his service; and then mentioned a road rather more to the east,
which led to a town, whence it would be easy to proceed into
Rousillon.

They now arrived at the village, and commenced their search for a
cottage, that would afford a night's lodging. In several, which they
entered, ignorance, poverty, and mirth seemed equally to prevail; and
the owners eyed St. Aubert with a mixture of curiosity and timidity.
Nothing like a bed could be found, and he had ceased to enquire for
one, when Emily joined him, who observed the languor of her father's
countenance, and lamented, that he had taken a road so ill provided
with the comforts necessary for an invalid. Other cottages, which they
examined, seemed somewhat less savage than the former, consisting of
two rooms, if such they could be called; the first of these occupied by
mules and pigs, the second by the family, which generally consisted of
six or eight children, with their parents, who slept on beds of skins and
dried beech leaves, spread upon a mud floor. Here, light was admitted,
and smoke discharged, through an aperture in the roof; and here the
scent of spirits (for the travelling smugglers, who haunted the Pyrénées,
had made this rude people familiar with the use of liquors) was generally perceptible enough. Emily turned from such scenes, and looked at
her father with anxious tenderness, which the young stranger seemed
to observe; for, drawing St. Aubert aside, he made him an offer of his
own bed. "It is a decent one," said he, "when compared with what we
have just seen, yet such as in other circumstances I should be ashamed
to offer you." St. Aubert acknowledged how much he felt himself
obliged by this kindness, but refused to accept it, till the young stranger

would take no denial. "Do not give me the pain of knowing, sir," said he, "that an invalid, like you, lies on hard skins, while I sleep in a bed. Besides, sir, your refusal wounds my pride; I must believe you think my offer unworthy your acceptance. Let me shew you the way. I have no doubt my landlady can accommodate this young lady also."

St. Aubert, at length, consented, that, if this could be done, he would accept his kindness, though he felt rather surprised, that the stranger had proved himself so deficient in gallantry, as to administer to the repose of an infirm man, rather than to that of a very lovely young woman, for he had not once offered the room for Emily. But she thought not of herself, and the animated smile she gave him, told how much she felt herself obliged for the preference of her father.

On their way, the stranger, whose name was Valancourt, stepped on first to speak to his hostess, and she came out to welcome St. Aubert into a cottage, much superior to any he had seen. This good woman seemed very willing to accommodate the strangers, who were soon compelled to accept the only two beds in the place. Eggs and milk were the only food the cottage afforded; but against scarcity of provisions St. Aubert had provided, and he requested Valancourt to stay, and partake with him of less homely fare; an invitation, which was readily accepted, and they passed an hour in intelligent conversation. St. Aubert was much pleased with the manly frankness, simplicity, and keen susceptibility to the grandeur of nature, which his new acquaintance discovered; and, indeed, he had often been heard to say, that, without a certain simplicity of heart, this taste could not exist in any strong degree.

The conversation was interrupted by a violent uproar without, in which the voice of the muleteer was heard above every other sound. Valancourt started from his seat, and went to enquire the occasion; but the dispute continued so long afterwards, that St. Aubert went himself, and found Michael quarrelling with the hostess, because she had refused to let his mules lie in a little room where he and three of her sons were to pass the night. The place was wretched enough, but there was no other for these people to sleep in; and, with somewhat more of delicacy than was usual among the inhabitants of this wild tract of country, she persisted in refusing to let the animals have the same *bed-chamber* with her children. This was a tender point with the muleteer; his honour was wounded when his mules were treated with disrespect, and he would have received a blow, perhaps, with more meekness. He declared that his beasts were as honest beasts, and as good beasts, as any in the whole province; and that they had a right to be well treated wherever they went. "They are as harmless as lambs," said he, "if people don't affront them. I never knew them behave themselves amiss above once or twice in my life, and then they had good reason for doing so. Once, indeed, they kicked at a boy's leg that lay asleep in the stable, and broke it; but I told them they were out there, and by St. Anthony! I believe they understood me, for they never did so again."

He concluded this eloquent harangue with protesting, that they should share with him, go where he would.

The dispute was at length settled by Valancourt, who drew the hostess aside, and desired she would let the muleteer and his beasts have the place in question to themselves, while her sons should have the bed of skins designed for him, for that he would wrap himself in his cloak, and sleep on the bench by the cottage door. But this she thought it her duty to oppose, and she felt it to be her inclination to disappoint the muleteer. Valancourt, however, was positive, and the tedious affair was at length settled.

It was late when St. Aubert and Emily retired to their rooms, and Valancourt to his station at the door, which, at this mild season, he preferred to a close cabin and a bed of skins. St. Aubert was somewhat surprised to find in his room volumes of Homer, Horace, and Petrarch; but the name of Valancourt, written in them, told him to whom they belonged.

CHAPTER IV

> In truth he was a strange and wayward wight,
> Fond of each gentle, and each dreadful scene,
> In darkness, and in storm he found delight;
> Nor less than when on ocean-wave serene
> The southern sun diffus'd his dazzling sheen.
> Even sad vicissitude amus'd his soul;
> And if a sigh would sometimes intervene,
> And down his cheek a tear of pity roll,
> A sigh, a tear, so sweet, he wish'd not to controul.
> THE MINSTREL

ST. AUBERT awoke at an early hour, refreshed by sleep, and desirous to set forward. He invited the stranger to breakfast with him; and, talking again of the road, Valancourt said, that, some months past, he had travelled as far as Beaujeu, which was a town of some consequence on the way to Rousillon. He recommended it to St. Aubert to take that route, and the latter determined to do so.

"The road from this hamlet," said Valancourt, "and that to Beaujeu, part at the distance of about a league and a half from hence; if you will give me leave, I will direct your muleteer so far. I must wander somewhere, and your company would make this a pleasanter ramble than any other I could take."

St. Aubert thankfully accepted his offer, and they set out together, the young stranger on foot, for he refused the invitation of St. Aubert to take a seat in his little carriage.

The road wound along the feet of the mountains through a pastoral valley, bright with verdure, and varied with groves of dwarf oak, beech, and sycamore, under whose branches herds of cattle reposed. The mountain-ash too, and the weeping birch, often threw their pendant foliage over the steeps above, where the scanty soil scarcely concealed their roots, and where their light branches waved to every breeze that fluttered from the mountains.

The travellers were frequently met at this early hour, for the sun had not yet risen upon the valley, by shepherds driving immense flocks from their folds to feed upon the hills. St. Aubert had set out thus early, not only that he might enjoy the first appearance of sunrise, but that he might inhale the first pure breath of morning, which above all things is refreshing to the spirits of the invalid. In these regions it was particularly so, where an abundance of wild flowers and aromatic herbs breathed forth their essence on the air.

The dawn, which softened the scenery with its peculiar grey tint, now dispersed, and Emily watched the progress of the day, first trembling on the tops of the highest cliffs, then touching them with splendid light, while their sides and the vale below were still wrapt in dewy mist. Meanwhile, the sullen grey of the eastern clouds began to blush, then to redden, and then to glow with a thousand colours, till the golden light darted over all the air, touched the lower points of the mountain's brow, and glanced in long sloping beams upon the valley and its stream. All nature seemed to have awakened from death into life; the spirit of St. Aubert was renovated. His heart was full; he wept, and his thoughts ascended to the Great Creator.

Emily wished to trip along the turf, so green and bright with dew, and to taste the full delight of that liberty, which the izard seemed to enjoy as he bounded along the brow of the cliffs; while Valancourt often stopped to speak with the travellers, and with social feeling to point out to them the peculiar objects of his admiration. St. Aubert was pleased with him: "Here is the real ingenuousness and ardour of youth," said he to himself; "this young man has never been at Paris."

He was sorry when they came to the spot where the roads parted, and his heart took a more affectionate leave of him than is usual after so short an acquaintance. Valancourt talked long by the side of the carriage; seemed more than once to be going, but still lingered, and appeared to search anxiously for topics of conversation to account for his delay. At length he took leave. As he went, St. Aubert observed him look with an earnest and pensive eye at Emily, who bowed to him with a countenance full of timid sweetness, while the carriage drove on. St. Aubert, for whatever reason, soon after looked from the window, and saw Valancourt standing upon the bank of the road, resting on his pike with folded arms, and following the carriage with his eyes. He waved his hand, and Valancourt, seeming to awake from his reverie, returned the salute, and started away.

The aspect of the country now began to change, and the travellers soon found themselves among mountains covered from their base nearly to their summits with forests of gloomy pine, except where a rock of granite shot up from the vale, and lost its snowy top in the clouds. The rivulet, which had hitherto accompanied them, now expanded into a river; and, flowing deeply and silently along, reflected, as in a mirror, the blackness of the impending shades. Sometimes a cliff was seen lifting its bold head above the woods and the vapours, that floated mid-way down the mountains; and sometimes a face of perpendicular marble rose from the water's edge, over which the larch threw his gigantic arms, here scathed with lightning, and there floating in luxuriant foliage.

They continued to travel over a rough and unfrequented road, seeing now and then at a distance the solitary shepherd, with his dog, stalking along the valley, and hearing only the dashing of torrents, which the woods concealed from the eye, the long sullen murmur of the breeze, as it swept over the pines, or the notes of the eagle and the vulture, which were seen towering round the beetling cliff.

Often, as the carriage moved slowly over uneven ground, St. Aubert alighted, and amused himself with examining the curious plants that grew on the banks of the road, and with which these regions abound; while Emily, wrapt in high enthusiasm, wandered away under the shades, listening in deep silence to the lonely murmur of the woods.

Neither village nor hamlet was seen for many leagues; the goatherd's or the hunter's cabin, perched among the cliffs of the rocks, were the only human habitations that appeared.

The travellers again took their dinner in the open air, on a pleasant spot in the valley, under the spreading shade of cedars; and then set forward towards Beaujeu.

The road now began to descend, and, leaving the pine forests behind, wound among rocky precipices. The evening twilight again fell over the scene, and the travellers were ignorant how far they might yet be from Beaujeu. St. Aubert, however, conjectured that the distance could not be very great, and comforted himself with the prospect of travelling on a more frequented road after reaching that town, where he designed to pass the night. Mingled woods, and rocks, and heathy mountains were now seen obscurely through the dusk; but soon even these imperfect images faded in darkness. Michael proceeded with caution, for he could scarcely distinguish the road; his mules, however, seemed to have more sagacity, and their steps were sure.

On turning the angle of a mountain, a light appeared at a distance, that illumined the rocks, and the horizon to a great extent. It was evidently a large fire, but whether accidental, or otherwise, there were no means of knowing. St. Aubert thought it was probably kindled by some of the numerous banditti, that infested the Pyrenées, and he became watchful and anxious to know whether the road passed near this fire. He had arms with him, which, on an emergency, might afford some protection, though certainly a very unequal one, against a band of robbers, so desperate too as those usually were who haunted these wild regions. While many reflections rose upon his mind, he heard a voice shouting from the road behind, and ordering the muleteer to stop. St. Aubert bade him proceed as fast as possible; but either Michael, or his mules were obstinate, for they did not quit the old pace. Horses' feet were now heard; a man rode up to the carriage, still ordering the driver to stop; and St. Aubert, who could no longer doubt his purpose, was with difficulty able to prepare a pistol for his defence, when his hand was upon the door of the chaise. The man staggered on his horse, the report of the pistol was followed by a groan, and St. Aubert's horror may be imagined, when in the next instant he thought he heard the faint voice of Valancourt. He now himself bade the muleteer stop; and, pronouncing the name of Valancourt, was answered in a voice, that no longer suffered him to doubt. St. Aubert, who instantly alighted and went to his assistance, found him still sitting on his horse, but bleeding profusely, and appearing to be in great pain, though he endeavoured to soften the terror of St. Aubert by assurances that he was not materially hurt, the wound being only in his arm. St. Aubert, with the muleteer, assisted him to dismount, and he sat down on the bank of the road, where St. Aubert tried to bind up his arm, but his hands trembled so excessively that he could not accomplish it; and, Michael being now gone in pursuit of the horse, which, on being disengaged from his rider, had galloped off, he called Emily to his assistance. Receiving no answer, he went to the carriage, and found her sunk on the seat in a fainting fit. Between the distress of this circumstance and that of leaving Valancourt bleeding, he scarcely knew what he did; he endeavoured, however, to raise her, and called to Michael to fetch water from the rivulet that flowed by the road, but Michael was gone beyond the reach of his voice. Valancourt, who heard these calls, and also the repeated name of Emily, instantly understood the subject of his distress; and, almost forgetting his own condition, he hastened to her relief. She was reviving when he reached the carriage; and then, understanding that anxiety for him had occasioned her indisposition, he assured her, in a voice that trembled, but not from anguish, that his wound was of no consequence. While he said this St. Aubert turned round, and perceiving that he was still bleeding, the subject of his alarm changed again, and he hastily formed some handkerchiefs into a bandage. This stopped the effusion of the blood; but St. Aubert, dreading the consequence of the wound, enquired repeatedly how far they were from Beaujeu; when, learning that it was at two leagues' distance, his distress increased, since he knew not how Valancourt, in his present state, would bear the motion of the carriage, and perceived that he was already faint from loss of blood. When he mentioned the subject of his anxiety, Valancourt entreated that he would not suffer himself to be thus alarmed on his account, for that he had no doubt he should be able to support himself very well; and then he talked of the accident as a slight one. The muleteer being now returned with Valancourt's horse, assisted him into the chaise; and, as Emily was now revived, they moved slowly on towards Beaujeu.

St. Aubert, when he had recovered from the terror occasioned him by this accident, expressed surprise on seeing Valancourt, who explained his unexpected appearance by saying, "You, sir, renewed my taste for society; when you had left the hamlet, it did indeed appear a solitude. I determined, therefore, since my object was merely amusement, to change the scene; and I took this road, because I knew it led through a more romantic tract of mountains than the spot I have left. Besides," added he, hesitating for an instant, "I will own, and why should I not? that I had some hope of overtaking you."

"And I have made you a very unexpected return for the compliment," said St. Aubert, who lamented again the rashness which had produced the accident, and explained the cause of his late alarm. But Valancourt seemed anxious only to remove from the minds of his companions every unpleasant feeling relative to himself; and, for that purpose, still struggled against a sense of pain, and tried to converse with gaiety. Emily meanwhile was silent, except when Valancourt particularly addressed her, and there was at those times a tremulous tone in his voice that spoke much.

They were now so near the fire, which had long flamed at a distance on the blackness of night, that it gleamed upon the road, and they could distinguish figures moving about the blaze. The way winding still nearer, they perceived in the valley one of those numerous bands of gipsies, which at that period particularly haunted the wilds of the Pyrenées, and lived partly by plundering the traveller. Emily looked with some degree of terror on the savage countenances of these people, shewn by the fire, which heightened the romantic effect of the scenery, as it threw a red dusky gleam upon the rocks and on the foliage of the trees, leaving heavy masses of shade and regions of obscurity, which the eye feared to penetrate.

They were preparing their supper; a large pot stood by the fire, over which several figures were busy. The blaze discovered a rude kind of tent, round which many children and dogs were playing, and the whole formed a picture highly grotesque. The travellers saw plainly their danger. Valancourt was silent, but laid his hand on one of St. Aubert's pistols; St. Aubert drew forth another, and Michael was ordered to proceed as fast as possible. They passed the place, however, without being attacked; the rovers being probably unprepared for the opportunity, and too busy about their supper to feel much interest, at the moment, in any thing besides.

After a league and a half more, passed in darkness, the travellers arrived at Beaujeu, and drove up to the only inn the place afforded; which, though superior to any they had seen since they entered the mountains, was bad enough.

The surgeon of the town was immediately sent for, if a surgeon he could be called, who prescribed for horses as well as for men, and shaved faces at least as dexterously as he set bones. After examining Valancourt's arm, and perceiving that the bullet had passed through the flesh without touching the bone, he dressed it, and left him with a solemn prescription of quiet, which his patient was not inclined to obey. The delight of ease had now succeeded to pain; for ease may be allowed to assume a positive quality when contrasted with anguish; and, his spirits thus re-animated, he wished to partake of the conversation of St. Aubert and Emily, who, released from so many apprehensions, were uncommonly cheerful. Late as it was, however, St. Aubert was obliged to go out with the landlord to buy meat for supper; and Emily, who, during this interval, had been absent as long as she could, upon excuses of looking to their accommodation, which she found rather better than she expected, was compelled to return, and converse with Valancourt alone. They talked of the character of the scenes they had passed, of the natural history of the country, of poetry, and of St. Aubert; a subject on which Emily always spoke and listened to with peculiar pleasure.

The travellers passed an agreeable evening, but St. Aubert was fatigued with his journey; and, as Valancourt seemed again sensible of pain, they separated soon after supper.

In the morning St. Aubert found that Valancourt had passed a restless night; that he was feverish, and his wound very painful. The surgeon, when he dressed it, advised him to remain quietly at Beaujeu; advice which was too reasonable to be rejected. St. Aubert, however, had no favourable opinion of this practitioner, and was anxious to commit Valancourt into more skilful hands; but learning, upon enquiry, that there was no town within several leagues which seemed more likely to afford better advice, he altered the plan of his journey, and determined to await the recovery of Valancourt, who, with somewhat more ceremony than sincerity, made many objections to this delay.

By order of his surgeon, Valancourt did not go out of the house that day; but St. Aubert and Emily surveyed with delight the environs of the town, situated at the feet of the Pyrenean Alps, that rose, some in abrupt precipices, and others swelling with woods of cedar, fir, and cypress, which stretched nearly to their highest summits. The cheerful green of the beech and mountain-ash was sometimes seen, like a gleam of light, amidst the dark verdure of the forest; and sometimes a torrent poured its sparkling flood, high among the woods.

Valancourt's indisposition detained the travellers at Beaujeu several days, during which interval St. Aubert had observed his disposition and his talents with the philosophic inquiry so natural to him. He saw a frank and generous nature, full of ardour, highly susceptible of whatever is grand and beautiful, but impetuous, wild, and somewhat romantic. Valancourt had known little of the world. His perceptions were clear, and his feelings just; his indignation of an unworthy, or his admiration of a generous action, were expressed in terms of equal vehemence. St. Aubert sometimes smiled at his warmth, but seldom checked it, and often repeated to himself, "This young man has never been at Paris." A sigh sometimes followed this silent ejaculation. He determined not to leave Valancourt till he should be perfectly recovered; and, as he was now well enough to travel, though not able to manage his horse, St. Aubert invited him to accompany him for a few days in the carriage. This he the more readily did, since he had discovered that Valancourt was of a family of the same name in Gascony, with whose respectability he was well acquainted. The latter accepted the offer with great pleasure, and they again set forward among these romantic wilds about Rousillon.

They travelled leisurely; stopping wherever a scene uncommonly grand appeared; frequently alighting to walk to an eminence, whither the mules could not go, from which the prospect opened in greater magnificence; and often sauntering over hillocks covered with lavender, wild thyme, juniper, and tamarisc; and under the shades of woods, between those boles they caught the long mountain-vista, sublime beyond any thing that Emily had ever imagined.

St. Aubert sometimes amused himself with botanizing, while

Valancourt and Emily strolled on; he pointing out to her notice the objects that particularly charmed him, and reciting beautiful passages from such of the Latin and Italian poets as he had heard her admire. In the pauses of conversation, when he thought himself not observed, he frequently fixed his eyes pensively on her countenance, which expressed with so much animation the taste and energy of her mind; and when he spoke again, there was a peculiar tenderness in the tone of his voice, that defeated any attempt to conceal his sentiments. By degrees these silent pauses became more frequent; till Emily, only, betrayed an anxiety to interrupt them; and she; who had been hitherto reserved, would now talk again, and again, of the woods and the vallies and the mountains, to avoid the danger of sympathy and silence.

From Beaujeu the road had constantly ascended, conducting the travellers into the higher regions of the air, where immense glaciers exhibited their frozen horrors, and eternal snow whitened the summits of the mountains. They often paused to contemplate these stupendous scenes, and, seated on some wild cliff, where only the ilex or the larch could flourish, looked over dark forests of fir, and precipices where human foot had never wandered, into the glen—so deep, that the thunder of the torrent, which was seen to foam along the bottom, was scarcely heard to murmur. Over these crags rose others of stupendous height, and fantastic shape; some shooting into cones; others impending far over their base, in huge masses of granite, along whose broken ridges was often lodged a weight of snow, that, trembling even to the vibration of a sound, threatened to bear destruction in its course to the vale. Around, on every side, far as the eye could penetrate, were seen only forms of grandeur—the long perspective of mountain-tops, tinged with ethereal blue, or white with snow; vallies of ice, and forests of gloomy fir. The serenity and clearness of the air in these high regions were particularly delightful to the travellers; it seemed to inspire them with a finer spirit, and diffused an indescribable complacency over their minds. They had no words to express the sublime emotions they felt. A solemn expression characterized the feelings of St. Aubert; tears often came to his eyes, and he frequently walked away from his companions. Valancourt now and then spoke, to point to Emily's notice some feature of the scene. The thinness of the atmosphere, through which every object came so distinctly to the eye, surprised and deluded her; who could scarcely believe that objects, which appeared so near, were, in reality, so distant. The deep silence of these solitudes was broken only at intervals by the scream of the vultures, seen cowering round some cliff below, or by the cry of the eagle sailing high in the air; except when the travellers listened to the hollow thunder that sometimes muttered at their feet. While, above, the deep blue of the heavens was unobscured by the lightest cloud, half way down the mountains, long billows of vapour were frequently seen rolling, now wholly excluding the country below, and now opening, and partially revealing its features. Emily delighted to observe the grandeur of these clouds as they changed in shape and tints, and to watch their various effect on the lower world, whose features, partly veiled, were continually assuming new forms of sublimity.

After traversing these regions for many leagues, they began to descend towards Rousillon, and features of beauty then mingled with the scene. Yet the travellers did not look back without some regret to the sublime objects they had quitted; though the eye, fatigued with the extension of its powers, was glad to repose on the verdure of woods and pastures, that now hung on the margin of the river below; to view again the humble cottage shaded by cedars, the playful group of mountaineer-children, and the flowery nooks that appeared among the hills.

As they descended, they saw at a distance, on the right, one of the grand passes of the Pyrenées into Spain, gleaming with its battlements and towers to the splendour of the setting rays, yellow tops of woods colouring the steeps below, while far above aspired the snowy points of the mountains, still reflecting a rosy hue.

St. Aubert began to look out for the little town he had been directed to by the people of Beaujeu, and where he meant to pass the night; but no habitation yet appeared. Of its distance Valancourt could not assist him to judge, for he had never been so far along this chain of Alps before. There was, however, a road to guide them; and there could be little doubt that it was the right one; for, since they had left Beaujeu, there had been no variety of tracks to perplex or mislead.

The sun now gave his last light, and St. Aubert bade the muleteer proceed with all possible dispatch. He found, indeed, the lassitude of illness return upon him, after a day of uncommon fatigue, both of body and mind, and he longed for repose. His anxiety was not soothed by observing a numerous train, consisting of men, horses, and loaded mules, winding down the steeps of an opposite mountain, appearing and disappearing at intervals among the woods, so that its numbers could not be judged of. Something bright, like arms, glanced in the setting ray, and the military dress was distinguishable upon the men who were in the van, and on others scattered among the troop that followed. As these wound into the vale, the rear of the party emerged from the woods, and exhibited a band of soldiers. St. Aubert's apprehensions now subsided; he had no doubt that the train before him consisted of smugglers, who, in conveying prohibited goods over the Pyrenées, had been encountered, and conquered by a party of troops.

The travellers had lingered so long among the sublimer scenes of these mountains, that they found themselves entirely mistaken in their calculation that they could reach Montigny at sunset; but, as they wound along the valley, they saw, on a rude Alpine bridge, that united two lofty crags of the glen, a group of mountaineer-children, amusing themselves with dropping pebbles into a torrent below, and watching the stones plunge into the water, that threw up its white spray high in the air as it received them, and returned a sullen sound, which the echoes of the mountains prolonged. Under the bridge was seen a perspective of the valley, with its cataract descending among the rocks, and a cottage on a cliff, overshadowed with pines. It appeared, that they could not be far from some small town. St. Aubert bade the muleteer stop, and then called to the children to enquire if he was near Montigny; but the distance, and the roaring of the waters, would not suffer his voice to be heard; and the crags, adjoining the bridge, were of such tremendous height and steepness, that to have climbed either would have been scarcely practicable to a person unacquainted with the ascent. St. Aubert, therefore, did not waste more moments in delay. They continued to travel long after twilight had obscured the road, which was so broken, that, now thinking it safer to walk than to ride, they all alighted. The moon was rising, but her light was yet too feeble to assist them. While they stepped carefully on, they heard the vesper-bell of a convent. The twilight would not permit them to distinguish anything like a building, but the sounds seemed to come from some woods, that overhung an acclivity to the right. Valancourt proposed to go in search of this convent. "If they will not accommodate us with a night's lodging," said he, "they may certainly inform us how far we are from Montigny, and direct us towards it." He was bounding forward, without waiting St. Aubert's reply, when the latter stopped him. "I am very weary," said St. Aubert, "and wish for nothing so much as for immediate rest. We will all go to the convent; your good looks would defeat our purpose; but when they see mine and Emily's exhausted countenances, they will scarcely deny us repose."

As he said this, he took Emily's arm within his, and, telling Michael to wait a while in the road with the carriage, they began to ascend towards the woods, guided by the bell of the convent. His steps were feeble, and Valancourt offered him his arm, which he accepted. The moon now threw a faint light over their path, and, soon after, enabled them to distinguish some towers rising above the tops of the woods. Still following the note of the bell, they entered the shade of those woods, lighted only by the moonbeams, that glided down between the leaves, and threw a tremulous uncertain gleam upon the steep track they were winding. The gloom and the silence that prevailed, except when the bell returned upon the air, together with the wildness of the surrounding scene, struck Emily with a degree of fear, which, however, the voice and conversation of Valancourt somewhat repressed. When they had been some time ascending, St. Aubert complained of weariness, and they stopped to rest upon a little green summit, where the trees opened, and admitted the moon-light. He sat down upon the turf, between Emily and Valancourt. The bell had now ceased, and the deep repose of the scene was undisturbed by any sound, for the low dull murmur of some distant torrents might be said to soothe, rather than to interrupt, the silence.

Before them, extended the valley they had quitted; its rocks, and woods to the left, just silvered by the rays, formed a contrast to the deep shadow, that involved the opposite cliffs, whose fringed summits only were tipped with light; while the distant perspective of the valley was lost in the yellow mist of moon-light. The travellers sat for some time wrapt in the complacency which such scenes inspire.

"These scenes," said Valancourt, at length, "soften the heart, like the notes of sweet music, and inspire that delicious melancholy which no person, who had felt it once, would resign for the gayest pleasures. They waken our best and purest feelings, disposing us to benevolence, pity, and friendship. Those whom I love—I always seem to love more in such an hour as this." His voice trembled, and he paused.

St. Aubert was silent; Emily perceived a warm tear fall upon the hand he held; she knew the object of his thoughts; hers too had, for some time, been occupied by the remembrance of her mother. He seemed by an effort to rouse himself. "Yes," said he, with an half-suppressed sigh, "the memory of those we love—of times for ever past! in such an hour as this steals upon the mind, like a strain of distant music in the stillness of night;—all tender and harmonious as this land-scape, sleeping in the mellow moon-light." After the pause of a moment, St. Aubert added, "I have always fancied, that I thought with more clearness, and precision, at such an hour than at any other, and that heart must be insensible in a great degree, that does not soften to its influence. But many such there are."

Valancourt sighed.

"Are there, indeed, many such?" said Emily.

"A few years hence, my Emily," replied St. Aubert, "and you may smile at the recollection of that question—if you do not weep to it. But come, I am somewhat refreshed, let us proceed."

Having emerged from the woods, they saw, upon a turfy hillock above, the convent of which they were in search. A high wall, that sur-rounded it, led them to an ancient gate, at which they knocked; and the poor monk, who opened it, conducted them into a small adjoining room, where he desired they would wait while he informed the superior of their request. In this interval, several friars came in separately to look at them; and at length the first monk returned, and they followed him to a room, where the superior was sitting in an arm-chair, with a large folio volume, printed in black letter, open on a desk before him. He received them with courtesy, though he did not rise from his seat; and, having asked them a few questions, granted their request. After a short conversation, formal and solemn on the part of the superior, they withdrew to the apartment where they were to sup, and Valancourt, whom one of the inferior friars civilly desired to accompany, went to seek Michael and his mules. They had not descended half way down the cliffs, before they heard the voice of the muleteer echoing far and wide. Sometimes he called on St. Aubert, and sometimes on Valancourt; who having, at length, convinced him that he had nothing to fear either for himself, or his master; and having disposed of him, for the night, in a cottage on the skirts of the woods, returned to sup with his friends, on such sober fare as the monks thought it prudent to set before them. While St. Aubert was too much indisposed to share it, Emily, in her anxiety for her father, forgot herself; and Valancourt, silent and thoughtful, yet never inattentive to them, appeared particularly solicitous to accommodate and relieve St. Aubert, who often observed, while his daughter was pressing him to eat, or adjusting the pillow she had placed in the back of his arm-chair, that Valancourt fixed on her a look of pensive tenderness, which he was not displeased to understand.

They separated at an early hour, and retired to their respective apartments. Emily was shown to hers by a nun of the convent, whom she was glad to dismiss, for her heart was melancholy, and her attention so much abstracted, that conversation with a stranger was painful. She thought her father daily declining, and attributed his present fatigue more to the feeble state of his frame, than to the difficulty of the journey. A train of gloomy ideas haunted her mind, till she fell asleep.

In about two hours after, she was awakened by the chiming of a bell, and then heard quick steps pass along the gallery, into which her chamber opened. She was so little accustomed to the manners of a convent, as to be alarmed by this circumstance; her fears, ever alive for her father, suggested that he was very ill, and she rose in haste to go to him. Having paused, however, to let the persons in the gallery pass before she opened her door, her thoughts, in the mean time, recovered from the confusion of sleep, and she understood that the bell was the call of the monks to prayers. It had now ceased, and, all being again still, she forbore to go to St. Aubert's room. Her mind was not disposed for immediate sleep, and the moon-light, that shone into her chamber, invited her to open the casement, and look out upon the country.

It was a still and beautiful night, the sky was unobscured by any cloud, and scarce a leaf of the woods beneath trembled in the air. As she listened, the mid-night hymn of the monks rose softly from a chapel, that stood on one of the lower cliffs, an holy strain, that seemed to ascend through the silence of night to heaven, and her thoughts ascended with it. From the consideration of His works, her mind arose to the adoration of the Deity, in His goodness and power; wherever she turned her view, whether on the sleeping earth, or to the vast regions of space, glowing with worlds beyond the reach of human thought, the sublimity of God, and the majesty of His presence appeared. Her eyes were filled with tears of awful love and admiration; and she felt that pure devotion, superior to all the distinctions of human system, which lifts the soul above this world, and seems to expand it into a nobler nature; such devotion as can, perhaps, only be experienced, when the mind, rescued, for a moment, from the humbleness of earthly consid-erations, aspires to contemplate His power in the sublimity of His works, and His goodness in the infinity of His blessings.

> Is it not now the hour,
> The holy hour, when to the cloudless height
> Of yon starred concave climbs the full-orbed moon,
> And to this nether world in solemn stillness,
> Gives sign, that, to the list'ning ear of Heaven
> Religion's voice should plead? The very babe
> Knows this, and, chance awak'd, his little hands
> Lifts to the gods, and on his innocent couch
> Calls down a blessing.*

The midnight chant of the monks soon after dropped into silence; but Emily remained at the casement, watching the setting moon, and the valley sinking into deep shade, and willing to prolong her present state of mind. At length she retired to her mattress, and sunk into tran-quil slumber.

CHAPTER V

> While in the rosy vale
> Love breath'd his infant sighs, from anguish free.
> THOMSON

ST. AUBERT, sufficiently restored by a night's repose to pursue his jour-ney, set out in the morning, with his family and Valancourt, for Rousillon, which he hoped to reach before night-fall. The scenes,

---

*CARACTACUS.

through which they now passed, were as wild and romantic, as any they had yet observed, with this difference, that beauty, every now and then, softened the landscape into smiles. Little woody recesses appeared among the mountains, covered with bright verdure and flowers; or a pastoral valley opened its grassy bosom in the shade of the cliffs, with flocks and herds loitering along the banks of a rivulet, that refreshed it with perpetual green. St. Aubert could not repent the having taken this fatiguing road, though he was this day, also, frequently obliged to alight, to walk along the rugged precipice, and to climb the steep and flinty mountain. The wonderful sublimity and variety of the prospects repaid him for all this, and the enthusiasm, with which they were viewed by his young companions, heightened his own, and awakened a remembrance of all the delightful emotions of his early days, when the sublime charms of nature were first unveiled to him. He found great pleasure in conversing with Valancourt, and in listening to his ingenuous remarks. The fire and simplicity of his manners seemed to render him a characteristic figure in the scenes around them; and St. Aubert discovered in his sentiments the justness and the dignity of an elevated mind, unbiassed by intercourse with the world. He perceived, that his opinions were formed, rather than imbibed; were more the result of thought, than of learning. Of the world he seemed to know nothing; for he believed well of all mankind, and this opinion gave him the reflected image of his own heart.

St. Aubert, as he sometimes lingered to examine the wild plants in his path, often looked forward with pleasure to Emily and Valancourt, as they strolled on together; he, with a countenance of animated delight, pointing to her attention some grand feature of the scene; and she, listening and observing with a look of tender seriousness, that spoke the elevation of her mind. They appeared like two lovers who had never strayed beyond these their native mountains; whose situation had secluded them from the frivolities of common life, whose ideas were simple and grand, like the landscapes among which they moved, and who knew no other happiness, than in the union of pure and affectionate hearts. St. Aubert smiled, and sighed at the romantic picture of felicity his fancy drew; and sighed again to think, that nature and simplicity were so little known to the world, as that their pleasures were thought romantic.

"The world," said he, pursuing this train of thought, "ridicules a passion which it seldom feels; its scenes, and its interests, distract the mind, deprave the taste, corrupt the heart, and love cannot exist in a heart that has lost the meek dignity of innocence. Virtue and taste are nearly the same, for virtue is little more than active taste, and the most delicate affections of each combine in real love. How then are we to look for love in great cities, where selfishness, dissipation, and insincerity supply the place of tenderness, simplicity and truth?"

It was near noon, when the travellers, having arrived at a piece of steep and dangerous road, alighted to walk. The road wound up an ascent, that was clothed with wood, and, instead of following the carriage, they entered the refreshing shade. A dewy coolness was diffused upon the air, which, with the bright verdure of turf, that grew under the trees, the mingled fragrance of flowers and of balm, thyme, and lavender, that enriched it, and the grandeur of the pines, beech, and chestnuts, that overshadowed them, rendered this a most delicious retreat. Sometimes, the thick foliage excluded all view of the country; at others, it admitted some partial catches of the distant scenery, which gave hints to the imagination to picture landscapes more interesting, more impressive, than any that had been presented to the eye. The wanderers often lingered to indulge in these reveries of fancy.

The pauses of silence, such as had formerly interrupted the conversations of Valancourt and Emily, were more frequent today than ever. Valancourt often dropped suddenly from the most animating vivacity into fits of deep musing, and there was, sometimes, an unaffected melancholy in his smile, which Emily could not avoid understanding, for her heart was interested in the sentiment it spoke.

St. Aubert was refreshed by the shades, and they continued to saunter under them, following, as nearly as they could guess, the direction of the road, till they perceived that they had totally lost it. They had continued near the brow of the precipice, allured by the scenery it exhibited, while the road wound far away over the cliff above. Valancourt called loudly to Michael, but heard no voice, except his own, echoing among the rocks, and his various efforts to regain the road were equally unsuccessful. While they were thus circumstanced, they perceived a shepherd's cabin, between the boles of the trees at some distance, and Valancourt bounded on first to ask assistance. When he reached it, he saw only two little children, at play, on the turf before the door. He looked into the hut, but no person was there, and the eldest of the boys told him that their father was with his flocks, and their mother was gone down into the vale, but would be back presently. As he stood, considering what was further to be done, on a sudden he heard Michael's voice roaring forth most manfully among the cliffs above, till he made their echoes ring. Valancourt immediately answered the call, and endeavoured to make his way through the thicket that clothed the steeps, following the direction of the sound. After much struggle over brambles and precipices, he reached Michael, and at length prevailed with him to be silent, and to listen to him. The road was at a considerable distance from the spot where St.

Aubert and Emily were; the carriage could not easily return to the entrance of the wood, and, since it would be very fatiguing for St. Aubert to climb the long and steep road to the place where it now stood, Valancourt was anxious to find a more easy ascent, by the way he had himself passed.

Meanwhile St. Aubert and Emily approached the cottage, and rested themselves on a rustic bench, fastened between two pines, which overshadowed it, till Valancourt, whose steps they had observed, should return.

The eldest of the children desisted from his play, and stood still to observe the strangers, while the younger continued his little gambols, and teased his brother to join in them. St. Aubert looked with pleasure upon this picture of infantine simplicity, till it brought to his remembrance his own boys, whom he had lost about the age of these, and their lamented mother; and he sunk into a thoughtfulness, which Emily observing, she immediately began to sing one of those simple and lively airs he was so fond of, and which she knew how to give with the most captivating sweetness. St. Aubert smiled on her through his tears, took her hand and pressed it affectionately, and then tried to dissipate the melancholy reflections that lingered in his mind.

While she sung, Valancourt approached, who was unwilling to interrupt her, and paused at a little distance to listen. When she had concluded, he joined the party, and told them, that he had found Michael, as well as a way, by which he thought they could ascend the cliff to the carriage. He pointed to the woody steeps above, which St. Aubert surveyed with an anxious eye. He was already wearied by his walk, and this ascent was formidable to him. He thought, however, it would be less toilsome than the long and broken road, and he determined to attempt it; but Emily, ever watchful of his ease, proposing that he should rest, and dine before they proceeded further, Valancourt went to the carriage for the refreshments deposited there.

On his return, he proposed removing a little higher up the mountain, to where the woods opened upon a grand and extensive prospect; and thither they were preparing to go, when they saw a young woman join the children, and caress and weep over them.

The travellers, interested by her distress, stopped to observe her. She took the youngest of the children in her arms, and, perceiving the strangers, hastily dried her tears, and proceeded to the cottage. St. Aubert, on enquiring the occasion of her sorrow, learned that her husband, who was a shepherd, and lived here in the summer months to watch over the flocks he led to feed upon these mountains, had lost, on the preceding night, his little all. A gang of gipsies, who had for some time infested the neighbourhood, had driven away several of his

master's sheep. "Jacques," added the shepherd's wife, "had saved a little money, and had bought a few sheep with it, and now they must go
to his master for those that are stolen; and what is worse than all, his
master, when he comes to know how it is, will trust him no longer with
the care of his flocks, for he is a hard man! and then what is to become
of our children!"

The innocent countenance of the woman, and the simplicity of her
manner in relating her grievance, inclined St. Aubert to believe her
story; and Valancourt, convinced that it was true, asked eagerly what
was the value of the stolen sheep; on hearing which he turned away
with a look of disappointment. St. Aubert put some money into her
hand, Emily too gave something from her little purse, and they walked
towards the cliff; but Valancourt lingered behind, and spoke to the
shepherd's wife, who was now weeping with gratitude and surprise. He
enquired how much money was yet wanting to replace the stolen
sheep, and found, that it was a sum very little short of all he had about
him. He was perplexed and distressed. "This sum then," said he to
himself, "would make this poor family completely happy—it is in my
power to give it—to make them completely happy! But what is to
become of me?—how shall I contrive to reach home with the little
money that will remain?" For a moment he stood, unwilling to forego
the luxury of raising a family from ruin to happiness, yet considering
the difficulties of pursuing his journey with so small a sum as would
be left.

While he was in this state of perplexity, the shepherd himself
appeared: his children ran to meet him; he took one of them in his
arms, and, with the other clinging to his coat, came forward with a loitering step. His forlorn and melancholy look determined Valancourt at
once; he threw down all the money he had, except a very few louis, and
bounded away after St. Aubert and Emily, who were proceeding slowly
up the steep. Valancourt had seldom felt his heart so light as at this
moment; his gay spirits danced with pleasure; every object around him
appeared more interesting, or beautiful, than before. St. Aubert
observed the uncommon vivacity of his countenance: "What has
pleased you so much?" said he. "O what a lovely day," replied
Valancourt, "how brightly the sun shines, how pure is this air, what
enchanting scenery!" "It is indeed enchanting," said St. Aubert, whom
early experience had taught to understand the nature of Valancourt's
present feelings. "What pity that the wealthy, who can command such
sunshine, should ever pass their days in gloom—in the cold shade of
selfishness! For you, my young friend, may the sun always shine as
brightly as at this moment; may your own conduct always give you the
sunshine of benevolence and reason united!"

Valancourt, highly flattered by this compliment, could make no reply but by a smile of gratitude.

They continued to wind under the woods, between the grassy knolls of the mountain, and, as they reached the shady summit, which he had pointed out, the whole party burst into an exclamation. Behind the spot where they stood, the rock rose perpendicularly in a massy wall to a considerable height, and then branched out into overhanging crags. Their grey tints were well contrasted by the bright hues of the plants and wild flowers, that grew in their fractured sides, and were deepened by the gloom of the pines and cedars, that waved above. The steeps below, over which the eye passed abruptly to the valley, were fringed with thickets of alpine shrubs; and, lower still, appeared the tufted tops of the chesnut woods, that clothed their base, among which peeped forth the shepherd's cottage, just left by the travellers, with its blueish smoke curling high in the air. On every side appeared the majestic summits of the Pyrenées, some exhibiting tremendous crags of marble, whose appearance was changing every instant, as the varying lights fell upon their surface; others, still higher, displaying only snowy points, while their lower steeps were covered almost invariably with forests of pine, larch, and oak, that stretched down to the vale. This was one of the narrow vallies, that open from the Pyrenées into the country of Rousillon, and whose green pastures, and cultivated beauty, form a decided and wonderful contrast to the romantic grandeur that environs it. Through a vista of the mountains appeared the lowlands of Rousillon, tinted with the blue haze of distance, as they united with the waters of the Mediterranean; where, on a promontory, which marked the boundary of the shore, stood a lonely beacon, over which were seen circling flights of sea-fowl. Beyond, appeared, now and then, a stealing sail, white with the sun-beam, and whose progress was perceivable by its approach to the light-house. Sometimes, too, was seen a sail so distant, that it served only to mark the line of separation between the sky and the waves.

On the other side of the valley, immediately opposite to the spot where the travellers rested, a rocky pass opened toward Gascony. Here no sign of cultivation appeared. The rocks of granite, that screened the glen, rose abruptly from their base, and stretched their barren points to the clouds, unvaried with woods, and uncheered even by a hunter's cabin. Sometimes, indeed, a gigantic larch threw its long shade over the precipice, and here and there a cliff reared on its brow a monumental cross, to tell the traveller the fate of him who had ventured thither before. This spot seemed the very haunt of banditti; and Emily, as she looked down upon it, almost expected to see them stealing out from some hollow cave to look for their prey. Soon after an object not less terrific struck her,—a gibbet standing on a point of rock near the entrance of the pass, and immediately over one of the crosses she had before observed. These were hieroglyphics that told a plain and dreadful story. She forbore to point it out to St. Aubert, but it threw a gloom over her spirits, and made her anxious to hasten forward, that they might with certainty reach Rousillon before night-fall. It was necessary, however, that St. Aubert should take some refreshment, and, seating themselves on the short dry turf, they opened the basket of provisions, while

> by breezy murmurs cool'd,
> Broad o'er *their* heads the verdant cedars wave,
> And high palmetos lift their graceful shade.
> ———————————————————— *they* draw
> Ethereal soul, there drink reviving gales
> Profusely breathing from the piney groves,
> And vales of fragrance; there at a distance hear
> The roaring floods, and cataracts.*

St. Aubert was revived by rest, and by the serene air of this summit; and Valancourt was so charmed with all around, and with the conversation of his companions, that he seemed to have forgotten he had any further to go. Having concluded their simple repast, they gave a long farewell look to the scene, and again began to ascend. St. Aubert rejoiced when he reached the carriage, which Emily entered with him; but Valancourt, willing to take a more extensive view of the enchanting country, into which they were about to descend, than he could do from a carriage, loosened his dogs, and once more bounded with them along the banks of the road. He often quitted it for points that promised a wider prospect, and the slow pace, at which the mules travelled, allowed him to overtake them with ease. Whenever a scene of uncommon magnificence appeared, he hastened to inform St. Aubert, who, though he was too much tired to walk himself, sometimes made the chaise wait, while Emily went to the neighbouring cliff.

It was evening when they descended the lower alps, that bind Rousillon, and form a majestic barrier round that charming country, leaving it open only on the east to the Mediterranean. The gay tints of cultivation once more beautified the landscape; for the lowlands were coloured with the richest hues, which a luxuriant climate, and an industrious people can awaken into life. Groves of orange and lemon perfumed the air, their ripe fruit glowing among the foliage; while, sloping to the plains, extensive vineyards spread their treasures. Beyond these, woods and pastures, and mingled towns and hamlets stretched

*THOMSON.

towards the sea, on whose bright surface gleamed many a distant sail; while, over the whole scene, was diffused the purple glow of evening. This landscape with the surrounding alps did, indeed, present a perfect picture of the lovely and the sublime, of "beauty sleeping in the lap of horror."

The travellers, having reached the plains, proceeded, between hedges of flowering myrtle and pomegranate, to the town of Arles, where they proposed to rest for the night. They met with simple, but neat accommodation, and would have passed a happy evening, after the toils and the delights of this day, had not the approaching separation thrown a gloom over their spirits. It was St. Aubert's plan to proceed, on the morrow, to the borders of the Mediterranean, and travel along its shores into Languedoc; and Valancourt, since he was now nearly recovered, and had no longer a pretence for continuing with his new friends, resolved to leave them here. St. Aubert, who was much pleased with him, invited him to go further, but did not repeat the invitation, and Valancourt had resolution enough to forego the temptation of accepting it, that he might prove himself not unworthy of the favour. On the following morning, therefore, they were to part, St. Aubert to pursue his way to Languedoc, and Valancourt to explore new scenes among the mountains, on his return home. During this evening he was often silent and thoughtful; St. Aubert's manner towards him was affectionate, though grave, and Emily was serious, though she made frequent efforts to appear cheerful. After one of the most melancholy evenings they had yet passed together, they separated for the night.

CHAPTER VI

> I care not, Fortune! what you me deny;
> You cannot rob me of free nature's grace;
> You cannot shut the windows of the sky,
> Through which Aurora shews her brightening face;
> You cannot bar my constant feet to trace
> The woods and lawns, by living stream, at eve:
> Let health my nerves and finer fibres brace,
> And I their toys to the great children leave:
> Of fancy, reason, virtue, nought can me bereave.
> THOMSON

IN the morning, Valancourt breakfasted with St. Aubert and Emily, neither of whom seemed much refreshed by sleep. The languor of illness still hung over St. Aubert, and to Emily's fears his disorder appeared to

be increasing fast upon him. She watched his looks with anxious affection, and their expression was always faithfully reflected in her own.

At the commencement of their acquaintance, Valancourt had made
known his name and family. St. Aubert was not a stranger to either, for
the family estates, which were now in the possession of an elder brother
of Valancourt, were little more than twenty miles distant from La
Vallée, and he had sometimes met the elder Valancourt on visits in the
neighbourhood. This knowledge had made him more willingly receive
his present companion; for, though his countenance and manners
would have won him the acquaintance of St. Aubert, who was very apt
to trust to the intelligence of his own eyes, with respect to countenances, he would not have accepted these, as sufficient introductions
to that of his daughter.

The breakfast was almost as silent as the supper of the preceding
night; but their musing was at length interrupted by the sound of the
carriage-wheels, which were to bear away St. Aubert and Emily.
Valancourt started from his chair, and went to the window; it was
indeed the carriage, and he returned to his seat without speaking. The
moment was now come when they must part. St. Aubert told
Valancourt, that he hoped he would never pass La Vallée without
favouring him with a visit; and Valancourt, eagerly thanking him,
assured him that he never would; as he said which he looked timidly at
Emily, who tried to smile away the seriousness of her spirits. They
passed a few minutes in interesting conversation, and St. Aubert then
led the way to the carriage, Emily and Valancourt following in silence.
The latter lingered at the door several minutes after they were seated,
and none of the party seemed to have courage enough to say—
Farewell. At length, St. Aubert pronounced the melancholy word,
which Emily passed to Valancourt, who returned it, with a dejected
smile, and the carriage drove on.

The travellers remained, for some time, in a state of tranquil pen-
siveness, which is not unpleasing. St. Aubert interrupted it by observing, "This is a very promising young man; it is many years since I have
been so much pleased with any person, on so short an acquaintance.
He brings back to my memory the days of my youth, when every scene
was new and delightful!" St. Aubert sighed, and sunk again into a
reverie; and, as Emily looked back upon the road they had passed,
Valancourt was seen, at the door of the little inn, following them with
his eyes. He perceived her, and waved his hand; and she returned the
adieu, till the winding road shut her from his sight.

"I remember when I was about his age," resumed St. Aubert, "and I
thought, and felt exactly as he does. The world was opening upon me
then, now—it is closing."

"My dear sir, do not think so gloomily," said Emily in a trembling voice, "I hope you have many, many years to live—for your own sake—for *my* sake."

"Ah, my Emily!" replied St. Aubert, "for thy sake! Well—I hope it is so." He wiped away a tear, that was stealing down his cheek, threw a smile upon his countenance, and said in a cheering voice, "There is something in the ardour and ingenuousness of youth, which is particularly pleasing to the contemplation of an old man, if his feelings have not been entirely corroded by the world. It is cheering and reviving, like the view of spring to a sick person; his mind catches somewhat of the spirit of the season, and his eyes are lighted up with a transient sunshine. Valancourt is this spring to me."

Emily, who pressed her father's hand affectionately, had never before listened with so much pleasure to the praises he bestowed; no, not even when he had bestowed them on herself.

They travelled on, among vineyards, woods, and pastures, delighted with the romantic beauty of the landscape, which was bounded, on one side, by the grandeur of the Pyrenées, and, on the other, by the ocean; and, soon after noon, they reached the town of Colioure, situated on the Mediterranean. Here they dined, and rested till towards the cool of day, when they pursued their way along the shores—those enchanting shores!—which extend to Languedoc. Emily gazed with enthusiasm on the vastness of the sea, its surface varying, as the lights and shadows fell, and on its woody banks, mellowed with autumnal tints.

St. Aubert was impatient to reach Perpignan, where he expected letters from M. Quesnel; and it was the expectation of these letters, that had induced him to leave Colioure, for his feeble frame had required immediate rest. After travelling a few miles, he fell asleep; and Emily, who had put two or three books into the carriage, on leaving La Vallée, had now the leisure for looking into them. She sought for one, in which Valancourt had been reading the day before, and hoped for the pleasure of re-tracing a page, over which the eyes of a beloved friend had lately passed, of dwelling on the passages, which he had admired, and of permitting them to speak to her in the language of his own mind, and to bring himself to her presence. On searching for the book, she could find it no where, but in its stead perceived a volume of Petrarch's poems, that had belonged to Valancourt, whose name was written in it, and from which he had frequently read passages to her, with all the pathetic expression, that characterized the feelings of the author. She hesitated in believing, what would have been sufficiently apparent to almost any other person, that he had purposely left this book, instead of the one she had lost, and that love had prompted the exchange; but, having opened it with impatient pleasure, and observed the lines of his pencil drawn along the various passages he had read aloud, and under others more descriptive of delicate tenderness than he had dared to trust his voice with, the conviction came, at length, to her mind. For some moments she was conscious only of being beloved; then, a recollection of all the variations of tone and countenance, with which he had recited these sonnets, and of the soul, which spoke in their expression, pressed to her memory, and she wept over the memorial of his affection.

They arrived at Perpignan soon after sunset, where St. Aubert found, as he had expected, letters from M. Quesnel, the contents of which so evidently and grievously affected him, that Emily was alarmed, and pressed him, as far as her delicacy would permit, to disclose the occasion of his concern; but he answered her only by tears, and immediately began to talk on other topics. Emily, though she forbore to press the one most interesting to her, was greatly affected by her father's manner, and passed a night of sleepless solicitude.

In the morning they pursued their journey along the coast towards Leucate, another town on the Mediterranean, situated on the borders of Languedoc and Rousillon. On the way, Emily renewed the subject of the preceding night, and appeared so deeply affected by St. Aubert's silence and dejection, that he relaxed from his reserve. "I was unwilling, my dear Emily," said he, "to throw a cloud over the pleasure you receive from these scenes, and meant, therefore, to conceal, for the present, some circumstances, with which, however, you must at length have been made acquainted. But your anxiety has defeated my purpose; you suffer as much from this, perhaps, as you will do from a knowledge of the facts I have to relate. M. Quesnel's visit proved an unhappy one to me; he came to tell me a part of the news he has now confirmed. You may have heard me mention a M. Motteville, of Paris, but you did not know that the chief of my personal property was invested in his hands. I had great confidence in him, and I am yet willing to believe, that he is not wholly unworthy of my esteem. A variety of circumstances have concurred to ruin him, and—I am ruined with him."

St. Aubert paused, to conceal his emotion.

"The letters I have just received from M. Quesnel," resumed he, struggling to speak with firmness, "enclosed others from Motteville, which confirmed all I dreaded."

"Must we then quit La Vallée?" said Emily, after a long pause of silence. "That is yet uncertain," replied St. Aubert, "it will depend upon the compromise Motteville is able to make with his creditors. My income, you know, was never large, and now it will be reduced to little indeed! It is for you, Emily, for you, my child, that I am most afflicted."

His last words faltered; Emily smiled tenderly upon him through her tears, and then, endeavouring to overcome her emotion, "My dear father," said she, "do not grieve for me, or for yourself; we may yet be happy;—if La Vallée remains for us, we must be happy. We will retain only one servant, and you shall scarcely perceive the change in your income. Be comforted, my dear sir; we shall not feel the want of those luxuries, which others value so highly, since we never had a taste for them; and poverty cannot deprive us of many consolations. It cannot rob us of the affection we have for each other, or degrade us in our own opinion, or in that of any person, whose opinion we ought to value."

St. Aubert concealed his face with his handkerchief, and was unable to speak; but Emily continued to urge to her father the truths, which himself had impressed upon her mind.

"Besides, my dear sir, poverty cannot deprive us of intellectual delights. It cannot deprive you of the comfort of affording me examples of fortitude and benevolence; nor me of the delight of consoling a beloved parent. It cannot deaden our taste for the grand, and the beautiful, or deny us the means of indulging it; for the scenes of nature— those sublime spectacles, so infinitely superior to all artificial luxuries! are open for the enjoyment of the poor, as well as of the rich. Of what, then, have we to complain, so long as we are not in want of necessaries? Pleasures, such as wealth cannot buy, will still be ours. We retain, then, the sublime luxuries of nature, and lose only the frivolous ones of art."

St. Aubert could not reply: he caught Emily to his bosom, their tears flowed together, but—they were not tears of sorrow. After this language of the heart, all other would have been feeble, and they remained silent for some time. Then, St. Aubert conversed as before; for, if his mind had not recovered its natural tranquillity, it at least assumed the appearance of it.

They reached the romantic town of Leucate early in the day, but St. Aubert was weary, and they determined to pass the night there. In the evening, he exerted himself so far as to walk with his daughter to view the environs that overlook the lake of Leucate, the Mediterranean, part of Rousillon, with the Pyrenées, and a wide extent of the luxuriant province of Languedoc, now blushing with the ripened vintage, which the peasants were beginning to gather. St. Aubert and Emily saw the busy groups, caught the joyous song, that was wafted on the breeze, and anticipated, with apparent pleasure, their next day's journey over this gay region. He designed, however, still to wind along the sea-shore. To return home immediately was partly his wish, but from this he was withheld by a desire to lengthen the pleasure, which the journey gave his daughter, and to try the effect of the sea air on his own disorder.

On the following day, therefore, they recommenced their journey through Languedoc, winding the shores of the Mediterranean; the Pyrenées still forming the magnificent back-ground of their prospects, while on their right was the ocean, and, on their left, wide extended plains melting into the blue horizon. St. Aubert was pleased, and conversed much with Emily, yet his cheerfulness was sometimes artificial, and sometimes a shade of melancholy would steal upon his countenance, and betray him. This was soon chased away by Emily's smile; who smiled, however, with an aching heart, for she saw that his misfortunes preyed upon his mind, and upon his enfeebled frame.

It was evening when they reached a small village of Upper Languedoc, where they meant to pass the night, but the place could not afford them beds; for here, too, it was the time of the vintage, and they were obliged to proceed to the next post. The languor of illness and of fatigue, which returned upon St. Aubert, required immediate repose, and the evening was now far advanced; but from necessity there was no appeal, and he ordered Michael to proceed.

The rich plains of Languedoc, which exhibited all the glories of the vintage, with the gaieties of a French festival, no longer awakened St. Aubert to pleasure, whose condition formed a mournful contrast to the hilarity and youthful beauty which surrounded him. As his languid eyes moved over the scene, he considered, that they would soon, perhaps, be closed for ever on this world. "Those distant and sublime mountains," said he secretly, as he gazed on a chain of the Pyrenées that stretched towards the west, "these luxuriant plains, this blue vault, the cheerful light of day, will be shut from my eyes! The song of the peasant, the cheering voice of man—will no longer sound for me!"

The intelligent eyes of Emily seemed to read what passed in the mind of her father, and she fixed them on his face, with an expression of such tender pity, as recalled his thoughts from every desultory object of regret, and he remembered only, that he must leave his daughter without protection. This reflection changed regret to agony; he sighed deeply, and remained silent, while she seemed to understand that sigh, for she pressed his hand affectionately, and then turned to the window to conceal her tears. The sun now threw a last yellow gleam on the waves of the Mediterranean, and the gloom of twilight spread fast over the scene, till only a melancholy ray appeared on the western horizon, marking the point where the sun had set amid the vapours of an autumnal evening. A cool breeze now came from the shore, and Emily let down the glass; but the air, which was refreshing to health, was as chilling to sickness, and St. Aubert desired, that the window might be drawn up. Increasing illness made him now more anxious than ever to finish the day's journey, and he stopped the muleteer to enquire how far they had yet to go to the next post. He replied, "Nine miles." "I feel I am unable to proceed much further," said St. Aubert; "enquire, as you go, if there is any house on the road that would accommodate us for the night." He sunk back in the carriage, and Michael, cracking his whip in the air, set off, and continued on the full gallop, till St. Aubert, almost fainting, called to him to stop. Emily looked anxiously from the window, and saw a peasant walking at some little distance on the road, for whom they waited, till he came up, when he was asked, if there was any house in the neighbourhood that accommodated travellers. He replied, that he knew of none. "There is a chateau, indeed, among those woods on the right," added he, "but I believe it receives nobody, and I cannot show you the way, for I am almost a stranger here." St. Aubert was going to ask him some further question concerning the chateau, but the man abruptly passed on. After some consideration, he ordered Michael to proceed slowly to the woods. Every moment now deepened the twilight, and increased the difficulty of finding the road. Another peasant soon after passed. "Which is the way to the chateau in the woods?" cried Michael.

"The chateau in the woods!" exclaimed the peasant—"Do you mean that with the turret, yonder?"

"I don't know as for the turret, as you call it," said Michael, "I mean that white piece of a building, that we see at a distance there, among the trees."

"Yes, that is the turret; why, who are you, that you are going thither?" said the man with surprise.

St. Aubert, on hearing this odd question, and observing the peculiar tone in which it was delivered, looked out from the carriage. "We are travellers," said he, "who are in search of a house of accommodation for the night; is there any hereabout?"

"None, Monsieur, unless you have a mind to try your luck yonder," replied the peasant, pointing to the woods, "but I would not advise you to go there."

"To whom does the chateau belong?"

"I scarcely know myself, Monsieur."

"It is uninhabited, then?" "No, not uninhabited; the steward and housekeeper are there, I believe."

On hearing this, St. Aubert determined to proceed to the chateau, and risque the refusal of being accommodated for the night; he therefore desired the countryman would shew Michael the way, and bade him expect reward for his trouble. The man was for a moment silent, and then said, that he was going on other business, but that the road could not be missed, if they went up an avenue to the right, to which he pointed. St. Aubert was going to speak, but the peasant wished him good night, and walked on.

The carriage now moved towards the avenue, which was guarded by a gate, and Michael having dismounted to open it, they entered between rows of ancient oak and chesnut, whose intermingled branches formed a lofty arch above. There was something so gloomy and desolate in the appearance of this avenue, and its lonely silence, that Emily almost shuddered as she passed along; and, recollecting the manner in which the peasant had mentioned the chateau, she gave a mysterious meaning to his words, such as she had not suspected when he uttered them. These apprehensions, however, she tried to check, considering that they were probably the effect of a melancholy imagination, which her father's situation, and a consideration of her own circumstances, had made sensible to every impression.

They passed slowly on, for they were now almost in darkness, which, together with the unevenness of the ground, and the frequent roots of old trees, that shot up above the soil, made it necessary to proceed with caution. On a sudden Michael stopped the carriage; and, as St. Aubert looked from the window to enquire the cause, he perceived a figure at some distance moving up the avenue. The dusk would not permit him to distinguish what it was, but he bade Michael go on.

"This seems a strange wild place," said Michael; "there is no house hereabout, don't your honour think we had better turn back?"

"Go a little farther, and if we see no house then, we will return to the road," replied St. Aubert.

Michael proceeded with reluctance, and the extreme slowness of his pace made St. Aubert look again from the window to hasten him, when again he saw the same figure. He was somewhat startled: probably the gloominess of the spot made him more liable to alarm than usual; however this might be, he now stopped Michael, and bade him call to the person in the avenue.

"Please your honour, he may be a robber," said Michael. "It does not please me," replied St. Aubert, who could not forbear smiling at the simplicity of his phrase, "and we will, therefore, return to the road, for I see no probability of meeting here with what we seek."

Michael turned about immediately, and was retracing his way with alacrity, when a voice was heard from among the trees on the left. It was not the voice of command, or distress, but a deep hollow tone, which seemed to be scarcely human. The man whipped his mules till they went as fast as possible, regardless of the darkness, the broken ground, and the necks of the whole party, nor once stopped till he reached the gate, which opened from the avenue into the high-road, where he went into a more moderate pace.

"I am very ill," said St. Aubert, taking his daughter's hand. "You are worse, then, sir!" said Emily, extremely alarmed by his manner, "you

are worse, and here is no assistance. Good God! what is to be done!"
He leaned his head on her shoulder, while she endeavoured to support
him with her arm, and Michael was again ordered to stop. When the
rattling of the wheels had ceased, music was heard on the air; it was to
Emily the voice of Hope. "Oh! we are near some human habitation!"
said she, "help may soon be had."

She listened anxiously; the sounds were distant, and seemed to come
from a remote part of the woods that bordered the road; and, as she
looked towards the spot whence they issued, she perceived in the faint
moon-light something like a chateau. It was difficult, however, to reach
this; St. Aubert was now too ill to bear the motion of the carriage;
Michael could not quit his mules; and Emily, who still supported her
father, feared to leave him, and also feared to venture alone to such a
distance, she knew not whither, or to whom. Something, however, it
was necessary to determine upon immediately; St. Aubert, therefore,
told Michael to proceed slowly; but they had not gone far, when he
fainted, and the carriage was again stopped. He lay quite senseless. —
"My dear, dear father!" cried Emily in great agony, who began to fear
that he was dying, "speak, if it is only one word to let me hear the sound
of your voice!" But no voice spoke in reply. In the agony of terror she
bade Michael bring water from the rivulet, that flowed along the road;
and, having received some in the man's hat, with trembling hands she
sprinkled it over her father's face, which, as the moon's rays now fell
upon it, seemed to bear the impression of death. Every emotion of selfish fear now gave way to a stronger influence, and, committing St.
Aubert to the care of Michael, who refused to go far from his mules, she
stepped from the carriage in search of the chateau she had seen at a distance. It was a still moon-light night, and the music, which yet sounded
on the air, directed her steps from the high road, up a shadowy lane,
that led to the woods. Her mind was for some time so entirely occupied
by anxiety and terror for her father, that she felt none for herself, till the
deepening gloom of the overhanging foliage, which now wholly
excluded the moon-light, and the wildness of the place, recalled her to
a sense of her adventurous situation. The music had ceased, and she
had no guide but chance. For a moment she paused in terrified perplexity, till a sense of her father's condition again overcoming every
consideration for herself, she proceeded. The lane terminated in the
woods, but she looked round in vain for a house, or a human being,
and as vainly listened for a sound to guide her. She hurried on, however, not knowing whither, avoiding the recesses of the woods, and
endeavouring to keep along their margin, till a rude kind of avenue,
which opened upon a moon-light spot, arrested her attention. The
wildness of this avenue brought to her recollection the one leading to

the turreted chateau, and she was inclined to believe, that this was a part of the same domain, and probably led to the same point. While she hesitated, whether to follow it or not, a sound of many voices in loud merriment burst upon her ear. It seemed not the laugh of cheerfulness, but of riot, and she stood appalled. While she paused, she heard a distant voice, calling from the way she had come, and not doubting but it was that of Michael, her first impulse was to hasten back; but a second thought changed her purpose; she believed that nothing less than the last extremity could have prevailed with Michael to quit his mules, and fearing that her father was now dying, she rushed forward, with a feeble hope of obtaining assistance from the people in the woods. Her heart beat with fearful expectation, as she drew near the spot whence the voices issued, and she often startled when her steps disturbed the fallen leaves. The sounds led her towards the moon-light glade she had before noticed; at a little distance from which she stopped, and saw, between the boles of the trees, a small circular level of green turf, surrounded by the woods, on which appeared a group of figures. On drawing nearer, she distinguished these, by their dress, to be peasants, and perceived several cottages scattered round the edge of the woods, which waved loftily over this spot. While she gazed, and endeavoured to overcome the apprehensions that withheld her steps, several peasant girls came out of a cottage; music instantly struck up, and the dance began. It was the joyous music of the vintage! the same she had before heard upon the air. Her heart, occupied with terror for her father, could not feel the contrast, which this gay scene offered to her own distress; she stepped hastily forward towards a group of elder peasants, who were seated at the door of a cottage, and, having explained her situation, entreated their assistance. Several of them rose with alacrity, and, offering any service in their power, followed Emily, who seemed to move on the wind, as fast as they could towards the road.

When she reached the carriage she found St. Aubert restored to animation. On the recovery of his senses, having heard from Michael whither his daughter was gone, anxiety for her overcame every regard for himself, and he had sent him in search of her. He was, however, still languid, and, perceiving himself unable to travel much farther, he renewed his enquiries for an inn, and concerning the chateau in the woods. "The chateau cannot accommodate you, sir," said a venerable peasant who had followed Emily from the woods, "it is scarcely inhabited; but, if you will do me the honour to visit my cottage, you shall be welcome to the best bed it affords."

St. Aubert was himself a Frenchman; he therefore was not surprised at French courtesy; but, ill as he was, he felt the value of the offer enhanced by the manner which accompanied it. He had too much delicacy to apologize, or to appear to hesitate about availing himself of the peasant's hospitality, but immediately accepted it with the same frankness with which it was offered.

The carriage again moved slowly on; Michael following the peasants up the lane, which Emily had just quitted, till they came to the moon-light glade. St. Aubert's spirits were so far restored by the courtesy of his host, and the near prospect of repose, that he looked with a sweet complacency upon the moon-light scene, surrounded by the shadowy woods, through which, here and there, an opening admitted the streaming splendour, discovering a cottage, or a sparkling rivulet. He listened, with no painful emotion, to the merry notes of the guitar and tamborine; and, though tears came to his eyes, when he saw the *debonnaire* dance of the peasants, they were not merely tears of mournful regret. With Emily it was otherwise; immediate terror for her father had now subsided into a gentle melancholy, which every note of joy, by awakening comparison, served to heighten.

The dance ceased on the approach of the carriage, which was a phenomenon in these sequestered woods, and the peasantry flocked round it with eager curiosity. On learning that it brought a sick stranger, several girls ran across the turf, and returned with wine and baskets of grapes, which they presented to the travellers, each with kind contention pressing for a preference. At length, the carriage stopped at a neat cottage, and his venerable conductor, having assisted St. Aubert to alight, led him and Emily to a small inner room, illuminated only by moon-beams, which the open casement admitted. St. Aubert, rejoicing in rest, seated himself in an arm-chair, and his senses were refreshed by the cool and balmy air, that lightly waved the embowering honeysuckles, and wafted their sweet breath into the apartment. His host, who was called La Voisin, quitted the room, but soon returned with fruits, cream, and all the pastoral luxury his cottage afforded; having set down which, with a smile of unfeigned welcome, he retired behind the chair of his guest. St. Aubert insisted on his taking a seat at the table, and, when the fruit had allayed the fever of his palate, and he found himself somewhat revived, he began to converse with his host, who communicated several particulars concerning himself and his family, which were interesting, because they were spoken from the heart, and delineated a picture of the sweet courtesies of family kindness. Emily sat by her father, holding his hand, and, while she listened to the old man, her heart swelled with the affectionate sympathy he described, and her tears fell to the mournful consideration, that death would probably soon deprive her of the dearest blessing she then possessed. The soft moon-light of an autumnal evening, and the distant music, which now sounded a plaintive strain, aided the melancholy of her mind. The old man continued to talk of his family, and St. Aubert remained silent. "I have only one daughter living," said La Voisin, "but she is happily married, and is every thing to me. When I lost my wife," he added with a sigh, "I came to live with Agnes, and her family; she has several children, who are all dancing on the green yonder, as merry as grasshoppers—and long may they be so! I hope to die among them, monsieur. I am old now, and cannot expect to live long, but there is some comfort in dying surrounded by one's children."

"My good friend," said St. Aubert, while his voice trembled, "I hope you will long live surrounded by them."

"Ah, sir! at my age I must not expect that!" replied the old man, and he paused: "I can scarcely wish it," he resumed, "for I trust that whenever I die I shall go to heaven, where my poor wife is gone before me. I can sometimes almost fancy I see her of a still moon-light night, walking among these shades she loved so well. Do you believe, monsieur, that we shall be permitted to revisit the earth, after we have quitted the body?"

Emily could no longer stifle the anguish of her heart; her tears fell fast upon her father's hand, which she yet held. He made an effort to speak, and at length said in a low voice, "I hope we shall be permitted to look down on those we have left on the earth, but I can only hope it. Futurity is much veiled from our eyes, and faith and hope are our only guides concerning it. We are not enjoined to believe, that disembodied spirits watch over the friends they have loved, but we may innocently hope it. It is a hope which I will never resign," continued he, while he wiped the tears from his daughter's eyes, "it will sweeten the bitter moments of death!" Tears fell slowly on his cheeks; La Voisin wept too, and there was a pause of silence. Then, La Voisin, renewing the subject, said, "But you believe, sir, that we shall meet in another world the relations we have loved in this; I must believe this." "Then do believe it," replied St. Aubert, "severe, indeed, would be the pangs of separation, if we believed it to be eternal. Look up, my dear Emily, we shall meet again!" He lifted his eyes towards heaven, and a gleam of moon-light, which fell upon his countenance, discovered peace and resignation, stealing on the lines of sorrow.

La Voisin felt that he had pursued the subject too far, and he dropped it, saying, "We are in darkness, I forgot to bring a light."

"No," said St. Aubert, "this is a light I love. Sit down, my good friend. Emily, my love, I find myself better than I have been all day; this air refreshes me. I can enjoy this tranquil hour, and that music, which floats so sweetly at a distance. Let me see you smile. Who touches that guitar so tastefully? are there two instruments, or is it an echo I hear?"

"It is an echo, monsieur, I fancy. That guitar is often heard at night, when all is still, but nobody knows who touches it, and it is sometimes accompanied by a voice so sweet, and so sad, one would almost think the woods were haunted." "They certainly are haunted," said St. Aubert with a smile, "but I believe it is by mortals." "I have sometimes heard it at midnight, when I could not sleep," rejoined La Voisin, not seeming to notice this remark, "almost under my window, and I never heard any music like it. It has often made me think of my poor wife till I cried. I have sometimes got up to the window to look if I could see anybody, but as soon as I opened the casement all was hushed, and nobody to be seen; and I have listened, and listened till I have been so timorous, that even the trembling of the leaves in the breeze has made me start. They say it often comes to warn people of their death, but I have heard it these many years, and outlived the warning."

Emily, though she smiled at the mention of this ridiculous superstition, could not, in the present tone of her spirits, wholly resist its contagion.

"Well, but, my good friend," said St. Aubert, "has nobody had courage to follow the sounds? If they had, they would probably have discovered who is the musician." "Yes, sir, they have followed them some way into the woods, but the music has still retreated, and seemed as distant as ever, and the people have at last been afraid of being led into harm, and would go no further. It is very seldom that I have heard these sounds so early in the evening. They usually come about midnight, when that bright planet, which is rising above the turret yonder, sets below the woods on the left."

"What turret?" asked St. Aubert with quickness, "I see none."

"Your pardon, monsieur, you do see one indeed, for the moon shines full upon it;—up the avenue yonder, a long way off; the chateau it belongs to is hid among the trees."

"Yes, my dear sir," said Emily, pointing, "don't you see something glitter above the dark woods? It is a fane, I fancy, which the rays fall upon."

"O yes, I see what you mean; and who does the chateau belong to?"

"The Marquis de Villeroi was its owner," replied La Voisin, emphatically.

"Ah!" said St. Aubert, with a deep sigh, "are we then so near Le-Blanc!" He appeared much agitated.

"It used to be the Marquis's favourite residence," resumed La Voisin, "but he took a dislike to the place, and has not been there for many years. We have heard lately that he is dead, and that it is fallen into other hands." St. Aubert, who had sat in deep musing, was roused by the last words. "Dead!" he exclaimed, "Good God! when did he die?"

"He is reported to have died about five weeks since," replied La Voisin. "Did you know the Marquis, sir?"

"This is very extraordinary!" said St. Aubert without attending to the question. "Why is it so, my dear sir?" said Emily, in a voice of timid curiosity. He made no reply, but sunk again into a reverie; and in a few moments, when he seemed to have recovered himself, asked who had succeeded to the estates. "I have forgot his title, monsieur," said La Voisin; "but my lord resides at Paris chiefly; I hear no talk of his coming hither."

"The chateau is shut up then, still?"

"Why, little better, sir; the old housekeeper, and her husband the steward, have the care of it, but they live generally in a cottage hard by."

"The chateau is spacious, I suppose," said Emily, "and must be desolate for the residence of only two persons."

"Desolate enough, mademoiselle," replied La Voisin, "I would not pass one night in the chateau, for the value of the whole domain."

"What is that?" said St. Aubert, roused again from thoughtfulness. As his host repeated his last sentence, a groan escaped from St. Aubert, and then, as if anxious to prevent it from being noticed, he hastily asked La Voisin how long he had lived in this neighbourhood. "Almost from my childhood, sir," replied his host.

"You remember the late marchioness, then?" said St. Aubert in an altered voice.

"Ah, monsieur!—that I do well. There are many besides me who remember her."

"Yes—" said St. Aubert, "and I am one of those."

"Alas, sir! you remember, then, a most beautiful and excellent lady. She deserved a better fate."

Tears stood in St. Aubert's eyes; "Enough," said he, in a voice almost stifled by the violence of his emotions,—"it is enough, my friend."

Emily, though extremely surprised by her father's manner, forbore to express her feelings by any question. La Voisin began to apologize, but St. Aubert interrupted him; "Apology is quite unnecessary," said he, "let us change the topic. You was speaking of the music we just now heard."

"I was, monsieur—but hark!—it comes again; listen to that voice!" They were all silent;

> At last a soft and solemn-breathing sound
> Rose, like a stream of rich distilled perfumes,
> And stole upon the air, that even Silence
> Was took ere she was 'ware, and wished she might
> Deny her nature, and be never more
> Still, to be so displaced.*

*MILTON.

In a few moments the voice died into air, and the instrument, which had been heard before, sounded in low symphony. St. Aubert now observed, that it produced a tone much more full and melodious than that of a guitar, and still more melancholy and soft than the lute. They continued to listen, but the sounds returned no more. "This is strange!" said St. Aubert, at length interrupting the silence. "Very strange!" said Emily. "It is so," rejoined La Voisin, and they were again silent.

After a long pause, "It is now about eighteen years since I first heard that music," said La Voisin; "I remember it was on a fine summer's night, much like this, but later, that I was walking in the woods, and alone. I remember, too, that my spirits were very low, for one of my boys was ill, and we feared we should lose him. I had been watching at his bed-side all the evening while his mother slept; for she had sat up with him the night before. I had been watching, and went out for a little fresh air, the day had been very sultry. As I walked under the shades and mused, I heard music at a distance, and thought it was Claude playing upon his flute, as he often did of a fine evening, at the cottage door. But, when I came to a place where the trees opened, (I shall never forget it!) and stood looking up at the north-lights, which shot up the heaven to a great height, I heard all of a sudden such sounds!—they came so as I cannot describe. It was like the music of angels, and I looked up again almost expecting to see them in the sky. When I came home, I told what I had heard, but they laughed at me, and said it must be some of the shepherds playing on their pipes, and I could not persuade them to the contrary. A few nights after, however, my wife herself heard the same sounds, and was as much surprised as I was, and father Denis frightened her sadly by saying, that it was music come to warn her of her child's death, and that music often came to houses where there was a dying person."

Emily, on hearing this, shrunk with a superstitious dread entirely new to her, and could scarcely conceal her agitation from St. Aubert.

"But the boy lived, monsieur, in spite of father Denis."

"Father Denis!" said St. Aubert, who had listened to "narrative old age" with patient attention, "are we near a convent, then?"

"Yes, sir; the convent of St. Clair stands at no great distance, on the sea shore yonder."

"Ah!" said St. Aubert, as if struck with some sudden remembrance, "the convent of St. Clair!" Emily observed the clouds of grief, mingled with a faint expression of horror, gathering on his brow; his countenance became fixed, and, touched as it now was by the silver whiteness of the moon-light, he resembled one of those marble statues of a monument, which seem to bend, in hopeless sorrow, over the ashes of the dead, shewn

by the blunted light
That the dim moon through painted casements lends.[*]

"But, my dear sir," said Emily, anxious to dissipate his thoughts, "you forget that repose is necessary to you. If our kind host will give me leave, I will prepare your bed, for I know how you like it to be made." St. Aubert, recollecting himself, and smiling affectionately, desired she would not add to her fatigue by that attention; and La Voisin, whose consideration for his guest had been suspended by the interests which his own narrative had recalled, now started from his seat, and, apologizing for not having called Agnes from the green, hurried out of the room.

In a few moments he returned with his daughter, a young woman of pleasing countenance, and Emily learned from her, what she had not before suspected, that, for their accommodation, it was necessary part of La Voisin's family should leave their beds; she lamented this circumstance, but Agnes, by her reply, fully proved that she inherited, at least, a share of her father's courteous hospitality. It was settled, that some of her children and Michael should sleep in the neighbouring cottage.

"If I am better, to-morrow, my dear," said St. Aubert when Emily returned to him, "I mean to set out at an early hour, that we may rest, during the heat of the day, and will travel towards home. In the present state of my health and spirits I cannot look on a longer journey with pleasure, and I am also very anxious to reach La Vallée." Emily, though she also desired to return, was grieved at her father's sudden wish to do so, which she thought indicated a greater degree of indisposition than he would acknowledge. St. Aubert now retired to rest, and Emily to her little chamber, but not to immediate repose. Her thoughts returned to the late conversation, concerning the state of departed spirits; a subject, at this time, particularly affecting to her, when she had every reason to believe that her dear father would ere long be numbered with them. She leaned pensively on the little open casement, and in deep thought fixed her eyes on the heaven, whose blue unclouded concave was studded thick with stars, the worlds, perhaps, of spirits, unsphered of mortal mould. As her eyes wandered along the boundless æther, her thoughts rose, as before, towards the sublimity of the Deity, and to the contemplation of futurity. No busy note of this world interrupted the course of her mind; the merry dance had ceased, and every cottager had retired to his home. The still air seemed scarcely to breathe upon the woods, and, now and then, the distant sound of a solitary sheep-bell, or of a closing casement, was all that broke on silence. At length,

---

[*]THE EMIGRANTS.

even this hint of human being was heard no more. Elevated and enwrapt, while her eyes were often wet with tears of sublime devotion and solemn awe, she continued at the casement, till the gloom of midnight hung over the earth, and the planet, which La Voisin had pointed out, sunk below the woods. She then recollected what he had said concerning this planet, and the mysterious music; and, as she lingered at the window, half hoping and half fearing that it would return, her mind was led to the remembrance of the extreme emotion her father had shewn on mention of the Marquis La Villeroi's death, and of the fate of the Marchioness, and she felt strongly interested concerning the remote cause of this emotion. Her surprise and curiosity were indeed the greater, because she did not recollect ever to have heard him mention the name of Villeroi.

No music, however, stole on the silence of the night, and Emily, perceiving the lateness of the hour, returned to a scene of fatigue, remembered that she was to rise early in the morning, and withdrew from the window to repose.

CHAPTER VII

> Let those deplore their doom,
> Whose hope still grovels in this dark sojourn.
> But lofty souls can look beyond the tomb,
> Can smile at fate, and wonder how they mourn.
> Shall Spring to these sad scenes no more return?
> Is yonder wave the sun's eternal bed?—
> Soon shall the orient with new lustre burn,
> And Spring shall soon her vital influence shed,
> Again attune the grove, again adorn the mead!
>   BEATTIE

EMILY, called, as she had requested, at an early hour, awoke, little refreshed by sleep, for uneasy dreams had pursued her, and marred the kindest blessing of the unhappy. But, when she opened her casement, looked out upon the woods, bright with the morning sun, and inspired the pure air, her mind was soothed. The scene was filled with that cheering freshness, which seems to breathe the very spirit of health, and she heard only sweet and *picturesque* sounds, if such an expression may be allowed—the matin-bell of a distant convent, the faint murmur of the sea-waves, the song of birds, and the far-off low of cattle, which she saw coming slowly on between the trunks of trees. Struck with the circumstances of imagery around her, she indulged the pensive tranquillity which they inspired; and while she leaned on her window, waiting till St. Aubert should descend to breakfast, her ideas arranged themselves in the following lines:

THE FIRST HOUR OF MORNING

How sweet to wind the forest's tangled shade,
   When early twilight, from the eastern bound,
Dawns on the sleeping landscape in the glade,
   And fades as morning spreads her blush around!

When ev'ry infant flower, that wept in night,
   Lifts its chill head soft glowing with a tear,
Expands its tender blossom to the light,
   And gives its incense to the genial air.

How fresh the breeze that wafts the rich perfume,
   And swells the melody of waking birds;
The hum of bees, beneath the verdant gloom,
   And woodman's song, and low of distant herds!

Then, doubtful gleams the mountain's hoary head,
   Seen through the parting foliage from afar;
And, farther still, the ocean's misty bed,
   With flitting sails, that partial sun-beams share.

But, vain the sylvan shade—the breath of May,
   The voice of music floating on the gale,
And forms, that beam through morning's dewy veil,
If health no longer bid the heart be gay!
O balmy hour! 'tis thine her wealth to give,
Here spread her blush, and bid the parent live!

Emily now heard persons moving below in the cottage, and presently the voice of Michael, who was talking to his mules, as he led them forth from a hut adjoining. As she left her room, St. Aubert, who was now risen, met her at the door, apparently as little restored by sleep as herself. She led him down stairs to the little parlour, in which they had supped on the preceding night, where they found a neat breakfast set out, while the host and his daughter waited to bid them good morrow.

"I envy you this cottage, my good friends," said St. Aubert, as he met them, "it is so pleasant, so quiet, and so neat; and this air, that one breathes—if any thing could restore lost health, it would surely be this air."

La Voisin bowed gratefully, and replied, with the gallantry of a Frenchman, "Our cottage may be envied, sir, since you and Mademoiselle have honoured it with your presence." St. Aubert gave him a friendly smile for his compliment, and sat down to a table, spread with cream, fruit, new cheese, butter, and coffee. Emily, who had observed her father with attention and thought he looked very ill, endeavoured to persuade him to defer travelling till the afternoon; but he seemed very anxious to be at home, and his anxiety he expressed repeatedly, and with an earnestness that was unusual with him. He now said, he found himself as well as he had been of late, and that he could bear travelling better in the cool hour of the morning, than at any other time. But, while he was talking with his venerable host, and thanking him for his kind attentions, Emily observed his countenance change, and, before she could reach him, he fell back in his chair. In a few moments he recovered from the sudden faintness that had come over him, but felt so ill, that he perceived himself unable to set out, and, having remained a little while, struggling against the pressure of indisposition, he begged he might be helped up stairs to bed. This request renewed all the terror which Emily had suffered on the preceding evening; but, though scarcely able to support herself, under the sudden shock it gave her, she tried to conceal her apprehensions from St. Aubert, and gave her trembling arm to assist him to the door of his chamber.

When he was once more in bed, he desired that Emily, who was then weeping in her own room, might be called; and, as she came, he waved his hand for every other person to quit the apartment. When they were alone, he held out his hand to her, and fixed his eyes upon her countenance, with an expression so full of tenderness and grief, that all her fortitude forsook her, and she burst into an agony of tears. St. Aubert seemed struggling to acquire firmness, but was still unable to speak; he could only press her hand, and check the tears that stood trembling in his eyes. At length he commanded his voice, "My dear child," said he, trying to smile through his anguish, "my dear Emily!" — and paused again. He raised his eyes to heaven, as if in prayer, and then, in a firmer tone, and with a look, in which the tenderness of the father was dignified by the pious solemnity of the saint, he said, "My dear child, I would soften the painful truth I have to tell you, but I find myself quite unequal to the art. Alas! I would, at this moment, conceal it from you, but that it would be most cruel to deceive you. It cannot be long before we must part; let us talk of it, that our thoughts and our prayers may prepare us to bear it." His voice faltered, while Emily, still weeping, pressed his hand close to her heart, which swelled with a convulsive sigh, but she could not look up.

"Let me not waste these moments," said St. Aubert, recovering himself, "I have much to say. There is a circumstance of solemn consequence, which I have to mention, and a solemn promise to obtain from you; when this is done I shall be easier. You have observed, my dear, how anxious I am to reach home, but know not all my reasons for this. Listen to what I am going to say.—Yet stay—before I say more give me this promise, a promise made to your dying father!"—St. Aubert was interrupted; Emily, struck by his last words, as if for the first time, with a conviction of his immediate danger, raised her head; her tears stopped, and, gazing at him for a moment with an expression of unutterable anguish, a slight convulsion seized her, and she sunk senseless in her chair. St. Aubert's cries brought La Voisin and his daughter to the room, and they administered every means in their power to restore her, but, for a considerable time, without effect. When she recovered, St. Aubert was so exhausted by the scene he had witnessed, that it was many minutes before he had strength to speak; he was, however, somewhat revived by a cordial, which Emily gave him; and, being again alone with her, he exerted himself to tranquilize her spirits, and to offer her all the comfort of which her situation admitted. She threw herself into his arms, wept on his neck, and grief made her so insensible to all he said, that he ceased to offer the alleviations, which he himself could not, at this moment, feel, and mingled his silent tears with hers. Recalled, at length, to a sense of duty, she tried to spare her father from farther view of her suffering; and, quitting his embrace, dried her tears, and said something, which she meant for consolation. "My dear Emily," replied St. Aubert, "my dear child, we must look up with humble confidence to that Being, who has protected and comforted us in every danger, and in every affliction we have known; to whose eye every moment of our lives has been exposed; he will not, he does not, forsake us now; I feel his consolations in my heart. I shall leave you, my child, still in his care; and, though I depart from this world, I shall be still in his presence. Nay, weep not again, my Emily. In death there is nothing new, or surprising, since we all know, that we are born to die; and nothing terrible to those, who can confide in an all-powerful God. Had my life been spared now, after a very few years, in the course of nature, I must have resigned it; old age, with all its train of infirmity, its privations and its sorrows, would have been mine; and then, at last, death would have come, and called forth the tears you now shed. Rather, my child, rejoice, that I am saved from such suffering, and that I am permitted to die with a mind unimpaired, and sensible of the comforts of faith and of resignation." St. Aubert paused, fatigued with speaking. Emily again endeavoured to assume an air of composure; and, in replying to what he had said, tried to soothe him with a belief, that he had not spoken in vain.

When he had reposed a while, he resumed the conversation. "Let me return," said he, "to a subject, which is very near my heart. I said I had a solemn promise to receive from you; let me receive it now, before

I explain the chief circumstance which it concerns; there are others, of which your peace requires that you should rest in ignorance. Promise, then, that you will perform exactly what I shall enjoin."

Emily, awed by the earnest solemnity of his manner, dried her tears, that had begun again to flow, in spite of her efforts to suppress them; and, looking eloquently at St. Aubert, bound herself to do whatever he should require by a vow, at which she shuddered, yet knew not why.

He proceeded: "I know you too well, my Emily, to believe, that you would break any promise, much less one thus solemnly given; your assurance gives me peace, and the observance of it is of the utmost importance to your tranquillity. Hear, then, what I am going to tell you. The closet, which adjoins my chamber at La Vallée, has a sliding board in the floor. You will know it by a remarkable knot in the wood, and by its being the next board, except one, to the wainscot, which fronts the door. At the distance of about a yard from that end, nearer the window, you will perceive a line across it, as if the plank had been joined;—the way to open it is this:—Press your foot upon the line; the end of the board will then sink, and you may slide it with ease beneath the other. Below, you will see a hollow place." St. Aubert paused for breath, and Emily sat fixed in deep attention. "Do you understand these directions, my dear?" said he. Emily, though scarcely able to speak, assured him that she did.

"When you return home, then," he added with a deep sigh—

At the mention of her return home, all the melancholy circumstances, that must attend this return, rushed upon her fancy; she burst into convulsive grief, and St. Aubert himself, affected beyond the resistance of the fortitude which he had, at first, summoned, wept with her. After some moments, he composed himself. "My dear child," said he, "be comforted. When I am gone, you will not be forsaken—I leave you only in the more immediate care of that Providence, which has never yet forsaken me. Do not afflict me with this excess of grief; rather teach me by your example to bear my own." He stopped again, and Emily, the more she endeavoured to restrain her emotion, found it the less possible to do so.

St. Aubert, who now spoke with pain, resumed the subject. "That closet, my dear,—when you return home, go to it; and, beneath the board I have described, you will find a packet of written papers. Attend to me now, for the promise you have given particularly relates to what I shall direct. These papers you must burn—and, solemnly I command you, *without examining them.*"

Emily's surprise, for a moment, overcame her grief, and she ventured to ask, why this must be? St. Aubert replied, that, if it had been right for him to explain his reasons, her late promise would have been unnecessarily exacted. "It is sufficient for you, my love, to have a deep sense of the importance of observing me in this instance." St. Aubert proceeded. "Under that board you will also find about two hundred louis d'ors, wrapped in a silk purse; indeed, it was to secure whatever money might be in the chateau, that this secret place was contrived, at a time when the province was over-run by troops of men, who took advantage of the tumults, and became plunderers.

"But I have yet another promise to receive from you, which is—that you will never, whatever may be your future circumstances, *sell* the chateau." St. Aubert even enjoined her, whenever she might marry, to make it an article in the contract, that the chateau should always be hers. He then gave her a more minute account of his present circumstances than he had yet done, adding, "The two hundred louis, with what money you will now find in my purse, is all the ready money I have to leave you. I have told you how I am circumstanced with M. Motteville, at Paris. Ah, my child! I leave you poor—but not destitute," he added, after a long pause. Emily could make no reply to any thing he now said, but knelt at the bed-side, with her face upon the quilt, weeping over the hand she held there.

After this conversation, the mind of St. Aubert appeared to be much more at ease; but, exhausted by the effort of speaking, he sunk into a kind of doze, and Emily continued to watch and weep beside him, till a gentle tap at the chamber-door roused her. It was La Voisin, come to say, that a confessor from the neighbouring convent was below, ready to attend St. Aubert. Emily would not suffer her father to be disturbed, but desired, that the priest might not leave the cottage. When St. Aubert awoke from this doze, his senses were confused, and it was some moments before he recovered them sufficiently to know, that it was Emily who sat beside him. He then moved his lips, and stretched forth his hand to her; as she received which, she sunk back in her chair, overcome by the impression of death on his countenance. In a few minutes he recovered his voice, and Emily then asked, if he wished to see the confessor; he replied, that he did; and, when the holy father appeared, she withdrew. They remained alone together above half an hour; when Emily was called in, she found St. Aubert more agitated than when she had left him, and she gazed, with a slight degree of resentment, at the friar, as the cause of this; who, however, looked mildly and mournfully at her, and turned away. St. Aubert, in a tremulous voice, said, he wished her to join in prayer with him, and asked if La Voisin would do so too. The old man and his daughter came; they both wept, and knelt with Emily round the bed, while the holy father read in a solemn voice the service for the dying. St. Aubert lay with a serene countenance, and seemed to join fervently in the devotion, while tears often stole from

beneath his closed eyelids, and Emily's sobs more than once interrupted the service.

When it was concluded, and extreme unction had been administered, the friar withdrew. St. Aubert then made a sign for La Voisin to
come nearer. He gave him his hand, and was, for a moment, silent. At
length, he said, in a trembling voice, "My good friend, our acquaintance has been short, but long enough to give you an opportunity of
shewing me much kind attention. I cannot doubt, that you will extend
this kindness to my daughter, when I am gone; she will have need of it.
I entrust her to your care during the few days she will remain here. I
need say no more—you know the feelings of a father, for you have children; mine would be, indeed, severe if I had less confidence in you."
He paused. La Voisin assured him, and his tears bore testimony to his
sincerity, that he would do all he could to soften her affliction, and that,
if St. Aubert wished it, he would even attend her into Gascony; an offer
so pleasing to St. Aubert, that he had scarcely words to acknowledge his
sense of the old man's kindness, or to tell him, that he accepted it. The
scene, that followed between St. Aubert and Emily, affected La Voisin
so much, that he quitted the chamber, and she was again left alone
with her father, whose spirits seemed fainting fast, but neither his
senses, or his voice, yet failed him; and, at intervals, he employed much
of these last awful moments in advising his daughter, as to her future
conduct. Perhaps, he never had thought more justly, or expressed himself more clearly, than he did now.

"Above all, my dear Emily," said he, "do not indulge in the pride of
fine feeling, the romantic error of amiable minds. Those, who really
possess sensibility, ought early to be taught, that it is a dangerous quality, which is continually extracting the excess of misery, or delight, from
every surrounding circumstance. And, since, in our passage through
this world, painful circumstances occur more frequently than pleasing
ones, and since our sense of evil is, I fear, more acute than our sense of
good, we become the victims of our feelings, unless we can in some
degree command them. I know you will say, (for you are young, my
Emily) I know you will say, that you are contented sometimes to suffer,
rather than to give up your refined sense of happiness, at others; but,
when your mind has been long harassed by vicissitude, you will be content to rest, and you will then recover from your delusion. You will perceive, that the phantom of happiness is exchanged for the substance;
for happiness arises in a state of peace, not of tumult. It is of a
temperate and uniform nature, and can no more exist in a heart, that
is continually alive to minute circumstances, than in one that is dead
to feeling. You see, my dear, that, though I would guard you against the
dangers of sensibility, I am not an advocate for apathy. At your age I

should have said *that* is a vice more hateful than all the errors of sensibility, and I say so still. I call it a *vice*, because it leads to positive evil; in this, however, it does no more than an ill-governed sensibility, which, by such a rule, might also be called a vice; but the evil of the former is of more general consequence. I have exhausted myself," said St. Aubert, feebly, "and have wearied you, my Emily; but, on a subject so important to your future comfort, I am anxious to be perfectly understood."

Emily assured him, that his advice was most precious to her, and that she would never forget it, or cease from endeavouring to profit by it. St. Aubert smiled affectionately and sorrowfully upon her. "I repeat it," said he, "I would not teach you to become insensible, if I could; I would only warn you of the evils of susceptibility, and point out how you may avoid them. Beware, my love, I conjure you, of that self-delusion, which has been fatal to the peace of so many persons; beware of priding yourself on the gracefulness of sensibility; if you yield to this vanity, your happiness is lost for ever. Always remember how much more valuable is the strength of fortitude, than the grace of sensibility. Do not, however, confound fortitude with apathy; apathy cannot know the virtue. Remember, too, that one act of beneficence, one act of real usefulness, is worth all the abstract sentiment in the world. Sentiment is a disgrace, instead of an ornament, unless it lead us to good actions. The miser, who thinks himself respectable, merely because he possesses wealth, and thus mistakes the means of doing good, for the actual accomplishment of it, is not more blameable than the man of sentiment, without active virtue. You may have observed persons, who delight so much in this sort of sensibility to sentiment, which excludes that to the calls of any practical virtue, that they turn from the distressed, and, because their sufferings are painful to be contemplated, do not endeavour to relieve them. How despicable is that humanity, which can be contented to pity, where it might assuage!"

St. Aubert, some time after, spoke of Madame Cheron, his sister. "Let me inform you of a circumstance, that nearly affects your welfare," he added. "We have, you know, had little intercourse for some years; but, as she is now your only female relation, I have thought it proper to consign you to her care, as you will see in my will, till you are of age, and to recommend you to her protection afterwards. She is not exactly the person, to whom I would have committed my Emily, but I had no alternative, and I believe her to be upon the whole—a good kind of woman. I need not recommend it to your prudence, my love, to endeavour to conciliate her kindness; you will do this for his sake, who has often wished to do so for yours."

Emily assured him, that, whatever he requested she would religiously perform to the utmost of her ability. "Alas!" added she, in a voice interrupted by sighs, "that will soon be all which remains for me; it will be almost my only consolation to fulfil your wishes."

St. Aubert looked up silently in her face, as if he would have spoken, but his spirit sunk a while, and his eyes became heavy and dull. She felt that look at her heart. "My dear father!" she exclaimed; and then, checking herself, pressed his hand closer, and hid her face with her handkerchief. Her tears were concealed, but St. Aubert heard her convulsive sobs. His spirits returned. "O my child!" said he, faintly, "let my consolations be yours. I die in peace; for I know, that I am about to return to the bosom of my Father, who will still be your Father, when I am gone. Always trust in him, my love, and he will support you in these moments, as he supports me."

Emily could only listen, and weep; but the extreme composure of his manner, and the faith and hope he expressed, somewhat soothed her anguish. Yet, whenever she looked upon his emaciated countenance, and saw the lines of death beginning to prevail over it—saw his sunk eyes, still bent on her, and their heavy lids pressing to a close, there was a pang in her heart, such as defied expression, though it required filial virtue, like hers, to forbear the attempt.

He desired once more to bless her; "Where are you, my dear?" said he, as he stretched forth his hands. Emily had turned to the window, that he might not perceive her anguish; she now understood, that his sight had failed him. When he had given her his blessing, and it seemed to be the last effort of expiring life, he sunk back on his pillow. She kissed his forehead; the damps of death had settled there, and, forgetting her fortitude for a moment, her tears mingled with them. St. Aubert lifted up his eyes; the spirit of a father returned to them, but it quickly vanished, and he spoke no more.

St. Aubert lingered till about three o'clock in the afternoon, and, thus gradually sinking into death, he expired without a struggle, or a sigh.

Emily was led from the chamber by La Voisin and his daughter, who did what they could to comfort her. The old man sat and wept with her. Agnes was more erroneously officious.

CHAPTER VIII

O'er him, whose doom thy virtues grieve,
Aerial forms shall sit at eve,
And bend the pensive head.

COLLINS.

THE monk, who had before appeared, returned in the evening to offer consolation to Emily, and brought a kind message from the lady abbess, inviting her to the convent. Emily, though she did not accept the offer, returned an answer expressive of her gratitude. The holy conversation of the friar, whose mild benevolence of manners bore some resemblance to those of St. Aubert, soothed the violence of her grief, and lifted her heart to the Being, who, extending through all place and all eternity, looks on the events of this little world as on the shadows of a moment, and beholds equally, and in the same instant, the soul that has passed the gates of death, and that, which still lingers in the body. "In the sight of God," said Emily, "my dear father now exists, as truly as he yesterday existed to me; it is to me only that he is dead; to God and to himself he yet lives!"

The good monk left her more tranquil than she had been since St. Aubert died; and, before she retired to her little cabin for the night, she trusted herself so far as to visit the corpse. Silent, and without weeping, she stood by its side. The features, placid and serene, told the nature of the last sensations, that had lingered in the now deserted frame. For a moment she turned away, in horror of the stillness in which death had fixed that countenance, never till now seen otherwise than animated; then gazed on it with a mixture of doubt and awful astonishment. Her reason could scarcely overcome an involuntary and unaccountable expectation of seeing that beloved countenance still susceptible. She continued to gaze wildly; took up the cold hand; spoke; still gazed, and then burst into a transport of grief. La Voisin, hearing her sobs, came into the room to lead her away, but she heard nothing, and only begged that he would leave her.

Again alone, she indulged her tears, and, when the gloom of evening obscured the chamber, and almost veiled from her eyes the object of her distress, she still hung over the body; till her spirits, at length, were exhausted, and she became tranquil. La Voisin again knocked at the door, and entreated that she would come to the common apartment. Before she went, she kissed the lips of St. Aubert, as she was wont to do when she bade him good night. Again she kissed them; her heart felt as if it would break, a few tears of agony started to her eyes, she looked up to heaven, then at St. Aubert, and left the room.

Retired to her lonely cabin, her melancholy thoughts still hovered round the body of her deceased parent; and, when she sunk into a kind of slumber, the images of her waking mind still haunted her fancy. She thought she saw her father approaching her with a benign countenance; then, smiling mournfully and pointing upwards, his lips moved, but, instead of words, she heard sweet music borne on the distant air, and presently saw his features glow with the mild rapture of a superior being. The strain seemed to swell louder, and she awoke. The vision was gone, but music yet came to her ear in strains such as angels might breathe. She doubted, listened, raised herself in the bed, and again listened. It was music, and not an illusion of her imagination. After a solemn steady harmony, it paused; then rose again, in mournful sweetness, and then died, in a cadence, that seemed to bear away the listening soul to heaven. She instantly remembered the music of the preceding night, with the strange circumstances, related by La Voisin, and the affecting conversation it had led to, concerning the state of departed spirits. All that St. Aubert had said, on that subject, now pressed upon her heart, and overwhelmed it. What a change in a few hours! He, who then could only conjecture, was now made acquainted with truth; was himself become one of the departed! As she listened, she was chilled with superstitious awe, her tears stopped; and she rose, and went to the window. All without was obscured in shade; but Emily, turning her eyes from the massy darkness of the woods, whose waving outline appeared on the horizon, saw, on the left, that effulgent planet, which the old man had pointed out, setting over the woods. She remembered what he had said concerning it, and, the music now coming at intervals on the air, she unclosed the casement to listen to the strains, that soon gradually sunk to a greater distance, and tried to discover whence they came. The obscurity prevented her from distinguishing any object on the green platform below; and the sounds became fainter and fainter, till they softened into silence. She listened, but they returned no more. Soon after, she observed the planet trembling between the fringed tops of the woods, and, in the next moment, sink behind them. Chilled with a melancholy awe, she retired once more to her bed, and, at length, forgot for a while her sorrows in sleep.

On the following morning, she was visited by a sister of the convent, who came, with kind offices and a second invitation from the lady abbess; and Emily, though she could not forsake the cottage, while the remains of her father were in it, consented, however painful such a visit must be, in the present state of her spirits, to pay her respects to the abbess, in the evening.

About an hour before sunset, La Voisin shewed her the way through the woods to the convent, which stood in a small bay of the Mediterranean, crowned by a woody amphitheatre; and Emily, had she been less unhappy, would have admired the extensive sea view, that appeared from the green slope, in front of the edifice, and the rich shores, hung with woods and pastures, that extended on either hand. But her thoughts were now occupied by one sad idea, and the features of nature were to her colourless and without form. The bell for vespers struck, as she passed the ancient gate of the convent, and seemed the

funereal note for St. Aubert. Little incidents affect a mind, enervated by
sorrow; Emily struggled against the sickening faintness, that came over
her, and was led into the presence of the abbess, who received her with
an air of maternal tenderness; an air of such gentle solicitude and consideration, as touched her with an instantaneous gratitude; her eyes
were filled with tears, and the words she would have spoken faltered on
her lips. The abbess led her to a seat, and sat down beside her, still
holding her hand and regarding her in silence, as Emily dried her tears
and attempted to speak. "Be composed, my daughter," said the abbess
in a soothing voice, "do not speak yet; I know all you would say. Your
spirits must be soothed. We are going to prayers;—will you attend our
evening service? It is comfortable, my child, to look up in our afflictions to a father, who sees and pities us, and who chastens in his
mercy."

Emily's tears flowed again, but a thousand sweet emotions mingled
with them. The abbess suffered her to weep without interruption, and
watched over her with a look of benignity, that might have characterized the countenance of a guardian angel. Emily, when she became
tranquil, was encouraged to speak without reserve, and to mention the
motive, that made her unwilling to quit the cottage, which the abbess
did not oppose even by a hint; but praised the filial piety of her conduct, and added a hope, that she would pass a few days at the convent,
before she returned to La Vallée. "You must allow yourself a little time
to recover from your first shock, my daughter, before you encounter a
second; I will not affect to conceal from you how much I know your
heart must suffer, on returning to the scene of your former happiness.
Here, you will have all, that quiet and sympathy and religion can give,
to restore your spirits. But come," added she, observing the tears swell
in Emily's eyes, "we will go to the chapel."

Emily followed to the parlour, where the nuns were assembled, to
whom the abbess committed her, saying, "This is a daughter, for whom
I have much esteem; be sisters to her."

They passed on in a train to the chapel, where the solemn devotion,
with which the service was performed, elevated her mind, and brought
to it the comforts of faith and resignation.

Twilight came on, before the abbess's kindness would suffer Emily to
depart, when she left the convent, with a heart much lighter than she
had entered it, and was reconducted by La Voisin through the woods,
the pensive gloom of which was in unison with the temper of her mind;
and she pursued the little wild path, in musing silence, till her guide
suddenly stopped, looked round, and then struck out of the path into
the high grass, saying he had mistaken the road. He now walked on
quickly, and Emily, proceeding with difficulty over the obscured and

uneven ground, was left at some distance, till her voice arrested him, who seemed unwilling to stop, and still hurried on. "If you are in doubt about the way," said Emily, "had we not better enquire it at the chateau yonder, between the trees?"

"No," replied La Voisin, "there is no occasion. When we reach that brook, ma'amselle, (you see the light upon the water there, beyond the woods) when we reach that brook, we shall be at home presently. I don't know how I happened to mistake the path; I seldom come this way after sunset."

"It is solitary enough," said Emily, "but you have no banditti here." "No, ma'amselle—no banditti."

"What are you afraid of then, my good friend? you are not superstitious?" "No, not superstitious; but, to tell you the truth, lady, nobody likes to go near that chateau, after dusk." "By whom is it inhabited," said Emily, "that it is so formidable?" "Why, ma'amselle, it is scarcely inhabited, for our lord the Marquis, and the lord of all these fine woods, too, is dead. He had not once been in it, for these many years, and his people, who have the care of it, live in a cottage close by." Emily now understood this to be the chateau, which La Voisin had formerly pointed out, as having belonged to the Marquis Villeroi, on the mention of which her father had appeared so much affected.

"Ah! it is a desolate place now," continued La Voisin, "and such a grand, fine place, as I remember it!" Emily enquired what had occasioned this lamentable change; but the old man was silent, and Emily, whose interest was awakened by the fear he had expressed, and above all by a recollection of her father's agitation, repeated the question, and added, "If you are neither afraid of the inhabitants, my good friend, nor are superstitious, how happens it, that you dread to pass near that chateau in the dark?"

"Perhaps, then, I am a little superstitious, ma'amselle; and, if you knew what I do, you might be so too. Strange things have happened there. Monsieur, your good father, appeared to have known the late Marchioness." "Pray inform me what did happen?" said Emily, with much emotion.

"Alas! ma'amselle," answered La Voisin, "enquire no further; it is not for me to lay open the domestic secrets of my lord."—Emily, surprised by the old man's words, and his manner of delivering them, forbore to repeat her question; a nearer interest, the remembrance of St. Aubert, occupied her thoughts, and she was led to recollect the music she heard on the preceding night, which she mentioned to La Voisin. "You was not alone, ma'amselle, in this," he replied, "I heard it too; but I have so often heard it, at the same hour, that I was scarcely surprised."

"You doubtless believe this music to have some connection with the chateau," said Emily suddenly, "and are, therefore, superstitious." "It may be so, ma'amselle, but there are other circumstances, belonging to that chateau, which I remember, and sadly too." A heavy sigh followed: but Emily's delicacy restrained the curiosity these words revived, and she enquired no further.

On reaching the cottage, all the violence of her grief returned; it seemed as if she had escaped its heavy pressure only while she was removed from the object of it. She passed immediately to the chamber, where the remains of her father were laid, and yielded to all the anguish of hopeless grief. La Voisin, at length, persuaded her to leave the room, and she returned to her own, where, exhausted by the sufferings of the day, she soon fell into deep sleep, and awoke considerably refreshed.

When the dreadful hour arrived, in which the remains of St. Aubert were to be taken from her for ever, she went alone to the chamber to look upon his countenance yet once again, and La Voisin, who had waited patiently below stairs, till her despair should subside, with the respect due to grief, forbore to interrupt the indulgence of it, till surprise, at the length of her stay, and then apprehension overcame his delicacy, and he went to lead her from the chamber. Having tapped gently at the door, without receiving an answer, he listened attentively, but all was still; no sigh, no sob of anguish was heard. Yet more alarmed by this silence, he opened the door, and found Emily lying senseless across the foot of the bed, near which stood the coffin. His calls procured assistance, and she was carried to her room, where proper applications, at length, restored her.

During her state of insensibility, La Voisin had given directions for the coffin to be closed, and he succeeded in persuading Emily to forbear revisiting the chamber. She, indeed, felt herself unequal to this, and also perceived the necessity of sparing her spirits, and recollecting fortitude sufficient to bear her through the approaching scene. St. Aubert had given a particular injunction, that his remains should be interred in the church of the convent of St. Clair, and, in mentioning the north chancel, near the ancient tomb of the Villerois, had pointed out the exact spot, where he wished to be laid. The superior had granted this place for the interment, and thither, therefore, the sad procession now moved, which was met, at the gates, by the venerable priest, followed by a train of friars. Every person, who heard the solemn chant of the anthem, and the peal of the organ, that struck up, when the body entered the church, and saw also the feeble steps, and the assumed tranquillity of Emily, gave her involuntary tears. She shed none, but walked, her face partly shaded by a thin black veil, between two persons, who supported her, preceded by the abbess, and followed by nuns, whose plaintive voices mellowed the swelling harmony of the dirge. When the procession came to the grave the music ceased. Emily drew the veil entirely over her face, and, in a momentary pause, between the anthem and the rest of the service, her sobs were distinctly audible. The holy father began the service, and Emily again commanded her feelings, till the coffin was let down, and she heard the earth rattle on its lid. Then, as she shuddered, a groan burst from her heart, and she leaned for support on the person who stood next to her. In a few moments she recovered; and, when she heard those affecting and sublime words: "His body is buried in peace, and his soul returns to Him that gave it," her anguish softened into tears.

The abbess led her from the church into her own parlour, and there administered all the consolations, that religion and gentle sympathy can give. Emily struggled against the pressure of grief; but the abbess, observing her attentively, ordered a bed to be prepared, and recommended her to retire to repose. She also kindly claimed her promise to remain a few days at the convent; and Emily, who had no wish to return to the cottage, the scene of all her sufferings, had leisure, now that no immediate care pressed upon her attention, to feel the indisposition, which disabled her from immediately travelling.

Meanwhile, the maternal kindness of the abbess, and the gentle attentions of the nuns did all, that was possible, towards soothing her spirits and restoring her health. But the latter was too deeply wounded, through the medium of her mind, to be quickly revived. She lingered for some weeks at the convent, under the influence of a slow fever, wishing to return home, yet unable to go thither; often even reluctant to leave the spot where her father's relics were deposited, and sometimes soothing herself with the consideration, that, if she died here, her remains would repose beside those of St. Aubert. In the meanwhile, she sent letters to Madame Cheron and to the old housekeeper, informing them of the sad event, that had taken place, and of her own situation. From her aunt she received an answer, abounding more in commonplace condolement, than in traits of real sorrow, which assured her, that a servant should be sent to conduct her to La Vallée, for that her own time was so much occupied by company, that she had no leisure to undertake so long a journey. However Emily might prefer La Vallée to Tholouse, she could not be insensible to the indecorous and unkind conduct of her aunt, in suffering her to return thither, where she had no longer a relation to console and protect her; a conduct, which was the more culpable, since St. Aubert had appointed Madame Cheron the guardian of his orphan daughter.

Madame Cheron's servant made the attendance of the good La Voisin unnecessary; and Emily, who felt sensibly her obligations to him, for all his kind attention to her late father, as well as to herself, was glad to spare him a long, and what, at his time of life, must have been a troublesome journey.

During her stay at the convent, the peace and sanctity that reigned within, the tranquil beauty of the scenery without, and the delicate attentions of the abbess and the nuns, were circumstances so soothing to her mind, that they almost tempted her to leave a world, where she had lost her dearest friends, and devote herself to the cloister, in a spot, rendered sacred to her by containing the tomb of St. Aubert. The pensive enthusiasm, too, so natural to her temper, had spread a beautiful illusion over the sanctified retirement of a nun, that almost hid from her view the selfishness of its security. But the touches, which a melancholy fancy, slightly tinctured with superstition, gave to the monastic scene, began to fade, as her spirits revived, and brought once more to her heart an image, which had only transiently been banished thence. By this she was silently awakened to hope and comfort and sweet affections; visions of happiness gleamed faintly at a distance, and, though she knew them to be illusions, she could not resolve to shut them out for ever. It was the remembrance of Valancourt, of his taste, his genius, and of the countenance which glowed with both, that, perhaps, alone determined her to return to the world. The grandeur and sublimity of the scenes, amidst which they had first met, had fascinated her fancy, and had imperceptibly contributed to render Valancourt more interesting by seeming to communicate to him somewhat of their own character. The esteem, too, which St. Aubert had repeatedly expressed for him, sanctioned this kindness; but, though his countenance and manner had continually expressed his admiration of her, he had not otherwise declared it; and even the hope of seeing him again was so distant, that she was scarcely conscious of it, still less that it influenced her conduct on this occasion.

It was several days after the arrival of Madame Cheron's servant before Emily was sufficiently recovered to undertake the journey to La Vallée. On the evening preceding her departure, she went to the cottage to take leave of La Voisin and his family, and to make them a return for their kindness. The old man she found sitting on a bench at his door, between his daughter, and his son-in-law, who was just returned from his daily labour, and who was playing upon a pipe, that, in tone, resembled an oboe. A flask of wine stood beside the old man, and, before him, a small table with fruit and bread, round which stood several of his grandsons, fine rosy children, who were taking their supper, as their mother distributed it. On the edge of the little green, that spread before the cottage, were cattle and a few sheep reposing under the trees. The landscape was touched with the mellow light of the evening sun, whose long slanting beams played through a vista of the woods, and lighted up the distant turrets of the chateau. She paused a moment, before she emerged from the shade, to gaze upon the happy group before her—on the complacency and ease of healthy age, depictured on the countenance of La Voisin; the maternal tenderness of Agnes, as she looked upon her children, and the innocency of infantine pleasures, reflected in their smiles. Emily looked again at the venerable old man, and at the cottage; the memory of her father rose with full force upon her mind, and she hastily stepped forward, afraid to trust herself with a longer pause. She took an affectionate and affecting leave of La Voisin and his family; he seemed to love her as his daughter, and shed tears; Emily shed many. She avoided going into the cottage, since she knew it would revive emotions, such as she could not now endure.

One painful scene yet awaited her, for she determined to visit again her father's grave; and that she might not be interrupted, or observed in the indulgence of her melancholy tenderness, she deferred her visit, till every inhabitant of the convent, except the nun who promised to bring her the key of the church, should be retired to rest. Emily remained in her chamber, till she heard the convent bell strike twelve, when the nun came, as she had appointed, with the key of a private door, that opened into the church, and they descended together the narrow winding stair-case, that led thither. The nun offered to accompany Emily to the grave, adding, "It is melancholy to go alone at this hour;" but the former, thanking her for the consideration, could not consent to have any witness of her sorrow; and the sister, having unlocked the door, gave her the lamp. "You will remember, sister," said she, "that in the east aisle, which you must pass, is a newly opened grave; hold the light to the ground, that you may not stumble over the loose earth." Emily, thanking her again, took the lamp, and, stepping into the church, sister Mariette departed. But Emily paused a moment at the door; a sudden fear came over her, and she returned to the foot of the stair-case, where, as she heard the steps of the nun ascending, and, while she held up the lamp, saw her black veil waving over the spiral balusters, she was tempted to call her back. While she hesitated, the veil disappeared, and, in the next moment, ashamed of her fears, she returned to the church. The cold air of the aisles chilled her, and their deep silence and extent, feebly shone upon by the moon-light, that streamed through a distant gothic window, would at any other time have awed her into superstition; now, grief occupied all her attention. She scarcely heard the whispering echoes of her own steps, or thought of the open grave, till she found herself almost on its brink. A friar of the convent had been buried there on the preceding evening, and, as she had sat alone in her chamber at twilight, she heard, at distance, the monks chanting the requiem for his soul. This brought freshly to her memory the circumstances of her father's death; and, as the voices, mingling with a low querulous peal of the organ, swelled faintly, gloomy and affecting visions had arisen upon her mind. Now she remembered them, and, turning aside to avoid the broken ground, these recollections made her pass on with quicker steps to the grave of St. Aubert, when in the moon-light, that fell athwart a remote part of the aisle, she thought she saw a shadow gliding between the pillars. She stopped to listen, and, not hearing any footstep, believed that her fancy had deceived her, and, no longer apprehensive of being observed, proceeded. St. Aubert was buried beneath a plain marble, bearing little more than his name and the date of his birth and death, near the foot of the stately monument of the Villerois. Emily remained at his grave, till a chime, that called the monks to early prayers, warned her to retire; then, she wept over it a last farewel, and forced herself from the spot. After this hour of melancholy indulgence, she was refreshed by a deeper sleep, than she had experienced for a long time, and, on awakening, her mind was more tranquil and resigned, than it had been since St. Aubert's death.

But, when the moment of her departure from the convent arrived, all her grief returned; the memory of the dead, and the kindness of the living attached her to the place; and for the sacred spot, where her father's remains were interred, she seemed to feel all those tender affections which we conceive for home. The abbess repeated many kind assurances of regard at their parting, and pressed her to return, if ever she should find her condition elsewhere unpleasant; many of the nuns also expressed unaffected regret at her departure, and Emily left the convent with many tears, and followed by sincere wishes for her happiness.

She had travelled several leagues, before the scenes of the country, through which she passed, had power to rouse her for a moment from the deep melancholy, into which she was sunk, and, when they did, it was only to remind her, that, on her last view of them, St. Aubert was at her side, and to call up to her remembrance the remarks he had delivered on similar scenery. Thus, without any particular occurrence, passed the day in languor and dejection. She slept that night in a town on the skirts of Languedoc, and, on the following morning, entered Gascony.

Towards the close of this day, Emily came within view of the plains in the neighbourhood of La Vallée, and the well-known objects of former times began to press upon her notice, and with them recollections, that awakened all her tenderness and grief. Often, while she looked through her tears upon the wild grandeur of the Pyrénées, now varied with the rich lights and shadows of evening, she remembered, that, when last she saw them, her father partook with her of the pleasure they inspired. Suddenly some scene, which he had particularly pointed out to her, would present itself, and the sick languor of despair would steal upon her heart. "There!" she would exclaim, "there are the very cliffs, there the wood of pines, which he looked at with such delight, as we passed this road together for the last time. There, too, under the crag of that mountain, is the cottage, peeping from among the cedars, which he bade me remember, and copy with my pencil. O my father, shall I never see you more!"

As she drew near the chateau, these melancholy memorials of past times multiplied. At length, the chateau itself appeared, amid the glowing beauty of St. Aubert's favourite landscape. This was an object, which called for fortitude, not for tears; Emily dried hers, and prepared to meet with calmness the trying moment of her return to that home, where there was no longer a parent to welcome her. "Yes," said she, "let me not forget the lessons he has taught me! How often he has pointed out the necessity of resisting even virtuous sorrow; how often we have admired together the greatness of a mind, that can at once suffer and reason! O my father! if you are permitted to look down upon your child, it will please you to see, that she remembers, and endeavours to practise, the precepts you have given her."

A turn on the road now allowed a nearer view of the chateau, the chimneys, tipped with light, rising from behind St. Aubert's favourite oaks, whose foliage partly concealed the lower part of the building. Emily could not suppress a heavy sigh. "This, too, was his favourite hour," said she, as she gazed upon the long evening shadows, stretched athwart the landscape. "How deep the repose, how lovely the scene! lovely and tranquil as in former days!"

Again she resisted the pressure of sorrow, till her ear caught the gay melody of the dance, which she had so often listened to, as she walked with St. Aubert, on the margin of the Garonne, when all her fortitude forsook her, and she continued to weep, till the carriage stopped at the little gate, that opened upon what was now her own territory. She raised her eyes on the sudden stopping of the carriage, and saw her father's old housekeeper coming to open the gate. Manchon also came running, and barking before her; and when his young mistress alighted, fawned, and played round her, gasping with joy.

"Dear ma'amselle!" said Theresa, and paused, and looked as if she would have offered something of condolement to Emily, whose tears now prevented reply. The dog still fawned and ran round her, and then flew towards the carriage, with a short quick bark. "Ah, ma'amselle!—

my poor master!" said Theresa, whose feelings were more awakened than her delicacy, "Manchon's gone to look for him." Emily sobbed aloud; and, on looking towards the carriage, which still stood with the door open, saw the animal spring into it, and instantly leap out, and then with his nose on the ground run round the horses.

"Don't cry so, ma'amselle," said Theresa, "it breaks my heart to see you." The dog now came running to Emily, then returned to the carriage, and then back again to her, whining and discontented. "Poor rogue!" said Theresa, "thou hast lost thy master, thou mayst well cry! But come, my dear young lady, be comforted. What shall I get to refresh you?" Emily gave her hand to the old servant, and tried to restrain her grief, while she made some kind enquiries concerning her health. But she still lingered in the walk which led to the chateau, for within was no person to meet her with the kiss of affection; her own heart no longer palpitated with impatient joy to meet again the well-known smile, and she dreaded to see objects, which would recall the full remembrance of her former happiness. She moved slowly towards the door, paused, went on, and paused again. How silent, how forsaken, how forlorn did the chateau appear! Trembling to enter it, yet blaming herself for delaying what she could not avoid, she, at length, passed into the hall; crossed it with a hurried step, as if afraid to look round, and opened the door of that room, which she was wont to call her own. The gloom of evening gave solemnity to its silent and deserted air. The chairs, the tables, every article of furniture, so familiar to her in happier times, spoke eloquently to her heart. She seated herself, without immediately observing it, in a window, which opened upon the garden, and where St. Aubert had often sat with her, watching the sun retire from the rich and extensive prospect, that appeared beyond the groves.

Having indulged her tears for some time, she became more composed; and, when Theresa, after seeing the baggage deposited in her lady's room, again appeared, she had so far recovered her spirits, as to be able to converse with her.

"I have made up the green bed for you, ma'amselle," said Theresa, as she set the coffee upon the table. "I thought you would like it better than your own now; but I little thought this day month, that you would come back alone. A-well-a-day! the news almost broke my heart, when it did come. Who would have believed, that my poor master, when he went from home, would never return again!" Emily hid her face with her handkerchief, and waved her hand.

"Do taste the coffee," said Theresa. "My dear young lady, be comforted—we must all die. My dear master is a saint above." Emily took the handkerchief from her face, and raised her eyes full of tears towards heaven; soon after she dried them, and, in a calm, but tremulous voice, began to enquire concerning some of her late father's pensioners.

"Alas-a-day!" said Theresa, as she poured out the coffee, and handed it to her mistress, "all that could come, have been here every day to enquire after you and my master." She then proceeded to tell, that some were dead whom they had left well; and others, who were ill, had recovered. "And see, ma'amselle," added Theresa, "there is old Mary coming up the garden now; she has looked every day these three years as if she would die, yet she is alive still. She has seen the chaise at the door, and knows you are come home."

The sight of this poor old woman would have been too much for Emily, and she begged Theresa would go and tell her, that she was too ill to see any person that night. "To-morrow I shall be better, perhaps; but give her this token of my remembrance."

Emily sat for some time, given up to sorrow. Not an object, on which her eye glanced, but awakened some remembrance, that led immediately to the subject of her grief. Her favourite plants, which St. Aubert had taught her to nurse; the little drawings, that adorned the room, which his taste had instructed her to execute; the books, that he had selected for her use, and which they had read together; her musical instruments, whose sounds he loved so well, and which he sometimes awakened himself—every object gave new force to sorrow. At length, she roused herself from this melancholy indulgence, and, summoning all her resolution, stepped forward to go into those forlorn rooms, which, though she dreaded to enter, she knew would yet more powerfully affect her, if she delayed to visit them.

Having passed through the green-house, her courage for a moment forsook her, when she opened the door of the library; and, perhaps, the shade, which evening and the foliage of the trees near the windows threw across the room, heightened the solemnity of her feelings on entering that apartment, where every thing spoke of her father. There was an arm chair, in which he used to sit; she shrunk when she observed it, for she had so often seen him seated there, and the idea of him rose so distinctly to her mind, that she almost fancied she saw him before her. But she checked the illusions of a distempered imagination, though she could not subdue a certain degree of awe, which now mingled with her emotions. She walked slowly to the chair, and seated herself in it; there was a reading-desk before it, on which lay a book open, as it had been left by her father. It was some moments before she recovered courage enough to examine it; and, when she looked at the open page, she immediately recollected, that St. Aubert, on the evening before his departure from the chateau, had read to her some passages from this his favourite author. The circumstance now affected her extremely; she looked at the page, wept, and looked again. To her the book appeared sacred and invaluable, and she would not have moved it, or closed the page, which he had left open, for the treasures of the Indies. Still she sat before the desk, and could not resolve to quit it, though the increasing gloom, and the profound silence of the apartment, revived a degree of painful awe. Her thoughts dwelt on the probable state of departed spirits, and she remembered the affecting conversation, which had passed between St. Aubert and La Voisin, on the night preceding his death.

As she mused she saw the door slowly open, and a rustling sound in a remote part of the room startled her. Through the dusk she thought she perceived something move. The subject she had been considering, and the present tone of her spirits, which made her imagination respond to every impression of her senses, gave her a sudden terror of something supernatural. She sat for a moment motionless, and then, her dissipated reason returning, "What should I fear?" said she. "If the spirits of those we love ever return to us, it is in kindness."

The silence, which again reigned, made her ashamed of her late fears, and she believed, that her imagination had deluded her, or that she had heard one of those unaccountable noises, which sometimes occur in old houses. The same sound, however, returned; and, distinguishing something moving towards her, and in the next instant press beside her into the chair, she shrieked; but her fleeting senses were instantly recalled, on perceiving that it was Manchon who sat by her, and who now licked her hands affectionately.

Perceiving her spirits unequal to the task she had assigned herself of visiting the deserted rooms of the chateau this night, when she left the library, she walked into the garden, and down to the terrace, that overhung the river. The sun was now set; but, under the dark branches of the almond trees, was seen the saffron glow of the west, spreading beyond the twilight of middle air. The bat flitted silently by; and, now and then, the mourning note of the nightingale was heard. The circumstances of the hour brought to her recollection some lines, which she had once heard St. Aubert recite on this very spot, and she had now a melancholy pleasure in repeating them.

SONNET

Now the bat circles on the breeze of eve,
That creeps, in shudd'ring fits, along the wave,
And trembles 'mid the woods, and through the cave
Whose lonely sighs the wanderer deceive;
For oft, when melancholy charms his mind,
He thinks the Spirit of the rock he hears,

Nor listens, but with sweetly-thrilling fears,
To the low, mystic murmurs of the wind!
Now the bat circles, and the twilight-dew
Falls silent round, and, o'er the mountain-cliff,
The gleaming wave, and far-discover'd skiff,
Spreads the gray veil of soft, harmonious hue.
So falls o'er Grief the dew of pity's tear
Dimming her lonely visions of despair.

Emily, wandering on, came to St. Aubert's favourite plane-tree, where so often, at this hour, they had sat beneath the shade together, and with her dear mother so often had conversed on the subject of a future state. How often, too, had her father expressed the comfort he derived from believing, that they should meet in another world! Emily, overcome by these recollections, left the plane-tree, and, as she leaned pensively on the wall of the terrace, she observed a group of peasants dancing gaily on the banks of the Garonne, which spread in broad expanse below, and reflected the evening light. What a contrast they formed to the desolate, unhappy Emily! They were gay and *debonnaire*, as they were wont to be when she, too, was gay—when St. Aubert used to listen to their merry music, with a countenance beaming pleasure and benevolence. Emily, having looked for a moment on this sprightly band, turned away, unable to bear the remembrances it excited; but where, alas! could she turn, and not meet new objects to give acuteness to grief?

As she walked slowly towards the house, she was met by Theresa. "Dear ma'amselle," said she, "I have been seeking you up and down this half hour, and was afraid some accident had happened to you. How can you like to wander about so in this night air! Do come into the house. Think what my poor master would have said, if he could see you. I am sure, when my dear lady died, no gentleman could take it more to heart than he did, yet you know he seldom shed a tear."

"Pray, Theresa, cease," said Emily, wishing to interrupt this ill-judged, but well-meaning harangue; Theresa's loquacity, however, was not to be silenced so easily. "And when you used to grieve so," she added, "he often told you how wrong it was—for that my mistress was happy. And, if she was happy, I am sure he is so too; for the prayers of the poor, they say, reach heaven." During this speech, Emily had walked silently into the chateau, and Theresa lighted her across the hall into the common sitting parlour, where she had laid the cloth, with one solitary knife and fork, for supper. Emily was in the room before she perceived that it was not her own apartment, but she checked the emotion which inclined her to leave it, and seated herself quietly by the little supper table. Her father's hat hung upon the opposite wall; while she gazed at it, a faintness came over her. Theresa looked at her, and then at the object, on which her eyes were settled, and went to remove it; but Emily waved her hand—"No," said she, "let it remain. I am going to my chamber." "Nay, ma'amselle, supper is ready." "I cannot take it," replied Emily, "I will go to my room, and try to sleep. Tomorrow I shall be better."

"This is poor doings!" said Theresa. "Dear lady! do take some food! I have dressed a pheasant, and a fine one it is. Old Monsieur Barreaux sent it this morning, for I saw him yesterday, and told him you were coming. And I know nobody that seemed more concerned, when he heard the sad news, then he."

"Did he?" said Emily, in a tender voice, while she felt her poor heart warmed for a moment by a ray of sympathy.

At length, her spirits were entirely overcome, and she retired to her room.

CHAPTER IX

> Can Music's voice, can Beauty's eye,
> Can Painting's glowing hand supply
> A charm so suited to my mind,
> As blows this hollow gust of wind?
> As drops this little weeping rill,
> Soft tinkling down the moss-grown hill;
> While, through the west, where sinks the crimson day,
> Meek Twilight slowly sails, and waves her banners gray?
>   MASON

EMILY, some time after her return to La Vallée, received letters from her aunt, Madame Cheron, in which, after some commonplace condolement and advice, she invited her to Tholouse, and added, that, as her late brother had entrusted Emily's *education* to her, she should consider herself bound to overlook her conduct. Emily, at this time, wished only to remain at La Vallée, in the scenes of her early happiness, now rendered infinitely dear to her, as the late residence of those, whom she had lost for ever, where she could weep unobserved, retrace their steps, and remember each minute particular of their manners. But she was equally anxious to avoid the displeasure of Madame Cheron.

Though her affection would not suffer her to question, even a moment, the propriety of St. Aubert's conduct in appointing Madame Cheron for her guardian, she was sensible, that this step had made her happiness depend, in a great degree, on the humour of her aunt. In her reply, she begged permission to remain, at present, at La Vallée, mentioning the extreme dejection of her spirits, and the necessity she felt for quiet and retirement to restore them. These she knew were not to be found at Madame Cheron's, whose inclinations led her into a life of dissipation, which her ample fortune encouraged; and, having given her answer, she felt somewhat more at ease.

In the first days of her affliction, she was visited by Monsieur Barreaux, a sincere mourner for St. Aubert. "I may well lament my friend," said he, "for I shall never meet with his resemblance. If I could have found such a man in what is called society, I should not have left it."

M. Barreaux's admiration of her father endeared him extremely to Emily, whose heart found almost its first relief in conversing of her parents, with a man, whom she so much revered, and who, though with such an ungracious appearance, possessed so much goodness of heart and delicacy of mind.

Several weeks passed away in quiet retirement, and Emily's affliction began to soften into melancholy. She could bear to read the books she had before read with her father; to sit in his chair in the library—to watch the flowers his hand had planted—to awaken the tones of that instrument his fingers had pressed, and sometimes even to play his favourite air.

When her mind had recovered from the first shock of affliction, perceiving the danger of yielding to indolence, and that activity alone could restore its tone, she scrupulously endeavoured to pass all her hours in employment. And it was now that she understood the full value of the education she had received from St. Aubert, for in cultivating her understanding he had secured her an asylum from indolence, without recourse to dissipation, and rich and varied amusement and information, independent of the society, from which her situation secluded her. Nor were the good effects of this education confined to selfish advantages, since, St. Aubert having nourished every amiable quality of her heart, it now expanded in benevolence to all around her, and taught her, when she could not remove the misfortunes of others, at least to soften them by sympathy and tenderness;—a benevolence that taught her to feel for all, that could suffer.

Madame Cheron returned no answer to Emily's letter, who began to hope, that she should be permitted to remain some time longer in her retirement, and her mind had now so far recovered its strength, that she ventured to view the scenes, which most powerfully recalled the images of past times. Among these was the fishing-house; and, to indulge still more the affectionate melancholy of the visit, she took thither her lute, that she might again hear there the tones, to which St.

Aubert and her mother had so often delighted to listen. She went alone, and at that still hour of the evening, which is so soothing to fancy and to grief. The last time she had been here she was in company with Monsieur and Madame St. Aubert, a few days preceding that, on which the latter was seized with a fatal illness. Now, when Emily again entered the woods, that surrounded the building, they awakened so forcibly the memory of former times, that her resolution yielded for a moment to excess of grief. She stopped, leaned for support against a tree, and wept for some minutes, before she had recovered herself sufficiently to proceed. The little path, that led to the building, was overgrown with grass and the flowers which St. Aubert had scattered carelessly along the border were almost choked with weeds—the tall thistle—the fox-glove, and the nettle. She often paused to look on the desolate spot, now so silent and forsaken, and when, with a trembling hand, she opened the door of the fishing-house, "Ah!" said she, "every thing—every thing remains as when I left it last—left it with those who never must return!" She went to a window, that overhung the rivulet, and, leaning over it, with her eyes fixed on the current, was soon lost in melancholy reverie. The lute she had brought lay forgotten beside her; the mournful sighing of the breeze, as it waved the high pines above, and its softer whispers among the osiers, that bowed upon the banks below, was a kind of music more in unison with her feelings. It did not vibrate on the chords of unhappy memory, but was soothing to the heart as the voice of Pity. She continued to muse, unconscious of the gloom of evening, and that the sun's last light trembled on the heights above, and would probably have remained so much longer, if a sudden footstep, without the building, had not alarmed her attention, and first made her recollect that she was unprotected. In the next moment, a door opened, and a stranger appeared, who stopped on perceiving Emily, and then began to apologize for his intrusion. But Emily, at the sound of his voice, lost her fear in a stronger emotion: its tones were familiar to her ear, and, though she could not readily distinguish through the dusk the features of the person who spoke, she felt a remembrance too strong to be distrusted.

He repeated his apology, and Emily then said something in reply, when the stranger eagerly advancing, exclaimed, "Good God! can it be—surely I am not mistaken—ma'amselle St. Aubert?—is it not?"

"It is indeed," said Emily, who was confirmed in her first conjecture, for she now distinguished the countenance of Valancourt, lighted up with still more than its usual animation. A thousand painful recollections crowded to her mind, and the effort, which she made to support herself, only served to increase her agitation. Valancourt, meanwhile, having enquired anxiously after her health, and expressed his hopes, that M. St. Aubert had found benefit from travelling, learned from the flood of tears, which she could no longer repress, the fatal truth. He led her to a seat, and sat down by her, while Emily continued to weep, and Valancourt to hold the hand, which she was unconscious he had taken, till it was wet with the tears, which grief for St. Aubert and sympathy for herself had called forth.

"I feel," said he at length, "I feel how insufficient all attempt at consolation must be on this subject. I can only mourn with you, for I cannot doubt the source of your tears. Would to God I were mistaken!"

Emily could still answer only by tears, till she rose, and begged they might leave the melancholy spot, when Valancourt, though he saw her feebleness, could not offer to detain her, but took her arm within his, and led her from the fishing-house. They walked silently through the woods, Valancourt anxious to know, yet fearing to ask any particulars concerning St. Aubert; and Emily too much distressed to converse. After some time, however, she acquired fortitude enough to speak of her father, and to give a brief account of the manner of his death; during which recital Valancourt's countenance betrayed strong emotion, and, when he heard that St. Aubert had died on the road, and that Emily had been left among strangers, he pressed her hand between his, and involuntarily exclaimed, "Why was I not there!" but in the next moment recollected himself, for he immediately returned to the mention of her father; till, perceiving that her spirits were exhausted, he gradually changed the subject, and spoke of himself. Emily thus learned that, after they had parted, he had wandered, for some time, along the shores of the Mediterranean, and had then returned through Languedoc into Gascony, which was his native province, and where he usually resided.

When he had concluded his little narrative, he sunk into a silence, which Emily was not disposed to interrupt, and it continued, till they reached the gate of the chateau, when he stopped, as if he had known this to be the limit of his walk. Here, saying, that it was his intention to return to Estuviere on the following day, he asked her if she would permit him to take leave of her in the morning; and Emily, perceiving that she could not reject an ordinary civility, without expressing by her refusal an expectation of something more, was compelled to answer, that she should be at home.

She passed a melancholy evening, during which the retrospect of all that had happened, since she had seen Valancourt, would rise to her imagination; and the scene of her father's death appeared in tints as fresh, as if it had passed on the preceding day. She remembered particularly the earnest and solemn manner, in which he had required her to destroy the manuscript papers, and, awakening from the lethargy, in which sorrow had held her, she was shocked to think she had not yet obeyed him, and determined, that another day should not reproach her with the neglect.

CHAPTER X

Can such things be,
And overcome us like a summer's cloud,
Without our special wonder?

MACBETH

ON the next morning, Emily ordered a fire to be lighted in the stove of the chamber, where St. Aubert used to sleep; and, as soon as she had breakfasted, went thither to burn the papers. Having fastened the door to prevent interruption, she opened the closet where they were concealed, as she entered which, she felt an emotion of unusual awe, and stood for some moments surveying it, trembling, and almost afraid to remove the board. There was a great chair in one corner of the closet, and, opposite to it, stood the table, at which she had seen her father sit, on the evening that preceded his departure, looking over, with so much emotion, what she believed to be these very papers.

The solitary life, which Emily had led of late, and the melancholy subjects, on which she had suffered her thoughts to dwell, had rendered her at times sensible to the "thick-coming fancies" of a mind greatly enervated. It was lamentable, that her excellent understanding should have yielded, even for a moment, to the reveries of superstition, or rather to those starts of imagination, which deceive the senses into what can be called nothing less than momentary madness. Instances of this temporary failure of mind had more than once occurred since her return home; particularly when, wandering through this lonely mansion in the evening twilight, she had been alarmed by appearances, which would have been unseen in her more cheerful days. To this infirm state of her nerves may be attributed what she imagined, when, her eyes glancing a second time on the arm-chair, which stood in an obscure part of the closet, the countenance of her dead father appeared there. Emily stood fixed for a moment to the floor, after which she left the closet. Her spirits, however, soon returned; she reproached herself with the weakness of thus suffering interruption in an act of serious importance, and again opened the door. By the directions which St. Aubert had given her, she readily found the board he had described in an opposite corner of the closet, near the window; she distinguished also the line he had mentioned, and, pressing it as he had bade her, it slid down, and disclosed the bundle of papers, together with some scattered ones, and the purse of louis. With a trembling hand she removed them, replaced the board, paused a moment, and was rising from the floor, when, on looking up, there appeared to her alarmed fancy the same countenance in the chair. The illusion, another instance of the unhappy effect which solitude and grief had gradually produced upon her mind, subdued her spirits; she rushed forward into the chamber, and sunk almost senseless into a chair. Returning reason soon overcame the dreadful, but pitiable attack of imagination, and she turned to the papers, though still with so little recollection, that her eyes involuntarily settled on the writing of some loose sheets, which lay open; and she was unconscious, that she was transgressing her father's strict injunction, till a sentence of dreadful import awakened her attention and her memory together. She hastily put the papers from her; but the words, which had roused equally her curiosity and terror, she could not dismiss from her thoughts. So powerfully had they affected her, that she even could not resolve to destroy the papers immediately; and the more she dwelt on the circumstance, the more it inflamed her imagination. Urged by the most forcible, and apparently the most necessary, curiosity to enquire farther, concerning the terrible and mysterious subject, to which she had seen an allusion, she began to lament her promise to destroy the papers. For a moment, she even doubted, whether it could justly be obeyed, in contradiction to such reasons as there appeared to be for further information. But the delusion was momentary.

"I have given a solemn promise," said she, "to observe a solemn injunction, and it is not my business to argue, but to obey. Let me hasten to remove the temptation, that would destroy my innocence, and embitter my life with the consciousness of irremediable guilt, while I have strength to reject it."

Thus re-animated with a sense of her duty, she completed the triumph of her integrity over temptation, more forcible than any she had ever known, and consigned the papers to the flames. Her eyes watched them as they slowly consumed, she shuddered at the recollection of the sentence she had just seen, and at the certainty, that the only opportunity of explaining it was then passing away for ever.

It was long after this, that she recollected the purse; and as she was depositing it, unopened, in a cabinet, perceiving that it contained something of a size larger than coin, she examined it. "His hand deposited them here," said she, as she kissed some pieces of the coin, and wetted them with her tears, "his hand—which is now dust!" At the bottom of the purse was a small packet, having taken out which, and unfolded paper after paper, she found to be an ivory case, containing the miniature of a—lady! She started—"The same," said she, "my father wept over!" On examining the countenance she could recollect no person that it resembled. It was of uncommon beauty, and was characterized by an expression of sweetness, shaded with sorrow, and tempered by resignation.

St. Aubert had given no directions concerning this picture, nor had even named it; she, therefore, thought herself justified in preserving it. More than once remembering his manner, when he had spoken of the Marchioness of Villeroi, she felt inclined to believe that this was her resemblance; yet there appeared no reason why he should have preserved a picture of that lady, or, having preserved it, why he should lament over it in a manner so striking and affecting as she had witnessed on the night preceding his departure.

Emily still gazed on the countenance, examining its features, but she knew not where to detect the charm that captivated her attention, and inspired sentiments of such love and pity. Dark brown hair played carelessly along the open forehead; the nose was rather inclined to aquiline; the lips spoke in a smile, but it was a melancholy one; the eyes were blue, and were directed upwards with an expression of peculiar meekness, while the soft cloud of the brow spoke of the fine sensibility of the temper.

Emily was roused from the musing mood into which the picture had thrown her, by the closing of the garden gate; and, on turning her eyes to the window, she saw Valancourt coming towards the chateau. Her spirits agitated by the subjects that had lately occupied her mind, she felt unprepared to see him, and remained a few moments in the chamber to recover herself.

When she met him in the parlour, she was struck with the change that appeared in his air and countenance since they had parted in Rousillon, which twilight and the distress she suffered on the preceding evening had prevented her from observing. But dejection and languor disappeared, for a moment, in the smile that now enlightened his countenance, on perceiving her. "You see," said he, "I have availed myself of the permission with which you honoured me — of bidding *you* farewell, whom I had the happiness of meeting only yesterday."

Emily smiled faintly, and, anxious to say something, asked if he had been long in Gascony. "A few days only," replied Valancourt, while a blush passed over his cheek. "I engaged in a long ramble after I had the misfortune of parting with the friends who had made my wanderings among the Pyrenées so delightful."

A tear came to Emily's eye, as Valancourt said this, which he observed; and, anxious to draw off her attention from the remembrance that had occasioned it, as well as shocked at his own thoughtlessness, he began to speak on other subjects, expressing his admiration of the chateau, and its prospects. Emily, who felt somewhat embarrassed how to support a conversation, was glad of such an opportunity to continue it on indifferent topics. They walked down to the terrace, where Valancourt was charmed with the river scenery, and the views over the opposite shores of Guienne.

As he leaned on the wall of the terrace, watching the rapid current of the Garonne, "I was a few weeks ago," said he, "at the source of this noble river; I had not then the happiness of knowing you, or I should have regretted your absence—it was a scene so exactly suited to your taste. It rises in a part of the Pyrenées, still wilder and more sublime, I think, than any we passed in the way to Rousillon." He then described its fall among the precipices of the mountains, where its waters, augmented by the streams that descend from the snowy summits around, rush into the Vallée d'Aran, between whose romantic heights it foams along, pursuing its way to the north west till it emerges upon the plains of Languedoc. Then, washing the walls of Tholouse, and turning again to the north west, it assumes a milder character, as it fertilizes the pastures of Gascony and Guienne, in its progress to the Bay of Biscay.

Emily and Valancourt talked of the scenes they had passed among the Pyrenean Alps; as he spoke of which there was often a tremulous tenderness in his voice, and sometimes he expatiated on them with all the fire of genius, sometimes would appear scarcely conscious of the topic, though he continued to speak. This subject recalled forcibly to Emily the idea of her father, whose image appeared in every landscape, which Valancourt particularized, whose remarks dwelt upon her memory, and whose enthusiasm still glowed in her heart. Her silence, at length, reminded Valancourt how nearly his conversation approached to the occasion of her grief, and he changed the subject, though for one scarcely less affecting to Emily. When he admired the grandeur of the plane-tree, that spread its wide branches over the terrace, and under whose shade they now sat, she remembered how often she had sat thus with St. Aubert, and heard him express the same admiration.

"This was a favourite tree with my dear father," said she; "he used to love to sit under its foliage with his family about him, in the fine evenings of summer."

Valancourt understood her feelings, and was silent; had she raised her eyes from the ground she would have seen tears in his. He rose, and leaned on the wall of the terrace, from which, in a few moments, he returned to his seat, then rose again, and appeared to be greatly agitated; while Emily found her spirits so much depressed, that several of her attempts to renew the conversation were ineffectual. Valancourt again sat down, but was still silent, and trembled. At length he said, with a hesitating voice, "This lovely scene!—I am going to leave—to leave you—perhaps for ever! These moments may never return; I cannot resolve to neglect, though I scarcely dare to avail myself of them. Let me, however, without offending the delicacy of your sorrow, venture to declare the admiration I must always feel of your goodness—O! that at some future period I might be permitted to call it love!"

Emily's emotion would not suffer her to reply; and Valancourt, who now ventured to look up, observing her countenance change, expected to see her faint, and made an involuntary effort to support her, which recalled Emily to a sense of her situation, and to an exertion of her spirits. Valancourt did not appear to notice her indisposition, but, when he spoke again, his voice told the tenderest love. "I will not presume," he added, "to intrude this subject longer upon your attention at this time, but I may, perhaps, be permitted to mention, that these parting moments would lose much of their bitterness if I might be allowed to hope the declaration I have made would not exclude me from your presence in future."

Emily made another effort to overcome the confusion of her thoughts, and to speak. She feared to trust the preference her heart acknowledged towards Valancourt, and to give him any encouragement for hope, on so short an acquaintance. For though in this narrow period she had observed much that was admirable in his taste and disposition, and though these observations had been sanctioned by the opinion of her father, they were not sufficient testimonies of his general worth to determine her upon a subject so infinitely important to her future happiness as that, which now solicited her attention. Yet, though the thought of dismissing Valancourt was so very painful to her, that she could scarcely endure to pause upon it, the consciousness of this made her fear the partiality of her judgment, and hesitate still more to encourage that suit, for which her own heart too tenderly pleaded. The family of Valancourt, if not his circumstances, had been known to her father, and known to be unexceptionable. Of his circumstances, Valancourt himself hinted as far as delicacy would permit, when he said he had at present little else to offer but an heart, that adored her. He had solicited only for a distant hope, and she could not resolve to forbid, though she scarcely dared to permit it; at length, she acquired courage to say, that she must think herself honoured by the good opinion of any person, whom her father had esteemed.

"And was I, then, thought worthy of his esteem?" said Valancourt, in a voice trembling with anxiety; then checking himself, he added, "But pardon the question; I scarcely know what I say. If I might dare to hope, that you think me not unworthy such honour, and might be permitted sometimes to enquire after your health, I should now leave you with comparative tranquillity."

Emily, after a moment's silence, said, "I will be ingenuous with you, for I know you will understand, and allow for my situation; you will consider it as a proof of my—my esteem that I am so. Though I live here in what was my father's house, I live here alone. I have, alas! no longer a parent—a parent, whose presence might sanction your visits. It is unnecessary for me to point out the impropriety of my receiving them."

"Nor will I affect to be insensible of this," replied Valancourt, adding mournfully—"but what is to console me for my candour? I distress you, and would now leave the subject, if I might carry with me a hope of being some time permitted to renew it, of being allowed to make myself known to your family."

Emily was again confused, and again hesitated what to reply; she felt most acutely the difficulty—the forlornness of her situation, which did not allow her a single relative, or friend, to whom she could turn for even a look, that might support and guide her in the present embarrassing circumstances. Madame Cheron, who was her only relative, and ought to have been this friend, was either occupied by her own amusements, or so resentful of the reluctance her niece had shewn to quit La Vallée, that she seemed totally to have abandoned her.

"Ah! I see," said Valancourt, after a long pause, during which Emily had begun, and left unfinished two or three sentences, "I see that I have nothing to hope; my fears were too just, you think me unworthy of your esteem. That fatal journey! which I considered as the happiest period of my life—those delightful days were to embitter all my future ones. How often I have looked back to them with hope and fear—yet never till this moment could I prevail with myself to regret their enchanting influence."

His voice faltered, and he abruptly quitted his seat and walked on the terrace. There was an expression of despair on his countenance, that affected Emily. The pleadings of her heart overcame, in some degree, her extreme timidity, and, when he resumed his seat, she said, in an accent that betrayed her tenderness, "You do both yourself and me injustice when you say I think you unworthy of my esteem; I will acknowledge that you have long possessed it, and—and——"

Valancourt waited impatiently for the conclusion of the sentence, but the words died on her lips. Her eyes, however, reflected all the emotions of her heart. Valancourt passed, in an instant, from the impatience of despair, to that of joy and tenderness. "O Emily!" he exclaimed, "my own Emily—teach me to sustain this moment! Let me seal it as the most sacred of my life!"

He pressed her hand to his lips, it was cold and trembling; and, raising his eyes, he saw the paleness of her countenance. Tears came to her relief, and Valancourt watched in anxious silence over her. In a few moments, she recovered herself, and smiling faintly through her tears, said, "Can you excuse this weakness? My spirits have not yet, I believe, recovered from the shock they lately received."

"I cannot excuse myself," said Valancourt, "but I will forbear to renew the subject, which may have contributed to agitate them, now that I can leave you with the sweet certainty of possessing your esteem."

Then, forgetting his resolution, he again spoke of himself. "You know not," said he, "the many anxious hours I have passed near you lately, when you believed me, if indeed you honoured me with a thought, far away. I have wandered, near the chateau, in the still hours of the night, when no eye could observe me. It was delightful to know I was so near you, and there was something particularly soothing in the thought, that I watched round your habitation, while you slept. These grounds are not entirely new to me. Once I ventured within the fence, and spent one of the happiest, and yet most melancholy hours of my life in walking under what I believed to be your window."

Emily enquired how long Valancourt had been in the neighbourhood. "Several days," he replied. "It was my design to avail myself of the permission M. St. Aubert had given me. I scarcely know how to account for it; but, though I anxiously wished to do this, my resolution always failed, when the moment approached, and I constantly deferred my visit. I lodged in a village at some distance, and wandered with my dogs, among the scenes of this charming country, wishing continually to meet you, yet not daring to visit you."

Having thus continued to converse, without perceiving the flight of time, Valancourt, at length, seemed to recollect himself. "I must go," said he mournfully, "but it is with the hope of seeing you again, of being permitted to pay my respects to your family; let me hear this hope confirmed by your voice." "My family will be happy to see any friend of my dear father," said Emily. Valancourt kissed her hand, and still lingered, unable to depart, while Emily sat silently, with her eyes bent on the ground; and Valancourt, as he gazed on her, considered that it would soon be impossible for him to recall, even to his memory, the exact resemblance of the beautiful countenance he then beheld; at this moment an hasty footstep approached from behind the plane-tree, and, turning her eyes, Emily saw Madame Cheron. She felt a blush steal upon her cheek, and her frame trembled with the emotion of her mind; but she instantly rose to meet her visitor. "So, niece!" said Madame Cheron, casting a look of surprise and enquiry on Valancourt, "so niece, how do you do? But I need not ask, your looks tell me you have already recovered your loss."

"My looks do me injustice then, Madame, my loss I know can never be recovered."

"Well—well! I will not argue with you; I see you have exactly your father's disposition; and let me tell you it would have been much happier for him, poor man! if it had been a different one."

A look of dignified displeasure, with which Emily regarded Madame Cheron, while she spoke, would have touched almost any other heart; she made no other reply, but introduced Valancourt, who could scarcely stifle the resentment he felt, and whose bow Madame Cheron returned with a slight curtsey, and a look of supercilious examination. After a few moments he took leave of Emily, in a manner, that hastily expressed his pain both at his own departure, and at leaving her to the society of Madame Cheron.

"Who is that young man?" said her aunt, in an accent which equally implied inquisitiveness and censure. "Some idle admirer of yours I suppose; but I believed niece you had a greater sense of propriety, than to have received the visits of any young man in your present unfriended situation. Let me tell you the world will observe those things, and it will talk, aye and very freely too."

Emily, extremely shocked at this coarse speech, attempted to interrupt it; but Madame Cheron would proceed, with all the self-importance of a person, to whom power is new.

"It is very necessary you should be under the eye of some person more able to guide you than yourself. I, indeed, have not much leisure for such a task; however, since your poor father made it his last request, that I should overlook your conduct—I must even take you under my care. But this let me tell you niece, that, unless you will determine to be very conformable to my direction, I shall not trouble myself longer about you."

Emily made no attempt to interrupt Madame Cheron a second time, grief and the pride of conscious innocence kept her silent, till her aunt said, "I am now come to take you with me to Tholouse; I am sorry to find, that your poor father died, after all, in such indifferent circumstances; however, I shall take you home with me. Ah! poor man, he was always more generous than provident, or he would not have left his daughter dependent on his relations."

"Nor has he done so, I hope, madam," said Emily calmly, "nor did his pecuniary misfortunes arise from that noble generosity, which always distinguished him. The affairs of M. de Motteville may, I trust, yet be settled without deeply injuring his creditors, and in the meantime I should be very happy to remain at La Vallée."

"No doubt you would," replied Madame Cheron, with a smile of irony, "and I shall no doubt consent to this, since I see how necessary tranquillity and retirement are to restore your spirits. I did not think you capable of so much duplicity, niece; when you pleaded this excuse for remaining here, I foolishly believed it to be a just one, nor expected to have found with you so agreeable a companion as this M. La Val——, I forget his name."

Emily could no longer endure these cruel indignities. "It was a just one, madam," said she; "and now, indeed, I feel more than ever the value of the retirement I then solicited; and, if the purport of your visit is only to add insult to the sorrows of your brother's child, she could well have spared it."

"I see that I have undertaken a very troublesome task," said Madame Cheron, colouring highly. "I am sure, madam," said Emily mildly, and endeavouring to restrain her tears, "I am sure my father did not mean it should be such. I have the happiness to reflect, that my conduct under his eye was such as he often delighted to approve. It would be very painful to me to disobey the sister of such a parent, and, if you believe the task will really be so troublesome, I must lament, that it is yours."

"Well! niece, fine speaking signifies little. I am willing, in consideration of my poor brother, to overlook the impropriety of your late conduct, and to try what your future will be."

Emily interrupted her, to beg she would explain what was the impropriety she alluded to.

"What impropriety! why that of receiving the visits of a lover unknown to your family," replied Madame Cheron, not considering the impropriety of which she had herself been guilty, in exposing her niece to the possibility of conduct so erroneous.

A faint blush passed over Emily's countenance; pride and anxiety struggled in her breast; and, till she recollected, that appearances did, in some degree, justify her aunt's suspicions, she could not resolve to humble herself so far as to enter into the defence of a conduct, which had been so innocent and undesigning on her part. She mentioned the manner of Valancourt's introduction to her father; the circumstances of his receiving the pistol-shot, and of their afterwards travelling together; with the accidental way, in which she had met him, on the preceding evening. She owned he had declared a partiality for her, and that he had asked permission to address her family.

"And who is this young adventurer, pray?" said Madame Cheron, "and what are his pretensions?" "These he must himself explain, madam," replied Emily. "Of his family my father was not ignorant, and I believe it is unexceptionable." She then proceeded to mention what she knew concerning it.

"O, then, this it seems is a younger brother," exclaimed her aunt, "and of course a beggar. A very fine tale indeed! And so my brother took a fancy to this young man after only a few days acquaintance!— but that was so like him! In his youth he was always taking these likes and dislikes, when no other person saw any reason for them at all; nay, indeed, I have often thought the people he disapproved were much more agreeable than those he admired;—but there is no accounting for tastes. He was always so much influenced by people's countenances; now I, for my part, have no notion of this, it is all ridiculous enthusiasm. What has a man's face to do with his character? Can a man of good character help having a disagreeable face?"—which last sentence Madame Cheron delivered with the decisive air of a person who congratulates herself on having made a grand discovery, and believes the question to be unanswerably settled.

Emily, desirous of concluding the conversation, enquired if her aunt would accept some refreshment, and Madame Cheron accompanied her to the chateau, but without desisting from a topic, which she discussed with so much complacency to herself, and severity to her niece.

"I am sorry to perceive, niece," said she, in allusion to somewhat that Emily had said, concerning physiognomy, "that you have a great many of your father's prejudices, and among them those sudden predilections for people from their looks. I can perceive, that you imagine yourself to be violently in love with this young adventurer, after an acquaintance of only a few days. There was something, too, so charmingly romantic in the manner of your meeting!"

Emily checked the tears, that trembled in her eyes, while she said, "When my conduct shall deserve this severity, madam, you will do well to exercise it; till then justice, if not tenderness, should surely restrain it. I have never willingly offended you; now I have lost my parents, you are the only person to whom I can look for kindness. Let me not lament more than ever the loss of such parents." The last words were almost stifled by her emotions, and she burst into tears. Remembering the delicacy and the tenderness of St. Aubert, the happy, happy days she had passed in these scenes, and contrasting them with the coarse and unfeeling behaviour of Madame Cheron, and with the future hours of mortification she must submit to in her presence—a degree of grief seized her, that almost reached despair. Madame Cheron, more offended by the reproof which Emily's words conveyed, than touched by the sorrow they expressed, said nothing, that might soften her grief; but, notwithstanding an apparent reluctance to receive her niece, she desired her company. The love of sway was her ruling passion, and she knew it would be highly gratified by taking into her house a young orphan, who had no appeal from her decisions, and on whom she could exercise without controul the capricious humour of the moment.

On entering the chateau, Madame Cheron expressed a desire, that she would put up what she thought necessary to take to Tholouse, as she meant to set off immediately. Emily now tried to persuade her to defer the journey, at least till the next day, and, at length, with much difficulty, prevailed.

The day passed in the exercise of petty tyranny on the part of Madame Cheron, and in mournful regret and melancholy anticipation on that of Emily, who, when her aunt retired to her apartment for the night, went to take leave of every other room in this her dear native home, which she was now quitting for she knew not how long, and for a world, to which she was wholly a stranger. She could not conquer a presentiment, which frequently occurred to her, this night—that she should never more return to La Vallée. Having passed a considerable time in what had been her father's study, having selected some of his favourite authors, to put up with her clothes, and shed many tears, as she wiped the dust from their covers, she seated herself in his chair before the reading desk, and sat lost in melancholy reflection, till Theresa opened the door to examine, as was her custom before she went to bed, if was all safe. She started, on observing her young lady, who bade her come in, and then gave her some directions for keeping the chateau in readiness for her reception at all times.

"Alas-a-day! that you should leave it!" said Theresa, "I think you would be happier here than where you are going, if one may judge." Emily made no reply to this remark; the sorrow Theresa proceeded to express at her departure affected her, but she found some comfort in the simple affection of this poor old servant, to whom she gave such directions as might best conduce to her comfort during her own absence.

Having dismissed Theresa to bed, Emily wandered through every lonely apartment of the chateau, lingering long in what had been her father's bed-room, indulging melancholy, yet not unpleasing, emotions, and, having often returned within the door to take another look at it, she withdrew to her own chamber. From her window she gazed upon the garden below, shewn faintly by the moon, rising over the tops of the palm-trees, and, at length, the calm beauty of the night increased a desire of indulging the mournful sweetness of bidding farewel to the beloved shades of her childhood, till she was tempted to descend. Throwing over her the light veil, in which she usually walked, she silently passed into the garden, and, hastening towards the distant groves, was glad to breathe once more the air of liberty, and to sigh unobserved. The deep repose of the scene, the rich scents, that floated on the breeze, the grandeur of the wide horizon and of the clear blue arch, soothed and gradually elevated her mind to that sublime complacency, which renders the vexations of this world so insignificant and mean in our eyes, that we wonder they have had power for a moment to disturb us. Emily forgot Madame Cheron and all the circumstances of her conduct, while her thoughts ascended to the contemplation of those unnumbered worlds, that lie scattered in the depths of æther, thousands of them hid from human eyes, and almost beyond the flight of human fancy. As her imagination soared through the regions of space, and aspired to that Great First Cause, which pervades and governs all being, the idea of her father scarcely ever left her; but it was a pleasing idea, since she resigned him to God in the full confidence of a pure and holy faith. She pursued her way through the groves to the terrace, often pausing as memory awakened the pang of affection, and as reason anticipated the exile, into which she was going.

And now the moon was high over the woods, touching their summits with yellow light, and darting between the foliage long level beams; while on the rapid Garonne below the trembling radiance was faintly obscured by the lightest vapour. Emily long watched the playing lustre, listened to the soothing murmur of the current, and the yet lighter sounds of the air, as it stirred, at intervals, the lofty palm-trees. "How delightful is the sweet breath of these groves," said she. "This lovely scene!—how often shall I remember and regret it, when I am far away. Alas! what events may occur before I see it again! O, peaceful, happy shades!—scenes of my infant delights, of parental tenderness now lost for ever!—why must I leave ye!—In your retreats I should still find safety and repose. Sweet hours of my childhood—I am now to leave even your last memorials! No objects, that would revive your impressions, will remain for me!"

Then drying her tears and looking up, her thoughts rose again to the sublime subject she had contemplated; the same divine complacency stole over her heart, and, hushing its throbs, inspired hope and confidence and resignation to the will of the Deity, whose works filled her mind with adoration.

Emily gazed long on the plane-tree, and then seated herself, for the last time, on the bench under its shade, where she had so often sat with her parents, and where, only a few hours before, she had conversed with Valancourt, at the remembrance of whom, thus revived, a mingled sensation of esteem, tenderness and anxiety rose in her breast. With this remembrance occurred a recollection of his late confession—that he had often wandered near her habitation in the night, having even passed the boundary of the garden, and it immediately occurred to her, that he might be at this moment in the grounds. The fear of meeting him, particularly after the declaration he had made, and of incurring a censure, which her aunt might so reasonably bestow, if it was known, that she was met by her lover, at this hour, made her instantly leave her beloved plane-tree, and walk towards the chateau. She cast an anxious eye around, and often stopped for a moment to examine the shadowy scene before she ventured to proceed, but she passed on without perceiving any person, till, having reached a clump of almond trees, not far from the house, she rested to take a retrospect of the garden, and to sigh forth another adieu. As her eyes wandered over the landscape she thought she perceived a person emerge from the groves, and pass slowly along a moon-light alley that led between them; but the distance, and the imperfect light would not suffer her to judge with any degree of certainty whether this was fancy or reality. She continued to gaze for some time on the spot, till on the dead stillness of the air she heard a sudden sound, and in the next instant fancied she distinguished footsteps near her. Wasting not another moment in conjecture, she hurried to the chateau, and, having reached it, retired to her chamber, where, as she closed her window she looked upon the garden, and then again thought she distinguished a figure, gliding between the almond trees she had just left. She immediately withdrew from the casement, and, though much agitated, sought in sleep the refreshment of a short oblivion.

CHAPTER XI

> I leave that flowery path for aye
> Of childhood, where I sported many a day,
> Warbling and sauntering carelessly along;
> Where every face was innocent and gay,
> Each vale romantic, tuneful every tongue,
> Sweet, wild, and artless all.
>
> THE MINSTREL

AT an early hour, the carriage, which was to take Emily and Madame Cheron to Tholouse, appeared at the door of the chateau, and Madame was already in the breakfast-room, when her niece entered it. The repast was silent and melancholy on the part of Emily; and Madame Cheron, whose vanity was piqued on observing her dejection, reproved her in a manner that did not contribute to remove it. It was with much reluctance, that Emily's request to take with her the dog, which had been a favourite of her father, was granted. Her aunt, impatient to be gone, ordered the carriage to draw up; and, while she passed to the hall door, Emily gave another look into the library, and another farewell glance over the garden, and then followed. Old Theresa stood at the door to take leave of her young lady. "God for ever keep you,

ma'amselle!" said she, while Emily gave her hand in silence, and could
answer only with a pressure of her hand, and a forced smile.

At the gate, which led out of the grounds, several of her father's pensioners were assembled to bid her farewell, to whom she would have
spoken, if her aunt would have suffered the driver to stop; and, having
distributed to them almost all the money she had about her, she sunk
back in the carriage, yielding to the melancholy of her heart. Soon
after, she caught, between the steep banks of the road, another view of
the chateau, peeping from among the high trees, and surrounded by
green slopes and tufted groves, the Garonne winding its way beneath
their shades, sometimes lost among the vineyards, and then rising in
greater majesty in the distant pastures. The towering precipices of the
Pyrenées, that rose to the south, gave Emily a thousand interesting recollections of her late journey; and these objects of her former enthusiastic admiration, now excited only sorrow and regret. Having gazed on
the chateau and its lovely scenery, till the banks again closed upon
them, her mind became too much occupied by mournful reflections,
to permit her to attend to the conversation, which Madame Cheron
had begun on some trivial topic, so that they soon travelled in profound
silence.

Valancourt, mean while, was returned to Estuviere, his heart occupied with the image of Emily; sometimes indulging in reveries of
future happiness, but more frequently shrinking with dread of the
opposition he might encounter from her family. He was the younger
son of an ancient family of Gascony; and, having lost his parents at an
early period of his life, the care of his education and of his small portion had devolved to his brother, the Count de Duvarney, his senior by
nearly twenty years. Valancourt had been educated in all the accomplishments of his age, and had an ardour of spirit, and a certain
grandeur of mind, that gave him particular excellence in the exercises
then thought heroic. His little fortune had been diminished by the necessary expences of his education; but M. La Valancourt, the elder,
seemed to think that his genius and accomplishments would amply
supply the deficiency of his inheritance. They offered flattering hopes
of promotion in the military profession, in those times almost the only
one in which a gentleman could engage without incurring a stain on
his name; and La Valancourt was of course enrolled in the army. The
general genius of his mind was but little understood by his brother.
That ardour for whatever is great and good in the moral world, as well
as in the natural one, displayed itself in his infant years; and the strong
indignation, which he felt and expressed at a criminal, or a mean
action, sometimes drew upon him the displeasure of his tutor; who
reprobated it under the general term of violence of temper; and who,

when haranguing on the virtues of mildness and moderation, seemed to forget the gentleness and compassion, which always appeared in his pupil towards objects of misfortune.

He had now obtained leave of absence from his regiment when he made the excursion into the Pyrenées, which was the means of introducing him to St. Aubert; and, as this permission was nearly expired, he was the more anxious to declare himself to Emily's family, from whom he reasonably apprehended opposition, since his fortune, though, with a moderate addition from hers, it would be sufficient to support them, would not satisfy the views, either of vanity, or ambition. Valancourt was not without the latter, but he saw golden visions of promotion in the army; and believed, that with Emily he could, in the mean time, be delighted to live within the limits of his humble income. His thoughts were now occupied in considering the means of making himself known to her family, to whom, however, he had yet no address, for he was entirely ignorant of Emily's precipitate departure from La Vallée, of whom he hoped to obtain it.

Meanwhile, the travellers pursued their journey; Emily making frequent efforts to appear cheerful, and too often relapsing into silence and dejection. Madame Cheron, attributing her melancholy solely to the circumstance of her being removed to a distance from her lover, and believing, that the sorrow, which her niece still expressed for the loss of St. Aubert, proceeded partly from an affectation of sensibility, endeavoured to make it appear ridiculous to her, that such deep regret should continue to be felt so long after the period usually allowed for grief.

At length, these unpleasant lectures were interrupted by the arrival of the travellers at Tholouse; and Emily, who had not been there for many years, and had only a very faint recollection of it, was surprised at the ostentatious style exhibited in her aunt's house and furniture; the more so, perhaps, because it was so totally different from the modest elegance, to which she had been accustomed. She followed Madame Cheron through a large hall, where several servants in rich liveries appeared, to a kind of saloon, fitted up with more shew than taste; and her aunt, complaining of fatigue, ordered supper immediately. "I am glad to find myself in my own house again," said she, throwing herself on a large settee, "and to have my own people about me. I detest travelling; though, indeed, I ought to like it, for what I see abroad always makes me delighted to return to my own chateau. What makes you so silent, child?—What is it that disturbs you now?"

Emily suppressed a starting tear, and tried to smile away the expression of an oppressed heart; she was thinking of *her* home, and felt too sensibly the arrogance and ostentatious vanity of Madame Cheron's conversation. "Can this be my father's sister!" said she to herself; and then the conviction that she was so, warming her heart with something like kindness towards her, she felt anxious to soften the harsh impression her mind had received of her aunt's character, and to shew a willingness to oblige her. The effort did not entirely fail; she listened with apparent chearfulness, while Madame Cheron expatiated on the splendour of her house, told of the numerous parties she entertained, and what she should expect of Emily, whose diffidence assumed the air of a reserve, which her aunt, believing it to be that of pride and ignorance united, now took occasion to reprehend. She knew nothing of the conduct of a mind, that fears to trust its own powers; which, possessing a nice judgment, and inclining to believe, that every other person perceives still more critically, fears to commit itself to censure, and seeks shelter in the obscurity of silence. Emily had frequently blushed at the fearless manners, which she had seen admired, and the brilliant nothings, which she had heard applauded; yet this applause, so far from encouraging her to imitate the conduct that had won it, rather made her shrink into the reserve, that would protect her from such absurdity.

Madame Cheron looked on her niece's diffidence with a feeling very near to contempt, and endeavoured to overcome it by reproof, rather than to encourage it by gentleness.

The entrance of supper somewhat interrupted the complacent discourse of Madame Cheron and the painful considerations, which it had forced upon Emily. When the repast, which was rendered ostentatious by the attendance of a great number of servants, and by a profusion of plate, was over, Madame Cheron retired to her chamber, and a female servant came to shew Emily to hers. Having passed up a large stair-case, and through several galleries, they came to a flight of back stairs, which led into a short passage in a remote part of the chateau, and there the servant opened the door of a small chamber, which she said was Ma'amselle Emily's, who, once more alone, indulged the tears she had long tried to restrain.

Those, who know, from experience, how much the heart becomes attached even to inanimate objects, to which it has been long accustomed, how unwillingly it resigns them; how with the sensations of an old friend it meets them, after temporary absence, will understand the forlornness of Emily's feelings, of Emily shut out from the only home she had known from her infancy, and thrown upon a scene, and among persons, disagreeable for more qualities than their novelty. Her father's favourite dog, now in the chamber, thus seemed to acquire the character and importance of a friend; and, as the animal fawned over her when she wept, and licked her hands, "Ah, poor Manchon!" said she, "I have nobody now to love me—but you!" and she wept the more.

After some time, her thoughts returning to her father's injunctions, she remembered how often he had blamed her for indulging useless sorrow; how often he had pointed out to her the necessity of fortitude and patience, assuring her, that the faculties of the mind strengthen by exertion, till they finally unnerve affliction, and triumph over it. These recollections dried her tears, gradually soothed her spirits, and inspired her with the sweet emulation of practising precepts, which her father had so frequently inculcated.

CHAPTER XII

Some pow'r impart the spear and shield,
At which the wizard passions fly,
By which the giant follies die.

COLLINS

MADAME Cheron's house stood at a little distance from the city of Tholouse, and was surrounded by extensive gardens, in which Emily, who had risen early, amused herself with wandering before breakfast. From a terrace, that extended along the highest part of them, was a wide view over Languedoc. On the distant horizon to the south, she discovered the wild summits of the Pyrenées, and her fancy immediately painted the green pastures of Gascony at their feet. Her heart pointed to her peaceful home—to the neighbourhood where Valancourt was—where St. Aubert had been; and her imagination, piercing the veil of distance, brought that home to her eyes in all its interesting and romantic beauty. She experienced an inexpressible pleasure in believing, that she beheld the country around it, though no feature could be distinguished, except the retiring chain of the Pyrenées; and, inattentive to the scene immediately before her, and to the flight of time, she continued to lean on the window of a pavilion, that terminated the terrace, with her eyes fixed on Gascony, and her mind occupied with the interesting ideas which the view of it awakened, till a servant came to tell her breakfast was ready. Her thoughts thus recalled to the surrounding objects, the straight walks, square parterres, and artificial fountains of the garden, could not fail, as she passed through it, to appear the worse, opposed to the negligent graces, and natural beauties of the grounds of La Vallée, upon which her recollection had been so intensely employed.

"Whither have you been rambling so early?" said Madame Cheron, as her niece entered the breakfast-room. "I don't approve of these solitary walks;" and Emily was surprised, when, having informed her aunt, that she had been no further than the gardens, she understood these to be included in the reproof. "I desire you will not walk there again at so early an hour unattended," said Madame Cheron; "my gardens are very extensive; and a young woman, who can make assignations by moonlight, at La Vallée, is not to be trusted to her own inclinations elsewhere."

Emily, extremely surprised and shocked, had scarcely power to beg an explanation of these words, and, when she did, her aunt absolutely refused to give it, though, by her severe looks, and half sentences, she appeared anxious to impress Emily with a belief, that she was well informed of some degrading circumstances of her conduct. Conscious innocence could not prevent a blush from stealing over Emily's cheek; she trembled, and looked confusedly under the bold eye of Madame Cheron, who blushed also; but hers was the blush of triumph, such as sometimes stains the countenance of a person, congratulating himself on the penetration which had taught him to suspect another, and who loses both pity for the supposed criminal, and indignation of his guilt, in the gratification of his own vanity.

Emily, not doubting that her aunt's mistake arose from the having observed her ramble in the garden on the night preceding her departure from La Vallée, now mentioned the motive of it, at which Madame Cheron smiled contemptuously, refusing either to accept this explanation, or to give her reasons for refusing it; and, soon after, she concluded the subject by saying, "I never trust people's assertions, I always judge of them by their actions; but I am willing to try what will be your behaviour in future."

Emily, less surprised by her aunt's moderation and mysterious silence, than by the accusation she had received, deeply considered the latter, and scarcely doubted, that it was Valancourt whom she had seen at night in the gardens of La Vallée, and that he had been observed there by Madame Cheron; who now passing from one painful topic only to revive another almost equally so, spoke of the situation of her niece's property, in the hands of M. Motteville. While she thus talked with ostentatious pity of Emily's misfortunes, she failed not to inculcate the duties of humility and gratitude, or to render Emily fully sensible of every cruel mortification, who soon perceived, that she was to be considered as a dependent, not only by her aunt, but by her aunt's servants.

She was now informed, that a large party were expected to dinner, on which account Madame Cheron repeated the lesson of the preceding night, concerning her conduct in company, and Emily wished, that she might have courage enough to practise it. Her aunt then proceeded to examine the simplicity of her dress, adding, that she expected to see her attired with gaiety and taste; after which she condescended to shew Emily the splendour of her chateau, and to point out the particular beauty, or elegance, which she thought distinguished each of her numerous suites of apartments. She then withdrew to her toilet, the throne of her homage, and Emily to her chamber, to unpack her books, and to try to charm her mind by reading, till the hour of dressing.

When the company arrived, Emily entered the saloon with an air of timidity, which all her efforts could not overcome, and which was increased by the consciousness of Madame Cheron's severe observation. Her mourning dress, the mild dejection of her beautiful countenance, and the retiring diffidence of her manner, rendered her a very interesting object to many of the company; among whom she distinguished Signor Montoni, and his friend Cavigni, the late visitors at M. Quesnel's, who now seemed to converse with Madame Cheron with the familiarity of old acquaintance, and she to attend to them with particular pleasure.

This Signor Montoni had an air of conscious superiority, animated by spirit, and strengthened by talents, to which every person seemed involuntarily to yield. The quickness of his perceptions was strikingly expressed on his countenance, yet that countenance could submit implicitly to occasion; and, more than once in this day, the triumph of art over nature might have been discerned in it. His visage was long, and rather narrow, yet he was called handsome; and it was, perhaps, the spirit and vigour of his soul, sparkling through his features, that triumphed for him. Emily felt admiration, but not the admiration that leads to esteem; for it was mixed with a degree of fear she knew not exactly wherefore.

Cavigni was gay and insinuating as formerly; and, though he paid almost incessant attention to Madame Cheron, he found some opportunities of conversing with Emily, to whom he directed, at first, the sallies of his wit, but now and then assumed an air of tenderness, which she observed, and shrunk from. Though she replied but little, the gentleness and sweetness of her manners encouraged him to talk, and she felt relieved when a young lady of the party, who spoke incessantly, obtruded herself on his notice. This lady, who possessed all the sprightliness of a Frenchwoman, with all her coquetry, affected to understand every subject, or rather there was no affectation in the case; for, never looking beyond the limits of her own ignorance, she believed she had nothing to learn. She attracted notice from all; amused some, disgusted others for a moment, and was then forgotten.

This day passed without any material occurrence; and Emily, though amused by the characters she had seen, was glad when she could retire to the recollections, which had acquired with her the character of duties.

A fortnight passed in a round of dissipation and company, and Emily, who attended Madame Cheron in all her visits, was sometimes entertained, but oftener wearied. She was struck by the apparent talents and knowledge displayed in the various conversations she listened to, and it was long before she discovered, that the talents were for the most part those of imposture, and the knowledge nothing more than was necessary to assist them. But what deceived her most, was the air of constant gaiety and good spirits, displayed by every visitor, and which she supposed to arise from content as constant, and from benevolence as ready. At length, from the over-acting of some, less accomplished than the others, she could perceive, that, though contentment and benevolence are the only sure sources of cheerfulness, the immoderate and feverish animation, usually exhibited in large parties, results partly from an insensibility to the cares, which benevolence must sometimes derive from the sufferings of others, and partly from a desire to display the appearance of that prosperity, which they know will command submission and attention to themselves.

Emily's pleasantest hours were passed in the pavilion of the terrace, to which she retired, when she could steal from observation, with a book to overcome, or a lute to indulge, her melancholy. There, as she sat with her eyes fixed on the far-distant Pyrenées, and her thoughts on Valancourt and the beloved scenes of Gascony, she would play the sweet and melancholy songs of her native province — the popular songs she had listened to from her childhood.

One evening, having excused herself from accompanying her aunt abroad, she thus withdrew to the pavilion, with books and her lute. It was the mild and beautiful evening of a sultry day, and the windows, which fronted the west, opened upon all the glory of a setting sun. Its rays illuminated, with strong splendour, the cliffs of the Pyrenées, and touched their snowy tops with a roseate hue, that remained, long after the sun had sunk below the horizon, and the shades of twilight had stolen over the landscape. Emily touched her lute with that fine melancholy expression, which came from her heart. The pensive hour and the scene, the evening light on the Garonne, that flowed at no great distance, and whose waves, as they passed towards La Vallée, she often viewed with a sigh, — these united circumstances disposed her mind to tenderness, and her thoughts were with Valancourt, of whom she had heard nothing since her arrival at Tholouse, and now that she was removed from him, and in uncertainty, she perceived all the interest he held in her heart. Before she saw Valancourt she had never met a mind and taste so accordant with her own, and, though Madame Cheron told her much of the arts of dissimulation, and that the elegance and propriety of thought, which she so much admired in her lover, were assumed for the purpose of pleasing her, she could scarcely doubt their truth. This possibility, however, faint as it was, was sufficient to harass her mind with anxiety, and she found, that few conditions are more painful than that of uncertainty, as to the merit of a beloved object; an uncertainty, which she would not have suffered, had her confidence in her own opinions been greater.

She was awakened from her musing by the sound of horses' feet along a road, that wound under the windows of the pavilion, and a gentleman passed on horseback, whose resemblance to Valancourt, in air and figure, for the twilight did not permit a view of his features, immediately struck her. She retired hastily from the lattice, fearing to be seen, yet wishing to observe further, while the stranger passed on without looking up, and, when she returned to the lattice, she saw him faintly through the twilight, winding under the high trees, that led to Tholouse. This little incident so much disturbed her spirits, that the temple and its scenery were no longer interesting to her, and, after walking awhile on the terrace, she returned to the chateau.

Madame Cheron, whether she had seen a rival admired, had lost at play, or had witnessed an entertainment more splendid than her own, was returned from her visit with a temper more than usually discomposed; and Emily was glad, when the hour arrived, in which she could retire to the solitude of her own apartment.

On the following morning, she was summoned to Madame Cheron, whose countenance was inflamed with resentment, and, as Emily advanced, she held out a letter to her.

"Do you know this hand?" said she, in a severe tone, and with a look that was intended to search her heart, while Emily examined the letter attentively, and assured her, that she did not.

"Do not provoke me," said her aunt; "you do know it, confess the truth immediately. I insist upon your confessing the truth instantly."

Emily was silent, and turned to leave the room, but Madame called her back. "O you are guilty, then," said she, "you do know the hand." "If you was before in doubt of this, madam," replied Emily calmly, "why did you accuse me of having told a falsehood." Madame Cheron did not blush; but her niece did, a moment after, when she heard the name of Valancourt. It was not, however, with the consciousness of deserving reproof, for, if she ever had seen his hand-writing, the present characters did not bring it to her recollection.

"It is useless to deny it," said Madame Cheron, "I see in your countenance, that you are no stranger to this letter; and, I dare say, you have received many such from this impertinent young man, without my knowledge, in my own house."

Emily, shocked at the indelicacy of this accusation, still more than by the vulgarity of the former, instantly forgot the pride, that had imposed silence, and endeavoured to vindicate herself from the aspersion, but Madame Cheron was not to be convinced.

"I cannot suppose," she resumed, "that this young man would have taken the liberty of writing to me, if you had not encouraged him to do so, and I must now"—"You will allow me to remind you, madam," said Emily timidly, "of some particulars of a conversation we had at La Vallée. I then told you truly, that I had only not forbade Monsieur Valancourt from addressing my family."

"I will not be interrupted," said Madame Cheron, interrupting her niece, "I was going to say—I—I—have forgot what I was going to say. But how happened it that you did not forbid him?" Emily was silent. "How happened it that you encouraged him to trouble me with this letter?—A young man that nobody knows;—an utter stranger in the place,—a young adventurer, no doubt, who is looking out for a good fortune. However, on that point he has mistaken his aim."

"His family was known to my father," said Emily modestly, and without appearing to be sensible of the last sentence.

"O! that is no recommendation at all," replied her aunt, with her usual readiness upon this topic; "he took such strange fancies to people! He was always judging persons by their countenances, and was continually deceived." "Yet it was but now, madam, that you judged me guilty by my countenance," said Emily, with a design of reproving Madame Cheron, to which she was induced by this disrespectful mention of her father.

"I called you here," resumed her aunt, colouring, "to tell you, that I will not be disturbed in my own house by any letters, or visits from young men, who may take a fancy to flatter you. This M. de Valantine—I think you call him, has the impertinence to beg I will permit him to pay his respects to me! I shall send him a proper answer. And for you, Emily, I repeat it once for all—if you are not contented to conform to my directions, and to my way of life, I shall give up the task of overlooking your conduct—I shall no longer trouble myself with your education, but shall send you to board in a convent."

"Dear madam," said Emily, bursting into tears, and overcome by the rude suspicions her aunt had expressed, "how have I deserved these reproofs?" She could say no more; and so very fearful was she of acting with any degree of impropriety in the affair itself, that, at the present moment, Madame Cheron might perhaps have prevailed with her to bind herself by a promise to renounce Valancourt for ever. Her mind, weakened by her terrors, would no longer suffer her to view him as she had formerly done; she feared the error of her own judgment, not that of Madame Cheron, and feared also, that, in her former conversation with him, at La Vallée, she had not conducted herself with sufficient reserve. She knew, that she did not deserve the coarse suspicions, which her aunt had thrown out, but a thousand scruples rose to torment her, such as would never have disturbed the peace of Madame Cheron. Thus rendered anxious to avoid every opportunity of erring, and willing to submit to any restrictions, that her aunt should think proper, she expressed an obedience, to which Madame Cheron did not give much confidence, and which she seemed to consider as the consequence of either fear, or artifice.

"Well, then," said she, "promise me that you will neither see this young man, nor write to him without my consent." "Dear madam," replied Emily, "can you suppose I would do either, unknown to you!" "I don't know what to suppose; there is no knowing how young women will act. It is difficult to place any confidence in them, for they have seldom sense enough to wish for the respect of the world."

"Alas, madam!" said Emily, "I am anxious for my own respect; my father taught me the value of that; he said if I deserved my own esteem, that the world would follow of course."

"My brother was a good kind of a man," replied Madame Cheron, "but he did not know the world. I am sure I have always felt a proper respect for myself, yet——" she stopped, but she might have added, that the world had not always shewn respect to her, and this without impeaching its judgment.

"Well!" resumed Madame Cheron, "you have not given me the promise, though, that I demand." Emily readily gave it, and, being then suffered to withdraw, she walked in the garden; tried to compose her spirits, and, at length, arrived at her favourite pavilion at the end of the terrace, where, seating herself at one of the embowered windows, that opened upon a balcony, the stillness and seclusion of the scene allowed her to recollect her thoughts, and to arrange them so as to form a clearer judgment of her former conduct. She endeavoured to review with exactness all the particulars of her conversation with Valancourt at La Vallée, had the satisfaction to observe nothing, that could alarm her delicate pride, and thus to be confirmed in the self-esteem, which was so necessary to her peace. Her mind then became tranquil, and she saw Valancourt amiable and intelligent, as he had formerly appeared, and Madame Cheron neither the one, or the other. The remembrance of her lover, however, brought with it many very painful emotions, for it by no means reconciled her to the thought of resigning him; and, Madame Cheron having already shewn how highly she disapproved of the attachment, she foresaw much suffering from the opposition of interests; yet with all this was mingled a degree of delight, which, in spite of reason, partook of hope. She determined, however, that no consideration should induce her to permit a clandestine correspondence, and to observe in her conversation with Valancourt, should they ever meet again, the same nicety of reserve, which had hitherto marked her conduct. As she repeated the words—"should we ever meet again!" she shrunk as if this was a circumstance, which had never before occurred to her, and tears came to her eyes, which she hastily dried, for she heard footsteps approaching, and then the door of the pavilion open, and, on turning, she saw—Valancourt. An emotion of mingled pleasure, surprise and apprehension pressed so suddenly upon her heart as almost to overcome her spirits; the colour left her cheeks, then returned brighter than before, and she was for a moment unable to speak, or to rise from her chair. His countenance was the mirror, in which she saw her own emotions reflected, and it roused her to self-command. The joy, which had animated his features, when he entered the pavilion, was suddenly repressed, as, approaching, he perceived her agitation, and, in a tremulous voice, enquired after her health. Recovered from her first surprise, she answered him with a tempered smile; but a variety of opposite emotions still assailed her heart, and struggled to subdue the mild dignity of her manner. It was difficult to tell which predominated—the joy of seeing Valancourt, or the terror of her aunt's displeasure, when she should hear of this meeting. After some short and embarrassed conversation, she led him into the gardens, and enquired if he had seen Madame Cheron. "No," said he, "I have not yet seen her, for they told me she was engaged, and as soon as I learned that you were in the gardens, I came hither." He paused a moment, in great agitation, and then added, "May I venture to tell you the purport of my visit, without incurring your displeasure, and to hope, that you will not accuse me of precipitation in now availing myself of the permission you once gave me of addressing your family?" Emily, who knew not what to reply, was spared from further perplexity, and was sensible only of fear, when on raising her eyes, she saw Madame Cheron turn into the avenue. As the consciousness of innocence returned, this fear was so far dissipated as to permit her to appear tranquil, and, instead of avoiding her aunt, she advanced with Valancourt to meet her. The look of haughty and impatient displeasure, with which Madame Cheron regarded them, made Emily shrink, who understood from a single glance, that this meeting was believed to have been more than accidental: having mentioned Valancourt's name, she became again too much agitated to remain with them, and returned into the chateau; where she awaited long, in a state of trembling anxiety, the conclusion of the conference. She knew not how to account for Valancourt's visit to her aunt, before he had received the permission he solicited, since she was ignorant of a circumstance, which would have rendered the request useless, even if Madame Cheron had been inclined to grant it. Valancourt, in the agitation of his spirits, had forgotten to date his letter, so that it was impossible for Madame Cheron to return an answer; and, when he recollected this circumstance, he was, perhaps, not so sorry for the omission as glad of the excuse it allowed him for waiting on her before she could send a refusal.

Madame Cheron had a long conversation with Valancourt, and, when she returned to the chateau, her countenance expressed ill-humour, but not the degree of severity, which Emily had apprehended. "I have dismissed this young man, at last," said she, "and I hope my house will never again be disturbed with similar visits. He assures me, that your interview was not preconcerted."

"Dear madam!" said Emily in extreme emotion, "you surely did not ask him the question!" "Most certainly I did; you could not suppose I should be so imprudent as to neglect it."

"Good God!" exclaimed Emily, "what an opinion must he form of me, since you, Madam, could express a suspicion of such ill conduct!"

"It is of very little consequence what opinion he may form of you," replied her aunt, "for I have put an end to the affair; but I believe he will not form a worse opinion of me for my prudent conduct. I let him see, that I was not to be trifled with, and that I had more delicacy, than to permit any clandestine correspondence to be carried on in my house."

Emily had frequently heard Madame Cheron use the word delicacy, but she was now more than usually perplexed to understand how she meant to apply it in this instance, in which her whole conduct appeared to merit the very reverse of the term.

"It was very inconsiderate of my brother," resumed Madame Cheron, "to leave the trouble of overlooking your conduct to me; I wish you was well settled in life. But if I find, that I am to be further troubled with such visitors as this M. Valancourt, I shall place you in a convent at once;—so remember the alternative. This young man has the impertinence to own to me,—he owns it! that his fortune is very small, and that he is chiefly dependent on an elder brother and on the profession he has chosen! He should have concealed these circumstances, at least, if he expected to succeed with me. Had he the presumption to suppose I would marry my niece to a person such as he describes himself!"

Emily dried her tears when she heard of the candid confession of Valancourt; and, though the circumstances it discovered were afflicting to her hopes, his artless conduct gave her a degree of pleasure, that overcame every other emotion. But she was compelled, even thus early in life, to observe, that good sense and noble integrity are not always sufficient to cope with folly and narrow cunning; and her heart was pure enough to allow her, even at this trying moment, to look with more pride on the defeat of the former, than with mortification on the conquests of the latter.

Madame Cheron pursued her triumph. "He has also thought proper to tell me, that he will receive his dismission from no person but yourself; this favour, however, I have absolutely refused him. He shall learn, that it is quite sufficient, that I disapprove him. And I take this opportunity of repeating,—that if you concert any means of interview unknown to me, you shall leave my house immediately."

"How little do you know me, madam, that you should think such an injunction necessary!" said Emily, trying to suppress her emotion, "how little of the dear parents, who educated me!"

Madame Cheron now went to dress for an engagement, which she had made for the evening; and Emily, who would gladly have been excused from attending her aunt, did not ask to remain at home lest her request should be attributed to an improper motive. When she retired to her own room, the little fortitude, which had supported her in the presence of her relation, forsook her; she remembered only that Valancourt, whose character appeared more amiable from every circumstance, that unfolded it, was banished from her presence, perhaps, for ever, and she passed the time in weeping, which, according to her aunt's direction, she ought to have employed in dressing. This important duty was, however, quickly dispatched; though, when she joined Madame Cheron at table, her eyes betrayed, that she had been in tears, and drew upon her a severe reproof.

Her efforts to appear cheerful did not entirely fail when she joined the company at the house of Madame Clairval, an elderly widow lady, who had lately come to reside at Tholouse, on an estate of her late husband. She had lived many years at Paris in a splendid style; had naturally a gay temper, and, since her residence at Tholouse, had given some of the most magnificent entertainments, that had been seen in that neighbourhood.

These excited not only the envy, but the trifling ambition of Madame Cheron, who, since she could not rival the splendour of her festivities, was desirous of being ranked in the number of her most intimate friends. For this purpose she paid her the most obsequious attention, and made a point of being disengaged, whenever she received an invitation from Madame Clairval, of whom she talked, wherever she went, and derived much self-consequence from impressing a belief on her general acquaintance, that they were on the most familiar footing.

The entertainments of this evening consisted of a ball and supper; it was a fancy ball, and the company danced in groups in the gardens, which were very extensive. The high and luxuriant trees, under which the groups assembled, were illuminated with a profusion of lamps, disposed with taste and fancy. The gay and various dresses of the company, some of whom were seated on the turf, conversing at their ease, observing the cotillons, taking refreshments, and sometimes touching sportively a guitar; the gallant manners of the gentlemen, the exquisitely capricious air of the ladies; the light fantastic steps of their dances; the musicians, with the lute, the hautboy, and the tabor, seated at the foot of an elm, and the sylvan scenery of woods around were circumstances, that unitedly formed a characteristic and striking picture of French festivity. Emily surveyed the gaiety of the scene with a melancholy kind of pleasure, and her emotion may be imagined when, as she stood with her aunt, looking at one of the groups, she perceived Valancourt; saw him dancing with a young and beautiful lady, saw him conversing with her with a mixture of attention and familiarity, such as she had seldom observed in his manner. She turned hastily from the scene, and attempted to draw away Madame Cheron, who was conversing with Signor Cavigni, and neither perceived Valancourt, or was willing to be interrupted. A faintness suddenly came over Emily, and, unable to support herself, she sat down on a turf bank beneath the trees, where several other persons were seated. One of these, observing the extreme paleness of her countenance, enquired if she was ill, and begged she would allow him to fetch her a glass of water, for which politeness she thanked him, but did not accept it. Her apprehension lest Valancourt should observe her emotion made her anxious to overcome it, and she succeeded so far as to re-compose her countenance. Madame Cheron was still conversing with Cavigni; and the Count Bauvillers, who had addressed Emily, made some observations upon the scene, to which she answered almost unconsciously, for her mind was still occupied with the idea of Valancourt, to whom it was with extreme uneasiness that she remained so near. Some remarks, however, which the Count made upon the dance obliged her to turn her eyes towards it, and, at that moment, Valancourt's met hers. Her colour faded again, she felt, that she was relapsing into faintness, and instantly averted her looks, but not before she had observed the altered countenance of Valancourt, on perceiving her. She would have left the spot immediately, had she not been conscious, that this conduct would have shewn him more obviously the interest he held in her heart; and, having tried to attend to the Count's conversation, and to join in it, she, at length, recovered her spirits. But, when he made some observation on Valancourt's partner, the fear of shewing that she was interested in the remark, would have betrayed it to him, had not the Count, while he spoke, looked towards the person of whom he was speaking. "The lady," said he, "dancing with that young Chevalier, who appears to be accomplished in every thing, but in dancing, is ranked among the beauties of Tholouse. She is handsome, and her fortune will be very large. I hope she will make a better choice in a partner for life than she has done in a partner for the dance, for I observe he has just put the set into great confusion; he does nothing but commit blunders. I am surprised, that, with his air and figure, he has not taken more care to accomplish himself in dancing."

Emily, whose heart trembled at every word, that was now uttered, endeavoured to turn the conversation from Valancourt, by enquiring the name of the lady, with whom he danced; but, before the Count could reply, the dance concluded, and Emily, perceiving that Valancourt was coming towards her, rose and joined Madame Cheron.

"Here is the Chevalier Valancourt, madam," said she in a whisper, "pray let us go." Her aunt immediately moved on, but not before Valancourt had reached them, who bowed lowly to Madame Cheron, and with an earnest and dejected look to Emily, with whom, notwithstanding all her effort, an air of more than common reserve prevailed. The presence of Madame Cheron prevented Valancourt from remaining, and he passed on with a countenance, whose melancholy reproached her for having increased it. Emily was called from the musing fit, into which she had fallen, by the Count Bauvillers, who was known to her aunt.

"I have your pardon to beg, ma'amselle," said he, "for a rudeness, which you will readily believe was quite unintentional. I did not know, that the Chevalier was your acquaintance, when I so freely criticised his dancing." Emily blushed and smiled, and Madame Cheron spared her the difficulty of replying. "If you mean the person, who has just passed us," said she, "I can assure you he is no acquaintance of either mine, or ma'amselle St. Aubert's: I know nothing of him."

"O! that is the Chevalier Valancourt," said Cavigni carelessly, and looking back. "You know him then?" said Madame Cheron. "I am not acquainted with him," replied Cavigni. "You don't know, then, the reason I have to call him impertinent;—he has had the presumption to admire my niece!"

"If every man deserves the title of impertinent, who admires ma'amselle St. Aubert," replied Cavigni, "I fear there are a great many impertinents, and I am willing to acknowledge myself one of the number."

"O Signor!" said Madame Cheron, with an affected smile, "I perceive you have learnt the art of complimenting, since you came into France. But it is cruel to compliment children, since they mistake flattery for truth."

Cavigni turned away his face for a moment, and then said with a studied air, "Whom then are we to compliment, madam? for it would be absurd to compliment a woman of refined understanding; *she* is above all praise." As he finished the sentence he gave Emily a sly look, and the smile, that had lurked in his eye, stole forth. She perfectly understood it, and blushed for Madame Cheron, who replied, "You are perfectly right, signor, no woman of understanding can endure compliment."

"I have heard Signor Montoni say," rejoined Cavigni, "that he never knew but one woman who deserved it."

"Well!" exclaimed Madame Cheron, with a short laugh, and a smile of unutterable complacency, "and who could she be?"

"O!" replied Cavigni, "it is impossible to mistake her, for certainly there is not more than one woman in the world, who has both the merit to deserve compliment and the wit to refuse it. Most women reverse the case entirely." He looked again at Emily, who blushed deeper than before for her aunt, and turned from him with displeasure.

"Well, signor!" said Madame Cheron, "I protest you are a Frenchman; I never heard a foreigner say any thing half so gallant as that!"

"True, madam," said the Count, who had been some time silent, and with a low bow, "but the gallantry of the compliment had been utterly lost, but for the ingenuity that discovered the application."

Madame Cheron did not perceive the meaning of this too satirical sentence, and she, therefore, escaped the pain, which Emily felt on her account. "O! here comes Signor Montoni himself," said her aunt, "I protest I will tell him all the fine things you have been saying to me." The Signor, however, passed at this moment into another walk. "Pray, who is it, that has so much engaged your friend this evening?" asked Madame Cheron, with an air of chagrin, "I have not seen him once."

"He had a very particular engagement with the Marquis La Rivière," replied Cavigni, "which has detained him, I perceive, till this moment, or he would have done himself the honour of paying his respects to you, madam, sooner, as he commissioned me to say. But, I know not how it is—your conversation is so fascinating—that it can charm even memory, I think, or I should certainly have delivered my friend's apology before."

"The apology, sir, would have been more satisfactory from himself," said Madame Cheron, whose vanity was more mortified by Montoni's neglect, than flattered by Cavigni's compliment. Her manner, at this moment, and Cavigni's late conversation, now awakened a suspicion in Emily's mind, which, notwithstanding that some recollections served to confirm it, appeared preposterous. She thought she perceived, that

Montoni was paying serious addresses to her aunt, and that she not only accepted them, but was jealously watchful of any appearance of neglect on his part.—That Madame Cheron at her years should elect a second husband was ridiculous, though her vanity made it not impossible; but that Montoni, with his discernment, his figure, and pretensions, should make a choice of Madame Cheron—appeared most wonderful. Her thoughts, however, did not dwell long on the subject; nearer interests pressed upon them; Valancourt, rejected of her aunt, and Valancourt dancing with a gay and beautiful partner, alternately tormented her mind. As she passed along the gardens she looked timidly forward, half fearing and half hoping that he might appear in the crowd; and the disappointment she felt on not seeing him, told her, that she had hoped more than she had feared.

Montoni soon after joined the party. He muttered over some short speech about regret for having been so long detained elsewhere, when he knew he should have the pleasure of seeing Madame Cheron here; and she, receiving the apology with the air of a pettish girl, addressed herself entirely to Cavigni, who looked archly at Montoni, as if he would have said, "I will not triumph over you too much; I will have the goodness to bear my honours meekly; but look sharp, Signor, or I shall certainly run away with your prize."

The supper was served in different pavilions in the gardens, as well as in one large saloon of the chateau, and with more of taste, than either of splendour, or even of plenty. Madame Cheron and her party supped with Madame Clairval in the saloon, and Emily, with difficulty, disguised her emotion, when she saw Valancourt placed at the same table with herself. There, Madame Cheron having surveyed him with high displeasure, said to some person who sat next to her, "Pray, who *is* that young man?" "It is the Chevalier Valancourt," was the answer. "Yes, I am not ignorant of his name, but who is this Chevalier Valancourt that thus intrudes himself at this table?" The attention of the person, to whom she spoke, was called off before she received a second reply. The table, at which they sat, was very long, and, Valancourt being seated, with his partner, near the bottom, and Emily near the top, the distance between them may account for his not immediately perceiving her. She avoided looking to that end of the table, but whenever her eyes happened to glance towards it, she observed him conversing with his beautiful companion, and the observation did not contribute to restore her peace, any more than the accounts she heard of the fortune and accomplishments of this same lady.

Madame Cheron, to whom these remarks were sometimes addressed, because they supported topics for trivial conversation, seemed indefatigable in her attempts to depreciate Valancourt, towards whom she felt all the petty resentment of a narrow pride. "I admire the lady," said she, "but I must condemn her choice of a partner." "Oh, the Chevalier Valancourt is one of the most accomplished young men we have," replied the lady, to whom this remark was addressed: "it is whispered, that Mademoiselle D'Emery, and her large fortune, are to be his."

"Impossible!" exclaimed Madame Cheron, reddening with vexation, "it is impossible that she can be so destitute of taste; he has so little the air of a person of condition, that, if I did not see him at the table of Madame Clairval, I should never have suspected him to be one. I have besides particular reasons for believing the report to be erroneous."

"I cannot doubt the truth of it," replied the lady gravely, disgusted by the abrupt contradiction she had received, concerning her opinion of Valancourt's merit. "You will, perhaps, doubt it," said Madame Cheron, "when I assure you, that it was only this morning that I rejected his suit." This was said without any intention of imposing the meaning it conveyed, but simply from a habit of considering herself to be the most important person in every affair that concerned her niece, and because literally she had rejected Valancourt. "Your reasons are indeed such as cannot be doubted," replied the lady, with an ironical smile. "Any more than the discernment of the Chevalier Valancourt," added Cavigni, who stood by the chair of Madame Cheron, and had heard her arrogate to herself, as he thought, a distinction which had been paid to her niece. "His discernment *may* be justly questioned, Signor," said Madame Cheron, who was not flattered by what she understood to be an encomium on Emily.

"Alas!" exclaimed Cavigni, surveying Madame Cheron with affected ecstasy, "how vain is that assertion, while that face—that shape—that air—combine to refute it! Unhappy Valancourt! his discernment has been his destruction."

Emily looked surprised and embarrassed; the lady, who had lately spoke, astonished, and Madame Cheron, who, though she did not perfectly understand this speech, was very ready to believe herself complimented by it, said smilingly, "O Signor! you are very gallant; but those, who hear you vindicate the Chevalier's discernment, will suppose that I am the object of it."

"They cannot doubt it," replied Cavigni, bowing low.

"And would not that be very mortifying, Signor?"

"Unquestionably it would," said Cavigni.

"I cannot endure the thought," said Madame Cheron.

"It is not to be endured," replied Cavigni.

"What can be done to prevent so humiliating a mistake?" rejoined Madame Cheron.

"Alas! I cannot assist you," replied Cavigni, with a deliberating air. "Your only chance of refuting the calumny, and of making people understand what you wish them to believe, is to persist in your first assertion; for, when they are told of the Chevalier's want of discernment, it is possible they may suppose he never presumed to distress you with his admiration.—But then again—that diffidence, which renders you so insensible to your own perfections—they will consider this, and Valancourt's taste will not be doubted, though you arraign it. In short, they will, in spite of your endeavours, continue to believe, what might very naturally have occurred to them without any hint of mine—that the Chevalier has taste enough to admire a beautiful woman."

"All this is very distressing!" said Madame Cheron, with a profound sigh.

"May I be allowed to ask what is so distressing?" said Madame Clairval, who was struck with the rueful countenance and doleful accent, with which this was delivered.

"It is a delicate subject," replied Madame Cheron, "a very mortifying one to me." "I am concerned to hear it," said Madame Clairval, "I hope nothing has occurred, this evening, particularly to distress you?" "Alas, yes! within this half hour; and I know not where the report may end;—my pride was never so shocked before, but I assure you the report is totally void of foundation." "Good God!" exclaimed Madame Clairval, "what can be done? Can you point out any way, by which I can assist, or console you?"

"The only way, by which you can do either," replied Madame Cheron, "is to contradict the report wherever you go."

"Well! but pray inform me what I am to contradict."

"It is so very humiliating, that I know not how to mention it," continued Madame Cheron, "but you shall judge. Do you observe that young man seated near the bottom of the table, who is conversing with Mademoiselle D'Emery?" "Yes, I perceive whom you mean." "You observe how little he has the air of a person of condition; I was saying just now, that I should not have thought him a gentleman, if I had not seen him at this table." "Well! but the report," said Madame Clairval, "let me understand the subject of your distress." "Ah! the subject of my distress," replied Madame Cheron; "this person, whom nobody knows—(I beg pardon, madam, I did not consider what I said)—this impertinent young man, having had the presumption to address my niece, has, I fear, given rise to a report, that he had declared himself my admirer. Now only consider how very mortifying such a report must be! You, I know, will feel for my situation. A woman of my condition!—think how degrading even the rumour of such an alliance must be."

"Degrading indeed, my poor friend!" said Madame Clairval. "You may rely upon it I will contradict the report wherever I go;" as she said which, she turned her attention upon another part of the company; and Cavigni, who had hitherto appeared a grave spectator of the scene, now fearing he should be unable to smother the laugh, that convulsed him, walked abruptly away.

"I perceive you do not know," said the lady who sat near Madame Cheron, "that the gentleman you have been speaking of is Madame Clairval's nephew!" "Impossible!" exclaimed Madame Cheron, who now began to perceive, that she had been totally mistaken in her judgment of Valancourt, and to praise him aloud with as much servility, as she had before censured him with frivolous malignity.

Emily, who, during the greater part of this conversation, had been so absorbed in thought as to be spared the pain of hearing it, was now extremely surprised by her aunt's praise of Valancourt, with whose relationship to Madame Clairval she was unacquainted; but she was not sorry when Madame Cheron, who, though she now tried to appear unconcerned, was really much embarrassed, prepared to withdraw immediately after supper. Montoni then came to hand Madame Cheron to her carriage, and Cavigni, with an arch solemnity of countenance, followed with Emily, who, as she wished them good night, and drew up the glass, saw Valancourt among the crowd at the gates. Before the carriage drove off, he disappeared. Madame Cheron forbore to mention him to Emily, and, as soon as they reached the chateau, they separated for the night.

On the following morning, as Emily sat at breakfast with her aunt, a letter was brought to her, of which she knew the handwriting upon the cover; and, as she received it with a trembling hand, Madame Cheron hastily enquired from whom it came. Emily, with her leave, broke the seal, and, observing the signature of Valancourt, gave it unread to her aunt, who received it with impatience; and, as she looked it over, Emily endeavoured to read on her countenance its contents. Having returned the letter to her niece, whose eyes asked if she might examine it, "Yes, read it, child," said Madame Cheron, in a manner less severe than she had expected, and Emily had, perhaps, never before so willingly obeyed her aunt. In this letter Valancourt said little of the interview of the preceding day, but concluded with declaring, that he would accept his dismission from Emily only, and with entreating, that she would allow him to wait upon her, on the approaching evening. When she read this, she was astonished at the moderation of Madame Cheron, and looked at her with timid expectation, as she said sorrowfully—"What am I to say, madam?"

"Why—we must see the young man, I believe," replied her aunt, "and hear what he has further to say for himself. You may tell him he may come." Emily dared scarcely credit what she heard. "Yet, stay," added Madame Cheron, "I will tell him so myself." She called for pen and ink; Emily still not daring to trust the emotions she felt, and almost sinking beneath them. Her surprise would have been less had she overheard, on the preceding evening, what Madame Cheron had not forgotten—that Valancourt was the nephew of Madame Clairval.

What were the particulars of her aunt's note Emily did not learn, but the result was a visit from Valancourt in the evening, whom Madame Cheron received alone, and they had a long conversation before Emily was called down. When she entered the room, her aunt was conversing with complacency, and she saw the eyes of Valancourt, as he impatiently rose, animated with hope.

"We have been talking over this affair," said Madame Cheron, "the Chevalier has been telling me, that the late Monsieur Clairval was the brother of the Countess de Duvarney, his mother. I only wish he had mentioned his relationship to Madame Clairval before; I certainly should have considered that circumstance as a sufficient introduction to my house." Valancourt bowed, and was going to address Emily, but her aunt prevented him. "I have, therefore, consented that you shall receive his visits; and, though I will not bind myself by any promise, or say, that I shall consider him as my nephew, yet I shall permit the intercourse, and shall look forward to any further connection as an event, which may possibly take place in a course of years, provided the Chevalier rises in his profession, or any circumstance occurs, which may make it prudent for him to take a wife. But Mons. Valancourt will observe, and you too, Emily, that, till that happens, I positively forbid any thoughts of marrying."

Emily's countenance, during this coarse speech, varied every instant, and, towards its conclusion, her distress had so much increased, that she was on the point of leaving the room. Valancourt, meanwhile, scarcely less embarrassed, did not dare to look at her, for whom he was thus distressed; but, when Madame Cheron was silent, he said, "Flattering, madam, as your approbation is to me—highly as I am honoured by it—I have yet so much to fear, that I scarcely dare to hope." "Pray, sir, explain yourself," said Madame Cheron; an unexpected requisition, which embarrassed Valancourt again, and almost overcame him with confusion, at circumstances, on which, had he been only a spectator of the scene, he would have smiled.

"Till I receive Mademoiselle St. Aubert's permission to accept your indulgence," said he, falteringly—"till she allows me to hope——"

"O! is that all?" interrupted Madame Cheron. "Well, I will take upon me to answer for her. But at the same time, sir, give me leave to observe to you, that I am her guardian, and that I expect, in every instance, that my will is hers."

As she said this, she rose and quitted the room, leaving Emily and Valancourt in a state of mutual embarrassment; and, when Valancourt's hopes enabled him to overcome his fears, and to address her with the zeal and sincerity so natural to him, it was a considerable time before she was sufficiently recovered to hear with distinctness his solicitations and enquiries.

The conduct of Madame Cheron in this affair had been entirely governed by selfish vanity. Valancourt, in his first interview, had with great candour laid open to her the true state of his present circumstances, and his future expectancies, and she, with more prudence than humanity, had absolutely and abruptly rejected his suit. She wished her niece to marry ambitiously, not because she desired to see her in possession of the happiness, which rank and wealth are usually believed to bestow, but because she desired to partake the importance, which such an alliance would give. When, therefore, she discovered that Valancourt was the nephew of a person of so much consequence as Madame Clairval, she became anxious for the connection, since the prospect it afforded of future fortune and distinction for Emily, promised the exaltation she coveted for herself. Her calculations concerning fortune in this alliance were guided rather by her wishes, than by any hint of Valancourt, or strong appearance of probability; and, when she rested her expectation on the wealth of Madame Clairval, she seemed totally to have forgotten, that the latter had a daughter. Valancourt, however, had not forgotten this circumstance, and the consideration of it had made him so modest in his expectations from Madame Clairval, that he had not even named the relationship in his first conversation with Madame Cheron. But, whatever might be the future fortune of Emily, the present distinction, which the connection would afford for herself, was certain, since the splendour of Madame Clairval's establishment was such as to excite the general envy and partial imitation of the neighbourhood. Thus had she consented to involve her niece in an engagement, to which she saw only a distant and uncertain conclusion, with as little consideration of her happiness, as when she had so precipitately forbade it: for though she herself possessed the means of rendering this union not only certain, but prudent, yet to do so was no part of her present intention.

From this period Valancourt made frequent visits to Madame Cheron, and Emily passed in his society the happiest hours she had known since the death of her father. They were both too much engaged by the present moments to give serious consideration to the future. They loved and were beloved, and saw not, that the very attachment, which formed the delight of their present days, might possibly occasion the sufferings of years. Meanwhile, Madame Cheron's intercourse with Madame Clairval became more frequent than before, and her vanity was already gratified by the opportunity of proclaiming, wherever she went, the attachment that subsisted between their nephew and niece.

Montoni was now also become a daily guest at the chateau, and Emily was compelled to observe, that he really was a suitor, and a favoured suitor, to her aunt.

Thus passed the winter months, not only in peace, but in happiness, to Valancourt and Emily; the station of his regiment being so near Tholouse, as to allow this frequent intercourse. The pavilion on the terrace was the favourite scene of their interviews, and there Emily, with Madame Cheron, would work, while Valancourt read aloud works of genius and taste, listened to her enthusiasm, expressed his own, and caught new opportunities of observing, that their minds were formed to constitute the happiness of each other, the same taste, the same noble and benevolent sentiments animating each.

CHAPTER XIII

> As when a shepherd of the Hebrid-Isles,
> Placed far amid the melancholy main,
> (Whether it be lone fancy him beguiles,
> Or that aerial beings sometimes deign
> To stand embodied to our senses plain)
> Sees on the naked hill, or valley low,
> The whilst in ocean Phœbus dips his wain,
> A vast assembly moving to and fro,
> Then all at once in air dissolves the wondrous show.
>
> CASTLE OF INDOLENCE

MADAME Cheron's avarice at length yielded to her vanity. Some very splendid entertainments, which Madame Clairval had given, and the general adulation, which was paid her, made the former more anxious than before to secure an alliance, that would so much exalt her in her own opinion and in that of the world. She proposed terms for the immediate marriage of her niece, and offered to give Emily a dower, provided Madame Clairval observed equal terms, on the part of her nephew. Madame Clairval listened to the proposal, and, considering that Emily was the apparent heiress of her aunt's wealth, accepted it. Meanwhile, Emily knew nothing of the transaction, till Madame Cheron informed her, that she must make preparation for the nuptials, which would be celebrated without further delay; then, astonished and wholly unable to account for this sudden conclusion, which Valancourt had not solicited (for he was ignorant of what had passed between the elder ladies, and had not dared to hope such good fortune), she decisively objected to it. Madame Cheron, however, quite as jealous of contradiction now, as she had been formerly, contended for a speedy marriage with as much vehemence as she had formerly opposed whatever had the most remote possibility of leading to it; and Emily's scruples disappeared, when she again saw Valancourt, who was now informed of the happiness, designed for him, and came to claim a promise of it from herself.

While preparations were making for these nuptials, Montoni became the acknowledged lover of Madame Cheron; and, though Madame Clairval was much displeased, when she heard of the approaching connection, and was willing to prevent that of Valancourt with Emily, her conscience told her, that she had no right thus to trifle with their peace, and Madame Clairval, though a woman of fashion, was far less advanced than her friend in the art of deriving satisfaction from distinction and admiration, rather than from conscience.

Emily observed with concern the ascendancy, which Montoni had acquired over Madame Cheron, as well as the increasing frequency of his visits; and her own opinion of this Italian was confirmed by that of Valancourt, who had always expressed a dislike of him. As she was, one morning, sitting at work in the pavilion, enjoying the pleasant freshness of spring, whose colours were now spread upon the landscape, and listening to Valancourt, who was reading, but who often laid aside the book to converse, she received a summons to attend Madame Cheron immediately, and had scarcely entered the dressing-room, when she observed with surprise the dejection of her aunt's countenance, and the contrasted gaiety of her dress. "So, niece!"—said Madame, and she stopped under some degree of embarrassment.—"I sent for you—I—I wished to see you; I have news to tell you. From this hour you must consider the Signor Montoni as your uncle—we were married this morning."

Astonished—not so much at the marriage, as at the secrecy with which it had been concluded, and the agitation with which it was announced, Emily, at length, attributed the privacy to the wish of Montoni, rather than of her aunt. His wife, however, intended, that the contrary should be believed, and therefore added, "you see I wished to avoid a bustle; but now the ceremony is over I shall do so no longer; and I wish to announce to my servants that they must receive the Signor Montoni for their master." Emily made a feeble attempt to congratulate her on these apparently imprudent nuptials. "I shall now celebrate my marriage with some splendour," continued Madame

Montoni, "and to save time I shall avail myself of the preparation that has been made for yours, which will, of course, be delayed a little while. Such of your wedding clothes as are ready I shall expect you will appear in, to do honour to this festival. I also wish you to inform Monsieur Valancourt, that I have changed my name, and he will acquaint Madame Clairval. In a few days I shall give a grand entertainment, at which I shall request their presence."

Emily was so lost in surprise and various thought, that she made Madame Montoni scarcely any reply, but, at her desire, she returned to inform Valancourt of what had passed. Surprise was not his predominant emotion on hearing of these hasty nuptials; and, when he learned, that they were to be the means of delaying his own, and that the very ornaments of the chateau, which had been prepared to grace the nuptial day of his Emily, were to be degraded to the celebration of Madame Montoni's, grief and indignation agitated him alternately. He could conceal neither from the observation of Emily, whose efforts to abstract him from these serious emotions, and to laugh at the apprehensive considerations, that assailed him, were ineffectual; and, when, at length, he took leave, there was an earnest tenderness in his manner, that extremely affected her; she even shed tears, when he disappeared at the end of the terrace, yet knew not exactly why she should do so.

Montoni now took possession of the chateau, and the command of its inhabitants, with the ease of a man, who had long considered it to be his own. His friend Cavigni, who had been extremely serviceable, in having paid Madame Cheron the attention and flattery, which she required, but from which Montoni too often revolted, had apartments assigned to him, and received from the domestics an equal degree of obedience with the master of the mansion.

Within a few days, Madame Montoni, as she had promised, gave a magnificent entertainment to a very numerous company, among whom was Valancourt; but at which Madame Clairval excused herself from attending. There was a concert, ball and supper. Valancourt was, of course, Emily's partner, and though, when he gave a look to the decorations of the apartments, he could not but remember, that they were designed for other festivities, than those they now contributed to celebrate, he endeavoured to check his concern by considering, that a little while only would elapse before they would be given to their original destination. During this evening, Madame Montoni danced, laughed and talked incessantly; while Montoni, silent, reserved and somewhat haughty, seemed weary of the parade, and of the frivolous company it had drawn together.

This was the first and the last entertainment, given in celebration of their nuptials. Montoni, though the severity of his temper and the gloominess of his pride prevented him from enjoying such festivities, was extremely willing to promote them. It was seldom, that he could meet in any company a man of more address, and still seldomer one of more understanding, than himself; the balance of advantage in such parties, or in the connections, which might arise from them, must, therefore, be on his side; and, knowing, as he did, the selfish purposes, for which they are generally frequented, he had no objection to mea- sure his talents of dissimulation with those of any other competitor for distinction and plunder. But his wife, who, when her own interest was immediately concerned, had sometimes more discernment than vanity, acquired a consciousness of her inferiority to other women, in personal attractions, which, uniting with the jealousy natural to the discovery, counteracted his readiness for mingling with all the parties Tholouse could afford. Till she had, as she supposed, the affections of an hus- band to lose, she had no motive for discovering the unwelcome truth, and it had never obtruded itself upon her; but, now that it influenced her policy, she opposed her husband's inclination for company, with the more eagerness, because she believed him to be really as well received in the female society of the place, as, during his addresses to her, he had affected to be.

A few weeks only had elapsed, since the marriage, when Madame Montoni informed Emily, that the Signor intended to return to Italy, as soon as the necessary preparation could be made for so long a journey. "We shall go to Venice," said she, "where the Signor has a fine man- sion, and from thence to his estate in Tuscany. Why do you look so grave, child?—You, who are so fond of a romantic country and fine views, will doubtless be delighted with this journey."

"Am I then to be of the party, madam?" said Emily, with extreme sur- prise and emotion. "Most certainly," replied her aunt, "how could you imagine we should leave you behind? But I see you are thinking of the Chevalier; he is not yet, I believe, informed of the journey, but he very soon will be so. Signor Montoni is gone to acquaint Madame Clairval of our journey, and to say, that the proposed connection between the families must from this time be thought of no more."

The unfeeling manner, in which Madame Montoni thus informed her niece, that she must be separated, perhaps for ever, from the man, with whom she was on the point of being united for life, added to the dismay, which she must otherwise have suffered at such intelligence. When she could speak, she asked the cause of the sudden change in Madame's sentiments towards Valancourt, but the only reply she could obtain was, that the Signor had forbade the connection, considering it to be greatly inferior to what Emily might reasonably expect.

"I now leave the affair entirely to the Signor," added Madame

Montoni, "but I must say, that M. Valancourt never was a favourite with me, and I was overpersuaded, or I should not have given my consent to the connection. I was weak enough—I am so foolish sometimes!—to suffer other people's uneasiness to affect me, and so my better judgment yielded to your affliction. But the Signor has very properly pointed out the folly of this, and he shall not have to reprove me a second time. I am determined, that you shall submit to those, who know how to guide you better than yourself—I am determined, that you shall be conformable."

Emily would have been astonished at the assertions of this eloquent speech, had not her mind been so overwhelmed by the sudden shock it had received, that she scarcely heard a word of what was latterly addressed to her. Whatever were the weaknesses of Madame Montoni, she might have avoided to accuse herself with those of compassion and tenderness to the feelings of others, and especially to those of Emily. It was the same ambition, that lately prevailed upon her to solicit an alliance with Madame Clairval's family, which induced her to withdraw from it, now that her marriage with Montoni had exalted her self-consequence, and, with it, her views for her niece.

Emily was, at this time, too much affected to employ either remonstrance, or entreaty on this topic; and when, at length, she attempted the latter, her emotion overcame her speech, and she retired to her apartment, to think, if in the present state of her mind to think was possible, upon this sudden and overwhelming subject. It was very long, before her spirits were sufficiently composed to permit the reflection, which, when it came, was dark and even terrible. She saw, that Montoni sought to aggrandise himself in his disposal of her, and it occurred, that his friend Cavigni was the person, for whom he was interested. The prospect of going to Italy was still rendered darker, when she considered the tumultuous situation of that country, then torn by civil commotion, where every petty state was at war with its neighbour, and even every castle liable to the attack of an invader. She considered the person, to whose immediate guidance she would be committed, and the vast distance, that was to separate her from Valancourt, and, at the recollection of him, every other image vanished from her mind, and every thought was again obscured by grief.

In this perturbed state she passed some hours, and, when she was summoned to dinner, she entreated permission to remain in her own apartment; but Madame Montoni was alone, and the request was refused. Emily and her aunt said little during the repast; the one occupied by her griefs, the other engrossed by the disappointment, which the unexpected absence of Montoni occasioned; for not only was her vanity piqued by the neglect, but her jealousy alarmed by what she considered as a mysterious engagement. When the cloth was drawn and they were alone, Emily renewed the mention of Valancourt; but her aunt, neither softened to pity, or awakened to remorse, became enraged, that her will should be opposed, and the authority of Montoni questioned, though this was done by Emily with her usual gentleness, who, after a long, and torturing conversation, retired in tears.

As she crossed the hall, a person entered it by the great door, whom, as her eyes hastily glanced that way, she imagined to be Montoni, and she was passing on with quicker steps, when she heard the well-known voice of Valancourt.

"Emily, O! my Emily!" cried he in a tone faltering with impatience, while she turned, and, as he advanced, was alarmed at the expression of his countenance and the eager desperation of his air. "In tears, Emily! I would speak with you," said he, "I have much to say; conduct me to where we may converse. But you tremble—you are ill! Let me lead you to a seat."

He observed the open door of an apartment, and hastily took her hand to lead her thither; but she attempted to withdraw it, and said, with a languid smile, "I am better already; if you wish to see my aunt she is in the dining-parlour." "I must speak with *you*, my Emily," replied Valancourt, "Good God! is it already come to this? Are you indeed so willing to resign me? But this is an improper place—I am overheard. Let me entreat your attention, if only for a few minutes."—"When you have seen my aunt," said Emily. "I was wretched enough when I came hither," exclaimed Valancourt, "do not increase my misery by this coldness—this cruel refusal."

The despondency, with which he spoke this, affected her almost to tears, but she persisted in refusing to hear him, till he had conversed with Madame Montoni. "Where is her husband, where, then, is Montoni?" said Valancourt, in an altered tone: "it is he, to whom I must speak."

Emily, terrified for the consequence of the indignation, that flashed in his eyes, tremblingly assured him, that Montoni was not at home, and entreated he would endeavour to moderate his resentment. At the tremulous accents of her voice, his eyes softened instantly from wildness into tenderness. "You are ill, Emily," said he, "they will destroy us both! Forgive me, that I dared to doubt your affection."

Emily no longer opposed him, as he led her into an adjoining parlour; the manner, in which he had named Montoni, had so much alarmed her for his own safety, that she was now only anxious to prevent the consequences of his just resentment. He listened to her entreaties, with attention, but replied to them only with looks of despondency and tenderness, concealing, as much as possible, the

sentiments he felt towards Montoni, that he might soothe the apprehensions, which distressed her. But she saw the veil he had spread over
his resentment, and, his assumed tranquillity only alarming her more,
she urged, at length, the impolicy of forcing an interview with
Montoni, and of taking any measure, which might render their separation irremediable. Valancourt yielded to these remonstrances, and her
affecting entreaties drew from him a promise, that, however Montoni
might persist in his design of disuniting them, he would not seek to
redress his wrongs by violence. "For my sake," said Emily, "let the consideration of what I should suffer deter you from such a mode of
revenge!" "For your sake, Emily," replied Valancourt, his eyes filling
with tears of tenderness and grief, while he gazed upon her. "Yes—
yes—I shall subdue myself. But, though I have given you my solemn
promise to do this, do not expect, that I can tamely submit to the
authority of Montoni; if I could, I should be unworthy of you. Yet, O
Emily! how long may he condemn me to live without you,—how long
may it be before you return to France!"

Emily endeavoured to soothe him with assurances of her unalterable
affection, and by representing, that, in little more than a year, she
should be her own mistress, as far as related to her aunt, from whose
guardianship her age would then release her; assurances, which gave
little consolation to Valancourt, who considered, that she would then
be in Italy and in the power of those, whose dominion over her would
not cease with their rights; but he affected to be consoled by them.
Emily, comforted by the promise she had obtained, and by his apparent composure, was about to leave him, when her aunt entered the
room. She threw a glance of sharp reproof upon her niece, who immediately withdrew, and of haughty displeasure upon Valancourt.

"This is not the conduct I should have expected from you, sir;" said
she, "I did not expect to see you in my house, after you had been
informed, that your visits were no longer agreeable, much less, that you
would seek a clandestine interview with my niece, and that she would
grant one."

Valancourt, perceiving it necessary to vindicate Emily from such a
design, explained, that the purpose of his own visit had been to request
an interview with Montoni, and he then entered upon the subject of it,
with the tempered spirit which the sex, rather than the respectability,
of Madame Montoni, demanded.

His expostulations were answered with severe rebuke; she lamented
again, that her prudence had ever yielded to what she termed compassion, and added, that she was so sensible of the folly of her former consent, that, to prevent the possibility of a repetition, she had committed
the affair entirely to the conduct of Signor Montoni.

The feeling eloquence of Valancourt, however, at length, made her sensible in some measure of her unworthy conduct, and she became susceptible to shame, but not remorse: she hated Valancourt, who awakened her to this painful sensation, and, in proportion as she grew dissatisfied with herself, her abhorrence of him increased. This was also the more inveterate, because his tempered words and manner were such as, without accusing her, compelled her to accuse herself, and neither left her a hope, that the odious portrait was the caricature of his prejudice, or afforded her an excuse for expressing the violent resentment, with which she contemplated it. At length, her anger rose to such an height, that Valancourt was compelled to leave the house abruptly, lest he should forfeit his own esteem by an intemperate reply. He was then convinced, that from Madame Montoni he had nothing to hope, for what of either pity, or justice could be expected from a person, who could feel the pain of guilt, without the humility of repentance?

To Montoni he looked with equal despondency, since it was nearly evident, that this plan of separation originated with him, and it was not probable, that he would relinquish his own views to entreaties, or remonstrances, which he must have foreseen and have been prepared to resist. Yet, remembering his promise to Emily, and more solicitous, concerning his love, than jealous of his consequence, Valancourt was careful to do nothing that might unnecessarily irritate Montoni; he wrote to him, therefore, not to demand an interview, but to solicit one, and, having done this, he endeavoured to wait with calmness his reply.

Madame Clairval was passive in the affair. When she gave her approbation to Valancourt's marriage, it was in the belief, that Emily would be the heiress of Madame Montoni's fortune; and, though, upon the nuptials of the latter, when she perceived the fallacy of this expectation, her conscience had withheld her from adopting any measure to prevent the union, her benevolence was not sufficiently active to impel her towards any step, that might now promote it. She was, on the contrary, secretly pleased, that Valancourt was released from an engagement, which she considered to be as inferior, in point of fortune, to his merit, as his alliance was thought by Montoni to be humiliating to the beauty of Emily; and, though her pride was wounded by this rejection of a member of her family, she disdained to shew resentment otherwise, than by silence.

Montoni, in his reply to Valancourt, said, that as an interview could neither remove the objections of the one, or overcome the wishes of the other, it would serve only to produce useless altercation between them. He, therefore, thought proper to refuse it.

In consideration of the policy, suggested by Emily, and of his promise to her, Valancourt restrained the impulse, that urged him to the house of Montoni, to demand what had been denied to his entreaties. He only repeated his solicitations to see him; seconding them with all the arguments his situation could suggest. Thus several days passed, in remonstrance, on one side, and inflexible denial, on the other; for, whether it was fear, or shame, or the hatred, which results from both, that made Montoni shun the man he had injured, he was peremptory in his refusal, and was neither softened to pity by the agony, which Valancourt's letters pourtrayed, or awakened to a repentance of his own injustice by the strong remonstrances he employed. At length, Valancourt's letters were returned unopened, and then, in the first moments of passionate despair, he forgot every promise to Emily, except the solemn one, which bound him to avoid violence, and hastened to Montoni's chateau, determined to see him by whatever other means might be necessary. Montoni was denied, and Valancourt, when he afterwards enquired for Madame, and Ma'amselle St. Aubert, was absolutely refused admittance by the servants. Not choosing to submit himself to a contest with these, he, at length, departed, and, returning home in a state of mind approaching to frenzy, wrote to Emily of what had passed, expressed without restraint all the agony of his heart, and entreated, that, since he must not otherwise hope to see her immediately, she would allow him an interview unknown to Montoni. Soon after he had dispatched this, his passions becoming more temperate, he was sensible of the error he had committed in having given Emily a new subject of distress in the strong mention of his own suffering, and would have given half the world, had it been his, to recover the letter. Emily, however, was spared the pain she must have received from it by the suspicious policy of Madame Montoni, who had ordered, that all letters, addressed to her niece, should be delivered to herself, and who, after having perused this and indulged the expressions of resentment, which Valancourt's mention of Montoni provoked, had consigned it to the flames.

Montoni, meanwhile, every day more impatient to leave France, gave repeated orders for dispatch to the servants employed in preparations for the journey, and to the persons, with whom he was transacting some particular business. He preserved a steady silence to the letters in which Valancourt, despairing of greater good, and having subdued the passion, that had transgressed against his policy, solicited only the indulgence of being allowed to bid Emily farewell. But, when the latter [Valancourt] learned, that she was really to set out in a very few days, and that it was designed he should see her no more, forgetting every consideration of prudence, he dared, in a second letter to Emily, to propose a clandestine marriage. This also was transmitted to Madame

Montoni, and the last day of Emily's stay at Tholouse arrived, without affording Valancourt even a line to soothe his sufferings, or a hope, that he should be allowed a parting interview.

During this period of torturing suspense to Valancourt, Emily was sunk into that kind of stupor, with which sudden and irremediable misfortune sometimes overwhelms the mind. Loving him with the tenderest affection, and having long been accustomed to consider him as the friend and companion of all her future days, she had no ideas of happiness, that were not connected with him. What, then, must have been her suffering, when thus suddenly they were to be separated, perhaps, for ever, certainly to be thrown into distant parts of the world, where they could scarcely hear of each other's existence; and all this in obedience to the will of a stranger, for such as Montoni, and of a person, who had but lately been anxious to hasten their nuptials! It was in vain, that she endeavoured to subdue her grief, and resign herself to an event, which she could not avoid. The silence of Valancourt afflicted more than it surprised her, since she attributed it to its just occasion; but, when the day, preceding that, on which she was to quit Tholouse, arrived, and she had heard no mention of his being permitted to take leave of her, grief overcame every consideration, that had made her reluctant to speak of him, and she enquired of Madame Montoni, whether this consolation had been refused. Her aunt informed her that it had, adding, that, after the provocation she had herself received from Valancourt, in their last interview, and the persecution, which the Signor had suffered from his letters, no entreaties should avail to procure it.

"If the Chevalier expected this favour from us," said she, "he should have conducted himself in a very different manner; he should have waited patiently, till he knew whether we were disposed to grant it, and not have come and reproved me, because I did not think proper to bestow my niece upon him,—and then have persisted in troubling the Signor, because he did not think proper to enter into any dispute about so childish an affair. His behaviour throughout has been extremely presumptuous and impertinent, and I desire, that I may never hear his name repeated, and that you will get the better of those foolish sorrows and whims, and look like other people, and not appear with that dismal countenance, as if you were ready to cry. For, though you say nothing, you cannot conceal your grief from my penetration. I can see you are ready to cry at this moment, though I am reproving you for it; aye, even now, in spite of my commands."

Emily, having turned away to hide her tears, quitted the room to indulge them, and the day was passed in an intensity of anguish, such as she had, perhaps, never known before. When she withdrew to her chamber for the night, she remained in the chair where she had placed herself, on entering the room, absorbed in her grief, till long after every member of the family, except herself, was retired to rest. She could not divest herself of a belief, that she had parted with Valancourt to meet no more; a belief, which did not arise merely from foreseen circumstances, for, though the length of the journey she was about to commence, the uncertainty as to the period of her return, together with the prohibitions she had received, seemed to justify it, she yielded also to an impression, which she mistook for a pre-sentiment, that she was going from Valancourt for ever. How dreadful to her imagination, too, was the distance that would separate them—the Alps, those tremendous barriers! would rise, and whole countries extend between the regions where each must exist! To live in adjoining provinces, to live even in the same country, though without seeing him, was comparative happiness to the conviction of this dreadful length of distance.

Her mind was, at length, so much agitated by the consideration of her state, and the belief, that she had seen Valancourt for the last time, that she suddenly became very faint, and, looking round the chamber for something, that might revive her, she observed the casements, and had just strength to throw one open, near which she seated herself. The air recalled her spirits, and the still moon-light, that fell upon the elms of a long avenue, fronting the window, somewhat soothed them, and determined her to try whether exercise and the open air would not relieve the intense pain that bound her temples. In the chateau all was still; and, passing down the great stair-case into the hall, from whence a passage led immediately to the garden, she softly and unheard, as she thought, unlocked the door, and entered the avenue. Emily passed on with steps now hurried, and now faltering, as, deceived by the shadows among the trees, she fancied she saw some person move in the distant perspective, and feared, that it was a spy of Madame Montoni. Her desire, however, to re-visit the pavilion, where she had passed so many happy hours with Valancourt, and had admired with him the extensive prospect over Languedoc and her native Gascony, overcame her apprehension of being observed, and she moved on towards the terrace, which, running along the upper garden, commanded the whole of the lower one, and communicated with it by a flight of marble steps, that terminated the avenue.

Having reached these steps, she paused a moment to look round, for her distance from the chateau now increased the fear, which the stillness and obscurity of the hour had awakened. But, perceiving nothing that could justify it, she ascended to the terrace, where the moon-light shewed the long broad walk, with the pavilion at its extremity, while the rays silvered the foliage of the high trees and shrubs, that bordered it on the right, and the tufted summits of those, that rose to a level with the balustrade on the left, from the garden below. Her distance from the chateau again alarming her, she paused to listen; the night was so calm, that no sound could have escaped her, but she heard only the plaintive sweetness of the nightingale, with the light shiver of the leaves, and she pursued her way towards the pavilion, having reached which, its obscurity did not prevent the emotion, that a fuller view of its well-known scene would have excited. The lattices were thrown back, and shewed beyond their embowered arch the moon-light landscape, shadowy and soft; its groves, and plains extending gradually and indistinctly to the eye, its distant mountains catching a stronger gleam, and the nearer river reflecting the moon, and trembling to her rays.

Emily, as she approached the lattice, was sensible of the features of this scene only as they served to bring Valancourt more immediately to her fancy. "Ah!" said she, with a heavy sigh, as she threw herself into a chair by the window, "how often have we sat together in this spot— often have looked upon that landscape! Never, never more shall we view it together—never—never more, perhaps, shall we look upon each other!"

Her tears were suddenly stopped by terror—a voice spoke near her in the pavilion; she shrieked—it spoke again, and she distinguished the well-known tones of Valancourt. It was indeed Valancourt who supported her in his arms! For some moments their emotion would not suffer either to speak. "Emily!" said Valancourt at length, as he pressed her hand in his. "Emily!" and he was again silent, but the accent, in which he had pronounced her name, expressed all his tenderness and sorrow.

"O my Emily!" he resumed, after a long pause, "I do then see you once again, and hear again the sound of that voice! I have haunted this place—these gardens, for many—many nights, with a faint, very faint hope of seeing you. This was the only chance that remained to me, and thank heaven! it has at length succeeded—I am not condemned to absolute despair!"

Emily said something, she scarcely knew what, expressive of her unalterable affection, and endeavoured to calm the agitation of his mind; but Valancourt could for some time only utter incoherent expressions of his emotions; and, when he was somewhat more composed, he said, "I came hither, soon after sunset, and have been watching in the gardens, and in this pavilion ever since; for, though I had now given up all hope of seeing you, I could not resolve to tear myself from a place so near to you, and should probably have lingered about the chateau till morning dawned. O how heavily the moments have passed, yet with what various emotion have they been marked, as I sometimes thought I heard footsteps, and fancied you were approaching, and then again—perceived only a dead and dreary silence! But, when you opened the door of the pavilion, and the darkness prevented my distinguishing with certainty, whether it was my love—my heart beat so strongly with hopes and fears, that I could not speak. The instant I heard the plaintive accents of your voice, my doubts vanished, but not my fears, till you spoke of me; then, losing the apprehension of alarming you in the excess of my emotion, I could no longer be silent. O Emily! these are moments, in which joy and grief struggle so powerfully for pre-eminence, that the heart can scarcely support the contest!"

Emily's heart acknowledged the truth of this assertion, but the joy she felt on thus meeting Valancourt, at the very moment when she was lamenting, that they must probably meet no more, soon melted into grief, as reflection stole over her thoughts, and imagination prompted visions of the future. She struggled to recover the calm dignity of mind, which was necessary to support her through this last interview, and which Valancourt found it utterly impossible to attain, for the transports of his joy changed abruptly into those of suffering, and he expressed in the most impassioned language his horror of this separation, and his despair of their ever meeting again. Emily wept silently as she listened to him, and then, trying to command her own distress, and to soothe his, she suggested every circumstance that could lead to hope. But the energy of his fears led him instantly to detect the friendly fallacies, which she endeavoured to impose on herself and him, and also to conjure up illusions too powerful for his reason.

"You are going from me," said he, "to a distant country, O how distant!—to new society, new friends, new admirers, with people too, who will try to make you forget me, and to promote new connections! How can I know this, and not know, that you will never return for me—never can be mine." His voice was stifled by sighs.

"You believe, then," said Emily, "that the pangs I suffer proceed from a trivial and temporary interest; you believe——"

"Suffer!" interrupted Valancourt, "suffer for me! O Emily—how sweet—how bitter are those words; what comfort, what anguish do they give! I ought not to doubt the steadiness of your affection, yet such is the inconsistency of real love, that it is always awake to suspicion, however unreasonable; always requiring new assurances from the object of its interest, and thus it is, that I always feel revived, as by a new conviction, when your words tell me I am dear to you; and, wanting these, I relapse into doubt, and too often into despondency." Then seeming to recollect himself, he exclaimed, "But what a wretch am I, thus to torture you, and in these moments, too! I, who ought to support and comfort you!"

This reflection overcame Valancourt with tenderness, but, relapsing into despondency, he again felt only for himself, and lamented again this cruel separation, in a voice and words so impassioned, that Emily could no longer struggle to repress her own grief, or to soothe his. Valancourt, between these emotions of love and pity, lost the power, and almost the wish, of repressing his agitation; and, in the intervals of convulsive sobs, he, at one moment, kissed away her tears, then told her cruelly, that possibly she might never again weep for him, and then tried to speak more calmly, but only exclaimed, "O Emily—my heart will break!—I cannot—cannot leave you! Now—I gaze upon that countenance, now I hold you in my arms! a little while, and all this will appear a dream. I shall look, and cannot see you; shall try to recollect your features—and the impression will be fled from my imagination;—to hear the tones of your voice, and even memory will be silent!—I cannot, cannot leave you! Why should we confide the happiness of our whole lives to the will of people, who have no right to interrupt, and, except in giving you to me, have no power to promote it? O Emily! venture to trust your own heart, venture to be mine for ever!" His voice trembled, and he was silent; Emily continued to weep, and was silent also, when Valancourt proceeded to propose an immediate marriage, and that, at an early hour on the following morning, she should quit Madame Montoni's house, and be conducted by him to the church of the Augustines, where a friar should await to unite them.

The silence, with which she listened to a proposal, dictated by love and despair, and enforced at a moment, when it seemed scarcely possible for her to oppose it;—when her heart was softened by the sorrows of a separation, that might be eternal, and her reason obscured by the illusions of love and terror, encouraged him to hope, that it would not be rejected. "Speak, my Emily!" said Valancourt eagerly, "let me hear your voice, let me hear you confirm my fate." She spoke not; her cheek was cold, and her senses seemed to fail her, but she did not faint. To Valancourt's terrified imagination she appeared to be dying; he called upon her name, rose to go to the chateau for assistance, and then, recollecting her situation, feared to go, or to leave her for a moment.

After a few minutes, she drew a deep sigh, and began to revive. The conflict she had suffered, between love and the duty she at present owed to her father's sister; her repugnance to a clandestine marriage, her fear of emerging on the world with embarrassments, such as might ultimately involve the object of her affection in misery and repentance;—all this various interest was too powerful for a mind, already enervated by sorrow, and her reason had suffered a transient suspension. But duty, and good sense, however hard the conflict, at length, triumphed over affection and mournful presentiment; above all, she dreaded to involve Valancourt in obscurity and vain regret, which she saw, or thought she saw, must be the too certain consequence of a marriage in their present circumstances; and she acted, perhaps, with somewhat more than female fortitude, when she resolved to endure a present, rather than provoke a distant misfortune.

With a candour, that proved how truly she esteemed and loved him, and which endeared her to him, if possible, more than ever, she told Valancourt all her reasons for rejecting his proposals. Those, which influenced her concerning his future welfare, he instantly refuted, or rather contradicted; but they awakened tender considerations for her, which the frenzy of passion and despair had concealed before, and love, which had but lately prompted him to propose a clandestine and immediate marriage, now induced him to renounce it. The triumph was almost too much for his heart; for Emily's sake, he endeavoured to stifle his grief, but the swelling anguish would not be restrained. "O Emily!" said he, "I must leave you—I *must* leave you, and I know it is for ever."

Convulsive sobs again interrupted his words, and they wept together in silence, till Emily, recollecting the danger of being discovered, and the impropriety of prolonging an interview, which might subject her to censure, summoned all her fortitude to utter a last farewell.

"Stay!" said Valancourt, "I conjure you stay, for I have much to tell you. The agitation of my mind has hitherto suffered me to speak only on the subject that occupied it;—I have forborne to mention a doubt of much importance, partly, lest it should appear as if I told it with an ungenerous view of alarming you into a compliance with my late proposal."

Emily, much agitated, did not leave Valancourt, but she led him from the pavilion, and, as they walked upon the terrace, he proceeded as follows:

"This Montoni: I have heard some strange hints concerning him. Are you certain he is of Madame Quesnel's family, and that his fortune is what it appears to be?"

"I have no reason to doubt either," replied Emily, in a voice of alarm. "Of the first, indeed, I cannot doubt, but I have no certain means of judging of the latter, and I entreat you will tell me all you have heard."

"That I certainly will, but it is very imperfect, and unsatisfactory information. I gathered it by accident from an Italian, who was speaking to another person of this Montoni. They were talking of his marriage; the Italian said, that if he was the person he meant, he was not likely to make Madame Cheron happy. He proceeded to speak of him in general terms of dislike, and then gave some particular hints, concerning his character, that excited my curiosity, and I ventured to ask him a few questions. He was reserved in his replies, but, after hesitating for some time, he owned, that he had understood abroad, that Montoni was a man of desperate fortune and character. He said something of a castle of Montoni's, situated among the Apennines, and of some strange circumstances, that might be mentioned, as to his former mode of life. I pressed him to inform me further, but I believe the strong interest I felt was visible in my manner, and alarmed him; for no entreaties could prevail with him to give any explanation of the circumstances he had alluded to, or to mention any thing further concerning Montoni. I observed to him, that, if Montoni was possessed of a castle in the Apennines, it appeared from such a circumstance, that he was of some family, and also seemed to contradict the report, that he was a man of entirely broken fortunes. He shook his head, and looked as if he could have said a great deal, but made no reply.

"A hope of learning something more satisfactory, or more positive, detained me in his company a considerable time, and I renewed the subject repeatedly, but the Italian wrapped himself up in reserve, said—that what he had mentioned he had caught only from a floating report, and that reports frequently arose from personal malice, and were very little to be depended upon. I forbore to press the subject farther, since it was obvious that he was alarmed for the consequence of what he had already said, and I was compelled to remain in uncertainty on a point where suspense is almost intolerable. Think, Emily, what I must suffer to see you depart for a foreign country, committed to the power of a man of such doubtful character as is this Montoni! But I will not alarm you unnecessarily;—it is possible, as the Italian said, at first, that this is not the Montoni he alluded to. Yet, Emily, consider well before you resolve to commit yourself to him. O! I must not trust myself to speak—or I shall renounce all the motives, which so lately influenced me to resign the hope of your becoming mine immediately."

Valancourt walked upon the terrace with hurried steps, while Emily remained leaning on the balustrade in deep thought. The information she had just received excited, perhaps, more alarm than it could justify, and raised once more the conflict of contrasted interests. She had never liked Montoni. The fire and keenness of his eye, its proud exultation, its bold fierceness, its sullen watchfulness, as occasion, and even slight occasion, had called forth the latent soul, she had often observed with emotion; while from the usual expression of his countenance she had always shrunk. From such observations she was the more inclined to believe, that it was this Montoni, of whom the Italian had uttered his suspicious hints. The thought of being solely in his power, in a foreign land, was terrifying to her, but it was not by terror alone that she was urged to an immediate marriage with Valancourt. The tenderest love had already pleaded his cause, but had been unable to overcome her opinion, as to her duty, her disinterested considerations for Valancourt, and the delicacy, which made her revolt from a clandestine union. It was not to be expected, that a vague terror would be more powerful, than the united influence of love and grief. But it recalled all their energy, and rendered a second conquest necessary.

With Valancourt, whose imagination was now awake to the suggestion of every passion; whose apprehensions for Emily had acquired strength by the mere mention of them, and became every instant more powerful, as his mind brooded over them—with Valancourt no second conquest was attainable. He thought he saw in the clearest light, and love assisted the fear, that this journey to Italy would involve Emily in misery; he determined, therefore, to persevere in opposing it, and in conjuring her to bestow upon him the title of her lawful protector.

"Emily!" said he, with solemn earnestness, "this is no time for scrupulous distinctions, for weighing the dubious and comparatively trifling circumstances, that may affect our future comfort. I now see, much more clearly than before, the train of serious dangers you are going to encounter with a man of Montoni's character. Those dark hints of the Italian spoke much, but not more than the idea I have of Montoni's disposition, as exhibited even in his countenance. I think I see at this moment all that could have been hinted, written there. He is the Italian, whom I fear, and I conjure you for your own sake, as well as for mine, to prevent the evils I shudder to foresee. O Emily! let my tenderness, my arms withhold you from them—give me the right to defend you!"

Emily only sighed, while Valancourt proceeded to remonstrate and to entreat with all the energy that love and apprehension could inspire. But, as his imagination magnified to her the possible evils she was going to meet, the mists of her own fancy began to dissipate, and allowed her to distinguish the exaggerated images, which imposed on his reason. She considered, that there was no proof of Montoni being the person, whom the stranger had meant; that, even if he was so, the Italian had noticed his character and broken fortunes merely from report; and that, though the countenance of Montoni seemed to give probability to a part of the rumour, it was not by such circumstances that an implicit belief of it could be justified. These considerations would probably not have arisen so distinctly to her mind, at this time, had not the terrors of Valancourt presented to her such obvious exaggerations of her danger, as incited her to distrust the fallacies of passion. But, while she endeavoured in the gentlest manner to convince him of his error, she plunged him into a new one. His voice and countenance changed to an expression of dark despair. "Emily!" said he, "this, this moment is the bitterest that is yet come to me. You do not—cannot love me!—It would be impossible for you to reason thus coolly, thus deliberately, if you did. I, *I* am torn with anguish at the prospect of our separation, and of the evils that may await you in consequence of it; I would encounter any hazards to prevent it—to save you. No! Emily, no!—you cannot love me."

"We have now little time to waste in exclamation, or assertion," said Emily, endeavouring to conceal her emotion: "if you are yet to learn how dear you are, and ever must be, to my heart, no assurances of mine can give you conviction."

The last words faltered on her lips, and her tears flowed fast. These words and tears brought, once more, and with instantaneous force, conviction of her love to Valancourt. He could only exclaim, "Emily! Emily!" and weep over the hand he pressed to his lips; but she, after some moments, again roused herself from the indulgence of sorrow, and said, "I must leave you; it is late, and my absence from the chateau may be discovered. Think of me—love me—when I am far away; the belief of this will be my comfort!"

"Think of you!—love you!" exclaimed Valancourt.

"Try to moderate these transports," said Emily, "for my sake, try."

"For your sake!"

"Yes, for my sake," replied Emily, in a tremulous voice, "I cannot leave you thus!"

"Then do not leave me!" said Valancourt, with quickness. "Why should we part, or part for longer than till to-morrow?"

"I am, indeed I am, unequal to these moments," replied Emily, "you tear my heart, but I never can consent to this hasty, imprudent proposal!"

"If we could command our time, my Emily, it should not be thus hasty; we must submit to circumstances."

"We must, indeed! I have already told you all my heart—my spirits are gone. You allowed the force of my objections, till your tenderness called up vague terrors, which have given us both unnecessary anguish. Spare me! do not oblige me to repeat the reasons I have already urged."

"Spare you!" cried Valancourt, "I am a wretch—a very wretch, that have felt only for myself!—I! who ought to have shewn the fortitude of a man, who ought to have supported you, I! have increased your sufferings by the conduct of a child! Forgive me, Emily! think of the distraction of my mind now that I am about to part with all that is dear to me—and forgive me! When you are gone, I shall recollect with bitter remorse what I have made you suffer, and shall wish in vain that I could see you, if only for a moment, that I might soothe your grief."

Tears again interrupted his voice, and Emily wept with him. "I will shew myself more worthy of your love," said Valancourt, at length; "I will not prolong these moments. My Emily—my own Emily! never forget me! God knows when we shall meet again! I resign you to his care.——O God!—O God!—protect and bless her!"

He pressed her hand to his heart. Emily sunk almost lifeless on his bosom, and neither wept, nor spoke. Valancourt, now commanding his own distress, tried to comfort and re-assure her, but she appeared totally unaffected by what he said, and a sigh, which she uttered, now and then, was all that proved she had not fainted.

He supported her slowly towards the chateau, weeping and speaking to her; but she answered only in sighs, till, having reached the gate, that terminated the avenue, she seemed to have recovered her consciousness, and, looking round, perceived how near they were to the chateau. "We must part here," said she, stopping, "Why prolong these moments? Teach me the fortitude I have forgot."

Valancourt struggled to assume a composed air. "Farewell, my love!" said he, in a voice of solemn tenderness—"trust me we shall meet again—meet for each other—meet to part no more!" His voice faltered, but, recovering it, he proceeded in a firmer tone. "You know not what I shall suffer, till I hear from you; I shall omit no opportunity of conveying to you my letters, yet I tremble to think how few may occur. And trust me, love, for your dear sake, I will try to bear this absence with fortitude. O how little I have shewn to-night!"

"Farewell!" said Emily faintly. "When you are gone, I shall think of many things I would have said to you." "And I of many—many!" said Valancourt; "I never left you yet, that I did not immediately remember some question, or some entreaty, or some circumstance, concerning my love, that I earnestly wished to mention, and feel wretched because I could not. O Emily! this countenance, on which I now gaze—will, in a moment, be gone from my eyes, and not all the efforts of fancy will be able to recall it with exactness. O! what an infinite difference between this moment and the next! *Now*, I am in your presence, can behold you! *then*, all will be a dreary blank—and I shall be a wanderer, exiled from my only home!"

Valancourt again pressed her to his heart, and held her there in silence, weeping. Tears once again calmed her oppressed mind. They again bade each other farewell, lingered a moment, and then parted. Valancourt seemed to force himself from the spot; he passed hastily up the avenue, and Emily, as she moved slowly towards the chateau, heard his distant steps. She listened to the sounds, as they sunk fainter and fainter, till the melancholy stillness of night alone remained; and then hurried to her chamber, to seek repose, which, alas! was fled from her wretchedness.

VOLUME 2

CHAPTER I

Where'er I roam, whatever realms I see,
My heart untravell'd still shall turn to thee.
GOLDSMITH

THE carriages were at the gates at an early hour; the bustle of the domestics, passing to and fro in the galleries, awakened Emily from harassing slumbers: her unquiet mind had, during the night, presented her with terrific images and obscure circumstances, concerning her affection and her future life. She now endeavoured to chase away the impressions they had left on her fancy; but from imaginary evils she awoke to the consciousness of real ones. Recollecting that she had parted with Valancourt, perhaps for ever, her heart sickened as memory revived. But she tried to dismiss the dismal forebodings that crowded on her mind, and to restrain the sorrow which she could not subdue; efforts which diffused over the settled melancholy of her countenance an expression of tempered resignation, as a thin veil, thrown over the features of beauty, renders them more interesting by a partial concealment. But Madame Montoni observed nothing in this countenance except its usual paleness, which attracted her censure. She told her niece, that she had been indulging in fanciful sorrows, and begged she would have more regard for decorum, than to let the world see that she could not renounce an improper attachment; at which Emily's pale cheek became flushed with crimson, but it was the blush of pride, and she made no answer. Soon after, Montoni entered the breakfast room, spoke little, and seemed impatient to be gone.

The windows of this room opened upon the garden. As Emily passed them, she saw the spot where she had parted with Valancourt on the preceding night: the remembrance pressed heavily on her heart, and she turned hastily away from the object that had awakened it.

The baggage being at length adjusted, the travellers entered their carriages, and Emily would have left the chateau without one sigh of

150

regret, had it not been situated in the neighbourhood of Valancourt's residence.

From a little eminence she looked back upon Tholouse, and the far-seen plains of Gascony, beyond which the broken summits of the Pyrenées appeared on the distant horizon, lighted up by a morning sun. "Dear pleasant mountains!" said she to herself, "how long may it be ere I see ye again, and how much may happen to make me miserable in the interval! Oh, could I now be certain, that I should ever return to ye, and find that Valancourt still lived for me, I should go in peace! He will still gaze on ye, gaze when I am far away!"

The trees, that impended over the high banks of the road and formed a line of perspective with the distant country, now threatened to exclude the view of them; but the blueish mountains still appeared beyond the dark foliage, and Emily continued to lean from the coach window, till at length the closing branches shut them from her sight.

Another object soon caught her attention. She had scarcely looked at a person who walked along the bank, with his hat, in which was the military feather, drawn over his eyes, before, at the sound of wheels, he suddenly turned, and she perceived that it was Valancourt himself, who waved his hand, sprung into the road, and through the window of the carriage put a letter into her hand. He endeavoured to smile through the despair that overspread his countenance as she passed on. The remembrance of that smile seemed impressed on Emily's mind for ever. She leaned from the window, and saw him on a knoll of the broken bank, leaning against the high trees that waved over him, and pursuing the carriage with his eyes. He waved his hand, and she continued to gaze till distance confused his figure, and at length another turn of the road entirely separated him from her sight.

Having stopped to take up Signor Cavigni at a chateau on the road, the travellers, of whom Emily was disrespectfully seated with Madame Montoni's woman in a second carriage, pursued their way over the plains of Languedoc. The presence of this servant restrained Emily from reading Valancourt's letter, for she did not choose to expose the emotions it might occasion to the observation of any person. Yet such was her wish to read this his last communication, that her trembling hand was every moment on the point of breaking the seal.

At length they reached the village, where they staid only to change horses, without alighting, and it was not till they stopped to dine, that Emily had an opportunity of reading the letter. Though she had never doubted the sincerity of Valancourt's affection, the fresh assurances she now received of it revived her spirits; she wept over his letter in tenderness, laid it by to be referred to when they should be particularly depressed, and then thought of him with much less anguish than she had done since they parted. Among some other requests, which were interesting to her, because expressive of his tenderness, and because a compliance with them seemed to annihilate for a while the pain of absence, he entreated she would always think of him at sunset. "You will then meet me in thought," said he; "I shall constantly watch the sunset, and I shall be happy in the belief, that your eyes are fixed upon the same object with mine, and that our minds are conversing. You know not, Emily, the comfort I promise myself from these moments; but I trust you will experience it."

It is unnecessary to say with what emotion Emily, on this evening, watched the declining sun, over a long extent of plains, on which she saw it set without interruption, and sink towards the province which Valancourt inhabited. After this hour her mind became far more tranquil and resigned, than it had been since the marriage of Montoni and her aunt.

During several days the travellers journeyed over the plains of Languedoc; and then entering Dauphiny, and winding for some time among the mountains of that romantic province, they quitted their carriages and began to ascend the Alps. And here such scenes of sublimity opened upon them as no colours of language must dare to paint! Emily's mind was even so much engaged with new and wonderful images, that they sometimes banished the idea of Valancourt, though they more frequently revived it. These brought to her recollection the prospects among the Pyrenées, which they had admired together, and had believed nothing could excel in grandeur. How often did she wish to express to him the new emotions which this astonishing scenery awakened, and that he could partake of them! Sometimes too she endeavoured to anticipate his remarks, and almost imagined him present. She seemed to have arisen into another world, and to have left every trifling thought, every trifling sentiment, in that below; those only of grandeur and sublimity now dilated her mind, and elevated the affections of her heart.

With what emotions of sublimity, softened by tenderness, did she meet Valancourt in thought, at the customary hour of sunset, when, wandering among the Alps, she watched the glorious orb sink amid their summits, his last tints die away on their snowy points, and a solemn obscurity steal over the scene! And when the last gleam had faded, she turned her eyes from the west with somewhat of the melancholy regret that is experienced after the departure of a beloved friend; while these lonely feelings were heightened by the spreading gloom, and by the low sounds, heard only when darkness confines attention, which make the general stillness more impressive—leaves shook by the air, the last sigh of the breeze that lingers after sunset, or the murmur of distant streams.

During the first days of this journey among the Alps, the scenery exhibited a wonderful mixture of solitude and inhabitation, of cultivation and barrenness. On the edge of tremendous precipices, and within the hollow of the cliffs, below which the clouds often floated, were seen villages, spires, and convent towers; while green pastures and vineyards spread their hues at the feet of perpendicular rocks of marble, or of granite, whose points, tufted with alpine shrubs, or exhibiting only massy crags, rose above each other, till they terminated in the snow-topt mountain, whence the torrent fell, that thundered along the valley.

The snow was not yet melted on the summit of Mount Cenis, over which the travellers passed; but Emily, as she looked upon its clear lake and extended plain, surrounded by broken cliffs, saw, in imagination, the verdant beauty it would exhibit when the snows should be gone, and the shepherds, leading up the midsummer flocks from Piedmont, to pasture on its flowery summit, should add Arcadian figures to Arcadian landscape.

As she descended on the Italian side, the precipices became still more tremendous, and the prospects still more wild and majestic, over which the shifting lights threw all the pomp of colouring. Emily delighted to observe the snowy tops of the mountains under the passing influence of the day, blushing with morning, glowing with the brightness of noon, or just tinted with the purple evening. The haunt of man could now only be discovered by the simple hut of the shepherd and the hunter, or by the rough pine bridge thrown across the torrent, to assist the latter in his chase of the chamois over crags where, but for this vestige of man, it would have been believed only the chamois or the wolf dared to venture. As Emily gazed upon one of these perilous bridges, with the cataract foaming beneath it, some images came to her mind, which she afterwards combined in the following

STORIED SONNET

The weary traveller, who, all night long,
Has climb'd among the Alps' tremendous steeps,
Skirting the pathless precipice, where throng
Wild forms of danger; as he onward creeps
If, chance, his anxious eye at distance sees
The mountain-shepherd's solitary home,
Peeping from forth the moon-illumin'd trees,
What sudden transports to his bosom come!
But, if between some hideous chasm yawn,
Where the cleft pine a doubtful bridge displays,
In dreadful silence, on the brink, forlorn
He stands, and views in the faint rays
Far, far below, the torrent's rising surge,

And listens to the wild impetuous roar;
Still eyes the depth, still shudders on the verge,
Fears to return, nor dares to venture o'er.
Desperate, at length the tottering plank he tries,
His weak steps slide, he shrieks, he sinks—he dies!

Emily, often as she travelled among the clouds, watched in silent awe their billowy surges rolling below; sometimes, wholly closing upon the scene, they appeared like a world of chaos, and, at others, spreading thinly, they opened and admitted partial catches of the landscape—the torrent, whose astounding roar had never failed, tumbling down the rocky chasm, huge cliffs white with snow, or the dark summits of the pine forests, that stretched mid-way down the mountains. But who may describe her rapture, when, having passed through a sea of vapour, she caught a first view of Italy; when, from the ridge of one of those tremendous precipices that hang upon Mount Cenis and guard the entrance of that enchanting country, she looked down through the lower clouds, and, as they floated away, saw the grassy vales of Piedmont at her feet, and, beyond, the plains of Lombardy extending to the farthest distance, at which appeared, on the faint horizon, the doubtful towers of Turin?

The solitary grandeur of the objects that immediately surrounded her, the mountain-region towering above, the deep precipices that fell beneath, the waving blackness of the forests of pine and oak, which skirted their feet, or hung within their recesses, the headlong torrents that, dashing among their cliffs, sometimes appeared like a cloud of mist, at others like a sheet of ice—these were features which received a higher character of sublimity from the reposing beauty of the Italian landscape below, stretching to the wide horizon, where the same melting blue tint seemed to unite earth and sky.

Madame Montoni only shuddered as she looked down precipices near whose edge the chairmen trotted lightly and swiftly, almost, as the chamois bounded, and from which Emily too recoiled; but with her fears were mingled such various emotions of delight, such admiration, astonishment, and awe, as she had never experienced before.

Meanwhile the carriers, having come to a landing-place, stopped to rest, and the travellers being seated on the point of a cliff, Montoni and Cavigni renewed a dispute concerning Hannibal's passage over the Alps, Montoni contending that he entered Italy by way of Mount Cenis, and Cavigni, that he passed over Mount St. Bernard. The subject brought to Emily's imagination the disasters he had suffered in this bold and perilous adventure. She saw his vast armies winding among the defiles, and over the tremendous cliffs of the mountains, which at night were lighted up by his fires, or by the torches which he caused to be carried when he pursued his indefatigable march. In the eye of fancy, she perceived the gleam of arms through the duskiness of night, the glitter of spears and helmets, and the banners floating dimly on the twilight; while now and then the blast of a distant trumpet echoed along the defile, and the signal was answered by a momentary clash of arms. She looked with horror upon the mountaineers, perched on the higher cliffs, assailing the troops below with broken fragments of the mountain; on soldiers and elephants tumbling headlong down the lower precipices; and, as she listened to the rebounding rocks, that followed their fall, the terrors of fancy yielded to those of reality, and she shuddered to behold herself on the dizzy height, whence she had pictured the descent of others.

Madame Montoni, meantime, as she looked upon Italy, was contemplating in imagination the splendour of palaces and the grandeur of castles, such as she believed she was going to be mistress of at Venice and in the Apennine, and she became, in idea, little less than a princess. Being no longer under the alarms which had deterred her from giving entertainments to the beauties of Tholouse, whom Montoni had mentioned with more *eclat* to his own vanity than credit to their discretion, or regard to truth, she determined to give concerts, though she had neither ear nor taste for music; *conversazioni*, though she had no talents for conversation; and to outvie, if possible, in the gaieties of her parties and the magnificence of her liveries, all the noblesse of Venice. This blissful reverie was somewhat obscured, when she recollected the Signor, her husband, who, though he was not averse to the profit which sometimes results from such parties, had always shewn a contempt of the frivolous parade that sometimes attends them; till she considered that his pride might be gratified by displaying, among his own friends, in his native city, the wealth which he had neglected in France; and she courted again the splendid illusions that had charmed her before.

The travellers, as they descended, gradually, exchanged the region of winter for the genial warmth and beauty of spring. The sky began to assume that serene and beautiful tint peculiar to the climate of Italy; patches of young verdure, fragrant shrubs and flowers looked gaily among the rocks, often fringing their rugged brows, or hanging in tufts from their broken sides; and the buds of the oak and mountain ash were expanding into foliage. Descending lower, the orange and the myrtle, every now and then, appeared in some sunny nook, with their yellow blossoms peeping from among the dark green of their leaves, and mingling with the scarlet flowers of the pomegranate and the paler ones of the arbutus, that ran mantling to the crags above; while, lower still, spread the pastures of Piedmont, where early flocks were cropping the luxuriant herbage of spring.

The river Doria, which, rising on the summit of Mount Cenis, had dashed for many leagues over the precipices that bordered the road, now began to assume a less impetuous, though scarcely less romantic character, as it approached the green vallies of Piedmont, into which the travellers descended with the evening sun; and Emily found herself once more amid the tranquil beauty of pastoral scenery; among flocks and herds, and slopes tufted with woods of lively verdure and with beautiful shrubs, such as she had often seen waving luxuriantly over the alps above. The verdure of the pasturage, now varied with the hues of early flowers, among which were yellow ranunculuses and pansey violets of delicious fragrance, she had never seen excelled. —Emily almost wished to become a peasant of Piedmont, to inhabit one of the pleasant embowered cottages which she saw peeping beneath the cliffs, and to pass her careless hours among these romantic landscapes. To the hours, the months, she was to pass under the dominion of Montoni, she looked with apprehension; while those which were departed she remembered with regret and sorrow.

In the present scenes her fancy often gave her the figure of Valancourt, whom she saw on a point of the cliffs, gazing with awe and admiration on the imagery around him; or wandering pensively along the vale below, frequently pausing to look back upon the scenery, and then, his countenance glowing with the poet's fire, pursuing his way to some overhanging height. When she again considered the time and the distance that were to separate them, that every step she now took lengthened this distance, her heart sunk, and the surrounding landscape charmed her no more.

The travellers, passing Novalesa, reached, after the evening had closed, the small and antient town of Susa, which had formerly guarded this pass of the Alps into Piedmont. The heights which command it had, since the invention of artillery, rendered its fortifications useless; but these romantic heights, seen by moon-light, with the town below, surrounded by its walls and watchtowers, and partially illumined, exhibited an interesting picture to Emily. Here they rested for the night at an inn, which had little accommodation to boast of; but the travellers brought with them the hunger that gives delicious flavour to the coarsest viands, and the weariness that ensures repose; and here Emily first caught a strain of Italian music, on Italian ground. As she sat after supper at a little window, that opened upon the country, observing an effect of the moon-light on the broken surface of the mountains, and remembering that on such a night as this she once had sat with her father and Valancourt, resting upon a cliff of the Pyrenées, she heard from below the long-drawn notes of a violin, of such tone and delicacy of expression, as harmonized exactly with the tender emotions she was indulging, and both charmed and surprised her. Cavigni, who approached the window, smiled at her surprise. "This is nothing extraordinary," said he, "you will hear the same, perhaps, at every inn on our way. It is one of our landlord's family who plays, I doubt not." Emily, as she listened, thought he could be scarcely less than a professor of music whom she heard; and the sweet and plaintive strains soon lulled her into a reverie, from which she was very unwillingly roused by the raillery of Cavigni, and by the voice of Montoni, who gave orders to a servant to have the carriages ready at an early hour on the following morning; and added, that he meant to dine at Turin.

Madame Montoni was exceedingly rejoiced to be once more on level ground; and, after giving a long detail of the various terrors she had suffered, which she forgot that she was describing to the companions of her dangers, she added a hope, that she should soon be beyond the view of these horrid mountains, "which all the world," said she, "should not tempt me to cross again." Complaining of fatigue she soon retired to rest, and Emily withdrew to her own room, when she understood from Annette, her aunt's woman, that Cavigni was nearly right in his conjecture concerning the musician, who had awakened the violin with so much taste, for that he was the son of a peasant inhabiting the neighbouring valley. "He is going to the Carnival at Venice," added Annette, "for they say he has a fine hand at playing, and will get a world of money; and the Carnival is just going to begin: but for my part, I should like to live among these pleasant woods and hills, better than in a town; and they say Ma'moiselle, we shall see no woods, or hills, or fields, at Venice, for that it is built in the very middle of the sea."

Emily agreed with the talkative Annette, that this young man was making a change for the worse, and could not forbear silently lamenting, that he should be drawn from the innocence and beauty of these scenes, to the corrupt ones of that voluptuous city.

When she was alone, unable to sleep, the landscapes of her native home, with Valancourt, and the circumstances of her departure, haunted her fancy; she drew pictures of social happiness amidst the grand simplicity of nature, such as she feared she had bade farewel to for ever; and then, the idea of this young Piedmontese, thus ignorantly sporting with his happiness, returned to her thoughts, and, glad to escape awhile from the pressure of nearer interests, she indulged her fancy in composing the following lines.

THE PIEDMONTESE

Ah, merry swain, who laugh'd along the vales,
And with your gay pipe made the mountains ring,
Why leave your cot, your woods, and thymy gales,
And friends belov'd, for aught that wealth can bring?
He goes to wake o'er moon-light seas the string,
Venetian gold his untaught fancy hails!
Yet oft of home his simple carols sing,
And his steps pause, as the last Alp he scales.
Once more he turns to view his native scene—
Far, far below, as roll the clouds away,
He spies his cabin 'mid the pine-tops green,
The well-known woods, clear brook, and pastures gay;
And thinks of friends and parents left behind,
Of sylvan revels, dance, and festive song;
And hears the faint reed swelling in the wind;
And his sad sighs the distant notes prolong!
Thus went the swain, till mountain-shadows fell,
And dimm'd the landscape to his aching sight;
And must he leave the vales he loves so well!
Can foreign wealth, and shows, his heart delight?
No, happy vales! your wild rocks still shall hear
His pipe, light sounding on the morning breeze;
Still shall he lead the flocks to streamlet clear,
And watch at eve beneath the western trees.
Away, Venetian gold—your charm is o'er!
And now his swift step seeks the lowland bow'rs,
Where, through the leaves, his cottage light *once more*
Guides him to happy friends, and jocund hours.
Ah, merry swain! that laugh along the vales,
And with your gay pipe make the mountains ring,
Your cot, your woods, your thymy-scented gales—
And friends belov'd—more joy than wealth can bring!

CHAPTER II

Titania. If you will patiently dance in our round,
And see our moon-light revels, go with us.
MIDSUMMER NIGHT'S DREAM

EARLY on the following morning, the travellers set out for Turin. The luxuriant plain, that extends from the feet of the Alps to that magnificent city, was not then, as now, shaded by an avenue of trees nine miles in length; but plantations of olives, mulberry and palms, festooned with vines, mingled with the pastoral scenery, through with the rapid Po, after its descent from the mountains, wandered to meet the humble Doria at Turin. As they advanced towards this city, the Alps, seen at some distance, began to appear in all their awful sublimity; chain rising over chain in long succession, their higher points darkened by the hovering clouds, sometimes hid, and at others seen shooting up far above them; while their lower steeps, broken into fantastic forms, were touched with blue and purplish tints, which, as they changed in light and shade, seemed to open new scenes to the eye. To the east stretched the plains of Lombardy, with the towers of Turin rising at a distance; and beyond, the Apennines, bounding the horizon.

The general magnificence of that city, with its vistas of churches and palaces, branching from the grand square, each opening to a landscape of the distant Alps or Apennines, was not only such as Emily had never seen in France, but such as she had never imagined.

Montoni, who had been often at Turin, and cared little about views of any kind, did not comply with his wife's request, that they might survey some of the palaces; but staying only till the necessary refreshments could be obtained, they set forward for Venice with all possible rapidity. Montoni's manner, during this journey, was grave, and even haughty; and towards Madame Montoni he was more especially reserved; but it was not the reserve of respect so much as of pride and discontent. Of Emily he took little notice. With Cavigni his conversations were commonly on political or military topics, such as the convulsed state of their country rendered at this time particularly interesting, Emily observed, that, at the mention of any daring exploit, Montoni's eyes lost their sullenness, and seemed instantaneously to gleam with fire; yet they still retained somewhat of a lurking cunning, and she sometimes thought that their fire partook more of the glare of malice than the brightness of valour, though the latter would well have harmonized with the high chivalric air of his figure, in which Cavigni, with all his gay and gallant manners, was his inferior.

On entering the Milanese, the gentlemen exchanged their French hats for the Italian cap of scarlet cloth, embroidered; and Emily was somewhat surprised to observe, that Montoni added to his the military plume, while Cavigni retained only the feather: which was usually worn with such caps: but she at length concluded, that Montoni assumed this ensign of a soldier for convenience, as a means of passing with more safety through a country over-run with parties of the military.

Over the beautiful plains of this country the devastations of war were frequently visible. Where the lands had not been suffered to lie uncultivated, they were often tracked with the steps of the spoiler; the vines were torn down from the branches that had supported them, the olives trampled upon the ground, and even the groves of mulberry trees had been hewn by the enemy to light fires that destroyed the hamlets and villages of their owners. Emily turned her eyes with a sigh from these painful vestiges of contention, to the Alps of the Grison, that over-looked them to the north, whose awful solitudes seemed to offer to per-secuted man a secure asylum.

The travellers frequently distinguished troops of soldiers moving at a distance; and they experienced, at the little inns on the road, the scarcity of provision and other inconveniences, which are a part of the consequence of intestine war; but they had never reason to be much alarmed for their immediate safety, and they passed on to Milan with little interruption of any kind, where they staid not to survey the grandeur of the city, or even to view its vast cathedral, which was then building.

Beyond Milan, the country wore the aspect of a ruder devastation; and though every thing seemed now quiet, the repose was like that of death, spread over features, which retain the impression of the last convulsions.

It was not till they had passed the eastern limits of the Milanese, that the travellers saw any troops since they had left Milan, when, as the evening was drawing to a close, they descried what appeared to be an army winding onward along the distant plains, whose spears and other arms caught the last rays of the sun. As the column advanced through a part of the road, contracted between two hillocks, some of the com-manders, on horseback, were distinguished on a small eminence, pointing and making signals for the march; while several of the officers were riding along the line directing its progress, according to the signs communicated by those above; and others, separating from the van-guard, which had emerged from the pass, were riding carelessly along the plains at some distance to the right of the army.

As they drew nearer, Montoni, distinguishing the feathers that waved in their caps, and the banners and liveries of the bands that followed them, thought he knew this to be the small army commanded by the famous captain Utaldo, with whom, as well as with some of the other chiefs, he was personally acquainted. He, therefore, gave orders that the carriages should draw up by the side of the road, to await their arrival, and give them the pass. A faint strain of martial music now stole by, and, gradually strengthening as the troops approached, Emily dis-tinguished the drums and trumpets, with the clash of cymbals and of arms, that were struck by a small party, in time to the march.

Montoni being now certain that these were the bands of the victori-ous Utaldo, leaned from the carriage window, and hailed their general by waving his cap in the air; which compliment the chief returned by raising his spear, and then letting it down again suddenly, while some of his officers, who were riding at a distance from the troops, came up to the carriage, and saluted Montoni as an old acquaintance. The captain himself soon after arriving, his bands halted while he conversed with Montoni, whom he appeared much rejoiced to see; and from what he said, Emily understood that this was a victorious army, returning into their own principality; while the numerous waggons, that accompanied them, contained the rich spoils of the enemy, their own wounded soldiers, and the prisoners they had taken in battle, who were to be ransomed when the peace, then negociating between the neighbouring states, should be ratified. The chiefs on the following day were to separate, and each, taking his share of the spoil, was to return with his own band to his castle. This was therefore to be an evening of uncommon and general festivity, in commemoration of the victory they had accomplished together, and of the farewell which the commanders were about to take of each other.

Emily, as these officers conversed with Montoni, observed with admiration, tinctured with awe, their high martial air, mingled with the haughtiness of the noblesse of those days, and heightened by the gallantry of their dress, by the plumes towering on their caps, the armorial coat, Persian sash, and ancient Spanish cloak. Utaldo, telling Montoni that his army were going to encamp for the night near a village at only a few miles distance, invited him to turn back and partake of their festivity, assuring the ladies also, that they should be pleasantly accommodated; but Montoni excused himself, adding, that it was his design to reach Verona that evening; and, after some conversation concerning the state of the country towards that city, they parted.

The travellers proceeded without any interruption; but it was some hours after sunset before they arrived at Verona, whose beautiful environs were therefore not seen by Emily till the following morning; when, leaving that pleasant town at an early hour, they set off for Padua, where they embarked on the Brenta for Venice. Here the scene was entirely changed; no vestiges of war, such as had deformed the plains of the Milanese, appeared; on the contrary, all was peace and elegance. The verdant banks of the Brenta exhibited a continued landscape of beauty, gaiety, and splendour. Emily gazed with admiration on the villas of the Venetian noblesse, with their cool porticos and colonnades, overhung with poplars and cypresses of majestic height and lively verdure; on their rich orangeries, whose blossoms perfumed the air, and on the luxuriant willows, that dipped their light leaves in the wave, and sheltered from the sun the gay parties whose music came at intervals on the breeze. The Carnival did, indeed, appear to extend from Venice along the whole line of these enchanting shores; the river was gay with boats passing to that city, exhibiting the fantastic diversity of a masquerade in the dresses of the people within them; and, towards evening, groups of dancers frequently were seen beneath the trees.

Cavigni, meanwhile, informed her of the names of the noblemen to whom the several villas they passed belonged, adding light sketches of their characters, such as served to amuse rather than to inform, exhibiting his own wit instead of the delineation of truth. Emily was sometimes diverted by his conversation; but his gaiety did not entertain Madame Montoni, as it had formerly done; she was frequently grave, and Montoni retained his usual reserve.

Nothing could exceed Emily's admiration on her first view of Venice, with its islets, palaces, and towers rising out of the sea, whose clear surface reflected the tremulous picture in all its colours. The sun, sinking in the west, tinted the waves and the lofty mountains of Friuli, which skirt the northern shores of the Adriatic, with a saffron glow, while on the marble porticos and colonnades of St. Mark were thrown the rich lights and shades of evening. As they glided on, the grander features of this city appeared more distinctly: its terraces, crowned with airy yet majestic fabrics, touched, as they now were, with the splendour of the setting sun, appeared as if they had been called up from the ocean by the wand of an enchanter, rather than reared by mortal hands.

The sun, soon after, sinking to the lower world, the shadow of the earth stole gradually over the waves, and then up the towering sides of the mountains of Friuli, till it extinguished even the last upward beams that had lingered on their summits, and the melancholy purple of evening drew over them, like a thin veil. How deep, how beautiful was the tranquillity that wrapped the scene! All nature seemed to repose; the finest emotions of the soul were alone awake. Emily's eyes filled with tears of admiration and sublime devotion, as she raised them over the sleeping world to the vast heavens, and heard the notes of solemn music, that stole over the waters from a distance. She listened in still rapture, and no person of the party broke the charm by an enquiry. The sounds seemed to grow on the air; for so smoothly did the barge glide along, that its motion was not perceivable, and the fairy city appeared approaching to welcome the strangers. They now distinguished a female voice, accompanied by a few instruments, singing a soft and mournful air; and its fine expression, as sometimes it seemed pleading with the impassioned tenderness of love, and then languishing into the cadence of hopeless grief, declared, that it flowed from no feigned sensibility. Ah! thought Emily, as she sighed and remembered Valancourt, those strains come from the heart!

She looked round, with anxious enquiry; the deep twilight, that had fallen over the scene, admitted only imperfect images to the eye, but, at some distance on the sea, she thought she perceived a gondola: a chorus of voices and instruments now swelled on the air—so sweet, so solemn! it seemed like the hymn of angels descending through the silence of night! Now it died away, and fancy almost beheld the holy choir reascending towards heaven; then again it swelled with the breeze, trembled awhile, and again died into silence. It brought to Emily's recollection some lines of her late father, and she repeated in a low voice,

> Oft I hear,
> Upon the silence of the midnight air,
> Celestial voices swell in holy chorus
> That bears the soul to heaven!

The deep stillness, that succeeded, was as expressive as the strain that had just ceased. It was uninterrupted for several minutes, till a general sigh seemed to release the company from their enchantment. Emily, however, long indulged the pleasing sadness, that had stolen upon her spirits; but the gay and busy scene that appeared, as the barge approached St. Mark's Place, at length roused her attention. The rising moon, which threw a shadowy light upon the terraces, and illumined the porticos and magnificent arcades that crowned them, discovered the various company, whose light steps, soft guitars, and softer voices, echoed through the colonnades.

The music they heard before now passed Montoni's barge, in one of the gondolas, of which several were seen skimming along the moon-light sea, full of gay parties, catching the cool breeze. Most of these had music, made sweeter by the waves over which it floated, and by the measured sound of oars, as they dashed the sparkling tide. Emily gazed, and listened, and thought herself in a fairy scene; even Madame Montoni was pleased; Montoni congratulated himself on his return to Venice, which he called the first city in the world, and Cavigni was more gay and animated than ever.

The barge passed on to the grand canal, where Montoni's mansion was situated. And here, other forms of beauty and of grandeur, such as her imagination had never painted, were unfolded to Emily in the palaces of Sansovino and Palladio, as she glided along the waves. The air bore no sounds, but those of sweetness, echoing along each margin of the canal, and from gondolas on its surface, while groups of masks were seen dancing on the moon-light terraces, and seemed almost to realize the romance of fairyland.

The barge stopped before the portico of a large house, from whence a servant of Montoni crossed the terrace, and immediately the party disembarked. From the portico they passed a noble hall to a stair-case of marble, which led to a saloon, fitted up in a style of magnificence that surprised Emily. The walls and ceilings were adorned with historical and allegorical paintings, in *fresco*; silver tripods, depending from chains of the same metal, illumined the apartment, the floor of which was covered with Indian mats painted in a variety of colours and devices; the couches and drapery of the lattices were of pale green silk, embroidered and fringed with green and gold. Balcony lattices opened upon the grand canal, whence rose a confusion of voices and of musical instruments, and the breeze that gave freshness to the apartment. Emily, considering the gloomy temper of Montoni, looked upon the splendid furniture of this house with surprise, and remembered the report of his being a man of broken fortune, with astonishment. "Ah!" said she to herself, "if Valancourt could but see this mansion, what peace would it give him! He would then be convinced that the report was groundless."

Madame Montoni seemed to assume the air of a princess; but Montoni was restless and discontented, and did not even observe the civility of bidding her welcome to her home.

Soon after his arrival, he ordered his gondola, and, with Cavigni, went out to mingle in the scenes of the evening. Madame then became serious and thoughtful. Emily, who was charmed with every thing she saw, endeavoured to enliven her; but reflection had not, with Madame Montoni, subdued caprice and ill-humour, and her answers discovered so much of both, that Emily gave up the attempt of diverting her, and withdrew to a lattice, to amuse herself with the scene without, so new and so enchanting.

The first object that attracted her notice was a group of dancers on the terrace below, led by a guitar and some other instruments. The girl, who struck the guitar, and another, who flourished a tambourine, passed on in a dancing step, and with a light grace and gaiety of heart, that would have subdued the goddess of spleen in her worst humour. After these came a group of fantastic figures, some dressed as gondolieri, others as minstrels, while others seemed to defy all description. They sung in parts, their voices accompanied by a few soft instruments. At a little distance from the portico they stopped, and Emily distinguished the verses of Ariosto. They sung of the wars of the Moors against Charlemagne, and then of the woes of Orlando: afterwards the measure changed, and the melancholy sweetness of Petrarch succeeded. The magic of his grief was assisted by all that Italian music and Italian expression, heightened by the enchantments of Venetian moonlight, could give.

Emily, as she listened, caught the pensive enthusiasm; her tears flowed silently, while her fancy bore her far away to France and to Valancourt. Each succeeding sonnet, more full of charming sadness than the last, seemed to bind the spell of melancholy: with extreme regret she saw the musicians move on, and her attention followed the strain till the last faint warble died in air. She then remained sunk in that pensive tranquillity which soft music leaves on the mind—a state like that produced by the view of a beautiful landscape by moon-light, or by the recollection of scenes marked with the tenderness of friends lost for ever, and with sorrows, which time has mellowed into mild regret. Such scenes are indeed, to the mind, like "those faint traces which the memory bears of music that is past."

Other sounds soon awakened her attention: it was the solemn harmony of horns, that swelled from a distance; and, observing the gondolas arrange themselves along the margin of the terraces, she threw on her veil, and, stepping into the balcony, discerned, in the distant perspective of the canal, something like a procession, floating on the light surface of the water: as it approached, the horns and other instruments mingled sweetly, and soon after the fabled deities of the city seemed to have arisen from the ocean; for Neptune, with Venice personified as his queen, came on the undulating waves, surrounded by tritons and sea-nymphs. The fantastic splendour of this spectacle, together with the grandeur of the surrounding palaces, appeared like the vision of a poet suddenly embodied, and the fanciful images, which it awakened in Emily's mind, lingered there long after the procession had passed away. She indulged herself in imagining what might be the manners and delights of a sea-nymph, till she almost wished to throw off the habit of mortality, and plunge into the green wave to participate them.

"How delightful," said she, "to live amidst the coral bowers and crystal caverns of the ocean, with my sister nymphs, and listen to the sounding waters above, and to the soft shells of the tritons! and then, after sunset, to skim on the surface of the waves round wild rocks and along sequestered shores, where, perhaps, some pensive wanderer comes to weep! Then would I soothe his sorrows with my sweet music, and offer him from a shell some of the delicious fruit that hangs round Neptune's palace."

She was recalled from her reverie to a mere mortal supper, and could not forbear smiling at the fancies she had been indulging, and at her conviction of the serious displeasure, which Madame Montoni would have expressed, could she have been made acquainted with them.

After supper, her aunt sat late, but Montoni did not return, and she at length retired to rest. If Emily had admired the magnificence of the saloon, she was not less surprised, on observing the half-furnished and forlorn appearance of the apartments she passed in the way to her chamber, whither she went through long suites of noble rooms, that seemed, from their desolate aspect, to have been unoccupied for many years. On the walls of some were the faded remains of tapestry; from others, painted in *fresco*, the damps had almost withdrawn both colours and design. At length she reached her own chamber, spacious, desolate, and lofty, like the rest, with high lattices that opened towards the Adriatic. It brought gloomy images to her mind, but the view of the Adriatic soon gave her others more airy, among which was that of the sea-nymph, whose delights she had before amused herself with picturing; and, anxious to escape from serious reflections, she now endeavoured to throw her fanciful ideas into a train, and concluded the hour with composing the following lines:

THE SEA-NYMPH

Down, down a thousand fathom deep,
Among the sounding seas I go;
Play round the foot of ev'ry steep
Whose cliffs above the ocean grow.

There, within their secret caves,
I hear the mighty rivers roar;
And guide their streams through Neptune's waves
To bless the green earth's inmost shore:

And bid the freshen'd waters glide,
For fern-crown'd nymphs of lake, or brook,
Through winding woods and pastures wide,
And many a wild, romantic nook.

For this the nymphs, at fall of eve,
Oft dance upon the flow'ry banks,
And sing my name, and garlands weave
To bear beneath the wave their thanks.

In coral bow'rs I love to lie,
And hear the surges roll above,
And through the waters view on high
The proud ships sail, and gay clouds move.

And oft at midnight's stillest hour,
When summer seas the vessel lave,
I love to prove my charmful pow'r
While floating on the moon-light wave.

And when deep sleep the crew has bound,
And the sad lover musing leans
O'er the ship's side, I breathe around
Such strains as speak no mortal means!

O'er the dim waves his searching eye
Sees but the vessel's lengthen'd shade;

Above—the moon and azure sky;
Entranc'd he hears, and half afraid!

Sometimes, a single note I swell,
That, softly sweet, at distance dies;
Then wake the magic of my shell,
And choral voices round me rise!

The trembling youth, charm'd by my strain,
Calls up the crew, who, silent, bend
O'er the high deck, but list in vain;
My song is hush'd, my wonders end!

Within the mountain's woody bay,
Where the tall bark at anchor rides,
At twilight hour, with tritons gay,
I dance upon the lapsing tides:

And with my sister-nymphs I sport,
Till the broad sun looks o'er the floods;
Then, swift we seek our crystal court,
Deep in the wave, 'mid Neptune's woods.

In cool arcades and glassy halls
We pass the sultry hours of noon,
Beyond wherever sun-beam falls,
Weaving sea-flowers in gay festoon.

The while we chant our ditties sweet
To some soft shell that warbles near;
Join'd by the murmuring currents, fleet,
That glide along our halls so clear.

There, the pale pearl and sapphire blue,
And ruby red, and em'rald green,
Dart from the domes a changing hue,
And sparry columns deck the scene.

When the dark storm scowls o'er the deep,
And long, long peals of thunder sound,
On some high cliff my watch I keep
O'er all the restless seas around:

Till on the ridgy wave afar
Comes the lone vessel, labouring slow,
Spreading the white foam in the air,
With sail and top-mast bending low.

Then, plunge I 'mid the ocean's roar,
My way by quiv'ring lightnings shewn,
To guide the bark to peaceful shore,
And hush the sailor's fearful groan.

And if too late I reach its side
To save it from the 'whelming surge,
I call my dolphins o'er the tide,
To bear the crew where isles emerge.

Their mournful spirits soon I cheer,
While round the desert coast I go,
With warbled songs they faintly hear,
Oft as the stormy gust sinks low.

My music leads to lofty groves,
That wild upon the sea-bank wave;
Where sweet fruits bloom, and fresh spring roves,
And closing boughs the tempest brave.

Then, from the air spirits obey
My potent voice they love so well,
And, on the clouds, paint visions gay,
While strains more sweet at distance swell.

And thus the lonely hours I cheat,
Soothing the ship-wreck'd sailor's heart,
Till from the waves the storms retreat,
And o'er the east the day-beams dart.

Neptune for this oft binds me fast
To rocks below, with coral chain,
Till all the tempest's over-past,
And drowning seamen cry in vain.

Whoe'er ye are that love my lay,
Come, when red sunset tints the wave,
To the still sands, where fairies play;
There, in cool seas, I love to lave.

CHAPTER III

He is a great observer, and he looks
Quite through the deeds of men: he loves no plays,
          he hears no music;
Seldom he smiles; and smiles in such a sort,
As if he mock'd himself, and scorn'd his spirit
That could be mov'd to smile at any thing.
Such men as he be never at heart's ease,
While they behold a greater than themselves.
                              JULIUS CAESAR

MONTONI and his companion did not return home, till many hours
after the dawn had blushed upon the Adriatic. The airy groups, which

had danced all night along the colonnade of St. Mark, dispersed before the morning, like so many spirits. Montoni had been otherwise engaged; his soul was little susceptible of light pleasures. He delighted in the energies of the passions; the difficulties and tempests of life, which wreck the happiness of others, roused and strengthened all the powers of his mind, and afforded him the highest enjoyments, of which his nature was capable. Without some object of strong interest, life was to him little more than a sleep; and, when pursuits of real interest failed, he substituted artificial ones, till habit changed their nature, and they ceased to be unreal. Of this kind was the habit of gaming, which he had adopted, first, for the purpose of relieving him from the languor of inaction, but had since pursued with the ardour of passion. In this occupation he had passed the night with Cavigni and a party of young men, who had more money than rank, and more vice than either. Montoni despised the greater part of these for the inferiority of their talents, rather than for their vicious inclinations, and associated with them only to make them the instruments of his purposes. Among these, however, were some of superior abilities, and a few whom Montoni admitted to his intimacy, but even towards these he still preserved a decisive and haughty air, which, while it imposed submission on weak and timid minds, roused the fierce hatred of strong ones. He had, of course, many and bitter enemies; but the rancour of their hatred proved the degree of his power; and, as power was his chief aim, he gloried more in such hatred, than it was possible he could in being esteemed. A feeling so tempered as that of esteem, he despised, and would have despised himself also had he thought himself capable of being flattered by it.

Among the few whom he distinguished, were the Signors Bertolini, Orsino, and Verezzi. The first was a man of gay temper, strong passions, dissipated, and of unbounded extravagance, but generous, brave, and unsuspicious. Orsino was reserved, and haughty; loving power more than ostentation; of a cruel and suspicious temper; quick to feel an injury, and relentless in avenging it; cunning and unsearchable in contrivance, patient and indefatigable in the execution of his schemes. He had a perfect command of feature and of his passions, of which he had scarcely any, but pride, revenge and avarice; and, in the gratification of these, few considerations had power to restrain him, few obstacles to withstand the depth of his stratagems. This man was the chief favourite of Montoni. Verezzi was a man of some talent, of fiery imagination, and the slave of alternate passions. He was gay, voluptuous, and daring; yet had neither perseverance or true courage, and was meanly selfish in all his aims. Quick to form schemes, and sanguine in his hope of success, he was the first to undertake, and to abandon, not only his own plans, but those adopted from other persons. Proud and impetuous, he revolted against all subordination; yet those who were acquainted with his character, and watched the turn of his passions, could lead him like a child.

Such were the friends whom Montoni introduced to his family and his table, on the day after his arrival at Venice. There were also of the party a Venetian nobleman, Count Morano, and a Signora Livona, whom Montoni had introduced to his wife, as a lady of distinguished merit, and who, having called in the morning to welcome her to Venice, had been requested to be of the dinner party.

Madame Montoni received with a very ill grace, the compliments of the Signors. She disliked them, because they were the friends of her husband; hated them, because she believed they had contributed to detain him abroad till so late an hour of the preceding morning; and envied them, since, conscious of her own want of influence, she was convinced, that he preferred their society to her own. The rank of Count Morano procured him that distinction which she refused to the rest of the company. The haughty sullenness of her countenance and manner, and the ostentatious extravagance of her dress, for she had not yet adopted the Venetian habit, were strikingly contrasted by the beauty, modesty, sweetness and simplicity of Emily, who observed, with more attention than pleasure, the party around her. The beauty and fascinating manners of Signora Livona, however, won her involuntary regard; while the sweetness of her accents and her air of gentle kindness awakened with Emily those pleasing affections, which so long had slumbered.

In the cool of the evening the party embarked in Montoni's gondola, and rowed out upon the sea. The red glow of sunset still touched the waves, and lingered in the west, where the melancholy gleam seemed slowly expiring, while the dark blue of the upper æther began to twinkle with stars. Emily sat, given up to pensive and sweet emotions. The smoothness of the water, over which she glided, its reflected images— a new heaven and trembling stars below the waves, with shadowy outlines of towers and porticos, conspired with the stillness of the hour, interrupted only by the passing wave, or the notes of distant music, to raise those emotions to enthusiasm. As she listened to the measured sound of the oars, and to the remote warblings that came in the breeze, her softened mind returned to the memory of St. Aubert and to Valancourt, and tears stole to her eyes. The rays of the moon, strengthening as the shadows deepened, soon after threw a silvery gleam upon her countenance, which was partly shaded by a thin black veil, and touched it with inimitable softness. Hers was the *contour* of a Madona, with the sensibility of a Magdalen; and the pensive uplifted eye, with the tear that glittered on her cheek, confirmed the expression of the character.

The last strain of distant music now died in air, for the gondola was far upon the waves, and the party determined to have music of their own. The Count Morano, who sat next to Emily, and who had been observing her for some time in silence, snatched up a lute, and struck the chords with the finger of harmony herself, while his voice, a fine tenor, accompanied them in a rondeau full of tender sadness. To him, indeed, might have been applied that beautiful exhortation of an English poet, had it then existed:

> Strike up, my master,
> But touch the strings with a religious softness!
> Teach sounds to languish through the night's dull ear
> Till Melancholy starts from off her couch,
> And Carelessness grows concert to attention!

With such powers of expression the Count sung the following

RONDEAU

> Soft as yon silver ray, that sleeps
> Upon the ocean's trembling tide;
> Soft as the air, that lightly sweeps
> Yon sail, that swells in stately pride:
>
> Soft as the surge's stealing note,
> That dies along the distant shores,
> Or warbled strain, that sinks remote —
> So soft the sigh my bosom pours!
>
> True as the wave to Cynthia's ray,
> True as the vessel to the breeze,
> True as the soul to music's sway,
> Or music to Venetian seas:
>
> Soft as yon silver beams, that sleep
> Upon the ocean's trembling breast;
> So soft, so true, fond Love shall weep,
> So soft, so true, with *thee* shall rest.

The cadence with which he returned from the last stanza to a repetition of the first; the fine modulation in which his voice stole upon the first line, and the pathetic energy with which it pronounced the last, were such as only exquisite taste could give. When he had concluded, he gave the lute with a sigh to Emily, who, to avoid any appearance of affectation, immediately began to play. She sung a melancholy little air, one of the popular songs of her native province, with a simplicity and pathos that made it enchanting. But its well-known melody brought so forcibly to her fancy the scenes and the persons, among which she had often heard it, that her spirits were overcome, her voice trembled and ceased—and the strings of the lute were struck with a disordered hand; till, ashamed of the emotion she had betrayed, she suddenly passed on to a song so gay and airy, that the steps of the dance seemed almost to echo to the notes. *Bravissimo!* burst instantly from the lips of her delighted auditors, and she was compelled to repeat the air. Among the compliments that followed, those of the Count were not the least audible, and they had not concluded, when Emily gave the instrument to Signora Livona, whose voice accompanied it with true Italian taste.

Afterwards, the Count, Emily, Cavigni, and the Signora, sung *canzonettes*, accompanied by a couple of lutes and a few other instruments. Sometimes the instruments suddenly ceased, and the voices dropped from the full swell of harmony into a low chant; then, after a deep pause, they rose by degrees, the instruments one by one striking up, till the loud and full chorus soared again to heaven!

Meanwhile, Montoni, who was weary of this harmony, was considering how he might disengage himself from his party, or withdraw with such of it as would be willing to play, to a Casino. In a pause of the music, he proposed returning to shore, a proposal which Orsino eagerly seconded, but which the Count and the other gentlemen as warmly opposed.

Montoni still meditated how he might excuse himself from longer attendance upon the Count, for to him only he thought excuse necessary, and how he might get to land, till the gondolieri of an empty boat, returning to Venice, hailed his people. Without troubling himself longer about an excuse, he seized this opportunity of going thither, and, committing the ladies to the care of his friends, departed with Orsino, while Emily, for the first time, saw him go with regret; for she considered his presence a protection, though she knew not what she should fear. He landed at St. Mark's, and, hurrying to a Casino, was soon lost amidst a crowd of gamesters.

Meanwhile, the Count having secretly dispatched a servant in Montoni's boat, for his own gondola and musicians, Emily heard, without knowing his project, the gay song of gondolieri approaching, as they sat on the stern of the boat, and saw the tremulous gleam of the moon-light wave, which their oars disturbed. Presently she heard the sound of instruments, and then a full symphony swelled on the air, and, the boats meeting, the gondolieri hailed each other. The Count then explaining himself, the party removed into his gondola, which was embellished with all that taste could bestow.

While they partook of a collation of fruits and ice, the whole band, following at a distance in the other boat, played the most sweet and enchanting strains, and the Count, who had again seated himself by Emily, paid her unremitted attention, and sometimes, in a low but impassioned voice, uttered compliments which she could not misunderstand. To avoid them she conversed with Signora Livona, and her manner to the Count assumed a mild reserve, which, though dignified, was too gentle to repress his assiduities: he could see, hear, speak to no person, but Emily, while Cavigni observed him now and then, with a look of displeasure, and Emily, with one of uneasiness. She now wished for nothing so much as to return to Venice, but it was near mid-night before the gondolas approached St. Mark's Place, where the voice of gaiety and song was loud. The busy hum of mingling sounds was heard at a considerable distance on the water, and, had not a bright moon-light discovered the city, with its terraces and towers, a stranger would almost have credited the fabled wonders of Neptune's court, and believed, that the tumult arose from beneath the waves.

They landed at St. Mark's, where the gaiety of the colonnades and the beauty of the night, made Madame Montoni willingly submit to the Count's solicitations to join the promenade, and afterwards to take a supper with the rest of the party, at his Casino. If any thing could have dissipated Emily's uneasiness, it would have been the grandeur, gaiety, and novelty of the surrounding scene, adorned with Palladio's palaces, and busy with parties of masqueraders.

At length they withdrew to the Casino, which was fitted up with infinite taste, and where a splendid banquet was prepared; but here Emily's reserve made the Count perceive, that it was necessary for his interest to win the favour of Madame Montoni, which, from the condescension she had already shewn to him, appeared to be an achievement of no great difficulty. He transferred, therefore, part of his attention from Emily to her aunt, who felt too much flattered by the distinction even to disguise her emotion; and, before the party broke up, he had entirely engaged the esteem of Madame Montoni. Whenever he addressed her, her ungracious countenance relaxed into smiles, and to whatever he proposed she assented. He invited her, with the rest of the party, to take coffee, in his box at the opera, on the following evening, and Emily heard the invitation accepted, with strong anxiety, concerning the means of excusing herself from attending Madame Montoni thither.

It was very late before their gondola was ordered, and Emily's surprise was extreme, when, on quitting the Casino, she beheld the broad sun rising out of the Adriatic, while St. Mark's Place was yet crowded with company. Sleep had long weighed heavily on her eyes, but now the fresh sea-breeze revived her, and she would have quitted the scene with regret, had not the Count been present, performing the duty, which he had imposed upon himself, of escorting them home. There they heard that Montoni was not yet returned; and his wife, retiring in displeasure to her apartment, at length released Emily from the fatigue of further attendance.

Montoni came home late in the morning, in a very ill humour, having lost considerably at play, and, before he withdrew to rest, had a private conference with Cavigni, whose manner, on the following day, seemed to tell, that the subject of it had not been pleasing to him.

In the evening, Madame Montoni, who, during the day, had observed a sullen silence towards her husband, received visits from some Venetian ladies, with whose sweet manners Emily was particularly charmed. They had an air of ease and kindness towards the strangers, as if they had been their familiar friends for years; and their conversation was by turns tender, sentimental and gay. Madame, though she had no taste for such conversation, and whose coarseness and selfishness sometimes exhibited a ludicrous contrast to their excessive refinement, could not remain wholly insensible to the captivations of their manner.

In a pause of conversation, a lady who was called Signora Herminia took up a lute, and began to play and sing, with as much easy gaiety, as if she had been alone. Her voice was uncommonly rich in tone, and various in expression; yet she appeared to be entirely unconscious of its powers, and meant nothing less than to display them. She sung from the gaiety of her heart, as she sat with her veil half thrown back, holding gracefully the lute, under the spreading foliage and flowers of some plants, that rose from baskets, and interlaced one of the lattices of the saloon. Emily, retiring a little from the company, sketched her figure, with the miniature scenery around her, and drew a very interesting picture, which, though it would not, perhaps, have borne criticism, had spirit and taste enough to awaken both the fancy and the heart. When she had finished it, she presented it to the beautiful original, who was delighted with the offering, as well as the sentiment it conveyed, and assured Emily, with a smile of captivating sweetness, that she should preserve it as a pledge of her friendship.

In the evening Cavigni joined the ladies, but Montoni had other engagements; and they embarked in the gondola for St. Mark's, where the same gay company seemed to flutter as on the preceding night. The cool breeze, the glassy sea, the gentle sound of its waves, and the sweeter murmur of distant music; the lofty porticos and arcades, and the happy groups that sauntered beneath them; these, with every feature and circumstance of the scene, united to charm Emily, no longer teased by the officious attentions of Count Morano. But, as she looked upon the moon-light sea, undulating along the walls of St. Mark, and, lingering for a moment over those walls, caught the sweet and melancholy song of some gondolier as he sat in his boat below, waiting for his master, her softened mind returned to the memory of her home, of her friends, and of all that was dear in her native country.

After walking some time, they sat down at the door of a Casino, and, while Cavigni was accommodating them with coffee and ice, were joined by Count Morano. He sought Emily with a look of impatient delight, who, remembering all the attention he had shewn her on the preceding evening, was compelled, as before, to shrink from his assiduities into a timid reserve, except when she conversed with Signora Herminia and the other ladies of her party.

It was near midnight before they withdrew to the opera, where Emily was not so charmed but that, when she remembered the scene she had just quitted, she felt how infinitely inferior all the splendour of art is to the sublimity of nature. Her heart was not now affected, tears of admiration did not start to her eyes, as when she viewed the vast expanse of ocean, the grandeur of the heavens, and listened to the rolling waters, and to the faint music that, at intervals, mingled with their roar. Remembering these, the scene before her faded into insignificance.

Of the evening, which passed on without any particular incident, she wished the conclusion, that she might escape from the attentions of the Count; and, as opposite qualities frequently attract each other in our thoughts, thus Emily, when she looked on Count Morano, remembered Valancourt, and a sigh sometimes followed the recollection.

Several weeks passed in the course of customary visits, during which nothing remarkable occurred. Emily was amused by the manners and scenes that surrounded her, so different from those of France, but where Count Morano, too frequently for her comfort, contrived to introduce himself. His manner, figure and accomplishments, which were generally admired, Emily would, perhaps, have admired also, had her heart been disengaged from Valancourt, and had the Count forborne to persecute her with officious attentions, during which she observed some traits in his character, that prejudiced her against whatever might otherwise be good in it.

Soon after his arrival at Venice, Montoni received a packet from M. Quesnel, in which the latter mentioned the death of his wife's uncle, at his villa on the Brenta; and that, in consequence of this event, he should hasten to take possession of that estate and of other effects bequeathed to him. This uncle was the brother of Madame Quesnel's late mother; Montoni was related to her by the father's side, and though he could have had neither claim nor expectation concerning these possessions, he could scarcely conceal the envy which M. Quesnel's letter excited.

Emily had observed with concern, that, since they left France, Montoni had not even affected kindness towards her aunt, and that, after treating her, at first, with neglect, he now met her with uniform ill-humour and reserve. She had never supposed, that her aunt's foibles could have escaped the discernment of Montoni, or that her mind or figure were of a kind to deserve his attention. Her surprise, therefore, at this match, had been extreme; but since he had made the choice, she did not suspect that he would so openly have discovered his contempt of it. But Montoni, who had been allured by the seeming wealth of Madame Cheron, was now severely disappointed by her comparative poverty, and highly exasperated by the deceit she had employed to conceal it, till concealment was no longer necessary. He had been deceived in an affair, wherein he meant to be the deceiver; out-witted by the superior cunning of a woman, whose understanding he despised, and to whom he had sacrificed his pride and his liberty, without saving himself from the ruin, which had impended over his head. Madame Montoni had contrived to have the greatest part of what she really did possess, settled upon herself: what remained, though it was totally inadequate both to her husband's expectations, and to his necessities, he had converted into money, and brought with him to Venice, that he might a little longer delude society, and make a last effort to regain the fortunes he had lost.

The hints which had been thrown out to Valancourt, concerning Montoni's character and condition, were too true; but it was now left to time and occasion, to unfold the circumstances, both of what had, and of what had not been hinted, and to time and occasion we commit them.

Madame Montoni was not of a nature to bear injuries' with meekness, or to resent them with dignity: her exasperated pride displayed itself in all the violence and acrimony of a little, or at least of an ill-regulated mind. She would not acknowledge, even to herself, that she had in any degree provoked contempt by her duplicity, but weakly persisted in believing, that she alone was to be pitied, and Montoni alone to be censured; for, as her mind had naturally little perception of moral obligation, she seldom understood its force but when it happened to be violated towards herself: her vanity had already been severely shocked by a discovery of Montoni's contempt; it remained to be farther reproved by a discovery of his circumstances. His mansion at Venice, though its furniture discovered a part of the truth to unprejudiced persons, told nothing to those who were blinded by a resolution to believe whatever they wished. Madame Montoni still thought herself little less than a princess, possessing a palace at Venice, and a castle among the Apennines. To the castle di Udolpho, indeed, Montoni sometimes talked of going for a few weeks to examine into its condition, and to receive some rents; for it appeared that he had not been there for two years, and that, during this period, it had been inhabited only by an old servant, whom he called his steward.

Emily listened to the mention of this journey with pleasure, for she not only expected from it new ideas, but a release from the persevering assiduities of Count Morano. In the country, too, she would have leisure to think of Valancourt, and to indulge the melancholy, which his image, and a recollection of the scenes of La Vallée, always blessed with the memory of her parents, awakened. The ideal scenes were dearer, and more soothing to her heart, than all the splendour of gay assemblies; they were a kind of talisman that expelled the poison of temporary evils, and supported her hopes of happy days: they appeared like a beautiful landscape, lighted up by a gleam of sun-shine, and seen through a perspective of dark and rugged rocks.

But Count Morano did not long confine himself to silent assiduities; he declared his passion to Emily, and made proposals to Montoni, who encouraged, though Emily rejected, him: with Montoni for his friend, and an abundance of vanity to delude him, he did not despair of success. Emily was astonished and highly disgusted at his perseverance, after she had explained her sentiments with a frankness that would not allow him to misunderstand them.

He now passed the greater part of his time at Montoni's, dining there almost daily, and attending Madame and Emily wherever they went; and all this, notwithstanding the uniform reserve of Emily, whose aunt seemed as anxious as Montoni to promote this marriage; and would never dispense with her attendance at any assembly where the Count proposed to be present.

Montoni now said nothing of his intended journey, of which Emily waited impatiently to hear; and he was seldom at home but when the Count, or Signor Orsino, was there, for between himself and Cavigni a coolness seemed to subsist, though the latter remained in his house. With Orsino, Montoni was frequently closeted for hours together, and, whatever might be the business, upon which they consulted, it appeared to be of consequence, since Montoni often sacrificed to it his favourite passion for play, and remained at home the whole night. There was somewhat of privacy, too, in the manner of Orsino's visits, which had never before occurred, and which excited not only surprise, but some degree of alarm in Emily's mind, who had unwillingly discovered much of his character when he had most endeavoured to disguise it. After these visits, Montoni was often more thoughtful than usual; sometimes the deep workings of his mind entirely abstracted him from surrounding objects, and threw a gloom over his visage that rendered it terrible; at others, his eyes seemed almost to flash fire, and all the energies of his soul appeared to be roused for some great enterprise. Emily observed these written characters of his thoughts with deep interest, and not without some degree of awe, when she considered that she was entirely in his power; but forbore even to hint her fears, or her observations, to Madame Montoni, who discerned nothing in her husband, at these times, but his usual sternness.

A second letter from M. Quesnel announced the arrival of himself and his lady at the Villa Miarenti; stated several circumstances of his good fortune, respecting the affair that had brought him into Italy; and concluded with an earnest request to see Montoni, his wife and niece, at his new estate.

Emily received, about the same period, a much more interesting letter, and which soothed for a while every anxiety of her heart. Valancourt, hoping she might be still at Venice, had trusted a letter to the ordinary post, that told her of his health, and of his unceasing and anxious affection. He had lingered at Tholouse for some time after her departure, that he might indulge the melancholy pleasure of wandering through the scenes where he had been accustomed to behold her, and had thence gone to his brother's chateau, which was in the neighbourhood of La Vallée. Having mentioned this, he added, "If the duty of attending my regiment did not require my departure, I know not when I should have resolution enough to quit the neighbourhood of a place which is endeared by the remembrance of you. The vicinity to La Vallée has alone detained me thus long at Estuviere: I frequently ride thither early in the morning, that I may wander, at leisure, through the day, among scenes, which were once your home, where I have been accustomed to see you, and to hear you converse. I have renewed my acquaintance with the good old Theresa, who rejoiced to see me, that she might talk of you: I need not say how much this circumstance attached me to her, or how eagerly I listened to her upon her favourite subject. You will guess the motive that first induced me to make myself known to Theresa: it was, indeed, no other than that of gaining admittance into the chateau and gardens, which my Emily had so lately inhabited: here, then, I wander, and meet your image under every shade: but chiefly I love to sit beneath the spreading branches of your favourite plane, where once, Emily, we sat together; where I first ventured to tell you, that I loved. O Emily! the remembrance of those moments overcomes me—I sit lost in reverie—I endeavour to see you dimly through my tears, in all the heaven of peace and innocence, such as you then appeared to me; to hear again the accents of that voice, which then thrilled my heart with tenderness and hope. I lean on the wall of the terrace, where we together watched the rapid current of the Garonne below, while I described the wild scenery about its source, but thought only of you. O Emily! are these moments passed for ever—will they never more return?"

In another part of his letter he wrote thus. "You see my letter is dated on many different days, and, if you look back to the first, you will perceive, that I began to write soon after your departure from France. To write was, indeed, the only employment that withdrew me from my own melancholy, and rendered your absence supportable, or rather, it seemed to destroy absence; for, when I was conversing with you on paper, and telling you every sentiment and affection of my heart, you almost appeared to be present. This employment has been from time to time my chief consolation, and I have deferred sending off my packet, merely for the comfort of prolonging it, though it was certain, that what I had written, was written to no purpose till you received it. Whenever my mind has been more than usually depressed I have come to pour forth its sorrows to you, and have always found consolation; and, when any little occurrence has interested my heart, and given a gleam of joy to my spirits, I have hastened to communicate it to you, and have received reflected satisfaction. Thus, my letter is a kind of picture of my life and of my thoughts for the last month, and thus, though it has been deeply interesting to me, while I wrote it, and I dare hope will, for the same reason, be not indifferent to you, yet to other readers it would seem to abound only in frivolities. Thus it is always, when we attempt to describe the finer movements of the heart, for they are too fine to be discerned, they can only be experienced, and are therefore passed over by the indifferent observer, while the interested one feels, that all description is imperfect and unnecessary, except as it may prove the sincerity of the writer, and soothe his own sufferings. You will pardon all this egotism—for I am a lover."

"I have just heard of a circumstance, which entirely destroys all my fairy paradise of ideal delight, and which will reconcile me to the necessity of returning to my regiment, for I must no longer wander beneath the beloved shades, where I have been accustomed to meet you in thought.—La Vallée is let! I have reason to believe this is without your knowledge, from what Theresa told me this morning, and, therefore, I mention the circumstance. She shed tears, while she related, that she was going to leave the service of her dear mistress, and the chateau where she had lived so many happy years; and all this, added she, without even a letter from Mademoiselle to soften the news; but it is all Mons. Quesnel's doings, and I dare say she does not even know what is going forward."

"Theresa added, That she had received a letter from him, informing her the chateau was let, and that, as her services would no longer be required, she must quit the place, on that day week, when the new tenant would arrive."

"Theresa had been surprised by a visit from M. Quesnel, some time before the receipt of this letter, who was accompanied by a stranger that viewed the premises with much curiosity."

Towards the conclusion of his letter, which is dated a week after this sentence, Valancourt adds, "I have received a summons from my regiment, and I join it without regret, since I am shut out from the scenes that are so interesting to my heart. I rode to La Vallée this morning, and heard that the new tenant was arrived, and that Theresa was gone. I should not treat the subject thus familiarly if I did not believe you to be uninformed of this disposal of your house; for your satisfaction I have endeavoured to learn something of the character and fortune of your tenant, but without success. He is a gentleman, they say, and this is all I can hear. The place, as I wandered round the boundaries, appeared more melancholy to my imagination, than I had ever seen it. I wished earnestly to have got admittance, that I might have taken another leave of your favourite plane-tree, and thought of you once more beneath its shade: but I forbore to tempt the curiosity of strangers: the fishing-house in the woods, however, was still open to me; thither I went, and passed an hour, which I cannot even look back upon without emotion. O Emily! surely we are not separated for ever—surely we shall live for each other!"

This letter brought many tears to Emily's eyes; tears of tenderness and satisfaction on learning that Valancourt was well, and that time and absence had in no degree effaced her image from his heart. There were passages in this letter which particularly affected her, such as those describing his visits to La Vallée, and the sentiments of delicate affection that its scenes had awakened. It was a considerable time before her mind was sufficiently abstracted from Valancourt to feel the force of his intelligence concerning La Vallée. That Mons. Quesnel should let it, without even consulting her on the measure, both surprised and shocked her, particularly as it proved the absolute authority he thought himself entitled to exercise in her affairs. It is true, he had proposed, before she left France, that the chateau should be let, during her absence, and to the economical prudence of this she had nothing to object; but the committing what had been her father's villa to the power and caprice of strangers, and the depriving herself of a sure home, should any unhappy circumstances make her look back to her home as an asylum, were considerations that made her, even then, strongly oppose the measure. Her father, too, in his last hour, had received from her a solemn promise never to dispose of La Vallée; and this she considered as in some degree violated if she suffered the place to be let. But it was now evident with how little respect M. Quesnel had regarded these objections, and how insignificant he considered every obstacle to pecuniary advantage. It appeared, also, that he had not even condescended to inform Montoni of the step he had taken, since no motive was evident for Montoni's concealing the circumstance from her, if it had been made known to him: this both displeased and surprised her; but the chief subjects of her uneasiness were—the temporary disposal of La Vallée, and the dismission of her father's old and faithful servant.—"Poor Theresa," said Emily, "thou hadst not saved much in thy servitude, for thou wast always tender towards the poor, and believd'st thou shouldst die in the family, where thy best years had been spent. Poor Theresa!—now thou art turned out in thy old age to seek thy bread!"

Emily wept bitterly as these thoughts passed over her mind, and she determined to consider what could be done for Theresa, and to talk very explicitly to M. Quesnel on the subject; but she much feared that his cold heart could feel only for itself. She determined also to enquire whether he had made any mention of her affairs, in his letter to Montoni, who soon gave her the opportunity she sought, by desiring that she would attend him in his study. She had little doubt, that the interview was intended for the purpose of communicating to her a part of M. Quesnel's letter concerning the transactions at La Vallée, and she obeyed him immediately. Montoni was alone.

"I have just been writing to Mons. Quesnel," said he when Emily appeared, "in reply to the letter I received from him a few days ago, and I wished to talk to you upon a subject that occupied part of it."

"I also wished to speak with you on this topic, sir," said Emily.

"It is a subject of some interest to you, undoubtedly," rejoined Montoni, "and I think you must see it in the light that I do; indeed it will not bear any other. I trust you will agree with me, that any objection founded on sentiment, as they call it, ought to yield to circumstances of solid advantage."

"Granting this, sir," replied Emily, modestly, "those of humanity ought surely to be attended to. But I fear it is now too late to deliberate upon this plan, and I must regret, that it is no longer in my power to reject it."

"It is too late," said Montoni; "but since it is so, I am pleased to observe, that you submit to reason and necessity without indulging useless complaint. I applaud this conduct exceedingly, the more, perhaps, since it discovers a strength of mind seldom observable in your sex. When you are older you will look back with gratitude to the friends who assisted in rescuing you from the romantic illusions of sentiment, and will perceive, that they are only the snares of childhood, and should be vanquished the moment you escape from the nursery. I have not closed my letter, and you may add a few lines to inform your uncle of your acquiescence. You will soon see him, for it is my intention to take you, with Madame Montoni, in a few days to Miarenti, and you can then talk over the affair."

Emily wrote on the opposite page of the paper as follows:

"It is now useless, sir, for me to remonstrate upon the circumstances of which Signor Montoni informs me that he has written. I could have wished, at least, that the affair had been concluded with less precipitation, that I might have taught myself to subdue some prejudices, as the Signor calls them, which still linger in my heart. As it is, I submit. In point of prudence nothing certainly can be objected; but, though I submit, I have yet much to say on some other points of the subject, when I shall have the honour of seeing you. In the meantime I entreat you will take care of Theresa, for the sake of,

Sir,
Your affectionate niece,
EMILY ST. AUBERT."

Montoni smiled satirically at what Emily had written, but did not object to it, and she withdrew to her own apartment, where she sat down to begin a letter to Valancourt, in which she related the particulars of her journey, and her arrival at Venice, described some of the most striking scenes in the passage over the Alps; her emotions on her first view of Italy; the manners and characters of the people around her, and some few circumstances of Montoni's conduct. But she avoided even naming Count Morano, much more the declaration he had made, since she well knew how tremblingly alive to fear is real love, how jealously watchful of every circumstance that may affect its interest; and she scrupulously avoided to give Valancourt even the slightest reason for believing he had a rival.

On the following day Count Morano dined again at Montoni's. He was in an uncommon flow of spirits, and Emily thought there was somewhat of exultation in his manner of addressing her, which she had never observed before. She endeavoured to repress this by more than her usual reserve, but the cold civility of her air now seemed rather to encourage than to depress him. He appeared watchful of an opportunity of speaking with her alone, and more than once solicited this; but Emily always replied, that she could hear nothing from him which he would be unwilling to repeat before the whole company.

In the evening, Madame Montoni and her party went out upon the sea, and as the Count led Emily to his *zendaletto*, he carried her hand to his lips, and thanked her for the condescension she had shown him. Emily, in extreme surprise and displeasure, hastily withdrew her hand, and concluded that he had spoken ironically; but, on reaching the steps of the terrace, and observing by the livery, that it was the Count's *zendaletto* which waited below, while the rest of the party, having arranged themselves in the gondolas, were moving on, she determined not to permit a separate conversation, and, wishing him a good evening, returned to the portico. The Count followed to expostulate and entreat, and Montoni, who then came out, rendered solicitation unnecessary, for, without condescending to speak, he took her hand, and led her to the *zendaletto*. Emily was not silent; she entreated Montoni, in a low voice, to consider the impropriety of these circumstances, and that he would spare her the mortification of submitting to them; he, however, was inflexible.

"This caprice is intolerable," said he, "and shall not be indulged: there is no impropriety in the case."

At this moment, Emily's dislike of Count Morano rose to abhorrence. That he should, with undaunted assurance, thus pursue her, notwithstanding all she had expressed on the subject of his addresses, and think, as it was evident he did, that her opinion of him was of no consequence, so long as his pretensions were sanctioned by Montoni, added indignation to the disgust which she had felt towards him. She was somewhat relieved by observing that Montoni was to be of the party, who seated himself on one side of her, while Morano placed himself on the other. There was a pause for some moments as the gondolieri prepared their oars, and Emily trembled from apprehension of the discourse that might follow this silence. At length she collected courage to break it herself, in the hope of preventing fine speeches from Morano, and reproof from Montoni. To some trivial remark which she made, the latter returned a short and disobliging reply; but Morano immediately followed with a general observation, which he contrived to end with a particular compliment, and, though Emily passed it without even the notice of a smile, he was not discouraged.

"I have been impatient," said he, addressing Emily, "to express my gratitude; to thank you for your goodness; but I must also thank Signor Montoni, who has allowed me this opportunity of doing so."

Emily regarded the Count with a look of mingled astonishment and displeasure.

"Why," continued he, "should you wish to diminish the delight of this moment by that air of cruel reserve?—Why seek to throw me again into the perplexities of doubt, by teaching your eyes to contradict the kindness of your late declaration? You cannot doubt the sincerity, the ardour of my passion; it is therefore unnecessary, charming Emily! surely unnecessary, any longer to attempt a disguise of your sentiments."

"If I ever had disguised them, sir," said Emily, with recollected spirit, "it would certainly be unnecessary any longer to do so. I had hoped, sir, that you would have spared me any farther necessity of alluding to them; but, since you do not grant this, hear me declare, and for the last time, that your perseverance has deprived you even of the esteem, which I was inclined to believe you merited."

"Astonishing!" exclaimed Montoni: "this is beyond even my expectation, though I have hitherto done justice to the caprice of the sex! But you will observe, Mademoiselle Emily, that I am no lover, though Count Morano is, and that I will not be made the amusement of your capricious moments. Here is the offer of an alliance, which would do honour to any family; yours, you will recollect, is not noble; you long resisted my remonstrances, but my honour is now engaged, and it shall not be trifled with.—You shall adhere to the declaration, which you have made me an agent to convey to the Count."

"I must certainly mistake you, sir," said Emily; "my answers on the subject have been uniform; it is unworthy of you to accuse me of caprice. If you have condescended to be my agent, it is an honour I did not solicit. I myself have constantly assured Count Morano, and you also, sir, that I never can accept the honour he offers me, and I now repeat the declaration."

The Count looked with an air of surprise and enquiry at Montoni, whose countenance also was marked with surprise, but it was surprise mingled with indignation.

"Here is confidence, as well as caprice!" said the latter. "Will you deny your own words, Madam?"

"Such a question is unworthy of an answer, sir;" said Emily blushing; "you will recollect yourself, and be sorry that you have asked it."

"Speak to the point," rejoined Montoni, in a voice of increasing vehemence. "Will you deny your own words; will you deny, that you acknowledged, only a few hours ago, that it was too late to recede from your engagements, and that you accepted the Count's hand?"

"I will deny all this, for no words of mine ever imported it."

"Astonishing! Will you deny what you wrote to Mons. Quesnel, your uncle? if you do, your own hand will bear testimony against you. What have you now to say?" continued Montoni, observing the silence and confusion of Emily.

"I now perceive, sir, that you are under a very great error, and that I have been equally mistaken."

"No more duplicity, I entreat; be open and candid, if it be possible."

"I have always been so, sir; and can claim no merit in such conduct, for I have had nothing to conceal."

"How is this, Signor?" cried Morano, with trembling emotion.

"Suspend your judgment, Count," replied Montoni, "the wiles of a female heart are unsearchable. Now, Madame, your *explanation.*"

"Excuse me, sir, if I withhold my explanation till you appear willing to give me your confidence; assertion at present can only subject me to insult."

"Your explanation, I entreat you!" said Morano.

"Well, well," rejoined Montoni, "I give you my confidence; let us hear this explanation."

"Let me lead to it then, by asking a question."

"As many as you please," said Montoni, contemptuously.

"What, then, was the subject of your letter to Mons. Quesnel?"

"The same that was the subject of your note to him, certainly. You did well to stipulate for my confidence before you demanded that question."

"I must beg you will be more explicit, sir; what was that subject?"

"What could it be, but the noble offer of Count Morano," said Montoni.

"Then, sir, we entirely misunderstood each other," replied Emily.

"We entirely misunderstood each other too, I suppose," rejoined Montoni, "in the conversation which preceded the writing of that note? I must do you the justice to own, that you are very ingenious at this same art of misunderstanding."

Emily tried to restrain the tears that came to her eyes, and to answer with becoming firmness. "Allow me, sir, to explain myself fully, or to be wholly silent."

"The explanation may now be dispensed with; it is anticipated. If Count Morano still thinks one necessary, I will give him an honest one—You have changed your intention since our last conversation; and, if he can have patience and humility enough to wait till to-morrow, he will probably find it changed again: but as I have neither the patience or the humility, which you expect from a lover, I warn you of the effect of my displeasure!"

"Montoni, you are too precipitate," said the Count, who had listened to this conversation in extreme agitation and impatience;—"Signora, I entreat your own explanation of this affair!"

"Signor Montoni has said justly," replied Emily, "that all explanation may now be dispensed with; after what has passed I cannot suffer myself to give one. It is sufficient for me, and for you, sir, that I repeat my late declaration; let me hope this is the last time it will be necessary for me to repeat it—I never can accept the honour of your alliance."

"Charming Emily!" exclaimed the Count in an impassioned tone, "let not resentment make you unjust; let me not suffer for the offence of Montoni!—Revoke——"

"Offence!" interrupted Montoni—"Count, this language is ridiculous, this submission is childish!—speak as becomes a man, not as the
slave of a pretty tyrant."

"You distract me, Signor; suffer me to plead my own cause; you have
already proved insufficient to it."

"All conversation on this subject, sir," said Emily, "is worse than useless, since it can bring only pain to each of us: if you would oblige me,
pursue it no farther."

"It is impossible, Madam, that I can thus easily resign the object of
a passion, which is the delight and torment of my life.—I must still
love—still pursue you with unremitting ardour;—when you shall be
convinced of the strength and constancy of my passion, your heart must
soften into pity and repentance."

"Is this generous, sir? is this manly? can it either deserve or obtain
the esteem you solicit, thus to continue a persecution from which I
have no present means of escaping?"

A gleam of moonlight that fell upon Morano's countenance,
revealed the strong emotions of his soul; and, glancing on Montoni discovered the dark resentment, which contrasted his features.

"By heaven this is too much!" suddenly exclaimed the Count;
"Signor Montoni, you treat me ill; it is from you that I shall look for
explanation."

"From me, sir! you shall have it;" muttered Montoni, "if your discernment is indeed so far obscured by passion, as to make explanation
necessary. And for you, Madam, you should learn, that a man of honour is not to be trifled with, though you may, perhaps, with impunity,
treat a *boy* like a puppet."

This sarcasm roused the pride of Morano, and the resentment which
he had felt at the indifference of Emily, being lost in indignation of the
insolence of Montoni, he determined to mortify him, by defending her.

"This also," said he, replying to Montoni's last words, "this also, shall
not pass unnoticed. I bid you learn, sir, that you have a stronger enemy
than a woman to contend with: I will protect Signora St. Aubert from
your threatened resentment. You have misled me, and would revenge
your disappointed views upon the innocent."

"Misled you!" retorted Montoni with quickness, "is my conduct—
my word"—then pausing, while he seemed endeavouring to restrain
the resentment, that flashed in his eyes, in the next moment he added,
in a subdued voice, "Count Morano, this is a language, a sort of conduct to which I am not accustomed: it is the conduct of a passionate
boy—as such, I pass it over in contempt."

"In contempt, Signor?"

"The respect I owe myself," rejoined Montoni, "requires, that I should converse more largely with you upon some points of the subject in dispute. Return with me to Venice, and I will condescend to convince you of your error."

"Condescend, sir! but I will not condescend to be so conversed with."

Montoni smiled contemptuously; and Emily, now terrified for the consequences of what she saw and heard, could no longer be silent. She explained the whole subject upon which she had mistaken Montoni in the morning, declaring, that she understood him to have consulted her solely concerning the disposal of La Vallée, and concluding with entreating, that he would write immediately to M. Quesnel, and rectify the mistake.

But Montoni either was, or affected to be, still incredulous; and Count Morano was still entangled in perplexity. While she was speaking, however, the attention of her auditors had been diverted from the immediate occasion of their resentment, and their passion consequently became less. Montoni desired the Count would order his servants to row back to Venice, that he might have some private conversation with him; and Morano, somewhat soothed by his softened voice and manner, and eager to examine into the full extent of his difficulties, complied.

Emily, comforted by this prospect of release, employed the present moments in endeavouring, with conciliating care, to prevent any fatal mischief between the persons who so lately had persecuted and insulted her.

Her spirits revived, when she heard once more the voice of song and laughter, resounding from the grand canal, and at length entered again between its stately piazzas. The *zendaletto* stopped at Montoni's mansion, and the Count hastily led her into the hall, where Montoni took his arm, and said something in a low voice, on which Morano kissed the hand he held, notwithstanding Emily's effort to disengage it, and, wishing her a good evening, with an accent and look she could not misunderstand, returned to his *zendaletto* with Montoni.

Emily, in her own apartment, considered with intense anxiety all the unjust and tyrannical conduct of Montoni, the dauntless perseverance of Morano, and her own desolate situation, removed from her friends and country. She looked in vain to Valancourt, confined by his profession to a distant kingdom, as her protector; but it gave her comfort to know, that there was, at least, one person in the world, who would sympathize in her afflictions, and whose wishes would fly eagerly to release her. Yet she determined not to give him unavailing pain by relating the reasons she had to regret the having rejected his better judgment concerning Montoni; reasons, however, which could not induce her to lament the delicacy and disinterested affection that had made her reject his proposal for a clandestine marriage. The approaching interview with her uncle she regarded with some degree of hope, for she determined to represent to him the distresses of her situation, and to entreat that he would allow her to return to France with him and Madame Quesnel. Then, suddenly remembering that her beloved La Vallée, her only home, was no longer at her command, her tears flowed anew, and she feared that she had little pity to expect from a man who, like M. Quesnel, could dispose of it without deigning to consult with her, and could dismiss an aged and faithful servant, destitute of either support or asylum. But, though it was certain, that she had herself no longer a home in France, and few, very few friends there, she determined to return, if possible, that she might be released from the power of Montoni, whose particularly oppressive conduct towards herself, and general character as to others, were justly terrible to her imagination. She had no wish to reside with her uncle, M. Quesnel, since his behaviour to her late father and to herself, had been uniformly such as to convince her, that in flying to him she could only obtain an exchange of oppressors; neither had she the slightest intention of consenting to the proposal of Valancourt for an immediate marriage, though this would give her a lawful and a generous protector, for the chief reasons, which had formerly influenced her conduct, still existed against it, while others, which seemed to justify the step, would not be done away; and his interest, his fame were at all times too dear to her, to suffer her to consent to a union, which, at this early period of their lives, would probably defeat both. One sure, and proper asylum, however, would still be open to her in France. She knew that she could board in the convent, where she had formerly experienced so much kindness, and which had an affecting and solemn claim upon her heart, since it contained the remains of her late father. Here she could remain in safety and tranquillity, till the term, for which La Vallée might be let, should expire; or, till the arrangement of M. Motteville's affairs enabled her so far to estimate the remains of her fortune, as to judge whether it would be prudent for her to reside there.

Concerning Montoni's conduct with respect to his letters to M. Quesnel, she had many doubts; however he might be at first mistaken on the subject, she much suspected that he wilfully persevered in his error, as a means of intimidating her into a compliance with his wishes of uniting her to Count Morano. Whether this was or was not the fact, she was extremely anxious to explain the affair to M. Quesnel, and looked forward with a mixture of impatience, hope and fear, to her approaching visit.

On the following day, Madame Montoni, being alone with Emily, introduced the mention of Count Morano, by expressing her surprise, that she had not joined the party on the water the preceding evening, and at her abrupt departure to Venice. Emily then related what had passed, expressed her concern for the mutual mistake that had occurred between Montoni and herself, and solicited her aunt's kind offices in urging him to give a decisive denial to the count's further addresses; but she soon perceived, that Madame Montoni had not been ignorant of the late conversation, when she introduced the present.

"You have no encouragement to expect from me," said her aunt, "in these notions. I have already given my opinion on the subject, and think Signor Montoni right in enforcing, by any means, your consent. If young persons will be blind to their interest, and obstinately oppose it, why, the greatest blessings they can have are friends, who will oppose their folly. Pray what pretensions of any kind do you think you have to such a match as is now offered you?"

"Not any whatever, Madam," replied Emily, "and, therefore, at least, suffer me to be happy in my humility."

"Nay, niece, it cannot be denied, that you have pride enough; my poor brother, your father, had his share of pride too; though, let me add, his fortune did not justify it."

Emily, somewhat embarrassed by the indignation, which this malevolent allusion to her father excited, and by the difficulty of rendering her answer as temperate as it should be reprehensive, hesitated for some moments, in a confusion, which highly gratified her aunt. At length she said, "My father's pride, Madam, had a noble object—the happiness which he knew could be derived only from goodness, knowledge and charity. As it never consisted in his superiority, in point of fortune, to some persons, it was not humbled by his inferiority, in that respect, to others. He never disdained those, who were wretched by poverty and misfortune; he did sometimes despise persons, who, with many opportunities of happiness, rendered themselves miserable by vanity, ignorance and cruelty. I shall think it my highest glory to emulate such pride."

"I do not pretend to understand any thing of these high-flown sentiments, niece; you have all that glory to yourself: I would teach you a little plain sense, and not have you so wise as to despise happiness."

"That would indeed not be wisdom, but folly," said Emily, "for wisdom can boast no higher attainment than happiness; but you will allow, Madam, that our ideas of happiness may differ. I cannot doubt, that you wish me to be happy, but I must fear you are mistaken in the means of making me so."

"I cannot boast of a learned education, niece, such as your father thought proper to give you, and, therefore, do not pretend to understand all these fine speeches about happiness. I must be contented to understand only common sense, and happy would it have been for you and your father, if that had been included in his education."

Emily was too much shocked by these reflections on her father's memory, to despise this speech as it deserved.

Madame Montoni was about to speak, but Emily quitted the room, and retired to her own, where the little spirit she had lately exerted yielded to grief and vexation, and left her only to her tears. From every review of her situation she could derive, indeed, only new sorrow. To the discovery, which had just been forced upon her, of Montoni's unworthiness, she had now to add, that of the cruel vanity, for the gratification of which her aunt was about to sacrifice her; of the effrontery and cunning, with which, at the time that she meditated the sacrifice, she boasted of her tenderness, or insulted her victim; and of the venomous envy, which, as it did not scruple to attack her father's character, could scarcely be expected to withhold from her own.

During the few days that intervened between this conversation and the departure for Miarenti, Montoni did not once address himself to Emily. His looks sufficiently declared his resentment; but that he should forbear to renew a mention of the subject of it, exceedingly surprised her, who was no less astonished, that, during three days, Count Morano neither visited Montoni, or was named by him. Several conjectures arose in her mind. Sometimes she feared that the dispute between them had been revived, and had ended fatally to the Count. Sometimes she was inclined to hope, that weariness, or disgust at her firm rejection of his suit had induced him to relinquish it; and, at others, she suspected that he had now recourse to stratagem, and forbore his visits, and prevailed with Montoni to forbear the repetition of his name, in the expectation that gratitude and generosity would prevail with her to give him the consent, which he could not hope from love.

Thus passed the time in vain conjecture, and alternate hopes and fears, till the day arrived when Montoni was to set out for the villa of Miarenti, which, like the preceding ones, neither brought the Count, or the mention of him.

Montoni having determined not to leave Venice, till towards evening, that he might avoid the heats, and catch the cool breezes of night, embarked about an hour before sunset, with his family, in a barge, for the Brenta. Emily sat alone near the stern of the vessel, and, as it floated slowly on, watched the gay and lofty city lessening from her view, till its palaces seemed to sink in the distant waves, while its loftier towers and domes, illumined by the declining sun, appeared on the horizon, like those far-seen clouds which, in more northern climes, often linger on the western verge, and catch the last light of a summer's evening. Soon after, even these grew dim, and faded in distance from her sight; but she still sat gazing on the vast scene of cloudless sky, and mighty waters, and listening in pleasing awe to the deep-sounding waves, while, as her eyes glanced over the Adriatic, towards the opposite shores, which were, however, far beyond the reach of sight, she thought of Greece, and, a thousand classical remembrances stealing to her mind, she experienced that pensive luxury which is felt on viewing the scenes of ancient story, and on comparing their present state of silence and solitude with that of their former grandeur and animation. The scenes of the Illiad illapsed in glowing colours to her fancy—scenes, once the haunt of heroes—now lonely, and in ruins; but which still shone, in the poet's strain, in all their youthful splendour.

As her imagination painted with melancholy touches, the deserted plains of Troy, such as they appeared in this after-day, she reanimated the landscape with the following little story.

STANZAS

O'er Ilion's plains, where once the warrior bled,
And once the poet rais'd his deathless strain,
O'er Ilion's plains a weary driver led
His stately camels: For the ruin'd fane

Wide round the lonely scene his glance he threw,
For now the red cloud faded in the west,
And twilight o'er the silent landscape drew
Her deep'ning veil; eastward his course he prest:

There, on the grey horizon's glimm'ring bound,
Rose the proud columns of deserted Troy,
And wandering shepherds now a shelter found
Within those walls, where princes wont to joy.

Beneath a lofty porch the driver pass'd,
Then, from his camels heav'd the heavy load;
Partook with them the simple, cool repast,
And in short vesper gave himself to God.

From distant lands with merchandise he came,
His all of wealth his patient servants bore;
Oft deep-drawn sighs his anxious wish proclaim
To reach, again, his happy cottage door;

For there, his wife, his little children, dwell;
Their smiles shall pay the toil of many an hour:
Ev'n now warm tears to expectation swell,
As fancy o'er his mind extends her pow'r.

A death-like stillness reign'd, where once the song,
The song of heroes, wak'd the midnight air,
Save, when a solemn murmur roll'd along,
That seem'd to say—"for future worlds prepare."

For Time's imperious voice was frequent heard
Shaking the marble temple to its fall,
(By hands he long had conquer'd, vainly rear'd),
And distant ruins answer'd to his call.

While Hamet slept, his camels round him lay,
Beneath him, all his store of wealth was piled;
And here, his cruse and empty wallet lay,
And there, the flute that chear'd him in the wild.

The robber Tartar on his slumber stole,
For o'er the waste, at eve, he watch'd his train;
Ah! who his thirst of plunder shall control?
Who calls on him for mercy—calls in vain!

A poison'd poignard in his belt he wore,
A crescent sword depended at his side,
The deathful quiver at his back he bore,
And infants—at his very look had died!

The moon's cold beam athwart the temple fell,
And to his sleeping prey the Tartar led;
But soft!—a startled camel shook his bell,
Then stretch'd his limbs, and rear'd his drowsy head.

Hamet awoke! the poignard glitter'd high!
Swift from his couch he sprung, and 'scap'd the blow;
When from an unknown hand the arrows fly,
That lay the ruffian, in his vengeance, low.

He groan'd, he died! from forth a column'd gate
A fearful shepherd, pale and silent, crept,
Who, as he watch'd his folded flock star-late,
Had mark'd the robber steal where Hamet slept.

He fear'd his own, and sav'd a stranger's life!
Poor Hamet clasp'd him to his grateful heart;
Then, rous'd his camels for the dusty strife,
And, with the shepherd, hasten'd to depart.

And now, Aurora breathes her fresh'ning gale,
And faintly trembles on the eastern cloud;
And now, the sun, from under twilight's veil,
Looks gaily forth, and melts her airy shroud.

Wide o'er the level plains, his slanting beams
Dart their long lines on Ilion's tower'd site;

> The distant Hellespont with morning gleams,
> And old Scamander winds his waves in light.
>
> All merry sound the camel bells, so gay,
> And merry beats fond Hamet's heart, for he,
> E'er the dim evening steals upon the day,
> His children, wife and happy home shall see.

As Emily approached the shores of Italy she began to discriminate the rich features and varied colouring of the landscape — the purple hills, groves of orange pine and cypress, shading magnificent villas, and towns rising among vineyards and plantations. The noble Brenta, pouring its broad waves into the sea, now appeared, and, when she reached its mouth, the barge stopped, that the horses might be fastened which were now to tow it up the stream. This done, Emily gave a last look to the Adriatic, and to the dim sail,

> That from the sky-mix'd wave
> Dawns on the sight,

and the barge slowly glided between the green and luxuriant slopes of the river. The grandeur of the Palladian villas, that adorn these shores, was considerably heightened by the setting rays, which threw strong contrasts of light and shade upon the porticos and long arcades, and beamed a mellow lustre upon the orangeries and the tall groves of pine and cypress, that overhung the buildings. The scent of oranges, of flowering myrtles, and other odoriferous plants was diffused upon the air, and often, from these embowered retreats, a strain of music stole on the calm, and "softened into silence."

The sun now sunk below the horizon, twilight fell over the landscape, and Emily, wrapt in musing silence, continued to watch its features gradually vanishing into obscurity. She remembered her many happy evenings, when with St. Aubert she had observed the shades of twilight steal over a scene as beautiful as this, from the gardens of La Vallée, and a tear fell to the memory of her father. Her spirits were softened into melancholy by the influence of the hour, by the low murmur of the wave passing under the vessel, and the stillness of the air, that trembled only at intervals with distant music: — why else should she, at these moments, have looked on her attachment to Valancourt with presages so very afflicting, since she had but lately received letters from him, that had soothed for a while all her anxieties? It now seemed to her oppressed mind, that she had taken leave of him for ever, and that the countries, which separated them, would never more be re-traced by her. She looked upon Count Morano with horror, as in some degree the cause of this; but apart from him, a conviction, if such that may be called, which arises from no proof, and which she knew not how to account for, seized her mind—that she should never see Valancourt again. Though she knew, that neither Morano's solicitations, nor Montoni's commands had lawful power to enforce her obedience, she regarded both with a superstitious dread, that they would finally prevail.

Lost in this melancholy reverie, and shedding frequent tears, Emily was at length roused by Montoni, and she followed him to the cabin, where refreshments were spread, and her aunt was seated alone. The countenance of Madame Montoni was inflamed with resentment, that appeared to be the consequence of some conversation she had held with her husband, who regarded her with a kind of sullen disdain, and both preserved, for some time, a haughty silence. Montoni then spoke to Emily of Mons. Quesnel: "You will not, I hope, persist in disclaiming your knowledge of the subject of my letter to him?"

"I had hoped, sir, that it was no longer necessary for me to disclaim it," said Emily, "I had hoped, from your silence, that you was convinced of your error."

"You have hoped impossibilities then," replied Montoni; "I might as reasonably have expected to find sincerity and uniformity of conduct in one of your sex, as you to convict me of error in this affair."

Emily blushed, and was silent; she now perceived too clearly, that she had hoped an impossibility, for, where no mistake had been committed no conviction could follow; and it was evident, that Montoni's conduct had not been the consequence of mistake, but of design.

Anxious to escape from conversation, which was both afflicting and humiliating to her, she soon returned to the deck, and resumed her station near the stern, without apprehension of cold, for no vapour rose from the water, and the air was dry and tranquil; here, at least, the benevolence of nature allowed her the quiet which Montoni had denied her elsewhere. It was now past midnight. The stars shed a kind of twilight, that served to shew the dark outline of the shores on either hand, and the grey surface of the river; till the moon rose from behind a high palm grove, and shed her mellow lustre over the scene. The vessel glided smoothly on: amid the stillness of the hour Emily heard, now and then, the solitary voice of the barge-men on the bank, as they spoke to their horses; while, from a remote part of the vessel, with melancholy song,

> The sailor sooth'd,
> Beneath the trembling moon, the midnight wave.

Emily, meanwhile, anticipated her reception by Mons. and Madame Quesnel; considered what she should say on the subject of La Vallée;

and then, to with-hold her mind from more anxious topics, tried to amuse herself by discriminating the faint-drawn features of the landscape, reposing in the moon-light. While her fancy thus wandered, she saw, at a distance, a building peeping between the moon-light trees, and, as the barge approached, heard voices speaking, and soon distinguished the lofty portico of a villa, overshadowed by groves of pine and sycamore, which she recollected to be the same, that had formerly been pointed out to her, as belonging to Madame Quesnel's relative.

The barge stopped at a flight of marble steps, which led up the bank to a lawn. Lights appeared between some pillars beyond the portico. Montoni sent forward his servant, and then disembarked with his family. They found Mons. and Madame Quesnel, with a few friends, seated on sofas in the portico, enjoying the cool breeze of the night, and eating fruits and ices, while some of their servants at a little distance, on the river's bank, were performing a simple serenade. Emily was now accustomed to the way of living in this warm country, and was not surprised to find Mons. and Madame Quesnel in their portico, two hours after midnight.

The usual salutations being over, the company seated themselves in the portico, and refreshments were brought them from the adjoining hall, where a banquet was spread, and servants attended. When the bustle of this meeting had subsided, and Emily had recovered from the little flutter into which it had thrown her spirits, she was struck with the singular beauty of the hall, so perfectly accommodated to the luxuries of the season. It was of white marble, and the roof, rising into an open cupola, was supported by columns of the same material. Two opposite sides of the apartment, terminating in open porticos, admitted to the hall a full view of the gardens, and of the river scenery; in the centre a fountain continually refreshed the air, and seemed to heighten the fragrance, that breathed from the surrounding orangeries, while its dashing waters gave an agreeable and soothing sound. Etruscan lamps, suspended from the pillars, diffused a brilliant light over the interior part of the hall, leaving the remoter porticos to the softer lustre of the moon.

Mons. Quesnel talked apart to Montoni of his own affairs, in his usual strain of self-importance; boasted of his new acquisitions, and then affected to pity some disappointments, which Montoni had lately sustained. Meanwhile, the latter, whose pride at least enabled him to despise such vanity as this, and whose discernment at once detected under this assumed pity, the frivolous malignity of Quesnel's mind, listened to him in contemptuous silence, till he named his niece, and then they left the portico, and walked away into the gardens.

Emily, however, still attended to Madame Quesnel, who spoke of France (for even the name of her native country was dear to her) and she found some pleasure in looking at a person, who had lately been in it. That country, too, was inhabited by Valancourt, and she listened to the mention of it, with a faint hope, that he also would be named. Madame Quesnel, who, when she was in France, had talked with rapture of Italy, now, that she was in Italy, talked with equal praise of France, and endeavoured to excite the wonder and the envy of her auditors by accounts of places, which they had not been happy enough to see. In these descriptions she not only imposed upon them, but upon herself, for she never thought a present pleasure equal to one, that was passed; and thus the delicious climate, the fragrant orangeries and all the luxuries, which surrounded her, slept unnoticed, while her fancy wandered over the distant scenes of a northern country.

Emily listened in vain for the name of Valancourt. Madame Montoni spoke in her turn of the delights of Venice, and of the pleasure she expected from visiting the fine castle of Montoni, on the Apennine; which latter mention, at least, was merely a retaliating boast, for Emily well knew, that her aunt had no taste for solitary grandeur, and, particularly, for such as the castle of Udolpho promised. Thus the party continued to converse, and, as far as civility would permit, to torture each other by mutual boasts, while they reclined on sofas in the portico, and were environed with delights both from nature and art, by which any honest minds would have been tempered to benevolence, and happy imaginations would have been soothed into enchantment.

The dawn, soon after, trembled in the eastern horizon, and the light tints of morning, gradually expanding, shewed the beautifully declining forms of the Italian mountains and the gleaming landscapes, stretched at their feet. Then the sun-beams, shooting up from behind the hills, spread over the scene that fine saffron tinge, which seems to impart repose to all it touches. The landscape no longer gleamed; all its glowing colours were revealed, except that its remoter features were still softened and united in the mist of distance, whose sweet effect was heightened to Emily by the dark verdure of the pines and cypresses, that over-arched the foreground of the river.

The market people, passing with their boats to Venice, now formed a moving picture on the Brenta. Most of these had little painted awnings, to shelter their owners from the sun-beams, which, together with the piles of fruit and flowers, displayed beneath, and the tasteful simplicity of the peasant girls, who watched the rural treasures, rendered them gay and striking objects. The swift movement of the boats down the current, the quick glance of oars in the water, and now and then the passing chorus of peasants, who reclined under the sail of their little bark, or the tones of some rustic instrument, played by a girl, as she sat near her sylvan cargo, heightened the animation and festivity of the scene.

When Montoni and M. Quesnel had joined the ladies, the party left the portico for the gardens, where the charming scenery soon withdrew Emily's thoughts from painful subjects. The majestic forms and rich verdure of cypresses she had never seen so perfect before: groves of cedar, lemon, and orange, the spiry clusters of the pine and poplar, the luxuriant chesnut and oriental plane, threw all their pomp of shade over these gardens; while bowers of flowering myrtle and other spicy shrubs mingled their fragrance with that of flowers, whose vivid and various colouring glowed with increased effect beneath the contrasted umbrage of the groves. The air also was continually refreshed by rivulets, which, with more taste than fashion, had been suffered to wander among the green recesses.

Emily often lingered behind the party, to contemplate the distant landscape, that closed a vista, or that gleamed beneath the dark foliage of the foreground;—the spiral summits of the mountains, touched with a purple tint, broken and steep above, but shelving gradually to their base; the open valley, marked by no formal lines of art; and the tall groves of cypress, pine and poplar, sometimes embellished by a ruined villa, whose broken columns appeared between the branches of a pine, that seemed to droop over their fall.

From other parts of the gardens, the character of the view was entirely changed, and the fine solitary beauty of the landscape shifted for the crowded features and varied colouring of inhabitation.

The sun was now gaining fast upon the sky, and the party quitted the gardens, and retired to repose.

CHAPTER IV

And poor Misfortune feels the lash of Vice.
THOMSON

EMILY seized the first opportunity of conversing alone with Mons. Quesnel, concerning La Vallée. His answers to her enquiries were concise, and delivered with the air of a man, who is conscious of possessing absolute power and impatient of hearing it questioned. He declared, that the disposal of the place was a necessary measure; and that she might consider herself indebted to his prudence for even the small income that remained for her. "But, however," added he, "when this Venetian Count (I have forgot his name) marries you, your present disagreeable state of dependence will cease. As a relation to you I rejoice in the circumstance, which is so fortunate for you, and, I may add, so unexpected by your friends."

For some moments Emily was chilled into silence by this speech; and, when she attempted to undeceive him, concerning the purport of the note she had inclosed in Montoni's letter, he appeared to have some private reason for disbelieving her assertion, and, for a considerable time, persevered in accusing her of capricious conduct. Being, at length, however, convinced that she really disliked Morano and had positively rejected his suit, his resentment was extravagant, and he expressed it in terms equally pointed and inhuman; for, secretly flattered by the prospect of a connection with a nobleman, whose title he had affected to forget, he was incapable of feeling pity for whatever sufferings of his niece might stand in the way of his ambition.

Emily saw at once in his manner all the difficulties, that awaited her, and, though no oppression could have power to make her renounce Valancourt for Morano, her fortitude now trembled at an encounter with the violent passions of her uncle.

She opposed his turbulence and indignation only by the mild dignity of a superior mind; but the gentle firmness of her conduct served to exasperate still more his resentment, since it compelled him to feel his own inferiority, and, when he left her, he declared, that, if she persisted in her folly, both himself and Montoni would abandon her to the contempt of the world.

The calmness she had assumed in his presence failed Emily, when alone, and she wept bitterly, and called frequently upon the name of her departed father, whose advice to her from his death-bed she then remembered. "Alas!" said she, "I do indeed perceive how much more valuable is the strength of fortitude than the grace of sensibility, and I will also endeavour to fulfil the promise I then made; I will not indulge in unavailing lamentation, but will try to endure, with firmness, the oppression I cannot elude."

Somewhat soothed by the consciousness of performing a part of St. Aubert's last request, and of endeavouring to pursue the conduct which he would have approved, she overcame her tears, and, when the company met at dinner, had recovered her usual serenity of countenance.

In the cool of the evening, the ladies took the *fresco* along the bank of the Brenta in Madame Quesnel's carriage. The state of Emily's mind was in melancholy contrast with the gay groups assembled beneath the shades that overhung this enchanting stream. Some were dancing under the trees, and others reclining on the grass, taking ices and coffee and calmly enjoying the effect of a beautiful evening, on a luxuriant landscape. Emily, when she looked at the snow-capt Apennines, ascending in the distance, thought of Montoni's castle, and suffered some terror, lest he should convey her thither, for the purpose of enforcing her obedience; but the thought vanished, when she considered, that she was as much in his power at Venice as she could be else-where.

It was moonlight before the party returned to the villa, where supper was spread in the airy hall, which had so much enchanted Emily's fancy, on the preceding night. The ladies seated themselves in the portico, till Mons. Quesnel, Montoni, and other gentlemen, should join them at table, and Emily endeavoured to resign herself to the tranquillity of the hour. Presently, a barge stopped at the steps that led into the gardens, and, soon after, she distinguished the voices of Montoni and Quesnel, and then that of Morano, who, in the next moment, appeared. His compliments she received in silence, and her cold air seemed at first to discompose him; but he soon recovered his usual gaiety of manner, though the officious kindness of M. and Madame Quesnel Emily perceived disgusted him. Such a degree of attention she had scarcely believed could be shewn by M. Quesnel, for she had never before seen him otherwise than in the presence of his inferiors or equals.

When she could retire to her own apartment, her mind almost involuntarily dwelt on the most probable means of prevailing with the Count to withdraw his suit, and to her liberal mind none appeared more probable, than that of acknowledging to him a prior attachment and throwing herself upon his generosity for a release. When, however, on the following day, he renewed his addresses, she shrunk from the adoption of the plan she had formed. There was something so repugnant to her just pride, in laying open the secret of her heart to such a man as Morano, and in suing to him for compassion, that she impatiently rejected this design and wondered, that she could have paused upon it for a moment. The rejection of his suit she repeated in the most decisive terms she could select, mingling with it a severe censure of his conduct; but, though the Count appeared mortified by this, he persevered in the most ardent professions of admiration, till he was interrupted and Emily released by the presence of Madame Quesnel.

During her stay at this pleasant villa, Emily was thus rendered miserable by the assiduities of Morano, together with the cruelly exerted authority of M. Quesnel and Montoni, who, with her aunt, seemed now more resolutely determined upon this marriage than they had even appeared to be at Venice. M. Quesnel, finding, that both argument and menace were ineffectual in enforcing an immediate conclusion to it, at length relinquished his endeavours, and trusted to the power of Montoni and to the course of events at Venice. Emily, indeed, looked to Venice with hope, for there she would be relieved in some measure from the persecution of Morano, who would no longer be an inhabitant of the same house with herself, and from that of Montoni, whose engagements would not permit him to be continually at home. But amidst the pressure of her own misfortunes, she did not forget those of poor Theresa, for whom she pleaded with courageous tenderness to Quesnel, who promised, in slight and general terms, that she should not be forgotten.

Montoni, in a long conversation with M. Quesnel, arranged the plan to be pursued respecting Emily, and M. Quesnel proposed to be at Venice, as soon as he should be informed, that the nuptials were concluded.

It was new to Emily to part with any person, with whom she was connected, without feelings of regret; the moment, however, in which she took leave of M. and Madame Quesnel, was, perhaps, the only satisfactory one she had known in their presence.

Morano returned in Montoni's barge, and Emily, as she watched her gradual approach to that magic city, saw at her side the only person, who occasioned her to view it with less than perfect delight. They arrived there about midnight, when Emily was released from the presence of the Count, who, with Montoni, went to a Casino, and she was suffered to retire to her own apartment.

On the following day, Montoni, in a short conversation, which he held with Emily, informed her, that he would no longer be *trifled* with, and that, since her marriage with the Count would be so highly advantageous to her, that folly only could object to it, and folly of such extent as was incapable of conviction, it should be celebrated without further delay, and, if that was necessary, without her consent.

Emily, who had hitherto tried remonstrance, had now recourse to supplication, for distress prevented her from foreseeing, that, with a man of Montoni's disposition, supplication would be equally useless. She afterwards enquired by what right he exerted this unlimited authority over her? a question, which her better judgment would have with-held her, in a calmer moment, from making, since it could avail her nothing, and would afford Montoni another opportunity of triumphing over her defenceless condition.

"By what right!" cried Montoni, with a malicious smile, "by the right of my will; if you can elude that, I will not enquire by what right you do so. I now remind you, for the last time, that you are a stranger, in a foreign country, and that it is your interest to make me your friend; you know the means; if you compel me to become your enemy—I will venture to tell you, that the punishment shall exceed your expectation. You may know *I* am not to be trifled with."

Emily continued, for some time after Montoni had left her, in a state of despair, or rather stupefaction; a consciousness of misery was all that remained in her mind. In this situation Madame Montoni found her, at the sound of whose voice Emily looked up, and her aunt, somewhat softened by the expression of despair, that fixed her countenance, spoke in a manner more kind than she had ever yet done. Emily's heart was touched; she shed tears, and, after weeping for some time, recovered sufficient composure to speak on the subject of her distress, and to endeavour to interest Madame Montoni in her behalf. But, though the compassion of her aunt had been surprised, her ambition was not to be overcome, and her present object was to be the aunt of a Countess. Emily's efforts, therefore, were as unsuccessful as they had been with Montoni, and she withdrew to her apartment to think and weep alone. How often did she remember the parting scene with Valancourt, and wish, that the Italian had mentioned Montoni's character with less reserve! When her mind, however, had recovered from the first shock of this behaviour, she considered, that it would be impossible for him to compel her alliance with Morano, if she persisted in refusing to repeat any part of the marriage ceremony; and she persevered in her resolution to await Montoni's threatened vengeance rather than give herself for life to a man, whom she must have despised for his present conduct, had she never even loved Valancourt; yet she trembled at the revenge she thus resolved to brave.

An affair, however, soon after occurred, which somewhat called off Montoni's attention from Emily. The mysterious visits of Orsino were renewed with more frequency since the return of the former to Venice. There were others, also, besides Orsino, admitted to these midnight councils, and among them Cavigni and Verezzi. Montoni became more reserved and austere in his manner than ever; and Emily, if her own interests had not made her regardless of his, might have perceived, that something extraordinary was working in his mind.

One night, on which a council was not held, Orsino came in great agitation of spirits, and dispatched his confidential servant to Montoni, who was at a Casino, desiring that he would return home immediately; but charging the servant not to mention his name. Montoni obeyed the summons, and, on meeting Orsino, was informed of the circumstances, that occasioned his visit and his visible alarm, with a part of which he was already acquainted.

A Venetian nobleman, who had, on some late occasion, provoked the hatred of Orsino, had been way-laid and poniarded by hired assassins: and, as the murdered person was of the first connections, the Senate had taken up the affair. One of the assassins was now apprehended, who had confessed, that Orsino was his employer in the atrocious deed; and the latter, informed of his danger, had now come to Montoni to consult on the measures necessary to favour his escape. He knew, that, at this time, the officers of the police were upon the watch

for him, all over the city; to leave it, at present, therefore, was impracticable, and Montoni consented to secrete him for a few days till the
vigilance of justice should relax, and then to assist him in quitting
Venice. He knew the danger he himself incurred by permitting Orsino
to remain in his house, but such was the nature of his obligations to this
man, that he did not think it prudent to refuse him an asylum.

Such was the person whom Montoni had admitted to his confidence, and for whom he felt as much friendship as was compatible
with his character.

While Orsino remained concealed in his house, Montoni was
unwilling to attract public observation by the nuptials of Count
Morano; but this obstacle was, in a few days, overcome by the departure of his criminal visitor, and he then informed Emily, that her marriage was to be celebrated on the following morning. To her repeated
assurances, that it should not take place, he replied only by a malignant
smile; and, telling her that the Count and a priest would be at his
house, early in the morning, he advised her no further to dare his
resentment, by opposition to his will and to her own interest. "I am now
going out for the evening," said he, "remember, that I shall give your
hand to Count Morano in the morning." Emily, having, ever since his
late threats, expected, that her trials would at length arrive to this crisis,
was less shocked by the declaration, than she otherwise would have
been, and she endeavoured to support herself by the belief, that the
marriage could not be valid, so long as she refused before the priest to
repeat any part of the ceremony. Yet, as the moment of trial
approached, her long-harassed spirits shrunk almost equally from the
encounter of his vengeance, and from the hand of Count Morano. She
was not even perfectly certain of the consequence of her steady refusal
at the altar, and she trembled, more than ever, at the power of
Montoni, which seemed unlimited as his will, for she saw, that he
would not scruple to transgress any law, if, by so doing, he could
accomplish his project.

While her mind was thus suffering and in a state little short of distraction, she was informed that Morano asked permission to see her,
and the servant had scarcely departed with an excuse, before she
repented that she had sent one. In the next moment, reverting to her
former design, and determining to try, whether expostulation and
entreaty would not succeed, where a refusal and a just disdain had
failed, she recalled the servant, and, sending a different message, prepared to go down to the Count.

The dignity and assumed composure with which she met him, and
the kind of pensive resignation, that softened her countenance, were
circumstances not likely to induce him to relinquish her, serving, as

they did, to heighten a passion, which had already intoxicated his judgment. He listened to all she said with an appearance of complacency and of a wish to oblige her; but his resolution remained invariably the same, and he endeavoured to win her admiration by every insinuating art he so well knew how to practise. Being, at length, assured, that she had nothing to hope from his justice, she repeated, in a solemn and impressive manner, her absolute rejection of his suit, and quitted him with an assurance, that her refusal would be effectually maintained against every circumstance, that could be imagined for subduing it. A just pride had restrained her tears in his presence, but now they flowed from the fulness of her heart. She often called upon the name of her late father, and often dwelt with unutterable anguish on the idea of Valancourt.

She did not go down to supper, but remained alone in her apartment, sometimes yielding to the influence of grief and terror, and, at others, endeavouring to fortify her mind against them, and to prepare herself to meet, with composed courage, the scene of the following morning, when all the stratagem of Morano and the violence of Montoni would be united against her.

The evening was far advanced, when Madame Montoni came to her chamber with some bridal ornaments, which the Count had sent to Emily. She had, this day, purposely avoided her niece; perhaps, because her usual insensibility failed her, and she feared to trust herself with a view of Emily's distress; or possibly, though her conscience was seldom audible, it now reproached her with her conduct to her brother's orphan child, whose happiness had been entrusted to her care by a dying father.

Emily could not look at these presents, and made a last, though almost hopeless, effort to interest the compassion of Madame Montoni, who, if she did feel any degree of pity, or remorse, successfully concealed it, and reproached her niece with folly in being miserable, concerning a marriage, which ought only to make her happy. "I am sure," said she, "if I was unmarried, and the Count had proposed to me, I should have been flattered by the distinction: and if I should have been so, I am sure, niece, you, who have no fortune, ought to feel yourself highly honoured, and shew a proper gratitude and humility towards the Count, for his condescension. I am often surprised, I must own, to observe how humbly he deports himself to you, notwithstanding the haughty airs you give yourself; I wonder he has patience to humour you so: if I was he, I know, I should often be ready to reprehend you, and make you know yourself a little better. I would not have flattered you, I can tell you, for it is this absurd flattery that makes you fancy yourself of so much consequence, that you think nobody can deserve you, and

I often tell the Count so, for I have no patience to hear him pay you such extravagant compliments, which you believe every word of!"

"Your patience, madam, cannot suffer more cruelly on such occasions, than my own," said Emily.

"O! that is all mere affectation," rejoined her aunt. "I know that his flattery delights you, and makes you so vain, that you think you may have the whole world at your feet. But you are very much mistaken; I can assure you, niece, you will not meet with many such suitors as the Count: every other person would have turned upon his heel, and left you to repent at your leisure, long ago."

"O that the Count had resembled every other person, then!" said Emily, with a heavy sigh.

"It is happy for you, that he does not," rejoined Madame Montoni; "and what I am now saying is from pure kindness. I am endeavouring to convince you of your good fortune, and to persuade you to submit to necessity with a good grace. It is nothing to me, you know, whether you like this marriage or not, for it must be; what I say, therefore, is from pure kindness. I wish to see you happy, and it is your own fault if you are not so. I would ask you, now, seriously and calmly, what kind of a match you can expect, since a Count cannot content your ambition?"

"I have no ambition whatever, madam," replied Emily, "my only wish is to remain in my present station."

"O! that is speaking quite from the purpose," said her aunt, "I see you are still thinking of Mons. Valancourt. Pray get rid of all those fantastic notions about love, and this ridiculous pride, and be something like a reasonable creature. But, however, this is nothing to the purpose—for your marriage with the Count takes place tomorrow, you know, whether you approve it or not. The Count will be trifled with no longer."

Emily made no attempt to reply to this curious speech; she felt it would be mean, and she knew it would be useless. Madame Montoni laid the Count's presents upon the table, on which Emily was leaning, and then, desiring she would be ready early in the morning, bade her good-night. "Good-night, madam," said Emily, with a deep sigh, as the door closed upon her aunt, and she was left once more to her own sad reflections. For some time she sat so lost in thought, as to be wholly unconscious where she was; at length, raising her head, and looking round the room, its gloom and profound stillness awed her. She fixed her eyes on the door, through which her aunt had disappeared, and listened anxiously for some sound, that might relieve the deep dejection of her spirits; but it was past midnight, and all the family except the servant, who sat up for Montoni, had retired to bed. Her mind, long harassed by distress, now yielded to imaginary terrors; she trembled to look into the obscurity of her spacious chamber, and feared she knew not what; a state of mind, which continued so long, that she would have called up Annette, her aunt's woman, had her fears permitted her to rise from her chair, and to cross the apartment.

These melancholy illusions at length began to disperse, and she retired to her bed, not to sleep, for that was scarcely possible, but to try, at least, to quiet her disturbed fancy, and to collect strength of spirits sufficient to bear her through the scene of the approaching morning.

CHAPTER V

Dark power! with shudd'ring, meek submitted thought
Be mine to read the visions old
Which thy awak'ning bards have told,
And, lest they meet my blasted view,
Hold each strange tale devoutly true.
COLLINS' ODE TO FEAR

EMILY was recalled from a kind of slumber, into which she had, at length, sunk, by a quick knocking at her chamber door. She started up in terror, for Montoni and Count Morano instantly came to her mind; but, having listened in silence for some time, and recognizing the voice of Annette, she rose and opened the door. "What brings you hither so early?" said Emily, trembling excessively. She was unable to support herself, and sat down on the bed.

"Dear ma'amselle!" said Annette, "do not look so pale. I am quite frightened to see you. Here is a fine bustle below stairs, all the servants running to and fro, and none of them fast enough! Here is a bustle, indeed, all of a sudden, and nobody knows for what!"

"Who is below besides them?" said Emily, "Annette, do not trifle with me!"

"Not for the world, ma'amselle, I would not trifle for the world; but one cannot help making one's remarks, and there is the Signor in such a bustle, as I never saw him before; and he has sent me to tell you, ma'am, to get ready immediately."

"Good God support me!" cried Emily, almost fainting, "Count Morano is below, then!"

"No, ma'amselle, he is not below that I know of," replied Annette, "only his *Excellenza* sent me to desire you would get ready directly to leave Venice, for that the gondolas would be at the steps of the canal in a few minutes: but I must hurry back to my lady, who is just at her wits end, and knows not which way to turn for haste."

"Explain, Annette, explain the meaning of all this before you go," said Emily, so overcome with surprise and timid hope, that she had scarcely breath to speak.

"Nay, ma'amselle, that is more than I can do. I only know that the Signor is just come home in a very ill humour, that he has had us all called out of our beds, and tells us we are all to leave Venice immediately."

"Is Count Morano to go with the Signor?" said Emily, "and whither are we going?"

"I know neither, ma'am, for certain; but I heard Ludovico say something about going, after we get to *Terra-firma*, to the Signor's castle among some mountains, that he talked of."

"The Apennines!" said Emily, eagerly, "O! then I have little to hope!"

"That is the very place, ma'am. But cheer up, and do not take it so much to heart, and think what a little time you have to get ready in, and how impatient the Signor is. Holy St. Mark! I hear the oars on the canal; and now they come nearer, and now they are dashing at the steps below; it is the gondola, sure enough."

Annette hastened from the room; and Emily prepared for this unexpected flight, as fast as her trembling hands would permit, not perceiving, that any change in her situation could possibly be for the worse. She had scarcely thrown her books and clothes into her travelling trunk, when, receiving a second summons, she went down to her aunt's dressing-room, where she found Montoni impatiently reproving his wife for delay. He went out, soon after, to give some further orders to his people, and Emily then enquired the occasion of this hasty journey; but her aunt appeared to be as ignorant as herself, and to undertake the journey with more reluctance.

The family at length embarked, but neither Count Morano, nor Cavigni, was of the party. Somewhat revived by observing this, Emily, when the gondolieri dashed their oars in the water, and put off from the steps of the portico, felt like a criminal, who receives a short reprieve. Her heart beat yet lighter, when they emerged from the canal into the ocean, and lighter still, when they skimmed past the walls of St. Mark, without having stopped to take up Count Morano.

The dawn now began to tint the horizon, and to break upon the shores of the Adriatic. Emily did not venture to ask any questions of Montoni, who sat, for some time, in gloomy silence, and then rolled himself up in his cloak, as if to sleep, while Madame Montoni did the same; but Emily, who could not sleep, undrew one of the little curtains of the gondola, and looked out upon the sea. The rising dawn now enlightened the mountain-tops of Friuli, but their lower sides, and the distant waves, that rolled at their feet, were still in deep shadow. Emily, sunk in tranquil melancholy, watched the strengthening light spreading upon the ocean, shewing successively Venice and her islets, and the shores of Italy, along which boats, with their pointed latin sails, began to move.

The gondolieri were frequently hailed, at this early hour, by the market-people, as they glided by towards Venice, and the *Lagune* soon displayed a gay scene of innumerable little barks, passing from *Terra-firma* with provisions. Emily gave a last look to that splendid city, but her mind was then occupied by considering the probable events, that awaited her, in the scenes, to which she was removing, and with conjectures, concerning the motive of this sudden journey. It appeared, upon calmer consideration, that Montoni was removing her to his secluded castle, because he could there, with more probability of success, attempt to terrify her into obedience; or, that, should its gloomy and sequestered scenes fail of this effect, her forced marriage with the Count could there be solemnized with the secrecy, which was necessary to the honour of Montoni. The little spirit, which this reprieve had recalled, now began to fail, and, when Emily reached the shore, her mind had sunk into all its former depression.

Montoni did not embark on the Brenta, but pursued his way in carriages across the country, towards the Apennine; during which journey, his manner to Emily was so particularly severe, that this alone would have confirmed her late conjecture, had any such confirmation been necessary. Her senses were now dead to the beautiful country, through which she travelled. Sometimes she was compelled to smile at the *naïveté* of Annette, in her remarks on what she saw, and sometimes to sigh, as a scene of peculiar beauty recalled Valancourt to her thoughts, who was indeed seldom absent from them, and of whom she could never hope to hear in the solitude, to which she was hastening.

At length, the travellers began to ascend among the Apennines. The immense pine-forests, which, at that period, overhung these mountains, and between which the road wound, excluded all view but of the cliffs aspiring above, except, that, now and then, an opening through the dark woods allowed the eye a momentary glimpse of the country below. The gloom of these shades, their solitary silence, except when the breeze swept over their summits, the tremendous precipices of the mountains, that came partially to the eye, each assisted to raise the solemnity of Emily's feelings into awe; she saw only images of gloomy grandeur, or of dreadful sublimity, around her; other images, equally gloomy and equally terrible, gleamed on her imagination. She was going she scarcely knew whither, under the dominion of a person, from whose arbitrary disposition she had already suffered so much, to marry, perhaps, a man who possessed neither her affection, or esteem; or to endure, beyond the hope of succour, whatever punishment revenge, and that Italian revenge, might dictate.—The more she considered what might be the motive of the journey, the more she became convinced, that it was for the purpose of concluding her nuptials with Count Morano, with that secrecy which her resolute resistance had made necessary to the honour, if not to the safety, of Montoni. From the deep solitudes, into which she was immerging, and from the gloomy castle, of which she had heard some mysterious hints, her sick heart recoiled in despair, and she experienced, that, though her mind was already occupied by peculiar distress, it was still alive to the influence of new and local circumstance; why else did she shudder at the idea of this desolate castle?

As the travellers still ascended among the pine forests, steep rose over steep, the mountains seemed to multiply, as they went, and what was the summit of one eminence proved to be only the base of another. At length, they reached a little plain, where the drivers stopped to rest the mules, whence a scene of such extent and magnificence opened below, as drew even from Madame Montoni a note of admiration. Emily lost, for a moment, her sorrows, in the immensity of nature. Beyond the amphitheatre of mountains, that stretched below, whose tops appeared as numerous almost, as the waves of the sea, and whose feet were concealed by the forests—extended the *Campagna* of Italy, where cities and rivers, and woods and all the glow of cultivation were mingled in gay confusion. The Adriatic bounded the horizon, into which the Po and the Brenta, after winding through the whole extent of the landscape, poured their fruitful waves. Emily gazed long on the splendours of the world she was quitting, of which the whole magnificence seemed thus given to her sight only to increase her regret on leaving it; for her, Valancourt alone was in that world; to him alone her heart turned, and for him alone fell her bitter tears.

From this sublime scene the travellers continued to ascend among the pines, till they entered a narrow pass of the mountains, which shut out every feature of the distant country, and, in its stead, exhibited only tremendous crags, impending over the road, where no vestige of humanity, or even of vegetation, appeared, except here and there the trunk and scathed branches of an oak, that hung nearly headlong from the rock, into which its strong roots had fastened. This pass, which led into the heart of the Apennine, at length opened to day, and a scene of mountains stretched in long perspective, as wild as any the travellers had yet passed. Still vast pine-forests hung upon their base, and crowned the ridgy precipice, that rose perpendicularly from the vale, while, above, the rolling mists caught the sun-beams, and touched their cliffs with all the magical colouring of light and shade. The scene seemed perpetually changing, and its features to assume new forms, as the winding road brought them to the eye in different attitudes; while the shifting vapours, now partially concealing their minuter beauties and now illuminating them with splendid tints, assisted the illusions of the sight.

Though the deep vallies between these mountains were, for the most part, clothed with pines, sometimes an abrupt opening presented a perspective of only barren rocks, with a cataract flashing from their summit among broken cliffs, till its waters, reaching the bottom, foamed along with unceasing fury; and sometimes pastoral scenes exhibited their "green delights" in the narrow vales, smiling amid surrounding horror. There herds and flocks of goats and sheep, browsing under the shade of hanging woods, and the shepherd's little cabin, reared on the margin of a clear stream, presented a sweet picture of repose.

Wild and romantic as were these scenes, their character had far less of the sublime, than had those of the Alps, which guard the entrance of Italy. Emily was often elevated, but seldom felt those emotions of indescribable awe which she had so continually experienced, in her passage over the Alps.

Towards the close of day, the road wound into a deep valley. Mountains, whose shaggy steeps appeared to be inaccessible, almost surrounded it. To the east, a vista opened, that exhibited the Apennines in their darkest horrors; and the long perspective of retiring summits, rising over each other, their ridges clothed with pines, exhibited a stronger image of grandeur, than any that Emily had yet seen. The sun had just sunk below the top of the mountains she was descending, whose long shadow stretched athwart the valley, but his sloping rays, shooting through an opening of the cliffs, touched with a yellow gleam the summits of the forest, that hung upon the opposite steeps, and streamed in full splendour upon the towers and battlements of a castle, that spread its extensive ramparts along the brow of a precipice above. The splendour of these illumined objects was heightened by the contrasted shade, which involved the valley below.

"There," said Montoni, speaking for the first time in several hours, "is Udolpho."

Emily gazed with melancholy awe upon the castle, which she understood to be Montoni's; for, though it was now lighted up by the setting sun, the gothic greatness of its features, and its mouldering walls of dark grey stone, rendered it a gloomy and sublime object. As she gazed, the light died away on its walls, leaving a melancholy purple tint, which spread deeper and deeper, as the thin vapour crept up the mountain, while the battlements above were still tipped with splendour. From those, too, the rays soon faded, and the whole edifice was invested with the solemn duskiness of evening. Silent, lonely, and sublime, it seemed to stand the sovereign of the scene, and to frown defiance on all, who dared to invade its solitary reign. As the twilight deepened, its features became more awful in obscurity, and Emily continued to gaze, till its clustering towers were alone seen, rising over the tops of the woods, beneath whose thick shade the carriages soon after began to ascend.

The extent and darkness of these tall woods awakened terrific images in her mind, and she almost expected to see banditti start up from under the trees. At length, the carriages emerged upon a heathy rock, and, soon after, reached the castle gates, where the deep tone of the portal bell, which was struck upon to give notice of their arrival, increased the fearful emotions, that had assailed Emily. While they waited till the servant within should come to open the gates, she anxiously surveyed the edifice: but the gloom, that overspread it, allowed her to distinguish little more than a part of its outline, with the massy walls of the ramparts, and to know, that it was vast, ancient and dreary. From the parts she saw, she judged of the heavy strength and extent of the whole. The gateway before her, leading into the courts, was of gigantic size, and was defended by two round towers, crowned by overhanging turrets, embattled, where, instead of banners, now waved long grass and wild plants, that had taken root among the mouldering stones, and which seemed to sigh, as the breeze rolled past, over the desolation around them. The towers were united by a curtain, pierced and embattled also, below which appeared the pointed arch of a huge portcullis, surmounting the gates: from these, the walls of the ramparts extended to other towers, overlooking the precipice, whose shattered outline, appearing on a gleam, that lingered in the west, told of the ravages of war. — Beyond these all was lost in the obscurity of evening.

While Emily gazed with awe upon the scene, footsteps were heard within the gates, and the undrawing of bolts; after which an ancient servant of the castle appeared, forcing back the huge folds of the portal, to admit his lord. As the carriage-wheels rolled heavily under the portcullis, Emily's heart sunk, and she seemed, as if she was going into her prison; the gloomy court, into which she passed, served to confirm the idea, and her imagination, ever awake to circumstance, suggested even more terrors, than her reason could justify.

Another gate delivered them into the second court, grass-grown, and more wild than the first, where, as she surveyed through the twilight its desolation — its lofty walls, overtopt with briony, moss and nightshade, and the embattled towers that rose above, — long-suffering and murder came to her thoughts. One of those instantaneous and unaccountable convictions, which sometimes conquer even strong minds, impressed her with its horror. The sentiment was not diminished, when she entered an extensive gothic hall, obscured by the gloom of evening, which a light, glimmering at a distance through a long perspective of arches, only rendered more striking. As a servant brought the lamp nearer, partial gleams fell upon the pillars and the pointed arches, forming a strong contrast with their shadows, that stretched along the pavement and the walls.

The sudden journey of Montoni had prevented his people from making any other preparations for his reception, than could be had in the short interval, since the arrival of the servant, who had been sent forward from Venice; and this, in some measure, may account for the air of extreme desolation, that everywhere appeared.

The servant, who came to light Montoni, bowed in silence, and the muscles of his countenance relaxed with no symptom of joy.— Montoni noticed the salutation by a slight motion of his hand, and passed on, while his lady, following, and looking round with a degree of surprise and discontent, which she seemed fearful of expressing, and Emily, surveying the extent and grandeur of the hall in timid wonder, approached a marble stair-case. The arches here opened to a lofty vault, from the centre of which hung a tripod lamp, which a servant was hastily lighting; and the rich fret-work of the roof, a corridor, leading into several upper apartments, and a painted window, stretching nearly from the pavement to the ceiling of the hall, became gradually visible.

Having crossed the foot of the stair-case, and passed through an ante-room, they entered a spacious apartment, whose walls, wainscoted with black larch-wood, the growth of the neighbouring mountains, were scarcely distinguishable from darkness itself. "Bring more light," said Montoni, as he entered. The servant, setting down his lamp, was withdrawing to obey him, when Madame Montoni observing, that the evening air of this mountainous region was cold, and that she should like a fire, Montoni ordered that wood might be brought.

While he paced the room with thoughtful steps, and Madame Montoni sat silently on a couch, at the upper end of it, waiting till the servant returned, Emily was observing the singular solemnity and desolation of the apartment, viewed, as it now was, by the glimmer of the single lamp, placed near a large Venetian mirror, that duskily reflected the scene, with the tall figure of Montoni passing slowly along, his arms folded, and his countenance shaded by the plume, that waved in his hat.

From the contemplation of this scene, Emily's mind proceeded to the apprehension of what she might suffer in it, till the remembrance of Valancourt, far, far distant! came to her heart, and softened it into sorrow. A heavy sigh escaped her: but, trying to conceal her tears, she walked away to one of the high windows, that opened upon the ramparts, below which, spread the woods she had passed in her approach to the castle. But the night-shade sat deeply on the mountains beyond, and their indented outline alone could be faintly traced on the horizon, where a red streak yet glimmered in the west. The valley between was sunk in darkness.

The scene within, upon which Emily turned on the opening of the door, was scarcely less gloomy. The old servant, who had received them at the gates, now entered, bending under a load of pine-branches, while two of Montoni's Venetian servants followed with lights.

"Your *Excellenza* is welcome to the castle," said the old man, as he raised himself from the hearth, where he had laid the wood: "it has been a lonely place a long while; but you will excuse it, Signor, knowing we had but short notice. It is near two years, come next feast of St. Mark, since your *Excellenza* was within these walls."

"You have a good memory, old Carlo," said Montoni: "it is thereabout; and how hast thou contrived to live so long?"

"A-well-a-day, sir, with much ado; the cold winds, that blow through the castle in winter, are almost too much for me; and I thought sometimes of asking your *Excellenza* to let me leave the mountains, and go down into the lowlands. But I don't know how it is—I am loth to quit these old walls I have lived in so long."

"Well, how have you gone on in the castle, since I left it?" said Montoni.

"Why much as usual, Signor, only it wants a good deal of repairing. There is the north tower—some of the battlements have tumbled down, and had liked one day to have knocked my poor wife (God rest her soul!) on the head. Your *Excellenza* must know"——

"Well, but the repairs," interrupted Montoni.

"Aye, the repairs," said Carlo: "a part of the roof of the great hall has fallen in, and all the winds from the mountains rushed through it last winter, and whistled through the whole castle so, that there was no keeping one's self warm, be where one would. There, my wife and I used to sit shivering over a great fire in one corner of the little hall, ready to die with cold, and"——

"But there are no more repairs wanted," said Montoni, impatiently.

"O Lord! Your *Excellenza*, yes—the wall of the rampart has tumbled down in three places; then, the stairs, that lead to the west gallery, have been a long time so bad, that it is dangerous to go up them; and the passage leading to the great oak chamber, that overhangs the north rampart—one night last winter I ventured to go there by myself, and your *Excellenza*"——

"Well, well, enough of this," said Montoni, with quickness: "I will talk more with thee to-morrow."

The fire was now lighted; Carlo swept the hearth, placed chairs, wiped the dust from a large marble table that stood near it, and then left the room.

Montoni and his family drew round the fire. Madame Montoni made several attempts at conversation, but his sullen answers repulsed her, while Emily sat endeavouring to acquire courage enough to speak to him. At length, in a tremulous voice, she said, "May I ask, sir, the motive of this sudden journey?"—After a long pause, she recovered sufficient courage to repeat the question.

"It does not suit me to answer enquiries," said Montoni, "nor does it become you to make them; time may unfold them all: but I desire I may be no further harassed, and I recommend it to you to retire to your chamber, and to endeavour to adopt a more rational conduct, than that of yielding to fancies, and to a sensibility, which, to call it by the gentlest name, is only a weakness."

Emily rose to withdraw. "Good night, madam," said she to her aunt, with an assumed composure, that could not disguise her emotion.

"Good night, my dear," said Madame Montoni, in a tone of kindness, which her niece had never before heard from her; and the unexpected endearment brought tears to Emily's eyes. She curtsied to Montoni, and was retiring; "But you do not know the way to your chamber," said her aunt. Montoni called the servant, who waited in the ante-room, and bade him send Madame Montoni's woman, with whom, in a few minutes, Emily withdrew.

"Do you know which is my room?" said she to Annette, as they crossed the hall.

"Yes, I believe I do, ma'amselle; but this is such a strange rambling place! I have been lost in it already: they call it the double chamber, over the south rampart, and I went up this great stair-case to it. My lady's room is at the other end of the castle."

Emily ascended the marble staircase, and came to the corridor, as they passed through which, Annette resumed her chat—"What a wild lonely place this is, ma'am! I shall be quite frightened to live in it. How often, and often have I wished myself in France again! I little thought, when I came with my lady to see the world, that I should ever be shut up in such a place as this, or I would never have left my own country! This way, ma'amselle, down this turning. I can almost believe in giants again, and such like, for this is just like one of their castles; and, some night or other, I suppose I shall see fairies too, hopping about in that great old hall, that looks more like a church, with its huge pillars, than any thing else."

"Yes," said Emily, smiling, and glad to escape from more serious thought, "if we come to the corridor, about midnight, and look down into the hall, we shall certainly see it illuminated with a thousand lamps, and the fairies tripping in gay circles to the sound of delicious music; for it is in such places as this, you know, that they come to hold their revels. But I am afraid, Annette, you will not be able to pay the necessary penance for such a sight: and, if once they hear your voice, the whole scene will vanish in an instant."

"O! if you will bear me company, ma'amselle, I will come to the corridor, this very night, and I promise you I will hold my tongue; it shall not be my fault if the show vanishes.—But do you think they will come?"

"I cannot promise that with certainty, but I will venture to say, it will not be your fault if the enchantment should vanish."

"Well, ma'amselle, that is saying more than I expected of you: but I am not so much afraid of fairies, as of ghosts, and they say there are a plentiful many of them about the castle: now I should be frightened to death, if I should chance to see any of them. But hush! ma'amselle, walk softly! I have thought, several times, something passed by me."

"Ridiculous!" said Emily, "you must not indulge such fancies."

"O ma'am! they are not fancies, for aught I know; Benedetto says these dismal galleries and halls are fit for nothing but ghosts to live in; and I verily believe, if I *live* long in them I shall turn to one myself!"

"I hope," said Emily, "you will not suffer Signor Montoni to hear of these weak fears; they would highly displease him."

"What, you know then, ma'amselle, all about it!" rejoined Annette. "No, no, I do know better than to do so; though, if the Signor can sleep sound, nobody else in the castle has any right to lie awake, I am sure." Emily did not appear to notice this remark.

"Down this passage, ma'amselle; this leads to a back stair-case. O! if I see any thing, I shall be frightened out of my wits!"

"That will scarcely be possible," said Emily, smiling, as she followed the winding of the passage, which opened into another gallery: and then Annette, perceiving that she had missed her way, while she had been so eloquently haranguing on ghosts and fairies, wandered about through other passages and galleries, till, at length, frightened by their intricacies and desolation, she called aloud for assistance: but they were beyond the hearing of the servants, who were on the other side of the castle, and Emily now opened the door of a chamber on the left.

"O! do not go in there, ma'amselle," said Annette, "you will only lose yourself further."

"Bring the light forward," said Emily, "we may possibly find our way through these rooms."

Annette stood at the door, in an attitude of hesitation, with the light held up to shew the chamber, but the feeble rays spread through not half of it. "Why do you hesitate?" said Emily, "let me see whither this room leads."

Annette advanced reluctantly. It opened into a suite of spacious and ancient apartments, some of which were hung with tapestry, and others wainscoted with cedar and black larch-wood. What furniture there was, seemed to be almost as old as the rooms, and retained an appearance of grandeur, though covered with dust, and dropping to pieces with the damps, and with age.

"How cold these rooms are, ma'amselle!" said Annette: "nobody has lived in them for many, many years, they say. Do let us go."

"They may open upon the great stair-case, perhaps," said Emily, passing on till she came to a chamber, hung with pictures, and took the light to examine that of a soldier on horseback in a field of battle.—He was darting his spear upon a man, who lay under the feet of the horse, and who held up one hand in a supplicating attitude. The soldier, whose beaver was up, regarded him with a look of vengeance, and the countenance, with that expression, struck Emily as resembling Montoni. She shuddered, and turned from it. Passing the light hastily over several other pictures, she came to one concealed by a veil of black silk. The singularity of the circumstance struck her, and she stopped before it, wishing to remove the veil, and examine what could thus carefully be concealed, but somewhat wanting courage. "Holy Virgin! what can this mean?" exclaimed Annette. "This is surely the picture they told me of at Venice."

"What picture?" said Emily. "Why a picture—a picture," replied Annette, hesitatingly—"but I never could make out exactly what it was about, either."

"Remove the veil, Annette."

"What! I, ma'amselle!—I! not for the world!" Emily, turning round, saw Annette's countenance grow pale. "And pray, what have you heard of this picture, to terrify you so, my good girl?" said she. "Nothing, ma'amselle: I have heard nothing, only let us find our way out."

"Certainly: but I wish first to examine the picture; take the light, Annette, while I lift the veil." Annette took the light, and immediately walked away with it, disregarding Emily's call to stay, who, not choosing to be left alone in the dark chamber, at length followed her. "What is the reason of this, Annette?" said Emily, when she overtook her, "what have you heard concerning that picture, which makes you so unwilling to stay when I bid you?"

"I don't know what is the reason, ma'amselle," replied Annette, "nor any thing about the picture, only I have heard there is something very dreadful belonging to it—and that it has been covered up in black *ever since*—and that nobody has looked at it for a great many years—and it somehow has to do with the owner of this castle before Signor Montoni came to the possession of it—and"——

"Well, Annette," said Emily, smiling, "I perceive it is as you say—that you know nothing about the picture."

"No, nothing, indeed, ma'amselle, for they made me promise never to tell: but"——

"Well," rejoined Emily, who observed that she was struggling between her inclination to reveal a secret, and her apprehension for the consequence, "I will enquire no further"——

"No, pray, ma'am, do not."

"Lest you should tell all," interrupted Emily.

Annette blushed, and Emily smiled, and they passed on to the extremity of this suite of apartments, and found themselves, after some further perplexity, once more at the top of the marble stair-case, where Annette left Emily, while she went to call one of the servants of the castle to shew them to the chamber, for which they had been seeking.

While she was absent, Emily's thoughts returned to the picture; an unwillingness to tamper with the integrity of a servant, had checked her enquiries on this subject, as well as concerning some alarming hints, which Annette had dropped respecting Montoni; though her curiosity was entirely awakened, and she had perceived, that her questions might easily be answered. She was now, however, inclined to go back to the apartment and examine the picture; but the loneliness of the hour and of the place, with the melancholy silence that reigned around her, conspired with a certain degree of awe, excited by the mystery attending this picture, to prevent her. She determined, however, when day-light should have re-animated her spirits, to go thither and remove the veil. As she leaned from the corridor, over the stair-case, and her eyes wandered round, she again observed, with wonder, the vast strength of the walls, now somewhat decayed, and the pillars of solid marble, that rose from the hall, and supported the roof.

A servant now appeared with Annette, and conducted Emily to her chamber, which was in a remote part of the castle, and at the very end of the corridor, from whence the suite of apartments opened, through which they had been wandering. The lonely aspect of her room made Emily unwilling that Annette should leave her immediately, and the dampness of it chilled her with more than fear. She begged Caterina, the servant of the castle, to bring some wood and light a fire.

"Aye, lady, it's many a year since a fire was lighted here," said Caterina.

"You need not tell us that, good woman," said Annette; "every room in the castle feels like a well. I wonder how you contrive to live here; for my part, I wish myself at Venice again." Emily waved her hand for Caterina to fetch the wood.

"I wonder, ma'am, why they call this the double chamber?" said Annette, while Emily surveyed it in silence and saw that it was lofty and spacious, like the others she had seen, and, like many of them, too, had its walls lined with dark larch-wood. The bed and other furniture was very ancient, and had an air of gloomy grandeur, like all that she had seen in the castle. One of the high casements, which she opened, over-looked a rampart, but the view beyond was hid in darkness.

In the presence of Annette, Emily tried to support her spirits, and to restrain the tears, which, every now and then, came to her eyes. She wished much to enquire when Count Morano was expected at the cas-tle, but an unwillingness to ask unnecessary questions, and to mention family concerns to a servant, withheld her. Meanwhile, Annette's thoughts were engaged upon another subject: she dearly loved the mar-vellous, and had heard of a circumstance, connected with the castle, that highly gratified this taste. Having been enjoined not to mention it, her inclination to tell it was so strong, that she was every instant on the point of speaking what she had heard. Such a strange circumstance, too, and to be obliged to conceal it, was a severe punishment; but she knew, that Montoni might impose one much severer, and she feared to incur it by offending him.

Caterina now brought the wood, and its bright blaze dispelled, for a while, the gloom of the chamber. She told Annette, that her lady had enquired for her, and Emily was once again left to her own sad reflec-tions. Her heart was not yet hardened against the stern manners of Montoni, and she was nearly as much shocked now, as she had been when she first witnessed them. The tenderness and affection, to which she had been accustomed, till she lost her parents, had made her par-ticularly sensible to any degree of unkindness, and such a reverse as this no apprehension had prepared her to support.

To call off her attention from subjects, that pressed heavily on her spirits, she rose and again examined her room and its furniture. As she walked round it, she passed a door, that was not quite shut, and, per-ceiving, that it was not the one, through which she entered, she brought the light forward to discover whither it led. She opened it, and, going forward, had nearly fallen down a steep, narrow stair-case that wound from it, between two stone walls. She wished to know to what it led, and was the more anxious, since it communicated so immediately with her apartment; but, in the present state of her spirits, she wanted courage to venture into the darkness alone. Closing the door, therefore, she endeavoured to fasten it, but, upon further examination, perceived, that it had no bolts on the chamber side, though it had two on the other. By placing a heavy chair against it, she in some measure remedied the defect; yet she was still alarmed at the thought of sleeping in this remote room alone, with a door opening she knew not whither, and which could not be perfectly fastened on the inside. Sometimes she wished to entreat of Madame Montoni, that Annette might have leave to remain with her all night, but was deterred by an apprehension of betraying what would be thought childish fears, and by an unwillingness to increase the apt terrors of Annette.

Her gloomy reflections were, soon after, interrupted by a footstep in the corridor, and she was glad to see Annette enter with some supper, sent by Madame Montoni. Having a table near the fire, she made the good girl sit down and sup with her; and, when their little repast was over, Annette, encouraged by her kindness and stirring the wood into a blaze, drew her chair upon the hearth, nearer to Emily, and said— "Did you ever hear, ma'amselle, of the strange accident, that made the Signor lord of this castle?"

"What wonderful story have you now to tell?" said Emily, concealing the curiosity, occasioned by the mysterious hints she had formerly heard on that subject.

"I have heard all about it, ma'amselle," said Annette, looking round the chamber and drawing closer to Emily; "Benedetto told it me as we travelled together: says he, 'Annette, you don't know about this castle here, that we are going to?' No, says I, Mr. Benedetto, pray what do you know? But, ma'amselle, you can keep a secret, or I would not tell it you for the world; for I promised never to tell, and they say, that the Signor does not like to have it talked of."

"If you promised to keep this secret," said Emily, "you do right not to mention it."

Annette paused a moment, and then said, "O, but to you, ma'amselle, to you I may tell it safely, I know."

Emily smiled, "I certainly shall keep it as faithfully as yourself, Annette."

Annette replied very gravely, that would do, and proceeded— "This castle, you must know, ma'amselle, is very old, and very strong, and has stood out many sieges, as they say. Now it was not Signor Montoni's always, nor his father's; no; but, by some law or other, it was to come to the Signor, if the lady died unmarried."

"What lady?" said Emily.

"I am not come to that yet," replied Annette, "it is the lady I am going to tell you about, ma'amselle: but, as I was saying, this lady lived in the castle, and had everything very grand about her, as you may suppose, ma'amselle. The Signor used often to come to see her, and was in love with her, and offered to marry her; for, though he was somehow related, that did not signify. But she was in love with somebody else, and would not have him, which made him very angry, as they say, and you know, ma'amselle, what an ill-looking gentleman he is, when he is angry. Perhaps she saw him in a passion, and therefore would not have him. But, as I was saying, she was very melancholy and unhappy, and all that, for a long while, and—— Holy Virgin! what noise is that? did not you hear a sound, ma'amselle?"

"It was only the wind," said Emily, "but do come to the end of your story."

"As I was saying—O, where was I?—as I was saying—she was very melancholy and unhappy a long while, and used to walk about upon the terrace, there, under the windows, by herself, and cry so! it would have done your heart good to hear her. That is—I don't mean good, but it would have made you cry too, as they tell me."

"Well, but, Annette, do tell me the substance of your tale."

"All in good time, ma'am; all this I heard before at Venice, but what is to come I never heard till to-day. This happened a great many years ago, when Signor Montoni was quite a young man. The lady—they called her Signora Laurentini, was very handsome, but she used to be in great passions, too, sometimes, as well as the Signor. Finding he could not make her listen to him—what does he do, but leave the castle, and never comes near it for a long time! but it was all one to her; she was just as unhappy whether he was here or not, till one evening, Holy St. Peter! ma'amselle," cried Annette, "look at that lamp, see how blue it burns!" She looked fearfully round the chamber. "Ridiculous girl!" said Emily, "why will you indulge those fancies? Pray let me hear the end of your story, I am weary."

Annette still kept her eyes on the lamp, and proceeded in a lower voice. "It was one evening, they say, at the latter end of the year, it might be about the middle of September, I suppose, or the beginning of October; nay, for that matter, it might be November, for that, too, is the latter end of the year, but that I cannot say for certain, because they did not tell me for certain themselves. However, it was at the latter end of the year, this grand lady walked out of the castle into the woods below, as she had often done before, all alone, only her maid was with her. The wind blew cold, and strewed the leaves about, and whistled dismally among those great old chesnut trees, that we passed, ma'am-selle, as we came to the castle—for Benedetto shewed me the trees as he was talking—the wind blew cold, and her woman would have persuaded her to return: but all would not do, for she was fond of walking in the woods, at evening time, and, if the leaves were falling about her, so much the better.

"Well, they saw her go down among the woods, but night came, and she did not return: ten o'clock, eleven o'clock, twelve o'clock came, and no lady! Well, the servants thought to be sure, some accident had befallen her, and they went out to seek her. They searched all night long, but could not find her, or any trace of her; and, from that day to this, ma'amselle, she has never been heard of."

"Is this true, Annette?" said Emily, in much surprise.

"True, ma'am!" said Annette, with a look of horror, "yes, it is true, indeed. But they do say," she added, lowering her voice, "they do say, that the Signora has been seen, several times since, walking in the woods and about the castle in the night: several of the old servants, who remained here some time after, declare they saw her; and, since then, she has been seen by some of the vassals, who have happened to be in the castle, at night. Carlo, the old steward, could tell such things, they say, if he would."

"How contradictory is this, Annette!" said Emily, "you say nothing has been since known of her, and yet she has been seen!"

"But all this was told me for a great secret," rejoined Annette, without noticing the remark, "and I am sure, ma'am, you would not hurt either me or Benedetto, so much as to go and tell it again." Emily remained silent, and Annette repeated her last sentence.

"You have nothing to fear from my indiscretion," replied Emily, "and let me advise you, my good Annette, be discreet yourself, and never mention what you have just told me to any other person. Signor Montoni, as you say, may be angry if he hears of it. But what inquiries were made concerning the lady?"

"O! a great deal, indeed, ma'amselle, for the Signor laid claim to the castle directly, as being the next heir, and they said, that is, the judges, or the senators, or somebody of that sort, said, he could not take possession of it till so many years were gone by, and then, if, after all, the lady could not be found, why she would be as good as dead, and the castle would be his own; and so it is his own. But the story went round, and many strange reports were spread, so very strange, ma'amselle, that I shall not tell them."

"That is stranger still, Annette," said Emily, smiling, and rousing herself from her reverie. "But, when Signora Laurentini was afterwards seen in the castle, did nobody speak to her?"

"Speak—speak to her!" cried Annette, with a look of terror; "no, to be sure."

"And why not?" rejoined Emily, willing to hear further.

"Holy Mother! speak to a spirit!"

"But what reason had they to conclude it was a spirit, unless they had approached, and spoken to it?"

"O ma'amselle, I cannot tell. How can you ask such shocking questions? But nobody ever saw it come in, or go out of the castle; and it was in one place now, and then the next minute in quite another part of the castle; and then it never spoke, and, if it was alive, what should it do in the castle if it never spoke? Several parts of the castle have never been gone into since, they say, for that very reason."

"What, because it never spoke?" said Emily, trying to laugh away the fears that began to steal upon her.—"No, ma'amselle, no;" replied Annette, rather angrily, "but because something has been seen there. They say, too, there is an old chapel adjoining the west side of the castle, where, any time at midnight, you may hear such groans!—it makes one shudder to think of them!—and strange sights have been seen there——"

"Pr'ythee, Annette, no more of these silly tales," said Emily.

"Silly tales, ma'amselle! O, but I will tell you one story about this, if you please, that Caterina told me. It was one cold winter's night that Caterina (she often came to the castle then, she says, to keep old Carlo and his wife company, and so he recommended her afterwards to the Signor, and she has lived here ever since) Caterina was sitting with them in the little hall, says Carlo, 'I wish we had some of those figs to roast, that lie in the store-closet, but it is a long way off, and I am loth to fetch them; do, Caterina,' says he, 'for you are young and nimble, do bring us some, the fire is in nice trim for roasting them; they lie,' says he, 'in such a corner of the store-room, at the end of the north-gallery; here, take the lamp,' says he, 'and mind, as you go up the great staircase, that the wind, through the roof, does not blow it out.' So, with that, Caterina took the lamp—Hush! ma'amselle, I surely heard a noise!"

Emily, whom Annette had now infected with her own terrors, listened attentively; but every thing was still, and Annette proceeded:

"Caterina went to the north-gallery, that is the wide gallery we passed, ma'am, before we came to the corridor, here. As she went with the lamp in her hand, thinking of nothing at all—— There, again!" cried Annette, suddenly—"I heard it again!—it was not fancy, ma'amselle!"

"Hush!" said Emily, trembling. They listened, and, continuing to sit quite still, Emily heard a low knocking against the wall. It came repeatedly. Annette then screamed loudly, and the chamber door slowly opened.—It was Caterina, come to tell Annette, that her lady wanted her. Emily, though she now perceived who it was, could not immediately overcome her terror; while Annette, half laughing, half crying, scolded Caterina heartily for thus alarming them; and was also terrified lest what she had told had been overheard.—Emily, whose mind was deeply impressed by the chief circumstance of Annette's relation, was unwilling to be left alone, in the present state of her spirits; but, to avoid offending Madame Montoni, and betraying her own weakness, she struggled to overcome the illusions of fear, and dismissed Annette for the night.

When she was alone, her thoughts recurred to the strange history of Signora Laurentini and then to her own strange situation, in the wild and solitary mountains of a foreign country, in the castle, and the power of a man, to whom, only a few preceding months, she was an entire stranger; who had already exercised an usurped authority over her, and whose character she now regarded, with a degree of terror, apparently justified by the fears of others. She knew, that he had invention equal to the conception and talents to the execution of any project, and she greatly feared he had a heart too void of feeling to oppose the perpetration of whatever his interest might suggest. She had long observed the unhappiness of Madame Montoni, and had often been witness to the stern and contemptuous behaviour she received from her husband. To these circumstances, which conspired to give her just cause for alarm, were now added those thousand nameless terrors, which exist only in active imaginations, and which set reason and examination equally at defiance.

Emily remembered all that Valancourt had told her, on the eve of her departure from Languedoc, respecting Montoni, and all that he had said to dissuade her from venturing on the journey. His fears had often since appeared to her prophetic — now they seemed confirmed. Her heart, as it gave her back the image of Valancourt, mourned in vain regret, but reason soon came with a consolation which, though feeble at first, acquired vigour from reflection. She considered, that, whatever might be her sufferings, she had withheld from involving him in misfortune, and that, whatever her future sorrows could be, she was, at least, free from self-reproach.

Her melancholy was assisted by the hollow sighings of the wind along the corridor and round the castle. The cheerful blaze of the wood had long been extinguished, and she sat with her eyes fixed on the dying embers, till a loud gust, that swept through the corridor, and shook the doors and casements, alarmed her, for its violence had moved the chair she had placed as a fastening, and the door, leading to the private stair-case, stood half open. Her curiosity and her fears were again awakened. She took the lamp to the top of the steps, and stood hesitating whether to go down; but again the profound stillness and the gloom of the place awed her, and, determining to enquire further, when day-light might assist the search, she closed the door, and placed against it a stronger guard.

She now retired to her bed, leaving the lamp burning on the table; but its gloomy light, instead of dispelling her fear, assisted it; for, by its uncertain rays, she almost fancied she saw shapes flit past her curtains and glide into the remote obscurity of her chamber.—The castle clock struck one before she closed her eyes to sleep.

CHAPTER VI

> I think it is the weakness of mine eyes,
> That shapes this monstrous apparition.
> It comes upon me!
>
> JULIUS CÆSAR

DAYLIGHT dispelled from Emily's mind the glooms of superstition, but not those of apprehension. The Count Morano was the first image, that occurred to her waking thoughts, and then came a train of anticipated evils, which she could neither conquer, nor avoid. She rose, and, to relieve her mind from the busy ideas, that tormented it, compelled herself to notice external objects. From her casement she looked out upon the wild grandeur of the scene, closed nearly on all sides by alpine steeps, whose tops, peeping over each other, faded from the eye in misty hues, while the promontories below were dark with woods, that swept down to their base, and stretched along the narrow vallies. The rich pomp of these woods was particularly delightful to Emily; and she viewed with astonishment the fortifications of the castle spreading along a vast extent of rock, and now partly in decay, the grandeur of the ramparts below, and the towers and battlements and various features of the fabric above. From these her sight wandered over the cliffs and woods into the valley, along which foamed a broad and rapid stream, seen falling among the crags of an opposite mountain, now flashing in the sun-beams, and now shadowed by over-arching pines, till it was entirely concealed by their thick foliage. Again it burst from beneath this darkness in one broad sheet of foam, and fell thundering into the vale. Nearer, towards the west, opened the mountain-vista, which Emily had viewed with such sublime emotion, on her approach to the castle: a thin dusky vapour, that rose from the valley, overspread its features with a sweet obscurity. As this ascended and caught the sun-beams, it kindled into a crimson tint, and touched with exquisite beauty the woods and cliffs, over which it passed to the summit of the mountains; then, as the veil drew up, it was delightful to watch the gleaming objects, that progressively disclosed themselves in the val-ley—the green turf—dark woods—little rocky recesses—a few peasants' huts—the foaming stream—a herd of cattle, and various images of pastoral beauty. Then, the pine-forests brightened, and then the broad breast of the mountains, till, at length, the mist settled round their summit, touching them with a ruddy glow. The features of the vista now appeared distinctly, and the broad deep shadows, that fell from the lower cliffs, gave strong effect to the streaming splendour above; while the mountains, gradually sinking in the perspective, appeared to shelve into the Adriatic sea, for such Emily imagined to be the gleam of blueish light, that terminated the view.

Thus she endeavoured to amuse her fancy, and was not unsuccessful. The breezy freshness of the morning, too, revived her. She raised her thoughts in prayer, which she felt always most disposed to do, when viewing the sublimity of nature, and her mind recovered its strength.

When she turned from the casement, her eyes glanced upon the door she had so carefully guarded, on the preceding night, and she now determined to examine whither it led; but, on advancing to remove the chairs, she perceived, that they were already moved a little way. Her surprise cannot be easily imagined, when, in the next minute, she perceived that the door was fastened.—She felt, as if she had seen an apparition. The door of the corridor was locked as she had left it, but this door, which could be secured only on the outside, must have been bolted, during the night. She became seriously uneasy at the thought of sleeping again in a chamber, thus liable to intrusion, so remote, too, as it was from the family, and she determined to mention the circumstance to Madame Montoni, and to request a change.

After some perplexity she found her way into the great hall, and to the room, which she had left, on the preceding night, where breakfast was spread, and her aunt was alone, for Montoni had been walking over the environs of the castle, examining the condition of its fortifications, and talking for some time with Carlo. Emily observed that her aunt had been weeping, and her heart softened towards her, with an affection, that shewed itself in her manner, rather than in words, while she carefully avoided the appearance of having noticed, that she was unhappy. She seized the opportunity of Montoni's absence to mention the circumstance of the door, to request that she might be allowed another apartment, and to enquire again, concerning the occasion of their sudden journey. On the first subject her aunt referred her to Montoni, positively refusing to interfere in the affair; on the last, she professed utter ignorance.

Emily, then, with a wish of making her aunt more reconciled to her situation, praised the grandeur of the castle and the surrounding scenery, and endeavoured to soften every unpleasing circumstance attending it. But, though misfortune had somewhat conquered the asperities of Madame Montoni's temper, and, by increasing her cares for herself, had taught her to feel in some degree for others, the capricious love of rule, which nature had planted and habit had nourished in her heart, was not subdued. She could not now deny herself the gratification of tyrannizing over the innocent and helpless Emily, by attempting to ridicule the taste she could not feel.

Her satirical discourse was, however, interrupted by the entrance of Montoni, and her countenance immediately assumed a mingled expression of fear and resentment, while he seated himself at the breakfast-table, as if unconscious of there being any person but himself in the room.

Emily, as she observed him in silence, saw, that his countenance was darker and sterner than usual. "O could I know," said she to herself, "what passes in that mind; could I know the thoughts, that are known there, I should no longer be condemned to this torturing suspense!" Their breakfast passed in silence, till Emily ventured to request, that another apartment might be allotted to her, and related the circumstance which made her wish it.

"I have no time to attend to these idle whims," said Montoni, "that chamber was prepared for you, and you must rest contented with it. It is not probable, that any person would take the trouble of going to that remote stair-case, for the purpose of fastening a door. If it was not fastened, when you entered the chamber, the wind, perhaps, shook the door and made the bolts slide. But I know not why I should undertake to account for so trifling an occurrence."

This explanation was by no means satisfactory to Emily, who had observed, that the bolts were rusted, and consequently could not be thus easily moved; but she forbore to say so, and repeated her request.

"If you will not release yourself from the slavery of these fears," said Montoni, sternly, "at least forbear to torment others by the mention of them. Conquer such whims, and endeavour to strengthen your mind. No existence is more contemptible than that, which is embittered by fear." As he said this, his eye glanced upon Madame Montoni, who coloured highly, but was still silent. Emily, wounded and disappointed, thought her fears were, in this instance, too reasonable to deserve ridicule; but, perceiving, that, however they might oppress her, she must endure them, she tried to withdraw her attention from the subject.

Carlo soon after entered with some fruit:

"Your *Excellenza* is tired after your long ramble," said he, as he set the fruit upon the table; "but you have more to see after breakfast. There is a place in the vaulted passage leading to——"

Montoni frowned upon him, and waved his hand for him to leave the room. Carlo stopped, looked down, and then added, as he advanced to the breakfast-table, and took up the basket of fruit, "I made bold, your *Excellenza*, to bring some cherries, here, for my honoured lady and my young mistress. Will your ladyship taste them, madam?" said Carlo, presenting the basket, "they are very fine ones, though I gathered them myself, and from an old tree, that catches all the south sun; they are as big as plums, your ladyship."

"Very well, old Carlo," said Madame Montoni; "I am obliged to you."

"And the young Signora, too, she may like some of them," rejoined Carlo, turning with the basket to Emily, "it will do me good to see her eat some."

"Thank you, Carlo," said Emily, taking some cherries, and smiling kindly.

"Come, come," said Montoni, impatiently, "enough of this. Leave the room, but be in waiting. I shall want you presently."

Carlo obeyed, and Montoni, soon after, went out to examine further into the state of the castle; while Emily remained with her aunt, patiently enduring her ill humour, and endeavouring, with much sweetness, to soothe her affliction, instead of resenting its effect.

When Madame Montoni retired to her dressing-room, Emily endeavoured to amuse herself by a view of the castle. Through a folding door, she passed from the great hall to the ramparts, which extended along the brow of the precipice, round three sides of the edifice; the fourth was guarded by the high walls of the courts, and by the gateway, through which she had passed, on the preceding evening. The grandeur of the broad ramparts, and the changing scenery they overlooked, excited her high admiration; for the extent of the terraces allowed the features of the country to be seen in such various points of view, that they appeared to form new landscapes. She often paused to examine the gothic magnificence of Udolpho, its proud irregularity, its lofty towers and battlements, its high-arched casements, and its slender watch-towers, perched upon the corners of turrets. Then she would lean on the wall of the terrace, and, shuddering, measure with her eye the precipice below, till the dark summits of the woods arrested it. Wherever she turned, appeared mountain-tops, forests of pine and narrow glens, opening among the Apennines and retiring from the sight into inaccessible regions.

While she thus leaned, Montoni, followed by two men, appeared, ascending a winding path, cut in the rock below. He stopped upon a cliff, and, pointing to the ramparts, turned to his followers, and talked with much eagerness of gesticulation.—Emily perceived, that one of these men was Carlo; the other was in the dress of a peasant, and he alone seemed to be receiving the directions of Montoni.

She withdrew from the walls, and pursued her walk, till she heard at a distance the sound of carriage wheels, and then the loud bell of the portal, when it instantly occurred to her, that Count Morano was arrived. As she hastily passed the folding doors from the terrace, towards her own apartment, several persons entered the hall by an opposite door. She saw them at the extremities of the arcades, and immediately retreated; but the agitation of her spirits, and the extent and duskiness of the hall, had prevented her from distinguishing the persons of the strangers. Her fears, however, had but one object, and they had called up that object to her fancy;—she believed that she had seen Count Morano.

When she thought that they had passed the hall, she ventured again to the door, and proceeded, unobserved, to her room, where she remained, agitated with apprehensions, and listening to every distant sound. At length, hearing voices on the rampart, she hastened to her window, and observed Montoni, with Signor Cavigni, walking below, conversing earnestly, and often stopping and turning towards each other, at which time their discourse seemed to be uncommonly interesting.

Of the several persons who had appeared in the hall, here was Cavigni alone: but Emily's alarm was soon after heightened by the steps of some one in the corridor, who, she apprehended, brought a message from the Count. In the next moment, Annette appeared.

"Ah! ma'amselle," said she, "here is the Signor Cavigni arrived! I am sure I rejoiced to see a christian person in this place; and then he is so good natured too, he always takes so much notice of me!—And here is also Signor Verezzi, and who do you think besides, ma'amselle?"

"I cannot guess, Annette; tell me quickly."

"Nay, ma'am, do guess once."

"Well, then," said Emily, with assumed composure, "it is—Count Morano, I suppose."

"Holy Virgin!" cried Annette, "are you ill, ma'amselle? you are going to faint! let me get some water."

Emily sunk into a chair. "Stay, Annette," said she, feebly, "do not leave me—I shall soon be better; open the casement.—The Count, you say—he is come then?"

"Who, I!—the Count! No, ma'amselle, I did not say so." "He is *not* come then?" said Emily eagerly. "No, ma'amselle."

"You are sure of it?"

"Lord bless me!" said Annette, "you recover very suddenly, ma'am! why, I thought you was dying, just now."

"But the Count—you are sure, is not come?"

"O yes, quite sure of that, ma'amselle. Why, I was looking out through the grate in the north turret, when the carriages drove into the court-yard, and I never expected to see such a goodly sight in this dismal old castle! but here are masters and servants, too, enough to make the place ring again. O! I was ready to leap through the rusty old bars for joy!—O! who would ever have thought of seeing a christian face in this huge dreary house? I could have kissed the very horses that brought them."

"Well, Annette, well, I am better now."

"Yes, ma'amselle, I see you are. O! all the servants will lead merry lives here, now; we shall have singing and dancing in the little hall, for the Signor cannot hear us there—and droll stories—Ludovico's come, ma'am; yes, there is Ludovico come with them! You remember Ludovico, ma'am—a tall, handsome young man—Signor Cavigni's lacquey—who always wears his cloak with such a grace, thrown round his left arm, and his hat set on so smartly, all on one side, and——"

"No," said Emily, who was wearied by her loquacity.

"What, ma'amselle, don't you remember Ludovico—who rowed the Cavaliero's gondola, at the last regatta, and won the prize? And who used to sing such sweet verses about Orlandos and about the Black-a-moors, too; and Charly—Charly—magne, yes, that was the name, all under my lattice, in the west portico, on the moon-light nights at Venice? O! I have listened to him!"——

"I fear, to thy peril, my good Annette," said Emily; "for it seems his verses have stolen thy heart. But let me advise you; if it is so, keep the secret; never let him know it."

"Ah—ma'amselle!—how can one keep such a secret as that?"

"Well, Annette, I am now so much better, that you may leave me."

"O, but, ma'amselle, I forgot to ask—how did you sleep in this dreary old chamber last night?"—"As well as usual."—"Did you hear no noises?"—"None."—"Nor see anything?"—"Nothing."—"Well, that is surprising!"—"Not in the least: and now tell me, why you ask these questions."

"O, ma'amselle! I would not tell you for the world, nor all I have heard about this chamber, either; it would frighten you so."

"If that is all, you have frightened me already, and may therefore tell me what you know, without hurting your conscience."

"O Lord! they say the room is haunted, and has been so these many years."

"It is by a ghost, then, who can draw bolts," said Emily, endeavouring to laugh away her apprehensions; "for I left the door open, last night, and found it fastened this morning."

Annette turned pale, and said not a word.

"Do you know whether any of the servants fastened this door in the morning, before I rose?"

"No, ma'am, that I will be bound they did not; but I don't know: shall I go and ask, ma'amselle?" said Annette, moving hastily towards the corridor.

"Stay, Annette, I have other questions to ask; tell me what you have heard concerning this room, and whither that stair-case leads."

"I will go and ask it all directly, ma'am; besides, I am sure my lady wants me. I cannot stay now, indeed, ma'am."

She hurried from the room, without waiting Emily's reply, whose heart, lightened by the certainty, that Morano was not arrived, allowed her to smile at the superstitious terror, which had seized on Annette; for, though she sometimes felt its influence herself, she could smile at it, when apparent in other persons.

Montoni having refused Emily another chamber, she determined to bear with patience the evil she could not remove, and, in order to make the room as comfortable as possible, unpacked her books, her sweet delight in happier days, and her soothing resource in the hours of moderate sorrow: but there were hours when even these failed of their effect; when the genius, the taste, the enthusiasm of the sublimest writers were felt no longer.

Her little library being arranged on a high chest, part of the furniture of the room, she took out her drawing utensils, and was tranquil enough to be pleased with the thought of sketching the sublime scenes, beheld from her windows; but she suddenly checked this pleasure, remembering how often she had soothed herself by the intention of obtaining amusement of this kind, and had been prevented by some new circumstance of misfortune.

"How can I suffer myself to be deluded by hope," said she, "and, because Count Morano is not yet arrived, feel a momentary happiness? Alas! what is it to me, whether he is here to-day, or to-morrow, if he comes at all? — and that he will come — it were weakness to doubt."

To withdraw her thoughts, however, from the subject of her misfortunes, she attempted to read, but her attention wandered from the page, and, at length, she threw aside the book, and determined to explore the adjoining chambers of the castle. Her imagination was pleased with the view of ancient grandeur, and an emotion of melancholy awe awakened all its powers, as she walked through rooms, obscure and desolate, where no footsteps had passed probably for many years, and remembered the strange history of the former possessor of the edifice. This brought to her recollection the veiled picture, which had attracted her curiosity, on the preceding night, and she resolved to examine it. As she passed through the chambers, that led to this, she found herself somewhat agitated; its connection with the late lady of the castle, and the conversation of Annette, together with the circumstance of the veil, throwing a mystery over the subject, that excited a faint degree of terror. But a terror of this nature, as it occupies and expands the mind, and elevates it to high expectation, is purely sublime, and leads us, by a kind of fascination, to seek even the object, from which we appear to shrink.

Emily passed on with faltering steps, and having paused a moment at the door, before she attempted to open it, she then hastily entered the chamber, and went towards the picture, which appeared to be enclosed in a frame of uncommon size, that hung in a dark part of the room. She paused again, and then, with a timid hand, lifted the veil; but instantly let it fall—perceiving that what it had concealed was no picture, and, before she could leave the chamber, she dropped senseless on the floor.

When she recovered her recollection, the remembrance of what she had seen had nearly deprived her of it a second time. She had scarcely strength to remove from the room, and regain her own; and, when arrived there, wanted courage to remain alone. Horror occupied her mind, and excluded, for a time, all sense of past, and dread of future misfortune: she seated herself near the casement, because from thence she heard voices, though distant, on the terrace, and might see people pass, and these, trifling as they were, were reviving circumstances. When her spirits had recovered their tone, she considered, whether she should mention what she had seen to Madame Montoni, and various and important motives urged her to do so, among which the least was the hope of the relief, which an overburdened mind finds in speaking of the subject of its interest. But she was aware of the terrible consequences, which such a communication might lead to; and, dreading the indiscretion of her aunt, at length, endeavoured to arm herself with resolution to observe a profound silence, on the subject. Montoni and Verezzi soon after passed under the casement, speaking cheerfully, and their voices revived her. Presently the Signors Bertolini and Cavigni joined the party on the terrace, and Emily, supposing that Madame Montoni was then alone, went to seek her; for the solitude of her chamber, and its proximity to that where she had received so severe a shock, again affected her spirits.

She found her aunt in her dressing-room, preparing for dinner. Emily's pale and affrighted countenance alarmed even Madame Montoni; but she had sufficient strength of mind to be silent on the subject, that still made her shudder, and which was ready to burst from her lips. In her aunt's apartment she remained, till they both descended to dinner. There she met the gentlemen lately arrived, who had a kind of busy seriousness in their looks, which was somewhat unusual with them, while their thoughts seemed too much occupied by some deep interest, to suffer them to bestow much attention either on Emily, or Madame Montoni. They spoke little, and Montoni less. Emily, as she now looked on him, shuddered. The horror of the chamber rushed on her mind. Several times the colour faded from her cheeks, and she feared, that illness would betray her emotions, and compel her to leave the room; but the strength of her resolution remedied the weakness of her frame; she obliged herself to converse, and even tried to look cheerful.

Montoni evidently laboured under some vexation, such as would probably have agitated a weaker mind, or a more susceptible heart, but which appeared, from the sternness of his countenance, only to bend up his faculties to energy and fortitude.

It was a comfortless and silent meal. The gloom of the castle seemed to have spread its contagion even over the gay countenance of Cavigni, and with this gloom was mingled a fierceness, such as she had seldom seen him indicate. Count Morano was not named, and what conversation there was, turned chiefly upon the wars, which at that time agitated the Italian states, the strength of the Venetian armies, and the characters of their generals.

After dinner, when the servants had withdrawn, Emily learned, that the cavalier, who had drawn upon himself the vengeance of Orsino, had since died of his wounds, and that strict search was still making for his murderer. The intelligence seemed to disturb Montoni, who mused, and then enquired, where Orsino had concealed himself. His guests, who all, except Cavigni, were ignorant, that Montoni had himself assisted him to escape from Venice, replied, that he had fled in the night with such precipitation and secrecy, that his most intimate companions knew not whither. Montoni blamed himself for having asked the question, for a second thought convinced him, that a man of Orsino's suspicious temper was not likely to trust any of the persons present with the knowledge of his asylum. He considered himself, however, as entitled to his utmost confidence, and did not doubt, that he should soon hear of him.

Emily retired with Madame Montoni, soon after the cloth was withdrawn, and left the cavaliers to their secret councils, but not before the significant frowns of Montoni had warned his wife to depart, who passed from the hall to the ramparts, and walked, for some time, in silence, which Emily did not interrupt, for her mind was also occupied by interests of its own. It required all her resolution, to forbear communicating to Madame Montoni the terrible subject, which still thrilled her every nerve with horror; and sometimes she was on the point of doing so, merely to obtain the relief of a moment; but she knew how wholly she was in the power of Montoni, and, considering, that the indiscretion of her aunt might prove fatal to them both, she compelled herself to endure a present and an inferior evil, rather than to tempt a future and a heavier one. A strange kind of presentiment frequently, on this day, occurred to her;—it seemed as if her fate rested here, and was by some invisible means connected with this castle.

"Let me not accelerate it," said she to herself: "for whatever I may be reserved, let me, at least, avoid self-reproach."

As she looked on the massy walls of the edifice, her melancholy spirits represented it to be her prison; and she started as at a new suggestion, when she considered how far distant she was from her native country, from her little peaceful home, and from her only friend—how remote was her hope of happiness, how feeble the expectation of again seeing him! Yet the idea of Valancourt, and her confidence in his faithful love, had hitherto been her only solace, and she struggled hard to retain them. A few tears of agony started to her eyes, which she turned aside to conceal.

While she afterwards leaned on the wall of the rampart, some peasants, at a little distance, were seen examining a breach, before which lay a heap of stones, as if to repair it, and a rusty old cannon, that appeared to have fallen from its station above. Madame Montoni stopped to speak to the men, and enquired what they were going to do. "To repair the fortifications, your ladyship," said one of them; a labour which she was somewhat surprised, that Montoni should think necessary, particularly since he had never spoken of the castle, as of a place, at which he meant to reside for any considerable time; but she passed on towards a lofty arch, that led from the south to the east rampart, and which adjoined the castle, on one side, while, on the other, it supported a small watch-tower, that entirely commanded the deep valley below. As she approached this arch, she saw, beyond it, winding along the woody descent of a distant mountain, a long troop of horse and foot, whom she knew to be soldiers, only by the glitter of their pikes and other arms, for the distance did not allow her to discover the colour of their liveries. As she gazed, the vanguard issued from the woods into the valley, but the train still continued to pour over the remote summit of the mountain, in endless succession; while, in the front, the military uniform became distinguishable, and the commanders, riding first, and seeming, by their gestures, to direct the march of those that followed, at length, approached very near to the castle.

Such a spectacle, in these solitary regions, both surprised and alarmed Madame Montoni, and she hastened towards some peasants, who were employed in raising bastions before the south rampart, where the rock was less abrupt than elsewhere. These men could give no satisfactory answers to her enquiries, but, being roused by them, gazed in stupid astonishment upon the long cavalcade. Madame Montoni, then thinking it necessary to communicate further the object of her alarm, sent Emily to say, that she wished to speak to Montoni; an errand her niece did not approve, for she dreaded his frowns, which she knew this message would provoke; but she obeyed in silence.

As she drew near the apartment, in which he sat with his guests, she heard them in earnest and loud dispute, and she paused a moment, trembling at the displeasure, which her sudden interruption would occasion. In the next, their voices sunk all together; she then ventured to open the door, and, while Montoni turned hastily and looked at her, without speaking, she delivered her message.

"Tell Madam Montoni I am engaged," said he.

Emily then thought it proper to mention the subject of her alarm. Montoni and his companions rose instantly and went to the windows, but, these not affording them a view of the troops, they at length proceeded to the ramparts, where Cavigni conjectured it to be a legion of *Condottieri,* on their march towards Modena.

One part of the cavalcade now extended along the valley, and another wound among the mountains towards the north, while some troops still lingered on the woody precipices, where the first had appeared, so that the great length of the procession seemed to include an whole army. While Montoni and his family watched its progress, they heard the sound of trumpets and the clash of cymbals in the vale, and then others, answering from the heights. Emily listened with emotion to the shrill blast, that woke the echoes of the mountains, and Montoni explained the signals, with which he appeared to be well acquainted, and which meant nothing hostile. The uniforms of the troops, and the kind of arms they bore, confirmed to him the conjecture of Cavigni, and he had the satisfaction to see them pass by, without even stopping to gaze upon his castle. He did not, however, leave the rampart, till the bases of the mountains had shut them from his view, and the last murmur of the trumpet floated away on the wind. Cavigni and Verezzi were inspirited by this spectacle, which seemed to have roused all the fire of their temper; Montoni turned into the castle in thoughtful silence.

Emily's mind had not yet sufficiently recovered from its late shock, to endure the loneliness of her chamber, and she remained upon the ramparts; for Madame Montoni had not invited her to her dressing-room, whither she had gone evidently in low spirits, and Emily, from her late experience, had lost all wish to explore the gloomy and mysterious recesses of the castle. The ramparts, therefore, were almost her only retreat, and here she lingered, till the gray haze of evening was again spread over the scene.

The cavaliers supped by themselves, and Madame Montoni remained in her apartment, whither Emily went, before she retired to her own. She found her aunt weeping, and in much agitation. The tenderness of Emily was naturally so soothing, that it seldom failed to give comfort to the drooping heart: but Madame Montoni's was torn, and the softest accents of Emily's voice were lost upon it. With her usual delicacy, she did not appear to observe her aunt's distress, but it gave an involuntary gentleness to her manners, and an air of solicitude to her countenance, which Madame Montoni was vexed to perceive, who seemed to feel the pity of her niece to be an insult to her pride, and dismissed her as soon as she properly could. Emily did not venture to mention again the reluctance she felt to her gloomy chamber, but she requested that Annette might be permitted to remain with her till she retired to rest; and the request was somewhat reluctantly granted. Annette, however, was now with the servants, and Emily withdrew alone.

With light and hasty steps she passed through the long galleries, while the feeble glimmer of the lamp she carried only shewed the gloom around her, and the passing air threatened to extinguish it. The lonely silence, that reigned in this part of the castle, awed her; now and then, indeed, she heard a faint peal of laughter rise from a remote part of the edifice, where the servants were assembled, but it was soon lost, and a kind of breathless stillness remained. As she passed the suite of rooms which she had visited in the morning, her eyes glanced fearfully on the door, and she almost fancied she heard murmuring sounds within, but she paused not a moment to enquire.

Having reached her own apartment, where no blazing wood on the hearth dissipated the gloom, she sat down with a book, to enliven her attention, till Annette should come, and a fire could be kindled. She continued to read till her light was nearly expired, but Annette did not appear, and the solitude and obscurity of her chamber again affected her spirits, the more, because of its nearness to the scene of horror, that she had witnessed in the morning. Gloomy and fantastic images came to her mind. She looked fearfully towards the door of the stair-case, and then, examining whether it was still fastened, found that it was so. Unable to conquer the uneasiness she felt at the prospect of sleeping again in this remote and insecure apartment, which some person seemed to have entered during the preceding night, her impatience to see Annette, whom she had bidden to enquire concerning this circumstance, became extremely painful. She wished also to question her, as to the object, which had excited so much horror in her own mind, and which Annette on the preceding evening had appeared to be in part acquainted with, though her words were very remote from the truth, and it appeared plainly to Emily, that the girl had been purposely misled by a false report: above all she was surprised, that the door of the chamber, which contained it, should be left unguarded. Such an instance of negligence almost surpassed belief. But her light was now expiring; the faint flashes it threw upon the walls called up all the terrors of fancy, and she rose to find her way to the habitable part of the castle, before it was quite extinguished.

As she opened the chamber door, she heard remote voices, and, soon after, saw a light issue upon the further end of the corridor, which Annette and another servant approached. "I am glad you are come," said Emily: "what has detained you so long? Pray light me a fire immediately."

"My lady wanted me, ma'amselle," replied Annette in some confusion; "I will go and get the wood."

"No," said Caterina, "that is my business," and left the room instantly, while Annette would have followed; but, being called back, she began to talk very loud, and laugh, and seemed afraid to trust a pause of silence.

Caterina soon returned with the wood, and then, when the cheerful blaze once more animated the room, and this servant had withdrawn, Emily asked Annette, whether she had made the enquiry she bade her. "Yes, ma'amselle," said Annette, "but not a soul knows any thing about the matter: and old Carlo—I watched him well, for they say he knows strange things—old Carlo looked so as I don't know how to tell, and he asked me again and again, if I was sure the door was ever unfastened. Lord, says I—am I sure I am alive? And as for me, ma'am, I am all astounded, as one may say, and would no more sleep in this chamber, than I would on the great cannon at the end of the east rampart."

"And what objection have you to that cannon, more than to any of the rest?" said Emily smiling: "the best would be rather a hard bed."

"Yes, ma'amselle, any of them would be hard enough for that matter; but they do say, that something has been seen in the dead of night, standing beside the great cannon, as if to guard it."

"Well! my good Annette, the people who tell such stories, are happy in having you for an auditor, for I perceive you believe them all."

"Dear ma'amselle! I will shew you the very cannon; you can see it from these windows!"

"Well," said Emily, "but that does not prove, that an apparition guards it."

"What! not if I shew you the very cannon! Dear ma'am, you will believe nothing."

"Nothing probably upon this subject, but what I see," said Emily.— "Well, ma'am, but you shall see it, if you will only step this way to the casement."—Emily could not forbear laughing, and Annette looked surprised. Perceiving her extreme aptitude to credit the marvellous, Emily forbore to mention the subject she had intended, lest it should overcome her with idle terrors, and she began to speak on a lively topic—the regattas of Venice.

"Aye, ma'amselle, those rowing matches," said Annette, "and the fine moon-light nights, are all, that are worth seeing in Venice. To be sure that moon is brighter than any I ever saw; and then to hear such sweet music, too, as Ludovico has often and often sung under the lattice by the west portico! Ma'amselle, it was Ludovico, that told me about that picture, which you wanted so to look at last night, and——"

"What picture?" said Emily, wishing Annette to explain herself.

"O! that terrible picture with the black veil over it."

"You never saw it, then?" said Emily.

"Who, I!—No, ma'amselle, I never did. But this morning," continued Annette, lowering her voice, and looking round the room, "this morning, as it was broad daylight, do you know, ma'am, I took a strange fancy to see it, as I had heard such odd hints about it, and I got as far as the door, and should have opened it, if it had not been locked!"

Emily, endeavouring to conceal the emotion this circumstance occasioned, enquired at what hour she went to the chamber, and found, that it was soon after herself had been there. She also asked further questions, and the answers convinced her, that Annette, and probably her informer, were ignorant of the terrible truth, though in Annette's account something very like the truth, now and then, mingled with the falsehood. Emily now began to fear, that her visit to the chamber had been observed, since the door had been closed, so immediately after her departure; and dreaded lest this should draw upon her the vengeance of Montoni. Her anxiety, also, was excited to know whence, and for what purpose, the delusive report, which had been imposed upon Annette, had originated, since Montoni could only have wished for silence and secrecy; but she felt, that the subject was too terrible for this lonely hour, and she compelled herself to leave it, to converse with Annette, whose chat, simple as it was, she preferred to the stillness of total solitude.

Thus they sat, till near midnight, but not without many hints from Annette, that she wished to go. The embers were now nearly burnt out; and Emily heard, at a distance, the thundering sound of the hall doors, as they were shut for the night. She, therefore, prepared for rest, but was still unwilling that Annette should leave her. At this instant, the great bell of the portal sounded. They listened in fearful expectation, when, after a long pause of silence, it sounded again. Soon after, they heard the noise of carriage wheels in the court-yard. Emily sunk almost lifeless in her chair; "It is the Count," said she.

"What, at this time of night, ma'am!" said Annette: "no, my dear lady. But, for that matter, it is a strange time of night for any body to come!"

"Nay, pr'ythee, good Annette, stay not talking," said Emily in a voice of agony—"Go, pr'ythee, go, and see who it is."

Annette left the room, and carried with her the light, leaving Emily in darkness, which a few moments before would have terrified her in this room, but was now scarcely observed by her. She listened and waited, in breathless expectation, and heard distant noises, but Annette did not return. Her patience, at length, exhausted, she tried to find her way to the corridor, but it was long before she could touch the door of the chamber, and, when she had opened it, the total darkness without made her fear to proceed. Voices were now heard, and Emily even thought she distinguished those of Count Morano, and Montoni. Soon after, she heard steps approaching, and then a ray of light streamed through the darkness, and Annette appeared, whom Emily went to meet.

"Yes, ma'amselle," said she, "you was right, it is the Count sure enough."

"It is he!" exclaimed Emily, lifting her eyes towards heaven and supporting herself by Annette's arm.

"Good Lord! my dear lady, don't be in such a *fluster*, and look so pale, we shall soon hear more."

"We shall, indeed!" said Emily, moving as fast as she was able towards her apartment. "I am not well; give me air." Annette opened a casement, and brought water. The faintness soon left Emily, but she desired Annette would not go till she heard from Montoni.

"Dear ma'amselle! he surely will not disturb you at this time of night; why he must think you are asleep."

"Stay with me till I am so, then," said Emily, who felt temporary relief from this suggestion, which appeared probable enough, though her fears had prevented its occurring to her. Annette, with secret reluctance, consented to stay, and Emily was now composed enough to ask her some questions; among others, whether she had seen the Count.

"Yes, ma'am, I saw him alight, for I went from hence to the grate in the north turret, that overlooks the inner court-yard, you know. There I saw the Count's carriage, and the Count in it, waiting at the great door,—for the porter was just gone to bed—with several men on horseback all by the light of the torches they carried." Emily was compelled to smile. "When the door was opened, the Count said something, that I could not make out, and then got out, and another gentleman with him. I thought, to be sure, the Signor was gone to bed, and I hastened away to my lady's dressing-room, to see what I could hear. But in the way I met Ludovico, and he told me that the Signor was up, counselling with his master and the other Signors, in the room at the end of the north gallery; and Ludovico held up his finger, and laid it on his lips, as much as to say—There is more going on, than you think of, Annette, but you must hold your tongue. And so I did hold my tongue, ma'amselle, and came away to tell you directly."

Emily enquired who the cavalier was, that accompanied the Count, and how Montoni received them; but Annette could not inform her.

"Ludovico," she added, "had just been to call Signor Montoni's valet, that he might tell him they were arrived, when I met him."

Emily sat musing, for some time, and then her anxiety was so much increased, that she desired Annette would go to the servants' hall, where it was possible she might hear something of the Count's intention, respecting his stay at the castle.

"Yes, ma'am," said Annette with readiness; "but how am I to find the way, if I leave the lamp with you?"

Emily said she would light her, and they immediately quitted the chamber. When they had reached the top of the great stair-case, Emily recollected, that she might be seen by the Count, and, to avoid the great hall, Annette conducted her through some private passages to a back stair-case, which led directly to that of the servants.

As she returned towards her chamber, Emily began to fear, that she might again lose herself in the intricacies of the castle, and again be shocked by some mysterious spectacle; and, though she was already perplexed by the numerous turnings, she feared to open one of the many doors that offered. While she stepped thoughtfully along, she fancied, that she heard a low moaning at no great distance, and, having paused a moment, she heard it again and distinctly. Several doors appeared on the right hand of the passage. She advanced, and listened. When she came to the second, she heard a voice, apparently in complaint, within, to which she continued to listen, afraid to open the door, and unwilling to leave it. Convulsive sobs followed, and then the piercing accents of an agonizing spirit burst forth. Emily stood appalled, and looked through the gloom, that surrounded her, in fearful expectation. The lamentations continued. Pity now began to subdue terror; it was possible she might administer comfort to the sufferer, at least, by expressing sympathy, and she laid her hand on the door. While she hesitated she thought she knew this voice, disguised as it was by tones of grief. Having, therefore, set down the lamp in the passage, she gently opened the door, within which all was dark, except that from an inner apartment a partial light appeared; and she stepped softly on. Before she reached it, the appearance of Madame Montoni, leaning on her dressing-table, weeping, and with a handkerchief held to her eyes, struck her, and she paused.

Some person was seated in a chair by the fire, but who it was she could not distinguish. He spoke, now and then, in a low voice, that did not allow Emily to hear what was uttered, but she thought, that Madame Montoni, at those times, wept the more, who was too much occupied by her own distress, to observe Emily, while the latter, though anxious to know what occasioned this, and who was the person admitted at so late an hour to her aunt's dressing-room, forbore to add to her sufferings by surprising her, or to take advantage of her situation, by listening to a private discourse. She, therefore, stepped softly back, and, after some further difficulty, found the way to her own chamber, where nearer interests, at length, excluded the surprise and concern she had felt, respecting Madame Montoni.

Annette, however, returned without satisfactory intelligence, for the servants, among whom she had been, were either entirely ignorant, or affected to be so, concerning the Count's intended stay at the castle. They could talk only of the steep and broken road they had just passed, and of the numerous dangers they had escaped and express wonder how their lord could choose to encounter all these, in the darkness of night; for they scarcely allowed, that the torches had served for any other purpose but that of shewing the dreariness of the mountains. Annette, finding she could gain no information, left them, making noisy petitions, for more wood on the fire and more supper on the table.

"And now, ma'amselle," added she, "I am so sleepy!—I am sure, if you was so sleepy, you would not desire me to sit up with you."

Emily, indeed, began to think it was cruel to wish it; she had also waited so long, without receiving a summons from Montoni, that it appeared he did not mean to disturb her, at this late hour, and she determined to dismiss Annette. But, when she again looked round her gloomy chamber, and recollected certain circumstances, fear seized her spirits, and she hesitated.

"And yet it were cruel of me to ask you to stay, till I am asleep, Annette," said she, "for I fear it will be very long before I forget myself in sleep."

"I dare say it will be very long, ma'amselle," said Annette.

"But, before you go," rejoined Emily, "let me ask you—Had Signor Montoni left Count Morano, when you quitted the hall?"

"O no, ma'am, they were alone together."

"Have you been in my aunt's dressing-room, since you left me?"

"No, ma'amselle, I called at the door as I passed, but it was fastened; so I thought my lady was gone to bed."

"Who, then, was with your lady just now?" said Emily, forgetting, in surprise, her usual prudence.

"Nobody, I believe, ma'am," replied Annette, "nobody has been with her, I believe, since I left you."

Emily took no further notice of the subject, and, after some struggle with imaginary fears, her good nature prevailed over them so far, that she dismissed Annette for the night. She then sat, musing upon her own circumstances and those of Madame Montoni, till her eye rested on the miniature picture, which she had found, after her father's death, among the papers he had enjoined her to destroy. It was open upon the table, before her, among some loose drawings, having, with them, been taken out of a little box by Emily, some hours before. The sight of it called up many interesting reflections, but the melancholy sweetness of the countenance soothed the emotions, which these had occasioned. It was the same style of countenance as that of her late father, and, while she gazed on it with fondness on this account, she even fancied a resemblance in the features. But this tranquillity was suddenly interrupted, when she recollected the words in the manuscript, that had been found with this picture, and which had formerly occasioned her so much doubt and horror. At length, she roused herself from the deep reverie, into which this remembrance had thrown her; but, when she rose to undress, the silence and solitude, to which she was left, at this midnight hour, for not even a distant sound was now heard, conspired with the impression the subject she had been considering had given to her mind, to appall her. Annette's hints, too, concerning this chamber, simple as they were, had not failed to affect her, since they followed a circumstance of peculiar horror, which she herself had witnessed, and since the scene of this was a chamber nearly adjoining her own.

The door of the stair-case was, perhaps, a subject of more reasonable alarm, and she now began to apprehend, such was the aptitude of her fears, that this stair-case had some private communication with the apartment, which she shuddered even to remember. Determined not to undress, she lay down to sleep in her clothes, with her late father's dog, the faithful *Manchon*, at the foot of the bed, whom she considered as a kind of guard.

Thus circumstanced, she tried to banish reflection, but her busy fancy would still hover over the subjects of her interest, and she heard the clock of the castle strike two, before she closed her eyes.

From the disturbed slumber, into which she then sunk, she was soon awakened by a noise, which seemed to arise within her chamber; but the silence, that prevailed, as she fearfully listened, inclined her to believe, that she had been alarmed by such sounds as sometimes occur in dreams, and she laid her head again upon the pillow.

A return of the noise again disturbed her; it seemed to come from that part of the room, which communicated with the private stair-case, and she instantly remembered the odd circumstance of the door having been fastened, during the preceding night, by some unknown hand. Her late alarming suspicion, concerning its communication, also occurred to her. Her heart became faint with terror. Half raising herself from the bed, and gently drawing aside the curtain, she looked towards the door of the stair-case, but the lamp, that burnt on the hearth, spread so feeble a light through the apartment, that the remote parts of it were lost in shadow. The noise, however, which, she was convinced, came from the door, continued. It seemed like that made by the undrawing of rusty bolts, and often ceased, and was then renewed more gently, as if the hand, that occasioned it, was restrained by a fear of discovery. While Emily kept her eyes fixed on the spot, she saw the door move, and then slowly open, and perceived something enter the room, but the extreme duskiness prevented her distinguishing what it was. Almost fainting with terror, she had yet sufficient command over herself, to check the shriek, that was escaping from her lips, and, letting the curtain drop from her hand, continued to observe in silence the motions of the mysterious form she saw. It seemed to glide along the remote obscurity of the apartment, then paused, and, as it approached the hearth, she perceived, in the stronger light, what appeared to be a human figure. Certain remembrances now struck upon her heart, and almost subdued the feeble remains of her spirits; she continued, however, to watch the figure, which remained for some time motionless, but then, advancing slowly towards the bed, stood silently at the feet, where the curtains, being a little open, allowed her still to see it; terror, however, had now deprived her of the power of discrimination, as well as of that of utterance.

Having continued there a moment, the form retreated towards the hearth, when it took the lamp, held it up, surveyed the chamber, for a few moments, and then again advanced towards the bed. The light at that instant awakening the dog, that had slept at Emily's feet, he barked loudly, and, jumping to the floor, flew at the stranger, who struck the animal smartly with a sheathed sword, and, springing towards the bed, Emily discovered—Count Morano!

She gazed at him for a moment in speechless affright, while he, throwing himself on his knee at the bed-side, besought her to fear nothing, and, having thrown down his sword, would have taken her hand, when the faculties, that terror had suspended, suddenly returned, and she sprung from the bed, in the dress, which surely a kind of prophetic apprehension had prevented her, on this night, from throwing aside.

Morano rose, followed her to the door, through which he had entered, and caught her hand, as she reached the top of the stair-case, but not before she had discovered, by the gleam of a lamp, another man half-way down the steps. She now screamed in despair, and, believing herself given up by Montoni, saw, indeed, no possibility of escape.

The Count, who still held her hand, led her back into the chamber.

"Why all this terror?" said he, in a tremulous voice. "Hear me, Emily: I come not to alarm you; no, by Heaven! I love you too well—too well for my own peace."

Emily looked at him for a moment, in fearful doubt.

"Then leave me, sir," said she, "leave me instantly."

"Hear me, Emily," resumed Morano, "hear me! I love, and am in despair—yes—in despair. How can I gaze upon you, and know, that it is, perhaps, for the last time, without suffering all the phrensy of despair? But it shall not be so; you shall be mine, in spite of Montoni and all his villany."

"In spite of Montoni!" cried Emily eagerly: "what is it I hear?"

"You hear, that Montoni is a villain," exclaimed Morano with vehemence,—"a villain who would have sold you to my love!—Who——"

"And is he less, who would have bought me?" said Emily, fixing on the Count an eye of calm contempt. "Leave the room, sir, instantly," she continued in a voice, trembling between joy and fear, "or I will alarm the family, and you may receive that from Signor Montoni's vengeance, which I have vainly supplicated from his pity." But Emily knew, that she was beyond the hearing of those, who might protect her.

"You can never hope any thing from his pity," said Morano, "he has used me infamously, and my vengeance shall pursue him. And for you, Emily, for you, he has new plans more profitable than the last, no doubt." The gleam of hope, which the Count's former speech had revived, was now nearly extinguished by the latter; and, while Emily's countenance betrayed the emotions of her mind, he endeavoured to take advantage of the discovery.

"I lose time," said he: "I came not to exclaim against Montoni; I came to solicit, to plead—to Emily; to tell her all I suffer, to entreat her to save me from despair, and herself from destruction. Emily! the schemes of Montoni are insearchable, but, I warn you, they are terrible; he has no principle, when interest, or ambition leads. Can I love you, and abandon you to his power? Fly, then, fly from this gloomy prison, with a lover, who adores you! I have bribed a servant of the castle to open the gates, and, before tomorrow's dawn, you shall be far on the way to Venice."

Emily, overcome by the sudden shock she had received, at the moment, too, when she had begun to hope for better days, now thought she saw destruction surround her on every side. Unable to reply, and almost to think, she threw herself into a chair, pale and breathless. That Montoni had formerly sold her to Morano, was very probable; that he had now withdrawn his consent to the marriage, was evident from the Count's present conduct; and it was nearly certain, that a scheme of stronger interest only could have induced the selfish Montoni to forego a plan, which he had hitherto so strenuously pursued. These reflections made her tremble at the hints, which Morano had just given, which she no longer hesitated to believe; and, while she shrunk from the new scenes of misery and oppression, that might await her in the castle of Udolpho, she was compelled to observe, that almost her only means of escaping them was by submitting herself to the protection of this man, with whom evils more certain and not less terrible appeared,—evils, upon which she could not endure to pause for an instant.

Her silence, though it was that of agony, encouraged the hopes of Morano, who watched her countenance with impatience, took again the resisting hand she had withdrawn, and, as he pressed it to his heart, again conjured her to determine immediately. "Every moment we lose, will make our departure more dangerous," said he: "these few moments lost may enable Montoni to overtake us."

"I beseech you, sir, be silent," said Emily faintly: "I am indeed very wretched, and wretched I must remain. Leave me—I command you, leave me to my fate."

"Never!" cried the Count vehemently: "let me perish first! But forgive my violence! the thought of losing you is madness. You cannot be ignorant of Montoni's character, you may be ignorant of his schemes—nay, you must be so, or you would not hesitate between my love and his power."

"Nor do I hesitate," said Emily.

"Let us go, then," said Morano, eagerly kissing her hand, and rising, "my carriage waits, below the castle walls."

"You mistake me, sir," said Emily. "Allow me to thank you for the interest you express in my welfare, and to decide by my own choice. I shall remain under the protection of Signor Montoni."

"Under his protection!" exclaimed Morano, proudly, "his *protection!* Emily, why will you suffer yourself to be thus deluded? I have already told you what you have to expect from his *protection.*"

"And pardon me, sir, if, in this instance, I doubt mere assertion, and, to be convinced, require something approaching to proof."

"I have now neither the time, or the means of adducing proof," replied the Count.

"Nor have I, sir, the inclination to listen to it, if you had."

"But you trifle with my patience and my distress," continued Morano. "Is a marriage with a man, who adores you, so very terrible in your eyes, that you would prefer to it all the misery, to which Montoni may condemn you in this remote prison? Some wretch must have stolen those affections, which ought to be mine, or you would not thus obstinately persist in refusing an offer, that would place you beyond the reach of oppression." Morano walked about the room, with quick steps, and a disturbed air.

"This discourse, Count Morano, sufficiently proves, that my affections ought not to be yours," said Emily, mildly, "and this conduct, that I should not be placed beyond the reach of oppression, so long as I remained in your power. If you wish me to believe otherwise, cease to oppress me any longer by your presence. If you refuse this, you will compel me to expose you to the resentment of Signor Montoni."

"Yes, let him come," cried Morano furiously, "and brave *my* resentment! Let him dare to face once more the man he has so courageously injured; danger shall teach him morality, and vengeance justice—let him come, and receive my sword in his heart!"

The vehemence, with which this was uttered, gave Emily new cause of alarm, who arose from her chair, but her trembling frame refused to support her, and she resumed her seat;—the words died on her lips, and, when she looked wistfully towards the door of the corridor, which was locked, she considered it was impossible for her to leave the apartment, before Morano would be apprised of, and able to counteract, her intention.

Without observing her agitation, he continued to pace the room in the utmost perturbation of spirits. His darkened countenance expressed all the rage of jealousy and revenge; and a person, who had seen his features under the smile of ineffable tenderness, which he so lately assumed, would now scarcely have believed them to be the same.

"Count Morano," said Emily, at length recovering her voice, "calm, I entreat you, these transports, and listen to reason, if you will not to pity. You have equally misplaced your love, and your hatred.—I never could have returned the affection, with which you honour me, and certainly have never encouraged it; neither has Signor Montoni injured you, for you must have known, that he had no right to dispose of my hand, had he even possessed the power to do so. Leave, then, leave the castle, while you may with safety. Spare yourself the dreadful consequences of an unjust revenge, and the remorse of having prolonged to me these moments of suffering."

"Is it for mine, or for Montoni's safety, that you are thus alarmed?" said Morano, coldly, and turning towards her with a look of acrimony.

"For both," replied Emily, in a trembling voice.

"Unjust revenge!" cried the Count, resuming the abrupt tones of passion. "Who, that looks upon that face, can imagine a punishment adequate to the injury he would have done me? Yes, I will leave the castle; but it shall not be alone. I have trifled too long. Since my prayers and my sufferings cannot prevail, force shall. I have people in waiting, who shall convey you to my carriage. Your voice will bring no succour; it cannot be heard from this remote part of the castle; submit, therefore, in silence, to go with me."

This was an unnecessary injunction, at present; for Emily was too certain, that her call would avail her nothing; and terror had so entirely disordered her thoughts, that she knew not how to plead to Morano, but sat, mute and trembling, in her chair, till he advanced to lift her from it, when she suddenly raised herself, and, with a repulsive gesture, and a countenance of forced serenity, said, "Count Morano! I am now in your power; but you will observe, that this is not the conduct which can win the esteem you appear so solicitous to obtain, and that you are preparing for yourself a load of remorse, in the miseries of a friendless orphan, which can never leave you. Do you believe your heart to be, indeed, so hardened, that you can look without emotion on the suffering, to which you would condemn me?"——

Emily was interrupted by the growling of the dog, who now came again from the bed, and Morano looked towards the door of the staircase, where no person appearing, he called aloud, "Cesario!"

"Emily," said the Count, "why will you reduce me to adopt this conduct? How much more willingly would I persuade, than compel you to become my wife! but, by Heaven! I will not leave you to be sold by Montoni. Yet a thought glances across my mind, that brings madness with it. I know not how to name it. It is preposterous—it cannot be.— Yet you tremble—you grow pale! It is! it is so;—you—you—love Montoni!" cried Morano, grasping Emily's wrist, and stamping his foot on the floor.

An involuntary air of surprise appeared on her countenance. "If you have indeed believed so," said she, "believe so still."

"That look, those words confirm it," exclaimed Morano, furiously. "No, no, no, Montoni had a richer prize in view, than gold. But he shall not live to triumph over me!—This very instant——"

He was interrupted by the loud barking of the dog.

"Stay, Count Morano," said Emily, terrified by his words, and by the fury expressed in his eyes, "I will save you from this error.—Of all men, Signor Montoni is not your rival; though, if I find all other means of saving myself vain, I will try whether my voice may not arouse his servants to my succour."

"Assertion," replied Morano, "at such a moment, is not to be depended upon. How could I suffer myself to doubt, even for an instant, that he could see you, and not love?—But my first care shall be to convey you from the castle. Cesario! ho,—Cesario!"

A man now appeared at the door of the stair-case, and other steps were heard ascending. Emily uttered a loud shriek, as Morano hurried her across the chamber, and, at the same moment, she heard a noise at the door, that opened upon the corridor. The Count paused an instant, as if his mind was suspended between love and the desire of vengeance; and, in that instant, the door gave way, and Montoni, followed by the old steward and several other persons, burst into the room.

"Draw!" cried Montoni to the Count, who did not pause for a second bidding, but, giving Emily into the hands of the people, that appeared from the stair-case, turned fiercely round. "This in thine heart, villain!" said he, as he made a thrust at Montoni with his sword, who parried the blow, and aimed another, while some of the persons, who had followed him into the room, endeavoured to part the combatants, and others rescued Emily from the hands of Morano's servants.

"Was it for this, Count Morano," said Montoni, in a cool sarcastic tone of voice, "that I received you under my roof, and permitted you, though my declared enemy, to remain under it for the night? Was it, that you might repay my hospitality with the treachery of a fiend, and rob me of my niece?"

"Who talks of treachery?" said Morano, in a tone of unrestrained vehemence. "Let him that does, shew an unblushing face of innocence. Montoni, you are a villain! If there is treachery in this affair, look to yourself as the author of it. *If*—do I say? *I*—whom you have wronged with unexampled baseness, whom you have injured almost beyond redress! But why do I use words?—Come on, coward, and receive justice at my hands!"

"Coward!" cried Montoni, bursting from the people who held him, and rushing on the Count, when they both retreated into the corridor, where the fight continued so desperately, that none of the spectators dared approach them, Montoni swearing, that the first who interfered, should fall by his sword.

Jealousy and revenge lent all their fury to Morano, while the superior skill and the temperance of Montoni enabled him to wound his adversary, whom his servants now attempted to seize, but he would not be restrained, and, regardless of his wound, continued to fight. He seemed to be insensible both of pain and loss of blood, and alive only to the energy of his passions. Montoni, on the contrary, persevered in the combat, with a fierce, yet wary, valour; he received the point of Morano's sword on his arm, but, almost in the same instant, severely wounded and disarmed him. The Count then fell back into the arms of his servant, while Montoni held his sword over him, and bade him ask his life. Morano, sinking under the anguish of his wound, had scarcely replied by a gesture, and by a few words, feebly articulated, that he would not—when he fainted; and Montoni was then going to have plunged the sword into his breast, as he lay senseless, but his arm was arrested by Cavigni. To the interruption he yielded without much difficulty, but his complexion changed almost to blackness, as he looked upon his fallen adversary, and ordered, that he should be carried instantly from the castle.

In the mean time, Emily, who had been with-held from leaving the chamber during the affray, now came forward into the corridor, and pleaded a cause of common humanity, with the feelings of the warmest benevolence, when she entreated Montoni to allow Morano the assistance in the castle, which his situation required. But Montoni, who had seldom listened to pity, now seemed rapacious of vengeance, and, with a monster's cruelty, again ordered his defeated enemy to be taken from the castle, in his present state, though there were only the woods, or a solitary neighbouring cottage, to shelter him from the night.

The Count's servants having declared, that they would not move him till he revived, Montoni's stood inactive, Cavigni remonstrating, and Emily, superior to Montoni's menaces, giving water to Morano, and directing the attendants to bind up his wound. At length, Montoni had leisure to feel pain from his own hurt, and he withdrew to examine it.

The Count, meanwhile, having slowly recovered, the first object he saw, on raising his eyes, was Emily, bending over him with a countenance strongly expressive of solicitude. He surveyed her with a look of anguish.

"I have deserved this," said he, "but not from Montoni. It is from you, Emily, that I have deserved punishment, yet I receive only pity!" He paused, for he had spoken with difficulty. After a moment, he proceeded. "I must resign you, but not to Montoni. Forgive me the sufferings I have already occasioned you! But for *that* villain—his infamy shall not go unpunished. Carry me from this place," said he to his servants. "I am in no condition to travel: you must, therefore, take me to the nearest cottage, for I will not pass the night under his roof, although I may expire on the way from it."

Cesario proposed to go out, and enquire for a cottage, that might receive his master, before he attempted to remove him: but Morano was impatient to be gone; the anguish of his mind seemed to be even greater than that of his wound, and he rejected, with disdain, the offer of Cavigni to entreat Montoni, that he might be suffered to pass the night in the castle. Cesario was now going to call up the carriage to the great gate, but the Count forbade him. "I cannot bear the motion of a carriage," said he: "call some others of my people, that they may assist in bearing me in their arms."

At length, however, Morano submitted to reason, and consented, that Cesario should first prepare some cottage to receive him. Emily, now that he had recovered his senses, was about to withdraw from the corridor, when a message from Montoni commanded her to do so, and also that the Count, if he was not already gone, should quit the castle immediately. Indignation flashed from Morano's eyes, and flushed his cheeks.

"Tell Montoni," said he, "that I shall go when it suits my own convenience; that I quit the castle, he dares to call his, as I would the nest of a serpent, and that this is not the last he shall hear from me. Tell him, I will not leave *another* murder on his conscience, if I can help it."

"Count Morano! do you know what you say?" said Cavigni.

"Yes, Signor, I know well what I say, and he will understand well what I mean. His conscience will assist his understanding, on this occasion."

"Count Morano," said Verezzi, who had hitherto silently observed him, "dare again to insult my friend, and I will plunge this sword in your body."

"It would be an action worthy the friend of a villain!" said Morano, as the strong impulse of his indignation enabled him to raise himself from the arms of his servants; but the energy was momentary, and he sunk back, exhausted by the effort. Montoni's people, meanwhile, held Verezzi, who seemed inclined, even in this instant, to execute his threat; and Cavigni, who was not so depraved as to abet the cowardly malignity of Verezzi, endeavoured to withdraw him from the corridor; and Emily, whom a compassionate interest had thus long detained, was now quitting it in new terror, when the supplicating voice of Morano arrested her, and, by a feeble gesture, he beckoned her to draw nearer. She advanced with timid steps, but the fainting languor of his countenance again awakened her pity, and overcame her terror.

"I am going from hence for ever," said he: "perhaps, I shall never see you again. I would carry with me your forgiveness, Emily; nay more — I would also carry your good wishes."

"You have my forgiveness, then," said Emily, "and my sincere wishes for your recovery."

"And only for my recovery?" said Morano, with a sigh. "For your general welfare," added Emily.

"Perhaps I ought to be contented with this," he resumed; "I certainly have not deserved more; but I would ask you, Emily, sometimes to think of me, and, forgetting my offence, to remember only the passion which occasioned it. I would ask, alas! impossibilities: I would ask you to love me! At this moment, when I am about to part with you, and that, perhaps, for ever, I am scarcely myself. Emily—may you never know the torture of a passion like mine! What do I say? O, that, for me, you might be sensible of such a passion!"

Emily looked impatient to be gone. "I entreat you, Count, to consult your own safety," said she, "and linger here no longer. I tremble for the consequences of Signor Verezzi's passion, and of Montoni's resentment, should he learn that you are still here."

Morano's face was overspread with a momentary crimson, his eyes sparkled, but he seemed endeavouring to conquer his emotion, and replied in a calm voice, "Since you are interested for my safety, I will regard it, and be gone. But, before I go, let me again hear you say, that you wish me well," said he, fixing on her an earnest and mournful look.

Emily repeated her assurances. He took her hand, which she scarcely attempted to withdraw, and put it to his lips. "Farewell, Count Morano!" said Emily; and she turned to go, when a second message arrived from Montoni, and she again conjured Morano, as he valued his life, to quit the castle immediately. He regarded her in silence, with a look of fixed despair. But she had no time to enforce her compassionate entreaties, and, not daring to disobey the second command of Montoni, she left the corridor, to attend him.

He was in the cedar parlour, that adjoined the great hall, laid upon a couch, and suffering a degree of anguish from his wound, which few persons could have disguised, as he did. His countenance, which was stern, but calm, expressed the dark passion of revenge, but no symptom of pain; bodily pain, indeed, he had always despised, and had yielded only to the strong and terrible energies of the soul. He was attended by old Carlo and by Signor Bertolini, but Madame Montoni was not with him.

Emily trembled, as she approached and received his severe rebuke, for not having obeyed his first summons; and perceived, also, that he attributed her stay in the corridor to a motive, that had not even occurred to her artless mind.

"This is an instance of female caprice," said he, "which I ought to have foreseen. Count Morano, whose suit you obstinately rejected, so long as it was countenanced by me, you favour, it seems, since you find I have dismissed him."

Emily looked astonished. "I do not comprehend you, sir," said she: "You certainly do not mean to imply, that the design of the Count to visit the double-chamber, was founded upon any approbation of mine."

"To that I reply nothing," said Montoni; "but it must certainly be a more than common interest, that made you plead so warmly in his cause, and that could detain you thus long in his presence, contrary to my express order—in the presence of a man, whom you have hitherto, on all occasions, most scrupulously shunned!"

"I fear, sir, it was a more than common interest, that detained me," said Emily calmly; "for of late I have been inclined to think, that of compassion is an uncommon one. But how could I, could *you*, sir, witness Count Morano's deplorable condition, and not wish to relieve it?"

"You add hypocrisy to caprice," said Montoni, frowning, "and an attempt at satire, to both; but, before you undertake to regulate the morals of other persons, you should learn and practise the virtues, which are indispensable to a woman—sincerity, uniformity of conduct and obedience."

Emily, who had always endeavoured to regulate her conduct by the nicest laws, and whose mind was finely sensible, not only of what is just in morals, but of whatever is beautiful in the female character, was shocked by these words; yet, in the next moment, her heart swelled with the consciousness of having deserved praise, instead of censure, and she was proudly silent. Montoni, acquainted with the delicacy of her mind, knew how keenly she would feel his rebuke; but he was a stranger to the luxury of conscious worth, and, therefore, did not foresee the energy of that sentiment, which now repelled his satire. Turning to a servant who had lately entered the room, he asked whether Morano had quitted the castle. The man answered, that his servants were then removing him, on a couch, to a neighbouring cottage. Montoni seemed somewhat appeased, on hearing this; and, when Ludovico appeared, a few moments after, and said, that Morano was gone, he told Emily she might retire to her apartment.

She withdrew willingly from his presence; but the thought of passing the remainder of the night in a chamber, which the door from the staircase made liable to the intrusion of any person, now alarmed her more than ever, and she determined to call at Madame Montoni's room, and request, that Annette might be permitted to be with her.

On reaching the great gallery, she heard voices seemingly in dispute, and, her spirits now apt to take alarm, she paused, but soon distinguished some words of Cavigni and Verezzi, and went towards them, in the hope of conciliating their difference. They were alone. Verezzi's face was still flushed with rage; and, as the first object of it was now removed from him, he appeared willing to transfer his resentment to Cavigni, who seemed to be expostulating, rather than disputing, with him.

Verezzi was protesting, that he would instantly inform Montoni of the insult, which Morano had thrown out against him, and above all, that, wherein he had accused him of murder.

"There is no answering," said Cavigni, "for the words of a man in a passion; little serious regard ought to be paid to them. If you persist in your resolution, the consequences may be fatal to both. We have now more serious interests to pursue, than those of a petty revenge."

Emily joined her entreaties to Cavigni's arguments, and they, at length, prevailed so far, as that Verezzi consented to retire, without seeing Montoni.

On calling at her aunt's apartment, she found it fastened. In a few minutes, however, it was opened by Madame Montoni herself.

It may be remembered, that it was by a door leading into the bedroom from a back passage, that Emily had secretly entered a few hours preceding. She now conjectured, by the calmness of Madame Montoni's air, that she was not apprised of the accident, which had befallen her husband, and was beginning to inform her of it, in the tenderest manner she could, when her aunt interrupted her, by saying, she was acquainted with the whole affair.

Emily knew indeed, that she had little reason to love Montoni, but could scarcely have believed her capable of such perfect apathy, as she now discovered towards him; having obtained permission, however, for Annette to sleep in her chamber, she went thither immediately.

A track of blood appeared along the corridor, leading to it; and on the spot, where the Count and Montoni had fought, the whole floor was stained. Emily shuddered, and leaned on Annette, as she passed. When she reached her apartment, she instantly determined, since the door of the stair-case had been left open, and that Annette was now with her, to explore whither it led,—a circumstance now materially connected with her own safety. Annette accordingly, half curious and half afraid, proposed to descend the stairs; but, on approaching the door, they perceived, that it was already fastened without, and their care was then directed to the securing it on the inside also, by placing against it as much of the heavy furniture of the room, as they could lift. Emily then retired to bed, and Annette continued on a chair by the hearth, where some feeble embers remained.

CHAPTER VII

Of aery tongues, that syllable men's names
On sands and shores and desert wildernesses.
                                        MILTON

IT is now necessary to mention some circumstances, which could not be related amidst the events of Emily's hasty departure from Venice, or together with those, which so rapidly succeeded to her arrival in the castle.

On the morning of her journey, Count Morano had gone at the appointed hour to the mansion of Montoni, to demand his bride. When he reached it, he was somewhat surprised by the silence and solitary air of the portico, where Montoni's lacqueys usually loitered; but surprise was soon changed to astonishment, and astonishment to the rage of disappointment, when the door was opened by an old woman, who told his servants, that her master and his family had left Venice, early in the morning, for *Terra-firma*. Scarcely believing what his servants told, he left his gondola, and rushed into the hall to enquire further. The old woman, who was the only person left in care of the mansion, persisted in her story, which the silent and deserted apartments soon convinced him was no fiction. He then seized her with a menacing air, as if he meant to wreak all his vengeance upon her, at the same time asking her twenty questions in a breath, and all these with a gesticulation so furious, that she was deprived of the power of answering them; then suddenly letting her go, he stamped about the hall, like a madman, cursing Montoni and his own folly.

When the good woman was at liberty, and had somewhat recovered from her fright, she told him all she knew of the affair, which was, indeed, very little, but enough to enable Morano to discover, that Montoni was gone to his castle on the Apennine. Thither he followed, as soon as his servants could complete the necessary preparation for the journey, accompanied by a friend, and attended by a number of his people, determined to obtain Emily, or a full revenge on Montoni. When his mind had recovered from the first effervescence of rage, and his thoughts became less obscured, his conscience hinted to him certain circumstances, which, in some measure, explained the conduct of Montoni: but how the latter could have been led to suspect an intention, which, he had believed, was known only to himself, he could not even guess. On this occasion, however, he had been partly betrayed by that sympathetic intelligence, which may be said to exist between bad minds, and which teaches one man to judge what another will do in the same circumstances. Thus it was with Montoni, who had now

The Mysteries of Udolpho

received indisputable proof of a truth, which he had some time suspected—that Morano's circumstances, instead of being affluent, as he
had been bidden to believe, were greatly involved. Montoni had been
interested in his suit, by motives entirely selfish, those of avarice and
pride; the last of which would have been gratified by an alliance with
a Venetian nobleman, the former by Emily's estate in Gascony, which
he had stipulated, as the price of his favour, should be delivered up to
him from the day of her marriage. In the meantime, he had been led
to suspect the consequence of the Count's boundless extravagance; but
it was not till the evening, preceding the intended nuptials, that he
obtained certain information of his distressed circumstances. He did
not hesitate then to infer, that Morano designed to defraud him of
Emily's estate; and in this supposition he was confirmed, and with
apparent reason, by the subsequent conduct of the Count, who, after
having appointed to meet him on that night, for the purpose of signing
the instrument, which was to secure to him his reward, failed in his
engagement. Such a circumstance, indeed, in a man of Morano's gay
and thoughtless character, and at a time when his mind was engaged
by the bustle of preparation for his nuptials, might have been attributed
to a cause less decisive, than design; but Montoni did not hesitate an
instant to interpret it his own way, and, after vainly waiting the Count's
arrival, for several hours, he gave orders for his people to be in readiness to set off at a moment's notice. By hastening to Udolpho he
intended to remove Emily from the reach of Morano, as well as to
break off the affair, without submitting himself to useless altercation:
and, if the Count meant what he called honourably, he would doubtless follow Emily, and sign the writings in question. If this was done, so
little consideration had Montoni for her welfare, that he would not
have scrupled to sacrifice her to a man of ruined fortune, since by that
means he could enrich himself; and he forbore to mention to her the
motive of his sudden journey, lest the hope it might revive should render her more intractable, when submission would be required.

With these considerations, he had left Venice; and, with others
totally different, Morano had, soon after, pursued his steps across the
rugged Apennines. When his arrival was announced at the castle,
Montoni did not believe, that he would have presumed to shew himself, unless he had meant to fulfil his engagement, and he, therefore,
readily admitted him; but the enraged countenance and expressions of
Morano, as he entered the apartment, instantly undeceived him; and,
when Montoni had explained, in part, the motives of his abrupt departure from Venice, the Count still persisted in demanding Emily, and
reproaching Montoni, without even naming the former stipulation.

Montoni, at length, weary of the dispute, deferred the settling of it till the morrow, and Morano retired with some hope, suggested by Montoni's apparent indecision. When, however, in the silence of his own apartment, he began to consider the past conversation, the character of Montoni, and some former instances of his duplicity, the hope, which he had admitted, vanished, and he determined not to neglect the present possibility of obtaining Emily by other means. To his confidential valet he told his design of carrying away Emily, and sent him back to Montoni's servants to find out one among them, who might enable him to execute it. The choice of this person he entrusted to the fellow's own discernment, and not imprudently; for he discovered a man, whom Montoni had, on some former occasion, treated harshly, and who was now ready to betray him. This man conducted Cesario round the castle, through a private passage, to the stair-case, that led to Emily's chamber; then shewed him a short way out of the building, and afterwards procured him the keys, that would secure his retreat. The man was well rewarded for his trouble; how the Count was rewarded for his treachery, had already appeared.

Meanwhile, old Carlo had overheard two of Morano's servants, who had been ordered to be in waiting with the carriage, beyond the castle walls, expressing their surprise at their master's sudden, and secret departure, for the valet had entrusted them with no more of Morano's designs, than it was necessary for them to execute. They, however, indulged themselves in surmises, and in expressing them to each other; and from these Carlo had drawn a just conclusion. But, before he ventured to disclose his apprehensions to Montoni, he endeavoured to obtain further confirmation of them, and, for this purpose, placed himself, with one of his fellow-servants, at the door of Emily's apartment, that opened upon the corridor. He did not watch long in vain, though the growling of the dog had once nearly betrayed him. When he was convinced, that Morano was in the room, and had listened long enough to his conversation, to understand his scheme, he immediately alarmed Montoni, and thus rescued Emily from the designs of the Count.

Montoni, on the following morning, appeared as usual, except that he wore his wounded arm in a sling; he went out upon the ramparts; overlooked the men employed in repairing them; gave orders for additional workmen, and then came into the castle to give audience to several persons, who were just arrived, and who were shewn into a private apartment, where he communicated with them, for near an hour. Carlo was then summoned, and ordered to conduct the strangers to a part of the castle, which, in former times, had been occupied by the upper servants of the family, and to provide them with every necessary refreshment. ——When he had done this, he was bidden to return to his master.

Meanwhile, the Count remained in a cottage in the skirts of the woods below, suffering under bodily and mental pain, and meditating deep revenge against Montoni. His servant, whom he had dispatched for a surgeon to the nearest town, which was, however, at a considerable distance, did not return till the following day, when, his wounds being examined and dressed, the practitioner refused to deliver any positive opinion, concerning the degree of danger attending them; but giving his patient a composing draught and ordering him to be quiet, remained at the cottage to watch the event.

Emily, for the remainder of the late eventful night, had been suffered to sleep, undisturbed; and, when her mind recovered from the confusion of slumber, and she remembered, that she was now released from the addresses of Count Morano, her spirits were suddenly relieved from a part of the terrible anxiety, that had long oppressed them; that which remained, arose chiefly from a recollection of Morano's assertions, concerning the schemes of Montoni. He had said, that plans of the latter, concerning Emily, were insearchable, yet that he knew them to be terrible. At the time he uttered this, she almost believed it to be designed for the purpose of prevailing with her to throw herself into his protection, and she still thought it might be chiefly so accounted for; but his assertions had left an impression on her mind, which a consideration of the character and former conduct of Montoni did not contribute to efface. She, however, checked her propensity to anticipate evil; and, determined to enjoy this respite from actual misfortune, tried to dismiss thought, took her instruments for drawing, and placed herself at a window, to select into a landscape some features of the scenery without.

As she was thus employed, she saw, walking on the rampart below, the men, who had so lately arrived at the castle. The sight of strangers surprised her, but still more, of strangers such as these. There was a singularity in their dress, and a certain fierceness in their air, that fixed all her attention. She withdrew from the casement, while they passed, but soon returned to observe them further. Their figures seemed so well suited to the wildness of the surrounding objects, that, as they stood surveying the castle, she sketched them for banditti, amid the mountain-view of her picture, when she had finished which, she was surprised to observe the spirit of her group. But she had copied from nature.

Carlo, when he had placed refreshment before these men in the apartment assigned to them, returned, as he was ordered, to Montoni, who was anxious to discover by what servant the keys of the castle had been delivered to Morano, on the preceding night. But this man, though he was too faithful to his master quietly to see him injured, would not betray a fellow-servant even to justice; he, therefore, pretended to be ignorant who it was, that had conspired with Count Morano, and related, as before, that he had only overheard some of the strangers describing the plot.

Montoni's suspicions naturally fell upon the porter, whom he ordered now to attend. Carlo hesitated, and then with slow steps went to seek him.

Barnardine, the porter, denied the accusation with a countenance so steady and undaunted, that Montoni could scarcely believe him guilty, though he knew not how to think him innocent. At length, the man was dismissed from his presence, and, though the real offender, escaped detection.

Montoni then went to his wife's apartment, whither Emily followed soon after, but, finding them in high dispute, was instantly leaving the room, when her aunt called her back, and desired her to stay. — "You shall be a witness," said she, "of my opposition. Now, sir, repeat the command, I have so often refused to obey."

Montoni turned, with a stern countenance, to Emily, and bade her quit the apartment, while his wife persisted in desiring, that she would stay. Emily was eager to escape from this scene of contention, and anxious, also, to serve her aunt; but she despaired of conciliating Montoni, in whose eyes the rising tempest of his soul flashed terribly.

"Leave the room," said he, in a voice of thunder. Emily obeyed, and, walking down to the rampart, which the strangers had now left, continued to meditate on the unhappy marriage of her father's sister, and on her own desolate situation, occasioned by the ridiculous imprudence of her, whom she had always wished to respect and love. Madame Montoni's conduct had, indeed, rendered it impossible for Emily to do either; but her gentle heart was touched by her distress, and, in the pity thus awakened, she forgot the injurious treatment she had received from her.

As she sauntered on the rampart, Annette appeared at the hall door, looked cautiously round, and then advanced to meet her.

"Dear ma'amselle, I have been looking for you all over the castle," said she. "If you will step this way, I will shew you a picture."

"A picture!" exclaimed Emily, and shuddered.

"Yes, ma'am, a picture of the late lady of this place. Old Carlo just now told me it was her, and I thought you would be curious to see it. As to my lady, you know, ma'amselle, one cannot talk about such things to her." ——

"And so," said Emily smilingly, "as you must talk of them to somebody——"

"Why, yes, ma'amselle; what can one do in such a place as this, if one must not talk? If I was in a dungeon, if they would let me talk—it would be some comfort; nay, I would talk, if it was only to the walls. But come, ma'amselle, we lose time—let me shew you to the picture."

"Is it veiled?" said Emily, pausing.

"Dear ma'amselle!" said Annette, fixing her eyes on Emily's face, "what makes you look so pale?—are you ill?"

"No, Annette, I am well enough, but I have no desire to see this picture; return into the hall."

"What! ma'am, not to see the lady of this castle?" said the girl—"the lady, who disappeared so strangely? Well! now, I would have run to the furthest mountain we can see, yonder, to have got a sight of such a picture; and, to speak my mind, that strange story is all, that makes me care about this old castle, though it makes me thrill all over, as it were, whenever I think of it."

"Yes, Annette, you love the wonderful; but do you know, that, unless you guard against this inclination, it will lead you into all the misery of superstition?"

Annette might have smiled in her turn, at this sage observation of Emily, who could tremble with ideal terrors, as much as herself, and listen almost as eagerly to the recital of a mysterious story. Annette urged her request.

"Are you sure it is a picture?" said Emily, "Have you seen it?—Is it veiled?"

"Holy Maria! ma'amselle, yes, no, yes. I am sure it is a picture—I have seen it, and it is not veiled!"

The tone and look of surprise, with which this was uttered, recalled Emily's prudence; who concealed her emotion under a smile, and bade Annette lead her to the picture. It was in an obscure chamber, adjoining that part of the castle, allotted to the servants. Several other portraits hung on the walls, covered, like this, with dust and cobweb.

"That is it, ma'amselle," said Annette, in a low voice, and pointing. Emily advanced, and surveyed the picture. It represented a lady in the flower of youth and beauty; her features were handsome and noble, full of strong expression, but had little of the captivating sweetness, that Emily had looked for, and still less of the pensive mildness she loved. It was a countenance, which spoke the language of passion, rather than that of sentiment; a haughty impatience of misfortune—not the placid melancholy of a spirit injured, yet resigned.

"How many years have passed, since this lady disappeared, Annette?" said Emily.

"Twenty years, ma'amselle, or thereabout, as they tell me; I know it is a long while ago." Emily continued to gaze upon the portrait.

"I think," resumed Annette, "the Signor would do well to hang it in a better place, than this old chamber. Now, in my mind, he ought to place the picture of a lady, who gave him all these riches, in the handsomest room in the castle. But he may have good reasons for what he does: and some people do say that he has lost his riches, as well as his gratitude. But hush, ma'am, not a word!" added Annette, laying her finger on her lips. Emily was too much absorbed in thought, to hear what she said.

"'Tis a handsome lady, I am sure," continued Annette: "the Signor need not be ashamed to put her in the great apartment, where the veiled picture hangs." Emily turned round. "But for that matter, she would be as little seen there, as here, for the door is always locked, I find."

"Let us leave this chamber," said Emily: "and let me caution you again, Annette; be guarded in your conversation, and never tell, that you know any thing of that picture."

"Holy Mother!" exclaimed Annette, "it is no secret; why all the servants have seen it already!"

Emily started. "How is this?" said she—"Have seen it! When?—how?"

"Dear, ma'amselle, there is nothing surprising in that; we had all a little more *curiousness* than you had."

"I thought you told me, the door was kept locked?" said Emily.

"If that was the case, ma'amselle," replied Annette, looking about her, "how could we get here?"

"Oh, you mean *this* picture," said Emily, with returning calmness. "Well, Annette, here is nothing more to engage my attention; we will go."

Emily, as she passed to her own apartment, saw Montoni go down to the hall, and she turned into her aunt's dressing-room, whom she found weeping and alone, grief and resentment struggling on her countenance. Pride had hitherto restrained complaint. Judging of Emily's disposition from her own, and from a consciousness of what her treatment of her deserved, she had believed, that her griefs would be cause of triumph to her niece, rather than of sympathy; that she would despise, not pity her. But she knew not the tenderness and benevolence of Emily's heart, that had always taught her to forget her own injuries in the misfortunes of her enemy. The sufferings of others, whoever they might be, called forth her ready compassion, which dissipated at once every obscuring cloud to goodness, that passion or prejudice might have raised in her mind.

Madame Montoni's sufferings, at length, rose above her pride, and, when Emily had before entered the room, she would have told them all, had not her husband prevented her; now that she was no longer restrained by his presence, she poured forth all her complaints to her niece.

"O Emily!" she exclaimed, "I am the most wretched of women—I am indeed cruelly treated! Who, with my prospects of happiness, could have foreseen such a wretched fate as this?—who could have thought, when I married such a man as the Signor, I should ever have to bewail my lot? But there is no judging what is for the best—there is no knowing what is for our good! The most flattering prospects often change—the best judgments may be deceived—who could have foreseen, when I married the Signor, that I should ever repent my *generosity*?"

Emily thought she might have foreseen it, but this was not a thought of triumph. She placed herself in a chair near her aunt, took her hand, and, with one of those looks of soft compassion, which might characterize the countenance of a guardian angel, spoke to her in the tenderest accents. But these did not soothe Madame Montoni, whom impatience to talk made unwilling to listen. She wanted to complain, not to be consoled; and it was by exclamations of complaint only, that Emily learned the particular circumstances of her affliction.

"Ungrateful man!" said Madame Montoni, "he has deceived me in every respect; and now he has taken me from my country and friends, to shut me up in this old castle; and, here he thinks he can compel me to do whatever he designs! But he shall find himself mistaken, he shall find that no threats can alter—But who would have believed! who would have supposed, that a man of his family and apparent wealth had absolutely no fortune?—no, scarcely a sequin of his own! I did all for the best; I thought he was a man of consequence, of great property, or I am sure I would never have married him,—ungrateful, artful man!" She paused to take breath.

"Dear Madam, be composed," said Emily: "the Signor may not be so rich as you had reason to expect, but surely he cannot be very poor, since this castle and the mansion at Venice are his. May I ask what are the circumstances, that particularly affect you?"

"What are the circumstances!" exclaimed Madame Montoni with resentment: "why is it not sufficient, that he had long ago ruined his own fortune by play, and that he has since lost what I brought him—and that now he would compel me to sign away my settlement (it was well I had the chief of my property settled on myself!) that he may lose this also, or throw it away in wild schemes, which nobody can understand but himself? And, and—is not all this sufficient?"

"It is, indeed," said Emily, "but you must recollect, dear madam, that I knew nothing of all this."

"Well, and is it not sufficient," rejoined her aunt, "that he is also absolutely ruined, that he is sunk deeply in debt, and that neither this castle, or the mansion at Venice, is his own, if all his debts, honourable and dishonourable, were paid!"

"I am shocked by what you tell me, madam," said Emily.

"And is it not enough," interrupted Madame Montoni, "that he has treated me with neglect, with cruelty, because I refused to relinquish my settlements, and, instead of being frightened by his menaces, resolutely defied him, and upbraided him with his shameful conduct? But I bore all meekly,—you know, niece, I never uttered a word of complaint, till now; no! That such a disposition as mine should be so imposed upon! That I, whose only faults are too much kindness, too much generosity, should be chained for life to such a vile, deceitful, cruel monster!"

Want of breath compelled Madame Montoni to stop. If any thing could have made Emily smile in these moments, it would have been this speech of her aunt, delivered in a voice very little below a scream, and with a vehemence of gesticulation and of countenance, that turned the whole into burlesque. Emily saw, that her misfortunes did not admit of real consolation, and, contemning the commonplace terms of superficial comfort, she was silent; while Madame Montoni, jealous of her own consequence, mistook this for the silence of indifference, or of contempt, and reproached her with want of duty and feeling.

"O! I suspected what all this boasted sensibility would prove to be!" rejoined she; "I thought it would not teach you to feel either duty, or affection, for your relations, who have treated you like their own daughter!"

"Pardon me, madam," said Emily, mildly, "it is not natural to me to boast, and if it was, I am sure I would not boast of sensibility—a quality, perhaps, more to be feared, than desired."

"Well, well, niece, I will not dispute with you. But, as I said, Montoni threatens me with violence, if I any longer refuse to sign away my settlements, and this was the subject of our contest, when you came into the room before. Now, I am determined no power on earth shall make me do this. Neither will I bear all this tamely. He shall hear his true character from me; I will tell him all he deserves, in spite of his threats and cruel treatment."

Emily seized a pause of Madame Montoni's voice, to speak. "Dear madam," said she, "but will not this serve to irritate the Signor unnecessarily? will it not provoke the harsh treatment you dread?"

"I do not care," replied Madame Montoni, "it does not signify: I will not submit to such usage. You would have me give up my settlements, too, I suppose!"

"No, madam, I do not exactly mean that."

"What is it you do mean then?"

"You spoke of reproaching the Signor,"—said Emily, with hesitation. "Why, does he not deserve reproaches?" said her aunt.

"Certainly he does; but will it be prudent in you, madam, to make them?"

"Prudent!" exclaimed Madame Montoni. "Is this a time to talk of prudence, when one is threatened with all sorts of violence?"

"It is to avoid that violence, that prudence is necessary," said Emily.

"Of prudence!" continued Madame Montoni, without attending to her, "of prudence towards a man, who does not scruple to break all the common ties of humanity in his conduct to me! And is it for me to consider prudence in my behaviour towards him! I am not so mean."

"It is for your own sake, not for the Signor's, madam," said Emily modestly, "that you should consult prudence. Your reproaches, however just, cannot punish him, but they may provoke him to further violence against you."

"What! would you have me submit, then, to whatever he commands—would you have me kneel down at his feet, and thank him for his cruelties? Would you have me give up my settlements?"

"How much you mistake me, madam!" said Emily, "I am unequal to advise you on a point so important as the last: but you will pardon me for saying, that, if you consult your own peace, you will try to conciliate Signor Montoni, rather than to irritate him by reproaches."

"Conciliate indeed! I tell you, niece, it is utterly impossible; I disdain to attempt it."

Emily was shocked to observe the perverted understanding and obstinate temper of Madame Montoni; but, not less grieved for her sufferings, she looked round for some alleviating circumstance to offer her. "Your situation is, perhaps, not so desperate, dear madam," said Emily, "as you may imagine. The Signor may represent his affairs to be worse than they are, for the purpose of pleading a stronger necessity for his possession of your settlement. Besides, so long as you keep this, you may look forward to it as a resource, at least, that will afford you a competence, should the Signor's future conduct compel you to sue for separation."

Madame Montoni impatiently interrupted her. "Unfeeling, cruel girl!" said she, "and so you would persuade me, that I have no reason to complain; that the Signor is in very flourishing circumstances, that my future prospects promise nothing but comfort, and that my griefs are as fanciful and romantic as your own! Is it the way to console me, to endeavour to persuade me out of my senses and my feelings, because you happen to have no feelings yourself? I thought I was opening my heart to a person, who could sympathize in my distress, but I find, that your people of sensibility can feel for nobody but themselves! You may retire to your chamber."

Emily, without replying, immediately left the room, with a mingled emotion of pity and contempt, and hastened to her own, where she yielded to the mournful reflections, which a knowledge of her aunt's situation had occasioned. The conversation of the Italian with Valancourt, in France, again occurred to her. His hints, respecting the broken fortunes of Montoni, were now completely justified; those, also, concerning his character, appeared not less so, though the particular circumstances, connected with his fame, to which the stranger had alluded, yet remained to be explained. Notwithstanding, that her own observations and the words of Count Morano had convinced her, that Montoni's situation was not what it formerly appeared to be, the intelligence she had just received from her aunt on this point, struck her with all the force of astonishment, which was not weakened, when she considered the present style of Montoni's living, the number of servants he maintained, and the new expences he was incurring, by repairing and fortifying his castle. Her anxiety for her aunt and for herself increased with reflection. Several assertions of Morano, which, on the preceding night, she had believed were prompted either by interest, or by resentment, now returned to her mind with the strength of truth. She could not doubt, that Montoni had formerly agreed to give her to the Count, for a pecuniary reward;—his character, and his distressed circumstances justified the belief; these, also, seemed to confirm Morano's assertion, that he now designed to dispose of her, more advantageously for himself, to a richer suitor.

Amidst the reproaches, which Morano had thrown out against Montoni, he had said—he would not quit the castle *he dared to call his*, nor willingly leave *another* murder on his conscience—hints, which might have no other origin than the passion of the moment: but Emily was now inclined to account for them more seriously, and she shuddered to think, that she was in the hands of a man, to whom it was even possible they could apply. At length, considering, that reflection could neither release her from her melancholy situation, or enable her to bear it with greater fortitude, she tried to divert her anxiety, and took down from her little library a volume of her favourite Ariosto; but his wild imagery and rich invention could not long enchant her attention; his spells did not reach her heart, and over her sleeping fancy they played, without awakening it.

She now put aside the book, and took her lute, for it was seldom that her sufferings refused to yield to the magic of sweet sounds; when they did so, she was oppressed by sorrow, that came from excess of tenderness and regret; and there were times, when music had increased such sorrow to a degree, that was scarcely endurable; when, if it had not suddenly ceased, she might have lost her reason. Such was the time, when she mourned for her father, and heard the midnight strains, that floated by her window near the convent in Languedoc, on the night that followed his death.

She continued to play, till Annette brought dinner into her chamber, at which Emily was surprised, and enquired whose order she obeyed. "My lady's, ma'amselle," replied Annette: "the Signor ordered her dinner to be carried to her own apartment, and so she has sent you yours. There have been sad doings between them, worse than ever, I think."

Emily, not appearing to notice what she said, sat down to the little table, that was spread for her. But Annette was not to be silenced thus easily. While she waited, she told of the arrival of the men, whom Emily had observed on the ramparts, and expressed much surprise at their strange appearance, as well as at the manner, in which they had been attended by Montoni's order. "Do they dine with the Signor, then?" said Emily.

"No, ma'amselle, they dined long ago, in an apartment at the north end of the castle, but I know not when they are to go, for the Signor told old Carlo to see them provided with every thing necessary. They have been walking all about the castle, and asking questions of the workmen on the ramparts. I never saw such strange-looking men in my life; I am frightened whenever I see them."

Emily enquired, if she had heard of Count Morano, and whether he was likely to recover: but Annette only knew, that he was lodged in a cottage in the wood below, and that every body said he must die. Emily's countenance discovered her emotion.

"Dear ma'amselle," said Annette, "to see how young ladies will disguise themselves, when they are in love! I thought you hated the Count, or I am sure I would not have told you; and I am sure you have cause enough to hate him."

"I hope I hate nobody," replied Emily, trying to smile; "but certainly I do not love Count Morano. I should be shocked to hear of any person dying by violent means."

"Yes, ma'amselle, but it is his own fault."

Emily looked displeased; and Annette, mistaking the cause of her displeasure, immediately began to excuse the Count, in her way. "To be sure, it was very ungenteel behaviour," said she, "to break into a lady's room, and then, when he found his discoursing was not agreeable to her, to refuse to go; and then, when the gentleman of the castle comes to desire him to walk about his business—to turn round, and draw his sword, and swear he'll run him through the body!—To be sure it was very ungenteel behaviour, but then he was disguised in love, and so did not know what he was about."

"Enough of this," said Emily, who now smiled without an effort; and Annette returned to a mention of the disagreement between Montoni, and her lady. "It is nothing new," said she: "we saw and heard enough of this at Venice, though I never told you of it, ma'amselle."

"Well, Annette, it was very prudent of you not to mention it then: be as prudent now; the subject is an unpleasant one."

"Ah dear, ma'amselle!—to see now how considerate you can be about some folks, who care so little about you! I cannot bear to see you so deceived, and I must tell you. But it is all for your own good, and not to spite my lady, though, to speak truth, I have little reason to love her; but——"

"You are not speaking thus of my aunt, I hope, Annette?" said Emily, gravely.

"Yes, ma'amselle, but I am, though; and if you knew as much as I do, you would not look so angry. I have often, and often, heard the Signor and her talking over your marriage with the Count, and she always advised him never to give up to your foolish whims, as she was pleased to call them, but to be resolute, and compel you to be obedient, whether you would, or no. And I am sure, my heart has ached a thousand times, and I have thought, when she was so unhappy herself, she might have felt a little for other people, and——"

"I thank you for your pity, Annette," said Emily, interrupting her: "but my aunt was unhappy then, and that disturbed her temper perhaps, or I think—I am sure—You may take away, Annette, I have done."

"Dear ma'amselle, you have eat nothing at all! Do try, and take a little bit more. Disturbed her temper truly! why, her temper is always disturbed, I think. And at Tholouse too I have heard my lady talking of you and Mons. Valancourt to Madame Merveille and Madame Vaison, often and often, in a very ill-natured way, as I thought, telling them what a deal of trouble she had to keep you in order, and what a fatigue and distress it was to her, and that she believed you would run away with Mons. Valancourt, if she was not to watch you closely; and that you connived at his coming about the house at night, and——"

"Good God!" exclaimed Emily, blushing deeply, "it is surely impossible my aunt could thus have represented me!"

"Indeed, ma'am, I say nothing more than the truth, and not all of that. But I thought, myself, she might have found something better to discourse about, than the faults of her own niece, even if you had been in fault, ma'amselle; but I did not believe a word of what she said. But my lady does not care what she says against any body, for that matter."

"However that may be, Annette," interrupted Emily, recovering her composure, "it does not become you to speak of the faults of my aunt to me. I know you have meant well, but—say no more.—I have quite dined."

Annette blushed, looked down, and then began slowly to clear the table.

"Is this, then, the reward of my ingenuousness?" said Emily, when she was alone; "the treatment I am to receive from a relation—an aunt—who ought to have been the guardian, not the slanderer of my reputation,—who, as a woman, ought to have respected the delicacy of female honour, and, as a relation, should have protected mine! But, to utter falsehoods on so nice a subject—to repay the openness, and, I may say with honest pride, the propriety of my conduct, with slanders—required a depravity of heart, such as I could scarcely have believed existed, such as I weep to find in a relation. O! what a contrast does her character present to that of my beloved father; while envy and low cunning form the chief traits of hers, his was distinguished by benevolence and philosophic wisdom! But now, let me only remember, if possible, that she is unfortunate."

Emily threw her veil over her, and went down to walk upon the ramparts, the only walk, indeed, which was open to her, though she often wished, that she might be permitted to ramble among the woods below, and still more, that she might sometimes explore the sublime scenes of the surrounding country. But, as Montoni would not suffer her to pass the gates of the castle, she tried to be contented with the romantic views she beheld from the walls. The peasants, who had been employed on the fortifications, had left their work, and the ramparts were silent and solitary. Their lonely appearance, together with the gloom of a lowering sky, assisted the musings of her mind, and threw over it a kind of melancholy tranquillity, such as she often loved to indulge. She turned to observe a fine effect of the sun, as his rays, suddenly streaming from behind a heavy cloud, lighted up the west towers of the castle, while the rest of the edifice was in deep shade, except, that, through a lofty gothic arch, adjoining the tower, which led to another terrace, the beams darted in full splendour, and shewed the three strangers she had observed in the morning. Perceiving them, she started, and a momentary fear came over her, as she looked up the long rampart, and saw no other persons. While she hesitated, they approached. The gate at the end of the terrace, whither they were advancing, she knew, was always locked, and she could not depart by the opposite extremity, without meeting them; but, before she passed them, she hastily drew a thin veil over her face, which did, indeed, but ill conceal her beauty. They looked earnestly at her, and spoke to each other in bad Italian, of which she caught only a few words; but the fierceness of their countenances, now that she was near enough to discriminate them, struck her yet more than the wild singularity of their air and dress had formerly done. It was the countenance and figure of him, who walked between the other two, that chiefly seized her attention, which expressed a sullen haughtiness and a kind of dark watchful villany, that gave a thrill of horror to her heart. All this was so legibly written on his features, as to be seen by a single glance, for she passed the group swiftly, and her timid eyes scarcely rested on them a moment. Having reached the terrace, she stopped, and perceived the strangers standing in the shadow of one of the turrets, gazing after her, and seemingly, by their action, in earnest conversation. She immediately left the rampart, and retired to her apartment.

In the evening, Montoni sat late, carousing with his guests in the cedar chamber. His recent triumph over Count Morano, or, perhaps, some other circumstance, contributed to elevate his spirits to an unusual height. He filled the goblet often, and gave a loose to merriment and talk. The gaiety of Cavigni, on the contrary, was somewhat clouded by anxiety. He kept a watchful eye upon Verezzi, whom, with the utmost difficulty, he had hitherto restrained from exasperating Montoni further against Morano, by a mention of his late taunting words.

One of the company exultingly recurred to the event of the preceding evening. Verezzi's eyes sparkled. The mention of Morano led to that of Emily, of whom they were all profuse in the praise, except Montoni, who sat silent, and then interrupted the subject.

When the servants had withdrawn, Montoni and his friends entered into close conversation, which was sometimes checked by the irascible temper of Verezzi, but in which Montoni displayed his conscious superiority, by that decisive look and manner, which always accompanied the vigour of his thought, and to which most of his companions submitted, as to a power, that they had no right to question, though of each other's self-importance they were jealously scrupulous. Amidst this conversation, one of them imprudently introduced again the name of Morano; and Verezzi, now more heated by wine, disregarded the expressive looks of Cavigni, and gave some dark hints of what had passed on the preceding night. These, however, Montoni did not appear to understand, for he continued silent in his chair, without discovering any emotion, while, the choler of Verezzi increasing with the apparent insensibility of Montoni, he at length told the suggestion of Morano, that this castle did not lawfully belong to him, and that he would not willingly leave another murder on his conscience.

"Am I to be insulted at my own table, and by my own friends?" said

Montoni, with a countenance pale in anger. "Why are the words of that madman repeated to me?" Verezzi, who had expected to hear Montoni's indignation poured forth against Morano, and answered by thanks to himself, looked with astonishment at Cavigni, who enjoyed his confusion. "Can you be weak enough to credit the assertions of a madman?" rejoined Montoni, "or, what is the same thing, a man possessed by the spirit of vengeance? But he has succeeded too well; you believe what he said."

"Signor," said Verezzi, "we believe only what we know." — "How!" interrupted Montoni, sternly: "produce your proof."

"We believe only what we know," repeated Verezzi, "and we know nothing of what Morano asserts." Montoni seemed to recover himself. "I am hasty, my friends," said he, "with respect to my honour; no man shall question it with impunity—you did not mean to question it. These foolish words are not worth your remembrance, or my resentment. Verezzi, here is to your first exploit."

"Success to your first exploit," re-echoed the whole company.

"Noble Signor," replied Verezzi, glad to find he had escaped Montoni's resentment, "with my good will, you shall build your ramparts of gold."

"Pass the goblet," cried Montoni. "We will drink to Signora St. Aubert," said Cavigni. "By your leave we will first drink to the lady of the castle," said Bertolini.—Montoni was silent. "To the lady of the castle," said his guests. He bowed his head.

"It much surprises me, Signor," said Bertolini, "that you have so long neglected this castle; it is a noble edifice."

"It suits our purpose," replied Montoni, "and *is* a noble edifice. You know not, it seems, by what mischance it came to me."

"It was a lucky mischance, be it what it may, Signor," replied Bertolini, smiling. "I would, that one so lucky had befallen me."

Montoni looked gravely at him. "If you will attend to what I say," he resumed, "you shall hear the story."

The countenances of Bertolini and Verezzi expressed something more than curiosity; Cavigni, who seemed to feel none, had probably heard the relation before.

"It is now near twenty years," said Montoni, "since this castle came into my possession. I inherit it by the female line. The lady, my predecessor, was only distantly related to me; I am the last of her family. She was beautiful and rich; I wooed her; but her heart was fixed upon another, and she rejected me. It is probable, however, that she was herself rejected of the person, whoever he might be, on whom she bestowed her favour, for a deep and settled melancholy took possession of her; and I have reason to believe she put a period to her own life. I was not at the castle at the time; but, as there are some singular and mysterious circumstances attending that event, I shall repeat them."

"Repeat them!" said a voice.

Montoni was silent; the guests looked at each other, to know who spoke; but they perceived, that each was making the same enquiry. Montoni, at length, recovered himself. "We are overheard," said he: "we will finish this subject another time. Pass the goblet."

The cavaliers looked round the wide chamber.

"Here is no person, but ourselves," said Verezzi: "pray, Signor, proceed."

"Did you hear any thing?" said Montoni.

"We did," said Bertolini.

"It could be only fancy," said Verezzi, looking round again. "We see no person besides ourselves; and the sound I thought I heard seemed within the room. Pray, Signor, go on."

Montoni paused a moment, and then proceeded in a lowered voice, while the cavaliers drew nearer to attend.

"Ye are to know, Signors, that the Lady Laurentini had for some months shewn symptoms of a dejected mind, nay, of a disturbed imagination. Her mood was very unequal; sometimes she was sunk in calm melancholy, and, at others, as I have been told, she betrayed all the symptoms of frantic madness. It was one night in the month of October, after she had recovered from one of those fits of excess, and had sunk again into her usual melancholy, that she retired alone to her chamber, and forbade all interruption. It was the chamber at the end of the corridor, Signors, where we had the affray, last night. From that hour, she was seen no more."

"How! seen no more!" said Bertolini, "was not her body found in the chamber?"

"Were her remains never found?" cried the rest of the company all together.

"Never!" replied Montoni.

"What reasons were there to suppose she destroyed herself, then?" said Bertolini.—"Aye, what reasons?" said Verezzi.—"How happened it, that her remains were never found? Although she killed herself, she could not bury herself." Montoni looked indignantly at Verezzi, who began to apologize. "Your pardon, Signor," said he: "I did not consider, that the lady was your relative, when I spoke of her so lightly."

Montoni accepted the apology.

"But the Signor will oblige us with the reasons, which urged him to believe, that the lady committed suicide."

"Those I will explain hereafter," said Montoni: "at present let me relate a most extraordinary circumstance. This conversation goes no further, Signors. Listen, then, to what I am going to say."

"Listen!" said a voice.

They were all again silent, and the countenance of Montoni changed. "This is no illusion of the fancy," said Cavigni, at length breaking the profound silence. — "No," said Bertolini; "I heard it myself, now. Yet here is no person in the room but ourselves!"

"This is very extraordinary," said Montoni, suddenly rising. "This is not to be borne; here is some deception, some trick. I will know what it means."

All the company rose from their chairs in confusion.

"It is very odd!" said Bertolini. "Here is really no stranger in the room. If it is a trick, Signor, you will do well to punish the author of it severely."

"A trick! what else can it be?" said Cavigni, affecting a laugh.

The servants were now summoned, and the chamber was searched, but no person was found. The surprise and consternation of the company increased. Montoni was discomposed. "We will leave this room," said he, "and the subject of our conversation also; it is too solemn." His guests were equally ready to quit the apartment; but the subject had roused their curiosity, and they entreated Montoni to withdraw to another chamber, and finish it; no entreaties could, however, prevail with him. Notwithstanding his efforts to appear at ease, he was visibly and greatly disordered.

"Why, Signor, you are not superstitious," cried Verezzi, jeeringly; "you, who have so often laughed at the credulity of others!"

"I am not superstitious," replied Montoni, regarding him with stern displeasure, "though I know how to despise the common-place sentences, which are frequently uttered against superstition. I will enquire further into this affair." He then left the room; and his guests, separating for the night, retired to their respective apartments.

CHAPTER VIII

He wears the rose of youth upon his cheek.
SHAKESPEARE

WE now return to Valancourt, who, it may be remembered, remained at Tholouse, some time after the departure of Emily, restless and miserable. Each morrow that approached, he designed should carry him from thence; yet to-morrow and to-morrow came, and still saw him lingering in the scene of his former happiness. He could not immediately tear himself from the spot, where he had been accustomed to converse with Emily, or from the objects they had viewed together, which appeared to him memorials of her affection, as well as a kind of surety for its faithfulness; and, next to the pain of bidding her adieu, was that of leaving the scenes which so powerfully awakened her image. Sometimes he had bribed a servant, who had been left in the care of Madame Montoni's chateau, to permit him to visit the gardens, and there he would wander, for hours together, rapt in a melancholy, not unpleasing. The terrace, and the pavilion at the end of it, where he had taken leave of Emily, on the eve of her departure from Tholouse, were his most favourite haunts. There, as he walked, or leaned from the window of the building, he would endeavour to recollect all she had said, on that night; to catch the tones of her voice, as they faintly vibrated on his memory, and to remember the exact expression of her countenance, which sometimes came suddenly to his fancy, like a vision; that beautiful countenance, which awakened, as by instantaneous magic, all the tenderness of his heart, and seemed to tell with irresistible eloquence—that he had lost her forever! At these moments, his hurried steps would have discovered to a spectator the despair of his heart. The character of Montoni, such as he had received from hints, and such as his fears represented it, would rise to his view, together with all the dangers it seemed to threaten to Emily and to his love. He blamed himself, that he had not urged these more forcibly to her, while it might have been in his power to detain her, and that he had suffered an absurd and criminal delicacy, as he termed it, to conquer so soon the reasonable arguments he had opposed to this journey. Any evil, that might have attended their marriage, seemed so inferior to those, which now threatened their love, or even to the sufferings, that absence occasioned, that he wondered how he could have ceased to urge his suit, till he had convinced her of its propriety; and he would certainly now have followed her to Italy, if he could have been spared from his regiment for so long a journey. His regiment, indeed, soon reminded him, that he had other duties to attend, than those of love.

A short time after his arrival at his brother's house, he was summoned to join his brother officers, and he accompanied a battalion to Paris; where a scene of novelty and gaiety opened upon him, such as, till then, he had only a faint idea of. But gaiety disgusted, and company fatigued, his sick mind; and he became an object of unceasing raillery to his companions, from whom, whenever he could steal an opportunity, he escaped, to think of Emily. The scenes around him, however, and the company with whom he was obliged to mingle, engaged his attention, though they failed to amuse his fancy, and thus gradually weakened the habit of yielding to lamentation, till it appeared less a duty to his love to indulge it. Among his brother-officers were many, who added to the ordinary character of a French soldier's gaiety some of those fascinating qualities, which too frequently throw a veil over folly, and sometimes even soften the features of vice into smiles. To these men the reserved and thoughtful manners of Valancourt were a kind of tacit censure on their own, for which they rallied him when present, and plotted against him when absent; they gloried in the thought of reducing him to their own level, and, considering it to be a spirited frolic, determined to accomplish it.

Valancourt was a stranger to the gradual progress of scheme and intrigue, against which he could not be on his guard. He had not been accustomed to receive ridicule, and he could ill endure its sting; he resented it, and this only drew upon him a louder laugh. To escape from such scenes, he fled into solitude, and there the image of Emily met him, and revived the pangs of love and despair. He then sought to renew those tasteful studies, which had been the delight of his early years; but his mind had lost the tranquillity, which is necessary for their enjoyment. To forget himself and the grief and anxiety, which the idea of her recalled, he would quit his solitude, and again mingle in the crowd—glad of a temporary relief, and rejoicing to snatch amusement for the moment.

Thus passed weeks after weeks, time gradually softening his sorrow, and habit strengthening his desire of amusement, till the scenes around him seemed to awaken into a new character, and Valancourt, to have fallen among them from the clouds.

His figure and address made him a welcome visitor, wherever he had been introduced, and he soon frequented the most gay and fashionable circles of Paris. Among these, was the assembly of the Countess Lacleur, a woman of eminent beauty and captivating manners. She had passed the spring of youth, but her wit prolonged the triumph of its reign, and they mutually assisted the fame of each other; for those, who were charmed by her loveliness, spoke with enthusiasm of her talents; and others, who admired her playful imagination, declared, that her personal graces were unrivalled. But her imagination was merely playful, and her wit, if such it could be called, was brilliant, rather than just; it dazzled, and its fallacy escaped the detection of the moment; for the accents, in which she pronounced it, and the smile, that accompanied them, were a spell upon the judgment of the auditors. Her *petits soupers* were the most tasteful of any in Paris, and were frequented by many of the second class of literati. She was fond of music, was herself a scientific performer, and had frequently concerts at her house. Valancourt, who passionately loved music, and who sometimes assisted at these concerts, admired her execution, but remembered with a sigh the eloquent simplicity of Emily's songs and the natural expression of her manner, which waited not to be approved by the judgment, but found their way at once to the heart.

Madame *La Comtesse* had often deep play at her house, which she affected to restrain, but secretly encouraged; and it was well known among her friends, that the splendour of her establishment was chiefly supplied from the profits of her tables. But her *petits soupers* were the most charming imaginable! Here were all the delicacies of the four quarters of the world, all the wit and the lighter efforts of genius, all the graces of conversation—the smiles of beauty, and the charm of music; and Valancourt passed his pleasantest, as well as most dangerous hours in these parties.

His brother, who remained with his family in Gascony, had contented himself with giving him letters of introduction to such of his relations, residing at Paris, as the latter was not already known to. All these were persons of some distinction; and, as neither the person, mind, or manners of Valancourt the younger threatened to disgrace their alliance, they received him with as much kindness as their nature, hardened by uninterrupted prosperity, would admit of; but their attentions did not extend to acts of real friendship; for they were too much occupied by their own pursuits, to feel any interest in his; and thus he was set down in the midst of Paris, in the pride of youth, with an open, unsuspicious temper and ardent affections, without one friend, to warn him of the dangers, to which he was exposed. Emily, who, had she been present, would have saved him from these evils by awakening his heart, and engaging him in worthy pursuits, now only increased his danger;—it was to lose the grief, which the remembrance of her occasioned, that he first sought amusement; and for this end he pursued it, till habit made it an object of abstract interest.

There was also a Marchioness Champfort, a young widow, at whose assemblies he passed much of his time. She was handsome, still more artful, gay and fond of intrigue. The society, which she drew round her, was less elegant and more vicious, than that of the Countess Lacleur: but, as she had address enough to throw a veil, though but a slight one, over the worst part of her character, she was still visited by many persons of what is called distinction. Valancourt was introduced to her parties by two of his brother officers, whose late ridicule he had now forgiven so far, that he could sometimes join in the laugh, which a mention of his former manners would renew.

The gaiety of the most splendid court in Europe, the magnificence of the palaces, entertainments, and equipages, that surrounded him— all conspired to dazzle his imagination, and re-animate his spirits, and the example and maxims of his military associates to delude his mind.

Emily's image, indeed, still lived there; but it was no longer the friend, the monitor, that saved him from himself, and to which he retired to weep the sweet, yet melancholy, tears of tenderness. When he had recourse to it, it assumed a countenance of mild reproach, that wrung his soul, and called forth tears of unmixed misery; his only escape from which was to forget the object of it, and he endeavoured, therefore, to think of Emily as seldom as he could.

Thus dangerously circumstanced was Valancourt, at the time, when Emily was suffering at Venice, from the persecuting addresses of Count Morano, and the unjust authority of Montoni; at which period we leave him.

CHAPTER IX

The image of a wicked, heinous fault
Lives in his eye; that close aspect of his
Does shew the mood of a much-troubled breast.
KING JOHN

LEAVING the gay scenes of Paris, we return to those of the gloomy Apennine, where Emily's thoughts were still faithful to Valancourt. Looking to him as to her only hope, she recollected, with jealous exactness, every assurance and every proof she had witnessed of his affection; read again and again the letters she had received from him; weighed, with intense anxiety, the force of every word, that spoke of his attachment; and dried her tears, as she trusted in his truth.

Montoni, meanwhile, had made strict enquiry concerning the strange circumstance of his alarm, without obtaining information; and was, at length, obliged to account for it by the reasonable supposition, that it was a mischievous trick played off by one of his domestics. His disagreements with Madame Montoni, on the subject of her settlements, were now more frequent than ever; he even confined her entirely to her own apartment, and did not scruple to threaten her with much greater severity, should she persevere in a refusal.

Reason, had she consulted it, would now have perplexed her in the choice of a conduct to be adopted. It would have pointed out the danger of irritating by further opposition a man, such as Montoni had proved himself to be, and to whose power she had so entirely committed herself; and it would also have told her, of what extreme importance to her future comfort it was, to reserve for herself those possessions, which would enable her to live independently of Montoni, should she ever escape from his immediate controul. But she was directed by a more decisive guide than reason—the spirit of revenge, which urged her to oppose violence to violence, and obstinacy to obstinacy.

Wholly confined to the solitude of her apartment, she was now reduced to solicit the society she had lately rejected; for Emily was the only person, except Annette, with whom she was permitted to converse.

Generously anxious for her peace, Emily, therefore, tried to persuade, when she could not convince, and sought by every gentle means to induce her to forbear that asperity of reply, which so greatly irritated Montoni. The pride of her aunt did sometimes soften to the soothing voice of Emily, and there even were moments, when she regarded her affectionate attentions with goodwill.

The scenes of terrible contention, to which Emily was frequently compelled to be witness, exhausted her spirits more than any circumstances, that had occurred since her departure from Tholouse. The gentleness and goodness of her parents, together with the scenes of her early happiness, often stole on her mind, like the visions of a higher world; while the characters and circumstances, now passing beneath her eye, excited both terror and surprise. She could scarcely have imagined, that passions so fierce and so various, as those which Montoni exhibited, could have been concentrated in one individual; yet what more surprised her, was, that, on great occasions, he could bend these passions, wild as they were, to the cause of his interest, and generally could disguise in his countenance their operation on his mind; but she had seen him too often, when he had thought it unnecessary to conceal his nature, to be deceived on such occasions.

Her present life appeared like the dream of a distempered imagination, or like one of those frightful fictions, in which the wild genius of the poets sometimes delighted. Reflection brought only regret, and anticipation terror. How often did she wish to "steal the lark's wing, and mount the swiftest gale," that Languedoc and repose might once more be hers!

Of Count Morano's health she made frequent enquiry; but Annette heard only vague reports of his danger, and that his surgeon had said he would never leave the cottage alive; while Emily could not but be shocked to think, that she, however innocently, might be the means of his death; and Annette, who did not fail to observe her emotion, interpreted it in her own way.

But a circumstance soon occurred, which entirely withdrew Annette's attention from this subject, and awakened the surprise and curiosity so natural to her. Coming one day to Emily's apartment, with a countenance full of importance, "What can all this mean, ma'amselle?" said she. "Would I was once safe in Languedoc again, they should never catch me going on my travels any more! I must think it a fine thing, truly, to come abroad, and see foreign parts! I little thought I was coming to be catched up in a old castle, among such dreary mountains, with the chance of being murdered, or, what is as good, having my throat cut!"

"What can all this mean, indeed, Annette?" said Emily, in astonishment.

"Aye, ma'amselle, you may look surprised; but you won't believe it, perhaps, till they have murdered you, too. You would not believe about the ghost I told you of, though I shewed you the very place, where it used to appear!—You will believe nothing, ma'amselle."

"Not till you speak more reasonably, Annette; for Heaven's sake, explain your meaning. You spoke of murder!"

"Aye, ma'amselle, they are coming to murder us all, perhaps; but what signifies explaining?—you will not believe."

Emily again desired her to relate what she had seen, or heard.

"O, I have seen enough, ma'am, and heard too much, as Ludovico can prove. Poor soul! they will murder him, too! I little thought, when he sung those sweet verses under my lattice, at Venice!"—— Emily looked impatient and displeased. "Well, ma'amselle, as I was saying, these preparations about the castle, and these strange-looking people, that are calling here every day, and the Signor's cruel usage of my lady, and his odd goings-on—all these, as I told Ludovico, can bode no good. And he bid me hold my tongue. So, says I, the Signor's strangely altered, Ludovico, in this gloomy castle, to what he was in France; there, all so gay! Nobody so gallant to my lady, then; and he could smile, too, upon a poor servant, sometimes, and jeer her, too, good-naturedly enough. I remember once, when he said to me, as I was going out of my lady's dressing-room—Annette, says he—"

"Never mind what the Signor said," interrupted Emily; "but tell me, at once, the circumstance, which has thus alarmed you."

"Aye, ma'amselle," rejoined Annette, "that is just what Ludovico said: says he, Never mind what the Signor says to you. So I told him what I thought about the Signor. He is so strangely altered, said I: for now he is so haughty, and so commanding, and so sharp with my lady; and, if he meets one, he'll scarcely look at one, unless it be to frown. So much the better, says Ludovico, so much the better. And to tell you the truth, ma'amselle, I thought this was a very ill-natured speech of Ludovico: but I went on. And then, says I, he is always knitting his brows; and if one speaks to him, he does not hear; and then he sits up counselling so, of a night, with the other Signors—there they are, till long past midnight, discoursing together! Aye, but says Ludovico, you don't know what they are counselling about. No, said I, but I can guess—it is about my young lady. Upon that, Ludovico burst out a-laughing, quite loud; so he put me in a huff, for I did not like that either I or you, ma'amselle, should be laughed at; and I turned away quick, but he stopped me. 'Don't be affronted, Annette,' said he, 'but I cannot help laughing'; and with that he laughed again. 'What!' says he, 'do you think the Signors sit up, night after night, only to counsel about thy young lady! No, no, there is something more in the wind than that. And these repairs about the castle, and these preparations about the ramparts—they are not making about young ladies.' Why, surely, said I, the Signor, my master, is not going to make war? 'Make war!' said Ludovico, 'what, upon the mountains and the woods? for here is no living soul to make war upon that I see.'

"What are these preparations for, then? said I; why surely nobody is coming to take away my master's castle! 'Then there are so many ill-looking fellows coming to the castle every day,' says Ludovico, without answering my question, 'and the Signor sees them all, and talks with them all, and they all stay in the neighbourhood! By holy St. Marco! some of them are the most cut-throat-looking dogs I ever set my eyes upon.'

"I asked Ludovico again, if he thought they were coming to take away my master's castle; and he said, No, he did not think they were, but he did not know for certain. 'Then yesterday,' said he, but you must not tell this, ma'amselle, 'yesterday, a party of these men came, and left all their horses in the castle stables, where, it seems, they are to stay, for the Signor ordered them all to be entertained with the best provender in the manger; but the men are, most of them, in the neighbouring cottages.'

"So, ma'amselle, I came to tell you all this, for I never heard any thing so strange in my life. But what can these ill-looking men be come about, if it is not to murder us? And the Signor knows this, or why should he be so civil to them? And why should he fortify the castle, and counsel so much with the other Signors, and be so thoughtful?"

"Is this all you have to tell, Annette?" said Emily. "Have you heard nothing else, that alarms you?"

"Nothing else, ma'amselle!" said Annette; "why, is not this enough?"

"Quite enough for my patience, Annette, but not quite enough to convince me we are all to be murdered, though I acknowledge here is sufficient food for curiosity." She forbore to speak her apprehensions, because she would not encourage Annette's wild terrors; but the present circumstances of the castle both surprised, and alarmed her. Annette, having told her tale, left the chamber, on the wing for new wonders.

In the evening, Emily had passed some melancholy hours with

Madame Montoni, and was retiring to rest, when she was alarmed by a strange and loud knocking at her chamber door, and then a heavy weight fell against it, that almost burst it open. She called to know who was there, and receiving no answer, repeated the call; but a chilling silence followed. It occurred to her—for, at this moment, she could not reason on the probability of circumstances—that some one of the strangers, lately arrived at the castle, had discovered her apartment, and was come with such intent, as their looks rendered too possible—to rob, perhaps to murder, her. The moment she admitted this possibility, terror supplied the place of conviction, and a kind of instinctive remembrance of her remote situation from the family heightened it to a degree, that almost overcame her senses. She looked at the door, which led to the staircase, expecting to see it open, and listening, in fearful silence, for a return of the noise, till she began to think it had proceeded from this door, and a wish of escaping through the opposite one rushed upon her mind. She went to the gallery door, and then, fearing to open it, lest some person might be silently lurking for her without, she stopped, but with her eyes fixed in expectation upon the opposite door of the stair-case. As thus she stood, she heard a faint breathing near her, and became convinced, that some person was on the other side of the door, which was already locked. She sought for other fastening, but there was none.

While she yet listened, the breathing was distinctly heard, and her terror was not soothed, when, looking round her wide and lonely chamber, she again considered her remote situation. As she stood hesitating whether to call for assistance, the continuance of the stillness surprised her; and her spirits would have revived, had she not continued to hear the faint breathing, that convinced her, the person, whoever it was, had not quitted the door.

At length, worn out with anxiety, she determined to call loudly for assistance from her casement, and was advancing to it, when, whether the terror of her mind gave her ideal sounds, or that real ones did come, she thought footsteps were ascending the private stair-case; and, expecting to see its door unclose, she forgot all other cause of alarm, and retreated towards the corridor. Here she endeavoured to make her escape, but, on opening the door, was very near falling over a person, who lay on the floor without. She screamed, and would have passed, but her trembling frame refused to support her; and the moment, in which she leaned against the wall of the gallery, allowed her leisure to observe the figure before her, and to recognise the features of Annette. Fear instantly yielded to surprise. She spoke in vain to the poor girl, who remained senseless on the floor, and then, losing all consciousness of her own weakness, hurried to her assistance.

When Annette recovered, she was helped by Emily into the chamber, but was still unable to speak, and looked round her, as if her eyes followed some person in the room. Emily tried to soothe her disturbed spirits, and forbore, at present, to ask her any questions; but the faculty of speech was never long with-held from Annette, and she explained, in broken sentences, and in her tedious way, the occasion of her disorder. She affirmed, and with a solemnity of conviction, that almost staggered the incredulity of Emily, that she had seen an apparition, as she was passing to her bedroom, through the corridor.

"I had heard strange stories of that chamber before," said Annette: "but as it was so near yours, ma'amselle, I would not tell them to you, because they would frighten you. The servants had told me, often and often, that it was haunted, and that was the reason why it was shut up: nay, for that matter, why the whole string of these rooms, here, are shut up. I quaked whenever I went by, and I must say, I did sometimes think I heard odd noises within it. But, as I said, as I was passing along the corridor, and not thinking a word about the matter, or even of the strange voice that the Signors heard the other night, all of a sudden comes a great light, and, looking behind me, there was a tall figure, (I saw it as plainly, ma'amselle, as I see you at this moment), a tall figure gliding along (Oh! I cannot describe how!) into the room, that is always shut up, and nobody has the key of it but the Signor, and the door shut directly."

"Then it doubtless was the Signor," said Emily.

"O no, ma'amselle, it could not be him, for I left him busy a-quarrelling in my lady's dressing-room!"

"You bring me strange tales, Annette," said Emily: "it was but this morning, that you would have terrified me with the apprehension of murder; and now you would persuade me, you have seen a ghost! These wonderful stories come too quickly."

"Nay, ma'amselle, I will say no more, only, if I had not been frightened, I should not have fainted dead away, so. I ran as fast as I could, to get to your door; but, what was worst of all, I could not call out; then I thought something must be strangely the matter with me, and directly I dropt down."

"Was it the chamber where the black veil hangs?" said Emily. "O! no, ma'amselle, it was one nearer to this. What shall I do, to get to my room? I would not go out into the corridor again, for the whole world!" Emily, whose spirits had been severely shocked, and who, therefore, did not like the thought of passing the night alone, told her she might sleep where she was. "O, no, ma'amselle," replied Annette, "I would not sleep in the room, now, for a thousand sequins!"

Wearied and disappointed, Emily first ridiculed, though she shared, her fears, and then tried to soothe them; but neither attempt succeeded, and the girl persisted in believing and affirming, that what she had seen was nothing human. It was not till some time after Emily had recovered her composure, that she recollected the steps she had heard on the stair-case—a remembrance, however, which made her insist that Annette should pass the night with her, and, with much difficulty, she, at length, prevailed, assisted by that part of the girl's fear, which concerned the corridor.

Early on the following morning, as Emily crossed the hall to the ramparts, she heard a noisy bustle in the court-yard, and the clatter of horses' hoofs. Such unusual sounds excited her curiosity; and, instead of going to the ramparts, she went to an upper casement, from whence she saw, in the court below, a large party of horsemen, dressed in a singular, but uniform, habit, and completely, though variously, armed. They wore a kind of short jacket, composed of black and scarlet, and several of them had a cloak, of plain black, which, covering the person entirely, hung down to the stirrups. As one of these cloaks glanced aside, she saw, beneath, daggers, apparently of different sizes, tucked into the horseman's belt. She further observed, that these were carried, in the same manner, by many of the horsemen without cloaks, most of whom bore also pikes, or javelins. On their heads, were the small Italian caps, some of which were distinguished by black feathers. Whether these caps gave a fierce air to the countenance, or that the countenances they surmounted had naturally such an appearance, Emily thought she had never, till then, seen an assemblage of faces so savage and terrific. While she gazed, she almost fancied herself surrounded by banditti; and a vague thought glanced athwart her fancy—that Montoni was the captain of the group before her, and that this castle was to be the place of rendezvous. The strange and horrible supposition was but momentary, though her reason could supply none more probable, and though she discovered, among the band, the strangers she had formerly noticed with so much alarm, who were now distinguished by the black plume.

While she continued gazing, Cavigni, Verezzi, and Bertolini came forth from the hall, habited like the rest, except that they wore hats, with a mixed plume of black and scarlet, and that their arms differed from those of the rest of the party. As they mounted their horses, Emily was struck with the exulting joy, expressed on the visage of Verezzi, while Cavigni was gay, yet with a shade of thought on his countenance; and, as he managed his horse with dexterity, his graceful and commanding figure, which exhibited the majesty of a hero, had never appeared to more advantage. Emily, as she observed him, thought he somewhat resembled Valancourt, in the spirit and dignity of his person;

but she looked in vain for the noble, benevolent countenance—the soul's intelligence, which overspread the features of the latter.

As she was hoping, she scarcely knew why, that Montoni would accompany the party, he appeared at the hall door, but un-accoutred. Having carefully observed the horsemen, conversed awhile with the cavaliers, and bidden them farewel, the band wheeled round the court, and, led by Verezzi, issued forth under the portcullis; Montoni following to the portal, and gazing after them for some time. Emily then retired from the casement, and, now certain of being unmolested, went to walk on the ramparts, from whence she soon after saw the party winding among the mountains to the west, appearing and disappearing between the woods, till distance confused their figures, consolidated their numbers, and only a dingy mass appeared moving along the heights.

Emily observed, that no workmen were on the ramparts, and that the repairs of the fortifications seemed to be completed. While she sauntered thoughtfully on, she heard distant footsteps, and, raising her eyes, saw several men lurking under the castle walls, who were evidently not workmen, but looked as if they would have accorded well with the party, which was gone. Wondering where Annette had hid herself so long, who might have explained some of the late circumstances, and then considering that Madame Montoni was probably risen, she went to her dressing-room, where she mentioned what had occurred; but Madame Montoni either would not, or could not, give any explanation of the event. The Signor's reserve to his wife, on this subject, was probably nothing more than usual; yet, to Emily, it gave an air of mystery to the whole affair, that seemed to hint, there was danger, if not villany, in his schemes.

Annette presently came, and, as usual, was full of alarm; to her lady's eager enquiries of what she had heard among the servants, she replied:

"Ah, madam! nobody knows what it is all about, but old Carlo; he knows well enough, I dare say, but he is as close as his master. Some say the Signor is going out to frighten the enemy, as they call it: but where is the enemy? Then others say, he is going to take away some body's castle: but I am sure he has room enough in his own, without taking other people's; and I am sure I should like it a great deal better, if there were more people to fill it."

"Ah! you will soon have your wish, I fear," replied Madame Montoni.

"No, madam, but such ill-looking fellows are not worth having. I mean such gallant, smart, merry fellows as Ludovico, who is always telling droll stories, to make one laugh. It was but yesterday, he told me such a *humoursome* tale! I can't help laughing at it now.—Says he——"

"Well, we can dispense with the story," said her lady. "Ah!" continued Annette, "he sees a great way further than other people! Now he sees into all the Signor's meaning, without knowing a word about the matter!"

"How is that?" said Madame Montoni.

"Why he says—but he made me promise not to tell, and I would not disoblige him for the world."

"What is it he made you promise not to tell?" said her lady, sternly. "I insist upon knowing immediately—what is it he made you promise?"

"O madam," cried Annette, "I would not tell for the universe!" "I insist upon your telling this instant," said Madame Montoni. "O dear madam! I would not tell for a hundred sequins! You would not have me forswear myself, madam!" exclaimed Annette.

"I will not wait another moment," said Madame Montoni. Annette was silent.

"The Signor shall be informed of this directly," rejoined her mistress: "he will make you discover all."

"It is Ludovico, who has discovered," said Annette: "but for mercy's sake, madam, don't tell the Signor, and you shall know all directly." Madame Montoni said, that she would not.

"Well then, madam, Ludovico says, that the Signor, my master, is—is—that is, he only thinks so, and any body, you know, madam, is free to think—that the Signor, my master, is—is——"

"Is what?" said her lady, impatiently.

"That the Signor, my master, is going to be—a great robber—that is—he is going to rob on his own account;—to be, (but I am sure I don't understand what he means) to be a—captain of—robbers."

"Art thou in thy senses, Annette?" said Madame Montoni; "or is this a trick to deceive me? Tell me, this instant, what Ludovico *did* say to thee;—no equivocation;—this instant."

"Nay, madam," cried Annette, "if this is all I am to get for having told the secret"—— Her mistress thus continued to insist, and Annette to protest, till Montoni, himself, appeared, who bade the latter leave the room, and she withdrew, trembling for the fate of her story. Emily also was retiring, but her aunt desired she would stay; and Montoni had so often made her a witness of their contention, that he no longer had scruples on that account.

"I insist upon knowing this instant, Signor, what all this means:" said his wife—"what are all these armed men, whom they tell me of, gone out about?" Montoni answered her only with a look of scorn; and Emily whispered something to her. "It does not signify," said her aunt: "I will know; and I will know, too, what the castle has been fortified for."

"Come, come," said Montoni, "other business brought me here. I must be trifled with no longer. I have immediate occasion for what I demand—those estates must be given up, without further contention; or I may find a way——"

"They never shall be given up," interrupted Madame Montoni: "they never shall enable you to carry on your wild schemes;—but what are these? I will know. Do you expect the castle to be attacked? Do you expect enemies? Am I to be shut up here, to be killed in a siege?"

"Sign the writings," said Montoni, "and you shall know more."

"What enemy can be coming?" continued his wife. "Have you entered into the service of the state? Am I to be blocked up here to die?"

"That may possibly happen," said Montoni, "unless you yield to my demand: for, come what may, you shall not quit the castle till then." Madame Montoni burst into loud lamentation, which she as suddenly checked, considering, that her husband's assertions might be only artifices, employed to extort her consent. She hinted this suspicion, and, in the next moment, told him also, that his designs were not so honourable as to serve the state, and that she believed he had only commenced a captain of banditti, to join the enemies of Venice, in plundering and laying waste the surrounding country.

Montoni looked at her for a moment with a steady and stern countenance; while Emily trembled, and his wife, for once, thought she had said too much. "You shall be removed, this night," said he, "to the east turret: there, perhaps, you may understand the danger of offending a man, who has an unlimited power over you."

Emily now fell at his feet, and, with tears of terror, supplicated for her aunt, who sat, trembling with fear, and indignation; now ready to pour forth execrations, and now to join the intercessions of Emily. Montoni, however, soon interrupted these entreaties with an horrible oath; and, as he burst from Emily, leaving his cloak, in her hand, she fell to the floor, with a force, that occasioned her a severe blow on the forehead. But he quitted the room, without attempting to raise her, whose attention was called from herself, by a deep groan from Madame Montoni, who continued otherwise unmoved in her chair, and had not fainted. Emily, hastening to her assistance, saw her eyes rolling, and her features convulsed.

Having spoken to her, without receiving an answer, she brought water, and supported her head, while she held it to her lips; but the increasing convulsions soon compelled Emily to call for assistance. On her way through the hall, in search of Annette, she met Montoni, whom she told what had happened, and conjured to return and comfort her aunt; but he turned silently away, with a look of indifference, and went out upon the ramparts. At length she found old Carlo and Annette, and they hastened to the dressing-room, where Madame Montoni had fallen on the floor, and was lying in strong convulsions. Having lifted her into the adjoining room, and laid her on the bed, the force of her disorder still made all their strength necessary to hold her, while Annette trembled and sobbed, and old Carlo looked silently and piteously on, as his feeble hands grasped those of his mistress, till, turning his eyes upon Emily, he exclaimed, "Good God! Signora, what is the matter?"

Emily looked calmly at him, and saw his enquiring eyes fixed on her: and Annette, looking up, screamed loudly; for Emily's face was stained with blood, which continued to fall slowly from her forehead: but her attention had been so entirely occupied by the scene before her, that she had felt no pain from the wound. She now held an handkerchief to her face, and, notwithstanding her faintness, continued to watch Madame Montoni, the violence of whose convulsions was abating, till at length they ceased, and left her in a kind of stupor.

"My aunt must remain quiet," said Emily. "Go, good Carlo; if we should want your assistance, I will send for you. In the mean time, if you have an opportunity, speak kindly of your mistress to your master."

"Alas!" said Carlo, "I have seen too much! I have little influence with the Signor. But do, dear young lady, take some care of yourself; that is an ugly wound, and you look sadly."

"Thank you, my friend, for your consideration," said Emily, smiling kindly: "the wound is trifling, it came by a fall."

Carlo shook his head, and left the room; and Emily, with Annette, continued to watch by her aunt. "Did my lady tell the Signor what Ludovico said, ma'amselle?" asked Annette in a whisper; but Emily quieted her fears on the subject.

"I thought what this quarrelling would come to," continued Annette: "I suppose the Signor has been beating my lady."

"No, no, Annette, you are totally mistaken, nothing extraordinary has happened."

"Why, extraordinary things happen here so often, ma'amselle, that there is nothing in them. Here is another legion of those ill-looking fellows, come to the castle, this morning."

"Hush! Annette, you will disturb my aunt; we will talk of that by and bye."

They continued watching silently, till Madame Montoni uttered a low sigh, when Emily took her hand, and spoke soothingly to her; but the former gazed with unconscious eyes, and it was long before she knew her niece. Her first words then enquired for Montoni; to which Emily replied by an entreaty, that she would compose her spirits, and consent to be kept quiet, adding, that, if she wished any message to be conveyed to him, she would herself deliver it. "No," said her aunt faintly, "no—I have nothing new to tell him. Does he persist in saying I shall be removed from my chamber?"

Emily replied, that he had not spoken, on the subject, since Madame Montoni heard him; and then she tried to divert her attention to some other topic; but her aunt seemed to be inattentive to what she said, and lost in secret thoughts. Emily, having brought her some refreshment, now left her to the care of Annette, and went in search of Montoni, whom she found on a remote part of the rampart, conversing among a group of the men described by Annette. They stood round him with fierce, yet subjugated, looks, while he, speaking earnestly, and pointing to the walls, did not perceive Emily, who remained at some distance, waiting till he should be at leisure, and observing involuntarily the appearance of one man, more savage than his fellows, who stood resting on his pike, and looking, over the shoulders of a comrade, at Montoni, to whom he listened with uncommon earnestness. This man was apparently of low condition; yet his looks appeared not to acknowledge the superiority of Montoni, as did those of his companions; and sometimes they even assumed an air of authority, which the decisive manner of the Signor could not repress. Some few words of Montoni then passed in the wind; and, as the men were separating, she heard him say, "This evening, then, begin the watch at sunset."

"At sunset, Signor," replied one or two of them, and walked away; while Emily approached Montoni, who appeared desirous of avoiding her: but, though she observed this, she had courage to proceed. She endeavoured to intercede once more for her aunt, represented to him her sufferings, and urged the danger of exposing her to a cold apartment in her present state. "She suffers by her own folly," said Montoni, "and is not to be pitied;—she knows how she may avoid these sufferings in future—if she is removed to the turret, it will be her own fault. Let her be obedient, and sign the writings you heard of, and I will think no more of it."

When Emily ventured still to plead, he sternly silenced and rebuked her for interfering in his domestic affairs, but, at length, dismissed her with this concession—That he would not remove Madame Montoni, on the ensuing night, but allow her till the next to consider, whether she would resign her settlements, or be imprisoned in the east turret of the castle, "where she shall find," he added, "a punishment she may not expect."

Emily then hastened to inform her aunt of this short respite and of the alternative, that awaited her, to which the latter made no reply, but appeared thoughtful, while Emily, in consideration of her extreme languor, wished to soothe her mind by leading it to less interesting topics: and, though these efforts were unsuccessful, and Madame Montoni became peevish, her resolution, on the contended point, seemed somewhat to relax, and Emily recommended, as her only means of safety, that she should submit to Montoni's demand. "You know not what you advise," said her aunt. "Do you understand, that these estates will descend to you at my death, if I persist in a refusal?"

"I was ignorant of that circumstance, madam," replied Emily, "but the knowledge of it cannot with-hold me from advising you to adopt the conduct, which not only your peace, but, I fear, your safety requires, and I entreat, that you will not suffer a consideration comparatively so trifling, to make you hesitate a moment in resigning them."

"Are you sincere, niece?" "Is it possible you can doubt it, madam?" Her aunt appeared to be affected. "You are not unworthy of these estates, niece," said she: "I would wish to keep them for your sake—you shew a virtue I did not expect."

"How have I deserved this reproof, madam?" said Emily sorrowfully.

"Reproof!" replied Madame Montoni: "I meant to praise your virtue."

"Alas! here is no exertion of virtue," rejoined Emily, "for here is no temptation to be overcome."

"Yet Monsieur Valancourt"—— said her aunt. "O, madam!" interrupted Emily, anticipating what she would have said, "do not let me glance on that subject: do not let my mind be stained with a wish so shockingly self-interested." She immediately changed the topic, and continued with Madame Montoni, till she withdrew to her apartment for the night.

At that hour, the castle was perfectly still, and every inhabitant of it, except herself, seemed to have retired to rest. As she passed along the wide and lonely galleries, dusky and silent, she felt forlorn and apprehensive of—she scarcely knew what; but when, entering the corridor, she recollected the incident of the preceding night, a dread seized her, lest a subject of alarm, similar to that, which had befallen Annette, should occur to her, and which, whether real, or ideal, would, she felt, have an almost equal effect upon her weakened spirits. The chamber, to which Annette had alluded, she did not exactly know, but understood it to be one of those she must pass in the way to her own; and, sending a fearful look forward into the gloom, she stepped lightly and cautiously along, till, coming to a door, from whence issued a low sound, she hesitated and paused; and, during the delay of that moment, her fears so much increased, that she had no power to move from the spot. Believing, that she heard a human voice within, she was somewhat revived; but, in the next moment, the door was opened, and a person, whom she conceived to be Montoni, appeared, who instantly started back, and closed it, though not before she had seen, by the light that burned in the chamber, another person, sitting in a melancholy attitude by the fire. Her terror vanished, but her astonishment only began, which was now roused by the mysterious secrecy of Montoni's manner, and by the discovery of a person, whom he thus visited at midnight, in an apartment, which had long been shut up, and of which such extraordinary reports were circulated.

While she thus continued hesitating, strongly prompted to watch Montoni's motions, yet fearing to irritate him by appearing to notice them, the door was again opened cautiously, and as instantly closed as before. She then stepped softly to her chamber, which was the next but one to this, but, having put down her lamp, returned to an obscure corner of the corridor, to observe the proceedings of this half-seen person, and to ascertain, whether it was indeed Montoni.

Having waited in silent expectation for a few minutes, with her eyes fixed on the door, it was again opened, and the same person appeared, whom she now knew to be Montoni. He looked cautiously round, without perceiving her, then, stepping forward, closed the door, and left the corridor. Soon after, Emily heard the door fastened on the inside, and she withdrew to her chamber, wondering at what she had witnessed.

It was now twelve o'clock. As she closed her casement, she heard footsteps on the terrace below, and saw imperfectly, through the gloom, several persons advancing, who passed under the casement. She then heard the clink of arms, and, in the next moment, the watch-word; when, recollecting the command she had overheard from Montoni, and the hour of the night, she understood, that these men were, for the first time, relieving guard in the castle. Having listened till all was again still, she retired to sleep.

CHAPTER X

And shall no lay of death
With pleasing murmur sooth
Her parted soul?
Shall no tear wet her grave?
SAYERS

ON the following morning, Emily went early to the apartment of Madame Montoni, who had slept well, and was much recovered. Her spirits had also returned with her health, and her resolution to oppose Montoni's demands revived, though it yet struggled with her fears, which Emily, who trembled for the consequence of further opposition, endeavoured to confirm.

Her aunt, as has been already shewn, had a disposition, which delighted in contradiction, and which taught her, when unpleasant circumstances were offered to her understanding, not to enquire into their truth, but to seek for arguments, by which she might make them appear false. Long habit had so entirely confirmed this natural propensity, that she was not conscious of possessing it. Emily's remonstrances and representations, therefore, roused her pride, instead of alarming, or convincing her judgment, and she still relied upon the discovery of some means, by which she might yet avoid submitting to the demand of her husband. Considering, that, if she could once escape from his castle, she might defy his power, and, obtaining a decisive separation, live in comfort on the estates, that yet remained for her, she mentioned this to her niece, who accorded with her in the wish, but differed from her, as to the probability of its completion. She represented the impossibility of passing the gates, secured and guarded as they were, and the extreme danger of committing her design to the discretion of a servant, who might either purposely betray, or accidentally disclose it.— Montoni's vengeance would also disdain restraint, if her intention was detected: and, though Emily wished, as fervently as she could do, to regain her freedom, and return to France, she consulted only Madame Montoni's safety, and persevered in advising her to relinquish her settlement, without braving further outrage.

The struggle of contrary emotions, however, continued to rage in her aunt's bosom, and she still brooded over the chance of effecting an escape. While she thus sat, Montoni entered the room, and, without noticing his wife's indisposition, said, that he came to remind her of the impolicy of trifling with him, and that he gave her only till the evening to determine, whether she would consent to his demand, or compel him, by a refusal, to remove her to the east turret. He added, that a party of cavaliers would dine with him, that day, and that he expected that she would sit at the head of the table, where Emily, also, must be present. Madame Montoni was now on the point of uttering an absolute refusal, but, suddenly considering, that her liberty, during this entertainment, though circumscribed, might favour her further plans, she acquiesced, with seeming reluctance, and Montoni, soon after, left the apartment. His command struck Emily with surprise and apprehension, who shrank from the thought of being exposed to the gaze of strangers, such as her fancy represented these to be, and the words of Count Morano, now again recollected, did not soothe her fears.

When she withdrew to prepare for dinner, she dressed herself with even more simplicity than usual, that she might escape observation—a policy, which did not avail her, for, as she re-passed to her aunt's apartment, she was met by Montoni, who censured what he called her prudish appearance, and insisted, that she should wear the most splendid dress she had, even that, which had been prepared for her intended nuptials with Count Morano, and which, it now appeared, her aunt had carefully brought with her from Venice. This was made, not in the Venetian, but, in the Neapolitan fashion, so as to set off the shape and figure, to the utmost advantage. In it, her beautiful chestnut tresses were negligently bound up in pearls, and suffered to fall back again on her neck. The simplicity of a better taste, than Madame Montoni's, was conspicuous in this dress, splendid as it was, and Emily's unaffected beauty never had appeared more captivatingly. She had now only to hope, that Montoni's order was prompted, not by any extraordinary design, but by an ostentation of displaying his family, richly attired, to the eyes of strangers; yet nothing less than his absolute command could have prevailed with her to wear a dress, that had been designed for such an offensive purpose, much less to have worn it on this occasion. As she descended to dinner, the emotion of her mind threw a faint blush over her countenance, and heightened its interesting expression; for timidity had made her linger in her apartment, till the utmost moment, and, when she entered the hall, in which a kind of state dinner was spread, Montoni and his guests were already seated at the table. She was then going to place herself by her aunt; but Montoni waved his hand, and two of the cavaliers rose, and seated her between them.

The eldest of these was a tall man, with strong Italian features, an aquiline nose, and dark penetrating eyes, that flashed with fire, when his mind was agitated, and, even in its state of rest, retained somewhat of the wildness of the passions. His visage was long and narrow, and his complexion of a sickly yellow.

The other, who appeared to be about forty, had features of a different cast, yet Italian, and his look was slow, subtle and penetrating; his eyes, of a dark grey, were small, and hollow; his complexion was a sunburnt brown, and the contour of his face, though inclined to oval, was irregular and ill-formed.

Eight other guests sat round the table, who were all dressed in an uniform, and had all an expression, more or less, of wild fierceness, of subtle design, or of licentious passions. As Emily timidly surveyed them, she remembered the scene of the preceding morning, and again almost fancied herself surrounded by banditti; then, looking back to the tranquillity of her early life, she felt scarcely less astonishment, than grief, at her present situation. The scene, in which they sat, assisted the illusion; it was an antient hall, gloomy from the style of its architecture, from its great extent, and because almost the only light it received was from one large gothic window, and from a pair of folding doors, which, being open, admitted likewise a view of the west rampart, with the wild mountains of the Apennine beyond.

The middle compartment of this hall rose into a vaulted roof, enriched with fretwork, and supported, on three sides, by pillars of marble; beyond these, long colonades retired in gloomy grandeur, till their extent was lost in twilight. The lightest footsteps of the servants, as they advanced through these, were returned in whispering echoes, and their figures, seen at a distance imperfectly through the dusk, frequently awakened Emily's imagination. She looked alternately at Montoni, at his guests and on the surrounding scene; and then, remembering her dear native province, her pleasant home and the simplicity and goodness of the friends, whom she had lost, grief and surprise again occupied her mind.

When her thoughts could return from these considerations, she fancied she observed an air of authority towards his guests, such as she had never before seen him assume, though he had always been distinguished by an haughty carriage; there was something also in the manners of the strangers, that seemed perfectly, though not servilely, to acknowledge his superiority.

During dinner, the conversation was chiefly on war and politics. They talked with energy of the state of Venice, its dangers, the character of the reigning Doge and of the chief senators; and then spoke of the state of Rome. When the repast was over, they rose, and, each filling his goblet with wine from the gilded ewer, that stood beside him, drank "Success to our exploits!" Montoni was lifting his goblet to his lips to drink this toast, when suddenly the wine hissed, rose to the brim, and, as he held the glass from him, it burst into a thousand pieces.

To him, who constantly used that sort of Venice glass, which had the quality of breaking, upon receiving poisoned liquor, a suspicion, that some of his guests had endeavoured to betray him, instantly occurred, and he ordered all the gates to be closed, drew his sword, and, looking round on them, who stood in silent amazement, exclaimed, "Here is a traitor among us; let those, that are innocent, assist in discovering the guilty."

Indignation flashed from the eyes of the cavaliers, who all drew their swords; and Madame Montoni, terrified at what might ensue, was hastening from the hall, when her husband commanded her to stay; but his further words could not now be distinguished, for the voice of every person rose together. His order, that all the servants should appear, was at length obeyed, and they declared their ignorance of any deceit—a protestation which could not be believed; for it was evident, that, as Montoni's liquor, and his only, had been poisoned, a deliberate design had been formed against his life, which could not have been carried so far towards its accomplishment, without the connivance of the servant, who had the care of the wine ewers.

This man, with another, whose face betrayed either the consciousness of guilt, or the fear of punishment, Montoni ordered to be chained instantly, and confined in a strong room, which had formerly been used as a prison. Thither, likewise, he would have sent all his guests, had he not foreseen the consequence of so bold and unjustifiable a proceeding. As to those, therefore, he contented himself with swearing, that no man should pass the gates, till this extraordinary affair had been investigated, and then sternly bade his wife retire to her apartment, whither he suffered Emily to attend her.

In about half an hour, he followed to the dressing-room; and Emily observed, with horror, his dark countenance and quivering lip, and heard him denounce vengeance on her aunt.

"It will avail you nothing," said he to his wife, "to deny the fact; I have proof of your guilt. Your only chance of mercy rests on a full confession;—there is nothing to hope from sullenness, or falsehood; your accomplice has confessed all."

Emily's fainting spirits were roused by astonishment, as she heard her aunt accused of a crime so atrocious, and she could not, for a moment, admit the possibility of her guilt. Meanwhile Madame Montoni's agitation did not permit her to reply; alternately her complexion varied from livid paleness to a crimson flush; and she trembled,—but, whether with fear, or with indignation, it were difficult to decide.

"Spare your words," said Montoni, seeing her about to speak, "your countenance makes full confession of your crime.—You shall be instantly removed to the east turret."

"This accusation," said Madame Montoni, speaking with difficulty, "is used only as an excuse for your cruelty; I disdain to reply to it. You do not believe me guilty."

"Signor!" said Emily solemnly, "this dreadful charge, I would answer with my life, is false. Nay, Signor," she added, observing the severity of his countenance, "this is no moment for restraint, on my part; I do not scruple to tell you, that you are deceived—most wickedly deceived, by the suggestion of some person, who aims at the ruin of my aunt:—it is impossible, that you could yourself have imagined a crime so hideous."

Montoni, his lips trembling more than before, replied only, "If you value your own safety," addressing Emily, "you will be silent. I shall know how to interpret your remonstrances, should you persevere in them."

Emily raised her eyes calmly to heaven. "Here is, indeed, then, nothing to hope!" said she.

"Peace!" cried Montoni, "or you shall find there is something to fear."

He turned to his wife, who had now recovered her spirits, and who vehemently and wildly remonstrated upon this mysterious suspicion: but Montoni's rage heightened with her indignation, and Emily, dreading the event of it, threw herself between them, and clasped his knees in silence, looking up in his face with an expression, that might have softened the heart of a fiend. Whether his was hardened by a conviction of Madame Montoni's guilt, or that a bare suspicion of it made him eager to exercise vengeance, he was totally and alike insensible to the distress of his wife, and to the pleading looks of Emily, whom he made no attempt to raise, but was vehemently menacing both, when he was called out of the room by some person at the door. As he shut the door, Emily heard him turn the lock and take out the key; so that Madame Montoni and herself were now prisoners; and she saw that his designs became more and more terrible. Her endeavours to explain his motives for this circumstance were almost as ineffectual as those to soothe the distress of her aunt, whose innocence she could not doubt; but she, at length, accounted for Montoni's readiness to suspect his wife by his own consciousness of cruelty towards her, and for the sudden violence of his present conduct against both, before even his suspicions could be completely formed, by his general eagerness to effect suddenly whatever he was led to desire and his carelessness of justice, or humanity, in accomplishing it.

Madame Montoni, after some time, again looked round, in search of a possibility of escape from the castle, and conversed with Emily on the subject, who was now willing to encounter any hazard, though she forbore to encourage a hope in her aunt, which she herself did not admit. How strongly the edifice was secured, and how vigilantly guarded, she knew too well; and trembled to commit their safety to the caprice of the servant, whose assistance they must solicit. Old Carlo was compassionate, but he seemed to be too much in his master's interest to be trusted by them; Annette could of herself do little, and Emily knew Ludovico only from her report. At present, however, these considerations were useless, Madame Montoni and her niece being shut up from all intercourse, even with the persons, whom there might be these reasons to reject.

In the hall, confusion and tumult still reigned. Emily, as she listened anxiously to the murmur, that sounded along the gallery, sometimes fancied she heard the clashing of swords, and, when she considered the nature of the provocation, given by Montoni, and his impetuosity, it appeared probable, that nothing less than arms would terminate the contention. Madame Montoni, having exhausted all her expressions of indignation, and Emily, hers of comfort, they remained silent, in that kind of breathless stillness, which, in nature, often succeeds to the uproar of conflicting elements; a stillness, like the morning, that dawns upon the ruins of an earthquake.

An uncertain kind of terror pervaded Emily's mind; the circumstances of the past hour still came dimly and confusedly to her memory; and her thoughts were various and rapid, though without tumult.

From this state of waking visions she was recalled by a knocking at the chamber-door, and, enquiring who was there, heard the whispering voice of Annette.

"Dear madam, let me come in, I have a great deal to say," said the poor girl.

"The door is locked," answered the lady.

"Yes, ma'am, but do pray open it."

"The Signor has the key," said Madame Montoni.

"O blessed Virgin! what will become of us?" exclaimed Annette.

"Assist us to escape," said her mistress. "Where is Ludovico?"

"Below in the hall, ma'am, amongst them all, fighting with the best of them!"

"Fighting! Who are fighting?" cried Madame Montoni.

"Why the Signor, ma'am, and all the Signors, and a great many more."

"Is any person much hurt?" said Emily, in a tremulous voice. "Hurt! Yes, ma'amselle,—there they lie bleeding, and the swords are clashing, and—O holy saints! Do let me in, ma'am, they are coming this way— I shall be murdered!"

"Fly!" cried Emily, "fly! we cannot open the door."

Annette repeated, that they were coming, and in the same moment fled.

"Be calm, madam," said Emily, turning to her aunt, "I entreat you to be calm, I am not frightened—not frightened in the least, do not you be alarmed."

"You can scarcely support yourself," replied her aunt; "Merciful God! what is it they mean to do with us?"

"They come, perhaps, to liberate us," said Emily, "Signor Montoni perhaps is—is conquered."

The belief of his death gave her spirits a sudden shock, and she grew faint as she saw him in imagination, expiring at her feet.

"They are coming!" cried Madame Montoni—"I hear their steps— they are at the door!"

Emily turned her languid eyes to the door, but terror deprived her of utterance. The key sounded in the lock; the door opened, and Montoni appeared, followed by three ruffian-like men. "Execute your orders," said he, turning to them, and pointing to his wife, who shrieked, but was immediately carried from the room; while Emily sunk, senseless, on a couch, by which she had endeavoured to support herself. When she recovered, she was alone, and recollected only, that Madame Montoni had been there, together with some unconnected particulars of the preceding transaction, which were, however, sufficient to renew all her terror. She looked wildly round the apartment, as if in search of some means of intelligence, concerning her aunt, while neither her own danger, or an idea of escaping from the room, immediately occurred.

When her recollection was more complete, she raised herself and went, but with only a faint hope, to examine whether the door was unfastened. It was so, and she then stepped timidly out into the gallery, but paused there, uncertain which way she should proceed. Her first wish was to gather some information, as to her aunt, and she, at length, turned her steps to go to the lesser hall, where Annette and the other servants usually waited.

Every where, as she passed, she heard, from a distance, the uproar of contention, and the figures and faces, which she met, hurrying along the passages, struck her mind with dismay. Emily might now have appeared, like an angel of light, encompassed by fiends. At length, she reached the lesser hall, which was silent and deserted, but, panting for breath, she sat down to recover herself. The total stillness of this place was as awful as the tumult, from which she had escaped: but she had now time to recall her scattered thoughts, to remember her personal danger, and to consider of some means of safety. She perceived, that it was useless to seek Madame Montoni, through the wide extent and intricacies of the castle, now, too, when every avenue seemed to be beset by ruffians; in this hall she could not resolve to stay, for she knew not how soon it might become their place of rendezvous; and, though she wished to go to her chamber, she dreaded again to encounter them on the way.

Thus she sat, trembling and hesitating, when a distant murmur broke on the silence, and grew louder and louder, till she distinguished voices and steps approaching. She then rose to go, but the sounds came along the only passage, by which she could depart, and she was compelled to await in the hall, the arrival of the persons, whose steps she heard. As these advanced, she distinguished groans, and then saw a man borne slowly along by four others. Her spirits faltered at the sight, and she leaned against the wall for support. The bearers, meanwhile, entered the hall, and, being too busily occupied to detain, or even notice Emily, she attempted to leave it, but her strength failed, and she again sat down on the bench. A damp chillness came over her; her sight became confused; she knew not what had passed, or where she was, yet the groans of the wounded person still vibrated on her heart. In a few moments, the tide of life seemed again to flow; she began to breathe more freely, and her senses revived. She had not fainted, nor had ever totally lost her consciousness, but had contrived to support herself on the bench; still without courage to turn her eyes upon the unfortunate object, which remained near her, and about whom the men were yet too much engaged to attend to her.

When her strength returned, she rose, and was suffered to leave the hall, though her anxiety, having produced some vain enquiries, concerning Madame Montoni, had thus made a discovery of herself. Towards her chamber she now hastened, as fast as her steps would bear her, for she still perceived, upon her passage, the sounds of confusion at a distance, and she endeavoured, by taking her way through some obscure rooms, to avoid encountering the persons, whose looks had terrified her before, as well as those parts of the castle, where the tumult might still rage.

At length, she reached her chamber, and, having secured the door of the corridor, felt herself, for a moment, in safety. A profound stillness reigned in this remote apartment, which not even the faint murmur of the most distant sounds now reached. She sat down, near one of the casements, and, as she gazed on the mountain-view beyond, the deep repose of its beauty struck her with all the force of contrast, and she could scarcely believe herself so near a scene of savage discord. The contending elements seemed to have retired from their natural spheres, and to have collected themselves into the minds of men, for there alone the tempest now reigned.

Emily tried to tranquillize her spirits, but anxiety made her constantly listen for some sound, and often look out upon the ramparts, where all, however, was lonely and still. As a sense of her own immediate danger had decreased, her apprehension concerning Madame Montoni heightened, who, she remembered, had been fiercely threatened with confinement in the east turret, and it was possible, that her husband had satisfied his present vengeance with this punishment. She, therefore, determined, when night should return, and the inhabitants of the castle should be asleep, to explore the way to the turret, which, as the direction it stood in was mentioned, appeared not very difficult to be done. She knew, indeed, that although her aunt might be there, she could afford her no effectual assistance, but it might give her some comfort even to know, that she was discovered, and to hear the sound of her niece's voice; for herself, any certainty, concerning

Madame Montoni's fate, appeared more tolerable, than this exhausting suspense.

Meanwhile, Annette did not appear, and Emily was surprised, and somewhat alarmed for her, whom, in the confusion of the late scene, various accidents might have befallen, and it was improbable, that she would have failed to come to her apartment, unless something unfortunate had happened.

Thus the hours passed in solitude, in silence, and in anxious conjecturing. Being not once disturbed by a message, or a sound, it appeared, that Montoni had wholly forgotten her, and it gave her some comfort to find, that she could be so unnoticed. She endeavoured to withdraw her thoughts from the anxiety, that preyed upon them, but they refused controul; she could neither read, or draw, and the tones of her lute were so utterly discordant with the present state of her feelings, that she could not endure them for a moment.

The sun, at length, set behind the western mountains; his fiery beams faded from the clouds, and then a dun melancholy purple drew over them, and gradually involved the features of the country below. Soon after, the sentinels passed on the rampart to commence the watch.

Twilight had now spread its gloom over every object; the dismal obscurity of her chamber recalled fearful thoughts, but she remembered, that to procure a light she must pass through a great extent of the castle, and, above all, through the halls, where she had already experienced so much horror. Darkness, indeed, in the present state of her spirits, made silence and solitude terrible to her; it would also prevent the possibility of her finding her way to the turret, and condemn her to remain in suspense, concerning the fate of her aunt; yet she dared not to venture forth for a lamp.

Continuing at the casement, that she might catch the last lingering gleam of evening, a thousand vague images of fear floated on her fancy. "What if some of these ruffians," said she, "should find out the private stair-case, and in the darkness of night steal into my chamber!" Then, recollecting the mysterious inhabitant of the neighbouring apartment, her terror changed its object. "He is not a prisoner," said she, "though he remains in one chamber, for Montoni did not fasten the door, when he left it; the unknown person himself did this; it is certain, therefore, he can come out when he pleases."

She paused, for, notwithstanding the terrors of darkness, she considered it to be very improbable, whoever he was, that he could have any interest in intruding upon her retirement; and again the subject of her emotion changed, when, remembering her nearness to the chamber, where the veil had formerly disclosed a dreadful spectacle, she doubted whether some passage might not communicate between it and the insecure door of the stair-case.

It was now entirely dark, and she left the casement. As she sat with her eyes fixed on the hearth, she thought she perceived there a spark of light; it twinkled and disappeared, and then again was visible. At length, with much care, she fanned the embers of a wood fire, that had been lighted in the morning, into flame, and, having communicated it to a lamp, which always stood in her room, felt a satisfaction not to be conceived, without a review of her situation. Her first care was to guard the door of the stair-case, for which purpose she placed against it all the furniture she could move, and she was thus employed, for some time, at the end of which she had another instance how much more oppressive misfortune is to the idle, than to the busy; for, having then leisure to think over all the circumstances of her present afflictions, she imagined a thousand evils for futurity, and these real and ideal subjects of distress alike wounded her mind.

Thus heavily moved the hours till midnight, when she counted the sullen notes of the great clock, as they rolled along the rampart, unmingled with any sound, except the distant foot-fall of a sentinel, who came to relieve guard. She now thought she might venture towards the turret, and, having gently opened the chamber door to examine the corridor, and to listen if any person was stirring in the castle, found all around in perfect stillness. Yet no sooner had she left the room, than she perceived a light flash on the walls of the corridor, and, without waiting to see by whom it was carried, she shrunk back, and closed her door. No one approaching, she conjectured, that it was Montoni going to pay his mid-night visit to her unknown neighbour, and she determined to wait, till he should have retired to his own apartment.

When the chimes had tolled another half hour, she once more opened the door, and, perceiving that no person was in the corridor, hastily crossed into a passage, that led along the south side of the castle towards the stair-case, whence she believed she could easily find her way to the turret. Often pausing on her way, listening apprehensively to the murmurs of the wind, and looking fearfully onward into the gloom of the long passages, she, at length, reached the stair-case; but there her perplexity began. Two passages appeared, of which she knew not how to prefer one, and was compelled, at last, to decide by chance, rather than by circumstances. That she entered, opened first into a wide gallery, along which she passed lightly and swiftly; for the lonely aspect of the place awed her, and she started at the echo of her own steps.

On a sudden, she thought she heard a voice, and, not distinguishing from whence it came, feared equally to proceed, or to return. For some moments, she stood in an attitude of listening expectation, shrinking almost from herself and scarcely daring to look round her. The voice came again, but, though it was now near her, terror did not allow her to judge exactly whence it proceeded. She thought, however, that it was the voice of complaint, and her belief was soon confirmed by a low moaning sound, that seemed to proceed from one of the chambers, opening into the gallery. It instantly occurred to her, that Madame Montoni might be there confined, and she advanced to the door to speak, but was checked by considering, that she was, perhaps, going to commit herself to a stranger, who might discover her to Montoni; for, though this person, whoever it was, seemed to be in affliction, it did not follow, that he was a prisoner.

While these thoughts passed over her mind, and left her still in hesitation, the voice spoke again, and, calling "Ludovico," she then perceived it to be that of Annette; on which, no longer hesitating, she went in joy to answer her.

"Ludovico!" cried Annette, sobbing—"Ludovico!"

"It is I," said Emily, trying to open the door. "How came you here? Who shut you up?"

"Ludovico!" repeated Annette—"O Ludovico!"

"It is not Ludovico, it is I—Mademoiselle Emily."

Annette ceased sobbing, and was silent.

"If you can open the door, let me in," said Emily, "here is no person to hurt you."

"Ludovico!—O, Ludovico!" cried Annette.

Emily now lost her patience, and her fear of being overheard increasing, she was even nearly about to leave the door, when she considered, that Annette might, possibly, know something of the situation of Madame Montoni, or direct her to the turret. At length, she obtained a reply, though little satisfactory, to her questions, for Annette knew nothing of Madame Montoni, and only conjured Emily to tell her what was become of Ludovico. Of him she had no information to give, and she again asked who had shut Annette up.

"Ludovico," said the poor girl, "Ludovico shut me up. When I ran away from the dressing-room door to-day, I went I scarcely knew where, for safety; and, in this gallery, here, I met Ludovico, who hurried me into this chamber, and locked me up to keep me out of harm, as he said. But he was in such a hurry himself, he hardly spoke ten words, but he told me he would come, and let me out, when all was quiet, and he took away the key with him. Now all these hours are passed, and I have neither seen, or heard a word of him; they have murdered him—I know they have!"

Emily suddenly remembered the wounded person, whom she had seen borne into the servants' hall, and she scarcely doubted, that he was

Ludovico, but she concealed the circumstance from Annette, and endeavoured to comfort her. Then, impatient to learn something of her aunt, she again enquired the way to the turret.

"O! you are not going, ma'amselle," said Annette, "for Heaven's sake, do not go, and leave me here by myself."

"Nay, Annette, you do not think I can wait in the gallery all night," replied Emily. "Direct me to the turret; in the morning I will endeavour to release you."

"O holy Mary!" exclaimed Annette, "am I to stay here by myself all night! I shall be frightened out of my senses, and I shall die of hunger; I have had nothing to eat since dinner!"

Emily could scarcely forbear smiling at the heterogeneous distresses of Annette, though she sincerely pitied them, and said what she could to soothe her. At length, she obtained something like a direction to the east turret, and quitted the door, from whence, after many intricacies and perplexities, she reached the steep and winding stairs of the turret, at the foot of which she stopped to rest, and to re-animate her courage with a sense of her duty. As she surveyed this dismal place, she perceived a door on the opposite side of the stair-case, and, anxious to know whether it would lead her to Madame Montoni, she tried to undraw the bolts, which fastened it. A fresher air came to her face, as she unclosed the door, which opened upon the east rampart, and the sudden current had nearly extinguished her light, which she now removed to a distance; and again, looking out upon the obscure terrace, she perceived only the faint outline of the walls and of some towers, while, above, heavy clouds, borne along the wind, seemed to mingle with the stars, and wrap the night in thicker darkness. As she gazed, now willing to defer the moment of certainty, from which she expected only confirmation of evil, a distant footstep reminded her, that she might be observed by the men on watch, and, hastily closing the door, she took her lamp, and passed up the stair-case. Trembling came upon her, as she ascended through the gloom. To her melancholy fancy this seemed to be a place of death, and the chilling silence, that reigned, confirmed its character. Her spirits faltered. "Perhaps," said she, "I am come hither only to learn a dreadful truth, or to witness some horrible spectacle; I feel that my senses would not survive such an addition of horror."

The image of her aunt murdered—murdered, perhaps, by the hand of Montoni, rose to her mind; she trembled, gasped for breath— repented that she had dared to venture hither, and checked her steps. But, after she had paused a few minutes, the consciousness of her duty returned, and she went on. Still all was silent. At length a track of blood, upon a stair, caught her eye; and instantly she perceived, that the wall and several other steps were stained. She paused, again struggled to support herself, and the lamp almost fell from her trembling hand. Still no sound was heard, no living being seemed to inhabit the turret; a thousand times she wished herself again in her chamber; dreaded to enquire farther—dreaded to encounter some horrible spectacle, and yet could not resolve, now that she was so near the termination of her efforts, to desist from them. Having again collected courage to proceed, after ascending about half way up the turret, she came to another door, but here again she stopped in hesitation; listened for sounds within, and then, summoning all her resolution, unclosed it, and entered a chamber, which, as her lamp shot its feeble rays through the darkness, seemed to exhibit only dew-stained and deserted walls. As she stood examining it, in fearful expectation of discovering the remains of her unfortunate aunt, she perceived something lying in an obscure corner of the room, and, struck with an horrible conviction, she became, for an instant, motionless and nearly insensible. Then, with a kind of desperate resolution, she hurried towards the object that excited her terror, when, perceiving the clothes of some person, on the floor, she caught hold of them, and found in her grasp the old uniform of a soldier, beneath which appeared a heap of pikes and other arms. Scarcely daring to trust her sight, she continued, for some moments, to gaze on the object of her late alarm, and then left the chamber, so much comforted and occupied by the conviction, that her aunt was not there, that she was going to descend the turret, without enquiring farther; when, on turning to do so, she observed upon some steps on the second flight an appearance of blood, and remembering, that there was yet another chamber to be explored, she again followed the windings of the ascent. Still, as she ascended, the track of blood glared upon the stairs.

It led her to the door of a landing-place, that terminated them, but she was unable to follow it farther. Now that she was so near the sought-for certainty, she dreaded to know it, even more than before, and had not fortitude sufficient to speak, or to attempt opening the door.

Having listened, in vain, for some sound, that might confirm, or destroy her fears, she, at length, laid her hand on the lock, and, finding it fastened, called on Madame Montoni; but only a chilling silence ensued.

"She is dead!" she cried,—"murdered!—her blood is on the stairs!"

Emily grew very faint; could support herself no longer, and had scarcely presence of mind to set down the lamp, and place herself on a step.

When her recollection returned, she spoke again at the door, and again attempted to open it, and, having lingered for some time, without receiving any answer, or hearing a sound, she descended the turret, and, with all the swiftness her feebleness would permit, sought her own apartment.

As she turned into the corridor, the door of a chamber opened, from whence Montoni came forth; but Emily, more terrified than ever to behold him, shrunk back into the passage soon enough to escape being noticed, and heard him close the door, which she had perceived was the same she formerly observed. Having here listened to his departing steps, till their faint sound was lost in distance, she ventured to her apartment, and, securing it once again, retired to her bed, leaving the lamp burning on the hearth. But sleep was fled from her harassed mind, to which images of horror alone occurred. She endeavoured to think it possible, that Madame Montoni had not been taken to the turret; but, when she recollected the former menaces of her husband and the terrible spirit of vengeance, which he had displayed on a late occasion; when she remembered his general character, the looks of the men, who had forced Madame Montoni from her apartment, and the written traces on the stairs of the turret—she could not doubt, that her aunt had been carried thither, and could scarcely hope, that she had not been carried to be murdered.

The grey of morning had long dawned through her casements, before Emily closed her eyes in sleep; when wearied nature, at length, yielded her a respite from suffering.

CHAPTER XI

Who rears the bloody hand?
SAYERS

EMILY remained in her chamber, on the following morning, without receiving any notice from Montoni, or seeing a human being, except the armed men, who sometimes passed on the terrace below. Having tasted no food since the dinner of the preceding day, extreme faintness made her feel the necessity of quitting the asylum of her apartment to obtain refreshment, and she was also very anxious to procure liberty for Annette. Willing, however, to defer venturing forth, as long as possible, and considering, whether she should apply to Montoni, or to the compassion of some other person, her excessive anxiety concerning her aunt, at length, overcame her abhorrence of his presence, and she determined to go to him, and to entreat, that he would suffer her to see Madame Montoni.

Meanwhile, it was too certain, from the absence of Annette, that some accident had befallen Ludovico, and that she was still in con-finement; Emily, therefore, resolved also to visit the chamber, where she had spoken to her, on the preceding night, and, if the poor girl was yet there, to inform Montoni of her situation.

It was near noon, before she ventured from her apartment, and went first to the south gallery, whither she passed without meeting a single person, or hearing a sound, except, now and then, the echo of a distant footstep.

It was unnecessary to call Annette, whose lamentations were audible upon the first approach to the gallery, and who, bewailing her own and Ludovico's fate, told Emily, that she should certainly be starved to death, if she was not let out immediately. Emily replied, that she was going to beg her release of Montoni; but the terrors of hunger now yielded to those of the Signor, and, when Emily left her, she was loudly entreating, that her place of refuge might be concealed from him.

As Emily drew near the great hall, the sounds she heard and the peo-ple she met in the passages renewed her alarm. The latter, however, were peaceable, and did not interrupt her, though they looked earnestly at her, as she passed, and sometimes spoke. On crossing the hall towards the cedar room, where Montoni usually sat, she perceived, on the pavement, fragments of swords, some tattered garments stained with blood, and almost expected to have seen among them a dead body; but from such a spectacle she was, at present, spared. As she approached the room, the sound of several voices issued from within, and a dread of appearing before many strangers, as well as of irritating Montoni by such an intrusion, made her pause and falter from her purpose. She looked up through the long arcades of the hall, in search of a servant, who might bear a message, but no one appeared, and the urgency of what she had to request made her still linger near the door. The voices within were not in contention, though she distinguished those of several of the guests of the preceding day; but still her resolu-tion failed, whenever she would have tapped at the door, and she had determined to walk in the hall, till some person should appear, who might call Montoni from the room, when, as she turned from the door, it was suddenly opened by himself. Emily trembled, and was confused, while he almost started with surprise, and all the terrors of his counte-nance unfolded themselves. She forgot all she would have said, and neither enquired for her aunt, or entreated for Annette, but stood silent and embarrassed.

After closing the door he reproved her for a meanness, of which she had not been guilty, and sternly questioned her what she had over-heard; an accusation, which revived her recollection so far, that she assured him she had not come thither with an intention to listen to his conversation, but to entreat his compassion for her aunt, and for Annette. Montoni seemed to doubt this assertion, for he regarded her with a scrutinizing look; and the doubt evidently arose from no trifling interest. Emily then further explained herself, and concluded with entreating him to inform her, where her aunt was placed, and to permit, that she might visit her; but he looked upon her only with a malignant smile, which instantaneously confirmed her worst fears for her aunt, and, at that moment, she had not courage to renew her entreaties.

"For Annette," said he, — "if you go to Carlo, he will release the girl; the foolish fellow, who shut her up, died yesterday." Emily shuddered. — "But my aunt, Signor" — said she, "O tell me of my aunt!"

"She is taken care of," replied Montoni hastily, "I have no time to answer idle questions."

He would have passed on, but Emily, in a voice of agony, that could not be wholly resisted, conjured him to tell her, where Madame Montoni was; while he paused, and she anxiously watched his countenance, a trumpet sounded, and, in the next moment, she heard the heavy gates of the portal open, and then the clattering of horses' hoofs in the court, with the confusion of many voices. She stood for a moment hesitating whether she should follow Montoni, who, at the sound of the trumpet, had passed through the hall, and, turning her eyes whence it came, she saw through the door, that opened beyond a long perspective of arches into the courts, a party of horsemen, whom she judged, as well as the distance and her embarrassment would allow, to be the same she had seen depart, a few days before. But she staid not to scrutinize, for, when the trumpet sounded again, the chevaliers rushed out of the cedar room, and men came running into the hall from every quarter of the castle. Emily once more hurried for shelter to her own apartment. Thither she was still pursued by images of horror. She re-considered Montoni's manner and words, when he had spoken of his wife, and they served only to confirm her most terrible suspicions. Tears refused any longer to relieve her distress, and she had sat for a considerable time absorbed in thought, when a knocking at the chamber door aroused her, on opening which she found old Carlo.

"Dear young lady," said he, "I have been so flurried, I never once thought of you till just now. I have brought you some fruit and wine, and I am sure you must stand in need of them by this time."

"Thank you, Carlo," said Emily, "this is very good of you. Did the Signor remind you of me?"

"No, Signora," replied Carlo, "his *Excellenza* has business enough on his hands." Emily then renewed her enquiries, concerning Madame Montoni, but Carlo had been employed at the other end of the castle, during the time, that she was removed, and he had heard nothing since, concerning her.

While he spoke, Emily looked steadily at him, for she scarcely knew whether he was really ignorant, or concealed his knowledge of the truth from a fear of offending his master. To several questions, concerning the contentions of yesterday, he gave very limited answers; but told, that the disputes were now amicably settled, and that the Signor believed himself to have been mistaken in his suspicions of his guests. "The fighting was about that, Signora," said Carlo; "but I trust I shall never see such another day in this castle, though strange things are about to be done."

On her enquiring his meaning, "Ah, Signora!" added he, "it is not for me to betray secrets, or tell all I think, but time will tell."

She then desired him to release Annette, and, having described the chamber in which the poor girl was confined, he promised to obey her immediately, and was departing, when she remembered to ask who were the persons just arrived. Her late conjecture was right; it was Verezzi, with his party.

Her spirits were somewhat soothed by this short conversation with Carlo; for, in her present circumstances, it afforded some comfort to hear the accents of compassion, and to meet the look of sympathy.

An hour passed before Annette appeared, who then came weeping and sobbing. "O Ludovico—Ludovico!" cried she.

"My poor Annette!" said Emily, and made her sit down.

"Who could have foreseen this, ma'amselle? O miserable, wretched, day—that ever I should live to see it!" and she continued to moan and lament, till Emily thought it necessary to check her excess of grief. "We are continually losing dear friends by death," said she, with a sigh, that came from her heart. "We must submit to the will of Heaven—our tears, alas! cannot recall the dead!"

Annette took the handkerchief from her face.

"You will meet Ludovico in a better world, I hope," added Emily.

"Yes—yes,—ma'amselle," sobbed Annette, "but I hope I shall meet him again in this—though he is so wounded!"

"Wounded!" exclaimed Emily, "does he live?"

"Yes, ma'am, but—but he has a terrible wound, and could not come to let me out. They thought him dead, at first, and he has not been rightly himself, till within this hour."

"Well, Annette, I rejoice to hear he lives."

"Lives! Holy Saints! why he will not die, surely!"

Emily said she hoped not, but this expression of hope Annette thought implied fear, and her own increased in proportion, as Emily endeavoured to encourage her. To enquiries, concerning Madame Montoni, she could give no satisfactory answers.

"I quite forgot to ask among the servants, ma'amselle," said she, "for I could think of nobody but poor Ludovico."

Annette's grief was now somewhat assuaged, and Emily sent her to make enquiries, concerning her lady, of whom, however, she could obtain no intelligence, some of the people she spoke with being really ignorant of her fate, and others having probably received orders to conceal it.

This day passed with Emily in continued grief and anxiety for her aunt; but she was unmolested by any notice from Montoni; and, now that Annette was liberated, she obtained food, without exposing herself to danger, or impertinence.

Two following days passed in the same manner, unmarked by any occurrence, during which she obtained no information of Madame Montoni. On the evening of the second, having dismissed Annette, and retired to bed, her mind became haunted by the most dismal images, such as her long anxiety, concerning her aunt, suggested; and, unable to forget herself, for a moment, or to vanquish the phantoms, that tormented her, she rose from her bed, and went to one of the casements of her chamber, to breathe a freer air.

All without was silent and dark, unless that could be called light, which was only the faint glimmer of the stars, shewing imperfectly the outline of the mountains, the western towers of the castle and the ramparts below, where a solitary sentinel was pacing. What an image of repose did this scene present! The fierce and terrible passions, too, which so often agitated the inhabitants of this edifice, seemed now hushed in sleep;—those mysterious workings, that rouse the elements of man's nature into tempest—were calm. Emily's heart was not so; but her sufferings, though deep, partook of the gentle character of her mind. Hers was a silent anguish, weeping, yet enduring; not the wild energy of passion, inflaming imagination, bearing down the barriers of reason and living in a world of its own.

The air refreshed her, and she continued at the casement, looking on the shadowy scene, over which the planets burned with a clear light, amid the deep blue æther, as they silently moved in their destined course. She remembered how often she had gazed on them with her dear father, how often he had pointed out their way in the heavens, and explained their laws; and these reflections led to others, which, in an almost equal degree, awakened her grief and astonishment.

They brought a retrospect of all the strange and mournful events, which had occurred since she lived in peace with her parents. And to Emily, who had been so tenderly educated, so tenderly loved, who once knew only goodness and happiness—to her, the late events and her present situation—in a foreign land—in a remote castle—surrounded by vice and violence—seemed more like the visions of a distempered imagination, than the circumstances of truth. She wept to think of what her parents would have suffered, could they have foreseen the events of her future life.

While she raised her streaming eyes to heaven, she observed the same planet, which she had seen in Languedoc, on the night, preceding her father's death, rise above the eastern towers of the castle, while she remembered the conversation, which had passed, concerning the probable state of departed souls; remembered, also, the solemn music she had heard, and to which the tenderness of her spirits had, in spite of her reason, given a superstitious meaning. At these recollections she wept again, and continued musing, when suddenly the notes of sweet music passed on the air. A superstitious dread stole over her; she stood listening, for some moments, in trembling expectation, and then endeavoured to re-collect her thoughts, and to reason herself into composure; but human reason cannot establish her laws on subjects, lost in the obscurity of imagination, any more than the eye can ascertain the form of objects, that only glimmer through the dimness of night.

Her surprise, on hearing such soothing and delicious sounds, was, at least, justifiable; for it was long—very long, since she had listened to any thing like melody. The fierce trumpet and the shrill fife were the only instruments she had heard, since her arrival at Udolpho.

When her mind was somewhat more composed, she tried to ascertain from what quarter the sounds proceeded, and thought they came from below; but whether from a room of the castle, or from the terrace, she could not with certainty judge. Fear and surprise now yielded to the enchantment of a strain, that floated on the silent night, with the most soft and melancholy sweetness. Suddenly, it seemed removed to a distance, trembled faintly, and then entirely ceased.

She continued to listen, sunk in that pleasing repose, which soft music leaves on the mind—but it came no more. Upon this strange circumstance her thoughts were long engaged, for strange it certainly was to hear music at midnight, when every inhabitant of the castle had long since retired to rest, and in a place, where nothing like harmony had been heard before, probably, for many years. Long-suffering had made her spirits peculiarly sensible to terror, and liable to be affected by the illusions of superstition.—It now seemed to her, as if her dead father had spoken to her in that strain, to inspire her with comfort and confidence, on the subject, which had then occupied her mind. Yet reason told her, that this was a wild conjecture, and she was inclined to dismiss it; but, with the inconsistency so natural, when imagination guides the thoughts, she then wavered towards a belief as wild. She remembered the singular event, connected with the castle, which had given it into the possession of its present owner; and, when she considered the mysterious manner, in which its late possessor had disappeared, and that she had never since been heard of, her mind was impressed with an high degree of solemn awe; so that, though there appeared no clue to connect that event with the late music, she was inclined fancifully to think they had some relation to each other. At this conjecture, a sudden chillness ran through her frame; she looked fearfully upon the duskiness of her chamber, and the dead silence, that prevailed there, heightened to her fancy its gloomy aspect.

At length, she left the casement, but her steps faltered, as she approached the bed, and she stopped and looked round. The single lamp, that burned in her spacious chamber, was expiring; for a moment, she shrunk from the darkness beyond; and then, ashamed of the weakness, which, however, she could not wholly conquer, went forward to the bed, where her mind did not soon know the soothings of sleep. She still mused on the late occurrence, and looked with anxiety to the next night, when, at the same hour, she determined to watch whether the music returned. "If those sounds were human," said she, "I shall probably hear them again."

CHAPTER XII

> Then, oh, you blessed ministers above,
> Keep me in patience; and, in ripen'd time,
> Unfold the evil which is here wrapt up
> In countenance.
>
> SHAKESPEARE

ANNETTE came almost breathless to Emily's apartment in the morning. "O ma'amselle!" said she, in broken sentences, "what news I have to tell! I have found out who the prisoner is—but he was no prisoner, neither;—he that was shut up in the chamber I told you of. I must think him a ghost, forsooth!"

"Who was the prisoner?" enquired Emily, while her thoughts glanced back to the circumstance of the preceding night.

"You mistake, ma'am," said Annette; "he was not a prisoner, after all."

"Who is the person, then?"

"Holy Saints!" rejoined Annette; "How I was surprised! I met him just now, on the rampart below, there. I never was so surprised in my life! Ah! ma'amselle! this is a strange place! I should never have done wondering, if I was to live here an hundred years. But, as I was saying, I met him just now on the rampart, and I was thinking of nobody less than of him."

"This trifling is insupportable," said Emily; "prythee, Annette, do not torture my patience any longer."

"Nay, ma'amselle, guess—guess who it was; it was somebody you know very well."

"I cannot guess," said Emily impatiently.

"Nay, ma'amselle, I'll tell you something to guess by—A tall Signor, with a longish face, who walks so stately, and used to wear such a high feather in his hat; and used often to look down upon the ground, when people spoke to him; and to look at people from under his eyebrows, as it were, all so dark and frowning. You have seen him, often and often, at Venice, ma'am. Then he was so intimate with the Signor, too. And, now I think of it, I wonder what he could be afraid of in this lonely old castle, that he should shut himself up for. But he is come abroad now, for I met him on the rampart just this minute. I trembled when I saw him, for I always was afraid of him, somehow; but I determined I would not let him see it; so I went up to him, and made him a low curtesy, 'You are welcome to the castle, Signor Orsino,' said I."

"O, it was Signor Orsino, then!" said Emily.

"Yes, ma'amselle, Signor Orsino, himself, who caused that Venetian gentleman to be killed, and has been popping about from place to place, ever since, as I hear."

"Good God!" exclaimed Emily, recovering from the shock of this intelligence; "and is *he* come to Udolpho! He does well to endeavour to conceal himself."

"Yes, ma'amselle, but if that was all, this desolate place would conceal him, without his shutting himself up in one room. Who would think of coming to look for him here? I am sure I should as soon think of going to look for any body in the other world."

"There is some truth in that," said Emily, who would now have concluded it was Orsino's music, which she had heard, on the preceding night, had she not known, that he had neither taste, or skill in the art. But, though she was unwilling to add to the number of Annette's surprises, by mentioning the subject of her own, she enquired, whether any person in the castle played on a musical instrument?

"O yes, ma'amselle! there is Benedetto plays the great drum to admiration; and then, there is Launcelot the trumpeter; nay, for that matter, Ludovico himself can play on the trumpet;—but he is ill now. I remember once"——

Emily interrupted her; "Have you heard no other music since you came to the castle—none last night?"

"Why, did *you* hear any last night, ma'amselle?"

Emily evaded this question, by repeating her own.

"Why, no, ma'am," replied Annette; "I never heard any music here, I must say, but the drums and the trumpet; and, as for last night, I did nothing but dream I saw my late lady's ghost."

"Your *late* lady's," said Emily in a tremulous voice; "you have heard more, then. Tell me—tell me all, Annette, I entreat; tell me the worst at once."

"Nay, ma'amselle, you know the worst already."

"I know nothing," said Emily.

"Yes, you do, ma'amselle; you know, that nobody knows any thing about her; and it is plain, therefore, she is gone, the way of the first lady of the castle—nobody ever knew any thing about her."

Emily leaned her head upon her hand, and was, for some time, silent; then, telling Annette she wished to be alone, the latter left the room.

The remark of Annette had revived Emily's terrible suspicion, concerning the fate of Madame Montoni; and she resolved to make another effort to obtain certainty on this subject, by applying to Montoni once more.

When Annette returned, a few hours after, she told Emily, that the porter of the castle wished very much to speak with her, for that he had something of importance to say; her spirits had, however, of late been so subject to alarm, that any new circumstance excited it; and this message from the porter, when her first surprise was over, made her look round for some lurking danger, the more suspiciously, perhaps, because she had frequently remarked the unpleasant air and countenance of this man. She now hesitated, whether to speak with him, doubting even, that this request was only a pretext to draw her into some danger; but a little reflection shewed her the improbability of this, and she blushed at her weak fears.

"I will speak to him, Annette," said she; "desire him to come to the corridor immediately."

Annette departed, and soon after returned.

"Barnardine, ma'amselle," said she, "dare not come to the corridor, lest he should be discovered, it is so far from his post; and he dare not even leave the gates for a moment now; but, if you will come to him at the portal, through some roundabout passages he told me of, without crossing the courts, he has that to tell, which will surprise you. But you must not come through the courts, lest the Signor should see you."

Emily, neither approving these "roundabout passages," nor the other part of the request, now positively refused to go. "Tell him," said she, "if he has any thing of consequence to impart, I will hear him in the corridor, whenever he has an opportunity of coming thither."

Annette went to deliver this message, and was absent a considerable time. When she returned, "It won't do, ma'amselle," said she. "Barnardine has been considering all this time what can be done, for it is as much as his place is worth to leave his post now. But, if you will come to the east rampart in the dusk of the evening, he can, perhaps, steal away, and tell you all he has to say."

Emily was surprised and alarmed, at the secrecy which this man seemed to think so necessary, and hesitated whether to meet him, till, considering, that he might mean to warn her of some serious danger, she resolved to go.

"Soon after sunset," said she, "I will be at the end of the east rampart. But then the watch will be set," she added, recollecting herself, "and how can Barnardine pass unobserved?"

"That is just what I said to him, ma'am, and he answered me, that he had the key of the gate, at the end of the rampart, that leads towards the courts, and could let himself through that way; and as for the sentinels, there were none at this end of the terrace, because the place is guarded enough by the high walls of the castle, and the east turret; and he said those at the other end were too far off to see him, if it was pretty duskyish."

"Well," said Emily, "I must hear what he has to tell; and, therefore, desire you will go with me to the terrace, this evening."

"He desired it might be pretty duskyish, ma'amselle," repeated Annette, "because of the watch."

Emily paused, and then said she would be on the terrace, an hour after sunset;—"and tell Barnardine," she added, "to be punctual to the time; for that I, also, may be observed by Signor Montoni. Where is the Signor? I would speak with him."

"He is in the cedar chamber, ma'am, counselling with the other Signors. He is going to give them a sort of treat to-day, to make up for what passed at the last, I suppose; the people are all very busy in the kitchen."

Emily now enquired, if Montoni expected any new guests? and Annette believed that he did not. "Poor Ludovico!" added she, "he would be as merry as the best of them, if he was well; but he may recover yet. Count Morano was wounded as bad, as he, and he is got well again, and is gone back to Venice."

"Is he so?" said Emily, "when did you hear this?"

"I heard it, last night, ma'amselle, but I forgot to tell it."

Emily asked some further questions, and then, desiring Annette would observe and inform her, when Montoni was alone, the girl went to deliver her message to Barnardine.

Montoni was, however, so much engaged, during the whole day, that Emily had no opportunity of seeking a release from her terrible suspense, concerning her aunt. Annette was employed in watching his steps, and in attending upon Ludovico, whom she, assisted by Caterina, nursed with the utmost care; and Emily was, of course, left much alone. Her thoughts dwelt often on the message of the porter, and were employed in conjecturing the subject, that occasioned it, which she sometimes imagined concerned the fate of Madame Montoni; at others, that it related to some personal danger, which threatened herself. The cautious secrecy which Barnardine observed in his conduct, inclined her to believe the latter.

As the hour of appointment drew near, her impatience increased. At length, the sun set; she heard the passing steps of the sentinels going to their posts; and waited only for Annette to accompany her to the terrace, who, soon after, came, and they descended together. When Emily expressed apprehensions of meeting Montoni, or some of his guests, "O, there is no fear of that, ma'amselle," said Annette, "they are all set in to feasting yet, and that Barnardine knows."

They reached the first terrace, where the sentinels demanded who passed; and Emily, having answered, walked on to the east rampart, at the entrance of which they were again stopped; and, having again replied, were permitted to proceed. But Emily did not like to expose herself to the discretion of these men, at such an hour; and, impatient to withdraw from the situation, she stepped hastily on in search of Barnardine. He was not yet come. She leaned pensively on the wall of the rampart, and waited for him. The gloom of twilight sat deep on the surrounding objects, blending in soft confusion the valley, the mountains, and the woods, whose tall heads, stirred by the evening breeze, gave the only sounds, that stole on silence, except a faint, faint chorus of distant voices, that arose from within the castle.

"What voices are those?" said Emily, as she fearfully listened.

"It is only the Signor and his guests, carousing," replied Annette.

"Good God!" thought Emily, "can this man's heart be so gay, when he has made another being so wretched; if, indeed, my aunt is yet suffered to feel her wretchedness? O! whatever are my own sufferings, may my heart never, never be hardened against those of others!"

She looked up, with a sensation of horror, to the east turret, near which she then stood; a light glimmered through the grates of the lower chamber, but those of the upper one were dark. Presently, she perceived a person moving with a lamp across the lower room; but this circumstance revived no hope, concerning Madame Montoni, whom she had vainly sought in that apartment, which had appeared to contain only soldiers' accoutrements. Emily, however, determined to attempt the outer door of the turret, as soon as Barnardine should withdraw; and, if it was unfastened, to make another effort to discover her aunt.

The moments passed, but still Barnardine did not appear; and Emily, becoming uneasy, hesitated whether to wait any longer. She would have sent Annette to the portal to hasten him, but feared to be left alone, for it was now almost dark, and a melancholy streak of red, that still lingered in the west, was the only vestige of departed day. The strong interest, however, which Barnardine's message had awakened, overcame other apprehensions, and still detained her.

While she was conjecturing with Annette what could thus occasion his absence, they heard a key turn in the lock of the gate near them, and presently saw a man advancing. It was Barnardine, of whom Emily hastily enquired what he had to communicate, and desired, that he would tell her quickly, "for I am chilled with this evening air," said she.

"You must dismiss your maid, lady," said the man in a voice, the deep tone of which shocked her, "what I have to tell is to you only."

Emily, after some hesitation, desired Annette to withdraw to a little distance. "Now, my friend, what would you say?"

He was silent a moment, as if considering, and then said,—

"That which would cost me my place, at least, if it came to the Signor's ears. You must promise, lady, that nothing shall ever make you tell a syllable of the matter; I have been trusted in this affair, and, if it was known, that I betrayed my trust, my life, perhaps, might answer it. But I was concerned for you, lady, and I resolved to tell you." He paused.——

Emily thanked him, assured him that he might repose on her discretion, and entreated him to dispatch.

"Annette told us in the hall how unhappy you was about Signora Montoni, and how much you wished to know what was become of her."

"Most true," said Emily eagerly, "and you can inform me. I conjure you tell me the worst, without hesitation." She rested her trembling arm upon the wall.

"I can tell you," said Barnardine, and paused.——

Emily had no power to enforce her entreaties.

"I *can* tell you," resumed Barnardine,—"but"——

"But what?" exclaimed Emily, recovering her resolution.

"Here I am, ma'amselle," said Annette, who, having heard the eager tone, in which Emily pronounced these words, came running towards her.

"Retire!" said Barnardine, sternly; "you are not wanted;" and, as Emily said nothing, Annette obeyed.

"I *can* tell you," repeated the porter,—"but I know not how—you was afflicted before."——

"I am prepared for the worst, my friend," said Emily, in a firm and solemn voice. "I can support any certainty better than this suspense."

"Well, Signora, if that is the case, you shall hear.—You know, I suppose, that the Signor and his lady used sometimes to disagree. It is none of my concerns to enquire what it was about, but I believe you know it was so."

"Well," said Emily, "proceed."

"The Signor, it seems, had lately been very wrath against her. I saw all, and heard all,—a great deal more than people thought for; but it was none of my business, so I said nothing. A few days ago, the Signor sent for me. 'Barnardine,' says he, 'you are—an honest man, I think I can trust you.' I assured his *Excellenza* that he could. 'Then,' says he, as near as I can remember, 'I have an affair in hand, which I want you to assist me in.'—Then he told me what I was to do; but that I shall say nothing about—it concerned only the Signora."

"O Heavens!" exclaimed Emily—"what have you done?"

Barnardine hesitated, and was silent.

"What fiend could tempt him, or you, to such an act!" cried Emily, chilled with horror, and scarcely able to support her fainting spirits.

"It was a fiend," said Barnardine in a gloomy tone of voice. They were now both silent;—Emily had not courage to enquire further, and Barnardine seemed to shrink from telling more. At length he said, "It is of no use to think of the past; the Signor was cruel enough, but he would be obeyed. What signified my refusing? He would have found others, who had no scruples."

"You have murdered her, then!" said Emily, in a hollow and inward voice—"I am talking with a murderer!" Barnardine stood silent; while Emily turned from him, and attempted to leave the place.

"Stay, lady!" said he, "You deserve to think so still—since you can believe me capable of such a deed."

"If you are innocent, tell me quickly," said Emily, in faint accents, "for I feel I shall not be able to hear you long."

"I will tell you no more," said he, and walked away. Emily had just strength enough to bid him stay, and then to call Annette, on whose arm she leaned, and they walked slowly up the rampart, till they heard steps behind them. It was Barnardine again.

"Send away the girl," said he, "and I will tell you more."

"She must not go," said Emily; "what you have to say, she may hear."

"May she so, lady?" said he. "You shall know no more, then;" and he was going, though slowly, when Emily's anxiety, overcoming the resentment and fear, which the man's behaviour had roused, she desired him to stay, and bade Annette retire.

"The Signora is alive," said he, "for me. She is my prisoner, though; his *Excellenza* has shut her up in the chamber over the great gates of the court, and I have the charge of her. I was going to have told you, you might see her—but now——"

Emily, relieved from an unutterable load of anguish by this speech, had now only to ask Barnardine's forgiveness, and to conjure, that he would let her visit her aunt.

He complied with less reluctance, than she expected, and told her, that, if she would repair, on the following night, when the Signor was retired to rest, to the postern-gate of the castle, she should, perhaps, see Madame Montoni.

Amid all the thankfulness, which Emily felt for this concession, she thought she observed a malicious triumph in his manner, when he pronounced the last words; but, in the next moment, she dismissed the thought, and, having again thanked him, commended her aunt to his pity, and assured him, that she would herself reward him, and would be punctual to her appointment, she bade him good night, and retired, unobserved, to her chamber. It was a considerable time, before the tumult of joy, which Barnardine's unexpected intelligence had occasioned, allowed Emily to think with clearness, or to be conscious of the real dangers, that still surrounded Madame Montoni and herself. When this agitation subsided, she perceived, that her aunt was yet the prisoner of a man, to whose vengeance, or avarice, she might fall a sacrifice; and, when she further considered the savage aspect of the person, who was appointed to guard Madame Montoni, her doom appeared to be already sealed, for the countenance of Barnardine seemed to bear the stamp of a murderer; and, when she had looked upon it, she felt inclined to believe, that there was no deed, however black, which he might not be prevailed upon to execute. These reflections brought to her remembrance the tone of voice, in which he had promised to grant her request to see his prisoner; and she mused upon it long in uneasiness and doubt. Sometimes, she even hesitated, whether to trust herself with him at the lonely hour he had appointed; and once, and only once, it struck her, that Madame Montoni might be already murdered, and that this ruffian was appointed to decoy herself to some secret place, where her life also was to be sacrificed to the avarice of Montoni, who then would claim securely the contested estates in Languedoc. The consideration of the enormity of such guilt did, at length, relieve her from the belief of its probability, but not from all the doubts and fears, which a recollection of Barnardine's manner had occasioned. From these subjects, her thoughts, at length, passed to others; and, as the evening advanced, she remembered, with somewhat more than surprise, the music she had heard, on the preceding night, and now awaited its return, with more than curiosity.

She distinguished, till a late hour, the distant carousals of Montoni and his companions—the loud contest, the dissolute laugh and the choral song, that made the halls re-echo. At length, she heard the heavy gates of the castle shut for the night, and those sounds instantly sunk into a silence, which was disturbed only by the whispering steps of persons, passing through the galleries to their remote rooms. Emily now judging it to be about the time, when she had heard the music, on the preceding night, dismissed Annette, and gently opened the casement to watch for its return. The planet she had so particularly noticed, at the recurrence of the music, was not yet risen; but, with superstitious weakness, she kept her eyes fixed on that part of the hemisphere, where it would rise, almost expecting, that, when it appeared, the sounds would return. At length, it came, serenely bright, over the eastern towers of the castle. Her heart trembled, when she perceived it, and she had scarcely courage to remain at the casement, lest the returning music should confirm her terror, and subdue the little strength she yet retained. The clock soon after struck one, and, knowing this to be about the time, when the sounds had occurred, she sat down in a chair, near the casement, and endeavoured to compose her spirits; but the anxiety of expectation yet disturbed them. Every thing, however, remained still; she heard only the solitary step of a sentinel, and the lulling murmur of the woods below, and she again leaned from the casement, and again looked, as if for intelligence, to the planet, which was now risen high above the towers.

Emily continued to listen, but no music came. "Those were surely no mortal sounds!" said she, recollecting their entrancing melody. "No inhabitant of this castle could utter such; and, where is the feeling, that could modulate such exquisite expression? We all know, that it has been affirmed celestial sounds have sometimes been heard on earth. Father Pierre and Father Antoine declared, that they had sometimes heard them in the stillness of night, when they alone were waking to offer their orisons to heaven. Nay, my dear father himself, once said, that, soon after my mother's death, as he lay watchful in grief, sounds of uncommon sweetness called him from his bed; and, on opening his window, he heard lofty music pass along the midnight air. It soothed him, he said; he looked up with confidence to heaven, and resigned her to his God."

Emily paused to weep at this recollection. "Perhaps," resumed she, "perhaps, those strains I heard were sent to comfort,—to encourage

me! Never shall I forget those I heard, at this hour, in Languedoc!
Perhaps, my father watches over me, at this moment!" She wept again
in tenderness. Thus passed the hour in watchfulness and solemn
thought; but no sounds returned; and, after remaining at the casement,
till the light tint of dawn began to edge the mountain-tops and steal
upon the night-shade, she concluded, that they would not return, and
retired reluctantly to repose.

VOLUME 3

CHAPTER I

I will advise you where to plant yourselves;
Acquaint you with the perfect spy o' the time,
The moment on 't; for 't must be done to-night.
                                                MACBETH

EMILY was somewhat surprised, on the following day, to find that
Annette had heard of Madame Montoni's confinement in the chamber
over the portal, as well as of her purposed visit there, on the approaching night. That the circumstance, which Barnardine had so solemnly
enjoined her to conceal, he had himself told to so indiscreet an hearer
as Annette, appeared very improbable, though he had now charged her
with a message, concerning the intended interview. He requested, that
Emily would meet him, unattended, on the terrace, at a little after midnight, when he himself would lead her to the place he had promised;
a proposal, from which she immediately shrunk, for a thousand vague
fears darted athwart her mind, such as had tormented her on the preceding night, and which she neither knew how to trust, or to dismiss. It
frequently occurred to her, that Barnardine might have deceived her,
concerning Madame Montoni, whose murderer, perhaps, he really
was; and that he had deceived her by order of Montoni, the more easily to draw her into some of the desperate designs of the latter. The terrible suspicion, that Madame Montoni no longer lived, thus came,
accompanied by one not less dreadful for herself. Unless the crime, by
which the aunt had suffered, was instigated merely by resentment,
unconnected with profit, a motive, upon which Montoni did not
appear very likely to act, its object must be unattained, till the niece was
also dead, to whom Montoni knew that his wife's estates must descend.
Emily remembered the words, which had informed her, that the contested estates in France would devolve to her, if Madame Montoni
died, without consigning them to her husband, and the former obstinate perseverance of her aunt made it too probable, that she had, to the

last, withheld them. At this instant, recollecting Barnardine's manner, on the preceding night, she now believed, what she had then fancied, that it expressed malignant triumph. She shuddered at the recollection, which confirmed her fears, and determined not to meet him on the terrace. Soon after, she was inclined to consider these suspicions as the extravagant exaggerations of a timid and harassed mind, and could not believe Montoni liable to such preposterous depravity as that of destroying, from one motive, his wife and her niece. She blamed herself for suffering her romantic imagination to carry her so far beyond the bounds of probability, and determined to endeavour to check its rapid flights, lest they should sometimes extend into madness. Still, however, she shrunk from the thought of meeting Barnardine, on the terrace, at midnight; and still the wish to be relieved from this terrible suspense, concerning her aunt, to see her, and to soothe her sufferings, made her hesitate what to do.

"Yet how is it possible, Annette, I can pass to the terrace at that hour?" said she, recollecting herself, "the sentinels will stop me, and Signor Montoni will hear of the affair."

"O ma'amselle! that is well thought of," replied Annette. "That is what Barnardine told me about. He gave me this key, and bade me say it unlocks the door at the end of the vaulted gallery, that opens near the end of the east rampart, so that you need not pass any of the men on watch. He bade me say, too, that his reason for requesting you to come to the terrace was, because he could take you to the place you want to go to, without opening the great doors of the hall, which grate so heavily."

Emily's spirits were somewhat calmed by this explanation, which seemed to be honestly given to Annette. "But why did he desire I would come alone, Annette?" said she.

"Why that was what I asked him myself, ma'amselle. Says I, Why is my young lady to come alone?—Surely I may come with her!—What harm can I do? But he said 'No—no—I tell you not,' in his gruff way. Nay, says I, I have been trusted in as great affairs as this, I warrant, and it's a hard matter if I can't keep a secret now. Still he would say nothing but—'No—no—no.' Well, says I, if you will only trust me, I will tell you a great secret, that was told me a month ago, and I have never opened my lips about it yet—so you need not be afraid of telling me. But all would not do. Then, ma'amselle, I went so far as to offer him a beautiful new sequin, that Ludovico gave me for a keep sake, and I would not have parted with it for all St. Marco's Place; but even that would not do! Now what can be the reason of this? But I know, you know, ma'am, who you are going to see."

"Pray did Barnardine tell you this?"

"He! No, ma'amselle, that he did not."

Emily enquired who did, but Annette shewed, that she *could* keep a secret.

During the remainder of the day, Emily's mind was agitated with doubts and fears and contrary determinations, on the subject of meeting this Barnardine on the rampart, and submitting herself to his guidance, she scarcely knew whither. Pity for her aunt and anxiety for herself alternately swayed her determination, and night came, before she had decided upon her conduct. She heard the castle clock strike eleven—twelve—and yet her mind wavered. The time, however, was now come, when she could hesitate no longer: and then the interest she felt for her aunt overcame other considerations, and, bidding Annette follow her to the outer door of the vaulted gallery, and there await her return, she descended from her chamber. The castle was perfectly still, and the great hall, where so lately she had witnessed a scene of dreadful contention, now returned only the whispering footsteps of the two solitary figures gliding fearfully between the pillars, and gleamed only to the feeble lamp they carried. Emily, deceived by the long shadows of the pillars and by the catching lights between, often stopped, imagining she saw some person, moving in the distant obscurity of the perspective; and, as she passed these pillars, she feared to turn her eyes toward them, almost expecting to see a figure start out from behind their broad shaft. She reached, however, the vaulted gallery, without interruption, but unclosed its outer door with a trembling hand, and, charging Annette not to quit it and to keep it a little open, that she might be heard if she called, she delivered to her the lamp, which she did not dare to take herself because of the men on watch, and, alone, stepped out upon the dark terrace. Every thing was so still, that she feared, lest her own light steps should be heard by the distant sentinels, and she walked cautiously towards the spot, where she had before met Barnardine, listening for a sound, and looking onward through the gloom in search of him. At length, she was startled by a deep voice, that spoke near her, and she paused, uncertain whether it was his, till it spoke again, and she then recognized the hollow tones of Barnardine, who had been punctual to the moment, and was at the appointed place, resting on the rampart wall. After chiding her for not coming sooner, and saying, that he had been waiting nearly half an hour, he desired Emily, who made no reply, to follow him to the door, through which he had entered the terrace.

While he unlocked it, she looked back to that she had left, and, observing the rays of the lamp stream through a small opening, was certain, that Annette was still there. But her remote situation could little befriend Emily, after she had quitted the terrace; and, when Barnardine unclosed the gate, the dismal aspect of the passage beyond, shewn by a torch burning on the pavement, made her shrink from following him alone, and she refused to go, unless Annette might accompany her. This, however, Barnardine absolutely refused to permit, mingling at the same time with his refusal such artful circumstances to heighten the pity and curiosity of Emily towards her aunt, that she, at length, consented to follow him alone to the portal.

He then took up the torch, and led her along the passage, at the extremity of which he unlocked another door, whence they descended, a few steps, into a chapel, which, as Barnardine held up the torch to light her, Emily observed to be in ruins, and she immediately recollected a former conversation of Annette, concerning it, with very unpleasant emotions. She looked fearfully on the almost roofless walls, green with damps, and on the gothic points of the windows, where the ivy and the briony had long supplied the place of glass, and ran mantling among the broken capitals of some columns, that had once supported the roof. Barnardine stumbled over the broken pavement, and his voice, as he uttered a sudden oath, was returned in hollow echoes, that made it more terrific. Emily's heart sunk; but she still followed him, and he turned out of what had been the principal aisle of the chapel. "Down these steps, lady," said Barnardine, as he descended a flight, which appeared to lead into the vaults; but Emily paused on the top, and demanded, in a tremulous tone, whither he was conducting her.

"To the portal," said Barnardine.

"Cannot we go through the chapel to the portal?" said Emily.

"No, Signora, that leads to the inner court, which I don't choose to unlock. This way, and we shall reach the outer court presently."

Emily still hesitated; fearing not only to go on, but, since she had gone thus far, to irritate Barnardine by refusing to go further.

"Come, lady," said the man, who had nearly reached the bottom of the flight, "make a little haste; I cannot wait here all night."

"Whither do these steps lead?" said Emily, yet pausing.

"To the portal," repeated Barnardine, in an angry tone, "I will wait no longer." As he said this, he moved on with the light, and Emily, fearing to provoke him by further delay, reluctantly followed. From the steps, they proceeded through a passage, adjoining the vaults, the walls of which were dropping with unwholesome dews, and the vapours, that crept along the ground, made the torch burn so dimly, that Emily expected every moment to see it extinguished, and Barnardine could scarcely find his way. As they advanced, these vapours thickened, and Barnardine, believing the torch was expiring, stopped for a moment to trim it. As he then rested against a pair of iron gates, that opened from the passage, Emily saw, by uncertain flashes of light, the vaults beyond, and, near her, heaps of earth, that seemed to surround an open grave. Such an object, in such a scene, would, at any time, have disturbed her; but now she was shocked by an instantaneous presentiment, that this was the grave of her unfortunate aunt, and that the treacherous Barnardine was leading herself to destruction. The obscure and terrible place, to which he had conducted her, seemed to justify the thought; it was a place suited for murder, a receptacle for the dead, where a deed of horror might be committed, and no vestige appear to proclaim it. Emily was so overwhelmed with terror, that, for a moment, she was unable to determine what conduct to pursue. She then considered, that it would be vain to attempt an escape from Barnardine, by flight, since the length and the intricacy of the way she had passed would soon enable him to overtake her, who was unacquainted with the turnings, and whose feebleness would not suffer her to run long with swiftness. She feared equally to irritate him by a disclosure of her suspicions, which a refusal to accompany him further certainly would do; and, since she was already as much in his power as it was possible she could be, if she proceeded, she, at length, determined to suppress, as far as she could, the appearance of apprehension, and to follow silently whither he designed to lead her. Pale with horror and anxiety, she now waited till Barnardine had trimmed the torch, and, as her sight glanced again upon the grave, she could not forbear enquiring, for whom it was prepared. He took his eyes from the torch, and fixed them upon her face without speaking. She faintly repeated the question, but the man, shaking the torch, passed on; and she followed, trembling, to a second flight of steps, having ascended which, a door delivered them into the first court of the castle. As they crossed it, the light shewed the high black walls around them, fringed with long grass and dank weeds, that found a scanty soil among the mouldering stones; the heavy buttresses, with, here and there, between them, a narrow grate, that admitted a freer circulation of air to the court, the massy iron gates, that led to the castle, whose clustering turrets appeared above, and, opposite, the huge towers and arch of the portal itself. In this scene the large, uncouth person of Barnardine, bearing the torch, formed a characteristic figure. This Barnardine was wrapt in a long dark cloak, which scarcely allowed the kind of half-boots, or sandals, that were laced upon his legs, to appear, and shewed only the point of a broad sword, which he usually wore, slung in a belt across his shoulders. On his head was a heavy flat velvet cap, somewhat resembling a turban, in which was a short feather; the visage beneath it shewed strong features, and a countenance furrowed with the lines of cunning and darkened by habitual discontent.

The view of the court, however, reanimated Emily, who, as she crossed silently towards the portal, began to hope, that her own fears, and not the treachery of Barnardine, had deceived her. She looked anxiously up at the first casement, that appeared above the lofty arch of the portcullis; but it was dark, and she enquired, whether it belonged to the chamber, where Madame Montoni was confined. Emily spoke low, and Barnardine, perhaps, did not hear her question, for he returned no answer; and they, soon after, entered the postern door of the gate-way, which brought them to the foot of a narrow stair-case, that wound up one of the towers.

"Up this stair-case the Signora lies," said Barnardine.

"Lies!" repeated Emily faintly, as she began to ascend.

"She lies in the upper chamber," said Barnardine.

As they passed up, the wind, which poured through the narrow cavities in the wall, made the torch flare, and it threw a stronger gleam upon the grim and sallow countenance of Barnardine, and discovered more fully the desolation of the place—the rough stone walls, the spiral stairs, black with age, and a suit of antient armour, with an iron visor, that hung upon the walls, and appeared a trophy of some former victory.

Having reached a landing-place, "You may wait here, lady," said he, applying a key to the door of a chamber, "while I go up, and tell the Signora you are coming."

"That ceremony is unnecessary," replied Emily, "my aunt will rejoice to see me."

"I am not so sure of that," said Barnardine, pointing to the room he had opened: "Come in here, lady, while I step up."

Emily, surprised and somewhat shocked, did not dare to oppose him further, but, as he was turning away with the torch, desired he would not leave her in darkness. He looked around, and, observing a tripod lamp, that stood on the stairs, lighted and gave it to Emily, who stepped forward into a large old chamber, and he closed the door. As she listened anxiously to his departing steps, she thought he descended, instead of ascending, the stairs; but the gusts of wind, that whistled round the portal, would not allow her to hear distinctly any other sound. Still, however, she listened, and, perceiving no step in the room above, where he had affirmed Madame Montoni to be, her anxiety increased, though she considered, that the thickness of the floor in this strong building might prevent any sound reaching her from the upper chamber. The next moment, in a pause of the wind, she distinguished Barnardine's step descending to the court, and then thought she heard his voice; but, the rising gust again overcoming other sounds, Emily, to be certain on this point, moved softly to the door, which, on attempting to open it, she discovered was fastened. All the horrid apprehensions, that had lately assailed her, returned at this instant with redoubled force, and no longer appeared like the exaggerations of a timid spirit, but seemed to have been sent to warn her of her fate. She now did not doubt, that Madame Montoni had been murdered, perhaps in this very chamber; or that she herself was brought hither for the same purpose. The countenance, the manners and the recollected words of Barnardine, when he had spoken of her aunt, confirmed her worst fears. For some moments, she was incapable of considering of any means, by which she might attempt an escape. Still she listened, but heard footsteps neither on the stairs, or in the room above; she thought, however, that she again distinguished Barnardine's voice below, and went to a grated window, that opened upon the court, to enquire further. Here, she plainly heard his hoarse accents, mingling with the blast, that swept by, but they were lost again so quickly, that their meaning could not be interpreted; and then the light of a torch, which seemed to issue from the portal below, flashed across the court, and the long shadow of a man, who was under the arch-way, appeared upon the pavement. Emily, from the hugeness of this sudden portrait, concluded it to be that of Barnardine; but other deep tones, which passed in the wind, soon convinced her he was not alone, and that his companion was not a person very liable to pity.

When her spirits had overcome the first shock of her situation, she held up the lamp to examine, if the chamber afforded a possibility of an escape. It was a spacious room, whose walls, wainscoted with rough oak, shewed no casement but the grated one, which Emily had left, and no other door than that, by which she had entered. The feeble rays of the lamp, however, did not allow her to see at once its full extent; she perceived no furniture, except, indeed, an iron chair, fastened in the centre of the chamber, immediately over which, depending on a chain from the ceiling, hung an iron ring. Having gazed upon these, for some time, with wonder and horror, she next observed iron bars below, made for the purpose of confining the feet, and on the arms of the chair were rings of the same metal. As she continued to survey them, she concluded, that they were instruments of torture, and it struck her, that some poor wretch had once been fastened in this chair, and had there been starved to death. She was chilled by the thought; but, what was her agony, when, in the next moment, it occurred to her, that her aunt might have been one of these victims, and that she herself might be the next! An acute pain seized her head, she was scarcely able to hold the lamp, and, looking round for support, was seating herself, unconsciously, in the iron chair itself; but suddenly perceiving where she was, she started from it in horror, and sprung towards a remote end of the room. Here again she looked round for a seat to sustain her, and perceived only a dark curtain, which, descending from the ceiling to the floor, was drawn along the whole side of the chamber. Ill as she was, the appearance of this curtain struck her, and she paused to gaze upon it, in wonder and apprehension.

It seemed to conceal a recess of the chamber; she wished, yet dreaded, to lift it, and to discover what it veiled: twice she was withheld by a recollection of the terrible spectacle her daring hand had formerly unveiled in an apartment of the castle, till, suddenly conjecturing, that it concealed the body of her murdered aunt, she seized it, in a fit of desperation, and drew it aside. Beyond, appeared a corpse, stretched on a kind of low couch, which was crimsoned with human blood, as was the floor beneath. The features, deformed by death, were ghastly and horrible, and more than one livid wound appeared in the face. Emily, bending over the body, gazed, for a moment, with an eager, frenzied eye; but, in the next, the lamp dropped from her hand, and she fell senseless at the foot of the couch.

When her senses returned, she found herself surrounded by men, among whom was Barnardine, who were lifting her from the floor, and then bore her along the chamber. She was sensible of what passed, but the extreme languor of her spirits did not permit her to speak, or move, or even to feel any distinct fear. They carried her down the stair-case, by which she had ascended; when, having reached the arch-way, they stopped, and one of the men, taking the torch from Barnardine, opened a small door, that was cut in the great gate, and, as he stepped out upon the road, the light he bore shewed several men on horseback, in waiting. Whether it was the freshness of the air, that revived Emily, or that the objects she now saw roused the spirit of alarm, she suddenly spoke, and made an ineffectual effort to disengage herself from the grasp of the ruffians, who held her.

Barnardine, meanwhile, called loudly for the torch, while distant voices answered, and several persons approached, and, in the same instant, a light flashed upon the court of the castle. Again he vociferated for the torch, and the men hurried Emily through the gate. At a short distance, under the shelter of the castle walls, she perceived the fellow, who had taken the light from the porter, holding it to a man, busily employed in altering the saddle of a horse, round which were several horsemen, looking on, whose harsh features received the full glare of the torch; while the broken ground beneath them, the opposite walls, with the tufted shrubs, that overhung their summits, and an embattled watch-tower above, were reddened with the gleam, which, fading gradually away, left the remoter ramparts and the woods below to the obscurity of night.

"What do you waste time for, there?" said Barnardine with an oath, as he approached the horsemen. "Dispatch—dispatch!"

"The saddle will be ready in a minute," replied the man who was buckling it, at whom Barnardine now swore again, for his negligence, and Emily, calling feebly for help, was hurried towards the horses, while the ruffians disputed on which to place her, the one designed for her not being ready. At this moment a cluster of lights issued from the great gates, and she immediately heard the shrill voice of Annette above those of several other persons, who advanced. In the same moment, she distinguished Montoni and Cavigni, followed by a number of ruffian-faced fellows, to whom she no longer looked with terror, but with hope, for, at this instant, she did not tremble at the thought of any dangers, that might await her within the castle, whence so lately, and so anxiously she had wished to escape. Those, which threatened her from without, had engrossed all her apprehensions.

A short contest ensued between the parties, in which that of Montoni, however, were presently victors, and the horsemen, perceiving that numbers were against them, and being, perhaps, not very warmly interested in the affair they had undertaken, galloped off, while Barnardine had run far enough to be lost in the darkness, and Emily was led back into the castle. As she re-passed the courts, the remembrance of what she had seen in the portal-chamber came, with all its horror, to her mind; and when, soon after, she heard the gate close, that shut her once more within the castle walls, she shuddered for herself, and, almost forgetting the danger she had escaped, could scarcely think, that any thing less precious than liberty and peace was to be found beyond them.

Montoni ordered Emily to await him in the cedar parlour, whither he soon followed, and then sternly questioned her on this mysterious affair. Though she now viewed him with horror, as the murderer of her aunt, and scarcely knew what she said in reply to his impatient enquiries, her answers and her manner convinced him, that she had not taken a voluntary part in the late scheme, and he dismissed her upon the appearance of his servants, whom he had ordered to attend, that he might enquire further into the affair, and discover those, who had been accomplices in it.

Emily had been some time in her apartment, before the tumult of her mind allowed her to remember several of the past circumstances. Then, again, the dead form, which the curtain in the portal-chamber had disclosed, came to her fancy, and she uttered a groan, which terrified Annette the more, as Emily forbore to satisfy her curiosity, on the subject of it, for she feared to trust her with so fatal a secret, lest her indiscretion should call down the immediate vengeance of Montoni on herself.

Thus compelled to bear within her own mind the whole horror of the secret, that oppressed it, her reason seemed to totter under the intolerable weight. She often fixed a wild and vacant look on Annette, and, when she spoke, either did not hear her, or answered from the purpose. Long fits of abstraction succeeded; Annette spoke repeatedly, but her voice seemed not to make any impression on the sense of the long agitated Emily, who sat fixed and silent, except that, now and then, she heaved a heavy sigh, but without tears.

Terrified at her condition, Annette, at length, left the room, to inform Montoni of it, who had just dismissed his servants, without having made any discoveries on the subject of his enquiry. The wild description, which this girl now gave of Emily, induced him to follow her immediately to the chamber.

At the sound of his voice, Emily turned her eyes, and a gleam of recollection seemed to shoot athwart her mind, for she immediately rose from her seat, and moved slowly to a remote part of the room. He spoke to her in accents somewhat softened from their usual harshness, but she regarded him with a kind of half curious, half terrified look, and answered only "yes," to whatever he said. Her mind still seemed to retain no other impression, than that of fear.

Of this disorder Annette could give no explanation, and Montoni, having attempted, for some time, to persuade Emily to talk, retired, after ordering Annette to remain with her, during the night, and to inform him, in the morning, of her condition.

When he was gone, Emily again came forward, and asked who it was, that had been there to disturb her. Annette said it was the Signor—Signor Montoni. Emily repeated the name after her, several times, as if she did not recollect it, and then suddenly groaned, and relapsed into abstraction.

With some difficulty, Annette led her to the bed, which Emily examined with an eager, frenzied eye, before she lay down, and then, pointing, turned with shuddering emotion, to Annette, who, now more terrified, went towards the door, that she might bring one of the female servants to pass the night with them; but Emily, observing her going, called her by name, and then in the naturally soft and plaintive tone of her voice, begged, that she, too, would not forsake her. — "For since my father died," added she, sighing, "every body forsakes me."

"Your father, ma'amselle!" said Annette, "he was dead before you knew me."

"He was, indeed!" rejoined Emily, and her tears began to flow. She now wept silently and long, after which, becoming quite calm, she at length sunk to sleep, Annette having had discretion enough not to interrupt her tears. This girl, as affectionate as she was simple, lost in these moments all her former fears of remaining in the chamber, and watched alone by Emily, during the whole night.

CHAPTER II

unfold
What worlds, or what vast regions, hold
Th' immortal mind, that hath forsook
Her mansion in this fleshly nook!
IL PENSEROSO

EMILY'S mind was refreshed by sleep. On waking in the morning, she looked with surprise on Annette, who sat sleeping in a chair beside the bed, and then endeavoured to recollect herself; but the circumstances of the preceding night were swept from her memory, which seemed to retain no trace of what had passed, and she was still gazing with surprise on Annette, when the latter awoke.

"O dear ma'amselle! do you know me?" cried she.

"Know you! Certainly," replied Emily, "you are Annette; but why are you sitting by me thus?"

"O you have been very ill, ma'amselle,—very ill indeed! and I am sure I thought——"

"This is very strange!" said Emily, still trying to recollect the past.— "But I think I do remember, that my fancy has been haunted by frightful dreams. Good God!" she added, suddenly starting—"surely it was nothing more than a dream!"

She fixed a terrified look upon Annette, who, intending to quiet her, said "Yes, ma'amselle, it was more than a dream, but it is all over now."

"She *is* murdered, then!" said Emily in an inward voice, and shuddering instantaneously. Annette screamed; for, being ignorant of the circumstance to which Emily referred, she attributed her manner to a disordered fancy; but, when she had explained to what her own speech alluded, Emily, recollecting the attempt that had been made to carry her off, asked if the contriver of it had been discovered. Annette replied, that he had not, though he might easily be guessed at; and then told Emily she might thank her for her deliverance, who, endeavouring to command the emotion, which the remembrance of her aunt had occasioned, appeared calmly to listen to Annette, though, in truth, she heard scarcely a word that was said.

"And so, ma'amselle," continued the latter, "I was determined to be even with Barnardine for refusing to tell me the secret, by finding it out myself; so I watched you, on the terrace, and, as soon as he had opened the door at the end, I stole out from the castle, to try to follow you; for, says I, I am sure no good can be planned, or why all this secrecy? So, sure enough, he had not bolted the door after him, and, when I opened it, I saw, by the glimmer of the torch, at the other end of the passage, which way you were going. I followed the light, at a distance, till you came to the vaults of the chapel, and there I was afraid to go further, for I had heard strange things about these vaults. But then, again, I was afraid to go back, all in darkness, by myself; so by the time Barnardine had trimmed the light, I had resolved to follow you, and I did so, till you came to the great court, and there I was afraid he would see me; so I stopped at the door again, and watched you across to the gates, and, when you was gone up the stairs, I whipt after. There, as I stood under the gate-way, I heard horses' feet without, and several men talking; and I heard them swearing at Barnardine for not bringing you out, and just then, he had like to have caught me, for he came down the stairs again, and I had hardly time to get out of his way. But I had heard enough of his secret now, and I determined to be even with him, and to save you, too, ma'amselle, for I guessed it to be some new scheme of Count Morano, though he was gone away. I ran into the castle, but I had hard work to find my way through the passage under the chapel, and what is very strange, I quite forgot to look for the ghosts they had told me about, though I would not go into that place again by myself for all the world! Luckily the Signor and Signor Cavigni were up, so we had soon a train at our heels, sufficient to frighten that Barnardine and his rogues, all together."

Annette ceased to speak, but Emily still appeared to listen. At length she said, suddenly, "I think I will go to him myself;—where is he?"

Annette asked who was meant.

"Signor Montoni," replied Emily. "I would speak with him;" and Annette, now remembering the order he had given, on the preceding night, respecting her young lady, rose, and said she would seek him herself.

This honest girl's suspicions of Count Morano were perfectly just; Emily, too, when she thought on the scheme, had attributed it to him; and Montoni, who had not a doubt on this subject, also, began to believe, that it was by the direction of Morano, that poison had formerly been mingled with his wine.

The professions of repentance, which Morano had made to Emily, under the anguish of his wound, were sincere at the moment he offered them; but he had mistaken the subject of his sorrow, for, while he thought he was condemning the cruelty of his late design, he was lamenting only the state of suffering, to which it had reduced him. As these sufferings abated, his former views revived, till, his health being re-established, he again found himself ready for enterprise and diffi-culty. The porter of the castle, who had served him, on a former occa-sion, willingly accepted a second bribe; and, having concerted the means of drawing Emily to the gates, Morano publicly left the hamlet, whither he had been carried after the affray, and withdrew with his peo-ple to another at several miles distance. From thence, on a night agreed upon by Barnardine, who had discovered from the thoughtless prattle of Annette, the most probable means of decoying Emily, the Count sent back his servants to the castle, while he awaited her arrival at the hamlet, with an intention of carrying her immediately to Venice. How this, his second scheme, was frustrated, has already appeared; but the violent, and various passions with which this Italian lover was now agi-tated, on his return to that city, can only be imagined.

Annette having made her report to Montoni of Emily's health and of her request to see him, he replied, that she might attend him in the cedar room, in about an hour. It was on the subject, that pressed so heavily on her mind, that Emily wished to speak to him, yet she did not distinctly know what good purpose this could answer, and sometimes she even recoiled in horror from the expectation of his presence. She wished, also, to petition, though she scarcely dared to believe the request would be granted, that he would permit her, since her aunt was no more, to return to her native country.

As the moment of interview approached, her agitation increased so much, that she almost resolved to excuse herself under what could scarcely be called a pretence of illness; and, when she considered what could be said, either concerning herself, or the fate of her aunt, she was equally hopeless as to the event of her entreaty, and terrified as to its effect upon the vengeful spirit of Montoni. Yet, to pretend ignorance of her death, appeared, in some degree, to be sharing its criminality, and, indeed, this event was the only ground, on which Emily could rest her petition for leaving Udolpho.

While her thoughts thus wavered, a message was brought, importing, that Montoni could not see her, till the next day; and her spirits were then relieved, for a moment, from an almost intolerable weight of apprehension. Annette said, she fancied the Chevaliers were going out to the wars again, for the court-yard was filled with horses, and she heard, that the rest of the party, who went out before, were expected at the castle. "And I heard one of the soldiers, too," added she, "say to his comrade, that he would warrant they'd bring home a rare deal of booty. — So, thinks I, if the Signor can, with a safe conscience, send his people out a-robbing — why it is no business of mine. I only wish I was once safe out of this castle; and, if it had not been for poor Ludovico's sake, I would have let Count Morano's people run away with us both, for it would have been serving you a good turn, ma'amselle, as well as myself."

Annette might have continued thus talking for hours for any interruption she would have received from Emily, who was silent, inattentive, absorbed in thought, and passed the whole of this day in a kind of solemn tranquillity, such as is often the result of faculties overstrained by suffering.

When night returned, Emily recollected the mysterious strains of music, that she had lately heard, in which she still felt some degree of interest, and of which she hoped to hear again the soothing sweetness. The influence of superstition now gained on the weakness of her long-harassed mind; she looked, with enthusiastic expectation, to the guardian spirit of her father, and, having dismissed Annette for the night, determined to watch alone for their return. It was not yet, however, near the time when she had heard the music on a former night, and anxious to call off her thoughts from distressing subjects, she sat down with one of the few books, that she had brought from France; but her mind, refusing controul, became restless and agitated, and she went often to the casement to listen for a sound. Once, she thought she heard a voice, but then, every thing without the casement remaining still, she concluded, that her fancy had deceived her.

Thus passed the time, till twelve o'clock, soon after which the distant sounds, that murmured through the castle, ceased, and sleep seemed to reign over all. Emily then seated herself at the casement, where she was soon recalled from the reverie, into which she sunk, by very unusual sounds, not of music, but like the low mourning of some person in distress. As she listened, her heart faltered in terror, and she became convinced, that the former sound was more than imaginary. Still, at intervals, she heard a kind of feeble lamentation, and sought to discover whence it came. There were several rooms underneath, adjoining the rampart, which had been long shut up, and, as the sound probably rose from one of these, she leaned from the casement to observe, whether any light was visible there. The chambers, as far as she could perceive, were quite dark, but, at a little distance, on the rampart below, she thought she saw something moving.

The faint twilight, which the stars shed, did not enable her to distinguish what it was; but she judged it to be a sentinel, on watch, and she removed her light to a remote part of the chamber, that she might escape notice, during her further observation.

The same object still appeared. Presently, it advanced along the rampart, towards her window, and she then distinguished something like a human form, but the silence, with which it moved, convinced her it was no sentinel. As it drew near, she hesitated whether to retire; a thrilling curiosity inclined her to stay, but a dread of she scarcely knew what warned her to withdraw.

While she paused, the figure came opposite to her casement, and was stationary. Every thing remained quiet; she had not heard even a foot-fall; and the solemnity of this silence, with the mysterious form she saw, subdued her spirits, so that she was moving from the casement, when, on a sudden, she observed the figure start away, and glide down the rampart, after which it was soon lost in the obscurity of night. Emily continued to gaze, for some time, on the way it had passed, and then retired within her chamber, musing on this strange circumstance, and scarcely doubting, that she had witnessed a supernatural appearance.

When her spirits recovered composure, she looked round for some other explanation. Remembering what she had heard of the daring enterprises of Montoni, it occurred to her, that she had just seen some unhappy person, who, having been plundered by his banditti, was brought hither a captive; and that the music she had formerly heard, came from him. Yet, if they had plundered him, it still appeared improbable, that they should have brought him to the castle, and it was also more consistent with the manners of banditti to murder those they rob, than to make them prisoners. But what, more than any other circumstance, contradicted the supposition, that it was a prisoner, was that it wandered on the terrace, without a guard: a consideration, which made her dismiss immediately her first surmise.

Afterwards, she was inclined to believe, that Count Morano had obtained admittance into the castle; but she soon recollected the difficulties and dangers, that must have opposed such an enterprise, and that, if he had so far succeeded, to come alone and in silence to her casement at midnight was not the conduct he would have adopted, particularly since the private stair-case, communicating with her apartment, was known to him; neither would he have uttered the dismal sounds she had heard.

Another suggestion represented, that this might be some person, who had designs upon the castle; but the mournful sounds destroyed, also, that probability. Thus, enquiry only perplexed her. Who, or what, it could be that haunted this lonely hour, complaining in such doleful accents and in such sweet music (for she was still inclined to believe, that the former strains and the late appearance were connected,) she had no means of ascertaining; and imagination again assumed her empire, and roused the mysteries of superstition.

She determined, however, to watch on the following night, when her doubts might, perhaps, be cleared up; and she almost resolved to address the figure, if it should appear again.

CHAPTER III

Such are those thick and gloomy shadows damp,
Oft seen in charnel-vaults and sepulchres,
Lingering, and sitting, by a new-made grave.

MILTON

ON the following day, Montoni sent a second excuse to Emily, who was surprised at the circumstance. "This is very strange!" said she to herself. "His conscience tells him the purport of my visit, and he defers it, to avoid an explanation." She now almost resolved to throw herself in his way, but terror checked the intention, and this day passed, as the preceding one, with Emily, except that a degree of awful expectation, concerning the approaching night, now somewhat disturbed the dreadful calmness that had pervaded her mind.

Towards evening, the second part of the band, which had made the first excursion among the mountains, returned to the castle, where, as they entered the courts, Emily, in her remote chamber, heard their loud shouts and strains of exultation, like the orgies of furies over some horrid sacrifice. She even feared they were about to commit some barbarous deed; a conjecture from which, however, Annette soon relieved her, by telling, that the people were only exulting over the plunder they had brought with them. This circumstance still further confirmed her in the belief, that Montoni had really commenced to be a captain of banditti, and meant to retrieve his broken fortunes by the plunder of travellers! Indeed, when she considered all the circumstances of his situation—in an armed, and almost inaccessible castle, retired far among the recesses of wild and solitary mountains, along whose distant skirts were scattered towns, and cities, whither wealthy travellers were continually passing—this appeared to be the situation of all others most suited for the success of schemes of rapine, and she yielded to the strange thought, that Montoni was become a captain of robbers. His character also, unprincipled, dauntless, cruel and enterprising, seemed to fit him for the situation. Delighting in the tumult and in the struggles of life, he was equally a stranger to pity and to fear; his very courage was a sort of animal ferocity; not the noble impulse of a principle, such as inspirits the mind against the oppressor, in the cause of the oppressed; but a constitutional hardiness of nerve, that cannot feel, and that, therefore, cannot fear.

Emily's supposition, however natural, was in part erroneous, for she was a stranger to the state of this country and to the circumstances, under which its frequent wars were partly conducted. The revenues of the many states of Italy being, at that time, insufficient to the support of standing armies, even during the short periods, which the turbulent habits both of the governments and the people permitted to pass in peace, an order of men arose not known in our age, and but faintly described in the history of their own. Of the soldiers, disbanded at the end of every war, few returned to the safe, but unprofitable occupations, then usual in peace. Sometimes they passed into other countries, and mingled with armies, which still kept the field. Sometimes they formed themselves into bands of robbers, and occupied remote fortresses, where their desperate character, the weakness of the governments which they offended, and the certainty, that they could be recalled to the armies, when their presence should be again wanted, prevented them from being much pursued by the civil power; and, sometimes, they attached themselves to the fortunes of a popular chief, by whom they were led into the service of any state, which could settle with him the price of their valour. From this latter practice arose their name—*Condottieri*; a term formidable all over Italy, for a period, which concluded in the earlier part of the seventeenth century, but of which it is not so easy to ascertain the commencement.

Contests between the smaller states were then, for the most part, affairs of enterprize alone, and the probabilities of success were estimated, not from the skill, but from the personal courage of the general, and the soldiers. The ability, which was necessary to the conduct of tedious operations, was little valued. It was enough to know how a party might be led towards their enemies, with the greatest secrecy, or conducted from them in the compactest order. The officer was to precipitate himself into a situation, where, but for his example, the soldiers might not have ventured; and, as the opposed parties knew little of each other's strength, the event of the day was frequently determined by the boldness of the first movements. In such services the *Condottieri* were eminent, and in these, where plunder always followed success, their characters acquired a mixture of intrepidity and profligacy, which awed even those whom they served.

When they were not thus engaged, their chief had usually his own fortress, in which, or in its neighbourhood, they enjoyed an irksome rest; and, though their wants were, at one time, partly supplied from the property of the inhabitants, the lavish distribution of their plunder at others, prevented them from being obnoxious; and the peasants of such districts gradually shared the character of their warlike visitors. The neighbouring governments sometimes professed, but seldom endeavoured, to suppress these military communities; both because it was difficult to do so, and because a disguised protection of them ensured, for the service of their wars, a body of men, who could not otherwise be so cheaply maintained, or so perfectly qualified. The commanders sometimes even relied so far upon this policy of the several powers, as to frequent their capitals; and Montoni, having met them in the gaming parties of Venice and Padua, conceived a desire to emulate their characters, before his ruined fortunes tempted him to adopt their practices. It was for the arrangement of his present plan of life, that the midnight councils were held at his mansion in Venice, and at which Orsino and some other members of the present community then assisted with suggestions, which they had since executed with the wreck of their fortunes.

On the return of night, Emily resumed her station at the casement. There was now a moon; and, as it rose over the tufted woods, its yellow light served to shew the lonely terrace and the surrounding objects, more distinctly, than the twilight of the stars had done, and promised Emily to assist her observations, should the mysterious form return. On this subject, she again wavered in conjecture, and hesitated whether to speak to the figure, to which a strong and almost irresistible interest urged her; but terror, at intervals, made her reluctant to do so.

"If this is a person who has designs upon the castle," said she, "my curiosity may prove fatal to me; yet the mysterious music, and the lamentations I heard, must surely have proceeded from him: if so, he cannot be an enemy."

She then thought of her unfortunate aunt, and, shuddering with grief and horror, the suggestions of imagination seized her mind with all the force of truth, and she believed, that the form she had seen was supernatural. She trembled, breathed with difficulty, an icy coldness touched her cheeks, and her fears for a while overcame her judgment. Her resolution now forsook her, and she determined, if the figure should appear, not to speak to it.

Thus the time passed, as she sat at her casement, awed by expectation, and by the gloom and stillness of midnight; for she saw obscurely in the moon-light only the mountains and woods, a cluster of towers, that formed the west angle of the castle, and the terrace below; and heard no sound, except, now and then, the lonely watch-word, passed by the centinels on duty, and afterwards the steps of the men who came to relieve guard, and whom she knew at a distance on the rampart by their pikes, that glittered in the moonbeam, and then, by the few short words, in which they hailed their fellows of the night. Emily retired within her chamber, while they passed the casement. When she returned to it, all was again quiet. It was now very late, she was wearied with watching, and began to doubt the reality of what she had seen on the preceding night; but she still lingered at the window, for her mind was too perturbed to admit of sleep. The moon shone with a clear lustre, that afforded her a complete view of the terrace; but she saw only a solitary centinel, pacing at one end of it; and, at length, tired with expectation, she withdrew to seek rest.

Such, however, was the impression, left on her mind by the music, and the complaining she had formerly heard, as well as by the figure, which she fancied she had seen, that she determined to repeat the watch, on the following night.

Montoni, on the next day, took no notice of Emily's appointed visit, but she, more anxious than before to see him, sent Annette to enquire, at what hour he would admit her. He mentioned eleven o'clock, and Emily was punctual to the moment; at which she called up all her fortitude to support the shock of his presence and the dreadful recollections it enforced. He was with several of his officers, in the cedar room; on observing whom she paused; and her agitation increased, while he continued to converse with them, apparently not observing her, till some of his officers, turning round, saw Emily, and uttered an exclamation. She was hastily retiring, when Montoni's voice arrested her, and, in a faultering accent, she said, — "I would speak with you, Signor Montoni, if you are at leisure."

"These are my friends," he replied, "whatever you would say, they may hear."

Emily, without replying, turned from the rude gaze of the chevaliers, and Montoni then followed her to the hall, whence he led her to a small room, of which he shut the door with violence. As she looked on his dark countenance, she again thought she saw the murderer of her aunt; and her mind was so convulsed with horror, that she had not power to recall thought enough to explain the purport of her visit; and to trust herself with the mention of Madame Montoni was more than she dared.

Montoni at length impatiently enquired what she had to say? "I have no time for trifling," he added, "my moments are important."

Emily then told him, that she wished to return to France, and came to beg, that he would permit her to do so. — But when he looked surprised, and enquired for the motive of the request, she hesitated, became paler than before, trembled, and had nearly sunk at his feet. He observed her emotion, with apparent indifference, and interrupted the silence by telling her, he must be gone. Emily, however, recalled her spirits sufficiently to enable her to repeat her request. And, when Montoni absolutely refused it, her slumbering mind was roused.

"I can no longer remain here with propriety, sir," said she, "and I may be allowed to ask, by what right you detain me."

"It is my will that you remain here," said Montoni, laying his hand on the door to go; "let that suffice you."

Emily, considering that she had no appeal from this will, forbore to dispute his right, and made a feeble effort to persuade him to be just. "While my aunt lived, sir," said she, in a tremulous voice, "my residence here was not improper; but now, that she is no more, I may surely be permitted to depart. My stay cannot benefit you, sir, and will only distress me."

"Who told you, that Madame Montoni was dead?" said Montoni, with an inquisitive eye. Emily hesitated, for nobody had told her so, and she did not dare to avow the having seen that spectacle in the portal-chamber, which had compelled her to the belief.

"Who told you so?" he repeated, more sternly.

"Alas! I know it too well," replied Emily: "spare me on this terrible subject!"

She sat down on a bench to support herself.

"If you wish to see her," said Montoni, "you may; she lies in the east turret."

He now left the room, without awaiting her reply, and returned to the cedar chamber, where such of the chevaliers as had not before seen Emily, began to rally him, on the discovery they had made; but Montoni did not appear disposed to bear this mirth, and they changed the subject.

Having talked with the subtle Orsino, on the plan of an excursion, which he meditated for a future day, his friend advised, that they should lie in wait for the enemy, which Verezzi impetuously opposed, reproached Orsino with want of spirit, and swore, that, if Montoni would let him lead on fifty men, he would conquer all that should oppose him.

Orsino smiled contemptuously; Montoni smiled too, but he also listened. Verezzi then proceeded with vehement declamation and assertion, till he was stopped by an argument of Orsino, which he knew not how to answer better than by invective. His fierce spirit detested the cunning caution of Orsino, whom he constantly opposed, and whose inveterate, though silent, hatred he had long ago incurred. And Montoni was a calm observer of both, whose different qualifications he knew, and how to bend their opposite character to the perfection of his own designs. But Verezzi, in the heat of opposition, now did not scruple to accuse Orsino of cowardice, at which the countenance of the latter, while he made no reply, was overspread with a livid paleness; and Montoni, who watched his lurking eye, saw him put his hand hastily into his bosom. But Verezzi, whose face, glowing with crimson, formed a striking contrast to the complexion of Orsino, remarked not the action, and continued boldly declaiming against cowards to Cavigni, who was slily laughing at his vehemence, and at the silent mortification of Orsino, when the latter, retiring a few steps behind, drew forth a stilletto to stab his adversary in the back. Montoni arrested his half-extended arm, and, with a significant look, made him return the poinard into his bosom, unseen by all except himself; for most of the party were disputing at a distant window, on the situation of a dell where they meant to form an ambuscade.

When Verezzi had turned round, the deadly hatred, expressed on the features of his opponent, raising, for the first time, a suspicion of his intention, he laid his hand on his sword, and then, seeming to recollect himself, strode up to Montoni.

"Signor," said he, with a significant look at Orsino, "we are not a band of assassins; if you have business for brave men employ me on this expedition: you shall have the last drop of my blood; if you have only work for cowards—keep him," pointing to Orsino, "and let me quit Udolpho."

Orsino, still more incensed, again drew forth his stilletto, and rushed towards Verezzi, who, at the same instant, advanced with his sword, when Montoni and the rest of the party interfered and separated them.

"This is the conduct of a boy," said Montoni to Verezzi, "not of a man: be more moderate in your speech."

"Moderation is the virtue of cowards," retorted Verezzi; "they are moderate in every thing—but in fear."

"I accept your words," said Montoni, turning upon him with a fierce and haughty look, and drawing his sword out of the scabbard.

"With all my heart," cried Verezzi, "though I did not mean them for you."

He directed a pass at Montoni; and, while they fought, the villain Orsino made another attempt to stab Verezzi, and was again prevented.

The combatants were, at length, separated; and, after a very long and violent dispute, reconciled. Montoni then left the room with Orsino, whom he detained in private consultation for a considerable time.

Emily, meanwhile, stunned by the last words of Montoni, forgot, for the moment, his declaration, that she should continue in the castle, while she thought of her unfortunate aunt, who, he had said, was laid in the east turret. In suffering the remains of his wife to lie thus long unburied, there appeared a degree of brutality more shocking than she had suspected even Montoni could practise.

After a long struggle, she determined to accept his permission to visit the turret, and to take a last look of her ill-fated aunt: with which design she returned to her chamber, and, while she waited for Annette to accompany her, endeavoured to acquire fortitude sufficient to support her through the approaching scene; for, though she trembled to encounter it, she knew that to remember the performance of this last act of duty would hereafter afford her consoling satisfaction.

Annette came, and Emily mentioned her purpose, from which the former endeavoured to dissuade her, though without effect, and Annette was, with much difficulty, prevailed upon to accompany her to the turret; but no consideration could make her promise to enter the chamber of death.

They now left the corridor, and, having reached the foot of the stair-case, which Emily had formerly ascended, Annette declared she would go no further, and Emily proceeded alone. When she saw the track of blood, which she had before observed, her spirits fainted, and, being compelled to rest on the stairs, she almost determined to proceed no further. The pause of a few moments restored her resolution, and she went on.

As she drew near the landing-place, upon which the upper chamber opened, she remembered, that the door was formerly fastened, and apprehended, that it might still be so. In this expectation, however, she was mistaken; for the door opened at once, into a dusky and silent chamber, round which she fearfully looked, and then slowly advanced, when a hollow voice spoke. Emily, who was unable to speak, or to move from the spot, uttered no sound of terror. The voice spoke again; and, then, thinking that it resembled that of Madame Montoni, Emily's spirits were instantly roused; she rushed towards a bed, that stood in a remote part of the room, and drew aside the curtains. Within, appeared a pale and emaciated face. She started back, then again advanced, shuddered as she took up the skeleton hand, that lay stretched upon the quilt; then let it drop, and then viewed the face with a long, unsettled gaze. It was that of Madame Montoni, though so changed by illness, that the resemblance of what it had been, could scarcely be traced in what it now appeared. She was still alive, and, raising her heavy eyes, she turned them on her niece.

"Where have you been so long?" said she, in the same hollow tone, "I thought you had forsaken me."

"Do you indeed live," said Emily, at length, "or is this but a terrible apparition?" She received no answer, and again she snatched up the hand. "This is substance," she exclaimed, "but it is cold—cold as marble!" She let it fall. "O, if you really live, speak!" said Emily, in a voice of desperation, "that I may not lose my senses—say you know me!"

"I do live," replied Madame Montoni, "but—I feel that I am about to die."

Emily clasped the hand she held, more eagerly, and groaned. They were both silent for some moments. Then Emily endeavoured to soothe her, and enquired what had reduced her to this present deplorable state.

Montoni, when he removed her to the turret under the improbable suspicion of having attempted his life, had ordered the men employed on the occasion, to observe a strict secrecy concerning her. To this he was influenced by a double motive. He meant to debar her from the comfort of Emily's visits, and to secure an opportunity of privately dispatching her, should any new circumstances occur to confirm the present suggestions of his suspecting mind. His consciousness of the hatred he deserved it was natural enough should at first lead him to attribute to her the attempt that had been made upon his life; and, though there was no other reason to believe that she was concerned in that atrocious design, his suspicions remained; he continued to confine her in the turret, under a strict guard; and, without pity or remorse, had suffered her to lie, forlorn and neglected, under a raging fever, till it had reduced her to the present state.

The track of blood, which Emily had seen on the stairs, had flowed from the unbound wound of one of the men employed to carry Madame Montoni, and which he had received in the late affray. At night these men, having contented themselves with securing the door of their prisoner's room, had retired from guard; and then it was, that Emily, at the time of her first enquiry, had found the turret so silent and deserted.

When she had attempted to open the door of the chamber, her aunt was sleeping, and this occasioned the silence, which had contributed to delude her into a belief, that she was no more; yet had her terror permitted her to persevere longer in the call, she would probably have awakened Madame Montoni, and have been spared much suffering. The spectacle in the portal-chamber, which afterwards confirmed Emily's horrible suspicion, was the corpse of a man, who had fallen in the affray, and the same which had been borne into the servants' hall, where she took refuge from the tumult. This man had lingered under his wounds for some days; and, soon after his death, his body had been removed on the couch, on which he died, for interment in the vault beneath the chapel, through which Emily and Barnardine had passed to the chamber.

Emily, after asking Madame Montoni a thousand questions concerning herself, left her, and sought Montoni; for the more solemn interest she felt for her aunt, made her now regardless of the resentment her remonstrances might draw upon herself, and of the improbability of his granting what she meant to entreat.

"Madame Montoni is now dying, sir," said Emily, as soon as she saw him—"Your resentment, surely will not pursue her to the last moment! Suffer her to be removed from that forlorn room to her own apartment, and to have necessary comforts administered."

"Of what service will that be, if she is dying?" said Montoni, with apparent indifference.

"The service, at least, of saving you, sir, from a few of those pangs of conscience you must suffer, when you shall be in the same situation," said Emily, with imprudent indignation, of which Montoni soon made her sensible, by commanding her to quit his presence. Then, forgetting her resentment, and impressed only by compassion for the piteous state of her aunt, dying without succour, she submitted to humble herself to Montoni, and to adopt every persuasive means, that might induce him to relent towards his wife.

For a considerable time he was proof against all she said, and all she looked; but at length the divinity of pity, beaming in Emily's eyes, seemed to touch his heart. He turned away, ashamed of his better feelings, half sullen and half relenting; but finally consented, that his wife should be removed to her own apartment, and that Emily should attend her. Dreading equally, that this relief might arrive too late, and that Montoni might retract his concession, Emily scarcely staid to thank him for it, but, assisted by Annette, she quickly prepared Madame Montoni's bed, and they carried her a cordial, that might enable her feeble frame to sustain the fatigue of a removal.

Madame was scarcely arrived in her own apartment, when an order was given by her husband, that she should remain in the turret; but Emily, thankful that she had made such dispatch, hastened to inform him of it, as well as that a second removal would instantly prove fatal, and he suffered his wife to continue where she was.

During this day, Emily never left Madame Montoni, except to prepare such little nourishing things as she judged necessary to sustain her, and which Madame Montoni received with quiet acquiescence, though she seemed sensible that they could not save her from approaching dissolution, and scarcely appeared to wish for life. Emily meanwhile watched over her with the most tender solicitude, no longer seeing her imperious aunt in the poor object before her, but the sister of her late beloved father, in a situation that called for all her compassion and kindness. When night came, she determined to sit up with her aunt, but this the latter positively forbade, commanding her to retire to rest, and Annette alone to remain in her chamber. Rest was, indeed, necessary to Emily, whose spirits and frame were equally wearied by the occurrences and exertions of the day; but she would not leave Madame Montoni, till after the turn of midnight, a period then thought so critical by the physicians.

Soon after twelve, having enjoined Annette to be wakeful, and to call her, should any change appear for the worse, Emily sorrowfully bade Madame Montoni good night, and withdrew to her chamber. Her spirits were more than usually depressed by the piteous condition of her aunt, whose recovery she scarcely dared to expect. To her own misfortunes she saw no period, inclosed as she was, in a remote castle, beyond the reach of any friends, had she possessed such, and beyond the pity even of strangers; while she knew herself to be in the power of a man capable of any action, which his interest, or his ambition, might suggest.

Occupied by melancholy reflections and by anticipations as sad, she did not retire immediately to rest, but leaned thoughtfully on her open casement. The scene before her of woods and mountains, reposing in the moon-light, formed a regretted contrast with the state of her mind; but the lonely murmur of these woods, and the view of this sleeping landscape, gradually soothed her emotions and softened her to tears.

She continued to weep, for some time, lost to every thing, but to a gentle sense of her misfortunes. When she, at length, took the handkerchief from her eyes, she perceived, before her, on the terrace below, the figure she had formerly observed, which stood fixed and silent, immediately opposite to her casement. On perceiving it, she started back, and terror for some time overcame curiosity;—at length, she returned to the casement, and still the figure was before it, which she now compelled herself to observe, but was utterly unable to speak, as she had formerly intended. The moon shone with a clear light, and it was, perhaps, the agitation of her mind, that prevented her distinguishing, with any degree of accuracy, the form before her. It was still stationary, and she began to doubt, whether it was really animated.

Her scattered thoughts were now so far returned as to remind her, that her light exposed her to dangerous observation, and she was stepping back to remove it, when she perceived the figure move, and then wave what seemed to be its arm, as if to beckon her; and, while she gazed, fixed in fear, it repeated the action. She now attempted to speak, but the words died on her lips, and she went from the casement to remove her light; as she was doing which, she heard, from without, a faint groan. Listening, but not daring to return, she presently heard it repeated.

"Good God!—what can this mean!" said she.

Again she listened, but the sound came no more; and, after a long interval of silence, she recovered courage enough to go to the casement, when she again saw the same appearance! It beckoned again, and again uttered a low sound.

"That groan was surely human!" said she. "I *will* speak." "Who is it," cried Emily in a faint voice, "that wanders at this late hour?"

The figure raised its head but suddenly started away, and glided down the terrace. She watched it, for a long while, passing swiftly in the moon-light, but heard no footstep, till a sentinel from the other extremity of the rampart walked slowly along. The man stopped under her window, and, looking up, called her by name. She was retiring precipitately, but, a second summons inducing her to reply, the soldier then respectfully asked if she had seen any thing pass. On her answering, that she had; he said no more, but walked away down the terrace, Emily following him with her eyes, till he was lost in the distance. But, as he was on guard, she knew he could not go beyond the rampart, and, therefore, resolved to await his return.

Soon after, his voice was heard, at a distance, calling loudly; and then a voice still more distant answered, and, in the next moment, the watch-word was given, and passed along the terrace. As the soldiers moved hastily under the casement, she called to enquire what had happened, but they passed without regarding her.

Emily's thoughts returning to the figure she had seen, "It cannot be a person, who has designs upon the castle," said she; "such an one would conduct himself very differently. He would not venture where sentinels were on watch, nor fix himself opposite to a window, where he perceived he must be observed; much less would he beckon, or utter a sound of complaint. Yet it cannot be a prisoner, for how could he obtain the opportunity to wander thus?"

If she had been subject to vanity, she might have supposed this figure to be some inhabitant of the castle, who wandered under her casement in the hope of seeing her, and of being allowed to declare his admiration; but this opinion never occurred to Emily, and, if it had, she would have dismissed it as improbable, on considering, that, when the opportunity of speaking had occurred, it had been suffered to pass in silence; and that, even at the moment in which she had spoken, the form had abruptly quitted the place.

While she mused, two sentinels walked up the rampart in earnest conversation, of which she caught a few words, and learned from these, that one of their comrades had fallen down senseless. Soon after, three other soldiers appeared slowly advancing from the bottom of the terrace, but she heard only a low voice, that came at intervals. As they drew near, she perceived this to be the voice of him, who walked in the middle, apparently supported by his comrades; and she again called to them, enquiring what had happened. At the sound of her voice, they stopped, and looked up, while she repeated her question, and was told, that Roberto, their fellow of the watch, had been seized with a fit, and that his cry, as he fell, had caused a false alarm.

"Is he subject to fits?" said Emily.

"Yes, Signora," replied Roberto; "but if I had not, what I saw was enough to have frightened the Pope himself."

"What was it?" enquired Emily, trembling.

"I cannot tell what it was, lady, or what I saw, or how it vanished," replied the soldier, who seemed to shudder at the recollection.

"Was it the person, whom you followed down the rampart, that has occasioned you this alarm?" said Emily, endeavouring to conceal her own.

"Person!" exclaimed the man, — "it was the devil, and this is not the first time I have seen him!"

"Nor will it be the last," observed one of his comrades, laughing.

"No, no, I warrant not," said another.

"Well," rejoined Roberto, "you may be as merry now, as you please; you was none so jocose the other night, Sebastian, when you was on watch with Launcelot."

"Launcelot need not talk of that," replied Sebastian, "let him remember how he stood trembling, and unable to give the *word*, till the man was gone. If the man had not come so silently upon us, I would have seized him, and soon made him tell who he was."

"What man?" enquired Emily.

"It was no man, lady," said Launcelot, who stood by, "but the devil himself, as my comrade says. What man, who does not live in the castle, could get within the walls at midnight? Why, I might just as well pretend to march to Venice, and get among all the Senators, when they are counselling; and I warrant I should have more chance of getting out again alive, than any fellow, that we should catch within the gates after dark. So I think I have proved plainly enough, that this can be nobody that lives out of the castle; and now I will prove, that it can be nobody that lives in the castle — for, if he did — why should he be afraid to be seen? So after this, I hope nobody will pretend to tell me it was anybody. No, I say again, by holy Pope! it was the devil, and Sebastian, there, knows this is not the first time we have seen him."

"When did you see the figure, then, before?" said Emily half smiling, who, though she thought the conversation somewhat too much, felt an interest, which would not permit her to conclude it.

"About a week ago, lady," said Sebastian, taking up the story.

"And where?"

"On the rampart, lady, higher up."

"Did you pursue it, that it fled?"

"No, Signora. Launcelot and I were on watch together, and every thing was so still, you might have heard a mouse stir, when, suddenly, Launcelot says — Sebastian! do you see nothing? I turned my head a little to the left, as it might be—thus. No, says I. Hush! said Launcelot,—look yonder—just by the last cannon on the rampart! I looked, and then thought I did see something move; but there being no light, but what the stars gave, I could not be certain. We stood quite silent, to watch it, and presently saw something pass along the castle wall just opposite to us!"

"Why did you not seize it, then?" cried a soldier, who had scarcely spoken till now.

"Aye, why did you not seize it?" said Roberto.

"You should have been there to have done that," replied Sebastian. "You would have been bold enough to have taken it by the throat, though it had been the devil himself; we could not take such a liberty, perhaps, because we are not so well acquainted with him, as you are. But, as I was saying, it stole by us so quickly, that we had not time to get rid of our surprise, before it was gone. Then, we knew it was in vain to follow. We kept constant watch all that night, but we saw it no more. Next morning, we told some of our comrades, who were on duty on other parts of the ramparts, what we had seen; but they had seen nothing, and laughed at us, and it was not till to-night, that the same figure walked again."

"Where did you lose it, friend?" said Emily to Roberto.

"When I left you, lady," replied the man, "you might see me go down the rampart, but it was not till I reached the east terrace, that I saw any thing. Then, the moon shining bright, I saw something like a shadow flitting before me, as it were, at some distance. I stopped, when I turned the corner of the east tower, where I had seen this figure not a moment before,—but it was gone! As I stood, looking through the old arch, which leads to the east rampart, and where I am sure it had passed, I heard, all of a sudden, such a sound!—It was not like a groan, or a cry, or a shout, or any thing I ever heard in my life. I heard it only once, and that was enough for me; for I know nothing that happened after, till I found my comrades, here, about me."

"Come," said Sebastian, "let us go to our posts—the moon is setting. Good night, lady!"

"Aye, let us go," rejoined Roberto. "Good night, lady."

"Good night; the holy mother guard you!" said Emily, as she closed her casement and retired to reflect upon the strange circumstance that had just occurred, connecting which with what had happened on former nights, she endeavoured to derive from the whole something more positive, than conjecture. But her imagination was inflamed, while her judgment was not enlightened, and the terrors of superstition again pervaded her mind.

CHAPTER IV

There is one within,
Besides the things, that we have heard and seen,
Recounts most horrid sights, seen by the watch.
JULIUS CÆSAR

IN the morning, Emily found Madame Montoni nearly in the same condition, as on the preceding night; she had slept little, and that little had not refreshed her; she smiled on her niece, and seemed cheered by her presence, but spoke only a few words, and never named Montoni, who, however, soon after, entered the room. His wife, when she understood that he was there, appeared much agitated, but was entirely silent, till Emily rose from a chair at the bed-side, when she begged, in a feeble voice, that she would not leave her.

The visit of Montoni was not to soothe his wife, whom he knew to be dying, or to console, or to ask her forgiveness, but to make a last effort to procure that signature, which would transfer her estates in Languedoc, after her death, to him rather than to Emily. This was a scene, that exhibited, on his part, his usual inhumanity, and, on that of Madame Montoni, a persevering spirit, contending with a feeble frame; while Emily repeatedly declared to him her willingness to resign all claim to those estates, rather than that the last hours of her aunt should be disturbed by contention. Montoni, however, did not leave the room, till his wife, exhausted by the obstinate dispute, had fainted, and she lay so long insensible, that Emily began to fear that the spark of life was extinguished. At length, she revived, and, looking feebly up at her niece, whose tears were falling over her, made an effort to speak, but her words were unintelligible, and Emily again apprehended she was dying. Afterwards, however, she recovered her speech, and, being somewhat restored by a cordial, conversed for a considerable time, on the subject of her estates in France, with clearness and precision. She directed her niece where to find some papers relative to them, which she had hitherto concealed from the search of Montoni, and earnestly charged her never to suffer these papers to escape her.

Soon after this conversation, Madame Montoni sunk into a dose, and continued slumbering, till evening, when she seemed better than she had been since her removal from the turret. Emily never left her, for a moment, till long after midnight, and even then would not have quitted the room, had not her aunt entreated, that she would retire to rest. She then obeyed, the more willingly, because her patient appeared somewhat recruited by sleep; and, giving Annette the same injunction, as on the preceding night, she withdrew to her own apartment. But her spirits were wakeful and agitated, and, finding it impossible to sleep, she determined to watch, once more, for the mysterious appearance, that had so much interested and alarmed her.

It was now the second watch of the night, and about the time when the figure had before appeared. Emily heard the passing steps of the sentinels, on the rampart, as they changed guard; and, when all was again silent, she took her station at the casement, leaving her lamp in a remote part of the chamber, that she might escape notice from without. The moon gave a faint and uncertain light, for heavy vapours surrounded it, and, often rolling over the disk, left the scene below in total darkness. It was in one of these moments of obscurity, that she observed a small and lambent flame, moving at some distance on the terrace. While she gazed, it disappeared, and, the moon again emerging from the lurid and heavy thunder clouds, she turned her attention to the heavens, where the vivid lightnings darted from cloud to cloud, and flashed silently on the woods below. She loved to catch, in the momentary gleam, the gloomy landscape. Sometimes, a cloud opened its light upon a distant mountain, and, while the sudden splendour illumined all its recesses of rock and wood, the rest of the scene remained in deep shadow; at others, partial features of the castle were revealed by the glimpse—the antient arch leading to the east rampart, the turret above, or the fortifications beyond; and then, perhaps, the whole edifice with all its towers, its dark massy walls and pointed casements would appear, and vanish in an instant.

Emily, looking again upon the rampart, perceived the flame she had seen before; it moved onward; and, soon after, she thought she heard a footstep. The light appeared and disappeared frequently, while, as she watched, it glided under her casements, and, at the same instant, she was certain, that a footstep passed, but the darkness did not permit her to distinguish any object except the flame. It moved away, and then, by a gleam of lightning, she perceived some person on the terrace. All the anxieties of the preceding night returned. This person advanced, and the playing flame alternately appeared and vanished. Emily wished to speak, to end her doubts, whether this figure were human or supernatural; but her courage failed as often as she attempted utterance, till the light moved again under the casement, and she faintly demanded, who passed.

"A friend," replied a voice.

"What friend?" said Emily, somewhat encouraged "who are you, and what is that light you carry?"

"I am Anthonio, one of the Signor's soldiers," replied the voice.

"And what is that tapering light you bear?" said Emily, "see how it darts upwards,—and now it vanishes!"

"This light, lady," said the soldier, "has appeared to-night as you see it, on the point of my lance, ever since I have been on watch; but what it means I cannot tell."

"This is very strange!" said Emily.

"My fellow-guard," continued the man, "has the same flame on his arms; he says he has sometimes seen it before. I never did; I am but lately come to the castle, for I have not been long a soldier."

"How does your comrade account for it?" said Emily.

"He says it is an omen, lady, and bodes no good."

"And what harm can it bode?" rejoined Emily.

"He knows not so much as that, lady."

Whether Emily was alarmed by this omen, or not, she certainly was relieved from much terror by discovering this man to be only a soldier on duty, and it immediately occurred to her, that it might be he, who had occasioned so much alarm on the preceding night. There were, however, some circumstances, that still required explanation. As far as she could judge by the faint moon-light, that had assisted her observation, the figure she had seen did not resemble this man either in shape or size; besides, she was certain it had carried no arms. The silence of its steps, if steps it had, the moaning sounds, too, which it had uttered, and its strange disappearance, were circumstances of mysterious import, that did not apply, with probability, to a soldier engaged in the duty of his guard.

She now enquired of the sentinel, whether he had seen any person besides his fellow watch, walking on the terrace, about midnight; and then briefly related what she had herself observed.

"I was not on guard that night, lady," replied the man, "but I heard of what happened. There are amongst us, who believe strange things. Strange stories, too, have long been told of this castle, but it is no business of mine to repeat them; and, for my part, I have no reason to complain; our Chief does nobly by us."

"I commend your prudence," said Emily. "Good night, and accept this from me," she added, throwing him a small piece of coin, and then closing the casement to put an end to the discourse.

When he was gone, she opened it again, listened with a gloomy pleasure to the distant thunder, that began to murmur among the mountains, and watched the arrowy lightnings, which broke over the remoter scene. The pealing thunder rolled onward, and then, reverbed by the mountains, other thunder seemed to answer from the opposite horizon; while the accumulating clouds, entirely concealing the moon, assumed a red sulphureous tinge, that foretold a violent storm.

Emily remained at her casement, till the vivid lightning, that now, every instant, revealed the wide horizon and the landscape below, made it no longer safe to do so, and she went to her couch; but, unable to compose her mind to sleep, still listened in silent awe to the tremendous sounds, that seemed to shake the castle to its foundation.

She had continued thus for a considerable time, when, amidst the uproar of the storm, she thought she heard a voice, and, raising herself to listen, saw the chamber door open, and Annette enter with a countenance of wild affright.

"She is dying, ma'amselle, my lady is dying!" said she.

Emily started up, and ran to Madame Montoni's room. When she entered, her aunt appeared to have fainted, for she was quite still, and insensible; and Emily with a strength of mind, that refused to yield to grief, while any duty required her activity, applied every means that seemed likely to restore her. But the last struggle was over—she was gone for ever.

When Emily perceived, that all her efforts were ineffectual, she interrogated the terrified Annette, and learned, that Madame Montoni had fallen into a doze soon after Emily's departure, in which she had continued, until a few minutes before her death.

"I wondered, ma'amselle," said Annette, "what was the reason my lady did not seem frightened at the thunder, when I was so terrified, and I went often to the bed to speak to her, but she appeared to be asleep; till presently I heard a strange noise, and, on going to her, saw she was dying."

Emily, at this recital, shed tears. She had no doubt but that the violent change in the air, which the tempest produced, had effected this fatal one, on the exhausted frame of Madame Montoni.

After some deliberation, she determined that Montoni should not be informed of this event till the morning, for she considered, that he might, perhaps, utter some inhuman expressions, such as in the present temper of her spirits she could not bear. With Annette alone, therefore, whom she encouraged by her own example, she performed some of the last solemn offices for the dead, and compelled herself to watch during the night, by the body of her deceased aunt. During this solemn period, rendered more awful by the tremendous storm that shook the air, she frequently addressed herself to Heaven for support and protection, and her pious prayers, we may believe, were accepted of the God, that giveth comfort.

CHAPTER V

The midnight clock has toll'd; and hark, the bell
Of Death beats slow! heard ye the note profound?
It pauses now; and now, with rising knell,
Flings to the hollow gale its sullen sound.

MASON

WHEN Montoni was informed of the death of his wife, and considered that she had died without giving him the signature so necessary to the accomplishment of his wishes, no sense of decency restrained the expression of his resentment. Emily anxiously avoided his presence, and watched, during two days and two nights, with little intermission, by the corpse of her late aunt. Her mind deeply impressed with the unhappy fate of this object, she forgot all her faults, her unjust and imperious conduct to herself; and, remembering only her sufferings, thought of her only with tender compassion. Sometimes, however, she could not avoid musing upon the strange infatuation that had proved so fatal to her aunt, and had involved herself in a labyrinth of misfortune, from which she saw no means of escaping,—the marriage with Montoni. But, when she considered this circumstance, it was "more in sorrow than in anger,"—more for the purpose of indulging lamentation, than reproach.

In her pious cares she was not disturbed by Montoni, who not only avoided the chamber, where the remains of his wife were laid, but that part of the castle adjoining to it, as if he had apprehended a contagion in death. He seemed to have given no orders respecting the funeral, and Emily began to fear he meant to offer a new insult to the memory of Madame Montoni; but from this apprehension she was relieved, when, on the evening of the second day, Annette informed her, that the interment was to take place that night. She knew, that Montoni would not attend; and it was so very grievous to her to think that the remains of her unfortunate aunt would pass to the grave without one relative, or friend to pay them the last decent rites, that she determined to be deterred by no considerations for herself, from observing this duty. She would otherwise have shrunk from the circumstance of following them to the cold vault, to which they were to be carried by men, whose air and countenances seemed to stamp them for murderers, at the midnight hour of silence and privacy, which Montoni had chosen for committing, if possible, to oblivion the reliques of a woman, whom his harsh conduct had, at least, contributed to destroy.

Emily, shuddering with emotions of horror and grief, assisted by Annette, prepared the corpse for interment; and, having wrapt it in cerements, and covered it with a winding-sheet, they watched beside it, till past midnight, when they heard the approaching footsteps of the men, who were to lay it in its earthy bed. It was with difficulty, that Emily overcame her emotion, when, the door of the chamber being thrown open, their gloomy countenances were seen by the glare of the torch they carried, and two of them, without speaking, lifted the body on their shoulders, while the third preceding them with the light, descended through the castle towards the grave, which was in the lower vault of the chapel within the castle walls.

They had to cross two courts, towards the east wing of the castle, which, adjoining the chapel, was, like it, in ruins: but the silence and gloom of these courts had now little power over Emily's mind, occupied as it was, with more mournful ideas; and she scarcely heard the low and dismal hooting of the night-birds, that roosted among the ivyed battlements of the ruin, or perceived the still flittings of the bat, which frequently crossed her way. But, when, having entered the chapel, and passed between the mouldering pillars of the aisles, the bearers stopped at a flight of steps, that led down to a low arched door, and, their comrade having descended to unlock it, she saw imperfectly the gloomy abyss beyond;—saw the corpse of her aunt carried down these steps, and the ruffian-like figure, that stood with a torch at the bottom to receive it—all her fortitude was lost in emotions of inexpressible grief and terror. She turned to lean upon Annette, who was cold and trembling like herself, and she lingered so long on the summit of the flight, that the gleam of the torch began to die away on the pillars of the chapel, and the men were almost beyond her view. Then, the gloom around her awakening other fears, and a sense of what she considered to be her duty overcoming her reluctance, she descended to the vaults, following the echo of footsteps and the faint ray, that pierced the darkness, till the harsh grating of a distant door, that was opened to receive the corpse, again appalled her.

After the pause of a moment, she went on, and, as she entered the vaults, saw between the arches, at some distance, the men lay down the body near the edge of an open grave, where stood another of Montoni's men and a priest, whom she did not observe, till he began the burial service; then, lifting her eyes from the ground, she saw the venerable figure of the friar, and heard him in a low voice, equally solemn and affecting, perform the service for the dead. At the moment, in which they let down the body into the earth, the scene was such as only the dark pencil of a Domenichino, perhaps, could have done justice to. The fierce features and wild dress of the *condottieri*, bending with their torches over the grave, into which the corpse was descending, were contrasted by the venerable figure of the monk, wrapt in long black garments, his cowl thrown back from his pale face, on which the light gleaming strongly shewed the lines of affliction softened by piety, and the few grey locks, which time had spared on his temples: while, beside him, stood the softer form of Emily, who leaned for support upon Annette; her face half averted, and shaded by a thin veil, that fell over her figure; and her mild and beautiful countenance fixed in grief so solemn as admitted not of tears, while she thus saw committed untimely to the earth her last relative and friend. The gleams, thrown between the arches of the vaults, where, here and there, the broken ground marked the spots in which other bodies had been recently interred, and the general obscurity beyond were circumstances, that alone would have led on the imagination of a spectator to scenes more horrible, than even that, which was pictured at the grave of the misguided and unfortunate Madame Montoni.

When the service was over, the friar regarded Emily with attention and surprise, and looked as if he wished to speak to her, but was restrained by the presence of the condottieri, who, as they now led the way to the courts, amused themselves with jokes upon his holy order, which he endured in silence, demanding only to be conducted safely to his convent, and to which Emily listened with concern and even horror. When they reached the court, the monk gave her his blessing, and, after a lingering look of pity, turned away to the portal, whither one of the men carried a torch; while Annette, lighting another, preceded Emily to her apartment. The appearance of the friar and the expression of tender compassion, with which he had regarded her, had interested Emily, who, though it was at her earnest supplication, that Montoni had consented to allow a priest to perform the last rites for his deceased wife, knew nothing concerning this person, till Annette now informed her, that he belonged to a monastery, situated among the mountains at a few miles distance. The Superior, who regarded Montoni and his associates, not only with aversion, but with terror, had probably feared to offend him by refusing his request, and had, therefore, ordered a monk to officiate at the funeral, who, with the meek spirit of a christian, had overcome his reluctance to enter the walls of such a castle, by the wish of performing what he considered to be his duty, and, as the chapel was built on consecrated ground, had not objected to commit to it the remains of the late unhappy Madame Montoni.

Several days passed with Emily in total seclusion, and in a state of mind partaking both of terror for herself, and grief for the departed. She, at length, determined to make other efforts to persuade Montoni to permit her return to France. Why he should wish to detain her, she could scarcely dare to conjecture; but it was too certain that he did so, and the absolute refusal he had formerly given to her departure allowed her little hope, that he would now consent to it. But the horror, which his presence inspired, made her defer, from day to day, the mention of this subject; and at last she was awakened from her inactivity only by a message from him, desiring her attendance at a certain hour. She began to hope he meant to resign, now that her aunt was no more, the authority he had usurped over her; till she recollected, that the estates, which had occasioned so much contention, were now hers, and she then feared Montoni was about to employ some stratagem for obtaining them, and that he would detain her his prisoner, till he succeeded. This thought, instead of overcoming her with despondency, roused all the latent powers of her fortitude into action; and the property, which she would willingly have resigned to secure the peace of her aunt, she resolved, that no common sufferings of her own should ever compel her to give to Montoni. For Valancourt's sake also she determined to preserve these estates, since they would afford that competency, by which she hoped to secure the comfort of their future lives. As she thought of this, she indulged the tenderness of tears, and anticipated the delight of that moment, when, with affectionate generosity, she might tell him they were his own. She saw the smile, that lighted up his features—the affectionate regard, which spoke at once his joy and thanks; and, at this instant, she believed she could brave any suffering, which the evil spirit of Montoni might be preparing for her. Remembering then, for the first time since her aunt's death, the papers relative to the estates in question, she determined to search for them, as soon as her interview with Montoni was over.

With these resolutions she met him at the appointed time, and waited to hear his intention before she renewed her request. With him were Orsino and another officer, and both were standing near a table, covered with papers, which he appeared to be examining.

"I sent for you, Emily," said Montoni, raising his head, "that you might be a witness in some business, which I am transacting with my friend Orsino. All that is required of you will be to sign your name to this paper:" he then took one up, hurried unintelligibly over some lines, and, laying it before her on the table, offered her a pen. She took it, and was going to write—when the design of Montoni came upon her mind like a flash of lightning; she trembled, let the pen fall, and refused to sign what she had not read. Montoni affected to laugh at her scruples, and, taking up the paper, again pretended to read; but Emily, who still trembled on perceiving her danger, and was astonished, that her own credulity had so nearly betrayed her, positively refused to sign any paper whatever. Montoni, for some time, persevered in affecting to ridicule this refusal; but, when he perceived by her steady perseverance, that she understood his design, he changed his manner, and bade her follow him to another room. There he told her, that he had been willing to spare himself and her the trouble of useless contest, in an affair, where his will was justice, and where she should find it law; and had, therefore, endeavoured to persuade, rather than to compel, her to the practice of her duty.

"I, as the husband of the late Signora Montoni," he added, "am the heir of all she possessed; the estates, therefore, which she refused to me in her life-time, can no longer be withheld, and, for your own sake, I would undeceive you, respecting a foolish assertion she once made to you in my hearing—that these estates would be yours, if she died without resigning them to me. She knew at that moment, she had no power to withhold them from me, after her decease; and I think you have more sense, than to provoke my resentment by advancing an unjust claim. I am not in the habit of flattering, and you will, therefore, receive, as sincere, the praise I bestow, when I say, that you possess an understanding superior to that of your sex; and that you have none of those contemptible foibles, that frequently mark the female character—such as avarice and the love of power, which latter makes women delight to contradict and to tease, when they cannot conquer. If I understand your disposition and your mind, you hold in sovereign contempt these common failings of your sex."

Montoni paused; and Emily remained silent and expecting; for she knew him too well, to believe he would condescend to such flattery, unless he thought it would promote his own interest; and, though he had forborne to name vanity among the foibles of women, it was evident, that he considered it to be a predominant one, since he designed to sacrifice to hers the character and understanding of her whole sex.

"Judging as I do," resumed Montoni, "I cannot believe you will oppose, where you know you cannot conquer, or, indeed, that you would wish to conquer, or be avaricious of any property, when you have not justice on your side. I think it proper, however, to acquaint you with the alternative. If you have a just opinion of the subject in question, you shall be allowed a safe conveyance to France, within a short period; but, if you are so unhappy as to be misled by the late assertion of the Signora, you shall remain my prisoner, till you are convinced of your error."

Emily calmly said,

"I am not so ignorant, Signor, of the laws on this subject, as to be misled by the assertion of any person. The law, in the present instance, gives me the estates in question, and my own hand shall never betray my right."

"I have been mistaken in my opinion of you, it appears," rejoined Montoni, sternly. "You speak boldly, and presumptuously, upon a subject, which you do not understand. For once, I am willing to pardon the conceit of ignorance; the weakness of your sex, too, from which, it seems, you are not exempt, claims some allowance; but, if you persist in this strain—you have every thing to fear from my justice."

"From your justice, Signor," rejoined Emily, "I have nothing to fear—I have only to hope."

Montoni looked at her with vexation, and seemed considering what to say. "I find that you are weak enough," he resumed, "to credit the idle assertion I alluded to! For your own sake I lament this; as to me, it is of little consequence. Your credulity can punish only yourself; and I must pity the weakness of mind, which leads you to so much suffering as you are compelling me to prepare for you."

"You may find, perhaps, Signor," said Emily, with mild dignity, "that the strength of my mind is equal to the justice of my cause; and that I can endure with fortitude, when it is in resistance of oppression."

"You speak like a heroine," said Montoni, contemptuously; "we shall see whether you can suffer like one."

Emily was silent, and he left the room.

Recollecting, that it was for Valancourt's sake she had thus resisted, she now smiled complacently upon the threatened sufferings, and retired to the spot, which her aunt had pointed out as the repository of the papers, relative to the estates, where she found them as described; and, since she knew of no better place of concealment, than this, returned them, without examining their contents, being fearful of discovery, while she should attempt a perusal.

To her own solitary chamber she once more returned, and there thought again of the late conversation with Montoni, and of the evil she might expect from opposition to his will. But his power did not appear so terrible to her imagination, as it was wont to do: a sacred pride was in her heart, that taught it to swell against the pressure of injustice, and almost to glory in the quiet sufferance of ills, in a cause, which had also the interest of Valancourt for its object. For the first time, she felt the full extent of her own superiority to Montoni, and despised the authority, which, till now, she had only feared.

As she sat musing, a peal of laughter rose from the terrace, and, on going to the casement, she saw, with inexpressible surprise, three ladies, dressed in the gala habit of Venice, walking with several gentlemen below. She gazed in an astonishment that made her remain at the window, regardless of being observed, till the group passed under it; and, one of the strangers looking up, she perceived the features of Signora Livona, with whose manners she had been so much charmed, the day after her arrival at Venice, and who had been there introduced at the table of Montoni. This discovery occasioned her an emotion of doubtful joy; for it was matter of joy and comfort to know, that a person, of a mind so gentle, as that of Signora Livona seemed to be, was near her; yet there was something so extraordinary in her being at this castle, circumstanced as it now was, and evidently, by the gaiety of her air, with her own consent, that a very painful surmise arose, concerning her character. But the thought was so shocking to Emily, whose affection the fascinating manners of the Signora had won, and appeared so improbable, when she remembered these manners, that she dismissed it almost instantly.

On Annette's appearance, however, she enquired, concerning these strangers; and the former was as eager to tell, as Emily was to learn. "They are just come, ma'amselle," said Annette, "with two Signors from Venice, and I was glad to see such Christian faces once again.— But what can they mean by coming here? They must surely be stark mad to come freely to such a place as this! Yet they do come freely, for they seem merry enough, I am sure."

"They were taken prisoners, perhaps?" said Emily.

"Taken prisoners!" exclaimed Annette; "no, indeed, ma'amselle, not they. I remember one of them very well at Venice: she came two or three times, to the Signor's, you know, ma'amselle, and it was said, but I did not believe a word of it—it was said, that the Signor liked her better than he should do. Then why, says I, bring her to my lady? Very true, said Ludovico; but he looked as if he knew more, too."

Emily desired Annette would endeavour to learn who these ladies were, as well as all she could concerning them; and she then changed the subject, and spoke of distant France.

"Ah, ma'amselle! we shall never see it more!" said Annette, almost weeping.—"I must come on my travels, forsooth!"

Emily tried to soothe and to cheer her, with a hope, in which she scarcely herself indulged.

"How—how, ma'amselle, could you leave France, and leave Mons. Valancourt, too?" said Annette, sobbing. "I—I—am sure, if Ludovico had been in France, I would never have left it."

"Why do you lament quitting France, then?" said Emily, trying to smile, "since, if you had remained there, you would not have found Ludovico."

"Ah, ma'amselle! I only wish I was out of this frightful castle, serving you in France, and I would care about nothing else!"

"Thank you, my good Annette, for your affectionate regard; the time will come, I hope, when you may remember the expression of that wish with pleasure."

Annette departed on her business, and Emily sought to lose the sense of her own cares, in the visionary scenes of the poet; but she had again to lament the irresistible force of circumstances over the taste and powers of the mind; and that it requires a spirit at ease to be sensible even to the abstract pleasures of pure intellect. The enthusiasm of genius, with all its pictured scenes, now appeared cold, and dim. As she mused upon the book before her, she involuntarily exclaimed, "Are these, indeed, the passages, that have so often given me exquisite delight?

Where did the charm exist?—Was it in my mind, or in the imagination of the poet? It lived in each," said she, pausing. "But the fire of the poet is vain, if the mind of his reader is not tempered like his own, however it may be inferior to his in power."

Emily would have pursued this train of thinking, because it relieved her from more painful reflection, but she found again, that thought cannot always be controlled by will; and hers returned to the consideration of her own situation.

In the evening, not choosing to venture down to the ramparts, where she would be exposed to the rude gaze of Montoni's associates, she walked for air in the gallery, adjoining her chamber; on reaching the further end of which she heard distant sounds of merriment and laughter. It was the wild uproar of riot, not the cheering gaiety of tempered mirth; and seemed to come from that part of the castle, where Montoni usually was. Such sounds, at this time, when her aunt had been so few days dead, particularly shocked her, consistent as they were with the late conduct of Montoni.

As she listened, she thought she distinguished female voices mingling with the laughter, and this confirmed her worst surmise, concerning the character of Signora Livona and her companions. It was evident, that they had not been brought hither by compulsion; and she beheld herself in the remote wilds of the Apennine, surrounded by men, whom she considered to be little less than ruffians, and their worst associates, amid scenes of vice, from which her soul recoiled in horror. It was at this moment, when the scenes of the present and the future opened to her imagination, that the image of Valancourt failed in its influence, and her resolution shook with dread. She thought she understood all the horrors, which Montoni was preparing for her, and shrunk from an encounter with such remorseless vengeance, as he could inflict. The disputed estates she now almost determined to yield at once, whenever he should again call upon her, that she might regain safety and freedom; but then, the remembrance of Valancourt would steal to her heart, and plunge her into the distractions of doubt.

She continued walking in the gallery, till evening threw its melancholy twilight through the painted casements, and deepened the gloom of the oak wainscoting around her; while the distant perspective of the corridor was so much obscured, as to be discernible only by the glimmering window, that terminated it.

Along the vaulted halls and passages below, peals of laughter echoed faintly, at intervals, to this remote part of the castle, and seemed to render the succeeding stillness more dreary. Emily, however, unwilling to return to her more forlorn chamber, whither Annette was not yet come, still paced the gallery. As she passed the door of the apartment, where she had once dared to lift the veil, which discovered to her a spectacle so horrible, that she had never after remembered it, but with emotions of indescribable awe, this remembrance suddenly recurred. It now brought with it reflections more terrible, than it had yet done, which the late conduct of Montoni occasioned; and, hastening to quit the gallery, while she had power to do so, she heard a sudden step behind her.—It might be that of Annette; but, turning fearfully to look, she saw, through the gloom, a tall figure following her, and all the horrors of that chamber rushed upon her mind. In the next moment, she found herself clasped in the arms of some person, and heard a deep voice murmur in her ear.

When she had power to speak, or to distinguish articulated sounds, she demanded who detained her.

"It is I," replied the voice—"Why are you thus alarmed?"

She looked on the face of the person who spoke, but the feeble light, that gleamed through the high casement at the end of the gallery, did not permit her to distinguish the features.

"Whoever you are," said Emily, in a trembling voice, "for heaven's sake let me go!"

"My charming Emily," said the man, "why will you shut yourself up in this obscure place, when there is so much gaiety below? Return with me to the cedar parlour, where you will be the fairest ornament of the party;—you shall not repent the exchange."

Emily disdained to reply, and still endeavoured to liberate herself.

"Promise, that you will come," he continued, "and I will release you immediately; but first give me a reward for so doing."

"Who are you?" demanded Emily, in a tone of mingled terror and indignation, while she still struggled for liberty—"who are you, that have the cruelty thus to insult me?"

"Why call me cruel?" said the man, "I would remove you from this dreary solitude to a merry party below. Do you not know me?"

Emily now faintly remembered, that he was one of the officers who were with Montoni when she attended him in the morning. "I thank you for the kindness of your intention," she replied, without appearing to understand him, "but I wish for nothing so much as that you would leave me."

"Charming Emily!" said he, "give up this foolish whim for solitude, and come with me to the company, and eclipse the beauties who make part of it; you, only, are worthy of my love." He attempted to kiss her hand, but the strong impulse of her indignation gave her power to liberate herself, and she fled towards the chamber. She closed the door, before he reached it, having secured which, she sunk in a chair, overcome by terror and by the exertion she had made, while she heard his voice, and his attempts to open the door, without having the power to raise herself. At length, she perceived him depart, and had remained, listening, for a considerable time, and was somewhat revived by not hearing any sound, when suddenly she remembered the door of the private stair-case, and that he might enter that way, since it was fastened only on the other side. She then employed herself in endeavouring to secure it, in the manner she had formerly done. It appeared to her, that Montoni had already commenced his scheme of vengeance, by withdrawing from her his protection, and she repented of the rashness, that had made her brave the power of such a man. To retain the estates seemed to be now utterly impossible, and to preserve her life, perhaps her honour, she resolved, if she should escape the horrors of this night, to give up all claims to the estates, on the morrow, provided Montoni would suffer her to depart from Udolpho.

When she had come to this decision, her mind became more composed, though she still anxiously listened, and often started at ideal sounds, that appeared to issue from the stair-case.

Having sat in darkness for some hours, during all which time Annette did not appear, she began to have serious apprehensions for her; but, not daring to venture down into the castle, was compelled to remain in uncertainty, as to the cause of this unusual absence.

Emily often stole to the stair-case door, to listen if any step approached, but still no sound alarmed her: determining, however, to watch, during the night, she once more rested on her dark and desolate couch, and bathed the pillow with innocent tears. She thought of her deceased parents and then of the absent Valancourt, and frequently called upon their names; for the profound stillness, that now reigned, was propitious to the musing sorrow of her mind.

While she thus remained, her ear suddenly caught the notes of distant music, to which she listened attentively, and, soon perceiving this to be the instrument she had formerly heard at midnight, she rose, and stepped softly to the casement, to which the sounds appeared to come from a lower room.

In a few moments, their soft melody was accompanied by a voice so full of pathos, that it evidently sang not of imaginary sorrows. Its sweet and peculiar tones she thought she had somewhere heard before; yet, if this was not fancy, it was, at most, a very faint recollection. It stole over her mind, amidst the anguish of her present suffering, like a celestial strain, soothing, and re-assuring her;—"Pleasant as the gale of spring, that sighs on the hunter's ear, when he awakens from dreams of joy, and has heard the music of the spirits of the hill."*

*OSSIAN. [A. R.]

But her emotion can scarcely be imagined, when she heard sung, with the taste and simplicity of true feeling, one of the popular airs of her native province, to which she had so often listened with delight, when a child, and which she had so often heard her father repeat! To this well-known song, never, till now, heard but in her native country, her heart melted, while the memory of past times returned. The pleasant, peaceful scenes of Gascony, the tenderness and goodness of her parents, the taste and simplicity of her former life—all rose to her fancy, and formed a picture, so sweet and glowing, so strikingly contrasted with the scenes, the characters and the dangers, which now surrounded her—that her mind could not bear to pause upon the retrospect, and shrunk at the acuteness of its own sufferings.

Her sighs were deep and convulsed; she could no longer listen to the strain, that had so often charmed her to tranquillity, and she withdrew from the casement to a remote part of the chamber. But she was not yet beyond the reach of the music; she heard the measure change, and the succeeding air called her again to the window, for she immediately recollected it to be the same she had formerly heard in the fishing-house in Gascony. Assisted, perhaps, by the mystery, which had then accompanied this strain, it had made so deep an impression on her memory, that she had never since entirely forgotten it; and the manner, in which it was now sung, convinced her, however unaccountable the circumstances appeared, that this was the same voice she had then heard. Surprise soon yielded to other emotions; a thought darted, like lightning, upon her mind, which discovered a train of hopes, that revived all her spirits. Yet these hopes were so new, so unexpected, so astonishing, that she did not dare to trust, though she could not resolve to discourage them. She sat down by the casement, breathless, and overcome with the alternate emotions of hope and fear; then rose again, leaned from the window, that she might catch a nearer sound, listened, now doubting and then believing, softly exclaimed the name of Valancourt, and then sunk again into the chair. Yes, it was possible, that Valancourt was near her, and she recollected circumstances, which induced her to believe it was his voice she had just heard. She remembered he had more than once said that the fishing-house, where she had formerly listened to this voice and air, and where she had seen pencilled sonnets, addressed to herself, had been his favourite haunt, before he had been made known to her; there, too, she had herself unexpectedly met him. It appeared, from these circumstances, more than probable, that he was the musician, who had formerly charmed her attention, and the author of the lines, which had expressed such tender admiration;—who else, indeed, could it be? She was unable, at that time, to form a conjecture, as to the writer, but, since her acquaintance with Valancourt, whenever he had mentioned the fishing-house to have been known to him, she had not scrupled to believe that he was the author of the sonnets.

As these considerations passed over her mind, joy, fear and tenderness contended at her heart; she leaned again from the casement to catch the sounds, which might confirm, or destroy her hope, though she did not recollect to have ever heard him sing; but the voice, and the instrument, now ceased.

She considered for a moment whether she should venture to speak: then, not choosing, lest it should be he, to mention his name, and yet too much interested to neglect the opportunity of enquiring, she called from the casement, "Is that song from Gascony?" Her anxious attention was not cheered by any reply; every thing remained silent. Her impatience increasing with her fears, she repeated the question; but still no sound was heard, except the sighings of the wind among the battlements above; and she endeavoured to console herself with a belief, that the stranger, whoever he was, had retired, before she had spoken, beyond the reach of her voice, which, it appeared certain, had Valancourt heard and recognized, he would instantly have replied to. Presently, however, she considered, that a motive of prudence, and not an accidental removal, might occasion his silence; but the surmise, that led to this reflection, suddenly changed her hope and joy to terror and grief; for, if Valancourt were in the castle, it was too probable, that he was here a prisoner, taken with some of his countrymen, many of whom were at that time engaged in the wars of Italy, or intercepted in some attempt to reach her. Had he even recollected Emily's voice, he would have feared, in these circumstances, to reply to it, in the presence of the men, who guarded his prison.

What so lately she had eagerly hoped she now believed she dreaded;—dreaded to know, that Valancourt was near her; and, while she was anxious to be relieved from her apprehension for his safety, she still was unconscious, that a hope of soon seeing him, struggled with the fear.

She remained listening at the casement, till the air began to freshen, and one high mountain in the east to glimmer with the morning; when, wearied with anxiety, she retired to her couch, where she found it utterly impossible to sleep, for joy, tenderness, doubt and apprehension, distracted her during the whole night. Now she rose from the couch, and opened the casement to listen; then she would pace the room with impatient steps, and, at length, return with despondence to her pillow. Never did hours appear to move so heavily, as those of this anxious night; after which she hoped that Annette might appear, and conclude her present state of torturing suspense.

CHAPTER VI

might we but hear
The folded flocks penn'd in their watled cotes,
Or sound of pastoral reed with oaten stops,
Or whistle from the lodge, or village cock
Count the night watches to his feathery dames,
'Twould be some solace yet, some little cheering
In this close dungeon of innumerous boughs.

MILTON

IN the morning, Emily was relieved from her fears for Annette, who came at an early hour.

"Here were fine doings in the castle, last night, ma'amselle," said she, as soon as she entered the room,—"fine doings, indeed! Was you not frightened, ma'amselle, at not seeing me?"

"I was alarmed both on your account and on my own," replied Emily—"What detained you?"

"Aye, I said so, I told him so; but it would not do. It was not my fault, indeed, ma'amselle, for I could not get out. That rogue Ludovico locked me up again."

"Locked you up!" said Emily, with displeasure, "Why do you permit Ludovico to lock you up?"

"Holy Saints!" exclaimed Annette, "how can I help it! If he will lock the door, ma'amselle, and take away the key, how am I to get out, unless I jump through the window? But that I should not mind so much, if the casements here were not all so high; one can hardly scramble up to them on the inside, and one should break one's neck, I suppose, going down on the outside. But you know, I dare say, ma'am, what a hurly-burly the castle was in, last night; you must have heard some of the uproar."

"What, were they disputing, then?" said Emily.

"No, ma'amselle, nor fighting, but almost as good, for I believe there was not one of the Signors sober; and what is more, not one of those fine ladies sober, either. I thought, when I saw them first, that all those fine silks and fine veils,—why, ma'amselle, their veils were worked with silver! and fine trimmings—boded no good—I guessed what they were!"

"Good God!" exclaimed Emily, "what will become of me!"

"Aye, ma'am, Ludovico said much the same thing of me. Good God! said he, Annette, what is to become of you, if you are to go running about the castle among all these drunken Signors?"

"O! says I, for that matter, I only want to go to my young lady's chamber, and I have only to go, you know, along the vaulted passage and across the great hall and up the marble stair-case and along the north gallery and through the west wing of the castle and I am in the corridor in a minute." "Are you so? says he, and what is to become of you, if you meet any of those noble cavaliers in the way?" "Well, says I, if you think there is danger, then, go with me, and guard me; I am never afraid when you are by." "What! says he, when I am scarcely recovered of one wound, shall I put myself in the way of getting another? for if any of the cavaliers meet you, they will fall a-fighting with me directly. No, no, says he, I will cut the way shorter, than through the vaulted passage and up the marble stair-case, and along the north gallery and through the west wing of the castle, for you shall stay here, Annette; you shall not go out of this room, to-night." "So, with that I says"——

"Well, well," said Emily, impatiently, and anxious to enquire on another subject, — "so he locked you up?"

"Yes, he did indeed, ma'amselle, notwithstanding all I could say to the contrary; and Caterina and I and he staid there all night. And in a few minutes after I was not so vexed, for there came Signor Verezzi roaring along the passage, like a mad bull, and he mistook Ludovico's hall, for old Carlo's; so he tried to burst open the door, and called out for more wine, for that he had drunk all the flasks dry, and was dying of thirst. So we were all as still as night, that he might suppose there was nobody in the room; but the Signor was as cunning as the best of us, and kept calling out at the door, 'Come forth, my antient hero!' said he, 'here is no enemy at the gate, that you need hide yourself: come forth, my valorous Signor Steward!' Just then old Carlo opened his door, and he came with a flask in his hand; for, as soon as the Signor saw him, he was as tame as could be, and followed him away as naturally as a dog does a butcher with a piece of meat in his basket. All this I saw through the key-hole. Well, Annette, said Ludovico, jeeringly, shall I let you out now? O no, says I, I would not"——

"I have some questions to ask you on another subject," interrupted Emily, quite wearied by this story. "Do you know whether there are any prisoners in the castle, and whether they are confined at this end of the edifice?"

"I was not in the way, ma'amselle," replied Annette, "when the first party came in from the mountains, and the last party is not come back yet, so I don't know, whether there are any prisoners; but it is expected back to-night, or to-morrow, and I shall know then, perhaps."

Emily enquired if she had ever heard the servants talk of prisoners.

"Ah ma'amselle!" said Annette archly, "now I dare say you are think-ing of Monsieur Valancourt, and that he may have come among the armies, which, they say, are come from our country, to fight against this state, and that he has met with some of *our* people, and is taken captive. O Lord! how glad I should be, if it was so!"

"Would you, indeed, be glad?" said Emily, in a tone of mournful reproach.

"To be sure I should, ma'am," replied Annette, "and would not you be glad too, to see Signor Valancourt? I don't know any chevalier I like better, I have a very great regard for the Signor, truly."

"Your regard for him cannot be doubted," said Emily, "since you wish to see him a prisoner."

"Why no, ma'amselle, not a prisoner either; but one must be glad to see him, you know. And it was only the other night I dreamt—I dreamt I saw him drive into the castle-yard all in a coach and six, and dressed out, with a laced coat and a sword, like a lord as he is."

Emily could not forbear smiling at Annette's ideas of Valancourt, and repeated her enquiry, whether she had heard the servants talk of prisoners.

"No, ma'amselle," replied she, "never; and lately they have done nothing but talk of the apparition, that has been walking about of a night on the ramparts, and that frightened the sentinels into fits. It came among them like a flash of fire, they say, and they all fell down in a row, till they came to themselves again; and then it was gone, and nothing to be seen but the old castle walls; so they helped one another up again as fast as they could. You would not believe, ma'amselle, though I shewed you the very cannon, where it used to appear."

"And are you, indeed, so simple, Annette," said Emily, smiling at this curious exaggeration of the circumstances she had witnessed, "as to credit these stories?"

"Credit them, ma'amselle! why all the world could not persuade me out of them. Roberto and Sebastian and half a dozen more of them went into fits! To be sure, there was no occasion for that; I said, myself, there was no need of that, for, says I, when the enemy comes, what a pretty figure they will cut, if they are to fall down in fits, all of a row! The enemy won't be so civil, perhaps, as to walk off, like the ghost, and leave them to help one another up, but will fall to, cutting and slashing, till he makes them all rise up dead men. No, no, says I, there is reason in all things: though I might have fallen down in a fit, that was no rule for them, being, because it is no business of mine to look gruff, and fight battles."

Emily endeavoured to correct the superstitious weakness of Annette, though she could not entirely subdue her own; to which the latter only replied, "Nay, ma'amselle, you will believe nothing; you are almost as bad as the Signor himself, who was in a great passion when they told of what had happened, and swore that the first man, who repeated such nonsense, should be thrown into the dungeon under the east turret. This was a hard punishment too, for only talking nonsense, as he called it, but I dare say he had other reasons for calling it so, than you have, ma'am."

Emily looked displeased, and made no reply. As she mused upon the recollected appearance, which had lately so much alarmed her, and considered the circumstances of the figure having stationed itself opposite to her casement, she was for a moment inclined to believe it was Valancourt, whom she had seen. Yet, if it was he, why did he not speak to her, when he had the opportunity of doing so—and, if he was a prisoner in the castle, and he could be here in no other character, how could he obtain the means of walking abroad on the rampart? Thus she was utterly unable to decide, whether the musician and the form she had observed, were the same, or, if they were, whether this was Valancourt. She, however, desired that Annette would endeavour to learn whether any prisoners were in the castle, and also their names.

"O dear, ma'amselle!" said Annette, "I forget to tell you what you bade me ask about, the ladies, as they call themselves, who are lately come to Udolpho. Why that Signora Livona, that the Signor brought to see my late lady at Venice, is his mistress now, and was little better then, I dare say. And Ludovico says (but pray be secret, ma'am) that his *Excellenza* introduced her only to impose upon the world, that had begun to make free with her character. So when people saw my lady notice her, they thought what they had heard must be scandal. The other two are the mistresses of Signor Verezzi and Signor Bertolini; and Signor Montoni invited them all to the castle; and so, yesterday, he gave a great entertainment; and there they were, all drinking Tuscany wine and all sorts, and laughing and singing, till they made the castle ring again. But I thought they were dismal sounds, so soon after my poor lady's death too; and they brought to my mind what she would have thought, if she had heard them—but she cannot hear them now, poor soul! said I."

Emily turned away to conceal her emotion, and then desired Annette to go, and make enquiry, concerning the prisoners, that might be in the castle, but conjured her to do it with caution, and on no account to mention her name, or that of Monsieur Valancourt.

"Now I think of it, ma'amselle," said Annette, "I do believe there are prisoners, for I overheard one of the Signor's men, yesterday, in the servants hall, talking something about ransoms, and saying what a fine thing it was for his *Excellenza* to catch up men, and they were as good booty as any other, because of the ransoms. And the other man was grumbling, and saying it was fine enough for the Signor, but none so fine for his soldiers, because, said he, we don't go shares there."

This information heightened Emily's impatience to know more, and Annette immediately departed on her enquiry.

The late resolution of Emily to resign her estates to Montoni, now gave way to new considerations; the possibility, that Valancourt was near her, revived her fortitude, and she determined to brave the threatened vengeance, at least, till she could be assured whether he was really in the castle. She was in this temper of mind, when she received a message from Montoni, requiring her attendance in the cedar parlour, which she obeyed with trembling, and, on her way thither, endeavoured to animate her fortitude with the idea of Valancourt.

Montoni was alone. "I sent for you," said he, "to give you another opportunity of retracting your late mistaken assertions concerning the Languedoc estates. I will condescend to advise, where I may command.—If you are really deluded by an opinion, that you have any right to these estates, at least, do not persist in the error—an error, which you may perceive, too late, has been fatal to you. Dare my resentment no further, but sign the papers."

"If I have no right in these estates, sir," said Emily, "of what service can it be to you, that I should sign any papers, concerning them? If the lands are yours by law, you certainly may possess them, without my interference, or my consent."

"I will have no more argument," said Montoni, with a look that made her tremble. "What had I but trouble to expect, when I condescended to reason with a baby! But I will be trifled with no longer: let the recollection of your aunt's sufferings, in consequence of her folly and obstinacy, teach you a lesson.—Sign the papers."

Emily's resolution was for a moment awed:—she shrunk at the recollections he revived, and from the vengeance he threatened; but then, the image of Valancourt, who so long had loved her, and who was now, perhaps, so near her, came to her heart, and, together with the strong feelings of indignation, with which she had always, from her infancy, regarded an act of injustice, inspired her with a noble, though imprudent, courage.

"Sign the papers," said Montoni, more impatiently than before.

"Never, sir," replied Emily; "that request would have proved to me the injustice of your claim, had I even been ignorant of my right."

Montoni turned pale with anger, while his quivering lip and lurking eye made her almost repent the boldness of her speech.

"Then all my vengeance falls upon you," he exclaimed, with an horrible oath. "And think not it shall be delayed. Neither the estates in Languedoc, or Gascony, shall be yours; you have dared to question my right,—now dare to question my power. I have a punishment which you think not of; it is terrible! This night—this very night"——

"This night!" repeated another voice.

Montoni paused, and turned half round, but, seeming to recollect himself, he proceeded in a lower tone.

"You have lately seen one terrible example of obstinacy and folly; yet this, it appears, has not been sufficient to deter you.—I could tell you of others—I could make you tremble at the bare recital."

He was interrupted by a groan, which seemed to rise from underneath the chamber they were in; and, as he threw a glance round it, impatience and rage flashed from his eyes, yet something like a shade of fear passed over his countenance. Emily sat down in a chair, near the door, for the various emotions she had suffered, now almost overcame her; but Montoni paused scarcely an instant, and, commanding his features, resumed his discourse in a lower, yet sterner voice.

"I say, I could give you other instances of my power and of my character, which it seems you do not understand, or you would not defy me.—I could tell you, that, when once my resolution is taken—— but I am talking to a baby. Let me, however, repeat, that terrible as are the examples I could recite, the recital could not now benefit you; for, though your repentance would put an immediate end to opposition, it would not now appease my indignation.—I will have vengeance as well as justice."

Another groan filled the pause which Montoni made.

"Leave the room instantly!" said he, seeming not to notice this strange occurrence. Without power to implore his pity, she rose to go, but found that she could not support herself; awe and terror overcame her, and she sunk again into the chair.

"Quit my presence!" cried Montoni. "This affectation of fear ill becomes the heroine who has just dared to brave my indignation."

"Did you hear nothing, Signor?" said Emily, trembling, and still unable to leave the room.

"I heard my own voice," rejoined Montoni, sternly.

"And nothing else?" said Emily, speaking with difficulty.—"There again! Do you hear nothing now?"

"Obey my order," repeated Montoni. "And for these fool's tricks—I will soon discover by whom they are practised."

Emily again rose, and exerted herself to the utmost to leave the room, while Montoni followed her; but, instead of calling aloud to his servants to search the chamber, as he had formerly done on a similar occurrence, passed to the ramparts.

As, in her way to the corridor, she rested for a moment at an open casement, Emily saw a party of Montoni's troops winding down a distant mountain, whom she noticed no further, than as they brought to her mind the wretched prisoners they were, perhaps, bringing to the castle. At length, having reached her apartment, she threw herself upon the couch, overcome with the new horrors of her situation. Her thoughts lost in tumult and perplexity, she could neither repent of, or approve, her late conduct; she could only remember, that she was in the power of a man, who had no principle of action—but his will; and the astonishment and terrors of superstition, which had, for a moment, so strongly assailed her, now yielded to those of reason.

She was, at length, roused from the reverie, which engaged her, by a confusion of distant voices, and a clattering of hoofs, that seemed to come, on the wind, from the courts. A sudden hope, that some good was approaching, seized her mind, till she remembered the troops she had observed from the casement, and concluded this to be the party, which Annette had said were expected at Udolpho.

Soon after, she heard voices faintly from the halls, and the noise of horses' feet sunk away in the wind; silence ensued. Emily listened anxiously for Annette's step in the corridor, but a pause of total stillness continued, till again the castle seemed to be all tumult and confusion. She heard the echoes of many footsteps, passing to and fro in the halls and avenues below, and then busy tongues were loud on the rampart. Having hurried to her casement, she perceived Montoni, with some of his officers, leaning on the walls, and pointing from them; while several soldiers were employed at the further end of the rampart about some cannon; and she continued to observe them, careless of the passing time.

Annette at length appeared, but brought no intelligence of Valancourt, "For, ma'amselle," said she, "all the people pretend to know nothing about any prisoners. But here is a fine piece of business! The rest of the party are just arrived, ma'am; they came scampering in, as if they would have broken their necks; one scarcely knew whether the man, or his horse would get within the gates first. And they have brought word—and such news! they have brought word, that a party of the enemy, as they call them, are coming towards the castle; so we shall have all the officers of justice, I suppose, besieging it! all those terrible-looking fellows one used to see at Venice."

"Thank God!" exclaimed Emily, fervently, "there is yet a hope left for me, then!"

"What mean you, ma'amselle? Do you wish to fall into the hands of those sad-looking men! Why I used to shudder as I passed them, and should have guessed what they were, if Ludovico had not told me."

"We cannot be in worse hands than at present," replied Emily, unguardedly; "but what reason have you to suppose these are officers of justice?"

"Why *our* people, ma'am, are all in such a fright, and a fuss; and I don't know any thing but the fear of justice, that could make them so. I used to think nothing on earth could fluster them, unless, indeed, it was a ghost, or so; but now, some of them are for hiding down in the vaults under the castle; but you must not tell the Signor this, ma'amselle, and I overheard two of them talking— Holy Mother! what makes you look so sad, ma'amselle? You don't hear what I say!"

"Yes, I do, Annette; pray proceed."

"Well, ma'amselle, all the castle is in such hurly-burly. Some of the men are loading the cannon, and some are examining the great gates, and the walls all round, and are hammering and patching up, just as if all those repairs had never been made, that were so long about. But what is to become of me and you, ma'amselle, and Ludovico? O! when I hear the sound of the cannon, I shall die with fright. If I could but catch the great gate open for one minute, I would be even with it for shutting me within these walls so long!—it should never see me again."

Emily caught the latter words of Annette. "O! if you could find it open, but for one moment!" she exclaimed, "my peace might yet be saved!" The heavy groan she uttered, and the wildness of her look, terrified Annette, still more than her words; who entreated Emily to explain the meaning of them, to whom it suddenly occurred, that Ludovico might be of some service, if there should be a possibility of escape, and who repeated the substance of what had passed between Montoni and herself, but conjured her to mention this to no person except to Ludovico. "It may, perhaps, be in his power," she added, "to effect our escape. Go to him, Annette, tell him what I have to apprehend, and what I have already suffered; but entreat him to be secret, and to lose no time in attempting to release us. If he is willing to undertake this he shall be amply rewarded. I cannot speak with him myself, for we might be observed, and then effectual care would be taken to prevent our flight. But be quick, Annette, and, above all, be discreet— I will await your return in this apartment."

The girl, whose honest heart had been much affected by the recital, was now as eager to obey, as Emily was to employ her, and she immediately quitted the room.

Emily's surprise increased, as she reflected upon Annette's intelligence. "Alas!" said she, "what can the officers of justice do against an armed castle? these cannot be such." Upon further consideration, however, she concluded, that, Montoni's bands having plundered the country round, the inhabitants had taken arms, and were coming with the officers of police and a party of soldiers, to force their way into the castle. "But they know not," thought she, "its strength, or the armed numbers within it. Alas! except from flight, I have nothing to hope!"

Montoni, though not precisely what Emily apprehended him to be—a captain of banditti—had employed his troops in enterprises not less daring, or less atrocious, than such a character would have undertaken. They had not only pillaged, whenever opportunity offered, the helpless traveller, but had attacked, and plundered the villas of several persons, which, being situated among the solitary recesses of the mountains, were totally unprepared for resistance. In these expeditions the commanders of the party did not appear, and the men, partly disguised, had sometimes been mistaken for common robbers, and, at others, for bands of the foreign enemy, who, at that period, invaded the country. But, though they had already pillaged several mansions, and brought home considerable treasures, they had ventured to approach only one castle, in the attack of which they were assisted by other troops of their own order; from this, however, they were vigorously repulsed, and pursued by some of the foreign enemy, who were in league with the besieged. Montoni's troops fled precipitately towards Udolpho, but were so closely tracked over the mountains, that, when they reached one of the heights in the neighbourhood of the castle, and looked back upon the road, they perceived the enemy winding among the cliffs below, and at not more than a league distant. Upon this discovery, they hastened forward with increased speed, to prepare Montoni for the enemy; and it was their arrival, which had thrown the castle into such confusion and tumult.

As Emily awaited anxiously some information from below, she now saw from her casements a body of troops pour over the neighbouring heights; and, though Annette had been gone a very short time, and had a difficult and dangerous business to accomplish, her impatience for intelligence became painful: she listened; opened her door; and often went out upon the corridor to meet her.

At length, she heard a footstep approach her chamber; and, on opening the door, saw, not Annette, but old Carlo! New fears rushed upon her mind. He said he came from the Signor, who had ordered him to inform her, that she must be ready to depart from Udolpho immediately, for that the castle was about to be besieged; and that mules were preparing to convey her, with her guides, to a place of safety.

"Of safety!" exclaimed Emily, thoughtlessly; "has, then, the Signor so much consideration for me?"

Carlo looked upon the ground, and made no reply. A thousand opposite emotions agitated Emily, successively, as she listened to old Carlo; those of joy, grief, distrust and apprehension, appeared, and vanished from her mind, with the quickness of lightning. One moment, it seemed impossible, that Montoni could take this measure merely for her preservation; and so very strange was his sending her from the castle at all, that she could attribute it only to the design of carrying into execution the new scheme of vengeance, with which he had menaced her. In the next instant, it appeared so desirable to quit the castle, under any circumstances, that she could not but rejoice in the prospect, believing that change must be for the better, till she remembered the probability of Valancourt being detained in it, when sorrow and regret usurped her mind, and she wished, much more fervently than she had yet done, that it might not be his voice which she had heard.

Carlo having reminded her, that she had no time to lose, for that the enemy were within sight of the castle, Emily entreated him to inform her whither she was to go; and, after some hesitation, he said he had received no orders to tell; but, on her repeating the question, replied, that he believed she was to be carried into Tuscany.

"To Tuscany!" exclaimed Emily—"and why thither?"

Carlo answered, that he knew nothing further, than that she was to be lodged in a cottage on the borders of Tuscany, at the feet of the Apennines—"Not a day's journey distant," said he.

Emily now dismissed him; and, with trembling hands, prepared the small package, that she meant to take with her; while she was employed about which Annette returned.

"O ma'amselle!" said she, "nothing can be done! Ludovico says the new porter is more watchful even than Barnardine was, and we might as well throw ourselves in the way of a dragon, as in his. Ludovico is almost as broken-hearted as you are, ma'am, on my account, he says, and I am sure I shall never live to hear the cannon fire twice!"

She now began to weep, but revived upon hearing of what had just occurred, and entreated Emily to take her with her.

"That I will do most willingly," replied Emily, "if Signor Montoni permits it;" to which Annette made no reply, but ran out of the room, and immediately sought Montoni, who was on the terrace, surrounded by his officers, where she began her petition. He sharply bade her go into the castle, and absolutely refused her request. Annette, however, not only pleaded for herself, but for Ludovico; and Montoni had ordered some of his men to take her from his presence, before she would retire.

In an agony of disappointment, she returned to Emily, who foreboded little good towards herself, from this refusal to Annette, and who, soon after, received a summons to repair to the great court, where the mules, with her guides, were in waiting. Emily here tried in vain to soothe the weeping Annette, who persisted in saying, that she should never see her dear young lady again; a fear, which her mistress secretly thought too well justified, but which she endeavoured to restrain, while, with apparent composure, she bade this affectionate servant farewell. Annette, however, followed to the courts, which were now thronged with people, busy in preparation for the enemy; and, having seen her mount her mule and depart, with her attendants, through the portal, turned into the castle and wept again.

Emily, meanwhile, as she looked back upon the gloomy courts of the castle, no longer silent as when she had first entered them, but resounding with the noise of preparation for their defence, as well as crowded with soldiers and workmen, hurrying to and fro; and, when she passed once more under the huge portcullis, which had formerly struck her with terror and dismay, and, looking round, saw no walls to confine her steps—felt, in spite of anticipation, the sudden joy of a prisoner, who unexpectedly finds himself at liberty. This emotion would not suffer her now to look impartially on the dangers that awaited her without; on mountains infested by hostile parties, who seized every opportunity for plunder; and on a journey commended under the guidance of men, whose countenances certainly did not speak favourably of their dispositions. In the present moments, she could only rejoice, that she was liberated from those walls, which she had entered with such dismal forebodings; and, remembering the superstitious presentiment, which had then seized her, she could now smile at the impression it had made upon her mind.

As she gazed, with these emotions, upon the turrets of the castle, rising high over the woods, among which she wound, the stranger, whom she believed to be confined there, returned to her remembrance, and anxiety and apprehension, lest he should be Valancourt, again passed like a cloud upon her joy. She recollected every circumstance, concerning this unknown person, since the night, when she had first heard him play the song of her native province;—circumstances, which she had so often recollected, and compared before, without extracting from them any thing like conviction, and which still only prompted her to believe, that Valancourt was a prisoner at Udolpho. It was possible, however, that the men, who were her conductors, might afford her information, on this subject; but, fearing to question them immediately, lest they should be unwilling to discover any circumstance to her in the presence of each other, she watched for an opportunity of speaking with them separately.

Soon after, a trumpet echoed faintly from a distance; the guides stopped, and looked toward the quarter whence it came, but the thick woods, which surrounded them, excluding all view of the country beyond, one of the men rode on to the point of an eminence, that afforded a more extensive prospect, to observe how near the enemy, whose trumpet he guessed this to be, were advanced; the other, meanwhile, remained with Emily, and to him she put some questions, concerning the stranger at Udolpho. Ugo, for this was his name, said, that there were several prisoners in the castle, but he neither recollected their persons, or the precise time of their arrival, and could therefore give her no information. There was a surliness in his manner, as he spoke, that made it probable he would not have satisfied her enquiries, even if he could have done so.

Having asked him what prisoners had been taken, about the time, as nearly as she could remember, when she had first heard the music, "All that week," said Ugo, "I was out with a party, upon the mountains, and knew nothing of what was doing at the castle. We had enough upon our hands, we had warm work of it."

Bertrand, the other man, being now returned, Emily enquired no further, and, when he had related to his companion what he had seen, they travelled on in deep silence; while Emily often caught, between the opening woods, partial glimpses of the castle above—the west towers, whose battlements were now crowded with archers, and the ramparts below, where soldiers were seen hurrying along, or busy upon the walls, preparing the cannon.

Having emerged from the woods, they wound along the valley in an opposite direction to that, from whence the enemy were approaching. Emily now had a full view of Udolpho, with its gray walls, towers and terraces, high over-topping the precipices and the dark woods, and glittering partially with the arms of the *condottieri*, as the sun's rays, streaming through an autumnal cloud, glanced upon a part of the edifice, whose remaining features stood in darkened majesty. She continued to gaze, through her tears, upon walls that, perhaps, confined Valancourt, and which now, as the cloud floated away, were lighted up with sudden splendour, and then, as suddenly were shrouded in gloom; while the passing gleam fell on the wood-tops below, and heightened the first tints of autumn, that had begun to steal upon the foliage. The winding mountains, at length, shut Udolpho from her view, and she turned, with mournful reluctance, to other objects. The melancholy sighing of the wind among the pines, that waved high over the steeps, and the distant thunder of a torrent assisted her musings, and conspired with the wild scenery around, to diffuse over her mind emotions solemn, yet not unpleasing, but which were soon interrupted by the distant roar of cannon, echoing among the mountains. The sounds rolled along the wind, and were repeated in faint and fainter reverberation, till they sunk in sullen murmurs. This was a signal, that the enemy had reached the castle, and fear for Valancourt again tormented Emily. She turned her anxious eyes towards that part of the country, where the edifice stood, but the intervening heights concealed it from her view; still, however, she saw the tall head of a mountain, which immediately fronted her late chamber, and on this she fixed her gaze, as if it could have told her of all that was passing in the scene it overlooked. The guides twice reminded her, that she was losing time and that they had far to go, before she could turn from this interesting object, and, even when she again moved onward, she often sent a look back, till only its blue point, brightening in a gleam of sunshine, appeared peeping over other mountains.

The sound of the cannon affected Ugo, as the blast of the trumpet does the war-horse; it called forth all the fire of his nature; he was impatient to be in the midst of the fight, and uttered frequent execrations against Montoni for having sent him to a distance. The feelings of his comrade seemed to be very opposite, and adapted rather to the cruelties, than to the dangers of war.

Emily asked frequent questions, concerning the place of her destination, but could only learn, that she was going to a cottage in Tuscany; and, whenever she mentioned the subject, she fancied she perceived, in the countenances of these men, an expression of malice and cunning, that alarmed her.

It was afternoon, when they had left the castle. During several hours, they travelled through regions of profound solitude, where no bleat of sheep, or bark of watch-dog, broke on silence, and they were now too far off to hear even the faint thunder of the cannon. Towards evening, they wound down precipices, black with forests of cypress, pine and cedar, into a glen so savage and secluded, that, if Solitude ever had local habitation, this might have been "her place of dearest residence." To Emily it appeared a spot exactly suited for the retreat of banditti, and, in her imagination, she already saw them lurking under the brow of some projecting rock, whence their shadows, lengthened by the setting sun, stretched across the road, and warned the traveller of his danger. She shuddered at the idea, and, looking at her conductors, to observe whether they were armed, thought she saw in them the banditti she dreaded!

It was in this glen, that they proposed to alight, "For," said Ugo, "night will come on presently, and then the wolves will make it dangerous to stop." This was a new subject of alarm to Emily, but inferior to what she suffered from the thought of being left in these wilds, at midnight, with two such men as her present conductors. Dark and dreadful hints of what might be Montoni's purpose in sending her hither, came to her mind. She endeavoured to dissuade the men from stopping, and enquired, with anxiety, how far they had yet to go.

"Many leagues yet," replied Bertrand. "As for you, Signora, you may do as you please about eating, but for us, we will make a hearty supper, while we can. We shall have need of it, I warrant, before we finish our journey. The sun's going down apace; let us alight under that rock, yonder."

His comrade assented, and, turning the mules out of the road, they advanced towards a cliff, overhung with cedars, Emily following in trembling silence. They lifted her from her mule, and, having seated themselves on the grass, at the foot of the rocks, drew some homely fare from a wallet, of which Emily tried to eat a little, the better to disguise her apprehensions.

The sun was now sunk behind the high mountains in the west, upon which a purple haze began to spread, and the gloom of twilight to draw over the surrounding objects. To the low and sullen murmur of the breeze, passing among the woods, she no longer listened with any degree of pleasure, for it conspired with the wildness of the scene and the evening hour, to depress her spirits.

Suspense had so much increased her anxiety, as to the prisoner at Udolpho, that, finding it impracticable to speak alone with Bertrand, on that subject, she renewed her questions in the presence of Ugo; but he either was, or pretended to be entirely ignorant, concerning the stranger. When he had dismissed the question, he talked with Ugo on some subject, which led to the mention of Signor Orsino and of the affair that had banished him from Venice; respecting which Emily had ventured to ask a few questions. Ugo appeared to be well acquainted with the circumstances of that tragical event, and related some minute particulars, that both shocked and surprised her; for it appeared very extraordinary how such particulars could be known to any, but to persons, present when the assassination was committed.

"He was of rank," said Bertrand, "or the State would not have troubled itself to enquire after his assassins. The Signor has been lucky hitherto; this is not the first affair of the kind he has had upon his hands; and to be sure, when a gentleman has no other way of getting redress—why he must take this."

"Aye," said Ugo, "and why is not this as good as another? This is the way to have justice done at once, without more ado. If you go to law, you must stay till the judges please, and may lose your cause, at last. Why the best way, then, is to make sure of your right, while you can, and execute justice yourself."

"Yes, yes," rejoined Bertrand, "if you wait till justice is done you—you may stay long enough. Why if I want a friend of mine properly served, how am I to get my revenge? Ten to one they will tell me he is in the right, and I am in the wrong. Or, if a fellow has got possession of property, which I think ought to be mine, why I may wait, till I starve, perhaps, before the law will give it me, and then, after all, the judge may say—the estate is his. What is to be done then?—Why the case is plain enough, I must take it at last."

Emily's horror at this conversation was heightened by a suspicion, that the latter part of it was pointed against herself, and that these men had been commissioned by Montoni to execute a similar kind of *justice*, in his cause.

"But I was speaking of Signor Orsino," resumed Bertrand, "he is one of those, who love to do justice at once. I remember, about ten years ago, the Signor had a quarrel with a cavaliero of Milan. The story was told me then, and it is still fresh in my head. They quarrelled about a lady, that the Signor liked, and she was perverse enough to prefer the gentleman of Milan, and even carried her whim so far as to marry him. This provoked the Signor, as well it might, for he had tried to talk reason to her a long while, and used to send people to serenade her, under her windows, of a night; and used to make verses about her, and would swear she was the handsomest lady in Milan—But all would not do— nothing would bring her to reason; and, as I said, she went so far at last, as to marry this other cavaliero. This made the Signor wrath, with a vengeance; he resolved to be even with her though, and he watched his opportunity, and did not wait long, for, soon after the marriage, they set out for Padua, nothing doubting, I warrant, of what was preparing for them. The cavaliero thought, to be sure, he was to be called to no account, but was to go off triumphant; but he was soon made to know another sort of story."

"What then, the lady had promised to have Signor Orsino?" said Ugo.

"Promised! No," replied Bertrand, "she had not wit enough even to tell him she liked him, as I heard, but the contrary, for she used to say, from the first, she never meant to have him. And this was what provoked the Signor, so, and with good reason, for, who likes to be told that he is disagreeable? and this was saying as good. It was enough to tell him this; she need not have gone, and married another."

"What, she married, then, on purpose to plague the Signor?" said Ugo.

"I don't know as for that," replied Bertrand, "they said, indeed, that she had had a regard for the other gentleman a great while; but that is nothing to the purpose, she should not have married him, and then the Signor would not have been so much provoked. She might have expected what was to follow; it was not to be supposed he would bear her ill usage tamely, and she might thank herself for what happened. But, as I said, they set out for Padua, she and her husband, and the road lay over some barren mountains like these. This suited the Signor's purpose well. He watched the time of their departure, and sent his men after them, with directions what to do. They kept their distance, till they saw their opportunity, and this did not happen, till the second day's journey, when, the gentleman having sent his servants forward to the next town, may be, to have horses in readiness, the Signor's men quickened their pace, and overtook the carriage, in a hollow, between two mountains, where the woods prevented the servants from seeing what passed, though they were then not far off. When we came up, we fired our tromboni, but missed."

Emily turned pale, at these words, and then hoped she had mistaken them; while Bertrand proceeded:

"The gentleman fired again, but he was soon made to alight, and it was as he turned to call his people, that he was struck. It was the most dexterous feat you ever saw — he was struck in the back with three stillettos at once. He fell, and was dispatched in a minute; but the lady escaped, for the servants had heard the firing, and came up before she could be taken care of. 'Bertrand,' said the Signor, when his men returned"——

"Bertrand!" exclaimed Emily, pale with horror, on whom not a syllable of this narrative had been lost.

"Bertrand, did I say?" rejoined the man, with some confusion — "No, Giovanni. But I have forgot where I was; — 'Bertrand,' said the Signor"——

"Bertrand, again!" said Emily, in a faltering voice, "Why do you repeat that name?"

Bertrand swore. "What signifies it," he proceeded, "what the man was called — Bertrand, or Giovanni — or Roberto? it's all one for that. You have put me out twice with that — question. 'Bertrand,' or Giovanni — or what you will — 'Bertrand,' said the Signor, 'if your comrades had done their duty, as well as you, I should not have lost the lady. Go, my honest fellow, and be happy with this.' He gave him a purse of gold — and little enough too, considering the service he had done him."

"Aye, aye," said Ugo, "little enough — little enough."

Emily now breathed with difficulty, and could scarcely support herself. When first she saw these men, their appearance and their connection with Montoni had been sufficient to impress her with distrust; but now, when one of them had betrayed himself to be a murderer, and she saw herself, at the approach of night, under his guidance, among wild and solitary mountains, and going she scarcely knew whither, the most agonizing terror seized her, which was the less supportable from the necessity she found herself under of concealing all symptoms of it from her companions. Reflecting on the character and the menaces of Montoni, it appeared not improbable, that he had delivered her to them, for the purpose of having her murdered, and of thus securing to himself, without further opposition, or delay, the estates, for which he had so long and so desperately contended. Yet, if this was his design, there appeared no necessity for sending her to such a distance from the castle; for, if any dread of discovery had made him unwilling to perpetrate the deed there, a much nearer place might have sufficed for the purpose of concealment. These considerations, however, did not immediately occur to Emily, with whom so many circumstances conspired to rouse terror, that she had no power to oppose it, or to enquire coolly into its grounds; and, if she had done so, still there were many appearances which would too well have justified her most terrible apprehensions. She did not now dare to speak to her conductors, at the sound of whose voices she trembled; and when, now and then, she stole a glance at them, their countenances, seen imperfectly through the gloom of evening, served to confirm her fears.

The sun had now been set some time; heavy clouds, whose lower skirts were tinged with sulphureous crimson, lingered in the west, and threw a reddish tint upon the pine forests, which sent forth a solemn sound, as the breeze rolled over them. The hollow moan struck upon Emily's heart, and served to render more gloomy and terrific every object around her,—the mountains, shaded in twilight— the gleaming torrent, hoarsely roaring—the black forests, and the deep glen, broken into rocky recesses, high overshadowed by cypress and sycamore and winding into long obscurity. To this glen, Emily, as she sent forth her anxious eye, thought there was no end; no hamlet, or even cottage, was seen, and still no distant bark of watch dog, or even faint, far-off halloo came on the wind. In a tremulous voice, she now ventured to remind the guides, that it was growing late, and to ask again how far they had to go: but they were too much occupied by their own discourse to attend to her question, which she forbore to repeat, lest it should provoke a surly answer. Having, however, soon after, finished their supper, the men collected the fragments into their wallet, and proceeded along this winding glen, in gloomy silence; while Emily again mused upon her own situation, and concerning the motives of Montoni for involving her in it. That it was for some evil purpose towards herself, she could not doubt; and it seemed, that, if he did not intend to destroy her, with a view of immediately seizing her estates, he meant to reserve her a while in concealment, for some more terrible design, for one that might equally gratify his avarice and still more his deep revenge. At this moment, remembering Signor Brochio and his behaviour in the corridor, a few preceding nights, the latter supposition, horrible as it was, strengthened in her belief. Yet, why remove her from the castle, where deeds of darkness had, she feared, been often executed with secrecy? —from chambers, perhaps

> With many a foul, and midnight murder stain'd.

The dread of what she might be going to encounter was now so excessive, that it sometimes threatened her senses; and, often as she went, she thought of her late father and of all he would have suffered, could he have foreseen the strange and dreadful events of her future life; and how anxiously he would have avoided that fatal confidence, which committed his daughter to the care of a woman so weak as was Madame Montoni. So romantic and improbable, indeed, did her present situation appear to Emily herself, particularly when she compared it with the repose and beauty of her early days, that there were moments, when she could almost have believed herself the victim of frightful visions, glaring upon a disordered fancy.

Restrained by the presence of her guides from expressing her terrors, their acuteness was, at length, lost in gloomy despair. The dreadful view of what might await her hereafter rendered her almost indifferent to the surrounding dangers. She now looked, with little emotion, on the wild dingles, and the gloomy road and mountains, whose outlines were only distinguishable through the dusk; —objects, which but lately had affected her spirits so much, as to awaken horrid views of the future, and to tinge these with their own gloom.

It was now so nearly dark, that the travellers, who proceeded only by the slowest pace, could scarcely discern their way. The clouds, which seemed charged with thunder, passed slowly along the heavens, shewing, at intervals, the trembling stars; while the groves of cypress and sycamore, that overhung the rocks, waved high in the breeze, as it swept over the glen, and then rushed among the distant woods. Emily shivered as it passed.

"Where is the torch?" said Ugo, "It grows dark."

"Not so dark yet," replied Bertrand, "but we may find our way, and 'tis best not light the torch, before we can help, for it may betray us, if any straggling party of the enemy is abroad."

Ugo muttered something, which Emily did not understand, and they proceeded in darkness, while she almost wished, that the enemy might discover them; for from change there was something to hope, since she could scarcely imagine any situation more dreadful than her present one.

As they moved slowly along, her attention was surprised by a thin tapering flame, that appeared, by fits, at the point of the pike, which Bertrand carried, resembling what she had observed on the lance of the sentinel, the night Madame Montoni died, and which he had said was an omen. The event immediately following it appeared to justify the assertion, and a superstitious impression had remained on Emily's mind, which the present appearance confirmed. She thought it was an omen of her own fate, and watched it successively vanish and return, in gloomy silence, which was at length interrupted by Bertrand.

"Let us light the torch," said he, "and get under shelter of the woods;—a storm is coming on—look at my lance."

He held it forth, with the flame tapering at its point.*

"Aye," said Ugo, "you are not one of those, that believe in omens: we have left cowards at the castle, who would turn pale at such a sight. I have often seen it before a thunder storm, it is an omen of that, and one is coming now, sure enough. The clouds flash fast already."

Emily was relieved by this conversation from some of the terrors of superstition, but those of reason increased, as, waiting while Ugo searched for a flint, to strike fire, she watched the pale lightning gleam over the woods they were about to enter, and illumine the harsh countenances of her companions. Ugo could not find a flint, and Bertrand became impatient, for the thunder sounded hollowly at a distance, and the lightning was more frequent. Sometimes, it revealed the nearer recesses of the woods, or, displaying some opening in their summits, illumined the ground beneath with partial splendour, the thick foliage of the trees preserving the surrounding scene in deep shadow.

At length, Ugo found a flint, and the torch was lighted. The men then dismounted, and, having assisted Emily, led the mules towards the woods, that skirted the glen, on the left, over broken ground, frequently interrupted with brush-wood and wild plants, which she was often obliged to make a circuit to avoid.

She could not approach these woods, without experiencing keener sense of her danger. Their deep silence, except when the wind swept among their branches, and impenetrable glooms shewn partially by the sudden flash, and then, by the red glare of the torch, which served only to make "darkness visible," were circumstances, that contributed to renew all her most terrible apprehensions; she thought, too, that, at this moment, the countenances of her conductors displayed more than their usual fierceness, mingled with a kind of lurking exultation, which they seemed endeavouring to disguise. To her affrighted fancy it occurred, that they were leading her into these woods to complete the will of Montoni by her murder. The horrid suggestion called a groan from her heart, which surprised her companions, who turned round quickly towards her, and she demanded why they led her thither, beseeching them to continue their way along the open glen,

---

*See the Abbé Berthelon on Electricity. [A. R.]

which she represented to be less dangerous than the woods, in a thunder storm.

"No, no," said Bertrand, "we know best where the danger lies. See how the clouds open over our heads. Besides, we can glide under cover of the woods with less hazard of being seen, should any of the enemy be wandering this way. By holy St. Peter and all the rest of them, I've as stout a heart as the best, as many a poor devil could tell, if he were alive again—but what can we do against numbers?"

"What are you whining about?" said Ugo, contemptuously, "who fears numbers! Let them come, though they were as many, as the Signor's castle could hold; I would shew the knaves what fighting is. For you—I would lay you quietly in a dry ditch, where you might peep out, and see me put the rogues to flight.—Who talks of fear!"

Bertrand replied, with an horrible oath, that he did not like such jesting, and a violent altercation ensued, which was, at length, silenced by the thunder, whose deep volley was heard afar, rolling onward till it burst over their heads in sounds, that seemed to shake the earth to its centre. The ruffians paused, and looked upon each other. Between the boles of the trees, the blue lightning flashed and quivered along the ground, while, as Emily looked under the boughs, the mountains beyond, frequently appeared to be clothed in livid flame. At this moment, perhaps, she felt less fear of the storm, than did either of her companions, for other terrors occupied her mind.

The men now rested under an enormous chesnut-tree, and fixed their pikes in the ground, at some distance, on the iron points of which Emily repeatedly observed the lightning play, and then glide down them into the earth.

"I would we were well in the Signor's castle!" said Bertrand, "I know not why he should send us on this business. Hark! how it rattles above, there! I could almost find in my heart to turn priest, and pray. Ugo, hast got a rosary?"

"No," replied Ugo, "I leave it to cowards like thee, to carry rosaries—I, carry a sword."

"And much good may it do thee in fighting against the storm!" said Bertrand.

Another peal, which was reverberated in tremendous echoes among the mountains, silenced them for a moment. As it rolled away, Ugo proposed going on. "We are only losing time here," said he, "for the thick boughs of the woods will shelter us as well as this chesnut-tree."

They again led the mules forward, between the boles of the trees, and over pathless grass, that concealed their high knotted roots. The rising wind was now heard contending with the thunder, as it rushed furiously among the branches above, and brightened the red flame of the torch, which threw a stronger light forward among the woods, and shewed their gloomy recesses to be suitable resorts for the wolves, of which Ugo had formerly spoken.

At length, the strength of the wind seemed to drive the storm before it, for the thunder rolled away into distance, and was only faintly heard. After travelling through the woods for nearly an hour, during which the elements seemed to have returned to repose, the travellers, gradually ascending from the glen, found themselves upon the open brow of a mountain, with a wide valley, extending in misty moon-light, at their feet, and above, the blue sky, trembling through the few thin clouds, that lingered after the storm, and were sinking slowly to the verge of the horizon.

Emily's spirits, now that she had quitted the woods, began to revive; for she considered, that, if these men had received an order to destroy her, they would probably have executed their barbarous purpose in the solitary wild, from whence they had just emerged, where the deed would have been shrouded from every human eye. Reassured by this reflection, and by the quiet demeanour of her guides, Emily, as they proceeded silently, in a kind of sheep track, that wound along the skirts of the woods, which ascended on the right, could not survey the sleeping beauty of the vale, to which they were declining, without a momentary sensation of pleasure. It seemed varied with woods, pastures, and sloping grounds, and was screened to the north and the east by an amphitheatre of the Apennines, whose outline on the horizon was here broken into varied and elegant forms; to the west and the south, the landscape extended indistinctly into the lowlands of Tuscany.

"There is the sea yonder," said Bertrand, as if he had known that Emily was examining the twilight view, "yonder in the west, though we cannot see it."

Emily already perceived a change in the climate, from that of the wild and mountainous tract she had left; and, as she continued descending, the air became perfumed by the breath of a thousand nameless flowers among the grass, called forth by the late rain. So soothingly beautiful was the scene around her, and so strikingly contrasted to the gloomy grandeur of those, to which she had long been confined, and to the manners of the people, who moved among them, that she could almost have fancied herself again at La Vallée, and, wondering why Montoni had sent her hither, could scarcely believe, that he had selected so enchanting a spot for any cruel design. It was, however, probably not the spot, but the persons, who happened to inhabit it, and to whose care he could safely commit the execution of his plans, whatever they might be, that had determined his choice.

She now ventured again to enquire, whether they were near the place of their destination, and was answered by Ugo, that they had not far to go. "Only to the wood of chesnuts in the valley yonder," said he, "there, by the brook, that sparkles with the moon; I wish I was once at rest there, with a flask of good wine, and a slice of Tuscany bacon."

Emily's spirits revived, when she heard, that the journey was so nearly concluded, and saw the wood of chesnuts in an open part of the vale, on the margin of the stream.

In a short time, they reached the entrance of the wood, and perceived, between the twinkling leaves, a light, streaming from a distant cottage window. They proceeded along the edge of the brook to where the trees, crowding over it, excluded the moon-beams, but a long line of light, from the cottage above, was seen on its dark tremulous surface. Bertrand now stepped on first, and Emily heard him knock, and call loudly at the door. As she reached it, the small upper casement, where the light appeared, was unclosed by a man, who, having enquired what they wanted, immediately descended, let them into a neat rustic cot, and called up his wife to set refreshments before the travellers. As this man conversed, rather apart, with Bertrand, Emily anxiously surveyed him. He was a tall, but not robust, peasant, of a sallow complexion, and had a shrewd and cunning eye; his countenance was not of a character to win the ready confidence of youth, and there was nothing in his manner, that might conciliate a stranger.

Ugo called impatiently for supper, and in a tone as if he knew his authority here to be unquestionable. "I expected you an hour ago," said the peasant, "for I have had Signor Montoni's letter these three hours, and I and my wife had given you up, and gone to bed. How did you fare in the storm?"

"Ill enough," replied Ugo, "ill enough and we are like to fare ill enough here, too, unless you will make more haste. Get us more wine, and let us see what you have to eat."

The peasant placed before them all, that his cottage afforded—ham, wine, figs, and grapes of such size and flavour, as Emily had seldom tasted.

After taking refreshment, she was shewn by the peasant's wife to her little bed-chamber, where she asked some questions concerning Montoni, to which the woman, whose name was Dorina, gave reserved answers, pretending ignorance of his *Excellenza*'s intention in sending Emily hither, but acknowledging that her husband had been apprized of the circumstance. Perceiving, that she could obtain no intelligence concerning her destination, Emily dismissed Dorina, and retired to repose; but all the busy scenes of her past and the anticipated ones of the future came to her anxious mind, and conspired with the sense of her new situation to banish sleep.

CHAPTER VII

Was nought around but images of rest,
Sleep-soothing groves, and quiet lawns between,
And flowery beds that slumbrous influence kest,*
From poppies breath'd, and banks of pleasant green,
Where never yet was creeping creature seen.
Meantime unnumbered glittering streamlets play'd,
And hurled every where their water's sheen,
That, as they bicker'd through the sunny glade,
Though restless still themselves, a lulling murmur made.
THOMSON

WHEN Emily, in the morning, opened her casement, she was surprised to observe the beauties, that surrounded it. The cottage was nearly embowered in the woods, which were chiefly of chesnut intermixed with some cypress, larch and sycamore. Beneath the dark and spreading branches, appeared, to the north, and to the east, the woody Apennines, rising in majestic amphitheatre, not black with pines, as she had been accustomed to see them, but their loftiest summits crowned with antient forests of chesnut, oak, and oriental plane, now animated with the rich tints of autumn, and which swept downward to the valley uninterruptedly, except where some bold rocky promontory looked out from among the foliage, and caught the passing gleam. Vineyards stretched along the feet of the mountains, where the elegant villas of the Tuscan nobility frequently adorned the scene, and overlooked slopes clothed with groves of olive, mulberry, orange and lemon. The plain, to which these declined, was coloured with the riches of cultivation, whose mingled hues were mellowed into harmony by an Italian sun. Vines, their purple clusters blushing between the russet foliage, hung in luxuriant festoons from the branches of standard fig and cherry trees, while pastures of verdure, such as Emily had seldom seen in Italy, enriched the banks of a stream that, after descending from the mountains, wound along the landscape, which it reflected, to a bay of the sea. There, far in the west, the waters, fading into the sky, assumed a tint of the faintest purple, and the line of separation between them was, now and then, discernible only by the progress of a sail, brightened with the sunbeam, along the horizon.

The cottage, which was shaded by the woods from the intenser rays of the sun, and was open only to his evening light, was covered entirely with vines, fig-trees and jessamine, whose flowers surpassed in size and fragrance any that Emily had seen. These and ripening clusters of grapes

*[Archaic variant of "cast"—ed.]

hung round her little casement. The turf, that grew under the woods, was inlaid with a variety of wild flowers and perfumed herbs, and, on the opposite margin of the stream, whose current diffused freshness beneath the shades, rose a grove of lemon and orange trees. This, though nearly opposite to Emily's window, did not interrupt her prospect, but rather heightened, by its dark verdure, the effect of the perspective; and to her this spot was a bower of sweets, whose charms communicated imperceptibly to her mind somewhat of their own serenity.

She was soon summoned to breakfast, by the peasant's daughter, a girl about seventeen, of a pleasant countenance, which, Emily was glad to observe, seemed animated with the pure affections of nature, though the others, that surrounded her, expressed, more or less, the worst qualities—cruelty, ferocity, cunning and duplicity; of the latter style of countenance, especially, were those of the peasant and his wife. Maddelina spoke little, but what she said was in a soft voice, and with an air of modesty and complacency, that interested Emily, who breakfasted at a separate table with Dorina, while Ugo and Bertrand were taking a repast of Tuscany bacon and wine with their host, near the cottage door; when they had finished which, Ugo, rising hastily, enquired for his mule, and Emily learned that he was to return to Udolpho, while Bertrand remained at the cottage; a circumstance, which, though it did not surprise, distressed her.

When Ugo was departed, Emily proposed to walk in the neighbouring woods; but, on being told, that she must not quit the cottage, without having Bertrand for her attendant, she withdrew to her own room. There, as her eyes settled on the towering Apennines, she recollected the terrific scenery they had exhibited and the horrors she had suffered, on the preceding night, particularly at the moment when Bertrand had betrayed himself to be an assassin; and these remembrances awakened a train of images, which, since they abstracted her from a consideration of her own situation, she pursued for some time, and then arranged in the following lines; pleased to have discovered any innocent means, by which she could beguile an hour of misfortune.

THE PILGRIM*

> Slow o'er the Apennine, with bleeding feet,
> A patient Pilgrim wound his lonely way,
> To deck the Lady of Loretto's seat
> With all the little wealth his zeal could pay.
> From mountain-tops cold died the evening ray,

---

*This poem and that entitled *The Traveller* in vol. ii, have already appeared in a periodical publication. [A. R.]

And, stretch'd in twilight, slept the vale below;
And now the last, last purple streaks of day
Along the melancholy West fade slow.
High o'er his head, the restless pines complain,
As on their summit rolls the breeze of night;
Beneath, the hoarse stream chides the rocks in vain:
The Pilgrim pauses on the dizzy height.
Then to the vale his cautious step he prest,
For there a hermit's cross was dimly seen,
Cresting the rock, and there his limbs might rest,
Cheer'd in the good man's cave, by faggot's sheen,
On leafy beds, nor guile his sleep molest.
Unhappy Luke! he trusts a treacherous clue!
Behind the cliff the lurking robber stood;
No friendly moon his giant shadow threw
Athwart the road, to save the Pilgrim's blood;
On as he went a vesper-hymn he sang,
The hymn, that nightly sooth'd him to repose.
Fierce on his harmless prey the ruffian sprang!
The Pilgrim bleeds to death, his eye-lids close.
Yet his meek spirit knew no vengeful care,
But, dying, for his murd'rer breath'd—a sainted pray'r!

Preferring the solitude of her room to the company of the persons below stairs, Emily dined above, and Maddelina was suffered to attend her, from whose simple conversation she learned, that the peasant and his wife were old inhabitants of this cottage, which had been purchased for them by Montoni, in reward of some service, rendered him, many years before, by Marco, to whom Carlo, the steward at the castle, was nearly related. "So many years ago, Signora," added Maddelina, "that I know nothing about it; but my father did the Signor a great good, for my mother has often said to him, this cottage was the least he ought to have had."

To the mention of this circumstance Emily listened with a painful interest, since it appeared to give a frightful colour to the character of Marco, whose service, thus rewarded by Montoni, she could scarcely doubt had been criminal; and, if so, had too much reason to believe, that she had been committed into his hands for some desperate purpose. "Did you ever hear how many years it is," said Emily, who was considering of Signora Laurentini's disappearance from Udolpho, "since your father performed the services you spoke of?"

"It was a little before he came to live at the cottage, Signora," replied Maddelina, "and that is about eighteen years ago."

This was near the period, when Signora Laurentini had been said to disappear, and it occurred to Emily, that Marco had assisted in that mysterious affair, and, perhaps, had been employed in a murder! This horrible suggestion fixed her in such profound reverie, that Maddelina quitted the room, unperceived by her, and she remained unconscious of all around her, for a considerable time. Tears, at length, came to her relief, after indulging which, her spirits becoming calmer, she ceased to tremble at a view of evils, that might never arrive; and had sufficient resolution to endeavour to withdraw her thoughts from the contemplation of her own interests. Remembering the few books, which even in the hurry of her departure from Udolpho she had put into her little package, she sat down with one of them at her pleasant casement, whence her eyes often wandered from the page to the landscape, whose beauty gradually soothed her mind into gentle melancholy.

Here, she remained alone, till evening, and saw the sun descend the western sky, throw all his pomp of light and shadow upon the mountains, and gleam upon the distant ocean and the stealing sails, as he sunk amidst the waves. Then, at the musing hour of twilight, her softened thoughts returned to Valancourt; she again recollected every circumstance, connected with the midnight music, and all that might assist her conjecture, concerning his imprisonment at the castle, and, becoming confirmed in the supposition, that it was his voice she had heard there, she looked back to that gloomy abode with emotions of grief and momentary regret.

Refreshed by the cool and fragrant air, and her spirits soothed to a state of gentle melancholy by the stilly murmur of the brook below and of the woods around, she lingered at her casement long after the sun had set, watching the valley sinking into obscurity, till only the grand outline of the surrounding mountains, shadowed upon the horizon, remained visible. But a clear moon-light, that succeeded, gave to the landscape, what time gives to the scenes of past life, when it softens all their harsher features, and throws over the whole the mellowing shade of distant contemplation. The scenes of La Vallée, in the early morn of her life, when she was protected and beloved by parents equally loved, appeared in Emily's memory tenderly beautiful, like the prospect before her, and awakened mournful comparisons. Unwilling to encounter the coarse behaviour of the peasant's wife, she remained supperless in her room, while she wept again over her forlorn and perilous situation, a review of which entirely overcame the small remains of her fortitude, and, reducing her to temporary despondence, she wished to be released from the heavy load of life, that had so long oppressed her, and prayed to Heaven to take her, in its mercy, to her parents.

Wearied with weeping, she, at length, lay down on her mattress, and sunk to sleep, but was soon awakened by a knocking at her chamber door, and, starting up in terror, she heard a voice calling her. The image of Bertrand, with a stilletto in his hand, appeared to her alarmed fancy, and she neither opened the door, or answered, but listened in profound silence, till, the voice repeating her name in the same low tone, she demanded who called. "It is I, Signora," replied the voice, which she now distinguished to be Maddelina's, "pray open the door. Don't be frightened, it is I."

"And what brings you here so late, Maddelina?" said Emily, as she let her in.

"Hush! Signora, for heaven's sake hush!—if we are overheard I shall never be forgiven. My father and mother and Bertrand are all gone to bed," continued Maddelina, as she gently shut the door, and crept forward, "and I have brought you some supper, for you had none, you know, Signora, below stairs. Here are some grapes and figs and half a cup of wine." Emily thanked her, but expressed apprehension lest this kindness should draw upon her the resentment of Dorina, when she perceived the fruit was gone. "Take it back, therefore, Maddelina," added Emily, "I shall suffer much less from the want of it, than I should do, if this act of good-nature was to subject you to your mother's displeasure."

"O Signora! there is no danger of that," replied Maddelina, "my mother cannot miss the fruit, for I saved it from my own supper. You will make me very unhappy, if you refuse to take it, Signora." Emily was so much affected by this instance of the good girl's generosity, that she remained for some time unable to reply, and Maddelina watched her in silence, till, mistaking the cause of her emotion, she said, "Do not weep so, Signora! My mother, to be sure, is a little cross, sometimes, but then it is soon over,—so don't take it so much to heart. She often scolds me, too, but then I have learned to bear it, and, when she has done, if I can but steal out into the woods, and play upon my sticcado, I forget it all directly."

Emily, smiling through her tears, told Maddelina, that she was a good girl, and then accepted her offering. She wished anxiously to know, whether Bertrand and Dorina had spoken of Montoni, or of his designs, concerning herself, in the presence of Maddelina, but disdained to tempt the innocent girl to a conduct so mean, as that of betraying the private conversations of her parents. When she was departing, Emily requested, that she would come to her room as often as she dared, without offending her mother, and Maddelina, after promising that she would do so, stole softly back again to her own chamber.

Thus several days passed, during which Emily remained in her own room, Maddelina attending her only at her repast, whose gentle countenance and manners soothed her more than any circumstance she had known for many months. Of her pleasant embowered chamber she now became fond, and began to experience in it those feelings of security, which we naturally attach to home. In this interval also, her mind, having been undisturbed by any new circumstance of disgust, or alarm, recovered its tone sufficiently to permit her the enjoyment of her books, among which she found some unfinished sketches of landscapes, several blank sheets of paper, with her drawing instruments, and she was thus enabled to amuse herself with selecting some of the lovely features of the prospect, that her window commanded, and combining them in scenes, to which her tasteful fancy gave a last grace. In these little sketches she generally placed interesting groups, characteristic of the scenery they animated, and often contrived to tell, with perspicuity, some simple and affecting story, when, as a tear fell over the pictured griefs, which her imagination drew, she would forget, for a moment, her real sufferings. Thus innocently she beguiled the heavy hours of misfortune, and, with meek patience, awaited the events of futurity.

A beautiful evening, that had succeeded to a sultry day, at length induced Emily to walk, though she knew that Bertrand must attend her, and, with Maddelina for her companion, she left the cottage, followed by Bertrand, who allowed her to choose her own way. The hour was cool and silent, and she could not look upon the country around her, without delight. How lovely, too, appeared the brilliant blue, that coloured all the upper region of the air, and, thence fading downward, was lost in the saffron glow of the horizon! Nor less so were the varied shades and warm colouring of the Apennines, as the evening sun threw his slanting rays athwart their broken surface. Emily followed the course of the stream, under the shades, that overhung its grassy margin. On the opposite banks, the pastures were animated with herds of cattle of a beautiful cream-colour; and, beyond, were groves of lemon and orange, with fruit glowing on the branches, frequent almost as the leaves, which partly concealed it. She pursued her way towards the sea, which reflected the warm glow of sunset, while the cliffs, that rose over its edge, were tinted with the last rays. The valley was terminated on the right by a lofty promontory, whose summit, impending over the waves, was crowned with a ruined tower, now serving for the purpose of a beacon, whose shattered battlements and the extended wings of some seafowl, that circled near it, were still illumined by the upward beams of the sun, though his disk was now sunk beneath the horizon; while the lower part of the ruin, the cliff on which it stood and the waves at its foot, were shaded with the first tints of twilight.

Having reached this headland, Emily gazed with solemn pleasure on the cliffs, that extended on either hand along the sequestered shores, some crowned with groves of pine, and others exhibiting only barren precipices of grayish marble, except where the crags were tufted with myrtle and other aromatic shrubs. The sea slept in a perfect calm; its waves, dying in murmurs on the shores, flowed with the gentlest undulation, while its clear surface reflected in softened beauty the vermeil tints of the west. Emily, as she looked upon the ocean, thought of France and of past times, and she wished, Oh! how ardently, and vainly—wished! that its waves would bear her to her distant, native home!

"Ah! that vessel," said she, "that vessel, which glides along so stately, with its tall sails reflected in the water is, perhaps, bound for France! Happy—happy bark!" She continued to gaze upon it, with warm emotion, till the gray of twilight obscured the distance, and veiled it from her view. The melancholy sound of the waves at her feet assisted the tenderness, that occasioned her tears, and this was the only sound, that broke upon the hour, till, having followed the windings of the beach, for some time, a chorus of voices passed her on the air. She paused a moment, wishing to hear more, yet fearing to be seen, and, for the first time, looked back to Bertrand, as her protector, who was following, at a short distance, in company with some other person. Reassured by this circumstance, she advanced towards the sounds, which seemed to arise from behind a high promontory, that projected athwart the beach. There was now a sudden pause in the music, and then one female voice was heard to sing in a kind of chant. Emily quickened her steps, and, winding round the rock, saw, within the sweeping bay, beyond, which was hung with woods from the borders of the beach to the very summit of the cliffs, two groups of peasants, one seated beneath the shades, and the other standing on the edge of the sea, round the girl, who was singing, and who held in her hand a chaplet of flowers, which she seemed about to drop into the waves.

Emily, listening with surprise and attention, distinguished the following invocation delivered in the pure and elegant tongue of Tuscany, and accompanied by a few pastoral instruments.

TO A SEA-NYMPH

O nymph! who loves to float on the green wave,
When Neptune sleeps beneath the moon-light hour,
Lull'd by the music's melancholy pow'r,
O nymph, arise from out thy pearly cave!

For Hesper beams amid the twilight shade,
And soon shall Cynthia tremble o'er the tide,
Gleam on these cliffs, that bound the ocean's pride,
And lonely silence all the air pervade.

Then, let thy tender voice at distance swell,
And steal along this solitary shore,
Sink on the breeze, till dying—heard no more—
Thou wak'st the sudden magic of thy shell.

While the long coast in echo sweet replies,
Thy soothing strains the pensive heart beguile,
And bid the visions of the future smile,
O nymph! from out thy pearly cave—arise!

(Chorus)—*Arise!*
(Semi-chorus)—*Arise!*

The last words being repeated by the surrounding group, the garland of flowers was thrown into the waves, and the chorus, sinking gradually into a chant, died away in silence.

"What can this mean, Maddelina?" said Emily, awakening from the pleasing trance, into which the music had lulled her. "This is the eve of a festival, Signora," replied Maddelina; "and the peasants then amuse themselves with all kinds of sports."

"But they talked of a sea-nymph," said Emily: "how came these good people to think of a sea-nymph?"

"O, Signora," rejoined Maddelina, mistaking the reason of Emily's surprise, "nobody *believes* in such things, but our old songs tell of them, and, when we are at our sports, we sometimes sing to them, and throw garlands into the sea."

Emily had been early taught to venerate Florence as the seat of literature and of the fine arts; but, that its taste for classic story should descend to the peasants of the country, occasioned her both surprise and admiration. The Arcadian air of the girls next attracted her attention. Their dress was a very short full petticoat of light green, with a boddice of white silk; the sleeves loose, and tied up at the shoulders with ribbons and bunches of flowers. Their hair, falling in ringlets on their necks, was also ornamented with flowers, and with a small straw hat, which, set rather backward and on one side of the head, gave an expression of gaiety and smartness to the whole figure. When the song had concluded, several of these girls approached Emily, and, inviting her to sit down among them, offered her, and Maddelina, whom they knew, grapes and figs.

Emily accepted their courtesy, much pleased with the gentleness and grace of their manners, which appeared to be perfectly natural to them; and when Bertrand, soon after, approached, and was hastily drawing her away, a peasant, holding up a flask, invited him to drink; a temptation, which Bertrand was seldom very valiant in resisting.

"Let the young lady join in the dance, my friend," said the peasant, "while we empty this flask. They are going to begin directly. Strike up! my lads, strike up your tambourines and merry flutes!"

They sounded gaily; and the younger peasants formed themselves into a circle, which Emily would readily have joined, had her spirits been in unison with their mirth. Maddelina, however, tripped it lightly, and Emily, as she looked on the happy group, lost the sense of her misfortunes in that of a benevolent pleasure. But the pensive melancholy of her mind returned, as she sat rather apart from the company, listening to the mellow music, which the breeze softened as it bore it away, and watching the moon, stealing its tremulous light over the waves and on the woody summits of the cliffs, that wound along these Tuscan shores.

Meanwhile, Bertrand was so well pleased with his first flask, that he very willingly commenced the attack on a second, and it was late before Emily, not without some apprehension, returned to the cottage.

After this evening, she frequently walked with Maddelina, but was never unattended by Bertrand; and her mind became by degrees as tranquil as the circumstances of her situation would permit. The quiet, in which she was suffered to live, encouraged her to hope, that she was not sent hither with an evil design; and, had it not appeared probable, that Valancourt was at this time an inhabitant of Udolpho, she would have wished to remain at the cottage, till an opportunity should offer of returning to her native country. But, concerning Montoni's motive for sending her into Tuscany, she was more than ever perplexed, nor could she believe that any consideration for her safety had influenced him on this occasion.

She had been some time at the cottage, before she recollected, that, in the hurry of leaving Udolpho, she had forgotten the papers committed to her by her late aunt, relative to the Languedoc estates; but, though this remembrance occasioned her much uneasiness, she had some hope, that, in the obscure place, where they were deposited, they would escape the detection of Montoni.

CHAPTER VIII

> My tongue hath but a heavier tale to say.
> I play the torturer, by small and small,
> To lengthen out the worst that must be spoken.
> RICHARD II

WE now return, for a moment, to Venice, where Count Morano was suffering under an accumulation of misfortunes. Soon after his arrival in that city, he had been arrested by order of the Senate, and, without knowing of what he was suspected, was conveyed to a place of confinement, whither the most strenuous enquiries of his friends had been unable to trace him. Who the enemy was, that had occasioned him this calamity, he had not been able to guess, unless, indeed, it was Montoni, on whom his suspicions rested, and not only with much apparent probability, but with justice.

In the affair of the poisoned cup, Montoni had suspected Morano; but, being unable to obtain the degree of proof, which was necessary to convict him of a guilty intention, he had recourse to means of other revenge, than he could hope to obtain by prosecution. He employed a person, in whom he believed he might confide, to drop a letter of accusation into the *Denunzie secrete*, or lions' mouths, which are fixed in a gallery of the Doge's palace, as receptacles for anonymous information, concerning persons, who may be disaffected towards the state. As, on these occasions, the accuser is not confronted with the accused, a man may falsely impeach his enemy, and accomplish an unjust revenge, without fear of punishment, or detection. That Montoni should have recourse to these diabolical means of ruining a person, whom he suspected of having attempted his life, is not in the least surprising. In the letter, which he had employed as the instrument of his revenge, he accused Morano of designs against the state, which he attempted to prove, with all the plausible simplicity of which he was master; and the Senate, with whom a suspicion was, at that time, almost equal to a proof, arrested the Count, in consequence of this accusation; and, without even hinting to him his crime, threw him into one of those secret prisons, which were the terror of the Venetians, and in which persons often languished, and sometimes died, without being discovered by their friends.

Morano had incurred the personal resentment of many members of the state; his habits of life had rendered him obnoxious to some; and his ambition, and the bold rivalship, which he discovered, on several public occasions,—to others; and it was not to be expected, that mercy would soften the rigour of a law, which was to be dispensed from the hands of his enemies.

Montoni, meantime, was beset by dangers of another kind. His castle was besieged by troops, who seemed willing to dare every thing, and to suffer patiently any hardships in pursuit of victory. The strength of the fortress, however, withstood their attack, and this, with the vigorous defence of the garrison and the scarcity of provision on these wild mountains, soon compelled the assailants to raise the siege.

When Udolpho was once more left to the quiet possession of Montoni, he dispatched Ugo into Tuscany for Emily, whom he had

sent from considerations of her personal safety, to a place of greater
security, than a castle, which was, at that time, liable to be overrun by
his enemies. Tranquillity being once more restored to Udolpho, he was
impatient to secure her again under his roof, and had commissioned
Ugo to assist Bertrand in guarding her back to the castle. Thus compelled to return, Emily bade the kind Maddelina farewell, with regret,
and, after about a fortnight's stay in Tuscany, where she had experienced an interval of quiet, which was absolutely necessary to sustain
her long-harassed spirits, began once more to ascend the Apennines,
from whose heights she gave a long and sorrowful look to the beautiful
country, that extended at their feet, and to the distant Mediterranean,
whose waves she had so often wished would bear her back to France.
The distress she felt, on her return towards the place of her former sufferings, was, however, softened by a conjecture, that Valancourt was
there, and she found some degree of comfort in the thought of being
near him, notwithstanding the consideration, that he was probably a
prisoner.

It was noon, when she had left the cottage, and the evening was
closed, long before she came within the neighbourhood of Udolpho.
There was a moon, but it shone only at intervals, for the night was
cloudy, and, lighted by the torch, which Ugo carried, the travellers
paced silently along, Emily musing on her situation, and Bertrand and
Ugo anticipating the comforts of a flask of wine and a good fire, for they
had perceived for some time the difference between the warm climate
of the lowlands of Tuscany and the nipping air of these upper regions.
Emily was, at length, roused from her reverie by the far-off sound of the
castle clock, to which she listened not without some degree of awe, as
it rolled away on the breeze. Another and another note succeeded, and
died in sullen murmur among the mountains:—to her mournful imagination it seemed a knell measuring out some fateful period for her.

"Aye, there is the old clock," said Bertrand, "there he is still; the cannon have not silenced him!"

"No," answered Ugo, "he crowed as loud as the best of them in the
midst of it all. There he was roaring out in the hottest fire I have seen
this many a day! I said that some of them would have a hit at the old
fellow, but he escaped, and the tower too."

The road winding round the base of a mountain, they now came
within view of the castle, which was shewn in the perspective of the valley by a gleam of moon-shine, and then vanished in shade; while even
a transient view of it had awakened the poignancy of Emily's feelings.
Its massy and gloomy walls gave her terrible ideas of imprisonment and
suffering: yet, as she advanced, some degree of hope mingled with her
terror; for, though this was certainly the residence of Montoni, it was

possibly, also, that of Valancourt, and she could not approach a place, where he might be, without experiencing somewhat of the joy of hope.

They continued to wind along the valley, and, soon after, she saw again the old walls and moon-lit towers, rising over the woods: the strong rays enabled her, also, to perceive the ravages, which the siege had made,—with the broken walls, and shattered battlements, for they were now at the foot of the steep, on which Udolpho stood. Massy fragments had rolled down among the woods, through which the travellers now began to ascend, and there mingled with the loose earth, and pieces of rock they had brought with them. The woods, too, had suffered much from the batteries above, for here the enemy had endeavoured to screen themselves from the fire of the ramparts. Many noble trees were levelled with the ground, and others, to a wide extent, were entirely stripped of their upper branches. "We had better dismount," said Ugo, "and lead the mules up the hill, or we shall get into some of the holes, which the balls have left. Here are plenty of them. Give me the torch," continued Ugo, after they had dismounted, "and take care you don't stumble over any thing, that lies in your way, for the ground is not yet cleared of the enemy."

"How!" exclaimed Emily, "are any of the enemy here, then?"

"Nay, I don't know for that, now," he replied, "but when I came away I saw one or two of them lying under the trees."

As they proceeded, the torch threw a gloomy light upon the ground, and far among the recesses of the woods, and Emily feared to look forward, lest some object of horror should meet her eye. The path was often strewn with broken heads of arrows, and with shattered remains of armour, such as at that period was mingled with the lighter dress of the soldiers. "Bring the light hither," said Bertrand, "I have stumbled over something, that rattles loud enough." Ugo holding up the torch, they perceived a steel breastplate on the ground, which Bertrand raised, and they saw, that it was pierced through, and that the lining was entirely covered with blood; but upon Emily's earnest entreaties, that they would proceed, Bertrand, uttering some joke upon the unfortunate person, to whom it had belonged, threw it hard upon the ground, and they passed on.

At every step she took, Emily feared to see some vestige of death. Coming soon after to an opening in the woods, Bertrand stopped to survey the ground, which was encumbered with massy trunks and branches of the trees, that had so lately adorned it, and seemed to have been a spot particularly fatal to the besiegers; for it was evident from the destruction of the trees, that here the hottest fire of the garrison had been directed. As Ugo held again forth the torch, steel glittered between the fallen trees; the ground beneath was covered with broken

arms, and with the torn vestments of soldiers, whose mangled forms
Emily almost expected to see; and she again entreated her companions
to proceed, who were, however, too intent in their examination, to
regard her, and she turned her eyes from this desolated scene to the
castle above, where she observed lights gliding along the ramparts.
Presently, the castle clock struck twelve, and then a trumpet sounded,
of which Emily enquired the occasion.

"O! they are only changing watch," replied Ugo. "I do not remember this trumpet," said Emily, "it is a new custom." "It is only an old one
revived, lady; we always use it in time of war. We have sounded it, at
midnight, ever since the place was besieged."

"Hark!" said Emily, as the trumpet sounded again; and, in the next
moment, she heard a faint clash of arms, and then the watchword
passed along the terrace above, and was answered from a distant part of
the castle; after which all was again still. She complained of cold, and
begged to go on. "Presently, lady," said Bertrand, turning over some
broken arms with the pike he usually carried. "What have we here?"

"Hark!" cried Emily, "what noise was that?"

"What noise was it?" said Ugo, starting up and listening.

"Hush!" repeated Emily. "It surely came from the ramparts above:"
and, on looking up, they perceived a light moving along the walls,
while, in the next instant, the breeze swelling, the voice sounded
louder than before.

"Who goes yonder?" cried a sentinel of the castle. "Speak or it will
be worse for you." Bertrand uttered a shout of joy. "Hah! my brave comrade, is it you?" said he, and he blew a shrill whistle, which signal was
answered by another from the soldier on watch; and the party, then
passing forward, soon after emerged from the woods upon the broken
road, that led immediately to the castle gates, and Emily saw, with
renewed terror, the whole of that stupendous structure. "Alas!" said she
to herself, "I am going again into my prison!"

"Here has been warm work, by St. Marco!" cried Bertrand, waving a
torch over the ground; "the balls have torn up the earth here with a
vengeance."

"Aye," replied Ugo, "they were fired from that redoubt, yonder, and
rare execution they did. The enemy made a furious attack upon the
great gates; but they might have guessed they could never carry it there;
for, besides the cannon from the walls, our archers, on the two round
towers, showered down upon them at such a rate, that, by holy Peter!
there was no standing it. I never saw a better sight in my life; I laughed,
till my sides aked, to see how the knaves scampered. Bertrand, my good
fellow, thou shouldst have been among them; I warrant thou wouldst
have won the race!"

"Hah! you are at your old tricks again," said Bertrand in a surly tone. "It is well for thee thou art so near the castle; thou knowest I have killed my man before now." Ugo replied only by a laugh, and then gave some further account of the siege, to which as Emily listened, she was struck by the strong contrast of the present scene with that which had so lately been acted here.

The mingled uproar of cannon, drums, and trumpets, the groans of the conquered, and the shouts of the conquerors were now sunk into a silence so profound, that it seemed as if death had triumphed alike over the vanquished and the victor. The shattered condition of one of the towers of the great gates by no means confirmed the *valiant* account just given by Ugo of the scampering party, who, it was evident, had not only made a stand, but had done much mischief before they took to flight; for this tower appeared, as far as Emily could judge by the dim moon-light that fell upon it, to be laid open, and the battlements were nearly demolished. While she gazed, a light glimmered through one of the lower loop-holes, and disappeared; but, in the next moment, she perceived through the broken wall, a soldier, with a lamp, ascending the narrow staircase, that wound within the tower, and, remembering that it was the same she had passed up, on the night, when Barnardine had deluded her with a promise of seeing Madame Montoni, fancy gave her somewhat of the terror she had then suffered. She was now very near the gates, over which the soldier having opened the door of the portal-chamber, the lamp he carried gave her a dusky view of that terrible apartment, and she almost sunk under the recollected horrors of the moment, when she had drawn aside the curtain, and discovered the object it was meant to conceal.

"Perhaps," said she to herself, "it is now used for a similar purpose; perhaps, that soldier goes, at this dead hour, to watch over the corpse of his friend!" The little remains of her fortitude now gave way to the united force of remembered and anticipated horrors, for the melancholy fate of Madame Montoni appeared to foretell her own. She considered, that, though the Languedoc estates, if she relinquished them, would satisfy Montoni's avarice, they might not appease his vengeance, which was seldom pacified but by a terrible sacrifice; and she even thought, that, were she to resign them, the fear of justice might urge him either to detain her a prisoner, or to take away her life.

They were now arrived at the gates, where Bertrand, observing the light glimmer through a small casement of the portal-chamber, called aloud; and the soldier, looking out, demanded who was there. "Here, I have brought you a prisoner," said Ugo, "open the gate, and let us in."

"Tell me first who it is, that demands entrance," replied the soldier. "What! my old comrade," cried Ugo, "don't you know me? not know

Ugo? I have brought home a prisoner here, bound hand and foot—a fellow, who has been drinking Tuscany wine, while we here have been fighting."

"You will not rest till you meet with your match," said Bertrand sullenly. "Hah! my comrade, is it you?" said the soldier—"I'll be with you directly."

Emily presently heard his steps descending the stairs within, and then the heavy chain fall, and the bolts undraw of a small postern door, which he opened to admit the party. He held the lamp low, to shew the step of the gate, and she found herself once more beneath the gloomy arch, and heard the door close, that seemed to shut her from the world for ever. In the next moment, she was in the first court of the castle, where she surveyed the spacious and solitary area, with a kind of calm despair; while the dead hour of the night, the gothic gloom of the surrounding buildings, and the hollow and imperfect echoes, which they returned, as Ugo and the soldier conversed together, assisted to increase the melancholy forebodings of her heart. Passing on to the second court, a distant sound broke feebly on the silence, and gradually swelling louder, as they advanced, Emily distinguished voices of revelry and laughter, but they were to her far other than sounds of joy. "Why, you have got some Tuscany wine among you, *here*," said Bertrand, "if one may judge by the uproar that is going forward. Ugo has taken a larger share of that than of fighting, I'll be sworn. Who is carousing at this late hour?"

"His *Excellenza* and the Signors," replied the soldier: "it is a sign you are a stranger at the castle, or you would not need to ask the question. They are brave spirits, that do without sleep—they generally pass the night in good cheer; would that we, who keep the watch, had a little of it! It is cold work, pacing the ramparts so many hours of the night, if one has no good liquor to warm one's heart."

"Courage, my lad, courage ought to warm your heart," said Ugo. "Courage!" replied the soldier sharply, with a menacing air, which Ugo perceiving, prevented his saying more, by returning to the subject of the carousal. "This is a new custom," said he; "when I left the castle, the Signors used to sit up counselling."

"Aye, and for that matter, carousing too," replied the soldier, "but, since the siege, they have done nothing but make merry: and if I was they, I would settle accounts with myself, for all my hard fighting, the same way."

They had now crossed the second court, and reached the hall door, when the soldier, bidding them good night, hastened back to his post; and, while they waited for admittance, Emily considered how she might avoid seeing Montoni, and retire unnoticed to her former apartment, for she shrunk from the thought of encountering either him, or any of his party, at this hour. The uproar within the castle was now so loud, that, though Ugo knocked repeatedly at the hall door, he was not heard by any of the servants, a circumstance, which increased Emily's alarm, while it allowed her time to deliberate on the means of retiring unobserved; for, though she might, perhaps, pass up the great stair-case unseen, it was impossible she could find the way to her chamber, without a light, the difficulty of procuring which, and the danger of wandering about the castle, without one, immediately struck her. Bertrand had only a torch, and she knew, that the servants never brought a taper to the door, for the hall was sufficiently lighted by the large tripod lamp, which hung in the vaulted roof; and, while she should wait till Annette could bring a taper, Montoni, or some of his companions, might discover her.

The door was now opened by Carlo; and Emily, having requested him to send Annette immediately with a light to the great gallery, where she determined to await her, passed on with hasty steps towards the stair-case; while Bertrand and Ugo, with the torch, followed old Carlo to the servants' hall, impatient for supper and the warm blaze of a wood fire. Emily, lighted only by the feeble rays, which the lamp above threw between the arches of this extensive hall, endeavoured to find her way to the stair-case, now hid in obscurity; while the shouts of merriment, that burst from a remote apartment, served, by heightening her terror, to increase her perplexity, and she expected, every instant, to see the door of that room open, and Montoni and his companions issue forth. Having, at length, reached the stair-case, and found her way to the top, she seated herself on the last stair, to await the arrival of Annette; for the profound darkness of the gallery deterred her from proceeding farther, and, while she listened for her footstep, she heard only distant sounds of revelry, which rose in sullen echoes from among the arcades below. Once she thought she heard a low sound from the dark gallery behind her; and, turning her eyes, fancied she saw something luminous move in it; and, since she could not, at this moment, subdue the weakness that caused her fears, she quitted her seat, and crept softly down a few stairs lower.

Annette not yet appearing, Emily now concluded, that she was gone to bed, and that nobody chose to call her up; and the prospect, that presented itself, of passing the night in darkness, in this place, or in some other equally forlorn (for she knew it would be impracticable to find her way through the intricacies of the galleries to her chamber), drew tears of mingled terror and despondency from her eyes.

While thus she sat, she fancied she heard again an odd sound from the gallery, and she listened, scarcely daring to breathe, but the increas-

ing voices below overcame every other sound. Soon after, she heard
Montoni and his companions burst into the hall, who spoke, as if they
were much intoxicated, and seemed to be advancing towards the stair-
case. She now remembered, that they must come this way to their
chambers, and, forgetting all the terrors of the gallery, hurried towards
it with an intention of secreting herself in some of the passages, that
opened beyond, and of endeavouring, when the Signors were retired,
to find her way to her own room, or to that of Annette, which was in a
remote part of the castle.

With extended arms, she crept along the gallery, still hearing the
voices of persons below, who seemed to stop in conversation at the foot
of the stair-case, and then pausing for a moment to listen, half fearful
of going further into the darkness of the gallery, where she still imagined, from the noise she had heard, that some person was lurking,
"They are already informed of my arrival," said she, "and Montoni is
coming himself to seek me! In the present state of his mind, his purpose must be desperate." Then, recollecting the scene, that had passed
in the corridor, on the night preceding her departure from the castle,
"O Valancourt!" said she, "I must then resign you for ever. To brave any
longer the injustice of Montoni, would not be fortitude, but rashness."
Still the voices below did not draw nearer, but they became louder, and
she distinguished those of Verezzi and Bertolini above the rest, while
the few words she caught made her listen more anxiously for others.
The conversation seemed to concern herself; and, having ventured to
step a few paces nearer to the stair-case, she discovered, that they were
disputing about her, each seeming to claim some former promise of
Montoni, who appeared, at first, inclined to appease and to persuade
them to return to their wine, but afterwards to be weary of the dispute,
and, saying that he left them to settle it as they could, was returning
with the rest of the party to the apartment he had just quitted. Verezzi
then stopped him. "Where is she? Signor," said he, in a voice of impatience: "tell us where she is." "I have already told you that I do not
know," replied Montoni, who seemed to be somewhat overcome with
wine; "but she is most probably gone to her apartment." Verezzi and
Bertolini now desisted from their enquiries, and sprang to the stair-case
together, while Emily, who, during this discourse, had trembled so
excessively, that she had with difficulty supported herself, seemed
inspired with new strength, the moment she heard the sound of their
steps, and ran along the gallery, dark as it was, with the fleetness of a
fawn. But, long before she reached its extremity, the light, which
Verezzi carried, flashed upon the walls; both appeared, and, instantly
perceiving Emily, pursued her. At this moment, Bertolini, whose steps,
though swift, were not steady, and whose impatience overcame what

little caution he had hitherto used, stumbled, and fell at his length. The lamp fell with him, and was presently expiring on the floor; but Verezzi, regardless of saving it, seized the advantage this accident gave him over his rival, and followed Emily, to whom, however, the light had shown one of the passages that branched from the gallery, and she instantly turned into it. Verezzi could just discern the way she had taken, and this he pursued; but the sound of her steps soon sunk in distance, while he, less acquainted with the passage, was obliged to proceed through the dark, with caution, lest he should fall down a flight of steps, such as in this extensive old castle frequently terminated an avenue. This passage at length brought Emily to the corridor, into which her own chamber opened, and, not hearing any footstep, she paused to take breath, and consider what was the safest design to be adopted. She had followed this passage, merely because it was the first that appeared, and now that she had reached the end of it, was as perplexed as before. Whither to go, or how further to find her way in the dark, she knew not; she was aware only that she must not seek her apartment, for there she would certainly be sought, and her danger increased every instant, while she remained near it. Her spirits and her breath, however, were so much exhausted, that she was compelled to rest, for a few minutes, at the end of the passage, and still she heard no steps approaching. As thus she stood, light glimmered under an opposite door of the gallery, and, from its situation, she knew, that it was the door of that mysterious chamber, where she had made a discovery so shocking, that she never remembered it but with the utmost horror. That there should be light in this chamber, and at this hour, excited her strong surprise, and she felt a momentary terror concerning it, which did not permit her to look again, for her spirits were now in such a state of weakness, that she almost expected to see the door slowly open, and some horrible object appear at it. Still she listened for a step along the passage, and looked up it, where, not a ray of light appearing, she concluded, that Verezzi had gone back for the lamp; and, believing that he would shortly be there, she again considered which way she should go, or rather which way she could find in the dark.

A faint ray still glimmered under the opposite door, but so great, and, perhaps, so just was her horror of that chamber, that she would not again have tempted its secrets, though she had been certain of obtaining the light so important to her safety. She was still breathing with difficulty, and resting at the end of the passage, when she heard a rustling sound, and then a low voice, so very near her, that it seemed close to her ear; but she had presence of mind to check her emotions, and to remain quite still; in the next moment, she perceived it to be the voice of Verezzi, who did not appear to know, that she was there, but to have spoken to himself. "The air is fresher here," said he: "this should be the corridor." Perhaps, he was one of those heroes, whose courage can defy an enemy better than darkness, and he tried to rally his spirits with the sound of his own voice. However this might be, he turned to the right, and proceeded, with the same stealing steps, towards Emily's apartment, apparently forgetting, that, in darkness, she could easily elude his search, even in her chamber; and, like an intoxicated person, he followed pertinaciously the one idea, that had possessed his imagination.

The moment she heard his steps steal away, she left her station and moved softly to the other end of the corridor, determined to trust again to chance, and to quit it by the first avenue she could find; but, before she could effect this, light broke upon the walls of the gallery, and, looking back, she saw Verezzi crossing it towards her chamber. She now glided into a passage, that opened on the left, without, as she thought, being perceived; but, in the next instant, another light, glimmering at the further end of this passage, threw her into new terror. While she stopped and hesitated which way to go, the pause allowed her to perceive, that it was Annette, who advanced, and she hurried to meet her: but her imprudence again alarmed Emily, on perceiving whom, she burst into a scream of joy, and it was some minutes, before she could be prevailed with to be silent, or to release her mistress from the ardent clasp, in which she held her. When, at length, Emily made Annette comprehend her danger, they hurried towards Annette's room, which was in a distant part of the castle. No apprehensions, however, could yet silence the latter. "Oh dear ma'amselle," said she, as they passed along, "what a terrified time have I had of it! Oh! I thought I should have died an hundred times! I never thought I should live to see you again! and I never was so glad to see any body in my whole life, as I am to see you now." "Hark!" cried Emily, "we are pursued; that was the echo of steps!" "No, ma'amselle," said Annette, "it was only the echo of a door shutting; sound runs along these vaulted passages so, that one is continually deceived by it; if one does but speak, or cough, it makes a noise as loud as a cannon." "Then there is the greater necessity for us to be silent," said Emily: "pr'ythee say no more, till we reach your chamber." Here, at length, they arrived, without interruption, and, Annette having fastened the door, Emily sat down on her little bed, to recover breath and composure. To her enquiry, whether Valancourt was among the prisoners in the castle, Annette replied, that she had not been able to hear, but that she knew there were several persons confined. She then proceeded, in her tedious way, to give an account of the siege, or rather a detail of her terrors and various sufferings, during the attack. "But," added she, "when I heard the shouts of victory from the ramparts, I thought we were all taken, and gave myself up for lost, instead of which, *we* had driven the enemy away. I went then to the north gallery, and saw a great many of them scampering away among the mountains; but the rampart walls were all in ruins, as one may say, and there was a dismal sight to see down among the woods below, where the poor fellows were lying in heaps, but were carried off presently by their comrades. While the siege was going on, the Signor was here, and there, and every where, at the same time, as Ludovico told me, for he would not let me see any thing hardly, and locked me up, as he has often done before, in a room in the middle of the castle, and used to bring me food, and come and talk with me as often as he could; and I must say, if it had not been for Ludovico, I should have died outright."

"Well, Annette," said Emily, "and how have affairs gone on, since the siege?"

"O! sad hurly burly doings, ma'amselle," replied Annette; "the Signors have done nothing but sit and drink and game, ever since. They sit up, all night, and play among themselves, for all those riches and fine things, they brought in, some time since, when they used to go out a-robbing, or as good, for days together; and then they have dreadful quarrels about who loses, and who wins. That fierce Signor Verezzi is always losing, as they tell me, and Signor Orsino wins from him, and this makes him very wroth, and they have had several hard set-to's about it. Then, all those fine ladies are at the castle still; and I declare I am frighted, whenever I meet any of them in the passages."——

"Surely, Annette," said Emily starting, "I heard a noise: listen." After a long pause, "No, ma'amselle," said Annette, "it was only the wind in the gallery; I often hear it, when it shakes the old doors, at the other end. But won't you go to bed, ma'amselle? you surely will not sit up starving, all night." Emily now laid herself down on the mattress, and desired Annette to leave the lamp burning on the hearth; having done which, the latter placed herself beside Emily, who, however, was not suffered to sleep, for she again thought she heard a noise from the passage; and Annette was again trying to convince her, that it was only the wind, when footsteps were distinctly heard near the door. Annette was now starting from the bed, but Emily prevailed with her to remain there, and listened with her in a state of terrible expectation. The steps still loitered at the door, when presently an attempt was made on the lock, and, in the next instant, a voice called. "For heaven's sake, Annette, do not answer," said Emily softly, "remain quite still; but I fear we must extinguish the lamp, or its glare will betray us." "Holy Virgin!" exclaimed Annette, forgetting her discretion, "I would not be in darkness now for the whole world." While she spoke, the voice became louder than before, and repeated Annette's name; "Blessed Virgin!"

cried she suddenly, "it is only Ludovico." She rose to open the door, but Emily prevented her, till they should be more certain, that it was he alone; with whom Annette, at length, talked for some time, and learned, that he was come to enquire after herself, whom he had let out of her room to go to Emily, and that he was now returned to lock her in again. Emily, fearful of being overheard, if they conversed any longer through the door, consented that it should be opened, and a young man appeared, whose open countenance confirmed the favourable opinion of him, which his care of Annette had already prompted her to form. She entreated his protection, should Verezzi make this requisite; and Ludovico offered to pass the night in an old chamber, adjoining, that opened from the gallery, and, on the first alarm, to come to their defence.

Emily was much soothed by this proposal; and Ludovico, having lighted his lamp, went to his station, while she, once more, endeavoured to repose on her mattress. But a variety of interests pressed upon her attention, and prevented sleep. She thought much on what Annette had told her of the dissolute manners of Montoni and his associates, and more of his present conduct towards herself, and of the danger, from which she had just escaped. From the view of her present situation she shrunk, as from a new picture of terror. She saw herself in a castle, inhabited by vice and violence, seated beyond the reach of law or justice, and in the power of a man, whose perseverance was equal to every occasion, and in whom passions, of which revenge was not the weakest, entirely supplied the place of principles. She was compelled, once more, to acknowledge, that it would be folly, and not fortitude, any longer to dare his power; and, resigning all hopes of future happiness with Valancourt, she determined, that, on the following morning, she would compromise with Montoni, and give up her estates, on condition, that he would permit her immediate return to France. Such considerations kept her waking for many hours; but, the night passed, without further alarm from Verezzi.

On the next morning, Emily had a long conversation with Ludovico, in which she heard circumstances concerning the castle, and received hints of the designs of Montoni, that considerably increased her alarms. On expressing her surprise, that Ludovico, who seemed to be so sensible of the evils of his situation, should continue in it, he informed her, that it was not his intention to do so, and she then ventured to ask him, if he would assist her to escape from the castle. Ludovico assured her of his readiness to attempt this, but strongly represented the difficulty of the enterprise, and the certain destruction which must ensue, should Montoni overtake them, before they had passed the mountains; he, however, promised to be watchful of every circumstance, that might contribute to the success of the attempt, and to think upon some plan of departure.

Emily now confided to him the name of Valancourt, and begged he would enquire for such a person among the prisoners in the castle; for the faint hope, which this conversation awakened, made her now recede from her resolution of an immediate compromise with Montoni. She determined, if possible, to delay this, till she heard further from Ludovico, and, if his designs were found to be impracticable, to resign the estates at once. Her thoughts were on this subject, when Montoni, who was now recovered from the intoxication of the preceding night, sent for her, and she immediately obeyed the summons. He was alone. "I find," said he, "that you were not in your chamber, last night; where were you?" Emily related to him some circumstances of her alarm, and entreated his protection from a repetition of them. "You know the terms of my protection," said he; "if you really value this, you will secure it." His open declaration, that he would only conditionally protect her, while she remained a prisoner in the castle, shewed Emily the necessity of an immediate compliance with his terms; but she first demanded, whether he would permit her immediately to depart, if she gave up her claim to the contested estates. In a very solemn manner he then assured her, that he would, and immediately laid before her a paper, which was to transfer the right of those estates to himself.

She was, for a considerable time, unable to sign it, and her heart was torn with contending interests, for she was about to resign the happiness of all her future years—the hope, which had sustained her in so many hours of adversity.

After hearing from Montoni a recapitulation of the conditions of her compliance, and a remonstrance, that his time was valuable, she put her hand to the paper; when she had done which, she fell back in her chair, but soon recovered, and desired, that he would give orders for her departure, and that he would allow Annette to accompany her. Montoni smiled. "It was necessary to deceive you," said he,—"there was no other way of making you act reasonably; you shall go, but it must not be at present. I must first secure these estates by possession: when that is done, you may return to France if you will."

The deliberate villany, with which he violated the solemn engagement he had just entered into, shocked Emily as much, as the certainty, that she had made a fruitless sacrifice, and must still remain his prisoner. She had no words to express what she felt, and knew, that it would have been useless, if she had. As she looked piteously at Montoni, he turned away, and at the same time desired she would withdraw to her apartment; but, unable to leave the room, she sat down in a chair near the door, and sighed heavily. She had neither words nor tears.

"Why will you indulge this childish grief?" said he. "Endeavour to strengthen your mind, to bear patiently what cannot now be avoided; you have no real evil to lament; be patient, and you will be sent back to France. At present retire to your apartment."

"I dare not go, sir," said she, "where I shall be liable to the intrusion of Signor Verezzi." "Have I not promised to protect you?" said Montoni. "You have promised, sir," —— replied Emily, after some hesitation. "And is not my promise sufficient?" added he sternly. "You will recollect your former promise, Signor," said Emily, trembling, "and may determine for me, whether I ought to rely upon this." "Will you provoke me to declare to you, that I will not protect you then?" said Montoni, in a tone of haughty displeasure. "If that will satisfy you, I will do it immediately. Withdraw to your chamber, before I retract my promise; you have nothing to fear there." Emily left the room, and moved slowly into the hall, where the fear of meeting Verezzi, or Bertolini, made her quicken her steps, though she could scarcely support herself; and soon after she reached once more her own apartment. Having looked fearfully round her, to examine if any person was there, and having searched every part of it, she fastened the door, and sat down by one of the casements. Here, while she looked out for some hope to support her fainting spirits, which had been so long harassed and oppressed, that, if she had not now struggled much against misfortune, they would have left her, perhaps, for ever, she endeavoured to believe, that Montoni did really intend to permit her return to France as soon as he had secured her property, and that he would, in the mean time, protect her from insult; but her chief hope rested with Ludovico, who, she doubted not, would be zealous in her cause, though he seemed almost to despair of success in it. One circumstance, however, she had to rejoice in. Her prudence, or rather her fears, had saved her from mentioning the name of Valancourt to Montoni, which she was several times on the point of doing, before she signed the paper, and of stipulating for his release, if he should be really a prisoner in the castle. Had she done this, Montoni's jealous fears would now probably have loaded Valancourt with new severities, and have suggested the advantage of holding him a captive for life.

Thus passed the melancholy day, as she had before passed many in this same chamber. When night drew on, she would have withdrawn herself to Annette's bed, had not a particular interest inclined her to remain in this chamber, in spite of her fears; for, when the castle should be still, and the customary hour arrived, she determined to watch for the music, which she had formerly heard. Though its sounds might not enable her positively to determine, whether Valancourt was there, they would perhaps strengthen her opinion that he was, and impart the comfort, so necessary to her present support.—But, on the other hand, if all should be silent—! She hardly dared to suffer her thoughts to glance that way, but waited, with impatient expectation, the approaching hour.

The night was stormy; the battlements of the castle appeared to rock in the wind, and, at intervals, long groans seemed to pass on the air, such as those, which often deceive the melancholy mind, in tempests, and amidst scenes of desolation. Emily heard, as formerly, the sentinels pass along the terrace to their posts, and, looking out from her casement, observed, that the watch was doubled; a precaution, which appeared necessary enough, when she threw her eyes on the walls, and saw their shattered condition. The well-known sounds of the soldiers' march, and of their distant voices, which passed her in the wind, and were lost again, recalled to her memory the melancholy sensation she had suffered, when she formerly heard the same sounds; and occasioned almost involuntary comparisons between her present, and her late situation. But this was no subject for congratulation, and she wisely checked the course of her thoughts, while, as the hour was not yet come, in which she had been accustomed to hear the music, she closed the casement, and endeavoured to await it in patience. The door of the stair-case she tried to secure, as usual, with some of the furniture of the room; but this expedient her fears now represented to her to be very inadequate to the power and perseverance of Verezzi; and she often looked at a large and heavy chest, that stood in the chamber, with wishes that she and Annette had strength enough to move it. While she blamed the long stay of this girl, who was still with Ludovico and some other of the servants, she trimmed her wood fire, to make the room appear less desolate, and sat down beside it with a book, which her eyes perused, while her thoughts wandered to Valancourt, and her own misfortunes. As she sat thus, she thought, in a pause of the wind, she distinguished music, and went to the casement to listen, but the loud swell of the gust overcame every other sound. When the wind sunk again, she heard distinctly, in the deep pause that succeeded, the sweet strings of a lute; but again the rising tempest bore away the notes, and again was succeeded by a solemn pause. Emily, trembling with hope and fear, opened her casement to listen, and to try whether her own voice could be heard by the musician; for to endure any longer this state of torturing suspense concerning Valancourt, seemed to be utterly impossible. There was a kind of breathless stillness in the chambers, that permitted her to distinguish from below the tender notes of the very lute she had formerly heard, and with it, a plaintive voice, made sweeter by the low rustling sound, that now began to creep along the wood-tops, till it was lost in the rising wind. Their tall heads then began to wave, while, through a forest of pine, on the left, the wind, groaning heavily, rolled onward over the woods below, bending them almost to their roots; and, as the long-resounding gale swept away, other woods, on the right, seemed to answer the "loud lament;" then, others, further still, softened it into a murmur, that died into silence. Emily listened, with mingled awe and expectation, hope and fear; and again the melting sweetness of the lute was heard, and the same solemn-breathing voice. Convinced that these came from an apartment underneath, she leaned far out of her window, that she might discover whether any light was there; but the casements below, as well as those above, were sunk so deep in the thick walls of the castle, that she could not see them, or even the faint ray, that probably glimmered through their bars. She then ventured to call; but the wind bore her voice to the other end of the terrace, and then the music was heard as before, in the pause of the gust. Suddenly, she thought she heard a noise in her chamber, and she drew herself within the casement; but, in a moment after, distinguishing Annette's voice at the door, she concluded it was her she had heard before, and she let her in. "Move softly, Annette, to the casement," said she, "and listen with me; the music is returned." They were silent till, the measure changing, Annette exclaimed, "Holy Virgin! I know that song well; it is a French song, one of the favourite songs of my dear country." This was the ballad Emily had heard on a former night, though not the one she had first listened to from the fishing-house in Gascony. "O! it is a Frenchman, that sings," said Annette: "it must be Monsieur Valancourt." "Hark! Annette, do not speak so loud," said Emily, "we may be overheard." "What! by the Chevalier?" said Annette. "No," replied Emily mournfully, "but by somebody, who may report us to the Signor. What reason have you to think it is Monsieur Valancourt, who sings? But hark! now the voice swells louder! Do you recollect those tones? I fear to trust my own judgment." "I never happened to hear the Chevalier sing, Mademoiselle," replied Annette, who, as Emily was disappointed to perceive, had no stronger reason for concluding this to be Valancourt, than that the musician must be a Frenchman. Soon after, she heard the song of the fishing-house, and distinguished her own name, which was repeated so distinctly, that Annette had heard it also. She trembled, sunk into a chair by the window, and Annette called aloud, "Monsieur Valancourt! Monsieur Valancourt!" while Emily endeavoured to check her, but she repeated the call more loudly than before, and the lute and the voice suddenly stopped. Emily listened, for some time, in a state of intolerable suspense; but, no answer being returned, "It does not signify,

Mademoiselle," said Annette; "it is the Chevalier, and I will speak to him." "No, Annette," said Emily, "I think I will speak myself; if it is he, he will know my voice, and speak again." "Who is it," said she, "that sings at this late hour?"

A long silence ensued, and, having repeated the question, she perceived some faint accents, mingling in the blast, that swept by; but the sounds were so distant, and passed so suddenly, that she could scarcely hear them, much less distinguish the words they uttered, or recognise the voice. After another pause, Emily called again; and again they heard a voice, but as faintly as before; and they perceived, that there were other circumstances, besides the strength, and direction of the wind, to content with; for the great depth, at which the casements were fixed in the castle walls, contributed, still more than the distance, to prevent articulated sounds from being understood, though general ones were easily heard. Emily, however, ventured to believe, from the circumstance of her voice alone having been answered, that the stranger was Valancourt, as well as that he knew her, and she gave herself up to speechless joy. Annette, however, was not speechless.—She renewed her calls, but received no answer; and Emily, fearing, that a further attempt, which certainly was, at present, highly dangerous, might expose them to the guards of the castle, while it could not perhaps terminate her suspense, insisted on Annette's dropping the enquiry for this night; though she determined herself to question Ludovico, on the subject, in the morning, more urgently than she had yet done. She was now enabled to say, that the stranger, whom she had formerly heard, was still in the castle, and to direct Ludovico to that part of it, in which he was confined.

Emily, attended by Annette, continued at the casement, for some time, but all remained still; they heard neither lute or voice again, and Emily was now as much oppressed by anxious joy, as she lately was by a sense of her misfortunes. With hasty steps she paced the room, now half calling on Valancourt's name, then suddenly stopping, and now going to the casement and listening, where, however, she heard nothing but the solemn waving of the woods. Sometimes her impatience to speak to Ludovico prompted her to send Annette to call him; but a sense of the impropriety of this at midnight restrained her. Annette, meanwhile, as impatient as her mistress, went as often to the casement to listen, and returned almost as much disappointed. She, at length, mentioned Signor Verezzi, and her fear, lest he should enter the chamber by the staircase, door. "But the night is now almost past, Mademoiselle," said she, recollecting herself; "there is the morning light, beginning to peep over those mountains yonder in the east."

Emily had forgotten, till this moment, that such a person existed as

Verezzi, and all the danger that had appeared to threaten her; but the mention of his name renewed her alarm, and she remembered the old chest, that she had wished to place against the door, which she now, with Annette, attempted to move, but it was so heavy, that they could not lift it from the floor. "What is in this great old chest, Mademoiselle," said Annette, "that makes it so weighty?" Emily having replied, "that she found it in the chamber, when she first came to the castle, and had never examined it."—"Then I will, ma'amselle," said Annette, and she tried to lift the lid; but this was held by a lock, for which she had no key, and which, indeed, appeared, from its peculiar construction, to open with a spring. The morning now glimmered through the casements, and the wind had sunk into a calm. Emily looked out upon the dusky woods, and on the twilight mountains, just stealing in the eye, and saw the whole scene, after the storm, lying in profound stillness, the woods motionless, and the clouds above, through which the dawn trembled, scarcely appearing to move along the heavens. One soldier was pacing the terrace beneath, with measured steps; and two, more distant, were sunk asleep on the walls, wearied with the night's watch. Having inhaled, for a while, the pure spirit of the air, and of vegetation, which the late rains had called forth; and having listened, once more, for a note of music, she now closed the casement, and retired to rest.

CHAPTER IX

> Thus on the chill Lapponian's dreary land,
> For many a long month lost in snow profound,
> When Sol from Cancer sends the seasons bland,
> And in their northern cave the storms hath bound;
> From silent mountains, straight, with startling sound,
> Torrents are hurl'd, green hills emerge, and lo,
> The trees with foliage, cliffs with flow'rs are crown'd;
> Pure rills through vales of verdure warbling go;
> And wonder, love, and joy, the peasant's heart o'erflow.
>   BEATTIE

SEVERAL of her succeeding days passed in suspense, for Ludovico could only learn from the soldiers, that there was a prisoner in the apartment, described to him by Emily, and that he was a Frenchman, whom they had taken in one of their skirmishes, with a party of his countrymen. During this interval, Emily escaped the persecutions of Bertolini, and Verezzi, by confining herself to her apartment; except that sometimes, in an evening, she ventured to walk in the adjoining corridor. Montoni appeared to respect his last promise, though he had prophaned his first; for to his protection only could she attribute her present repose; and in this she was now so secure, that she did not wish to leave the castle, till she could obtain some certainty concerning Valancourt; for which she waited, indeed, without any sacrifice of her own comfort, since no circumstance had occurred to make her escape probable.

On the fourth day, Ludovico informed her, that he had hopes of being admitted to the presence of the prisoner; it being the turn of a soldier, with whom he had been for some time familiar, to attend him on the following night. He was not deceived in his hope; for, under pretence of carrying in a pitcher of water, he entered the prison, though, his prudence having prevented him from telling the sentinel the real motive of his visit, he was obliged to make his conference with the prisoner a very short one.

Emily awaited the result in her own apartment, Ludovico having promised to accompany Annette to the corridor, in the evening; where, after several hours impatiently counted, he arrived. Emily, having then uttered the name of Valancourt, could articulate no more, but hesitated in trembling expectation. "The Chevalier would not entrust me with his name, Signora," replied Ludovico; "but, when I just mentioned yours, he seemed overwhelmed with joy, though he was not so much surprised as I expected." "Does he then remember me?" she exclaimed.

"O! it is Mons. Valancourt," said Annette, and looked impatiently at Ludovico, who understood her look, and replied to Emily: "Yes, lady, the Chevalier does, indeed, remember you, and, I am sure, has a very great regard for you, and I made bold to say you had for him. He then enquired how you came to know he was in the castle, and whether you ordered me to speak to him. The first question I could not answer, but the second I did; and then he went off into his ecstasies again. I was afraid his joy would have betrayed him to the sentinel at the door."

"But how does he look, Ludovico?" interrupted Emily: "is he not melancholy and ill with this long confinement?"—"Why, as to melancholy, I saw no symptom of that, lady, while I was with him, for he seemed in the finest spirits I ever saw any body in, in all my life. His countenance was all joy, and, if one may judge from that, he was very well; but I did not ask him." "Did he send me no message?" said Emily. "O yes, Signora, and something besides," replied Ludovico, who searched his pockets. "Surely, I have not lost it," added he. "The Chevalier said, he would have written, madam, if he had had pen and ink, and was going to have sent a very long message, when the sentinel entered the room, but not before he had given me this." Ludovico then drew forth a miniature from his bosom, which Emily received with a trembling hand, and perceived to be a portrait of herself—the very picture, which her mother had lost so strangely in the fishing-house at La Vallée.

Tears of mingled joy and tenderness flowed to her eyes, while Ludovico proceeded—" 'Tell your lady,' said the Chevalier, as he gave me the picture, 'that this has been my companion, and only solace in all my misfortunes. Tell her, that I have worn it next my heart, and that I sent it her as the pledge of an affection, which can never die; that I would not part with it, but to her, for the wealth of worlds, and that I now part with it, only in the hope of soon receiving it from her hands. Tell her'—Just then, Signora, the sentinel came in, and the Chevalier said no more; but he had before asked me to contrive an interview for him with you; and when I told him, how little hope I had of prevailing with the guard to assist me, he said, that was not, perhaps, of so much consequence as I imagined, and bade me contrive to bring back your answer, and he would inform me of more than he chose to do then. So this, I think, lady, is the whole of what passed."

"How, Ludovico, shall I reward you for your zeal?" said Emily: "but, indeed, I do not now possess the means. When can you see the Chevalier again?" "That is uncertain, Signora," replied he. "It depends upon who stands guard next: there are not more than one or two among them, from whom I would dare to ask admittance to the prison-chamber."

"I need not bid you remember, Ludovico," resumed Emily, "how very much interested I am in your seeing the Chevalier soon; and, when you do so, tell him, that I have received the picture, and, with the sentiments he wished. Tell him I have suffered much, and still suffer—" She paused. "But shall I tell him you will see him, lady?" said Ludovico. "Most certainly I will," replied Emily. "But when, Signora, and where?" "That must depend upon circumstances," returned Emily. "The place, and the hour, must be regulated by his opportunities."

"As to the place, mademoiselle," said Annette, "there is no other place in the castle, besides this corridor, where *we* can see him in safety, you know; and, as for the hour,—it must be when all the Signors are asleep, if that ever happens!" "You may mention these circumstances to the Chevalier, Ludovico," said she, checking the flippancy of Annette, "and leave them to his judgment and opportunity. Tell him, my heart is unchanged. But, above all, let him see you again as soon as possible; and, Ludovico, I think it is needless to tell you I shall very anxiously look for you." Having then wished her good night, Ludovico descended the staircase, and Emily retired to rest, but not to sleep, for joy now rendered her as wakeful, as she had ever been from grief. Montoni and his castle had all vanished from her mind, like the frightful vision of a necromancer, and she wandered, once more, in fairy scenes of unfading happiness:

> As when, beneath the beam
> Of summer moons, the distant woods among,
> Or by some flood, all silver'd with the gleam,
> The soft embodied Fays thro' airy portals stream.

A week elapsed, before Ludovico again visited the prison; for the sentinels, during that period, were men, in whom he could not confide, and he feared to awaken curiosity, by asking to see their prisoner. In this interval, he communicated to Emily terrific reports of what was passing in the castle; of riots, quarrels, and of carousals more alarming than either; while from some circumstances, which he mentioned, she not only doubted, whether Montoni meant ever to release her, but greatly feared, that he had designs, concerning her,—such as she had formerly dreaded. Her name was frequently mentioned in the conversations, which Bertolini and Verezzi held together, and, at those times, they were frequently in contention. Montoni had lost large sums to Verezzi, so that there was a dreadful possibility of his designing her to be a substitute for the debt; but, as she was ignorant, that he had formerly encouraged the hopes of Bertolini also, concerning herself, after the latter had done him some signal service, she knew not how to account for these contentions between Bertolini and Verezzi. The cause of them, however, appeared to be of little consequence, for she thought she saw destruction approaching in many forms, and her entreaties to Ludovico to contrive an escape and to see the prisoner again, were more urgent than ever.

At length, he informed her, that he had again visited the Chevalier, who had directed him to confide in the guard of the prison, from whom he had already received some instances of kindness, and who had promised to permit his going into the castle for half an hour, on the ensuing night, when Montoni and his companions should be engaged at their carousals. "This was kind, to be sure," added Ludovico: "but Sebastian knows he runs no risque in letting the Chevalier out, for, if he can get beyond the bars and iron doors of the castle, he must be cunning indeed. But the Chevalier desired me, Signora, to go to you immediately, and to beg you would allow him to visit you, this night, if it was only for a moment, for that he could no longer live under the same roof, without seeing you; the hour, he said, he could not mention, for it must depend on circumstances (just as you said, Signora); and the place he desired you would appoint, as knowing which was best for your own safety."

Emily was now so much agitated by the near prospect of meeting

Valancourt, that it was some time, before she could give any answer to
Ludovico, or consider of the place of meeting; when she did, she saw
none, that promised so much security, as the corridor, near her own
apartment, which she was checked from leaving, by the apprehension
of meeting any of Montoni's guests, on their way to their rooms; and
she dismissed the scruples, which delicacy opposed, now that a serious
danger was to be avoided by encountering them. It was settled, therefore, that the Chevalier should meet her in the corridor, at that hour of
the night, which Ludovico, who was to be upon the watch, should
judge safest: and Emily, as may be imagined, passed this interval in a
tumult of hope and joy, anxiety and impatience. Never, since her residence in the castle, had she watched, with so much pleasure, the sun
set behind the mountains, and twilight shade, and darkness veil the
scene, as on this evening. She counted the notes of the great clock, and
listened to the steps of the sentinels, as they changed the watch, only to
rejoice, that another hour was gone. "O, Valancourt!" said she, "after
all I have suffered; after our long, long separation, when I thought I
should never—never see you more—we are still to meet again! O! I
have endured grief, and anxiety, and terror, and let me, then, not sink
beneath this joy!" These were moments, when it was impossible for her
to feel emotions of regret, or melancholy, for any ordinary interests;—
even the reflection, that she had resigned the estates, which would
have been a provision for herself and Valancourt for life, threw only a
light and transient shade upon her spirits. The idea of Valancourt, and
that she should see him so soon, alone occupied her heart.

At length the clock struck twelve; she opened the door to listen, if
any noise was in the castle, and heard only distant shouts of riot and
laughter, echoed feebly along the gallery. She guessed, that the Signor
and his guests were at the banquet. "They are now engaged for the
night," said she; "and Valancourt will soon be here." Having softly
closed the door, she paced the room with impatient steps, and often
went to the casement to listen for the lute; but all was silent, and, her
agitation every moment increasing, she was at length unable to support
herself, and sat down by the window. Annette, whom she detained, was,
in the meantime, as loquacious as usual; but Emily heard scarcely any
thing she said, and having at length risen to the casement, she distinguished the chords of the lute, struck with an expressive hand, and then
the voice, she had formerly listened to, accompanied it.

> Now rising love they fann'd, now pleasing dole
> They breath'd in tender musings through the heart;
> And now a graver, sacred strain they stole,
> As when seraphic hands an hymn impart!

Emily wept in doubtful joy and tenderness; and, when the strain ceased, she considered it as a signal, that Valancourt was about to leave the prison. Soon after, she heard steps in the corridor;—they were the light, quick steps of hope; she could scarcely support herself, as they approached, but opening the door of the apartment, she advanced to meet Valancourt, and, in the next moment, sunk in the arms of a stranger. His voice—his countenance instantly convinced her, and she fainted away.

On reviving, she found herself supported by the stranger, who was watching over her recovery, with a countenance of ineffable tenderness and anxiety. She had no spirits for reply, or enquiry; she asked no questions, but burst into tears, and disengaged herself from his arms; when the expression of his countenance changed to surprise and disappointment, and he turned to Ludovico, for an explanation; Annette soon gave the information, which Ludovico could not. "O, sir!" said she, in a voice, interrupted with sobs; "O, sir! you are not the other Chevalier. We expected Monsieur Valancourt, but you are not he! O Ludovico! how could you deceive us so? my poor lady will never recover it— never!" The stranger, who now appeared much agitated, attempted to speak, but his words faltered; and then striking his hand against his forehead, as if in sudden despair, he walked abruptly to the other end of the corridor.

Suddenly, Annette dried her tears, and spoke to Ludovico. "But, perhaps," said she, "after all, the other Chevalier is not this: perhaps the Chevalier Valancourt is still below." Emily raised her head. "No," replied Ludovico, "Monsieur Valancourt never was below, if this gentleman is not he." "If you, sir," said Ludovico, addressing the stranger, "would but have had the goodness to trust me with your name, this mistake had been avoided." "Most true," replied the stranger, speaking in broken Italian, "but it was of the utmost consequence to me, that my name should be concealed from Montoni. Madam," added he then, addressing Emily in French, "will you permit me to apologize for the pain I have occasioned you, and to explain to you alone my name, and the circumstance, which has led me into this error? I am of France;— I am your countryman;—we are met in a foreign land." Emily tried to compose her spirits; yet she hesitated to grant his request. At length, desiring, that Ludovico would wait on the stair-case, and detaining Annette, she told the stranger, that her woman understood very little Italian, and begged he would communicate what he wished to say, in that language.—Having withdrawn to a distant part of the corridor, he said, with a long-drawn sigh, "You, madam, are no stranger to me, though I am so unhappy as to be unknown to you.—My name is Du Pont; I am of France, of Gascony, your native province, and have long admired,—and, why should I affect to disguise it?—have long loved you." He paused, but, in the next moment, proceeded. "My family, madam, is probably not unknown to you, for we lived within a few miles of La Vallée, and I have, sometimes, had the happiness of meeting you, on visits in the neighbourhood. I will not offend you by repeating how much you interested me; how much I loved to wander in the scenes you frequented; how often I visited your favourite fishing-house, and lamented the circumstance, which, at that time, forbade me to reveal my passion. I will not explain how I surrendered to temptation, and became possessed of a treasure, which was to me inestimable; a treasure, which I committed to your messenger, a few days ago, with expectations very different from my present ones. I will say nothing of these circumstances, for I know they will avail me little; let me only supplicate from you forgiveness, and the picture, which I so unwarily returned. Your generosity will pardon the theft, and restore the prize. My crime has been my punishment; for the portrait I stole has contributed to nourish a passion, which must still be my torment."

Emily now interrupted him. "I think, sir, I may leave it to your integrity to determine, whether, after what has just appeared, concerning Mons. Valancourt, I ought to return the picture. I think you will acknowledge, that this would not be generosity; and you will allow me to add, that it would be doing myself an injustice. I must consider myself honoured by your good opinion, but"—and she hesitated,— "the mistake of this evening makes it unnecessary for me to say more."

"It does, madam,—alas! it does!" said the stranger, who, after a long pause, proceeded.—"But you will allow me to shew my disinterestedness, though not my love, and will accept the services I offer. Yet, alas! what services can I offer? I am myself a prisoner, a sufferer, like you. But, dear as liberty is to me, I would not seek it through half the hazards I would encounter to deliver you from this recess of vice. Accept the offered services of a friend; do not refuse me the reward of having, at least, attempted to deserve your thanks."

"You deserve them already, sir," said Emily; "the wish deserves my warmest thanks. But you will excuse me for reminding you of the danger you incur by prolonging this interview. It will be a great consolation to me to remember, whether your friendly attempts to release me succeed or not, that I have a countryman, who would so generously protect me."—Monsieur Du Pont took her hand, which she but feebly attempted to withdraw, and pressed it respectfully to his lips. "Allow me to breathe another fervent sigh for your happiness," said he, "and to applaud myself for an affection, which I cannot conquer." As he said this, Emily heard a noise from her apartment, and, turning round, saw the door from the stair-case open, and a man rush into her chamber. "I will teach you to conquer it," cried he, as he advanced into the corridor, and drew a stiletto, which he aimed at Du Pont, who was unarmed, but who, stepping back, avoided the blow, and then sprung upon Verezzi, from whom he wrenched the stiletto. While they struggled in each other's grasp, Emily, followed by Annette, ran further into the corridor, calling on Ludovico, who was, however, gone from the stair-case, and, as she advanced, terrified and uncertain what to do, a distant noise, that seemed to arise from the hall, reminded her of the danger she was incurring; and, sending Annette forward in search of Ludovico, she returned to the spot where Du Pont and Verezzi were still struggling for victory. It was her own cause which was to be decided with that of the former, whose conduct, independently of this circumstance, would, however, have interested her in his success, even had she not disliked and dreaded Verezzi. She threw herself in a chair, and supplicated them to desist from further violence, till, at length, Du Pont forced Verezzi to the floor, where he lay stunned by the violence of his fall; and she then entreated Du Pont to escape from the room, before Montoni, or his party, should appear; but he still refused to leave her unprotected; and, while Emily, now more terrified for him, than for herself, enforced the entreaty, they heard steps ascending the private stair-case.

"O you are lost!" cried she, "these are Montoni's people." Du Pont made no reply, but supported Emily, while, with a steady, though eager, countenance, he awaited their appearance, and, in the next moment, Ludovico, alone, mounted the landing-place. Throwing an hasty glance round the chamber, "Follow me," said he, "as you value your lives; we have not an instant to lose!"

Emily enquired what had occurred, and whither they were to go?

"I cannot stay to tell you now, Signora," replied Ludovico: "fly! fly!"

She immediately followed him, accompanied by Mons. Du Pont, down the stair-case, and along a vaulted passage, when suddenly she recollected Annette, and enquired for her. "She awaits us further on, Signora," said Ludovico, almost breathless with haste; "the gates were open, a moment since, to a party just come in from the mountains: they will be shut, I fear, before we can reach them! Through this door, Signora," added Ludovico, holding down the lamp, "take care, here are two steps."

Emily followed, trembling still more, than before she had understood, that her escape from the castle, depended upon the present moment; while Du Pont supported her, and endeavoured, as they passed along, to cheer her spirits.

"Speak low, Signor," said Ludovico, "these passages send echoes all round the castle."

"Take care of the light," cried Emily, "you go so fast, that the air will extinguish it."

Ludovico now opened another door, where they found Annette, and the party then descended a short flight of steps into a passage, which, Ludovico said, led round the inner court of the castle, and opened into the outer one. As they advanced, confused and tumultuous sounds, that seemed to come from the inner court, alarmed Emily. "Nay, Signora," said Ludovico, "our only hope is in that tumult; while the Signor's people are busied about the men, who are just arrived, we may, perhaps, pass unnoticed through the gates. But hush!" he added, as they approached the small door, that opened into the outer court, "if you will remain here a moment, I will go to see whether the gates are open, and any body is in the way. Pray extinguish the light, Signor, if you hear me talking," continued Ludovico, delivering the lamp to Du Pont, "and remain quite still."

Saying this, he stepped out upon the court, and they closed the door, listening anxiously to his departing steps. No voice, however, was heard in the court, which he was crossing, though a confusion of many voices yet issued from the inner one. "We shall soon be beyond the walls," said Du Pont softly to Emily, "support yourself a little longer, Madam, and all will be well."

But soon they heard Ludovico speaking loud, and the voice also of some other person, and Du Pont immediately extinguished the lamp. "Ah! it is too late!" exclaimed Emily, "what is to become of us?" They listened again, and then perceived, that Ludovico was talking with a sentinel, whose voices were heard also by Emily's favourite dog, that had followed her from the chamber, and now barked loudly. "This dog will betray us!" said Du Pont, "I will hold him." "I fear he has already betrayed us!" replied Emily. Du Pont, however, caught him up, and, again listening to what was going on without, they heard Ludovico say, "I'll watch the gates the while."

"Stay a minute," replied the sentinel, "and you need not have the trouble, for the horses will be sent round to the outer stables, then the gates will be shut, and I can leave my post." "I don't mind the trouble, comrade," said Ludovico, "you will do such another good turn for me, some time. Go—go, and fetch the wine; the rogues, that are just come in, will drink it all else."

The soldier hesitated, and then called aloud to the people in the second court, to know why they did not send out the horses, that the gates might be shut; but they were too much engaged, to attend to him, even if they had heard his voice.

"Aye—aye," said Ludovico, "they know better than that; they are sharing it all among them; if you wait till the horses come out, you must wait till the wine is drunk. I have had my share already, but, since you do not care about yours, I see no reason why I should not have that too."

"Hold, hold, not so fast," cried the sentinel, "do watch then, for a moment: I'll be with you presently."

"Don't hurry yourself," said Ludovico, coolly, "I have kept guard before now. But you may leave me your trombone,* that, if the castle should be attacked, you know, I may be able to defend the pass, like a hero."

"There, my good fellow," returned the soldier, "there, take it—it has seen service, though it could do little in defending the castle. I'll tell you a good story, though, about this same trombone."

"You'll tell it better when you have had the wine," said Ludovico. "There! they are coming out from the court already."

"I'll have the wine, though," said the sentinel, running off. "I won't keep you a minute."

"Take your time, I am in no haste," replied Ludovico, who was already hurrying across the court, when the soldier came back. "Whither so fast, friend—whither so fast?" said the latter. "What! is this the way you keep watch! I must stand to my post myself, I see."

"Aye, well," replied Ludovico, "you have saved me the trouble of following you further, for I wanted to tell you, if you have a mind to drink the Tuscany wine, you must go to Sebastian, he is dealing it out; the other that Federico has, is not worth having. But you are not likely to have any, I see, for they are all coming out."

"By St. Peter! so they are," said the soldier, and again ran off, while Ludovico, once more at liberty, hastened to the door of the passage, where Emily was sinking under the anxiety this long discourse had occasioned; but, on his telling them the court was clear, they followed him to the gates, without waiting another instant, yet not before he had seized two horses, that had strayed from the second court, and were picking a scanty meal among the grass, which grew between the pavement of the first.

They passed, without interruption, the dreadful gates, and took the road that led down among the woods, Emily, Monsieur Du Pont and Annette on foot, and Ludovico, who was mounted on one horse, leading the other. Having reached them, they stopped, while Emily and Annette were placed on horseback with their two protectors, when, Ludovico leading the way, they set off as fast as the broken road, and the feeble light, which a rising moon threw among the foliage, would permit.

*A kind of blunderbuss. [A. R.]

Emily was so much astonished by this sudden departure, that she scarcely dared to believe herself awake; and she yet much doubted whether this adventure would terminate in escape,—a doubt, which had too much probability to justify it; for, before they quitted the woods, they heard shouts in the wind, and, on emerging from them, saw lights moving quickly near the castle above. Du Pont whipped his horse, and with some difficulty compelled him to go faster.

"Ah! poor beast," said Ludovico, "he is weary enough;—he has been out all day; but, Signor, we must fly for it, now; for yonder are lights coming this way."

Having given his own horse a lash, they now both set off on a full gallop; and, when they again looked back, the lights were so distant as scarcely to be discerned, and the voices were sunk into silence. The travellers then abated their pace, and, consulting whither they should direct their course, it was determined they should descend into Tuscany, and endeavour to reach the Mediterranean, where they could readily embark for France. Thither Du Pont meant to attend Emily, if he should learn, that the regiment he had accompanied into Italy, was returned to his native country.

They were now in the road, which Emily had travelled with Ugo and Bertrand; but Ludovico, who was the only one of the party, acquainted with the passes of these mountains, said, that, a little further on, a bye-road, branching from this, would lead them down into Tuscany with very little difficulty; and that, at a few leagues distance, was a small town, where necessaries could be procured for their journey.

"But, I hope," added he, "we shall meet with no straggling parties of banditti; some of them are abroad, I know. However, I have got a good trombone, which will be of some service, if we should encounter any of those brave spirits. You have no arms, Signor?" "Yes," replied Du Pont, "I have the villain's stilletto, who would have stabbed me—but let us rejoice in our escape from Udolpho, nor torment ourselves with looking out for dangers, that may never arrive."

The moon was now risen high over the woods, that hung upon the sides of the narrow glen, through which they wandered, and afforded them light sufficient to distinguish their way, and to avoid the loose and broken stones, that frequently crossed it. They now travelled leisurely, and in profound silence; for they had scarcely yet recovered from the astonishment, into which this sudden escape had thrown them.— Emily's mind, especially, was sunk, after the various emotions it had suffered, into a kind of musing stillness, which the reposing beauty of the surrounding scene and the creeping murmur of the night-breeze among the foliage above contributed to prolong. She thought of Valancourt and of France, with hope, and she would have thought of them with joy, had not the first events of this evening harassed her spirits too much, to permit her now to feel so lively a sensation. Meanwhile, Emily was alone the object of Du Pont's melancholy consideration; yet, with the despondency he suffered, as he mused on his recent disappointment, was mingled a sweet pleasure, occasioned by her presence, though they did not now exchange a single word. Annette thought of this wonderful escape, of the bustle in which Montoni and his people must be, now that their flight was discovered; of her native country, whither she hoped she was returning, and of her marriage with Ludovico, to which there no longer appeared any impediment, for poverty she did not consider such. Ludovico, on his part, congratulated himself, on having rescued his Annette and Signora Emily from the danger, that had surrounded them; on his own liberation from people, whose manners he had long detested; on the freedom he had given to Monsieur Du Pont; on his prospect of happiness with the object of his affections, and not a little on the address, with which he had deceived the sentinel, and conducted the whole of this affair.

Thus variously engaged in thought, the travellers passed on silently, for above an hour, a question only being, now and then, asked by Du Pont, concerning the road, or a remark uttered by Annette, respecting objects, seen imperfectly in the twilight. At length, lights were perceived twinkling on the side of a mountain, and Ludovico had no doubt, that they proceeded from the town he had mentioned, while his companions, satisfied by this assurance, sunk again into silence. Annette was the first who interrupted this. "Holy Peter!" said she, "What shall we do for money on our journey? for I know neither I, or my lady, have a single sequin; the Signor took care of that!"

This remark produced a serious enquiry, which ended in as serious an embarrassment, for Du Pont had been rifled of nearly all his money, when he was taken prisoner; the remainder he had given to the sentinel, who had enabled him occasionally to leave his prison-chamber; and Ludovico, who had for some time found a difficulty, in procuring any part of the wages due to him, had now scarcely cash sufficient to procure necessary refreshment at the first town, in which they should arrive.

Their poverty was the more distressing, since it would detain them among the mountains, where, even in a town, they could scarcely consider themselves safe from Montoni. The travellers, however, had only to proceed and dare the future; and they continued their way through lonely wilds and dusky vallies, where the overhanging foliage now admitted, and then excluded the moon-light;—wilds so desolate, that they appeared, on the first glance, as if no human being had ever trode them before. Even the road, in which the party were, did but slightly contradict this error, for the high grass and other luxuriant vegetation, with which it was overgrown, told how very seldom the foot of a traveller had passed it.

At length, from a distance, was heard the faint tinkling of a sheep-bell; and, soon after, the bleat of flocks, and the party then knew, that they were near some human habitation, for the light, which Ludovico had fancied to proceed from a town, had long been concealed by intervening mountains. Cheered by this hope, they quickened their pace along the narrow pass they were winding, and it opened upon one of those pastoral vallies of the Apennines, which might be painted for a scene of Arcadia, and whose beauty and simplicity are finely contrasted by the grandeur of the snow-topt mountains above.

The morning light, now glimmering in the horizon, shewed faintly, at a little distance, upon the brow of a hill, which seemed to peep from "under the opening eye-lids of the morn," the town they were in search of, and which they soon after reached. It was not without some difficulty, that they there found a house, which could afford shelter for themselves and their horses; and Emily desired they might not rest longer than was necessary for refreshment. Her appearance excited some surprise, for she was without a hat, having had time only to throw on her veil before she left the castle, a circumstance, that compelled her to regret again the want of money, without which it was impossible to procure this necessary article of dress.

Ludovico, on examining his purse, found it even insufficient to supply present refreshment, and Du Pont, at length, ventured to inform the landlord, whose countenance was simple and honest, of their exact situation, and requested, that he would assist them to pursue their journey; a purpose, which he promised to comply with, as far as he was able, when he learned that they were prisoners escaping from Montoni, whom he had too much reason to hate. But, though he consented to lend them fresh horses to carry them to the next town, he was too poor himself to trust them with money, and they were again lamenting their poverty, when Ludovico, who had been with his tired horses to the hovel, which served for a stable, entered the room, half frantic with joy, in which his auditors soon participated. On removing the saddle from one of the horses, he had found beneath it a small bag, containing, no doubt, the booty of one of the *condottieri*, who had returned from a plundering excursion, just before Ludovico left the castle, and whose horse having strayed from the inner court, while his master was engaged in drinking, had brought away the treasure, which the ruffian had considered the reward of his exploit.

On counting over this, Du Pont found, that it would be more than sufficient to carry them all to France, where he now determined to accompany Emily, whether he should obtain intelligence of his regiment, or not; for, though he had as much confidence in the integrity of Ludovico, as his small knowledge of him allowed, he could not endure the thought of committing her to his care for the voyage; nor, perhaps, had he resolution enough to deny himself the dangerous pleasure, which he might derive from her presence.

He now consulted them, concerning the sea-port, to which they should direct their way, and Ludovico, better informed of the geography of the country, said, that Leghorn was the nearest port of consequence, which Du Pont knew also to be the most likely of any in Italy to assist their plan, since from thence vessels of all nations were continually departing. Thither, therefore, it was determined, that they should proceed.

Emily, having purchased a little straw hat, such as was worn by the peasant girls of Tuscany, and some other little necessary equipments for the journey, and the travellers, having exchanged their tired horses for others better able to carry them, re-commenced their joyous way, as the sun was rising over the mountains, and, after travelling through this romantic country, for several hours, began to descend into the vale of Arno. And here Emily beheld all the charms of sylvan and pastoral landscape united, adorned with the elegant villas of the Florentine nobles, and diversified with the various riches of cultivation. How vivid the shrubs, that embowered the slopes, with the woods, that stretched amphitheatrically along the mountains! and, above all, how elegant the outline of these waving Apennines, now softening from the wildness, which their interior regions exhibited! At a distance, in the east, Emily discovered Florence, with its towers rising on the brilliant horizon, and its luxuriant plain, spreading to the feet of the Apennines, speckled with gardens and magnificent villas, or coloured with groves of orange and lemon, with vines, corn, and plantations of olives and mulberry; while, to the west, the vale opened to the waters of the Mediterranean, so distant, that they were known only by a blueish line, that appeared upon the horizon, and by the light marine vapour, which just stained the æther above.

With a full heart, Emily hailed the waves, that were to bear her back to her native country, the remembrance of which, however, brought with it a pang; for she had there no home to receive, no parents to welcome her, but was going, like a forlorn pilgrim, to weep over the sad spot, where he, who *was* her father, lay interred. Nor were her spirits cheered, when she considered how long it would probably be before she should see Valancourt, who might be stationed with his regiment in a distant part of France, and that, when they did meet, it would be only to lament the successful villany of Montoni; yet, still she would have felt inexpressible delight at the thought of being once more in the same country with Valancourt, had it even been certain, that she could not see him.

The intense heat, for it was now noon, obliged the travellers to look out for a shady recess, where they might rest, for a few hours, and the neighbouring thickets, abounding with wild grapes, raspberries, and figs, promised them grateful refreshment. Soon after, they turned from the road into a grove, whose thick foliage entirely excluded the sunbeams, and where a spring, gushing from the rock, gave coolness to the air; and, having alighted and turned the horses to graze, Annette and Ludovico ran to gather fruit from the surrounding thickets, of which they soon returned with an abundance. The travellers, seated under the shade of a pine and cypress grove and on turf, enriched with such a profusion of fragrant flowers, as Emily had scarcely ever seen, even among the Pyrenées, took their simple repast, and viewed, with new delight, beneath the dark umbrage of gigantic pines, the glowing landscape stretching to the sea.

Emily and Du Pont gradually became thoughtful and silent; but Annette was all joy and loquacity, and Ludovico was gay, without forgetting the respectful distance, which was due to his companions. The repast being over, Du Pont recommended Emily to endeavour to sleep, during these sultry hours, and, desiring the servants would do the same, said he would watch the while; but Ludovico wished to spare him this trouble; and Emily and Annette, wearied with travelling, tried to repose, while he stood guard with his trombone.

When Emily, refreshed by slumber, awoke, she found the sentinel asleep on his post and Du Pont awake, but lost in melancholy thought. As the sun was yet too high to allow them to continue their journey, and as it was necessary, that Ludovico, after the toils and trouble he had suffered, should finish his sleep, Emily took this opportunity of enquiring by what accident Du Pont became Montoni's prisoner, and he, pleased with the interest this enquiry expressed and with the excuse it gave him for talking to her of himself, immediately answered her curiosity.

"I came into Italy, madam," said Du Pont, "in the service of my country. In an adventure among the mountains our party, engaging with the bands of Montoni, was routed, and I, with a few of my comrades, was taken prisoner. When they told me, whose captive I was, the name of Montoni struck me, for I remembered, that Madame Cheron, your aunt, had married an Italian of that name, and that you had accompanied them into Italy. It was not, however, till some time after, that I became convinced this was the same Montoni, or learned that you, madam, was under the same roof with myself. I will not pain you by describing what were my emotions upon this discovery, which I owed to a sentinel, whom I had so far won to my interest, that he granted me many indulgences, one of which was very important to me, and somewhat dangerous to himself; but he persisted in refusing to convey any letter, or notice of my situation to you, for he justly dreaded a discovery and the consequent vengeance of Montoni. He however enabled me to see you more than once. You are surprised, madam, and I will explain myself. My health and spirits suffered extremely from want of air and exercise, and, at length, I gained so far upon the pity, or the avarice of the man, that he gave me the means of walking on the terrace."

Emily now listened, with very anxious attention, to the narrative of Du Pont, who proceeded:

"In granting this indulgence, he knew, that he had nothing to apprehend from a chance of my escaping from a castle, which was vigilantly guarded, and the nearest terrace of which rose over a perpendicular rock; he shewed me also," continued Du Pont, "a door concealed in the cedar wainscot of the apartment where I was confined, which he instructed me how to open; and which, leading into a passage, formed within the thickness of the wall, that extended far along the castle, finally opened in an obscure corner of the eastern rampart. I have since been informed, that there are many passages of the same kind concealed within the prodigious walls of that edifice, and which were, undoubtedly, contrived for the purpose of facilitating escapes in time of war. Through this avenue, at the dead of night, I often stole to the terrace, where I walked with the utmost caution, lest my steps should betray me to the sentinels on duty in distant parts; for this end of it, being guarded by high buildings, was not watched by soldiers. In one of these midnight wanderings, I saw light in a casement that overlooked the rampart, and which, I observed, was immediately over my prison-chamber. It occurred to me, that you might be in that apartment, and, with the hope of seeing you, I placed myself opposite to the window."

Emily, remembering the figure that had formerly appeared on the terrace, and which had occasioned her so much anxiety, exclaimed, "It was you then, Monsieur Du Pont, who occasioned me much foolish terror; my spirits were, at that time, so much weakened by long suffering, that they took alarm at every hint." Du Pont, after lamenting, that he had occasioned her any apprehension, added, "As I rested on the wall, opposite to your casement, the consideration of your melancholy situation and of my own called from me involuntary sounds of lamentation, which drew you, I fancy, to the casement; I saw there a person, whom I believed to be you. O! I will say nothing of my emotion at that moment; I wished to speak, but prudence restrained me, till the distant foot-step of a sentinel compelled me suddenly to quit my station.

"It was some time, before I had another opportunity of walking, for I could only leave my prison, when it happened to be the turn of one man to guard me; meanwhile I became convinced from some circumstances related by him, that your apartment was over mine, and, when again I ventured forth, I returned to your casement, where again I saw you, but without daring to speak. I waved my hand, and you suddenly disappeared; then it was, that I forgot my prudence, and yielded to lamentation; again you appeared—you spoke—I heard the well-known accent of your voice! and, at that moment, my discretion would have forsaken me again, had I not heard also the approaching steps of a soldier, when I instantly quitted the place, though not before the man had seen me. He followed down the terrace and gained so fast upon me, that I was compelled to make use of a stratagem, ridiculous enough, to save myself. I had heard of the superstition of many of these men, and I uttered a strange noise, with a hope, that my pursuer would mistake it for something supernatural, and desist from pursuit. Luckily for myself I succeeded; the man, it seems, was subject to fits, and the terror he suffered threw him into one, by which accident I secured my retreat. A sense of the danger I had escaped, and the increased watchfulness, which my appearance had occasioned among the sentinels, deterred me ever after from walking on the terrace; but, in the stillness of night, I frequently beguiled myself with an old lute, procured for me by a soldier, which I sometimes accompanied with my voice, and sometimes, I will acknowledge, with a hope of making myself heard by you; but it was only a few evenings ago, that this hope was answered. I then thought I heard a voice in the wind, calling me; yet, even then I feared to reply, lest the sentinel at the prison door should hear me. Was I right, madam, in this conjecture—was it you who spoke?"

"Yes," said Emily, with an involuntary sigh, "you was right indeed."

Du Pont, observing the painful emotions, which this question revived, now changed the subject. "In one of my excursions through the passage, which I have mentioned, I overheard a singular conversation," said he.

"In the passage!" said Emily, with surprise.

"I heard it in the passage," said Du Pont, "but it proceeded from an apartment, adjoining the wall, within which the passage wound, and the shell of the wall was there so thin, and was also somewhat decayed, that I could distinctly hear every word, spoken on the other side. It happened that Montoni and his companions were assembled in the room, and Montoni began to relate the extraordinary history of the lady, his predecessor, in the castle. He did, indeed, mention some very surprising circumstances, and whether they were strictly true, his conscience must decide; I fear it will determine against him. But you, madam, have doubtless heard the report, which he designs should circulate, on the subject of that lady's mysterious fate."

"I have, sir," replied Emily, "and I perceive, that you doubt it."

"I doubted it before the period I am speaking of," rejoined Du Pont;—"but some circumstances, mentioned by Montoni, greatly contributed to my suspicions. The account I then heard, almost convinced me, that he was a murderer. I trembled for you;—the more so that I had heard the guests mention your name in a manner, that threatened your repose; and, knowing, that the most impious men are often the most superstitious, I determined to try whether I could not awaken their consciences, and awe them from the commission of the crime I dreaded. I listened closely to Montoni, and, in the most striking passages of his story, I joined my voice, and repeated his last words, in a disguised and hollow tone."

"But was you not afraid of being discovered?" said Emily.

"I was not," replied Du Pont; "for I knew, that, if Montoni had been acquainted with the secret of this passage, he would not have confined me in the apartment, to which it led. I knew also, from better authority, that he was ignorant of it. The party, for some time, appeared inattentive to my voice; but, at length, were so much alarmed, that they quitted the apartment; and, having heard Montoni order his servants to search it, I returned to my prison, which was very distant from this part of the passage." "I remember perfectly to have heard of the conversation you mention," said Emily; "it spread a general alarm among Montoni's people, and I will own I was weak enough to partake of it."

Monsieur Du Pont and Emily thus continued to converse of Montoni, and then of France, and of the plan of their voyage; when Emily told him, that it was her intention to retire to a convent in Languedoc, where she had been formerly treated with much kindness, and from thence to write to her relation Monsieur Quesnel, and inform him of her conduct. There, she designed to wait, till La Vallée should again be her own, whither she hoped her income would some time permit her to return; for Du Pont now taught her to expect, that the estate, of which Montoni had attempted to defraud her, was not irrecoverably lost, and he again congratulated her on her escape from Montoni, who, he had not a doubt, meant to have detained her for life. The possibility of recovering her aunt's estates for Valancourt and herself lighted up a joy in Emily's heart, such as she had not known for many months; but she endeavoured to conceal this from Monsieur Du Pont, lest it should lead him to a painful remembrance of his rival.

They continued to converse, till the sun was declining in the west, when Du Pont awoke Ludovico, and they set forward on their journey. Gradually descending the lower slopes of the valley, they reached the Arno, and wound along its pastoral margin, for many miles, delighted with the scenery around them, and with the remembrances, which its classic waves revived. At a distance, they heard the gay song of the peasants among the vineyards, and observed the setting sun tint the waves with yellow lustre, and twilight draw a dusky purple over the mountains, which, at length, deepened into night. Then the *lucciola*, the fire-fly of Tuscany, was seen to flash its sudden sparks among the foliage, while the *cicala*, with its shrill note, became more clamorous than even during the noon-day heat, loving best the hour when the English beetle, with less offensive sound,

> winds
> His small but sullen horn,
> As oft he rises 'midst the twilight path,
> Against the pilgrim borne in heedless hum.*

The travellers crossed the Arno by moon-light, at a ferry, and, learning that Pisa was distant only a few miles down the river, they wished to have proceeded thither in a boat, but, as none could be procured, they set out on their wearied horses for that city. As they approached it, the vale expanded into a plain, variegated with vineyards, corn, olives and mulberry groves; but it was late, before they reached its gates, where Emily was surprised to hear the busy sound of footsteps and the tones of musical instruments, as well as to see the lively groups, that filled the streets, and she almost fancied herself again at Venice; but here was no moon-light sea—no gay gondolas, dashing the waves,—no *Palladian* palaces, to throw enchantment over the fancy and lead it into the wilds of fairy story. The Arno rolled through the town, but no music trembled from balconies over its waters; it gave only the busy voices of sailors on board vessels just arrived from the Mediterranean; the melancholy heaving of the anchor, and the shrill boatswain's whistle;—sounds, which, since that period, have there sunk almost into silence. They then served to remind Du Pont, that it was probable he might hear of a vessel, sailing soon to France from this port, and thus be spared the trouble of going to Leghorn. As soon as Emily had reached the inn, he went therefore to the quay, to make his enquiries; but, after all the endeavours of himself and Ludovico, they could hear of no bark, destined immediately for France, and the travellers returned to their resting-place. Here also, Du Pont endeavoured to learn where his regiment

---

*COLLINS. [A. R.]

then lay, but could acquire no information concerning it. The travellers retired early to rest, after the fatigues of this day; and, on the following, rose early, and, without pausing to view the celebrated antiquities of the place, or the wonders of its hanging tower, pursued their journey in the cooler hours, through a charming country, rich with wine, and corn and oil. The Apennines, no longer awful, or even grand, here softened into the beauty of sylvan and pastoral landscape; and Emily, as she descended them, looked down delighted on Leghorn, and its spacious bay, filled with vessels, and crowned with these beautiful hills.

She was no less surprised and amused, on entering this town, to find it crowded with persons in the dresses of all nations; a scene, which reminded her of a Venetian masquerade, such as she had witnessed at the time of the Carnival; but here, was bustle, without gaiety, and noise instead of music, while elegance was to be looked for only in the waving outlines of the surrounding hills.

Monsieur Du Pont, immediately on their arrival, went down to the quay, where he heard of several French vessels, and of one, that was to sail, in a few days, for Marseilles, from whence another vessel could be procured, without difficulty, to take them across the gulf of Lyons towards Narbonne, on the coast not many leagues from which city he understood the convent was seated, to which Emily wished to retire. He, therefore, immediately engaged with the captain to take them to Marseilles, and Emily was delighted to hear, that her passage to France was secured. Her mind was now relieved from the terror of pursuit, and the pleasing hope of soon seeing her native country—that country which held Valancourt, restored to her spirits a degree of cheerfulness, such as she had scarcely known, since the death of her father. At Leghorn also, Du Pont heard of his regiment, and that it had embarked for France; a circumstance, which gave him great satisfaction, for he could now accompany Emily thither, without reproach to his conscience, or apprehension of displeasure from his commander. During these days, he scrupulously forbore to distress her by a mention of his passion, and she was compelled to esteem and pity, though she could not love him. He endeavoured to amuse her by shewing the environs of the town, and they often walked together on the seashore, and on the busy quays, where Emily was frequently interested by the arrival and departure of vessels, participating in the joy of meeting friends, and, sometimes, shedding a sympathetic tear to the sorrow of those, that were separating. It was after having witnessed a scene of the latter kind, that she arranged the following stanzas:

THE MARINER

Soft came the breath of spring; smooth flow'd the tide;
And blue the heaven in its mirror smil'd;
The white sail trembled, swell'd, expanded wide,
The busy sailors at the anchor toil'd.

With anxious friends, that shed the parting tear,
The deck was throng'd—how swift the moments fly!
The vessel heaves, the farewel signs appear;
Mute is each tongue, and eloquent each eye!

The last dread moment comes!—The sailor-youth
Hides the big drop, then smiles amid his pain,
Sooths his sad bride, and vows eternal truth,
"Farewel, my love—we shall—shall meet again!"

Long on the stern, with waving hand, he stood;
The crowded shore sinks, lessening, from his view,
As gradual glides the bark along the flood;
His bride is seen no more—"Adieu!—adieu!"

The breeze of Eve moans low, her smile is o'er,
Dim steals her twilight down the crimson'd west,
He climbs the top-most mast, to seek once more
The far-seen coast, where all his wishes rest.

He views its dark line on the distant sky,
And Fancy leads him to his little home,
He sees his weeping love, he hears her sigh,
He sooths her griefs, and tells of joys to come.

Eve yields to night, the breeze to wintry gales,
In one vast shade the seas and shores repose;
He turns his aching eyes,—his spirit fails,
The chill tear falls;—sad to the deck he goes!

The storm of midnight swells, the sails are furl'd,
Deep sounds the lead, but finds no friendly shore,
Fast o'er the waves the wretched bark is hurl'd,
"O Ellen, Ellen! we must meet no more!"

Lightnings, that shew the vast and foamy deep,
The rending thunders, as they onward roll,
The loud, loud winds, that o'er the billows sweep—
Shake the firm nerve, appall the bravest soul!

Ah! what avails the seamen's toiling care!
The straining cordage bursts, the mast is riv'n;
The sounds of terror groan along the air,
Then sink afar;—the bark on rocks is driv'n!

Fierce o'er the wreck the whelming waters pass'd,
The helpless crew sunk in the roaring main!
Henry's faint accents trembled in the blast—
"Farewel, my love!—we ne'er shall meet again!"

Oft, at the calm and silent evening hour,
When summer-breezes linger on the wave,
A melancholy voice is heard to pour
Its lonely sweetness o'er poor Henry's grave!

And oft, at midnight, airy strains are heard
Around the grove, where Ellen's form is laid;
Nor is the dirge by village-maidens fear'd,
For lovers' spirits guard the holy shade!

CHAPTER X

Oh! the joy
Of young ideas, painted on the mind
In the warm glowing colours fancy spreads
On objects not yet known, when all is new,
And all is lovely!

SACRED DRAMAS

WE now return to Languedoc and to the mention of Count De Villefort, the nobleman, who succeeded to an estate of the Marquis De Villeroi situated near the monastery of St. Claire. It may be recollected, that this chateau was uninhabited, when St. Aubert and his daughter were in the neighbourhood, and that the former was much affected on discovering himself to be so near Chateau-le-Blanc, a place, concerning which the good old La Voisin afterwards dropped some hints, that had alarmed Emily's curiosity.

It was in the year 1584, the beginning of that, in which St. Aubert died, that Francis Beauveau, Count De Villefort, came into possession of the mansion and extensive domain called Chateau-le-Blanc, situated in the province of Languedoc, on the shore of the Mediterranean. This estate, which, during some centuries, had belonged to his family, now descended to him, on the decease of his relative, the Marquis De Villeroi, who had been latterly a man of reserved manners and austere character; circumstances, which, together with the duties of his profession, that often called him into the field, had prevented any degree of intimacy with his cousin, the Count De Villefort. For many years, they had known little of each other, and the Count received the first intelligence of his death, which happened in a distant part of France, together with the instruments, that gave him possession of the domain

Chateau-le-Blanc; but it was not till the following year, that he determined to visit that estate, when he designed to pass the autumn there. The scenes of Chateau-le-Blanc often came to his remembrance, heightened by the touches, which a warm imagination gives to the recollection of early pleasures; for, many years before, in the life-time of the Marchioness, and at that age when the mind is particularly sensible to impressions of gaiety and delight, he had once visited this spot, and, though he had passed a long intervening period amidst the vexations and tumults of public affairs, which too frequently corrode the heart, and vitiate the taste, the shades of Languedoc and the grandeur of its distant scenery had never been remembered by him with indifference.

During many years, the chateau had been abandoned by the late Marquis, and, being inhabited only by an old steward and his wife, had been suffered to fall much into decay. To superintend the repairs, that would be requisite to make it a comfortable residence, had been a principal motive with the Count for passing the autumnal months in Languedoc; and neither the remonstrances, or the tears of the Countess, for, on urgent occasions, she could weep, were powerful enough to overcome his determination. She prepared, therefore, to obey the command, which she could not conquer, and to resign the gay assemblies of Paris,—where her beauty was generally unrivalled and won the applause, to which her wit had but feeble claim—for the twilight canopy of woods, the lonely grandeur of mountains and the solemnity of gothic halls and of long, long galleries, which echoed only the solitary step of a domestic, or the measured clink, that ascended from the great clock—the ancient monitor of the hall below. From these melancholy expectations she endeavoured to relieve her spirits by recollecting all that she had ever heard, concerning the joyous vintage of the plains of Languedoc; but there, alas! no airy forms would bound to the gay melody of Parisian dances, and a view of the rustic festivities of peasants could afford little pleasure to a heart, in which even the feelings of ordinary benevolence had long since decayed under the corruptions of luxury.

The Count had a son and a daughter, the children of a former marriage, who, he designed, should accompany him to the south of France; Henri, who was in his twentieth year, was in the French service; and Blanche, who was not yet eighteen, had been hitherto confined to the convent, where she had been placed immediately on her father's second marriage. The present Countess, who had neither sufficient ability, or inclination, to superintend the education of her daughter-in-law, had advised this step, and the dread of superior beauty had since urged her to employ every art, that might prevail on the

Count to prolong the period of Blanche's seclusion; it was, therefore, with extreme mortification, that she now understood he would no longer submit on this subject, yet it afforded her some consolation to consider, that, though the Lady Blanche would emerge from her convent, the shades of the country would, for some time, veil her beauty from the public eye.

On the morning, which commenced the journey, the postillions stopped at the convent, by the Count's order, to take up Blanche, whose heart beat with delight, at the prospect of novelty and freedom now before her. As the time of her departure drew nigh, her impatience had increased, and the last night, during which she counted every note of every hour, had appeared the most tedious of any she had ever known. The morning light, at length, dawned; the matin-bell rang; she heard the nuns descending from their chambers, and she started from a sleepless pillow to welcome the day, which was to emancipate her from the severities of a cloister, and introduce her to a world, where pleasure was ever smiling, and goodness ever blessed—where, in short, nothing but pleasure and goodness reigned! When the bell of the great gate rang, and the sound was followed by that of carriage wheels, she ran, with a palpitating heart, to her lattice, and, perceiving her father's carriage in the court below, danced, with airy steps, along the gallery, where she was met by a nun with a summons from the abbess. In the next moment, she was in the parlour, and in the presence of the Countess who now appeared to her as an angel, that was to lead her into happiness. But the emotions of the Countess, on beholding her, were not in unison with those of Blanche, who had never appeared so lovely as at this moment, when her countenance, animated by the lightning smile of joy, glowed with the beauty of happy innocence.

After conversing for a few minutes with the abbess, the Countess rose to go. This was the moment, which Blanche had anticipated with such eager expectation, the summit from which she looked down upon the fairy-land of happiness, and surveyed all its enchantment; was it a moment, then, for tears of regret? Yet it was so. She turned, with an altered and dejected countenance, to her young companions, who were come to bid her farewell, and wept! Even my lady abbess, so stately and so solemn, she saluted with a degree of sorrow, which, an hour before, she would have believed it impossible to feel, and which may be accounted for by considering how reluctantly we all part, even with unpleasing objects, when the separation is consciously for ever. Again, she kissed the poor nuns and then followed the Countess from that spot with tears, which she expected to leave only with smiles.

But the presence of her father and the variety of objects, on the road, soon engaged her attention, and dissipated the shade, which tender regret had thrown upon her spirits. Inattentive to a conversation, which was passing between the Countess and a Mademoiselle Bearn, her friend, Blanche sat, lost in pleasing reverie, as she watched the clouds floating silently along the blue expanse, now veiling the sun and stretching their shadows along the distant scene, and then disclosing all his brightness. The journey continued to give Blanche inexpressible delight, for new scenes of nature were every instant opening to her view, and her fancy became stored with gay and beautiful imagery.

It was on the evening of the seventh day, that the travellers came within view of Chateau-le-Blanc, the romantic beauty of whose situation strongly impressed the imagination of Blanche, who observed, with sublime astonishment, the Pyrenean mountains, which had been seen only at a distance during the day, now rising within a few leagues, with their wild cliffs and immense precipices, which the evening clouds, floating round them, now disclosed, and again veiled. The setting rays, that tinged their snowy summits with a roseate hue, touched their lower points with various colouring, while the blueish tint, that pervaded their shadowy recesses, gave the strength of contrast to the splendour of light. The plains of Languedoc, blushing with the purple vine and diversified with groves of mulberry, almond and olives, spread far to the north and the east; to the south, appeared the Mediterranean, clear as crystal, and blue as the heavens it reflected, bearing on its bosom vessels, whose white sails caught the sun-beams, and gave animation to the scene. On a high promontory, washed by the waters of the Mediterranean, stood her father's mansion, almost secluded from the eye by woods of intermingled pine, oak and chesnut, which crowned the eminence, and sloped towards the plains, on one side; while, on the other, they extended to a considerable distance along the sea-shores.

As Blanche drew nearer, the gothic features of this antient mansion successively appeared—first an embattled turret, rising above the trees—then the broken arch of an immense gate-way, retiring beyond them; and she almost fancied herself approaching a castle, such as is often celebrated in early story, where the knights look out from the battlements on some champion below, who, clothed in black armour, comes, with his companions, to rescue the fair lady of his love from the oppression of his rival; a sort of legends, to which she had once or twice obtained access in the library of her convent, that, like many others, belonging to the monks, was stored with these reliques of romantic fiction.

The carriages stopped at a gate, which led into the domain of the chateau, but which was now fastened; and the great bell, that had formerly served to announce the arrival of strangers, having long since fallen from its station, a servant climbed over a ruined part of the adjoining wall, to give notice to those within of the arrival of their lord.

As Blanche leaned from the coach window, she resigned herself to the sweet and gentle emotions, which the hour and the scenery awakened. The sun had now left the earth, and twilight began to darken the mountains; while the distant waters, reflecting the blush that still glowed in the west, appeared like a line of light, skirting the horizon. The low murmur of waves, breaking on the shore, came in the breeze, and, now and then, the melancholy dashing of oars was feebly heard from a distance. She was suffered to indulge her pensive mood, for the thoughts of the rest of the party were silently engaged upon the subjects of their several interests. Meanwhile, the Countess, reflecting, with regret, upon the gay parties she had left at Paris, surveyed, with disgust, what she thought the gloomy woods and solitary wildness of the scene; and, shrinking from the prospect of being shut up in an old castle, was prepared to meet every object with displeasure. The feelings of Henri were somewhat similar to those of the Countess; he gave a mournful sigh to the delights of the capital, and to the remembrance of a lady, who, he believed, had engaged his affections, and who had certainly fascinated his imagination; but the surrounding country, and the mode of life, on which he was entering, had, for him, at least, the charm of novelty, and his regret was softened by the gay expectations of youth.

The gates being at length unbarred, the carriage moved slowly on, under spreading chesnuts, that almost excluded the remains of day, following what had been formerly a road, but which now, overgrown with luxuriant vegetation, could be traced only by the boundary, formed by trees, on either side, and which wound for near half a mile among the woods, before it reached the chateau. This was the very avenue that St. Aubert and Emily had formerly entered, on their first arrival in the neighbourhood, with the hope of finding a house, that would receive them, for the night, and had so abruptly quitted, on perceiving the wildness of the place, and a figure, which the postillion had fancied was a robber.

"What a dismal place is this!" exclaimed the Countess, as the carriage penetrated the deeper recesses of the woods. "Surely, my lord, you do not mean to pass all the autumn in this barbarous spot! One ought to bring hither a cup of the waters of Lethe, that the remembrance of pleasanter scenes may not heighten, at least, the natural dreariness of these."

"I shall be governed by circumstances, madam," said the Count, "this barbarous spot was inhabited by my ancestors."

The carriage now stopped at the chateau, where, at the door of the great hall, appeared the old steward and the Parisian servants, who had been sent to prepare the chateau, waiting to receive their lord. Lady Blanche now perceived, that the edifice was not built entirely in the gothic style, but that it had additions of a more modern date; the large and gloomy hall, however, into which she now entered, was entirely gothic, and sumptuous tapestry, which it was now too dark to distinguish, hung upon the walls, and depictured scenes from some of the antient Provençal romances. A vast gothic window, embroidered with *clematis* and eglantine, that ascended to the south, led the eye, now that the casements were thrown open, through this verdant shade, over a sloping lawn, to the tops of dark woods, that hung upon the brow of the promontory. Beyond, appeared the waters of the Mediterranean, stretching far to the south, and to the east, where they were lost in the horizon; while, to the north-east, they were bounded by the luxuriant shores of Languedoc and Provence, enriched with wood, and gay with vines and sloping pastures; and, to the south-west, by the majestic Pyrenées, now fading from the eye, beneath the gradual gloom.

Blanche, as she crossed the hall, stopped a moment to observe this lovely prospect, which the evening twilight obscured, yet did not conceal. But she was quickly awakened from the complacent delight, which this scene had diffused upon her mind, by the Countess, who, discontented with every object around, and impatient for refreshment and repose, hastened forward to a large parlour, whose cedar wainscot, narrow, pointed casements, and dark ceiling of carved cypress wood, gave it an aspect of peculiar gloom, which the dingy green velvet of the chairs and couches, fringed with tarnished gold, had once been designed to enliven.

While the Countess enquired for refreshment, the Count, attended by his son, went to look over some part of the chateau, and Lady Blanche reluctantly remained to witness the discontent and ill-humour of her step-mother.

"How long have you lived in this desolate place?" said her ladyship, to the old house keeper, who came to pay her duty.

"Above twenty years, your ladyship, on the next feast of St. Jerome."

"How happened it, that you have lived here so long, and almost alone, too? I understood, that the chateau had been shut up for some years?"

"Yes, madam, it was for many years after my late lord, the Count, went to the wars; but it is above twenty years, since I and my husband came into his service. The place is so large, and has of late been so lonely, that we were lost in it, and, after some time, we went to live in a cottage at the end of the woods, near some of the tenants, and came to look after the chateau, every now and then. When my lord returned to France from the wars, he took a dislike to the place, and never came to live here again, and so he was satisfied with our remaining at the cottage. Alas—alas! how the chateau is changed from what it once was! What delight my late lady used to take in it! I well remember when she came here a bride, and how fine it was. Now, it has been neglected so long, and is gone into such decay! I shall never see those days again!"

The Countess appearing to be somewhat offended by the thoughtless simplicity, with which the old woman regretted former times, Dorothée added—"But the chateau will now be inhabited, and cheerful again; not all the world could tempt me to live in it alone."

"Well, the experiment will not be made, I believe," said the Countess, displeased that her own silence had been unable to awe the loquacity of this rustic old housekeeper, now spared from further attendance by the entrance of the Count, who said he had been viewing part of the chateau, and found, that it would require considerable repairs and some alterations, before it would be perfectly comfortable, as a place of residence. "I am sorry to hear it, my lord," replied the Countess. "And why sorry, madam?" "Because the place will ill repay your trouble; and were it even a paradise, it would be insufferable at such a distance from Paris."

The Count made no reply, but walked abruptly to a window. "There are windows, my lord, but they neither admit entertainment, or light; they shew only a scene of savage nature."

"I am at a loss, madam," said the Count, "to conjecture what you mean by savage nature. Do those plains, or those woods, or that fine expanse of water, deserve the name?"

"Those mountains certainly do, my lord," rejoined the Countess, pointing to the Pyrenées, "and this chateau, though not a work of rude nature, is, to my taste, at least, one of savage art." The Count coloured highly. "This place, madam, was the work of my ancestors," said he, "and you must allow me to say, that your present conversation discovers neither good taste, or good manners." Blanche, now shocked at an altercation, which appeared to be increasing to a serious disagreement, rose to leave the room, when her mother's woman entered it; and the Countess, immediately desiring to be shewn to her own apartment, withdrew, attended by Mademoiselle Bearn.

Lady Blanche, it being not yet dark, took this opportunity of exploring new scenes, and, leaving the parlour, she passed from the hall into a wide gallery, whose walls were decorated by marble pilasters, which supported an arched roof, composed of a rich mosaic work. Through a distant window, that seemed to terminate the gallery, were seen the purple clouds of evening and a landscape, whose features, thinly veiled in twilight, no longer appeared distinctly, but, blended into one grand mass, stretched to the horizon, coloured only with a tint of solemn grey.

The gallery terminated in a saloon, to which the window she had seen through an open door, belonged; but the increasing dusk permitted her only an imperfect view of this apartment, which seemed to be magnificent and of modern architecture; though it had been either suffered to fall into decay, or had never been properly finished. The windows, which were numerous and large, descended low, and afforded a very extensive, and what Blanche's fancy represented to be, a very lovely prospect; and she stood for some time, surveying the grey obscurity and depicturing imaginary woods and mountains, vallies and rivers, on this scene of night; her solemn sensations rather assisted, than interrupted, by the distant bark of a watch-dog, and by the breeze, as it trembled upon the light foliage of the shrubs. Now and then, appeared for a moment, among the woods, a cottage light; and, at length, was heard, afar off, the evening bell of a convent, dying on the air. When she withdrew her thoughts from these subjects of fanciful delight, the gloom and silence of the saloon somewhat awed her; and, having sought the door of the gallery, and pursued, for a considerable time, a dark passage, she came to a hall, but one totally different from that she had formerly seen. By the twilight, admitted through an open portico, she could just distinguish this apartment to be of very light and airy architecture, and that it was paved with white marble, pillars of which supported the roof, that rose into arches built in the Moorish style. While Blanche stood on the steps of this portico, the moon rose over the sea, and gradually disclosed, in partial light, the beauties of the eminence, on which she stood, whence a lawn, now rude and overgrown with high grass, sloped to the woods, that, almost surrounding the chateau, extended in a grand sweep down the southern sides of the promontory to the very margin of the ocean. Beyond the woods, on the north-side, appeared a long tract of the plains of Languedoc; and, to the east, the landscape she had before dimly seen, with the towers of a monastery, illumined by the moon, rising over dark groves.

The soft and shadowy tint, that overspread the scene, the waves, undulating in the moon-light, and their low and measured murmurs on the beach, were circumstances, that united to elevate the unaccustomed mind of Blanche to enthusiasm.

"And have I lived in this glorious world so long," said she, "and never till now beheld such a prospect—never experienced these delights! Every peasant girl, on my father's domain, has viewed from her infancy the face of nature; has ranged, at liberty, her romantic wilds, while I have been shut in a cloister from the view of these beautiful appearances, which were designed to enchant all eyes, and awaken all hearts. How can the poor nuns and friars feel the full fervour of devotion, if they never see the sun rise, or set? Never, till this evening, did I know what true devotion is; for, never before did I see the sun sink below the vast earth! To-morrow, for the first time in my life, I will see it rise. O, who would live in Paris, to look upon black walls and dirty streets, when, in the country, they might gaze on the blue heavens, and all the green earth!"

This enthusiastic soliloquy was interrupted by a rustling noise in the hall; and, while the loneliness of the place made her sensible to fear, she thought she perceived something moving between the pillars. For a moment, she continued silently observing it, till, ashamed of her ridiculous apprehensions, she recollected courage enough to demand who was there. "O my young lady, is it you?" said the old housekeeper, who was come to shut the windows, "I am glad it is you." The manner, in which she spoke this, with a faint breath, rather surprised Blanche, who said, "You seemed frightened, Dorothée, what is the matter?"

"No, not frightened, ma'amselle," replied Dorothée, hesitating and trying to appear composed, "but I am old, and—a little matter startles me." The Lady Blanche smiled at the distinction. "I am glad, that my lord the Count is come to live at the chateau, ma'amselle," continued Dorothée, "for it has been many a year deserted, and dreary enough; now, the place will look a little as it used to do, when my poor lady was alive." Blanche enquired how long it was, since the Marchioness died? "Alas! my lady," replied Dorothée, "so long—that I have ceased to count the years! The place, to my mind, has mourned ever since, and I am sure my lord's vassals have! But you have lost yourself, ma'amselle,—shall I shew you to the other side of the chateau?"

Blanche enquired how long this part of the edifice had been built. "Soon after my lord's marriage, ma'am," replied Dorothée. "The place was large enough without this addition, for many rooms of the old building were even then never made use of, and my lord had a princely household too; but he thought the antient mansion gloomy, and gloomy enough it is!" Lady Blanche now desired to be shewn to the inhabited part of the chateau; and, as the passages were entirely dark, Dorothée conducted her along the edge of the lawn to the opposite side of the edifice, where, a door opening into the great hall, she was met by Mademoiselle Bearn. "Where have you been so long?" said she, "I had begun to think some wonderful adventure had befallen you, and that the giant of this enchanted castle, or the ghost, which, no doubt, haunts it, had conveyed you through a trap-door into some subterranean vault, whence you was never to return."

"No," replied Blanche, laughingly, "you seem to love adventures so well, that I leave them for you to achieve."

"Well, I am willing to achieve them, provided I am allowed to describe them."

"My dear Mademoiselle Bearn," said Henri, as he met her at the door of the parlour, "no ghost of these days would be so savage as to impose silence on you. Our ghosts are more civilized than to condemn a lady to a purgatory severer even, than their own, be it what it may."

Mademoiselle Bearn replied only by a laugh; and, the Count now entering the room, supper was served, during which he spoke little, frequently appeared to be abstracted from the company, and more than once remarked, that the place was greatly altered, since he had last seen it. "Many years have intervened since that period," said he; "and, though the grand features of the scenery admit of no change, they impress me with sensations very different from those I formerly experienced."

"Did these scenes, sir," said Blanche, "ever appear more lovely, than they do now? To me this seems hardly possible." The Count, regarding her with a melancholy smile, said, "They once were as delightful to me, as they are now to you; the landscape is not changed, but time has changed me; from my mind the illusion, which gave spirit to the colouring of nature, is fading fast! If you live, my dear Blanche, to revisit this spot, at the distance of many years, you will, perhaps, remember and understand the feelings of your father."

Lady Blanche, affected by these words, remained silent; she looked forward to the period, which the Count anticipated, and considering, that he, who now spoke, would then probably be no more, her eyes, bent to the ground, were filled with tears. She gave her hand to her father, who, smiling affectionately, rose from his chair, and went to a window to conceal his emotion.

The fatigues of the day made the party separate at an early hour, when Blanche retired through a long oak gallery to her chamber, whose spacious and lofty walls, high antiquated casements, and, what was the effect of these, its gloomy air, did not reconcile her to its remote situation, in this antient building. The furniture, also, was of antient date; the bed was of blue damask, trimmed with tarnished gold lace, and its lofty tester rose in the form of a canopy, whence the curtains descended, like those of such tents as are sometimes represented in old pictures, and, indeed, much resembling those, exhibited on the faded tapestry, with which the chamber was hung. To Blanche, every object here was matter of curiosity; and, taking the light from her woman to examine the tapestry, she perceived, that it represented scenes from the wars of Troy, though the almost colourless worsted now mocked the glowing actions they once had painted. She laughed at the ludicrous absurdity she observed, till, recollecting, that the hands, which had wove it, were, like the poet, whose thoughts of fire they had attempted to express, long since mouldered into dust, a train of melancholy ideas passed over her mind, and she almost wept.

Having given her woman a strict injunction to awaken her, before sun-rise, she dismissed her; and then, to dissipate the gloom, which reflection had cast upon her spirits, opened one of the high casements, and was again cheered by the face of living nature. The shadowy earth, the air, and ocean—all was still. Along the deep serene of the heavens, a few light clouds floated slowly, through whose skirts the stars now seemed to tremble, and now to emerge with purer splendour. Blanche's thoughts arose involuntarily to the Great Author of the sublime objects she contemplated, and she breathed a prayer of finer devotion, than any she had ever uttered beneath the vaulted roof of a cloister. At this casement, she remained till the glooms of midnight were stretched over the prospect. She then retired to her pillow, and, "with gay visions of to-morrow," to those sweet slumbers, which health and happy innocence only know.

> To-morrow to fresh woods and pastures new.

CHAPTER XI

> What transport to retrace our early plays,
> Our easy bliss, when each thing joy supplied
> The woods, the mountains and the warbling maze
> Of the wild brooks!
>
> THOMSON

BLANCHE'S slumbers continued, till long after the hour, which she had so impatiently anticipated, for her woman, fatigued with travelling, did not call her, till breakfast was nearly ready. Her disappointment, however, was instantly forgotten, when, on opening the casement, she saw, on one hand, the wide sea sparkling in the morning rays, with its stealing sails and glancing oars; and, on the other, the fresh woods, the plains far-stretching and the blue mountains, all glowing with the splendour of day.

As she inspired the pure breeze, health spread a deeper blush upon her countenance, and pleasure danced in her eyes.

"Who could first invent convents!" said she, "and who could first persuade people to go into them? and to make religion a pretence, too, where all that should inspire it, is so carefully shut out! God is best pleased with the homage of a grateful heart, and, when we view his glories, we feel most grateful. I never felt so much devotion, during the many dull years I was in the convent, as I have done in the few hours, that I have been here, where I need only look on all around me—to adore God in my inmost heart!"

Saying this, she left the window, bounded along the gallery, and, in the next moment, was in the breakfast room, where the Count was already seated. The cheerfulness of a bright sunshine had dispersed the melancholy glooms of his reflections, a pleasant smile was on his countenance, and he spoke in an enlivening voice to Blanche, whose heart echoed back the tones. Henri and, soon after, the Countess with Mademoiselle Bearn appeared, and the whole party seemed to acknowledge the influence of the scene; even the Countess was so much re-animated as to receive the civilities of her husband with complacency, and but once forgot her good-humour, which was when she asked whether they had any neighbours, who were likely to make *this barbarous spot* more tolerable, and whether the Count believed it possible for her to exist here, without some amusement?

Soon after breakfast the party dispersed; the Count, ordering his steward to attend him in the library, went to survey the condition of his premises, and to visit some of his tenants; Henri hastened with alacrity to the shore to examine a boat, that was to bear them on a little voyage in the evening and to superintend the adjustment of a silk awning; while the Countess, attended by Mademoiselle Bearn, retired to an apartment on the modern side of the chateau, which was fitted up with airy elegance; and, as the windows opened upon balconies, that fronted the sea, she was there saved from a view of the *horrid* Pyrenées. Here, while she reclined on a sofa, and, casting her languid eyes over the ocean, which appeared beyond the wood-tops, indulged in the luxuries of *ennui*, her companion read aloud a sentimental novel, on some fashionable system of philosophy, for the Countess was herself somewhat of a *philosopher*, especially as to *infidelity*, and among a certain circle her opinions were waited for with impatience, and received as doctrines.

The Lady Blanche, meanwhile, hastened to indulge, amidst the wild wood-walks around the chateau, her new enthusiasm, where, as she wandered under the shades, her gay spirits gradually yielded to pensive complacency. Now, she moved with solemn steps, beneath the gloom of thickly interwoven branches, where the fresh dew still hung upon every flower, that peeped from among the grass; and now tripped sportively along the path, on which the sunbeams darted and the chequered foliage trembled—where the tender greens of the beech, the acacia and the mountain-ash, mingling with the solemn tints of the cedar, the pine and cypress, exhibited as fine a contrast of colouring, as the majestic oak and oriental plane did of form, to the feathery lightness of the cork tree and the waving grace of the poplar.

Having reached a rustic seat, within a deep recess of the woods, she rested awhile, and, as her eyes caught, through a distant opening, a glimpse of the blue waters of the Mediterranean, with the white sail, gliding on its bosom, or of the broad mountain, glowing beneath the mid-day sun, her mind experienced somewhat of that exquisite delight, which awakens the fancy, and leads to poetry. The hum of bees alone broke the stillness around her, as, with other insects of various hues, they sported gaily in the shade, or sipped sweets from the fresh flowers: and, while Blanche watched a butter-fly, flitting from bud to bud, she indulged herself in imagining the pleasures of its short day, till she had composed the following stanzas.

THE BUTTER-FLY TO HIS LOVE

What bowery dell, with fragrant breath,
Courts thee to stay thy airy flight;
Nor seek again the purple heath,
So oft the scene of gay delight?

Long I've watch'd i' the lily's bell,
Whose whiteness stole the morning's beam;
No fluttering sounds thy coming tell,
No waving wings, at distance, gleam.

But fountain fresh, nor breathing grove,
Nor sunny mead, nor blossom'd tree,
So sweet as lily's cell shall prove,—
The bower of constant love and me.

When April buds begin to blow,
The prim-rose, and the hare-bell blue,
That on the verdant moss bank grow,
With violet cups, that weep in dew;

When wanton gales breathe through the shade,
And shake the blooms, and steal their sweets,
And swell the song of ev'ry glade,
I range the forest's green retreats:

There, through the tangled wood-walks play,
Where no rude urchin paces near,
Where sparely peeps the sultry day,
And light dews freshen all the air.

High on a sun-beam oft I sport
O'er bower and fountain, vale and hill;
Oft ev'ry blushing flow'ret court,
That hangs its head o'er winding rill.

But these I'll leave to be thy guide,
And shew thee, where the jasmine spreads

Her snowy leaf, where may-flow'rs hide,
And rose-buds rear their peeping heads.

With me the mountain's summit scale,
And taste the wild-thyme's honied bloom,
Whose fragrance, floating on the gale,
Oft leads me to the cedar's gloom.

Yet, yet, no sound comes in the breeze!
What shade thus dares to tempt thy stay?
Once, me alone thou wish'd to please,
And with me only thou wouldst stray.

But, while thy long delay I mourn,
And chide the sweet shades for their guile,
Thou may'st be true, and they forlorn,
And fairy favours court thy smile.

The tiny queen of fairy-land,
Who knows thy speed, hath sent thee far,
To bring, or ere the night-watch stand,
Rich essence for her shadowy car:

Perchance her acorn-cups to fill
With nectar from the Indian rose,
Or gather, near some haunted rill,
May-dews, that lull to sleep Love's woes:

Or, o'er the mountains, bade thee fly,
To tell her fairy love to speed,
When ev'ning steals upon the sky,
To dance along the twilight mead.

But now I see thee sailing low,
Gay as the brightest flow'rs of spring,
Thy coat of blue and jet I know,
And well thy gold and purple wing.

Borne on the gale, thou com'st to me;
O! welcome, welcome to my home!
In lily's cell we'll live in glee,
Together o'er the mountains roam!

When Lady Blanche returned to the chateau, instead of going to the apartment of the Countess, she amused herself with wandering over that part of the edifice, which she had not yet examined, of which the most antient first attracted her curiosity; for, though what she had seen of the modern was gay and elegant, there was something in the former more interesting to her imagination. Having passed up the great stair-case, and through the oak gallery, she entered upon a long suite of chambers, whose walls were either hung with tapestry, or wainscoted with cedar, the furniture of which looked almost as antient as the rooms themselves; the spacious fire-places, where no mark of social cheer remained, presented an image of cold desolation; and the whole suite had so much the air of neglect and desertion, that it seemed, as if the venerable persons, whose portraits hung upon the walls, had been the last to inhabit them.

On leaving these rooms, she found herself in another gallery, one end of which was terminated by a back stair-case, and the other by a door, that seemed to communicate with the north-side of the chateau, but which being fastened, she descended the stair-case, and, opening a door in the wall, a few steps down, found herself in a small square room, that formed part of the west turret of the castle. Three windows presented each a separate and beautiful prospect; that to the north, overlooking Languedoc; another to the west, the hills ascending towards the Pyrenées, whose awful summits crowned the landscape; and a third, fronting the south, gave the Mediterranean, and a part of the wild shores of Rousillon, to the eye.

Having left the turret, and descended the narrow stair-case, she found herself in a dusky passage, where she wandered, unable to find her way, till impatience yielded to apprehension, and she called for assistance. Presently steps approached, and light glimmered through a door at the other extremity of the passage, which was opened with caution by some person, who did not venture beyond it, and whom Blanche observed in silence, till the door was closing, when she called aloud, and, hastening towards it, perceived the old housekeeper.

"Dear ma'amselle! is it you?" said Dorothée, "How could you find your way hither?" Had Blanche been less occupied by her own fears, she would probably have observed the strong expressions of terror and surprise on Dorothée's countenance, who now led her through a long succession of passages and rooms, that looked as if they had been un-inhabited for a century, till they reached that appropriated to the housekeeper, where Dorothée entreated she would sit down and take refreshment. Blanche accepted the sweet meats, offered to her, mentioned her discovery of the pleasant turret, and her wish to appropriate it to her own use. Whether Dorothée's taste was not so sensible to the beauties of landscape as her young lady's, or that the constant view of lovely scenery had deadened it, she forbore to praise the subject of Blanche's enthusiasm, which, however, her silence did not repress. To Lady Blanche's enquiry of whither the door she had found fastened at the end of the gallery led, she replied, that it opened to a suite of rooms, which had not been entered, during many years, "For," added she, "my late lady died in one of them, and I could never find in my heart to go into them since."

Blanche, though she wished to see these chambers, forbore, on observing that Dorothée's eyes were filled with tears, to ask her to unlock them, and, soon after, went to dress for dinner, at which the whole party met in good spirits and good humour, except the Countess, whose vacant mind, overcome by the languor of idleness, would neither suffer her to be happy herself, or to contribute to the happiness of others. Mademoiselle Bearn, attempting to be witty, directed her *badinage* against Henri, who answered, because he could not well avoid it, rather than from any inclination to notice her, whose liveliness sometimes amused, but whose conceit and insensibility often disgusted him.

The cheerfulness, with which Blanche rejoined the party, vanished, on her reaching the margin of the sea; she gazed with apprehension upon the immense expanse of waters, which, at a distance, she had beheld only with delight and astonishment, and it was by a strong effort, that she so far overcame her fears as to follow her father into the boat.

As she silently surveyed the vast horizon, bending round the distant verge of the ocean, an emotion of sublimest rapture struggled to overcome a sense of personal danger. A light breeze played on the water, and on the silk awning of the boat, and waved the foliage of the receding woods, that crowned the cliffs, for many miles, and which the Count surveyed with the pride of conscious property, as well as with the eye of taste.

At some distance, among these woods, stood a pavilion, which had once been the scene of social gaiety, and which its situation still made one of romantic beauty. Thither, the Count had ordered coffee and other refreshment to be carried, and thither the sailors now steered their course, following the windings of the shore round many a woody promontory and circling bay; while the pensive tones of horns and other wind instruments, played by the attendants in a distant boat, echoed among the rocks, and died along the waves. Blanche had now subdued her fears; a delightful tranquillity stole over her mind, and held her in silence; and she was too happy even to remember the convent, or her former sorrows, as subjects of comparison with her present felicity.

The Countess felt less unhappy than she had done, since the moment of her leaving Paris; for her mind was now under some degree of restraint; she feared to indulge its wayward humours, and even wished to recover the Count's good opinion. On his family, and on the surrounding scene, he looked with tempered pleasure and benevolent satisfaction, while his son exhibited the gay spirits of youth, anticipating new delights, and regretless of those, that were passed.

After near an hour's rowing, the party landed, and ascended a little path, overgrown with vegetation. At a little distance from the point of the eminence, within the shadowy recess of the woods, appeared the pavilion, which Blanche perceived, as she caught a glimpse of its portico between the trees, to be built of variegated marble. As she followed the Countess, she often turned her eyes with rapture towards the ocean, seen beneath the dark foliage, far below, and from thence upon the deep woods, whose silence and impenetrable gloom awakened emotions more solemn, but scarcely less delightful.

The pavilion had been prepared, as far as was possible, on a very short notice, for the reception of its visitors; but the faded colours of its painted walls and ceiling, and the decayed drapery of its once magnificent furniture, declared how long it had been neglected, and abandoned to the empire of the changing seasons. While the party partook of a collation of fruit and coffee, the horns, placed in a distant part of the woods, where an echo sweetened and prolonged their melancholy tones, broke softly on the stillness of the scene. This spot seemed to attract even the admiration of the Countess, or, perhaps, it was merely the pleasure of planning furniture and decorations, that made her dwell so long on the necessity of repairing and adorning it; while the Count, never happier than when he saw her mind engaged by natural and simple objects, acquiesced in all her designs, concerning the pavilion. The paintings on the walls and coved ceiling were to be renewed, the canopies and sofas were to be of light green damask; marble statues of wood-nymphs, bearing on their heads baskets of living flowers, were to adorn the recesses between the windows, which, descending to the ground, were to admit to every part of the room, and it was of octagonal form, the various landscape. One window opened upon a romantic glade, where the eye roved among the woody recesses, and the scene was bounded only by a lengthened pomp of groves; from another, the woods receding disclosed the distant summits of the Pyrenées; a third fronted an avenue, beyond which the grey towers of Chateau-le-Blanc, and a picturesque part of its ruin were seen partially among the foliage; while a fourth gave, between the trees, a glimpse of the green pastures and villages, that diversify the banks of the Aude. The Mediterranean, with the bold cliffs, that overlooked its shores, were the grand objects of a fifth window, and the others gave, in different points of view, the wild scenery of the woods.

After wandering, for some time, in these, the party returned to the shore and embarked; and, the beauty of the evening tempting them to extend their excursion, they proceeded further up the bay. A dead calm had succeeded the light breeze, that wafted them hither, and the men took to their oars. Around, the waters were spread into one vast expanse of polished mirror, reflecting the grey cliffs and feathery woods, that over-hung its surface, the glow of the western horizon and the dark clouds, that came slowly from the east. Blanche loved to see the dipping oars imprint the water, and to watch the spreading circles they left, which gave a tremulous motion to the reflected landscape, without destroying the harmony of its features.

Above the darkness of the woods, her eye now caught a cluster of high towers, touched with the splendour of the setting rays; and, soon after, the horns being then silent, she heard the faint swell of choral voices from a distance.

"What voices are those, upon the air?" said the Count, looking round, and listening; but the strain had ceased. "It seemed to be a vesper-hymn, which I have often heard in my convent," said Blanche.

"We are near the monastery, then," observed the Count; and, the boat soon after doubling a lofty head-land, the monastery of St. Claire appeared, seated near the margin of the sea, where the cliffs, suddenly sinking, formed a low shore within a small bay, almost encircled with woods, among which partial features of the edifice were seen;—the great gate and gothic window of the hall, the cloisters and the side of a chapel more remote; while a venerable arch, which had once led to a part of the fabric, now demolished, stood a majestic ruin detached from the main building, beyond which appeared a grand perspective of the woods. On the grey walls, the moss had fastened, and, round the pointed windows of the chapel, the ivy and the briony hung in many a fantastic wreath.

All without was silent and forsaken; but, while Blanche gazed with admiration on this venerable pile, whose effect was heightened by the strong lights and shadows thrown athwart it by a cloudy sunset, a sound of many voices, slowly chanting, arose from within. The Count bade his men rest on their oars. The monks were singing the hymn of vespers, and some female voices mingled with the strain, which rose by soft degrees, till the high organ and the choral sounds swelled into full and solemn harmony. The strain, soon after, dropped into sudden silence, and was renewed in a low and still more solemn key, till, at length, the holy chorus died away, and was heard no more.—Blanche sighed, tears trembled in her eyes, and her thoughts seemed wafted with the sounds to heaven. While a rapt stillness prevailed in the boat, a train of friars, and then of nuns, veiled in white, issued from the cloisters, and passed, under the shade of the woods, to the main body of the edifice.

The Countess was the first of her party to awaken from this pause of silence.

"These dismal hymns and friars make one quite melancholy," said she; "twilight is coming on; pray let us return, or it will be dark before we get home."

The Count, looking up, now perceived, that the twilight of evening was anticipated by an approaching storm. In the east a tempest was collecting; a heavy gloom came on, opposing and contrasting the glowing splendour of the setting sun. The clamorous sea-fowl skimmed in fleet circles upon the surface of the sea, dipping their light pinions in the wave, as they fled away in search of shelter. The boatmen pulled hard at their oars; but the thunder, that now muttered at a distance, and the heavy drops, that began to dimple the water, made the Count determine to put back to the monastery for shelter, and the course of the boat was immediately changed. As the clouds approached the west, their lurid darkness changed to a deep ruddy glow, which, by reflection, seemed to fire the tops of the woods and the shattered towers of the monastery.

The appearance of the heavens alarmed the Countess and Mademoiselle Bearn, whose expressions of apprehension distressed the Count, and perplexed his men; while Blanche continued silent, now agitated with fear, and now with admiration, as she viewed the grandeur of the clouds, and their effect on the scenery, and listened to the long, long peals of thunder, that rolled through the air.

The boat having reached the lawn before the monastery, the Count sent a servant to announce his arrival, and to entreat shelter of the Superior, who, soon after, appeared at the great gate, attended by several monks, while the servant returned with a message, expressive at once of hospitality and pride, but of pride disguised in submission. The party immediately disembarked, and, having hastily crossed the lawn — for the shower was now heavy — were received at the gate by the Superior, who, as they entered, stretched forth his hands and gave his blessing; and they passed into the great hall, where the lady abbess waited, attended by several nuns, clothed, like herself, in black, and veiled in white. The veil of the abbess was, however, thrown half back, and discovered a countenance, whose chaste dignity was sweetened by the smile of welcome, with which she addressed the Countess, whom she led, with Blanche and Mademoiselle Bearn, into the convent parlour, while the Count and Henri were conducted by the Superior to the refectory.

The Countess, fatigued and discontented, received the politeness of the abbess with careless haughtiness, and had followed her, with indolent steps, to the parlour, over which the painted casements and wainscot of larch-wood threw, at all times, a melancholy shade, and where the gloom of evening now loured almost to darkness.

While the lady abbess ordered refreshment, and conversed with the

Countess, Blanche withdrew to a window, the lower panes of which, being without painting, allowed her to observe the progress of the storm over the Mediterranean, whose dark waves, that had so lately slept, now came boldly swelling, in long succession, to the shore, where they burst in white foam, and threw up a high spray over the rocks. A red sulphureous tint overspread the long line of clouds, that hung above the western horizon, beneath whose dark skirts the sun looking out, illumined the distant shores of Languedoc, as well as the tufted summits of the nearer woods, and shed a partial gleam on the western waves. The rest of the scene was in deep gloom, except where a sun-beam, darting between the clouds, glanced on the white wings of the sea-fowl, that circled high among them, or touched the swelling sail of a vessel, which was seen labouring in the storm. Blanche, for some time, anxiously watched the progress of the bark, as it threw the waves in foam around it, and, as the lightnings flashed, looked to the opening heavens, with many a sigh for the fate of the poor mariners.

The sun, at length, set, and the heavy clouds, which had long impended, dropped over the splendour of his course; the vessel, however, was yet dimly seen, and Blanche continued to observe it, till the quick succession of flashes, lighting up the gloom of the whole horizon, warned her to retire from the window, and she joined the Abbess, who, having exhausted all her topics of conversation with the Countess, had now leisure to notice her.

But their discourse was interrupted by tremendous peals of thunder; and the bell of the monastery soon after ringing out, summoned the inhabitants to prayer. As Blanche passed the window, she gave another look to the ocean, where, by the momentary flash, that illumined the vast body of the waters, she distinguished the vessel she had observed before, amidst a sea of foam, breaking the billows, the mast now bowing to the waves, and then rising high in air.

She sighed fervently as she gazed, and then followed the Lady Abbess and the Countess to the chapel. Meanwhile, some of the Count's servants, having gone by land to the chateau for carriages, returned soon after vespers had concluded, when, the storm being somewhat abated, the Count and his family returned home. Blanche was surprised to discover how much the windings of the shore had deceived her, concerning the distance of the chateau from the monastery, whose vesper bell she had heard, on the preceding evening, from the windows of the west saloon, and whose towers she would also have seen from thence, had not twilight veiled them.

On their arrival at the chateau, the Countess, affecting more fatigue, than she really felt, withdrew to her apartment, and the Count, with his daughter and Henri, went to the supper-room, where they had not been long, when they heard, in a pause of the gust, a firing of guns, which the Count understanding to be signals of distress from some vessel in the storm, went to a window, that opened towards the Mediterranean, to observe further; but the sea was now involved in utter darkness, and the loud howlings of the tempest had again overcome every other sound. Blanche, remembering the bark, which she had before seen, now joined her father, with trembling anxiety. In a few moments, the report of guns was again borne along the wind, and as suddenly wafted away; a tremendous burst of thunder followed, and, in the flash, that had preceded it, and which seemed to quiver over the whole surface of the waters, a vessel was discovered, tossing amidst the white foam of the waves at some distance from the shore. Impenetrable darkness again involved the scene, but soon a second flash shewed the bark, with one sail unfurled, driving towards the coast. Blanche hung upon her father's arm, with looks full of the agony of united terror and pity, which were unnecessary to awaken the heart of the Count, who gazed upon the sea with a piteous expression, and, perceiving, that no boat could live in the storm, forbore to send one; but he gave orders to his people to carry torches out upon the cliffs, hoping they might prove a kind of beacon to the vessel, or, at least, warn the crew of the rocks they were approaching. While Henri went out to direct on what part of the cliffs the lights should appear, Blanche remained with her father, at the window, catching, every now and then, as the lightnings flashed, a glimpse of the vessel; and she soon saw, with reviving hope, the torches flaming on the blackness of night, and, as they waved over the cliffs, casting a red gleam on the gasping billows. When the firing of guns was repeated, the torches were tossed high in the air, as if answering the signal, and the firing was then redoubled; but, though the wind bore the sound away, she fancied, as the lightnings glanced, that the vessel was much nearer the shore.

The Count's servants were now seen, running to and fro, on the rocks; some venturing almost to the point of the crags, and bending over, held out their torches fastened to long poles; while others, whose steps could be traced only by the course of the lights, descended the steep and dangerous path, that wound to the margin of the sea, and, with loud halloos, hailed the mariners, whose shrill whistle, and then feeble voices, were heard, at intervals, mingling with the storm. Sudden shouts from the people on the rocks increased the anxiety of Blanche to an almost intolerable degree: but her suspense, concerning the fate of the mariners, was soon over, when Henri, running breathless into the room, told that the vessel was anchored in the bay below, but in so shattered a condition, that it was feared she would part before the crew could disembark. The Count immediately gave orders for his own boats to assist in bringing them to shore, and that such of these unfortunate strangers as could not be accommodated in the adjacent hamlet should be entertained at the chateau. Among the latter, were Emily St. Aubert, Monsieur Du Pont, Ludovico and Annette, who, having embarked at Leghorn and reached Marseilles, were from thence crossing the Gulf of Lyons, when this storm overtook them. They were received by the Count with his usual benignity, who, though Emily wished to have proceeded immediately to the monastery of St. Claire, would not allow her to leave the chateau, that night; and, indeed, the terror and fatigue she had suffered would scarcely have permitted her to go farther.

In Monsieur Du Pont the Count discovered an old acquaintance, and much joy and congratulation passed between them, after which Emily was introduced by name to the Count's family, whose hospitable benevolence dissipated the little embarrassment, which her situation had occasioned her, and the party were soon seated at the supper-table. The unaffected kindness of Blanche and the lively joy she expressed on the escape of the strangers, for whom her pity had been so much interested, gradually revived Emily's languid spirits; and Du Pont, relieved from his terrors for her and for himself, felt the full contrast, between his late situation on a dark and tremendous ocean, and his present one, in a cheerful mansion, where he was surrounded with plenty, elegance and smiles of welcome.

Annette, meanwhile, in the servants' hall, was telling of all the dangers she had encountered, and congratulating herself so heartily upon her own and Ludovico's escape, and on her present comforts, that she often made all that part of the chateau ring with merriment and laughter. Ludovico's spirits were as gay as her own, but he had discretion enough to restrain them, and tried to check hers, though in vain, till her laughter, at length, ascended to *my lady's* chamber, who sent to enquire what occasioned so much uproar in the chateau, and to command silence.

Emily withdrew early to seek the repose she so much required, but her pillow was long a sleepless one. On this her return to her native country, many interesting remembrances were awakened; all the events and sufferings she had experienced, since she quitted it, came in long succession to her fancy, and were chased only by the image of Valancourt, with whom to believe herself once more in the same land, after they had been so long, and so distantly separated, gave her emotions of indescribable joy, but which afterwards yielded to anxiety and apprehension, when she considered the long period, that had elapsed, since any letter had passed between them, and how much might have happened in this interval to affect her future peace. But the thought,

that Valancourt might be now no more, or, if living, might have forgotten her, was so very terrible to her heart, that she would scarcely suffer herself to pause upon the possibility. She determined to inform
him, on the following day, of her arrival in France, which it was
scarcely possible he could know but by a letter from herself, and, after
soothing her spirits with the hope of soon hearing, that he was well, and
unchanged in his affections, she, at length, sunk to repose.

CHAPTER XII

Oft woo'd the gleam of Cynthia, silver-bright,
In cloisters dim, far from the haunts of folly,
With freedom by my side, and soft-ey'd melancholy.
                                    GRAY

THE Lady Blanche was so much interested for Emily, that, upon hearing she was going to reside in the neighbouring convent, she requested
the Count would invite her to lengthen her stay at the chateau. "And
you know, my dear sir," added Blanche, "how delighted I shall be with
such a companion; for, at present, I have no friend to walk, or to read
with, since Mademoiselle Bearn is my mamma's friend only."

The Count smiled at the youthful simplicity, with which his daughter yielded to first impressions; and, though he chose to warn her of
their danger, he silently applauded the benevolence, that could thus
readily expand in confidence to a stranger. He had observed Emily,
with attention, on the preceding evening, and was as much pleased
with her, as it was possible he could be with any person, on so short an
acquaintance. The mention, made of her by Mons. Du Pont, had also
given him a favourable impression of Emily; but, extremely cautious as
to those, whom he introduced to the intimacy of his daughter, he determined, on hearing that the former was no stranger at the convent of St.
Claire, to visit the abbess, and, if her account corresponded with his
wish, to invite Emily to pass some time at the chateau. On this subject,
he was influenced by a consideration of the Lady Blanche's welfare,
still more than by either a wish to oblige her, or to befriend the orphan
Emily, for whom, however, he felt considerably interested.

On the following morning, Emily was too much fatigued to appear;
but Mons. Du Pont was at the breakfast-table, when the Count entered
the room, who pressed him, as his former acquaintance, and the son of
a very old friend, to prolong his stay at the chateau; an invitation,
which Du Pont willingly accepted, since it would allow him to be near
Emily; and, though he was not conscious of encouraging a hope, that

she would ever return his affection, he had not fortitude enough to attempt, at present, to overcome it.

Emily, when she was somewhat recovered, wandered with her new friend over the grounds belonging to the chateau, as much delighted with the surrounding views, as Blanche, in the benevolence of her heart, had wished; from thence she perceived, beyond the woods, the towers of the monastery, and remarked, that it was to this convent she designed to go.

"Ah!" said Blanche with surprise, "I am but just released from a convent, and would you go into one? If you could know what pleasure I feel in wandering here, at liberty,—and in seeing the sky and the fields, and the woods all round me, I think you would not." Emily, smiling at the warmth, with which the Lady Blanche spoke, observed, that she did not mean to confine herself to a convent for life.

"No, you may not intend it now," said Blanche; "but you do not know to what the nuns may persuade you to consent: I know how kind they will appear, and how happy, for I have seen too much of their art."

When they returned to the chateau, Lady Blanche conducted Emily to her favourite turret, and from thence they rambled through the ancient chambers, which Blanche had visited before. Emily was amused by observing the structure of these apartments, and the fashion of their old but still magnificent furniture, and by comparing them with those of the castle of Udolpho, which were yet more antique and grotesque. She was also interested by Dorothée the house-keeper, who attended them, whose appearance was almost as antique as the objects around her, and who seemed no less interested by Emily, on whom she frequently gazed with so much deep attention, as scarcely to hear what was said to her.

While Emily looked from one of the casements, she perceived, with surprise, some objects, that were familiar to her memory;—the fields and woods, with the gleaming brook, which she had passed with La Voisin, one evening, soon after the death of Monsieur St. Aubert, in her way from the monastery to her cottage; and she now knew this to be the chateau, which he had then avoided, and concerning which he had dropped some remarkable hints.

Shocked by this discovery, yet scarcely knowing why, she mused for some time in silence, and remembered the emotion, which her father had betrayed on finding himself so near this mansion, and some other circumstances of his conduct, that now greatly interested her. The music, too, which she had formerly heard, and, respecting which La Voisin had given such an odd account, occurred to her, and, desirous of knowing more concerning it, she asked Dorothée whether it returned at midnight, as usual, and whether the musician had yet been discovered.

"Yes, ma'amselle," replied Dorothée, "that music is still heard, but the musician has never been found out, nor ever will, I believe; though there are some people, who can guess."

"Indeed!" said Emily, "then why do they not pursue the enquiry?"

"Ah, young lady! enquiry enough has been made—but who can pursue a spirit?"

Emily smiled, and, remembering how lately she had suffered herself to be led away by superstition, determined now to resist its contagion; yet, in spight of her efforts, she felt awe mingle with her curiosity, on this subject; and Blanche, who had hitherto listened in silence, now enquired what this music was, and how long it had been heard.

"Ever since the death of my lady, madam," replied Dorothée.

"Why, the place is not haunted, surely?" said Blanche, between jesting and seriousness.

"I have heard that music almost ever since my dear lady died," continued Dorothée, "and never before then. But that is nothing to some things I could tell of."

"Do, pray, tell them, then," said Lady Blanche, now more in earnest than in jest. "I am much interested, for I have heard sister Henriette, and sister Sophie, in the convent, tell of such strange appearances, which they themselves had witnessed!"

"You never heard, my lady, I suppose, what made us leave the chateau, and go and live in a cottage," said Dorothée. "Never!" replied Blanche with impatience.

"Nor the reason, that my lord, the Marquis"—Dorothée checked herself, hesitated, and then endeavoured to change the topic; but the curiosity of Blanche was too much awakened to suffer the subject thus easily to escape her, and she pressed the old house-keeper to proceed with her account, upon whom, however, no entreaties could prevail; and it was evident, that she was alarmed for the imprudence, into which she had already betrayed herself.

"I perceive," said Emily, smiling, "that all old mansions are haunted; I am lately come from a place of wonders; but unluckily, since I left it, I have heard almost all of them explained."

Blanche was silent; Dorothée looked grave, and sighed; and Emily felt herself still inclined to believe more of the wonderful, than she chose to acknowledge. Just then, she remembered the spectacle she had witnessed in a chamber of Udolpho, and, by an odd kind of coincidence, the alarming words, that had accidentally met her eye in the MS. papers, which she had destroyed, in obedience to the command of her father; and she shuddered at the meaning they seemed to impart, almost as much as at the horrible appearance, disclosed by the black veil.

The Lady Blanche, meanwhile, unable to prevail with Dorothée to explain the subject of her late hints, had desired, on reaching the door, that terminated the gallery, and which she found fastened on the preceding day, to see the suite of rooms beyond. "Dear young lady," said the housekeeper, "I have told you my reason for not opening them; I have never seen them, since my dear lady died; and it would go hard with me to see them now. Pray, madam, do not ask me again."

"Certainly I will not," replied Blanche, "if that is really your objection."

"Alas! it is," said the old woman: "we all loved her well, and I shall always grieve for her. Time runs round! it is now many years, since she died; but I remember every thing, that happened then, as if it was but yesterday. Many things, that have passed of late years, are gone quite from my memory, while those so long ago, I can see as if in a glass." She paused, but afterwards, as they walked up the gallery, added to Emily, "This young lady sometimes brings the late Marchioness to my mind; I can remember, when she looked just as blooming, and very like her, when she smiles. Poor lady! how gay she was, when she first came to the chateau!"

"And was she not gay, afterwards?" said Blanche.

Dorothée shook her head; and Emily observed her, with eyes strongly expressive of the interest she now felt. "Let us sit down in this window," said the Lady Blanche, on reaching the opposite end of the gallery: "and pray, Dorothée, if it is not painful to you, tell us something more about the Marchioness. I should like to look into the glass you spoke of just now, and see a few of the circumstances, which you say often pass over it."

"No, my lady," replied Dorothée; "if you knew as much as I do, you would not, for you would find there a dismal train of them; I often wish I could shut them out, but they will rise to my mind. I see my dear lady on her death-bed,—her very look,—and remember all she said—it was a terrible scene!"

"Why was it so terrible?" said Emily with emotion.

"Ah, dear young lady! is not death always terrible?" replied Dorothée.

To some further enquiries of Blanche Dorothée was silent; and Emily, observing the tears in her eyes, forbore to urge the subject, and endeavoured to withdraw the attention of her young friend to some object in the gardens, where the Count, with the Countess and Monsieur Du Pont, appearing, they went down to join them.

When he perceived Emily, he advanced to meet her, and presented her to the Countess, in a manner so benign, that it recalled most powerfully to her mind the idea of her late father, and she felt more gratitude to him, than embarrassment towards the Countess, who, however, received her with one of those fascinating smiles, which her caprice sometimes allowed her to assume, and which was now the result of a conversation the Count had held with her, concerning Emily. Whatever this might be, or whatever had passed in his conversation with the lady abbess, whom he had just visited, esteem and kindness were strongly apparent in his manner, when he addressed Emily, who experienced that sweet emotion, which arises from the consciousness of possessing the approbation of the good; for to the Count's worth she had been inclined to yield her confidence almost from the first moment, in which she had seen him.

Before she could finish her acknowledgments for the hospitality she had received, and mention of her design of going immediately to the convent, she was interrupted by an invitation to lengthen her stay at the chateau, which was pressed by the Count and the Countess, with an appearance of such friendly sincerity, that, though she much wished to see her old friends at the monastery, and to sigh, once more, over her father's grave, she consented to remain a few days at the chateau.

To the abbess, however, she immediately wrote, mentioning her arrival in Languedoc and her wish to be received into the convent, as a boarder; she also sent letters to Monsieur Quesnel and to Valancourt, whom she merely informed of her arrival in France; and, as she knew not where the latter might be stationed, she directed her letter to his brother's seat in Gascony.

In the evening, Lady Blanche and Mons. Du Pont walked with Emily to the cottage of La Voisin, which she had now a melancholy pleasure in approaching, for time had softened her grief for the loss of St. Aubert, though it could not annihilate it, and she felt a soothing sadness in indulging the recollections, which this scene recalled. La Voisin was still living, and seemed to enjoy, as much as formerly, the tranquil evening of a blameless life. He was sitting at the door of his cottage, watching some of his grandchildren, playing on the grass before him, and, now and then, with a laugh, or a commendation, encouraging their sports. He immediately recollected Emily, whom he was much pleased to see, and she was as rejoiced to hear, that he had not lost one of his family, since her departure.

"Yes, ma'amselle," said the old man, "we all live merrily together still, thank God! and I believe there is not a happier family to be found in Languedoc, than ours."

Emily did not trust herself in the chamber, where St. Aubert died; and, after half an hour's conversation with La Voisin and his family, she left the cottage.

During these the first days of her stay at Chateau-le-Blanc, she was often affected, by observing the deep, but silent melancholy, which, at times, stole over Du Pont; and Emily, pitying the self-delusion, which disarmed him of the will to depart, determined to withdraw herself as soon as the respect she owed the Count and Countess De Villefort would permit. The dejection of his friend soon alarmed the anxiety of the Count, to whom Du Pont, at length, confided the secret of his hopeless affection, which, however, the former could only commiserate, though he secretly determined to befriend his suit, if an opportunity of doing so should ever occur. Considering the dangerous situation of Du Pont, he but feebly opposed his intention of leaving Chateau-le-Blanc, on the following day, but drew from him a promise of a longer visit, when he could return with safety to his peace. Emily herself, though she could not encourage his affection, esteemed him both for the many virtues he possessed, and for the services she had received from him; and it was not without tender emotions of gratitude and pity, that she now saw him depart for his family seat in Gascony; while he took leave of her with a countenance so expressive of love and grief, as to interest the Count more warmly in his cause than before.

In a few days, Emily also left the chateau, but not before the Count and Countess had received her promise to repeat her visit very soon; and she was welcomed by the abbess, with the same maternal kindness she had formerly experienced, and by the nuns, with much expression of regard. The well-known scenes of the convent occasioned her many melancholy recollections, but with these were mingled others, that inspired gratitude for having escaped the various dangers, that had pursued her, since she quitted it, and for the good, which she yet possessed; and, though she once more wept over her father's grave, with tears of tender affection, her grief was softened from its former acuteness.

Some time after her return to the monastery, she received a letter from her uncle, Mons. Quesnel, in answer to information that she had arrived in France, and to her enquiries, concerning such of her affairs as he had undertaken to conduct during her absence, especially as to the period for which La Vallée had been let, whither it was her wish to return, if it should appear, that her income would permit her to do so. The reply of Mons. Quesnel was cold and formal, as she expected, expressing neither concern for the evils she suffered, nor pleasure, that she was now removed from them; nor did he allow the opportunity to pass, of reproving her for her rejection of Count Morano, whom he affected still to believe a man of honour and fortune; nor of vehemently declaiming against Montoni, to whom he had always, till now, felt himself to be inferior. On Emily's pecuniary concerns, he was not very explicit; he informed her, however, that the term, for which La Vallée had been engaged, was nearly expired; but, without inviting her to his own house, added, that her circumstances would by no means allow her to reside there, and earnestly advised her to remain, for the present, in the convent of St. Claire.

To her enquiries respecting poor old Theresa, her late father's servant, he gave no answer. In the postscript to his letter, Monsieur Quesnel mentioned M. Motteville, in whose hands the late St. Aubert had placed the chief of his personal property, as being likely to arrange his affairs nearly to the satisfaction of his creditors, and that Emily would recover much more of her fortune, than she had formerly reason to expect. The letter also inclosed to Emily an order upon a merchant at Narbonne, for a small sum of money.

The tranquillity of the monastery, and the liberty she was suffered to enjoy, in wandering among the woods and shores of this delightful province, gradually restored her spirits to their natural tone, except that anxiety would sometimes intrude, concerning Valancourt, as the time approached, when it was possible that she might receive an answer to her letter.

CHAPTER XIII

> As when a wave, that from a cloud impends,
> And, swell'd with tempests, on the ship descends,
> White are the decks with foam; the winds aloud,
> Howl o'er the masts, and sing through ev'ry shroud:
> Pale, trembling, tir'd, the sailors freeze with fears,
> And instant death on ev'ry wave appears.
>
> POPE'S HOMER

THE Lady Blanche, meanwhile, who was left much alone, became impatient for the company of her new friend, whom she wished to observe sharing in the delight she received from the beautiful scenery around. She had now no person, to whom she could express her admiration and communicate her pleasures, no eye, that sparkled to her smile, or countenance, that reflected her happiness; and she became spiritless and pensive. The Count, observing her dissatisfaction, readily yielded to her entreaties, and reminded Emily of her promised visit; but the silence of Valancourt, which was now prolonged far beyond the period, when a letter might have arrived from Estuviere, oppressed Emily with severe anxiety, and, rendering her averse to society, she would willingly have deferred her acceptance of this invitation, till her spirits should be relieved. The Count and his family, however, pressed to see her; and, as the circumstances, that prompted her wish for solitude, could not be explained, there was an appearance of caprice in her refusal, which she could not persevere in, without offending the friends, whose esteem she valued. At length, therefore, she returned upon a second visit to Chateau-le-Blanc. Here the friendly manner of Count De Villefort encouraged Emily to mention to him her situation, respecting the estates of her late aunt, and to consult him on the means of recovering them. He had little doubt, that the law would decide in her favour, and, advising her to apply to it, offered first to write to an advocate at Avignon, on whose opinion he thought he could rely. His kindness was gratefully accepted by Emily, who, soothed by the courtesy she daily experienced, would have been once more happy, could she have been assured of Valancourt's welfare and unaltered affection. She had now been above a week at the chateau, without receiving intelligence of him, and, though she knew, that, if he was absent from his brother's residence, it was scarcely probable her letter had yet reached him, she could not forbear to admit doubts and fears, that destroyed her peace. Again she would consider of all, that might have happened in the long period, since her first seclusion at Udolpho, and her mind was sometimes so overwhelmed with an apprehension, that Valancourt was no more, or that he lived no longer for her, that the company even of Blanche became intolerably oppressive, and she would sit alone in her apartment for hours together, when the engagements of the family allowed her to do so, without incivility.

In one of these solitary hours, she unlocked a little box, which contained some letters of Valancourt, with some drawings she had sketched, during her stay in Tuscany, the latter of which were no longer interesting to her; but, in the letters, she now, with melancholy indulgence, meant to retrace the tenderness, that had so often soothed her, and rendered her, for a moment, insensible of the distance, which separated her from the writer. But their effect was now changed; the affection they expressed appealed so forcibly to her heart, when she considered that it had, perhaps, yielded to the powers of time and absence, and even the view of the hand-writing recalled so many painful recollections, that she found herself unable to go through the first she had opened, and sat musing, with her cheek resting on her arm, and tears stealing from her eyes, when old Dorothée entered the room to inform her, that dinner would be ready, an hour before the usual time. Emily started on perceiving her, and hastily put up the papers, but not before Dorothée had observed both her agitation and her tears.

"Ah, ma'amselle!" said she, "you, who are so young,—have you reason for sorrow?"

Emily tried to smile, but was unable to speak.

"Alas! dear young lady, when you come to my age, you will not weep at trifles; and surely you have nothing serious, to grieve you."

"No, Dorothée, nothing of any consequence," replied Emily. Dorothée, now stooping to pick up something, that had dropped from among the papers, suddenly exclaimed, "Holy Mary! what is it I see?" and then, trembling, sat down in a chair, that stood by the table.

"What is it you do see?" said Emily, alarmed by her manner, and looking round the room.

"It is herself," said Dorothée, "her very self! just as she looked a little before she died!"

Emily, still more alarmed, began now to fear, that Dorothée was seized with sudden phrensy, but entreated her to explain herself.

"That picture!" said she, "where did you find it, lady? it is my blessed mistress herself!"

She laid on the table the miniature, which Emily had long ago found among the papers her father had enjoined her to destroy, and over which she had once seen him shed such tender and affecting tears; and, recollecting all the various circumstances of his conduct, that had long perplexed her, her emotions increased to an excess, which deprived her of all power to ask the questions she trembled to have answered, and she could only enquire, whether Dorothée was certain the picture resembled the late marchioness.

"O, ma'amselle!" said she, "how came it to strike me so, the instant I saw it, if it was not my lady's likeness? Ah!" added she, taking up the miniature, "these are her own blue eyes—looking so sweet and so mild; and there is her very look, such as I have often seen it, when she had sat thinking for a long while, and then, the tears would often steal down her cheeks—but she never would complain! It was that look so meek, as it were, and resigned, that used to break my heart and make me love her so!"

"Dorothée!" said Emily solemnly, "I am interested in the cause of that grief, more so, perhaps, than you may imagine; and I entreat, that you will no longer refuse to indulge my curiosity;—it is not a common one."

As Emily said this, she remembered the papers, with which the picture had been found, and had scarcely a doubt, that they had concerned the Marchioness de Villeroi; but with this supposition came a scruple, whether she ought to enquire further on a subject, which might prove to be the same, that her father had so carefully endeavoured to conceal. Her curiosity, concerning the Marchioness, powerful as it was, it is probable she would now have resisted, as she had formerly done, on unwarily observing the few terrible words in the papers, which had never since been erased from her memory, had she been certain that the history of that lady was the subject of those papers, or, that such simple particulars only as it was probable Dorothée could relate were included in her father's command. What was known to her could be no secret to many other persons; and, since it appeared very unlikely, that St. Aubert should attempt to conceal what Emily might learn by ordinary means, she at length concluded, that, if the papers had related to the story of the Marchioness, it was not those circumstances of it, which Dorothée could disclose, that he had thought sufficiently important to wish to have concealed. She, therefore, no longer hesitated to make the enquiries, that might lead to the gratification of her curiosity.

"Ah, ma'amselle!" said Dorothée, "it is a sad story, and cannot be told now: but what am I saying? I never will tell it. Many years have passed, since it happened; and I never loved to talk of the Marchioness to any body, but my husband. He lived in the family, at that time, as well as myself, and he knew many particulars from me, which nobody else did; for I was about the person of my lady in her last illness, and saw and heard as much, or more than my lord himself. Sweet saint! how patient she was! When she died, I thought I could have died with her!"

"Dorothée," said Emily, interrupting her, "what you shall tell, you may depend upon it, shall never be disclosed by me. I have, I repeat it, particular reasons for wishing to be informed on this subject, and am willing to bind myself, in the most solemn manner, never to mention what you shall wish me to conceal."

Dorothée seemed surprised at the earnestness of Emily's manner, and, after regarding her for some moments, in silence, said, "Young lady! that look of yours pleads for you—it is so like my dear mistress's, that I can almost fancy I see her before me; if you were her daughter, you could not remind me of her more. But dinner will be ready—had you not better go down?"

"You will first promise to grant my request," said Emily.

"And ought not you first to tell me, ma'amselle, how this picture fell into your hands, and the reasons you say you have for curiosity about my lady?"

"Why, no, Dorothée," replied Emily, recollecting herself, "I have also particular reasons for observing silence, on these subjects, at least, till I know further; and, remember, I do not promise ever to speak upon them; therefore, do not let me induce you to satisfy my curiosity, from an expectation, that I shall gratify yours. What I may judge proper to conceal, does not concern myself alone, or I should have less scruple in revealing it: let a confidence in my honour alone persuade you to disclose what I request."

"Well, lady!" replied Dorothée, after a long pause, during which her eyes were fixed upon Emily, "you seem so much interested,—and this picture and that face of yours make me think you have some reason to be so,—that I will trust you—and tell some things, that I never told before to any body, but my husband, though there are people, who have suspected as much. I will tell you the particulars of my lady's death, too, and some of my own suspicions; but you must first promise me by all the saints"——

Emily, interrupting her, solemnly promised never to reveal what should be confided to her, without Dorothée's consent.

"But there is the horn, ma'amselle, sounding for dinner," said Dorothée; "I must be gone."

"When shall I see you again?" enquired Emily.

Dorothée mused, and then replied, "Why, madam, it may make people curious, if it is known I am so much in your apartment, and that I should be sorry for; so I will come when I am least likely to be observed. I have little leisure in the day, and I shall have a good deal to say; so, if you please, ma'am, I will come, when the family are all in bed."

"That will suit me very well," replied Emily: "Remember, then, to-night"——

"Aye, that is well remembered," said Dorothée, "I fear I cannot come to-night, madam, for there will be the dance of the vintage, and it will be late, before the servants go to rest; for, when they once set in to dance, they will keep it up, in the cool of the air, till morning; at least, it used to be so in my time."

"Ah! is it the dance of the vintage?" said Emily, with a deep sigh, remembering, that it was on the evening of this festival, in the preceding year, that St. Aubert and herself had arrived in the neighbourhood of Chateau-le-Blanc. She paused a moment, overcome by the sudden recollection, and then, recovering herself, added—"But this dance is in the open woods; you, therefore, will not be wanted, and can easily come to me."

Dorothée replied, that she had been accustomed to be present at the dance of the vintage, and she did not wish to be absent now; "but if I can get away, madam, I will," said she.

Emily then hastened to the dining-room, where the Count conducted himself with the courtesy, which is inseparable from true dignity, and of which the Countess frequently practised little, though her manner to Emily was an exception to her usual habit. But, if she retained few of the ornamental virtues, she cherished other qualities, which she seemed to consider invaluable. She had dismissed the grace of modesty, but then she knew perfectly well how to manage the stare of assurance; her manners had little of the tempered sweetness, which is necessary to render the female character interesting, but she could occasionally throw into them an affectation of spirits, which seemed to triumph over every person, who approached her. In the country, however, she generally affected an elegant languor, that persuaded her almost to faint, when her favourite read to her a story of fictitious sorrow; but her countenance suffered no change, when living objects of distress solicited her charity, and her heart beat with no transport to the thought of giving them instant relief;—she was a stranger to the highest luxury, of which, perhaps, the human mind can be sensible, for her benevolence had never yet called smiles upon the face of misery.

In the evening, the Count, with all his family, except the Countess and Mademoiselle Bearn, went to the woods to witness the festivity of the peasants. The scene was in a glade, where the trees, opening, formed a circle round the turf they highly overshadowed; between their branches, vines, loaded with ripe clusters, were hung in gay festoons; and, beneath, were tables, with fruit, wine, cheese and other rural fare,—and seats for the Count and his family. At a little distance, were benches for the elder peasants, few of whom, however, could forbear to join the jocund dance, which began soon after sunset, when several of sixty tripped it with almost as much glee and airy lightness, as those of sixteen.

The musicians, who sat carelessly on the grass, at the foot of a tree, seemed inspired by the sound of their own instruments, which were chiefly flutes and a kind of long guitar. Behind, stood a boy, flourishing a tamborine, and dancing a solo, except that, as he sometimes gaily tossed the instrument, he tripped among the other dancers, when his antic gestures called forth a broader laugh, and heightened the rustic spirit of the scene.

The Count was highly delighted with the happiness he witnessed, to which his bounty had largely contributed, and the Lady Blanche joined the dance with a young gentleman of her father's party. Du Pont requested Emily's hand, but her spirits were too much depressed, to permit her to engage in the present festivity, which called to her remembrance that of the preceding year, when St. Aubert was living, and of the melancholy scenes, which had immediately followed it.

Overcome by these recollections, she, at length, left the spot, and walked slowly into the woods, where the softened music, floating at a distance, soothed her melancholy mind. The moon threw a mellow light among the foliage; the air was balmy and cool, and Emily, lost in thought, strolled on, without observing whither, till she perceived the sounds sinking afar off, and an awful stillness round her, except that, sometimes, the nightingale beguiled the silence with

Liquid notes, that close the eye of day.

At length, she found herself near the avenue, which, on the night of her father's arrival, Michael had attempted to pass in search of a house, which was still nearly as wild and desolate as it had then appeared; for the Count had been so much engaged in directing other improvements, that he had neglected to give orders, concerning this extensive approach, and the road was yet broken, and the trees overloaded with their own luxuriance.

As she stood surveying it, and remembering the emotions, which she had formerly suffered there, she suddenly recollected the figure, that had been seen stealing among the trees, and which had returned no answer to Michael's repeated calls; and she experienced somewhat of the fear, that had then assailed her, for it did not appear improbable, that these deep woods were occasionally the haunt of banditti. She, therefore, turned back, and was hastily pursuing her way to the dancers, when she heard steps approaching from the avenue; and, being still beyond the call of the peasants on the green, for she could neither hear their voices, or their music, she quickened her pace; but the persons following gained fast upon her, and, at length, distinguishing the voice of Henri, she walked leisurely, till he came up. He expressed some surprise at meeting her so far from the company; and, on her saying, that the pleasant moon-light had beguiled her to walk farther than she intended, an exclamation burst from the lips of his companion, and she thought she heard Valancourt speak! It was, indeed, he! and the meeting was such as may be imagined, between persons so affectionate, and so long separated as they had been.

In the joy of these moments, Emily forgot all her past sufferings, and Valancourt seemed to have forgotten, that any person but Emily existed; while Henri was a silent and astonished spectator of the scene.

Valancourt asked a thousand questions, concerning herself and Montoni, which there was now no time to answer; but she learned, that her letter had been forwarded to him, at Paris, which he had previously quitted, and was returning to Gascony, whither the letter also returned, which, at length, informed him of Emily's arrival, and on the receipt of which he had immediately set out for Languedoc. On reaching the monastery, whence she had dated her letter, he found, to his extreme disappointment, that the gates were already closed for the night; and believing, that he should not see Emily, till the morrow, he was returning to his little inn, with the intention of writing to her, when he was overtaken by Henri, with whom he had been intimate at Paris, and was led to her, whom he was secretly lamenting that he should not see, till the following day.

Emily, with Valancourt and Henri, now returned to the green, where the latter presented Valancourt to the Count, who, she fancied, received him with less than his usual benignity, though it appeared, that they were not strangers to each other. He was invited, however, to partake of the diversions of the evening; and, when he had paid his respects to the Count, and while the dancers continued their festivity, he seated himself by Emily, and conversed, without restraint. The lights, which were hung among the trees, under which they sat, allowed her a more perfect view of the countenance she had so frequently in absence endeavoured to recollect, and she perceived, with some regret, that it was not the same as when last she saw it. There was all its wonted intelligence and fire; but it had lost much of the simplicity, and somewhat of the open benevolence, that used to characterise it. Still, however, it was an interesting countenance; but Emily thought she perceived, at intervals, anxiety contract, and melancholy fix the features of Valancourt; sometimes, too, he fell into a momentary musing, and then appeared anxious to dissipate thought; while, at others, as he fixed his eyes on Emily, a kind of sudden distraction seemed to cross his mind. In her he perceived the same goodness and beautiful simplicity, that had charmed him, on their first acquaintance. The bloom of her countenance was somewhat faded, but all its sweetness remained, and it was rendered more interesting, than ever, by the faint expression of melancholy, that sometimes mingled with her smile.

At his request, she related the most important circumstances, that had occurred to her, since she left France, and emotions of pity and indignation alternately prevailed in his mind, when he heard how much she had suffered from the villany of Montoni. More than once, when she was speaking of his conduct, of which the guilt was rather softened, than exaggerated, by her representation, he started from his seat, and walked away, apparently overcome as much by self accusation as by resentment. Her sufferings alone were mentioned in the few words, which he could address to her, and he listened not to the account, which she was careful to give as distinctly as possible, of the present loss of Madame Montoni's estates, and of the little reason there was to expect their restoration. At length, Valancourt remained lost in thought, and then some secret cause seemed to overcome him with anguish. Again he abruptly left her. When he returned, she perceived, that he had been weeping, and tenderly begged, that he would compose himself. "My sufferings are all passed now," said she, "for I have escaped from the tyranny of Montoni, and I see you well—let me also see you happy."

Valancourt was more agitated, than before. "I am unworthy of you, Emily," said he, "I am unworthy of you;"—words, by his manner of uttering which Emily was then more shocked than by their import. She fixed on him a mournful and enquiring eye. "Do not look thus on me," said he, turning away and pressing her hand; "I cannot bear those looks."

"I would ask," said Emily, in a gentle, but agitated voice, "the meaning of your words; but I perceive, that the question would distress you now. Let us talk on other subjects. To-morrow, perhaps, you may be more composed. Observe those moon light woods, and the towers, which appear obscurely in the perspective. You used to be a great admirer of landscape, and I have heard you say, that the faculty of deriving consolation, under misfortune, from the sublime prospects, which neither oppression, or poverty with-hold from us, was the peculiar blessing of the innocent." Valancourt was deeply affected. "Yes," replied he, "I had once a taste for innocent and elegant delights—I had once an uncorrupted heart." Then, checking himself, he added, "Do you remember our journey together in the Pyrenées?"

"Can I forget it?" said Emily.—"Would that I could!" he replied;—"that was the happiest period of my life. I then loved, with enthusiasm, whatever was truly great, or good." It was some time before Emily could repress her tears, and try to command her emotions. "If you wish to forget that journey," said she, "it must certainly be my wish to forget it also." She paused, and then added, "You make me very uneasy; but this is not the time for further enquiry;—yet, how can I bear to believe, even for a moment, that you are less worthy of my esteem than formerly? I have still sufficient confidence in your candour, to believe, that, when I shall ask for an explanation, you will give it me."—"Yes," said Valancourt, "yes, Emily: I have not yet lost my candour: if I had, I could better have disguised my emotions, on learning what were your sufferings—your virtues, while I—I—but I will say no more. I did not mean to have said even so much—I have been surprised into the self-accusation. Tell me, Emily, that you will not forget that journey—will not wish to forget it, and I will be calm. I would not lose the remembrance of it for the whole earth."

"How contradictory is this!" said Emily;—"but we may be overheard. My recollection of it shall depend upon yours; I will endeavour to forget, or to recollect it, as you may do. Let us join the Count."—"Tell me first," said Valancourt, "that you forgive the uneasiness I have occasioned you, this evening, and that you will still love me."—"I sincerely forgive you," replied Emily. "You best know whether I shall continue to love you, for you know whether you deserve my esteem. At present, I will believe that you do. It is unnecessary to say," added she, observing his dejection, "how much pain it would give me to believe otherwise.—The young lady, who approaches, is the Count's daughter."

Valancourt and Emily now joined the Lady Blanche; and the party, soon after, sat down with the Count, his son, and the Chevalier Du Pont, at a banquet, spread under a gay awning, beneath the trees. At the table also were seated several of the most venerable of the Count's tenants, and it was a festive repast to all but Valancourt and Emily. When the Count retired to the chateau, he did not invite Valancourt to accompany him, who, therefore, took leave of Emily, and retired to his solitary inn for the night: meanwhile, she soon withdrew to her own apartment, where she mused, with deep anxiety and concern, on his behaviour, and on the Count's reception of him. Her attention was thus so wholly engaged, that she forgot Dorothée and her appointment, till morning was far advanced, when, knowing that the good old woman would not come, she retired, for a few hours, to repose.

On the following day, when the Count had accidentally joined Emily in one of the walks, they talked of the festival of the preceding evening, and this led him to a mention of Valancourt. "That is a young man of talents," said he; "you were formerly acquainted with him, I perceive." Emily said, that she was. "He was introduced to me, at Paris," said the Count, "and I was much pleased with him, on our first acquaintance." He paused, and Emily trembled, between the desire of hearing more and the fear of shewing the Count, that she felt an interest on the subject. "May I ask," said he, at length, "how long you have known Monsieur Valancourt?"—"Will you allow me to ask your reason for the question, sir?" said she; "and I will answer it immediately."—"Certainly," said the Count, "that is but just. I will tell you my reason. I cannot but perceive, that Monsieur Valancourt admires you; in that, however, there is nothing extraordinary; every person, who sees you, must do the same. I am above using common-place compliments; I speak with sincerity. What I fear, is, that he is a favoured admirer."—"Why do you fear it, sir?" said Emily, endeavouring to conceal her emotion.—"Because," replied the Count, "I think him not worthy of your favour." Emily, greatly agitated, entreated further explanation. "I will give it," said he, "if you will believe, that nothing but a strong interest in your welfare could induce me to hazard that assertion."—"I must believe so, sir," replied Emily.

"But let us rest under these trees," said the Count, observing the paleness of her countenance; "here is a seat—you are fatigued." They sat down, and the Count proceeded. "Many young ladies, circumstanced as you are, would think my conduct, on this occasion, and on so short an acquaintance, impertinent, instead of friendly; from what I have observed of your temper and understanding, I do not fear such a return from you. Our acquaintance has been short, but long enough to make me esteem you, and feel a lively interest in your happiness. You deserve to be very happy, and I trust that you will be so." Emily sighed softly, and bowed her thanks. The Count paused again. "I am unpleasantly circumstanced," said he; "but an opportunity of rendering you important service shall overcome inferior considerations. Will you inform me of the manner of your first acquaintance with the Chevalier Valancourt, if the subject is not too painful?"

Emily briefly related the accident of their meeting in the presence of her father, and then so earnestly entreated the Count not to hesitate in declaring what he knew, that he perceived the violent emotion, against which she was contending, and, regarding her with a look of tender compassion, considered how he might communicate his information with least pain to his anxious auditor.

"The Chevalier and my son," said he, "were introduced to each other, at the table of a brother officer, at whose house I also met him, and invited him to my own, whenever he should be disengaged. I did not then know, that he had formed an acquaintance with a set of men, a disgrace to their species, who live by plunder and pass their lives in continual debauchery. I knew several of the Chevalier's family, resident at Paris, and considered them as sufficient pledges for his introduction to my own. But you are ill; I will leave the subject."—"No, sir," said Emily, "I beg you will proceed: I am only distressed."—"*Only!*" said the Count, with emphasis; "however, I will proceed. I soon learned, that these, his associates, had drawn him into a course of dissipation, from which he appeared to have neither the power, nor the inclination, to extricate himself. He lost large sums at the gaming-table; he became infatuated with play; and was ruined. I spoke tenderly of this to his friends, who assured me, that they had remonstrated with him, till they were weary. I afterwards learned, that, in consideration of his talents for play, which were generally successful, when unopposed by the tricks of villany,—that in consideration of these, the party had initiated him into the secrets of their trade, and allotted him a share of their profits." "Impossible!" said Emily suddenly; "but—pardon me, sir, I scarcely know what I say; allow for the distress of my mind. I must, indeed, I must believe, that you have not been truly informed. The Chevalier had, doubtless, enemies, who misrepresented him."—"I should be most happy to believe so," replied the Count, "but I cannot. Nothing short of conviction, and a regard for your happiness, could have urged me to repeat these unpleasant reports."

Emily was silent. She recollected Valancourt's sayings, on the preceding evening, which discovered the pangs of self-reproach, and seemed to confirm all that the Count had related. Yet she had not fortitude enough to dare conviction. Her heart was overwhelmed with anguish at the mere suspicion of his guilt, and she could not endure a belief of it. After a silence, the Count said, "I perceive, and can allow for, your want of conviction. It is necessary I should give some proof of what I have asserted; but this I cannot do, without subjecting one, who is very dear to me, to danger."—"What is the danger you apprehend, sir?" said Emily; "if I can prevent it, you may safely confide in my honour."—"On your honour I am certain I can rely," said the Count; "but can I trust your fortitude? Do you think you can resist the solicitation of a favoured admirer, when he pleads, in affliction, for the name of one, who has robbed him of a blessing?"—"I shall not be exposed to such a temptation, sir," said Emily, with modest pride, "for I cannot favour one, whom I must no longer esteem. I, however, readily give my word." Tears, in the mean time, contradicted her first assertion; and she felt, that time and effort only could eradicate an affection, which had been formed on virtuous esteem, and cherished by habit and difficulty.

"I will trust you then," said the Count, "for conviction is necessary to your peace, and cannot, I perceive, be obtained, without this confidence. My son has too often been an eye-witness of the Chevalier's ill conduct; he was very near being drawn in by it; he was, indeed, drawn in to the commission of many follies, but I rescued him from guilt and destruction. Judge then, Mademoiselle St. Aubert, whether a father, who had nearly lost his only son by the example of the Chevalier, has not, from conviction, reason to warn those, whom he esteems, against trusting their happiness in such hands. I have myself seen the Chevalier engaged in deep play with men, whom I almost shuddered to look upon. If you still doubt, I will refer you to my son."

"I must not doubt what you have yourself witnessed," replied Emily, sinking with grief, "or what you assert. But the Chevalier has, perhaps, been drawn only into a transient folly, which he may never repeat. If you had known the justness of his former principles, you would allow for my present incredulity."

"Alas!" observed the Count, "it is difficult to believe that, which will make us wretched. But I will not soothe you by flattering and false hopes. We all know how fascinating the vice of gaming is, and how difficult it is, also, to conquer habits; the Chevalier might, perhaps, reform for a while, but he would soon relapse into dissipation—for I fear, not only the bonds of habit would be powerful, but that his morals are corrupted. And—why should I conceal from you, that play is not his only vice? he appears to have a taste for every vicious pleasure."

The Count hesitated and paused; while Emily endeavoured to support herself, as, with increasing perturbation, she expected what he might further say. A long pause of silence ensued, during which he was visibly agitated; at length, he said, "It would be a cruel delicacy, that could prevail with me to be silent—and I will inform you, that the Chevalier's extravagance has brought him twice into the prisons of Paris, from whence he was last extricated, as I was told upon authority, which I cannot doubt, by a well-known Parisian Countess, with whom he continued to reside, when I left Paris."

He paused again; and, looking at Emily, perceived her countenance change, and that she was falling from the seat; he caught her, but she had fainted, and he called loudly for assistance. They were, however, beyond the hearing of his servants at the chateau, and he feared to leave her while he went thither for assistance, yet knew not how otherwise to obtain it; till a fountain at no great distance caught his eye, and he endeavoured to support Emily against the tree, under which she had been sitting, while he went thither for water. But, again he was perplexed, for he had nothing near him, in which water could be brought; but while, with increased anxiety, he watched her, he thought he perceived in her countenance symptoms of returning life.

It was long, however, before she revived, and then she found herself supported—not by the Count, but by Valancourt, who was observing her with looks of earnest apprehension, and who now spoke to her in a tone, tremulous with his anxiety. At the sound of his well-known voice, she raised her eyes, but presently closed them, and a faintness again came over her.

The Count, with a look somewhat stern, waved him to withdraw; but he only sighed heavily, and called on the name of Emily, as he again held the water, that had been brought, to her lips. On the Count's repeating his action, and accompanying it with words, Valancourt answered him with a look of deep resentment, and refused to leave the place, till she should revive, or to resign her for a moment to the care of any person. In the next instant, his conscience seemed to inform him of what had been the subject of the Count's conversation with Emily, and indignation flashed in his eyes; but it was quickly repressed, and succeeded by an expression of serious anguish, that induced the Count to regard him with more pity than resentment, and the view of which so much affected Emily, when she again revived, that she yielded to the weakness of tears. But she soon restrained them, and, exerting her resolution to appear recovered, she rose, thanked the Count and Henri, with whom Valancourt had entered the garden, for their care, and moved towards the chateau, without noticing Valancourt, who, heart-struck by her manner, exclaimed in a low voice—"Good God! how have I deserved this?—what has been said, to occasion this change?"

Emily, without replying, but with increased emotion, quickened her steps. "What has thus disordered you, Emily?" said he, as he still walked by her side: "give me a few moments' conversation, I entreat you;—I am very miserable!"

Though this was spoken in a low voice, it was overheard by the Count, who immediately replied, that Mademoiselle St. Aubert was then too much indisposed, to attend to any conversation, but that he would venture to promise she would see Monsieur Valancourt on the morrow, if she was better.

Valancourt's cheek was crimsoned: he looked haughtily at the Count, and then at Emily, with successive expressions of surprise, grief and supplication, which she could neither misunderstand, or resist, and she said languidly—"I shall be better tomorrow, and if you wish to accept the Count's permission, I will see you then."

"See me!" exclaimed Valancourt, as he threw a glance of mingled pride and resentment upon the Count; and then, seeming to recollect himself, he added—"But I will come, madam; I will accept the Count's *permission*."

When they reached the door of the chateau, he lingered a moment, for his resentment was now fled; and then, with a look so expressive of tenderness and grief, that Emily's heart was not proof against it, he bade her good morning, and, bowing slightly to the Count, disappeared.

Emily withdrew to her own apartment, under such oppression of heart as she had seldom known, when she endeavoured to recollect all that the Count had told, to examine the probability of the circumstances he himself believed, and to consider of her future conduct towards Valancourt. But, when she attempted to think, her mind refused controul, and she could only feel that she was miserable. One moment, she sunk under the conviction, that Valancourt was no longer the same, whom she had so tenderly loved, the idea of whom had hitherto supported her under affliction, and cheered her with the hope of happier days,—but a fallen, a worthless character, whom she must teach herself to despise—if she could not forget. Then, unable to endure this terrible supposition, she rejected it, and disdained to believe him capable of conduct, such as the Count had described, to whom she believed he had been misrepresented by some artful enemy; and there were moments, when she even ventured to doubt the integrity of the Count himself, and to suspect, that he was influenced by some selfish motive, to break her connection with Valancourt. But this was the error of an instant, only; the Count's character, which she had heard spoken of by Du Pont and many other persons, and had herself observed, enabled her to judge, and forbade the supposition; had her confidence, indeed, been less, there appeared to be no temptation to betray him into conduct so treacherous, and so cruel. Nor did reflection suffer her to preserve the hope, that Valancourt had been misrepresented to the Count, who had said, that he spoke chiefly from his own observation, and from his son's experience. She must part from Valancourt, therefore, for ever—for what of either happiness or tranquillity could she expect with a man, whose tastes were degenerated into low inclinations, and to whom vice was become habitual? whom she must no longer esteem, though the remembrance of what he once was, and the long habit of loving him, would render it very difficult for her to despise him.

"O Valancourt!" she would exclaim, "having been separated so long—do we meet, only to be miserable—only to part for ever?"

Amidst all the tumult of her mind, she remembered pertinaciously the seeming candour and simplicity of his conduct, on the preceding night; and, had she dared to trust her own heart, it would have led her to hope much from this. Still she could not resolve to dismiss him for ever, without obtaining further proof of his ill conduct; yet she saw no probability of procuring it, if, indeed, proof more positive was possible. Something, however, it was necessary to decide upon, and she almost determined to be guided in her opinion solely by the manner, with which Valancourt should receive her hints concerning his late conduct.

Thus passed the hours till dinner-time, when Emily, struggling against the pressure of her grief, dried her tears, and joined the family at table, where the Count preserved towards her the most delicate attention; but the Countess and Mademoiselle Bearn, having looked, for a moment, with surprise, on her dejected countenance, began, as usual, to talk of trifles, while the eyes of Lady Blanche asked much of her friend, who could only reply by a mournful smile.

Emily withdrew as soon after dinner as possible, and was followed by the Lady Blanche, whose anxious enquiries, however, she found herself quite unequal to answer, and whom she entreated to spare her on the subject of her distress. To converse on any topic, was now, indeed, so extremely painful to her, that she soon gave up the attempt, and Blanche left her, with pity of the sorrow, which she perceived she had no power to assuage.

Emily secretly determined to go to her convent in a day or two; for company, especially that of the Countess and Mademoiselle Bearn, was intolerable to her, in the present state of her spirits; and, in the retirement of the convent, as well as the kindness of the abbess, she hoped to recover the command of her mind, and to teach it resignation to the event, which, she too plainly perceived, was approaching.

To have lost Valancourt by death, or to have seen him married to a rival, would, she thought, have given her less anguish, than a conviction of his unworthiness, which must terminate in misery to himself, and which robbed her even of the solitary image her heart so long had cherished. These painful reflections were interrupted, for a moment, by a note from Valancourt, written in evident distraction of mind, entreating, that she would permit him to see her on the approaching evening, instead of the following morning; a request, which occasioned her so much agitation, that she was unable to answer it. She wished to see him, and to terminate her present state of suspense, yet shrunk from the interview, and, incapable of deciding for herself, she, at length, sent to beg a few moments' conversation with the Count in his library, where she delivered to him the note, and requested his advice. After reading it, he said, that, if she believed herself well enough to support the interview, his opinion was, that, for the relief of both parties, it ought to take place, that evening.

"His affection for you is, undoubtedly, a very sincere one," added the Count; "and he appears so much distressed, and you, my amiable friend, are so ill at ease—that the sooner the affair is decided, the better."

Emily replied, therefore, to Valancourt, that she would see him, and then exerted herself in endeavours to attain fortitude and composure, to bear her through the approaching scene—a scene so afflictingly the reverse of any, to which she had looked forward!

VOLUME 4

CHAPTER I

Is all the council that we two have shared,
     the hours that we have spent,
When we have chid the hasty-footed time
For parting us—Oh! and is all forgot?

And will you rend our ancient love asunder?
      MIDSUMMER NIGHT'S DREAM

IN the evening, when Emily was at length informed, that Count De Villefort requested to see her, she guessed that Valancourt was below, and, endeavouring to assume composure and to recollect all her spirits, she rose and left the apartment; but on reaching the door of the library, where she imagined him to be, her emotion returned with such energy, that, fearing to trust herself in the room, she returned into the hall, where she continued for a considerable time, unable to command her agitated spirits.

When she could recall them, she found in the library Valancourt, seated with the Count, who both rose on her entrance; but she did not dare to look at Valancourt, and the Count, having led her to a chair, immediately withdrew.

Emily remained with her eyes fixed on the floor, under such oppression of heart, that she could not speak, and with difficulty breathed; while Valancourt threw himself into a chair beside her, and, sighing heavily, continued silent, when, had she raised her eyes, she would have perceived the violent emotions, with which he was agitated.

At length, in a tremulous voice, he said, "I have solicited to see you this evening, that I might, at least, be spared the further torture of suspense, which your altered manner had occasioned me, and which the hints I have just received from the Count have in part explained. I perceive I have enemies, Emily, who envied me my late happiness, and who have been busy in searching out the means to destroy it: I perceive, too, that time and absence have weakened the affection you once felt for me, and that you can now easily be taught to forget me."

His last words faltered, and Emily, less able to speak than before, continued silent.

"O what a meeting is this!" exclaimed Valancourt, starting from his seat, and pacing the room with hurried steps, "what a meeting is this, after our long—long separation!" Again he sat down, and, after the struggle of a moment, he added in a firm but despairing tone, "This is too much—I cannot bear it! Emily, will you not speak to me?"

He covered his face with his hand, as if to conceal his emotion, and took Emily's, which she did not withdraw. Her tears could no longer be restrained; and, when he raised his eyes and perceived that she was weeping, all his tenderness returned, and a gleam of hope appeared to cross his mind, for he exclaimed, "O! you do pity me, then, you do love me! Yes, you are still my own Emily—let me believe those tears, that tell me so!"

Emily now made an effort to recover her firmness, and, hastily drying them, "Yes," said she, "I do pity you—I weep for you—but, ought I to think of you with affection? You may remember, that yester-evening I said, I had still sufficient confidence in your candour to believe, that, when I should request an explanation of your words, you would give it. This explanation is now unnecessary, I understand them too well; but prove, at least, that your candour is deserving of the confidence I give it, when I ask you, whether you are conscious of being the same estimable Valancourt—whom I once loved."

"Once loved!" cried he,—"the same—the same!" He paused in extreme emotion, and then added, in a voice at once solemn, and dejected,—"No—I am not the same!—I am lost—I am no longer worthy of you!"

He again concealed his face. Emily was too much affected by this honest confession to reply immediately, and, while she struggled to overcome the pleadings of her heart, and to act with the decisive firmness, which was necessary for her future peace, she perceived all the danger of trusting long to her resolution, in the presence of Valancourt, and was anxious to conclude an interview, that tortured them both; yet, when she considered, that this was probably their last meeting, her fortitude sunk at once, and she experienced only emotions of tenderness and of despondency.

Valancourt, meanwhile, lost in emotions of remorse and grief, which he had neither the power, or the will to express, sat insensible almost of the presence of Emily, his features still concealed, and his breast agitated by convulsive sighs.

"Spare me the necessity," said Emily, recollecting her fortitude, "spare me the necessity of mentioning those circumstances of your conduct, which oblige me to break our connection forever.—We must part, I now see you for the last time."

"Impossible!" cried Valancourt, roused from his deep silence, "You cannot mean what you say!—you cannot mean to throw me from you forever!"

"We must part," repeated Emily, with emphasis,—"and that forever! Your own conduct has made this necessary."

"This is the Count's determination," said he haughtily, "not yours, and I shall enquire by what authority he interferes between us." He now rose, and walked about the room in great emotion.

"Let me save you from this error," said Emily, not less agitated—"it is my determination, and, if you reflect a moment on your late conduct, you will perceive, that my future peace requires it."

"Your future peace requires, that we should part—part forever!" said Valancourt, "How little did I ever expect to hear you say so!"

"And how little did I expect, that it would be necessary for me to say so!" rejoined Emily, while her voice softened into tenderness, and her tears flowed again.—"That you—you, Valancourt, would ever fall from my esteem!"

He was silent a moment, as if overwhelmed by the consciousness of no longer deserving this esteem, as well as the certainty of having lost it, and then, with impassioned grief, lamented the criminality of his late conduct and the misery to which it had reduced him, till, overcome by a recollection of the past and a conviction of the future, he burst into tears, and uttered only deep and broken sighs.

The remorse he had expressed, and the distress he suffered could not be witnessed by Emily with indifference, and, had she not called to her recollection all the circumstances, of which Count De Villefort had informed her, and all he had said of the danger of confiding in repentance, formed under the influence of passion, she might perhaps have trusted to the assurances of her heart, and have forgotten his misconduct in the tenderness, which that repentance excited.

Valancourt, returning to the chair beside her, at length, said, in a calm voice, "'Tis true, I am fallen—fallen from my own esteem! but could you, Emily, so soon, so suddenly resign, if you had not before ceased to love me, or, if your conduct was not governed by the designs, I will say, the selfish designs of another person! Would you not otherwise be willing to hope for my reformation—and could you bear, by estranging me from you, to abandon me to misery—to myself!"—Emily wept aloud.—"No, Emily—no—you would not do this, if you still loved me. You would find your own happiness in saving mine."

"There are too many probabilities against that hope," said Emily, "to

justify me in trusting the comfort of my whole life to it. May I not also
ask, whether you could wish me to do this, if you really loved me?"

"Really loved you!" exclaimed Valancourt—"is it possible you can
doubt my love! Yet it is reasonable, that you should do so, since you see,
that I am less ready to suffer the horror of parting with you, than that of
involving you in my ruin. Yes, Emily—I am ruined—irreparably
ruined—I am involved in debts, which I can never discharge!" Valancourt's look, which was wild, as he spoke this, soon settled into an
expression of gloomy despair; and Emily, while she was compelled to
admire his sincerity, saw, with unutterable anguish, new reasons for fear
in the suddenness of his feelings and the extent of the misery, in which
they might involve him. After some minutes, she seemed to contend
against her grief and to struggle for fortitude to conclude the interview.
"I will not prolong these moments," said she, "by a conversation, which
can answer no good purpose. Valancourt, farewell!"

"You are not going?" said he, wildly interrupting her—"You will not
leave me thus—you will not abandon me even before my mind has
suggested any possibility of compromise between the last indulgence of
my despair and the endurance of my loss!" Emily was terrified by the
sternness of his look, and said, in a soothing voice, "You have yourself
acknowledged, that it is necessary we should part;—if you wish, that I
should believe you love me, you will repeat the acknowledgment."—
"Never—never," cried he—"I was distracted when I made it. O!
Emily—this is too much;—though you are not deceived as to my faults,
you must be deluded into this exasperation against them. The Count is
the barrier between us; but he shall not long remain so."

"You are, indeed, distracted," said Emily, "the Count is not your
enemy; on the contrary, he is my friend, and that might, in some
degree, induce you to consider him as yours."—"Your friend!" said
Valancourt, hastily, "how long has he been your friend, that he can so
easily make you forget your lover? Was it he, who recommended to
your favour the Monsieur Du Pont, who, you say, accompanied you
from Italy, and who, I say, has stolen your affections? But I have no
right to question you;—you are your own mistress. Du Pont, perhaps,
may not long triumph over my fallen fortunes!" Emily, more frightened
than before by the frantic looks of Valancourt, said, in a tone scarcely
audible, "For heaven's sake be reasonable—be composed. Monsieur
Du Pont is not your rival, nor is the Count his advocate. You have no
rival; nor, except yourself, an enemy. My heart is wrung with anguish,
which must increase while your frantic behaviour shews me, more than
ever, that you are no longer the Valancourt I have been accustomed to
love."

He made no reply, but sat with his arms rested on the table and his face concealed by his hands; while Emily stood, silent and trembling, wretched for herself and dreading to leave him in this state of mind.

"O excess of misery!" he suddenly exclaimed, "that I can never lament my sufferings, without accusing myself, nor remember you, without recollecting the folly and the vice, by which I have lost you! Why was I forced to Paris, and why did I yield to allurements, which were to make me despicable for ever! O! why cannot I look back, without interruption, to those days of innocence and peace, the days of our early love!"—The recollection seemed to melt his heart, and the frenzy of despair yielded to tears. After a long pause, turning towards her and taking her hand, he said, in a softened voice, "Emily, can you bear that we should part—can you resolve to give up an heart, that loves you like mine—an heart, which, though it has erred—widely erred, is not irretrievable from error, as, you well know, it never can be retrievable from love?" Emily made no reply, but with her tears. "Can you," continued he, "can you forget all our former days of happiness and confidence— when I had not a thought, that I might wish to conceal from you— when I had no taste—no pleasures, in which you did not participate?"

"O do not lead me to the remembrance of those days," said Emily, "unless you can teach me to forget the present; I do not mean to reproach you; if I did, I should be spared these tears; but why will you render your present sufferings more conspicuous, by contrasting them with your former virtues?"

"Those virtues," said Valancourt, "might, perhaps, again be mine, if your affection, which nurtured them, was unchanged;—but I fear, indeed, I see, that you can no longer love me; else the happy hours, which we have passed together, would plead for me, and you could not look back upon them unmoved. Yet, why should I torture myself with the remembrance—why do I linger here? Am I not ruined—would it not be madness to involve you in my misfortunes, even if your heart was still my own? I will not distress you further. Yet, before I go," added he, in a solemn voice, "let me repeat, that, whatever may be my destiny—whatever I may be doomed to suffer, I must always love you— most fondly love you! I am going, Emily, I am going to leave you—to leave you, forever!" As he spoke the last words, his voice trembled, and he threw himself again into the chair, from which he had risen. Emily was utterly unable to leave the room, or to say farewell. All impression of his criminal conduct and almost of his follies was obliterated from her mind, and she was sensible only of pity and grief.

"My fortitude is gone," said Valancourt at length; "I can no longer even struggle to recall it. I cannot now leave you—I cannot bid you an eternal farewell; say, at least, that you will see me once again." Emily's heart was somewhat relieved by the request, and she endeavoured to believe, that she ought not to refuse it. Yet she was embarrassed by recollecting, that she was a visitor in the house of the Count, who could not be pleased by the return of Valancourt. Other considerations, however, soon overcame this, and she granted his request, on the condition, that he would neither think of the Count, as his enemy, nor Du Pont as his rival. He then left her, with a heart, so much lightened by this short respite, that he almost lost every former sense of misfortune.

Emily withdrew to her own room, that she might compose her spirits and remove the traces of her tears, which would encourage the censorious remarks of the Countess and her favourite, as well as excite the curiosity of the rest of the family. She found it, however, impossible to tranquillize her mind, from which she could not expel the remembrance of the late scene with Valancourt, or the consciousness, that she was to see him again, on the morrow. This meeting now appeared more terrible to her than the last, for the ingenuous confession he had made of his ill conduct and his embarrassed circumstances, with the strength and tenderness of affection, which this confession discovered, had deeply impressed her, and, in spite of all she had heard and believed to his disadvantage, her esteem began to return. It frequently appeared to her impossible, that he could have been guilty of the depravities, reported of him, which, if not inconsistent with his warmth and impetuosity, were entirely so with his candour and sensibility. Whatever was the criminality, which had given rise to the reports, she could not now believe them to be wholly true, nor that his heart was finally closed against the charms of virtue. The deep consciousness, which he felt as well as expressed of his errors, seemed to justify the opinion; and, as she understood not the instability of youthful dispositions, when opposed by habit, and that professions frequently deceive those, who make, as well as those, who hear them, she might have yielded to the flattering persuasions of her own heart and the pleadings of Valancourt, had she not been guided by the superior prudence of the Count. He represented to her, in a clear light, the danger of her present situation, that of listening to promises of amendment, made under the influence of strong passion, and the slight hope, which could attach to a connection, whose chance of happiness rested upon the retrieval of ruined circumstances and the reform of corrupted habits. On these accounts, he lamented, that Emily had consented to a second interview, for he saw how much it would shake her resolution and increase the difficulty of her conquest.

Her mind was now so entirely occupied by nearer interests, that she forgot the old housekeeper and the promised history, which so lately had excited her curiosity, but which Dorothée was probably not very anxious to disclose, for night came; the hours passed; and she did not appear in Emily's chamber. With the latter it was a sleepless and dismal night; the more she suffered her memory to dwell on the late scenes with Valancourt, the more her resolution declined, and she was obliged to recollect all the arguments, which the Count had made use of to strengthen it, and all the precepts, which she had received from her deceased father, on the subject of self-command, to enable her to act, with prudence and dignity, on this the most severe occasion of her life. There were moments, when all her fortitude forsook her, and when, remembering the confidence of former times, she thought it impossible, that she could renounce Valancourt. His reformation then appeared certain; the arguments of Count De Villefort were forgotten; she readily believed all she wished, and was willing to encounter any evil, rather than that of an immediate separation.

Thus passed the night in ineffectual struggles between affection and reason, and she rose, in the morning, with a mind, weakened and irresolute, and a frame, trembling with illness.

CHAPTER II

Come, weep with me;—past hope, past cure, past help!
ROMEO AND JULIET

VALANCOURT, meanwhile, suffered the tortures of remorse and despair. The sight of Emily had renewed all the ardour, with which he first loved her, and which had suffered a temporary abatement from absence and the passing scenes of busy life. When, on the receipt of her letter, he set out for Languedoc, he then knew, that his own folly had involved him in ruin, and it was no part of his design to conceal this from her. But he lamented only the delay which his ill-conduct must give to their marriage, and did not foresee, that the information could induce her to break their connection forever. While the prospect of this separation overwhelmed his mind, before stung with self-reproach, he awaited their second interview, in a state little short of distraction, yet was still inclined to hope, that his pleadings might prevail upon her not to exact it. In the morning, he sent to know at what hour she would see him; and his note arrived, when she was with the Count, who had sought an opportunity of again conversing with her of Valancourt; for he perceived the extreme distress of her mind, and feared, more than ever, that her fortitude would desert her. Emily having dismissed the messenger, the Count returned to the subject of their late conversation, urging his fear of Valancourt's entreaties, and again pointing out to her the lengthened misery, that must ensue, if she should refuse to encounter some present uneasiness. His repeated arguments could, indeed, alone have protected her from the affection she still felt for Valancourt, and she resolved to be governed by them.

The hour of interview, at length, arrived. Emily went to it, at least, with composure of manner, but Valancourt was so much agitated, that he could not speak, for several minutes, and his first words were alternately those of lamentation, entreaty, and self-reproach. Afterward, he said, "Emily, I have loved you—I do love you, better than my life; but I am ruined by my own conduct. Yet I would seek to entangle you in a connection, that must be miserable for you, rather than subject myself to the punishment, which is my due, the loss of you. I am a wretch, but I will be a villain no longer.—I will not endeavour to shake your resolution by the pleadings of a selfish passion. I resign you, Emily, and will endeavour to find consolation in considering, that, though I am miserable, you, at least, may be happy. The merit of the sacrifice is, indeed, not my own, for I should never have attained strength of mind to surrender you, if your prudence had not demanded it."

He paused a moment, while Emily attempted to conceal the tears, which came to her eyes. She would have said, "You speak now, as you were wont to do," but she checked herself.—"Forgive me, Emily," said he, "all the sufferings I have occasioned you, and, sometimes, when you think of the wretched Valancourt, remember, that his only consolation would be to believe, that you are no longer unhappy by his folly." The tears now fell fast upon her cheek, and he was relapsing into the phrensy of despair, when Emily endeavoured to recall her fortitude and to terminate an interview, which only seemed to increase the distress of both. Perceiving her tears and that she was rising to go, Valancourt struggled, once more, to overcome his own feelings and to soothe hers. "The remembrance of this sorrow," said he, "shall in future be my protection. O! never again will example, or temptation have power to seduce me to evil, exalted as I shall be by the recollection of your grief for me."

Emily was somewhat comforted by this assurance. "We are now parting for ever," said she; "but, if my happiness is dear to you, you will always remember, that nothing can contribute to it more, than to believe, that you have recovered your own esteem." Valancourt took her hand;—his eyes were covered with tears, and the farewell he would have spoken was lost in sighs. After a few moments, Emily said, with difficulty and emotion, "Farewell, Valancourt, may you be happy!" She repeated her "farewell," and attempted to withdraw her hand, but he still held it and bathed it with his tears. "Why prolong these moments?" said Emily, in a voice scarcely audible, "they are too painful to us both." "This is too—too much," exclaimed Valancourt, resigning her hand

and throwing himself into a chair, where he covered his face with his hands and was overcome, for some moments, by convulsive sighs. After a long pause, during which Emily wept in silence, and Valancourt seemed struggling with his grief, she again rose to take leave of him. Then, endeavouring to recover his composure, "I am again afflicting you," said he, "but let the anguish I suffer plead for me." He then added, in a solemn voice, which frequently trembled with the agitation of his heart, "Farewell, Emily, you will always be the only object of my tenderness. Sometimes you will think of the unhappy Valancourt, and it will be with pity, though it may not be with esteem. O! what is the whole world to me, without you—without your esteem!" He checked himself—"I am falling again into the error I have just lamented. I must not intrude longer upon your patience, or I shall relapse into despair."

He once more bade Emily adieu, pressed her hand to his lips, looked at her, for the last time, and hurried out of the room.

Emily remained in the chair, where he had left her, oppressed with a pain at her heart, which scarcely permitted her to breathe, and listening to his departing steps, sinking fainter and fainter, as he crossed the hall. She was, at length, roused by the voice of the Countess in the garden, and, her attention being then awakened, the first object, which struck her sight, was the vacant chair, where Valancourt had sat. The tears, which had been, for some time, repressed by the kind of astonishment, that followed his departure, now came to her relief, and she was, at length, sufficiently composed to return to her own room.

CHAPTER III

This is no mortal business, nor no sound
That the earth owes!
SHAKESPEARE

WE now return to the mention of Montoni, whose rage and disappointment were soon lost in nearer interests, than any, which the unhappy Emily had awakened. His depredations having exceeded their usual limits, and reached an extent, at which neither the timidity of the then commercial senate of Venice, nor their hope of his occasional assistance would permit them to connive, the same effort, it was resolved, should complete the suppression of his power and the correction of his outrages. While a corps of considerable strength was upon the point of receiving orders to march for Udolpho, a young officer, prompted partly by resentment, for some injury, received from Montoni, and partly by the hope of distinction, solicited an interview with the Minister, who directed the enterprise. To him he represented, that the situation of Udolpho rendered it too strong to be taken by open force, except after some tedious operations; that Montoni had lately shewn how capable he was of adding to its strength all the advantages, which could be derived from the skill of a commander; that so considerable a body of troops, as that allotted to the expedition, could not approach Udolpho without his knowledge, and that it was not for the honour of the republic to have a large part of its regular force employed, for such a time as the siege of Udolpho would require, upon the attack of a handful of banditti. The object of the expedition, he thought, might be accomplished much more safely and speedily by mingling contrivance with force. It was possible to meet Montoni and his party, without their walls, and to attack them then; or, by approaching the fortress, with the secrecy, consistent with the march of smaller bodies of troops, to take advantage either of the treachery, or negligence of some of his party, and to rush unexpectedly upon the whole even in the castle of Udolpho.

This advice was seriously attended to, and the officer, who gave it, received the command of the troops, demanded for his purpose. His first efforts were accordingly those of contrivance alone. In the neighbourhood of Udolpho, he waited, till he had secured the assistance of several of the condottieri, of whom he found none, that he addressed, unwilling to punish their imperious master and to secure their own pardon from the senate. He learned also the number of Montoni's troops, and that it had been much increased, since his late successes. The conclusion of his plan was soon effected. Having returned with his party, who received the watch-word and other assistance from their friends within, Montoni and his officers were surprised by one division, who had been directed to their apartment, while the other maintained the slight combat, which preceded the surrender of the whole garrison. Among the persons, seized with Montoni, was Orsino, the assassin, who had joined him on his first arrival at Udolpho, and whose concealment had been made known to the senate by Count Morano, after the unsuccessful attempt of the latter to carry off Emily. It was, indeed, partly for the purpose of capturing this man, by whom one of the senate had been murdered, that the expedition was undertaken, and its success was so acceptable to them, that Morano was instantly released, notwithstanding the political suspicions, which Montoni, by his secret accusation, had excited against him. The celerity and ease, with which this whole transaction was completed, prevented it from attracting curiosity, or even from obtaining a place in any of the published records of that time; so that Emily, who remained in Languedoc, was ignorant of the defeat and signal humiliation of her late persecutor.

Her mind was now occupied with sufferings, which no effort of reason had yet been able to controul. Count De Villefort, who sincerely attempted whatever benevolence could suggest for softening them, sometimes allowed her the solitude she wished for, sometimes led her into friendly parties, and constantly protected her, as much as possible, from the shrewd enquiries and critical conversation of the Countess. He often invited her to make excursions, with him and his daughter, during which he conversed entirely on questions, suitable to her taste, without appearing to consult it, and thus endeavoured gradually to withdraw her from the subject of her grief, and to awake other interests in her mind. Emily, to whom he appeared as the enlightened friend and protector of her youth, soon felt for him the tender affection of a daughter, and her heart expanded to her young friend Blanche, as to a sister, whose kindness and simplicity compensated for the want of more brilliant qualities. It was long before she could sufficiently abstract her mind from Valancourt to listen to the story, promised by old Dorothée, concerning which her curiosity had once been so deeply interested; but Dorothée, at length, reminded her of it, and Emily desired, that she would come, that night, to her chamber.

Still her thoughts were employed by considerations, which weakened her curiosity, and Dorothée's tap at the door, soon after twelve, surprised her almost as much as if it had not been appointed. "I am come, at last, lady," said she; "I wonder what it is makes my old limbs shake so, to-night. I thought, once or twice, I should have dropped, as I was a-coming." Emily seated her in a chair, and desired, that she would compose her spirits, before she entered upon the subject, that had brought her thither. "Alas," said Dorothée, "it is thinking of that, I believe, which has disturbed me so. In my way hither too, I passed the chamber, where my dear lady died, and every thing was so still and gloomy about me, that I almost fancied I saw her, as she appeared upon her death-bed."

Emily now drew her chair near to Dorothée, who went on. "It is about twenty years since my lady Marchioness came a bride to the chateau. O! I well remember how she looked, when she came into the great hall, where we servants were all assembled to welcome her, and how happy my lord the Marquis seemed. Ah! who would have thought then!—But, as I was saying, ma'amselle, I thought the Marchioness, with all her sweet looks, did not look happy at heart, and so I told my husband, and he said it was all fancy; so I said no more, but I made my remarks, for all that. My lady Marchioness was then about your age, and, as I have often thought, very like you. Well! my lord the Marquis kept open house, for a long time, and gave such entertainments and there were such gay doings as have never been in the chateau since. I was younger, ma'amselle, then, than I am now, and was as gay as the best of them. I remember I danced with Philip, the butler, in a pink gown, with yellow ribbons, and a coif, not such as they wear now, but plaited high, with ribbons all about it. It was very becoming truly;—my lord, the Marquis, noticed me. Ah! he was a good-natured gentleman then—who would have thought that he!"——

"But the Marchioness, Dorothée," said Emily, "you was telling me of her."

"O yes, my lady Marchioness, I thought she did not seem happy at heart, and once, soon after the marriage, I caught her crying in her chamber; but, when she saw me, she dried her eyes, and pretended to smile. I did not dare then to ask what was the matter; but, the next time I saw her crying, I did, and she seemed displeased;—so I said no more. I found out, some time after, how it was. Her father, it seems, had commanded her to marry my lord, the Marquis, for his money, and there was another nobleman, or else a chevalier, that she liked better and that was very fond of her, and she fretted for the loss of him, I fancy, but she never told me so. My lady always tried to conceal her tears from the Marquis, for I have often seen her, after she has been so sorrowful, look so calm and sweet, when he came into the room! But my lord, all of a sudden, grew gloomy and fretful, and very unkind sometimes to my lady. This afflicted her very much, as I saw, for she never complained, and she used to try so sweetly to oblige him and to bring him into a good humour, that my heart has often ached to see it. But he used to be stubborn, and give her harsh answers, and then, when she found it all in vain, she would go to her own room, and cry so! I used to hear her in the anti-room, poor dear lady! but I seldom ventured to go to her. I used, sometimes, to think my lord was jealous. To be sure my lady was greatly admired, but she was too good to deserve suspicion. Among the many chevaliers, that visited at the chateau, there was one, that I always thought seemed just suited for my lady; he was so courteous, yet so spirited, and there was such a grace, as it were, in all he did, or said. I always observed, that, whenever he had been there, the Marquis was more gloomy and my lady more thoughtful, and it came into my head, that this was the chevalier she ought to have married, but I never could learn for certain."

"What was the chevalier's name, Dorothée?" said Emily.

"Why that I will not tell even to you, ma'amselle, for evil may come of it. I once heard from a person, who is since dead, that the Marchioness was not in law the wife of the Marquis, for that she had before been privately married to the gentleman she was so much attached to, and was afterwards afraid to own it to her father, who was a very stern man; but this seems very unlikely, and I never gave much faith to it. As I was saying, the Marquis was most out of humour, as I thought, when the chevalier I spoke of had been at the chateau, and, at last, his ill treatment of my lady made her quite miserable. He would see hardly any visitors at the castle, and made her live almost by herself. I was her constant attendant, and saw all she suffered, but still she never complained.

"After matters had gone on thus, for near a year, my lady was taken ill, and I thought her long fretting had made her so,—but, alas! I fear it was worse than that."

"Worse! Dorothée," said Emily, "can that be possible?"

"I fear it was so, madam, there were strange appearances. But I will only tell what happened. My lord, the Marquis——"

"Hush, Dorothée, what sounds were those?" said Emily.

Dorothée changed countenance, and, while they both listened, they heard, on the stillness of the night, music of uncommon sweetness.

"I have surely heard that voice before!" said Emily, at length.

"I have often heard it, and at this same hour," said Dorothée, solemnly, "and, if spirits ever bring music—that is surely the music of one!"

Emily, as the sounds drew nearer, knew them to be the same she had formerly heard at the time of her father's death, and, whether it was the remembrance they now revived of that melancholy event, or that she was struck with superstitious awe, it is certain she was so much affected, that she had nearly fainted.

"I think I once told you, madam," said Dorothée, "that I first heard this music, soon after my lady's death! I well remember the night!"——

"Hark! it comes again!" said Emily, "let us open the window, and listen."

They did so; but, soon, the sounds floated gradually away into distance, and all was again still; they seemed to have sunk among the woods, whose tufted tops were visible upon the clear horizon, while every other feature of the scene was involved in the night-shade, which, however, allowed the eye an indistinct view of some objects in the garden below.

As Emily leaned on the window, gazing with a kind of thrilling awe upon the obscurity beneath, and then upon the cloudless arch above, enlightened only by the stars, Dorothée, in a low voice, resumed her narrative.

"I was saying, ma'amselle, that I well remember when first I heard that music. It was one night, soon after my lady's death, that I had sat up later than usual, and I don't know how it was, but I had been thinking a great deal about my poor mistress, and of the sad scene I had lately witnessed. The chateau was quite still, and I was in the chamber at a good distance from the rest of the servants, and this, with the mournful things I had been thinking of, I suppose, made me low spirited, for I felt very lonely and forlorn, as it were, and listened often, wishing to hear a sound in the chateau, for you know, ma'amselle, when one can hear people moving, one does not so much mind, about one's fears. But all the servants were gone to bed, and I sat, thinking and thinking, till I was almost afraid to look round the room, and my poor lady's countenance often came to my mind, such as I had seen her when she was dying, and, once or twice, I almost thought I saw her before me,—when suddenly I heard such sweet music! It seemed just at my window, and I shall never forget what I felt. I had not power to move from my chair, but then, when I thought it was my dear lady's voice, the tears came to my eyes. I had often heard her sing, in her lifetime, and to be sure she had a very fine voice; it had made me cry to hear her, many a time, when she has sat in her oriel, of an evening, playing upon her lute such sad songs, and singing so. O! it went to one's heart! I have listened in the ante-chamber, for the hour together, and she would sometimes sit playing, with the window open, when it was summer time, till it was quite dark, and when I have gone in, to shut it, she has hardly seemed to know what hour it was. But, as I said, madam," continued Dorothée, "when first I heard the music, that came just now, I thought it was my late lady's, and I have often thought so again, when I have heard it, as I have done at intervals, ever since. Sometimes, many months have gone by, but still it has returned."

"It is extraordinary," observed Emily, "that no person has yet discovered the musician."

"Aye, ma'amselle, if it had been any thing earthly it would have been discovered long ago, but who could have courage to follow a spirit, and if they had, what good could it do?—for spirits, *you know*, ma'am, can take any shape, or no shape, and they will be here, one minute, and, the next perhaps, in a quite different place!"

"Pray resume your story of the Marchioness," said Emily, "and acquaint me with the manner of her death."

"I will, ma'am," said Dorothée, "but shall we leave the window?"

"This cool air refreshes me," replied Emily, "and I love to hear it creep along the woods, and to look upon this dusky landscape. You was speaking of my lord, the Marquis, when the music interrupted us."

"Yes, madam, my lord, the Marquis, became more and more gloomy; and my lady grew worse and worse, till, one night, she was taken very ill, indeed. I was called up, and, when I came to her bedside, I was shocked to see her countenance—it was so changed! She looked piteously up at me, and desired I would call the Marquis again, for he was not yet come, and tell him she had something particular to

say to him. At last, he came, and he did, to be sure, seem very sorry to
see her, but he said very little. My lady told him she felt herself to be
dying, and wished to speak with him alone, and then I left the room,
but I shall never forget his look as I went.

"When I returned, I ventured to remind my lord about sending for a
doctor, for I supposed he had forgot to do so, in his grief; but my lady
said it was then too late; but my lord, so far from thinking so, seemed
to think light of her disorder—till she was seized with such terrible
pains! O, I never shall forget her shriek! My lord then sent off a man
and horse for the doctor, and walked about the room and all over the
chateau in the greatest distress; and I staid by my dear lady, and did
what I could to ease her sufferings. She had intervals of ease, and in
one of these she sent for my lord again; when he came, I was going, but
she desired I would not leave her. O! I shall never forget what a scene
passed—I can hardly bear to think of it now! My lord was almost distracted, for my lady behaved with so much goodness, and took such
pains to comfort him, that, if he ever had suffered a suspicion to enter
his head, he must now have been convinced he was wrong. And to be
sure he did seem to be overwhelmed with the thought of his treatment
of her, and this affected her so much, that she fainted away.

"We then got my lord out of the room; he went into his library, and
threw himself on the floor, and there he staid, and would hear no reason, that was talked to him. When my lady recovered, she enquired for
him, but, afterwards, said she could not bear to see his grief, and
desired we would let her die quietly. She died in my arms, ma'amselle,
and she went off as peacefully as a child, for all the violence of her disorder was passed."

Dorothée paused, and wept, and Emily wept with her; for she was
much affected by the goodness of the late Marchioness, and by the
meek patience, with which she had suffered.

"When the doctor came," resumed Dorothée, "alas! he came too
late; he appeared greatly shocked to see her, for soon after her death a
frightful blackness spread all over her face. When he had sent the attendants out of the room, he asked me several odd questions about the
Marchioness, particularly concerning the manner, in which she had
been seized, and he often shook his head at my answers, and seemed
to mean more, than he chose to say. But I understood him too well.
However, I kept my remarks to myself, and only told them to my husband, who bade me hold my tongue. Some of the other servants, however, suspected what I did, and strange reports were whispered about
the neighbourhood, but nobody dared to make any stir about them.
When my lord heard that my lady was dead, he shut himself up, and
would see nobody but the doctor, who used to be with him alone,

sometimes for an hour together; and, after that, the doctor never talked with me again about my lady. When she was buried in the church of the convent, at a little distance yonder, if the moon was up you might see the towers here, ma'amselle, all my lord's vassals followed the funeral, and there was not a dry eye among them, for she had done a deal of good among the poor. My lord, the Marquis, I never saw any body so melancholy as he was afterwards, and sometimes he would be in such fits of violence, that we almost thought he had lost his senses. He did not stay long at the chateau, but joined his regiment, and, soon after, all the servants, except my husband and I, received notice to go, for my lord went to the wars. I never saw him after, for he would not return to the chateau, though it is such a fine place, and never finished those fine rooms he was building on the west side of it, and it has, in a manner, been shut up ever since, till my lord the Count came here."

"The death of the Marchioness appears extraordinary," said Emily, who was anxious to know more than she dared to ask.

"Yes, madam," replied Dorothée, "it was extraordinary; I have told you all I saw, and you may easily guess what I think. I cannot say more, because I would not spread reports, that might offend my lord the Count."

"You are very right," said Emily;—"where did the Marquis die?"— "In the north of France, I believe, ma'amselle," replied Dorothée. "I was very glad, when I heard my lord the Count was coming, for this had been a sad desolate place, these many years, and we heard such strange noises, sometimes, after my lady's death, that, as I told you before, my husband and I left it for a neighbouring cottage. And now, lady, I have told you all this sad history, and all my thoughts, and you have promised, you know, never to give the least hint about it."—"I have," said Emily, "and I will be faithful to my promise, Dorothée;— what you have told has interested me more than you can imagine. I only wish I could prevail upon you to tell the name of the chevalier, whom you thought so deserving of the Marchioness."

Dorothée, however, steadily refused to do this, and then returned to the notice of Emily's likeness to the late Marchioness. "There is another picture of her," added she, "hanging in a room of the suite, which was shut up. It was drawn, as I have heard, before she was married, and is much more like you than the miniature." When Emily expressed a strong desire to see this, Dorothée replied, that she did not like to open those rooms; but Emily reminded her, that the Count had talked the other day of ordering them to be opened; of which Dorothée seemed to consider much, and then she owned, that she should feel less, if she went into them with Emily first, than otherwise, and at length promised to shew the picture.

The night was too far advanced and Emily was too much affected by the narrative of the scenes, which had passed in those apartments, to wish to visit them at this hour, but she requested that Dorothée would return on the following night, when they were not likely to be observed, and conduct her thither. Besides her wish to examine the portrait, she felt a thrilling curiosity to see the chamber, in which the Marchioness had died, and which Dorothée had said remained, with the bed and furniture, just as when the corpse was removed for interment. The solemn emotions, which the expectation of viewing such a scene had awakened, were in unison with the present tone of her mind, depressed by severe disappointment. Cheerful objects rather added to, than removed this depression; but, perhaps, she yielded too much to her melancholy inclination, and imprudently lamented the misfortune, which no virtue of her own could have taught her to avoid, though no effort of reason could make her look unmoved upon the self-degradation of him, whom she had once esteemed and loved.

Dorothée promised to return, on the following night, with the keys of the chambers, and then wished Emily good repose, and departed. Emily, however, continued at the window, musing upon the melancholy fate of the Marchioness and listening, in awful expectation, for a return of the music. But the stillness of the night remained long unbroken, except by the murmuring sounds of the woods, as they waved in the breeze, and then by the distant bell of the convent, striking one. She now withdrew from the window, and, as she sat at her bed-side, indulging melancholy reveries, which the loneliness of the hour assisted, the stillness was suddenly interrupted not by music, but by very uncommon sounds, that seemed to come either from the room, adjoining her own, or from one below. The terrible catastrophe, that had been related to her, together with the mysterious circumstances, said to have since occurred in the chateau, had so much shocked her spirits, that she now sunk, for a moment, under the weakness of superstition. The sounds, however, did not return, and she retired, to forget in sleep the disastrous story she had heard.

CHAPTER IV

Now it is the time of night,
That, the graves all gaping wide,
Every one lets forth his sprite,
In the church-way path to glide.
SHAKESPEARE

ON the next night, about the same hour as before, Dorothée came to Emily's chamber, with the keys of that suite of rooms, which had been particularly appropriated to the late Marchioness. These extended along the north side of the chateau, forming part of the old building; and, as Emily's room was in the south, they had to pass over a great extent of the castle, and by the chambers of several of the family, whose observations Dorothée was anxious to avoid, since it might excite enquiry, and raise reports, such as would displease the Count. She, therefore, requested, that Emily would wait half an hour, before they ventured forth, that they might be certain all the servants were gone to bed. It was nearly one, before the chateau was perfectly still, or Dorothée thought it prudent to leave the chamber. In this interval, her spirits seemed to be greatly affected by the remembrance of past events, and by the prospect of entering again upon places, where these had occurred, and in which she had not been for so many years. Emily too was affected, but her feelings had more of solemnity, and less of fear. From the silence, into which reflection and expectation had thrown them, they, at length, roused themselves, and left the chamber. Dorothée, at first, carried the lamp, but her hand trembled so much with infirmity and alarm, that Emily took it from her, and offered her arm, to support her feeble steps.

They had to descend the great stair-case, and, after passing over a wide extent of the chateau, to ascend another, which led to the suite of rooms they were in quest of. They stepped cautiously along the open corridor, that ran round the great hall, and into which the chambers of the Count, Countess, and the Lady Blanche, opened, and, from thence, descending the chief stair-case, they crossed the hall itself. Proceeding through the servants hall, where the dying embers of a wood fire still glimmered on the hearth, and the supper table was surrounded by chairs, that obstructed their passage, they came to the foot of the back stair-case. Old Dorothée here paused, and looked around; "Let us listen," said she, "if any thing is stirring; Ma'amselle, do you hear any voice?" "None," said Emily, "there certainly is no person up in the chateau, besides ourselves." — "No, ma'amselle," said Dorothée, "but I have never been here at this hour before, and, after what I know, my fears are not wonderful." — "What do you know?" said Emily. — "O, ma'amselle, we have no time for talking now; let us go on. That door on the left is the one we must open."

They proceeded, and, having reached the top of the stair-case, Dorothée applied the key to the lock. "Ah," said she, as she endeavoured to turn it, "so many years have passed since this was opened, that I fear it will not move." Emily was more successful, and they presently entered a spacious and ancient chamber.

"Alas!" exclaimed Dorothée, as she entered, "the last time I passed through this door—I followed my poor lady's corpse!"

Emily, struck with the circumstance, and affected by the dusky and solemn air of the apartment, remained silent, and they passed on through a long suite of rooms, till they came to one more spacious than the rest, and rich in the remains of faded magnificence.

"Let us rest here awhile, madam," said Dorothée faintly, "we are going into the chamber, where my lady died! that door opens into it. Ah, ma'amselle! why did you persuade me to come?"

Emily drew one of the massy arm-chairs, with which the apartment was furnished, and begged Dorothée would sit down, and try to compose her spirits.

"How the sight of this place brings all that passed formerly to my mind!" said Dorothée; "it seems as if it was but yesterday since all that sad affair happened!"

"Hark! what noise is that?" said Emily.

Dorothée, half starting from her chair, looked round the apartment, and they listened—but, every thing remaining still, the old woman spoke again upon the subject of her sorrow. "This saloon, ma'amselle, was in my lady's time the finest apartment in the chateau, and it was fitted up according to her own taste. All this grand furniture, but you can now hardly see what it is for the dust, and our light is none of the best— ah! how I have seen this room lighted up in my lady's time!—all this grand furniture came from Paris, and was made after the fashion of some in the Louvre there, except those large glasses, and they came from some outlandish place, and that rich tapestry. How the colours are faded already!—since I saw it last!"

"I understood, that was twenty years ago," observed Emily.

"Thereabout, madam," said Dorothée, "and well remembered, but all the time between then and now seems as nothing. That tapestry used to be greatly admired at, it tells the stories out of some famous book, or other, but I have forgot the name."

Emily now rose to examine the figures it exhibited, and discovered, by verses in the Provençal tongue, wrought underneath each scene, that it exhibited stories from some of the most celebrated ancient romances.

Dorothée's spirits being now more composed, she rose, and unlocked the door that led into the late Marchioness's apartment, and Emily passed into a lofty chamber, hung round with dark arras, and so spacious, that the lamp she held up did not shew its extent; while Dorothée, when she entered, had dropped into a chair, where, sighing deeply, she scarcely trusted herself with the view of a scene so affecting to her. It was some time before Emily perceived, through the dusk, the bed on which the Marchioness was said to have died; when, advancing to the upper end of the room, she discovered the high canopied tester of dark green damask, with the curtains descending to the floor in the fashion of a tent, half drawn, and remaining apparently, as they had been left twenty years before; and over the whole bedding was thrown a counterpane, or pall, of black velvet, that hung down to the floor. Emily shuddered, as she held the lamp over it, and looked within the dark curtains, where she almost expected to have seen a human face, and, suddenly remembering the horror she had suffered upon discovering the dying Madame Montoni in the turret-chamber of Udolpho, her spirits fainted, and she was turning from the bed, when Dorothée, who had now reached it, exclaimed, "Holy Virgin! methinks I see my lady stretched upon that pall—as when last I saw her!"

Emily, shocked by this exclamation, looked involuntarily again within the curtains, but the blackness of the pall only appeared; while Dorothée was compelled to support herself upon the side of the bed, and presently tears brought her some relief.

"Ah!" said she, after she had wept awhile, "it was here I sat on that terrible night, and held my lady's hand, and heard her last words, and saw all her sufferings—*here* she died in my arms!"

"Do not indulge these painful recollections," said Emily, "let us go. Shew me the picture you mentioned, if it will not too much affect you."

"It hangs in the oriel," said Dorothée rising, and going towards a small door near the bed's head, which she opened, and Emily followed with the light, into the closet of the late Marchioness.

"Alas! there she is, ma'amselle," said Dorothée, pointing to a portrait of a lady, "there is her very self! just as she looked when she came first to the chateau. You see, madam, she was all blooming like you, then— and so soon to be cut off!"

While Dorothée spoke, Emily was attentively examining the picture, which bore a strong resemblance to the miniature, though the expression of the countenance in each was somewhat different; but still she thought she perceived something of that pensive melancholy in the portrait, which so strongly characterised the miniature.

"Pray, ma'amselle, stand beside the picture, that I may look at you together," said Dorothée, who, when the request was complied with, exclaimed again at the resemblance. Emily also, as she gazed upon it, thought that she had somewhere seen a person very like it, though she could not now recollect who this was.

In this closet were many memorials of the departed Marchioness; a robe and several articles of her dress were scattered upon the chairs, as if they had just been thrown off. On the floor were a pair of black satin slippers, and, on the dressing-table, a pair of gloves and a long black veil, which, as Emily took it up to examine, she perceived was dropping to pieces with age.

"Ah!" said Dorothée, observing the veil, "my lady's hand laid it there; it has never been moved since!"

Emily, shuddering, immediately laid it down again. "I well remember seeing her take it off," continued Dorothée, "it was on the night before her death, when she had returned from a little walk I had persuaded her to take in the gardens, and she seemed refreshed by it. I told her how much better she looked, and I remember what a languid smile she gave me; but, alas! she little thought, or I either, that she was to die, that night."

Dorothée wept again, and then, taking up the veil, threw it suddenly over Emily, who shuddered to find it wrapped round her, descending even to her feet, and, as she endeavoured to throw it off, Dorothée intreated that she would keep it on for one moment. "I thought," added she, "how like you would look to my dear mistress in that veil; — may your life, ma'amselle, be a happier one than hers!"

Emily, having disengaged herself from the veil, laid it again on the dressing-table, and surveyed the closet, where every object, on which her eye fixed, seemed to speak of the Marchioness. In a large oriel window of painted glass, stood a table, with a silver crucifix, and a prayer-book open; and Emily remembered with emotion what Dorothée had mentioned concerning her custom of playing on her lute in this window, before she observed the lute itself, lying on a corner of the table, as if it had been carelessly placed there by the hand, that had so often awakened it.

"This is a sad forlorn place!" said Dorothée, "for, when my dear lady died, I had no heart to put it to rights, or the chamber either; and my lord never came into the rooms after, so they remain just as they did when my lady was removed for interment."

While Dorothée spoke, Emily was still looking on the lute, which was a Spanish one, and remarkably large; and then, with a hesitating hand, she took it up, and passed her fingers over the chords. They were out of tune, but uttered a deep and full sound. Dorothée started at their well-known tones, and, seeing the lute in Emily's hand, said, "This is the lute my lady Marchioness loved so! I remember when last she played upon it—it was on the night that she died. I came as usual to undress her, and, as I entered the bed-chamber, I heard the sound of music from the oriel, and perceiving it was my lady's, who was sitting there, I stepped softly to the door, which stood a little open, to listen; for the music—though it was mournful—was so sweet! There I saw her, with the lute in her hand, looking upwards, and the tears fell upon her cheeks, while she sung a vesper hymn, so soft, and so solemn! and her voice trembled, as it were, and then she would stop for a moment, and wipe away her tears, and go on again, lower than before. O! I had often listened to my lady, but never heard any thing so sweet as this; it made me cry, almost, to hear it. She had been at prayers, I fancy, for there was the book open on the table beside her—aye, and there it lies open still! Pray, let us leave the oriel, ma'amselle," added Dorothée, "this is a heart-breaking place!"

Having returned into the chamber, she desired to look once more upon the bed, when, as they came opposite to the open door, leading into the saloon, Emily, in the partial gleam, which the lamp threw into it, thought she saw something glide along into the obscurer part of the room. Her spirits had been much affected by the surrounding scene, or it is probable this circumstance, whether real or imaginary, would not have affected her in the degree it did; but she endeavoured to conceal her emotion from Dorothée, who, however, observing her countenance change, enquired if she was ill.

"Let us go," said Emily, faintly, "the air of these rooms is unwholesome;" but, when she attempted to do so, considering that she must pass through the apartment where the phantom of her terror had appeared, this terror increased, and, too faint to support herself, she sat down on the side of the bed.

Dorothée, believing that she was only affected by a consideration of the melancholy catastrophe, which had happened on this spot, endeavoured to cheer her; and then, as they sat together on the bed, she began to relate other particulars concerning it, and this without reflecting, that it might increase Emily's emotion, but because they were particularly interesting to herself. "A little before my lady's death," said she, "when the pains were gone off, she called me to her, and stretching out her hand to me, I sat down just there—where the curtain falls upon the bed. How well I remember her look at the time—death was in it!—I can almost fancy I see her now.—There she lay, ma'amselle—her face was upon the pillow there! This black counterpane was not upon the bed then; it was laid on, after her death, and she was laid out upon it."

Emily turned to look within the dusky curtains, as if she could have seen the countenance of which Dorothée spoke. The edge of the white pillow only appeared above the blackness of the pall, but, as her eyes wandered over the pall itself, she fancied she saw it move. Without speaking, she caught Dorothée's arm, who, surprised by the action, and by the look of terror that accompanied it, turned her eyes from Emily to the bed, where, in the next moment she, too, saw the pall slowly lifted, and fall again.

Emily attempted to go, but Dorothée stood fixed and gazing upon the bed; and, at length, said—"It is only the wind, that waves it, ma'am-selle; we have left all the doors open: see how the air waves the lamp, too.—It is only the wind."

She had scarcely uttered these words, when the pall was more violently agitated than before; but Emily, somewhat ashamed of her terrors, stepped back to the bed, willing to be convinced that the wind only had occasioned her alarm; when, as she gazed within the curtains, the pall moved again, and, in the next moment, the apparition of a human countenance rose above it.

Screaming with terror, they both fled, and got out of the chamber as fast as their trembling limbs would bear them, leaving open the doors of all the rooms, through which they passed. When they reached the stair-case, Dorothée threw open a chamber door, where some of the female servants slept, and sunk breathless on the bed; while Emily, deprived of all presence of mind, made only a feeble attempt to conceal the occasion of her terror from the astonished servants; and, though Dorothée, when she could speak, endeavoured to laugh at her own fright, and was joined by Emily, no remonstrances could prevail with the servants, who had quickly taken the alarm, to pass even the remainder of the night in a room so near to these terrific chambers.

Dorothée having accompanied Emily to her own apartment, they then began to talk over, with some degree of coolness, the strange circumstance, that had just occurred; and Emily would almost have doubted her own perceptions, had not those of Dorothée attested their truth. Having now mentioned what she had observed in the outer chamber, she asked the housekeeper, whether she was certain no door had been left unfastened, by which a person might secretly have entered the apartments? Dorothée replied, that she had constantly kept the keys of the several doors in her own possession; that, when she had gone her rounds through the castle, as she frequently did, to examine if all was safe, she had tried these doors among the rest, and had always found them fastened. It was, therefore, impossible, she added, that any person could have got admittance into the apartments; and, if they could—it was very improbable they should have chose to sleep in a place so cold and forlorn.

Emily observed, that their visit to these chambers had, perhaps, been watched, and that some person, for a frolic, had followed them into the rooms, with a design to frighten them, and, while they were in the oriel, had taken the opportunity of concealing himself in the bed.

Dorothée allowed, that this was possible, till she recollected, that, on entering the apartments, she had turned the key of the outer door, and this, which had been done to prevent their visit being noticed by any of the family, who might happen to be up, must effectually have excluded every person, except themselves, from the chambers; and she now persisted in affirming, that the ghastly countenance she had seen was nothing human, but some dreadful apparition.

Emily was very solemnly affected. Of whatever nature might be the appearance she had witnessed, whether human or supernatural, the fate of the deceased Marchioness was a truth not to be doubted; and this unaccountable circumstance, occurring in the very scene of her sufferings, affected Emily's imagination with a superstitious awe, to which, after having detected the fallacies at Udolpho, she might not have yielded, had she been ignorant of the unhappy story, related by the housekeeper. Her she now solemnly conjured to conceal the occurrence of this night, and to make light of the terror she had already betrayed, that the Count might not be distressed by reports, which would certainly spread alarm and confusion among his family. "Time," she added, "may explain this mysterious affair; meanwhile let us watch the event in silence."

Dorothée readily acquiesced; but she now recollected that she had left all the doors of the north suite of rooms open, and, not having courage to return alone to lock even the outer one, Emily, after some effort, so far conquered her own fears, that she offered to accompany her to the foot of the back stair-case, and to wait there while Dorothée ascended, whose resolution being re-assured by this circumstance, she consented to go, and they left Emily's apartment together.

No sound disturbed the stillness, as they passed along the halls and galleries; but, on reaching the foot of the back stair-case, Dorothée's resolution failed again; having, however, paused a moment to listen, and no sound being heard above, she ascended, leaving Emily below, and, scarcely suffering her eye to glance within the first chamber, she fastened the door, which shut up the whole suite of apartments, and returned to Emily.

As they stepped along the passage, leading into the great hall, a sound of lamentation was heard, which seemed to come from the hall itself, and they stopped in new alarm to listen, when Emily presently distinguished the voice of Annette, whom she found crossing the hall, with another female servant, and so terrified by the report, which the other maids had spread, that, believing she could be safe only where her lady was, she was going for refuge to her apartment. Emily's endeavours to laugh, or to argue her out of these terrors, were equally vain, and, in compassion to her distress, she consented that she should remain in her room during the night.

CHAPTER V

Hail, mildly-pleasing Solitude!
Companion of the wise and good—

Thine is the balmy breath of morn,
Just as the dew-bent rose is born.

But chief when evening scenes decay
And the faint landscape swims away,
Thine is the doubtful, soft decline,
And that best hour of musing thine.
THOMSON

EMILY'S injunctions to Annette to be silent on the subject of her terror were ineffectual, and the occurrence of the preceding night spread such alarm among the servants, who now all affirmed, that they had frequently heard unaccountable noises in the chateau, that a report soon reached the Count of the north side of the castle being haunted. He treated this, at first, with ridicule, but, perceiving, that it was productive of serious evil, in the confusion it occasioned among his household, he forbade any person to repeat it, on pain of punishment.

The arrival of a party of his friends soon withdrew his thoughts entirely from this subject, and his servants had now little leisure to brood over it, except, indeed, in the evenings after supper, when they all assembled in their hall, and related stories of ghosts, till they feared to look round the room; started, if the echo of a closing door murmured along the passage, and refused to go singly to any part of the castle.

On these occasions Annette made a distinguished figure. When she told not only of all the wonders she had witnessed, but of all that she had imagined, in the castle of Udolpho, with the story of the strange disappearance of Signora Laurentini, she made no trifling impression on the mind of her attentive auditors. Her suspicions, concerning Montoni, she would also have freely disclosed, had not Ludovico, who was now in the service of the Count, prudently checked her loquacity, whenever it pointed to that subject.

Among the visitors at the chateau was the Baron de Saint Foix, an old friend of the Count, and his son, the Chevalier St. Foix, a sensible and amiable young man, who, having in the preceding year seen the Lady Blanche, at Paris, had become her declared admirer. The friendship, which the Count had long entertained for his father, and the equality of their circumstances made him secretly approve of the connection; but, thinking his daughter at this time too young to fix her choice for life, and wishing to prove the sincerity and strength of the Chevalier's attachment, he then rejected his suit, though without forbidding his future hope. This young man now came, with the Baron, his father, to claim the reward of a steady affection, a claim, which the Count admitted and which Blanche did not reject.

While these visitors were at the chateau, it became a scene of gaiety and splendour. The pavilion in the woods was fitted up and frequented, in the fine evenings, as a supper-room, when the hour usually concluded with a concert, at which the Count and Countess, who were scientific performers, and the Chevaliers Henri and St. Foix, with the Lady Blanche and Emily, whose voices and fine taste compensated for the want of more skilful execution, usually assisted. Several of the Count's servants performed on horns and other instruments, some of which, placed at a little distance among the woods, spoke, in sweet response, to the harmony, that proceeded from the pavilion.

At any other period, these parties would have been delightful to Emily; but her spirits were now oppressed with a melancholy, which she perceived that no kind of what is called amusement had power to dissipate, and which the tender and, frequently, pathetic, melody of these concerts sometimes increased to a very painful degree.

She was particularly fond of walking in the woods, that hung on a promontory, overlooking the sea. Their luxuriant shade was soothing to her pensive mind, and, in the partial views, which they afforded of the Mediterranean, with its winding shores and passing sails, tranquil beauty was united with grandeur. The paths were rude and frequently overgrown with vegetation, but their tasteful owner would suffer little to be done to them, and scarcely a single branch to be lopped from the venerable trees. On an eminence, in one of the most sequestered parts of these woods, was a rustic seat, formed of the trunk of a decayed oak, which had once been a noble tree, and of which many lofty branches still flourishing united with beech and pines to over-canopy the spot. Beneath their deep umbrage, the eye passed over the tops of other woods, to the Mediterranean, and, to the left, through an opening, was seen a ruined watch-tower, standing on a point of rock, near the sea, and rising from among the tufted foliage.

Hither Emily often came alone in the silence of evening, and, soothed by the scenery and by the faint murmur, that rose from the waves, would sit, till darkness obliged her to return to the chateau. Frequently, also, she visited the watch-tower, which commanded the entire prospect, and, when she leaned against its broken walls, and thought of Valancourt, she not once imagined, what was so true, that this tower had been almost as frequently his resort, as her own, since his estrangement from the neighbouring chateau.

One evening, she lingered here to a late hour. She had sat on the steps of the building, watching, in tranquil melancholy, the gradual effect of evening over the extensive prospect, till the gray waters of the Mediterranean and the massy woods were almost the only features of the scene, that remained visible; when, as she gazed alternately on these, and on the mild blue of the heavens, where the first pale star of evening appeared, she personified the hour in the following lines:—

SONG OF THE EVENING HOUR

Last of the Hours, that track the fading Day,
I move along the realms of twilight air,
And hear, remote, the choral song decay
Of sister-nymphs, who dance around his car.

Then, as I follow through the azure void,
His partial splendour from my straining eye
Sinks in the depth of space; my only guide
His faint ray dawning on the farthest sky;

Save that sweet, lingering strain of gayer Hours,
Whose close my voice prolongs in dying notes,
While mortals on the green earth own its pow'rs,
As downward on the evening gale it floats.

When fades along the West the Sun's last beam,
As, weary, to the nether world he goes,
And mountain-summits catch the purple gleam,
And slumbering ocean faint and fainter glows,

Silent upon the globe's broad shade I steal,
And o'er its dry turf shed the cooling dews,
And ev'ry fever'd herb and flow'ret heal,
And all their fragrance on the air diffuse.

Where'er I move, a tranquil pleasure reigns;
O'er all the scene the dusky tints I send,
That forests wild and mountains, stretching plains
And peopled towns, in soft confusion blend.

Wide o'er the world I waft the fresh'ning wind,
Low breathing through the woods and twilight vale,
In whispers soft, that woo the pensive mind
Of him, who loves my lonely steps to hail.

His tender oaten reed I watch to hear,
Stealing its sweetness o'er some plaining rill,
Or soothing ocean's wave, when storms are near,
Or swelling in the breeze from distant hill!

I wake the fairy elves, who shun the light;
When, from their blossom'd beds, they slily peep,

And spy my pale star, leading on the night,—
Forth to their games and revelry they leap;

Send all the prison'd sweets abroad in air,
That with them slumber'd in the flow'ret's cell;
Then to the shores and moon-light brooks repair,
Till the high larks their matin-carol swell.

The wood-nymphs hail my airs and temper'd shade,
With ditties soft and lightly sportive dance,
On river margin of some bow'ry glade,
And strew their fresh buds as my steps advance:

But, swift I pass, and distant regions trace,
For moon-beams silver all the eastern cloud,
And Day's last crimson vestige fades apace;
Down the steep west I fly from Midnight's shroud.

The moon was now rising out of the sea. She watched its gradual progress, the extending line of radiance it threw upon the waters, the sparkling oars, the sail faintly silvered, and the wood-tops and the battlements of the watch-tower, at whose foot she was sitting, just tinted with the rays. Emily's spirits were in harmony with this scene. As she sat meditating, sounds stole by her on the air, which she immediately knew to be the music and the voice she had formerly heard at midnight, and the emotion of awe, which she felt, was not unmixed with terror, when she considered her remote and lonely situation. The sounds drew nearer. She would have risen to leave the place, but they seemed to come from the way she must have taken towards the chateau, and she awaited the event in trembling expectation. The sounds continued to approach, for some time, and then ceased. Emily sat listening, gazing and unable to move, when she saw a figure emerge from the shade of the woods and pass along the bank, at some little distance before her. It went swiftly, and her spirits were so overcome with awe, that, though she saw, she did not much observe it.

Having left the spot, with a resolution never again to visit it alone, at so late an hour, she began to approach the chateau, when she heard voices calling her from the part of the wood, which was nearest to it. They were the shouts of the Count's servants, who were sent to search for her; and when she entered the supper-room, where he sat with Henri and Blanche, he gently reproached her with a look, which she blushed to have deserved.

This little occurrence deeply impressed her mind, and, when she withdrew to her own room, it recalled so forcibly the circumstances she had witnessed, a few nights before, that she had scarcely courage to remain alone. She watched to a late hour, when, no sound having renewed her fears, she, at length, sunk to repose. But this was of short continuance, for she was disturbed by a loud and unusual noise, that seemed to come from the gallery, into which her chamber opened. Groans were distinctly heard, and, immediately after, a dead weight fell against the door, with a violence, that threatened to burst it open. She called loudly to know who was there, but received no answer, though, at intervals, she still thought she heard something like a low moaning. Fear deprived her of the power to move. Soon after, she heard footsteps in a remote part of the gallery, and, as they approached, she called more loudly than before, till the steps paused at her door. She then distinguished the voices of several of the servants, who seemed too much engaged by some circumstance without, to attend to her calls; but, Annette soon after entering the room for water, Emily understood, that one of the maids had fainted, whom she immediately desired them to bring into her room, where she assisted to restore her. When this girl had recovered her speech, she affirmed, that, as she was passing up the back stair-case, in the way to her chamber, she had seen an apparition on the second landing-place; she held the lamp low, she said, that she might pick her way, several of the stairs being infirm and even decayed, and it was upon raising her eyes, that she saw this appearance. It stood for a moment in the corner of the landing-place, which she was approaching, and then, gliding up the stairs, vanished at the door of the apartment, that had been lately opened. She heard afterwards a hollow sound.

"Then the devil has got a key to that apartment," said Dorothée, "for it could be nobody but he; I locked the door myself!"

The girl, springing down the stairs and passing up the great stair-case, had run, with a faint scream, till she reached the gallery, where she fell, groaning, at Emily's door.

Gently chiding her for the alarm she had occasioned, Emily tried to make her ashamed of her fears; but the girl persisted in saying, that she had seen an apparition, till she went to her own room, whither she was accompanied by all the servants present, except Dorothée, who, at Emily's request, remained with her during the night. Emily was perplexed, and Dorothée was terrified, and mentioned many occurrences of former times, which had long since confirmed her superstitions; among these, according to her belief, she had once witnessed an appearance, like that just described, and on the very same spot, and it was the remembrance of it, that had made her pause, when she was going to ascend the stairs with Emily, and which had increased her reluctance to open the north apartments. Whatever might be Emily's opinions, she did not disclose them, but listened attentively to all that Dorothée communicated, which occasioned her much thought and perplexity.

From this night the terror of the servants increased to such an excess, that several of them determined to leave the chateau, and requested their discharge of the Count, who, if he had any faith in the subject of their alarm, thought proper to dissemble it, and, anxious to avoid the inconvenience that threatened him, employed ridicule and then argument to convince them they had nothing to apprehend from supernatural agency. But fear had rendered their minds inaccessible to reason; and it was now, that Ludovico proved at once his courage and his gratitude for the kindness he had received from the Count, by offering to watch, during a night, in the suite of rooms, reputed to be haunted. He feared, he said, no spirits, and, if any thing of human form appeared — he would prove that he dreaded that as little.

The Count paused upon the offer, while the servants, who heard it, looked upon one another in doubt and amazement, and Annette, terrified for the safety of Ludovico, employed tears and entreaties to dissuade him from his purpose.

"You are a bold fellow," said the Count, smiling, "Think well of what you are going to encounter, before you finally determine upon it. However, if you persevere in your resolution, I will accept your offer, and your intrepidity shall not go unrewarded."

"I desire no reward, your *Excellenza*," replied Ludovico, "but your approbation. Your *Excellenza* has been sufficiently good to me already; but I wish to have arms, that I may be equal to my enemy, if he should appear."

"Your sword cannot defend you against a ghost," replied the Count, throwing a glance of irony upon the other servants, "neither can bars, or bolts; for a spirit, you know, can glide through a keyhole as easily as through a door."

"Give me a sword, my lord Count," said Ludovico, "and I will lay all the spirits, that shall attack me, in the red sea."

"Well," said the Count, "you shall have a sword, and good cheer, too; and your brave comrades here will, perhaps, have courage enough to remain another night in the chateau, since your boldness will certainly, for this night, at least, confine all the malice of the spectre to yourself."

Curiosity now struggled with fear in the minds of several of his fellow servants, and, at length, they resolved to await the event of Ludovico's rashness.

Emily was surprised and concerned, when she heard of his intention, and was frequently inclined to mention what she had witnessed in the north apartments to the Count, for she could not entirely divest herself of fears for Ludovico's safety, though her reason represented these to be absurd. The necessity, however, of concealing the secret, with which Dorothée had entrusted her, and which must have been mentioned, with the late occurrence, in excuse for her having so privately visited the north apartments, kept her entirely silent on the subject of her apprehension; and she tried only to soothe Annette, who held, that Ludovico was certainly to be destroyed; and who was much less affected by Emily's consolatory efforts, than by the manner of old Dorothée, who often, as she exclaimed Ludovico, sighed, and threw up her eyes to heaven.

CHAPTER VI

Ye gods of quiet, and of sleep profound!
Whose soft dominion o'er this castle sways,
And all the widely-silent places round,
Forgive me, if my trembling pen displays
What never yet was sung in mortal lays.
THOMSON

THE Count gave orders for the north apartments to be opened and prepared for the reception of Ludovico; but Dorothée, remembering what she had lately witnessed there, feared to obey, and, not one of the other servants daring to venture thither, the rooms remained shut up till the time when Ludovico was to retire thither for the night, an hour, for which the whole household waited with impatience.

After supper, Ludovico, by the order of the Count, attended him in his closet, where they remained alone for near half an hour, and, on leaving which, his Lord delivered to him a sword.

"It has seen service in mortal quarrels," said the Count, jocosely, "you will use it honourably, no doubt, in a spiritual one. Tomorrow, let me hear that there is not one ghost remaining in the chateau."

Ludovico received it with a respectful bow. "You shall be obeyed, my Lord," said he; "I will engage, that no spectre shall disturb the peace of the chateau after this night."

They now returned to the supper-room, where the Count's guests awaited to accompany him and Ludovico to the door of the north apartments, and Dorothée, being summoned for the keys, delivered them to Ludovico, who then led the way, followed by most of the inhabitants of the chateau. Having reached the back stair-case, several of the servants shrunk back, and refused to go further, but the rest followed him to the top of the stair-case, where a broad landing-place allowed them to flock round him, while he applied the key to the door, during which they watched him with as much eager curiosity as if he had been performing some magical rite.

Ludovico, unaccustomed to the lock, could not turn it, and

Dorothée, who had lingered far behind, was called forward, under whose hand the door opened slowly, and, her eye glancing within the dusky chamber, she uttered a sudden shriek, and retreated. At this signal of alarm, the greater part of the crowd hurried down the stairs, and the Count, Henri and Ludovico were left alone to pursue the enquiry, who instantly rushed into the apartment, Ludovico with a drawn sword, which he had just time to draw from the scabbard, the Count with the lamp in his hand, and Henri carrying a basket, containing provisions for the courageous adventurer.

Having looked hastily round the first room, where nothing appeared to justify alarm, they passed on to the second; and, here too all being quiet, they proceeded to a third with a more tempered step. The Count had now leisure to smile at the discomposure, into which he had been surprised, and to ask Ludovico in which room he designed to pass the night.

"There are several chambers beyond these, your *Excellenza*," said Ludovico, pointing to a door, "and in one of them is a bed, they say. I will pass the night there, and when I am weary of watching, I can lie down."

"Good;" said the Count; "let us go on. You see these rooms shew nothing, but damp walls and decaying furniture. I have been so much engaged since I came to the chateau, that I have not looked into them till now. Remember, Ludovico, to tell the housekeeper, to-morrow, to throw open these windows. The damask hangings are dropping to pieces, I will have them taken down, and this antique furniture removed."

"Dear sir!" said Henri, "here is an arm-chair so massy with gilding, that it resembles one of the state chairs at the Louvre, more than any thing else."

"Yes," said the Count, stopping a moment to survey it, "there is a history belonging to that chair, but I have not time to tell it. — Let us pass on. This suite runs to a greater extent than I had imagined; it is many years since I was in them. But where is the bed-room you speak of, Ludovico? — these are only ante-chambers to the great drawing-room. I remember them in their splendour!"

"The bed, my Lord," replied Ludovico, "they told me, was in a room that opens beyond the saloon, and terminates the suite."

"O, here is the saloon," said the Count, as they entered the spacious apartment, in which Emily and Dorothée had rested. He here stood for a moment, surveying the reliques of faded grandeur, which it exhibited — the sumptuous tapestry — the long and low sophas of velvet, with frames heavily carved and gilded — the floor inlaid with small squares of fine marble, and covered in the centre with a piece of very rich tapestry-work—the casements of painted glass, and the large Venetian mirrors, of a size and quality, such as at that period France could not make, which reflected, on every side, the spacious apartment. These had formerly also reflected a gay and brilliant scene, for this had been the state-room of the chateau, and here the Marchioness had held the assemblies, that made part of the festivities of her nuptials. If the wand of a magician could have recalled the vanished groups, many of them vanished even from the earth! that once had passed over these polished mirrors, what a varied and contrasted picture would they have exhibited with the present! Now, instead of a blaze of lights, and a splendid and busy crowd, they reflected only the rays of the one glimmering lamp, which the Count held up, and which scarcely served to shew the three forlorn figures, that stood surveying the room, and the spacious and dusky walls around them.

"Ah!" said the Count to Henri, awaking from his deep reverie, "how the scene is changed since last I saw it! I was a young man, then, and the Marchioness was alive and in her bloom; many other persons were here, too, who are now no more! There stood the orchestra; here we tripped in many a sprightly maze—the walls echoing to the dance! Now, they resound only one feeble voice—and even that will, ere long, be heard no more! My son, remember, that I was once as young as yourself, and that you must pass away like those, who have preceded you—like those, who, as they sung and danced in this once gay apartment, forgot, that years are made up of moments, and that every step they took carried them nearer to their graves. But such reflections are useless, I had almost said criminal, unless they teach us to prepare for eternity, since, otherwise, they cloud our present happiness, without guiding us to a future one. But enough of this; let us go on."

Ludovico now opened the door of the bed-room, and the Count, as he entered, was struck with the funereal appearance, which the dark arras gave to it. He approached the bed, with an emotion of solemnity, and, perceiving it to be covered with the pall of black velvet, paused; "What can this mean?" said he, as he gazed upon it.

"I have heard, my Lord," said Ludovico, as he stood at the feet, looking within the canopied curtains, "that the Lady Marchioness de Villeroi died in this chamber, and remained here till she was removed to be buried; and this, perhaps, Signor, may account for the pall."

The Count made no reply, but stood for a few moments engaged in thought, and evidently much affected. Then, turning to Ludovico, he asked him with a serious air, whether he thought his courage would support him through the night? "If you doubt this," added the Count, "do not be ashamed to own it; I will release you from your engagement, without exposing you to the triumphs of your fellow-servants."

Ludovico paused; pride, and something very like fear, seemed struggling in his breast; pride, however, was victorious;—he blushed, and his hesitation ceased.

"No, my Lord," said he, "I will go through with what I have begun; and I am grateful for your consideration. On that hearth I will make a fire, and, with the good cheer in this basket, I doubt not I shall do well."

"Be it so," said the Count; "but how will you beguile the tediousness of the night, if you do not sleep?"

"When I am weary, my Lord," replied Ludovico, "I shall not fear to sleep; in the meanwhile, I have a book, that will entertain me."

"Well," said the Count, "I hope nothing will disturb you; but if you should be seriously alarmed in the night, come to my apartment. I have too much confidence in your good sense and courage, to believe you will be alarmed on slight grounds; or suffer the gloom of this chamber, or its remote situation, to overcome you with ideal terrors. To-morrow, I shall have to thank you for an important service; these rooms shall then be thrown open, and my people will be convinced of their error. Good night, Ludovico; let me see you early in the morning, and remember what I lately said to you."

"I will, my Lord; good night to your *Excellenza*; let me attend you with the light."

He lighted the Count and Henri through the chambers to the outer door; on the landing-place stood a lamp, which one of the affrighted servants had left, and Henri, as he took it up, again bade Ludovico good night, who, having respectfully returned the wish, closed the door upon them, and fastened it. Then, as he retired to the bed-chamber, he examined the rooms, through which he passed, with more minuteness than he had done before, for he apprehended, that some person might have concealed himself in them, for the purpose of frightening him. No one, however, but himself, was in these chambers, and, leaving open the doors, through which he passed, he came again to the great drawing-room, whose spaciousness and silent gloom somewhat awed him. For a moment he stood, looking back through the long suite of rooms he had quitted, and, as he turned, perceiving a light and his own figure, reflected in one of the large mirrors, he started. Other objects too were seen obscurely on its dark surface, but he paused not to examine them, and returned hastily into the bed-room, as he surveyed which, he observed the door of the oriel, and opened it. All within was still. On looking round, his eye was arrested by the portrait of the deceased Marchioness, upon which he gazed, for a considerable time, with great attention and some surprise; and then, having examined the closet, he returned into the bed-room, where he kindled a wood fire, the bright blaze of which revived his spirits, which had begun to yield to the gloom and silence of the place, for gusts of wind alone broke at intervals this silence. He now drew a small table and a chair near the fire, took a bottle of wine, and some cold provision out of his basket, and regaled himself. When he had finished his repast, he laid his sword upon the table, and, not feeling disposed to sleep, drew from his pocket the book he had spoken of. — It was a volume of old Provençal tales. Having stirred the fire into a brighter blaze, trimmed his lamp, and drawn his chair upon the hearth, he began to read, and his attention was soon wholly occupied by the scenes, which the page disclosed.

The Count, meanwhile, had returned to the supper-room, whither those of the party, who had attended him to the north apartment, had retreated, upon hearing Dorothée's scream, and who were now earnest in their enquiries concerning those chambers. The Count rallied his guests on their precipitate retreat, and on the superstitious inclination which had occasioned it, and this led to the question, Whether the spirit, after it has quitted the body, is ever permitted to revisit the earth; and if it is, whether it was possible for spirits to become visible to the sense. The Baron was of opinion, that the first was probable, and the last was possible, and he endeavoured to justify this opinion by respectable authorities, both ancient and modern, which he quoted. The Count, however, was decidedly against him, and a long conversation ensued, in which the usual arguments on these subjects were on both sides brought forward with skill, and discussed with candour, but without converting either party to the opinion of his opponent. The effect of their conversation on their auditors was various. Though the Count had much the superiority of the Baron in point of argument, he had considerably fewer adherents; for that love, so natural to the human mind, of whatever is able to distend its faculties with wonder and astonishment, attached the majority of the company to the side of the Baron; and, though many of the Count's propositions were unanswerable, his opponents were inclined to believe this the consequence of their own want of knowledge, on so abstracted a subject, rather than that arguments did not exist, which were forcible enough to conquer his.

Blanche was pale with attention, till the ridicule in her father's glance called a blush upon her countenance, and she then endeavoured to forget the superstitious tales she had been told in her convent. Meanwhile, Emily had been listening with deep attention to the discussion of what was to her a very interesting question, and, remembering the appearance she had witnessed in the apartment of the late Marchioness, she was frequently chilled with awe. Several times she was on the point of mentioning what she had seen, but the fear of giving pain to the Count, and the dread of his ridicule, restrained her;

and, awaiting in anxious expectation the event of Ludovico's intrepidity, she determined that her future silence should depend upon it.

When the party had separated for the night, and the Count retired to his dressing-room, the remembrance of the desolate scenes he had lately witnessed in his own mansion deeply affected him, but at length he was aroused from his reverie and his silence. "What music is that I hear?"—said he suddenly to his valet, "Who plays at this late hour?"

The man made no reply, and the Count continued to listen, and then added, "That is no common musician; he touches the instrument with a delicate hand; who is it, Pierre?"

"My lord!" said the man, hesitatingly.

"Who plays that instrument?" repeated the Count.

"Does not your lordship know, then?" said the valet.

"What mean you?" said the Count, somewhat sternly.

"Nothing, my Lord, I meant nothing," rejoined the man submissively—"Only—that music—goes about the house at midnight often, and I thought your lordship might have heard it before."

"Music goes about the house at midnight! Poor fellow!—does nobody dance to the music, too?"

"It is not in the chateau, I believe, my Lord; the sounds come from the woods, they say, though they seem so near;—but then a spirit can do any thing!"

"Ah, poor fellow!" said the Count, "I perceive you are as silly as the rest of them; to-morrow, you will be convinced of your ridiculous error. But hark!—what voice is that?"

"O my Lord! that is the voice we often hear with the music."

"Often!" said the Count, "How often, pray? It is a very fine one."

"Why, my Lord, I myself have not heard it more than two or three times, but there are those who have lived here longer, that have heard it often enough."

"What a swell was that!" exclaimed the Count, as he still listened, "And now, what a dying cadence! This is surely something more than mortal!"

"That is what they say, my Lord," said the valet; "they say it is nothing mortal, that utters it; and if I might say my thoughts"—

"Peace!" said the Count, and he listened till the strain died away.

"This is strange!" said he, as he turned from the window, "Close the casements, Pierre."

Pierre obeyed, and the Count soon after dismissed him, but did not so soon lose the remembrance of the music, which long vibrated in his fancy in tones of melting sweetness, while surprise and perplexity engaged his thoughts.

Ludovico, meanwhile, in his remote chamber, heard, now and then, the faint echo of a closing door, as the family retired to rest, and then the hall clock, at a great distance, strike twelve. "It is midnight," said he, and he looked suspiciously round the spacious chamber. The fire on the hearth was now nearly expiring, for his attention having been engaged by the book before him, he had forgotten every thing besides; but he soon added fresh wood, not because he was cold, though the night was stormy, but because he was cheerless; and, having again trimmed his lamp, he poured out a glass of wine, drew his chair nearer to the crackling blaze, tried to be deaf to the wind, that howled mournfully at the casements, endeavoured to abstract his mind from the melancholy, that was stealing upon him, and again took up his book. It had been lent to him by Dorothée, who had formerly picked it up in an obscure corner of the Marquis's library, and who, having opened it and perceived some of the marvels it related, had carefully preserved it for her own entertainment, its condition giving her some excuse for detaining it from its proper station. The damp corner into which it had fallen, had caused the cover to be disfigured and mouldy, and the leaves to be so discoloured with spots, that it was not without difficulty the letters could be traced. The fictions of the Provençal writers, whether drawn from the Arabian legends, brought by the Saracens into Spain, or recounting the chivalric exploits performed by the crusaders, whom the Troubadors accompanied to the east, were generally splendid and always marvellous, both in scenery and incident; and it is not wonderful, that Dorothée and Ludovico should be fascinated by inventions, which had captivated the careless imagination in every rank of society, in a former age. Some of the tales, however, in the book now before Ludovico, were of simple structure, and exhibited nothing of the magnificent machinery and heroic manners, which usually characterized the fables of the twelfth century, and of this description was the one he now happened to open, which, in its original style, was of great length, but which may be thus shortly related. The reader will perceive, that it is strongly tinctured with the superstition of the times.

THE PROVENÇAL TALE

"There lived, in the province of Bretagne, a noble Baron, famous for his magnificence and courtly hospitalities. His castle was graced with ladies of exquisite beauty, and thronged with illustrious knights; for the honour he paid to feats of chivalry invited the brave of distant countries to enter his lists, and his court was more splendid than those of many princes. Eight minstrels were retained in his service, who used to sing to their harps romantic fictions, taken from the Arabians, or adventures of chivalry, that befel knights during the crusades, or the martial deeds of the Baron, their lord;—while he, surrounded by his knights and ladies, banqueted in the great hall of his castle, where the costly tapestry, that adorned the walls with pictured exploits of his ancestors, the casements of painted glass, enriched with armorial bearings, the gorgeous banners, that waved along the roof, the sumptuous canopies, the profusion of gold and silver, that glittered on the sideboards, the numerous dishes, that covered the tables, the number and gay liveries of the attendants, with the chivalric and splendid attire of the guests, united to form a scene of magnificence, such as we may not hope to see in these *degenerate days*.

"Of the Baron, the following adventure is related. One night, having retired late from the banquet to his chamber, and dismissed his attendants, he was surprised by the appearance of a stranger of a noble air, but of a sorrowful and dejected countenance. Believing, that this person had been secreted in the apartment, since it appeared impossible he could have lately passed the anti-room, unobserved by the pages in waiting, who would have prevented this intrusion on their lord, the Baron, calling loudly for his people, drew his sword, which he had not yet taken from his side, and stood upon his defence. The stranger slowly advancing, told him, that there was nothing to fear; that he came with no hostile design, but to communicate to him a terrible secret, which it was necessary for him to know.

"The Baron, appeased by the courteous manners of the stranger, after surveying him, for some time, in silence, returned his sword into the scabbard, and desired him to explain the means, by which he had obtained access to the chamber, and the purpose of this extraordinary visit.

"Without answering either of these enquiries, the stranger said, that he could not then explain himself, but that, if the Baron would follow him to the edge of the forest, at a short distance from the castle walls, he would there convince him, that he had something of importance to disclose.

"This proposal again alarmed the Baron, who could scarcely believe, that the stranger meant to draw him to so solitary a spot, at this hour of the night, without harbouring a design against his life, and he refused to go, observing, at the same time, that, if the stranger's purpose was an honourable one, he would not persist in refusing to reveal the occasion of his visit, in the apartment where they were.

"While he spoke this, he viewed the stranger still more attentively than before, but observed no change in his countenance, or any symptom, that might intimate a consciousness of evil design. He was habited like a knight, was of a tall and majestic stature, and of dignified and courteous manners. Still, however, he refused to communicate the subject of his errand in any place, but that he had mentioned, and, at the same time, gave hints concerning the secret he would disclose, that awakened a degree of solemn curiosity in the Baron, which, at length, induced him to consent to follow the stranger, on certain conditions.

"'Sir knight,' said he, 'I will attend you to the forest, and will take with me only four of my people, who shall witness our conference.'

"To this, however, the Knight objected.

"'What I would disclose,' said he, with solemnity, 'is to you alone. There are only three living persons, to whom the circumstance is known; it is of more consequence to you and your house, than I shall now explain. In future years, you will look back to this night with satisfaction or repentance, accordingly as you now determine. As you would hereafter prosper—follow me; I pledge you the honour of a knight, that no evil shall befall you;—if you are contented to dare futurity—remain in your chamber, and I will depart as I came.'

"'Sir knight,' replied the Baron, 'how is it possible, that my future peace can depend upon my present determination?'

"'That is not now to be told,' said the stranger, 'I have explained myself to the utmost. It is late; if you follow me it must be quickly;—you will do well to consider the alternative.'

"The Baron mused, and, as he looked upon the knight, he perceived his countenance assume a singular solemnity."

[Here Ludovico thought he heard a noise, and he threw a glance round the chamber, and then held up the lamp to assist his observation; but, not perceiving any thing to confirm his alarm, he took up the book again and pursued the story.]

"The Baron paced his apartment, for some time, in silence, impressed by the last words of the stranger, whose extraordinary request he feared to grant, and feared, also, to refuse. At length, he said, 'Sir knight, you are utterly unknown to me; tell me yourself,—is it reasonable, that I should trust myself alone with a stranger, at this hour, in a solitary forest? Tell me, at least, who you are, and who assisted to secrete you in this chamber.'

"The knight frowned at these latter words, and was a moment silent; then, with a countenance somewhat stern, he said,

"'I am an English knight; I am called Sir Bevys of Lancaster,—and my deeds are not unknown at the Holy City, whence I was returning to my native land, when I was benighted in the neighbouring forest.'

"'Your name is not unknown to fame,' said the Baron, 'I have heard of it.' (The Knight looked haughtily.) 'But why, since my castle is known to entertain all true knights, did not your herald announce you? Why did you not appear at the banquet, where your presence would

have been welcomed, instead of hiding yourself in my castle, and stealing to my chamber, at midnight?'

"The stranger frowned, and turned away in silence; but the Baron
repeated the questions.

"'I come not,' said the Knight, 'to answer enquiries, but to reveal
facts. If you would know more, follow me, and again I pledge the honour of a Knight, that you shall return in safety.—Be quick in your determination—I must be gone.'

"After some further hesitation, the Baron determined to follow the
stranger, and to see the result of his extraordinary request; he, therefore,
again drew forth his sword, and, taking up a lamp, bade the Knight lead
on. The latter obeyed, and, opening the door of the chamber, they
passed into the anti-room, where the Baron, surprised to find all his
pages asleep, stopped, and, with hasty violence, was going to reprimand
them for their carelessness, when the Knight waved his hand, and
looked so expressively upon the Baron, that the latter restrained his
resentment, and passed on.

"The Knight, having descended a stair-case, opened a secret door,
which the Baron had believed was known only to himself, and, proceeding through several narrow and winding passages, came, at length,
to a small gate, that opened beyond the walls of the castle. Meanwhile,
the Baron followed in silence and amazement, on perceiving that these
secret passages were so well known to a stranger, and felt inclined to
return from an adventure, that appeared to partake of treachery, as well
as danger. Then, considering that he was armed, and observing the
courteous and noble air of his conductor, his courage returned, he
blushed, that it had failed him for a moment, and he resolved to trace
the mystery to its source.

"He now found himself on the heathy platform, before the great
gates of his castle, where, on looking up, he perceived lights glimmering in the different casements of the guests, who were retiring to sleep;
and, while he shivered in the blast, and looked on the dark and desolate scene around him, he thought of the comforts of his warm chamber, rendered cheerful by the blaze of wood, and felt, for a moment,
the full contrast of his present situation."

[Here Ludovico paused a moment, and, looking at his own fire, gave
it a brightening stir.]

"The wind was strong, and the Baron watched his lamp with anxiety,
expecting every moment to see it extinguished; but, though the flame
wavered, it did not expire, and he still followed the stranger, who often
sighed as he went, but did not speak.

"When they reached the borders of the forest, the Knight turned, and raised his head, as if he meant to address the Baron, but then, closing his lips in silence, he walked on.

"As they entered, beneath the dark and spreading boughs, the Baron, affected by the solemnity of the scene, hesitated whether to proceed, and demanded how much further they were to go. The Knight replied only by a gesture, and the Baron, with hesitating steps and a suspicious eye, followed through an obscure and intricate path, till, having proceeded a considerable way, he again demanded whither they were going, and refused to proceed unless he was informed.

"As he said this, he looked at his own sword, and at the Knight alternately, who shook his head, and whose dejected countenance disarmed the Baron, for a moment, of suspicion.

"'A little further is the place, whither I would lead you,' said the stranger; 'no evil shall befall you—I have sworn it on the honour of a knight.'

"The Baron, re-assured, again followed in silence, and they soon arrived at a deep recess of the forest, where the dark and lofty chesnuts entirely excluded the sky, and which was so overgrown with underwood, that they proceeded with difficulty. The Knight sighed deeply as he passed, and sometimes paused; and having, at length, reached a spot, where the trees crowded into a knot, he turned, and, with a terrific look, pointing to the ground, the Baron saw there the body of a man, stretched at its length, and weltering in blood; a ghastly wound was on the forehead, and death appeared already to have contracted the features.

"The Baron, on perceiving the spectacle, started in horror, looked at the Knight for explanation, and was then going to raise the body and examine if there were yet any remains of life; but the stranger, waving his hand, fixed upon him a look so earnest and mournful, as not only much surprised him, but made him desist.

"But, what were the Baron's emotions, when, on holding the lamp near the features of the corpse, he discovered the exact resemblance of the stranger his conductor, to whom he now looked up in astonishment and enquiry? As he gazed, he perceived the countenance of the Knight change, and begin to fade, till his whole form gradually vanished from his astonished sense! While the Baron stood, fixed to the spot, a voice was heard to utter these words:——"

[Ludovico started, and laid down the book, for he thought he heard a voice in the chamber, and he looked toward the bed, where, however, he saw only the dark curtains and the pall. He listened, scarcely daring to draw his breath, but heard only the distant roaring of the sea in the storm, and the blast, that rushed by the casements; when, concluding, that he had been deceived by its sighings, he took up his book to finish the story.]

"While the Baron stood, fixed to the spot, a voice was heard to utter these words:——

"The body of Sir Bevys of Lancaster, a noble knight of England, lies before you. He was, this night, waylaid and murdered, as he journeyed from the Holy City towards his native land. Respect the honour of knighthood and the law of humanity; inter the body in christian ground, and cause his murderers to be punished. As ye observe, or neglect this, shall peace and happiness, or war and misery, light upon you and your house for ever!"

"The Baron, when he recovered from the awe and astonishment, into which this adventure had thrown him, returned to his castle, whither he caused the body of Sir Bevys to be removed; and, on the following day, it was interred, with the honours of knighthood, in the chapel of the castle, attended by all the noble knights and ladies, who graced the court of Baron de Brunne."

Ludovico, having finished this story, laid aside the book, for he felt drowsy, and, after putting more wood on the fire and taking another glass of wine, he reposed himself in the arm-chair on the hearth. In his dream he still beheld the chamber where he really was, and, once or twice, started from imperfect slumbers, imagining he saw a man's face, looking over the high back of his armchair. This idea had so strongly impressed him, that, when he raised his eyes, he almost expected to meet other eyes, fixed upon his own, and he quitted his seat and looked behind the chair, before he felt perfectly convinced, that no person was there.

Thus closed the hour.

CHAPTER VII

> Enjoy the honey-heavy dew of slumber;
> Thou hast no figures, nor no fantasies,
> Which busy care draws in the brains of men;
> Therefore thou sleep'st so sound.
>
> SHAKESPEARE

THE Count, who had slept little during the night, rose early, and, anxious to speak with Ludovico, went to the north apartment; but, the outer door having been fastened, on the preceding night, he was obliged to knock loudly for admittance. Neither the knocking, or his voice was heard; but, considering the distance of this door from the bed-room, and that Ludovico, wearied with watching, had probably fallen into a deep sleep, the Count was not surprised on receiving no answer, and, leaving the door, he went down to walk in his grounds.

It was a gray autumnal morning. The sun, rising over Provence, gave only a feeble light, as his rays struggled through the vapours that ascended from the sea, and floated heavily over the wood-tops, which were now varied with many a mellow tint of autumn. The storm was passed, but the waves were yet violently agitated, and their course was traced by long lines of foam, while not a breeze fluttered in the sails of the vessels, near the shore, that were weighing anchor to depart. The still gloom of the hour was pleasing to the Count, and he pursued his way through the woods, sunk in deep thought.

Emily also rose at an early hour, and took her customary walk along the brow of the promontory, that overhung the Mediterranean. Her mind was now not occupied with the occurrences of the chateau, and Valancourt was the subject of her mournful thoughts; whom she had not yet taught herself to consider with indifference, though her judgment constantly reproached her for the affection, that lingered in her heart, after her esteem for him was departed. Remembrance frequently gave her his parting look and the tones of his voice, when he had bade her a last farewel; and, some accidental associations now recalling these circumstances to her fancy, with peculiar energy, she shed bitter tears to the recollection.

Having reached the watch-tower, she seated herself on the broken steps, and, in melancholy dejection, watched the waves, half hid in vapour, as they came rolling towards the shore, and threw up their light spray round the rocks below. Their hollow murmur and the obscuring mists, that came in wreaths up the cliffs, gave a solemnity to the scene, which was in harmony with the temper of her mind, and she sat, given up to the remembrance of past times, till this became too painful, and she abruptly quitted the place. On passing the little gate of the watch-tower, she observed letters, engraved on the stone postern, which she paused to examine, and, though they appeared to have been rudely cut with a pen-knife, the characters were familiar to her; at length, recognizing the hand-writing of Valancourt, she read, with trembling anxiety the following lines, entitled

SHIPWRECK

'Tis solemn midnight! On this lonely steep,
Beneath this watch-tow'r's desolated wall,
Where mystic shapes the wonderer appall,
I rest; and view below the desert deep,
As through tempestuous clouds the moon's cold light
Gleams on the wave. Viewless, the winds of night

With loud mysterious force the billows sweep,
And sullen roar the surges, far below.
In the still pauses of the gust I hear
The voice of spirits, rising sweet and slow,
And oft among the clouds their forms appear.
But hark! what shriek of death comes in the gale,
And in the distant ray what glimmering sail
Bends to the storm?—Now sinks the note of fear!
Ah! wretched mariners!—no more shall day
Unclose his cheering eye to light ye on your way!

From these lines it appeared, that Valancourt had visited the tower; that he had probably been here on the preceding night, for it was such an one as they described, and that he had left the building very lately, since it had not long been light, and without light it was impossible these letters could have been cut. It was thus even probable, that he might be yet in the gardens.

As these reflections passed rapidly over the mind of Emily, they called up a variety of contending emotions, that almost overcame her spirits; but her first impulse was to avoid him, and, immediately leaving the tower, she returned, with hasty steps, towards the chateau. As she passed along, she remembered the music she had lately heard near the tower, with the figure, which had appeared, and, in this moment of agitation, she was inclined to believe, that she had then heard and seen Valancourt; but other recollections soon convinced her of her error. On turning into a thicker part of the woods, she perceived a person, walking slowly in the gloom at some little distance, and, her mind engaged by the idea of him, she started and paused, imagining this to be Valancourt. The person advanced with quicker steps, and, before she could recover recollection enough to avoid him, he spoke, and she then knew the voice of the Count, who expressed some surprise, on finding her walking at so early an hour, and made a feeble effort to rally her on her love of solitude. But he soon perceived this to be more a subject of concern than of light laughter, and, changing his manner, affectionately expostulated with Emily, on thus indulging unavailing regret; who, though she acknowledged the justness of all he said, could not restrain her tears, while she did so, and he presently quitted the topic. Expressing surprise at not having yet heard from his friend, the Advocate at Avignon, in answer to the questions proposed to him, respecting the estates of the late Madame Montoni, he, with friendly zeal, endeavoured to cheer Emily with hopes of establishing her claim to them; while she felt, that the estates could now contribute little to the happiness of a life, in which Valancourt had no longer an interest.

When they returned to the chateau, Emily retired to her apartment, and Count De Villefort to the door of the north chambers. This was still fastened, but, being now determined to arouse Ludovico, he renewed his calls more loudly than before, after which a total silence ensued, and the Count, finding all his efforts to be heard ineffectual, at length began to fear, that some accident had befallen Ludovico, whom terror of an imaginary being might have deprived of his senses. He, therefore, left the door with an intention of summoning his servants to force it open, some of whom he now heard moving in the lower part of the chateau.

To the Count's enquiries, whether they had seen or heard Ludovico, they replied in affright, that not one of them had ventured on the north side of the chateau, since the preceding night.

"He sleeps soundly then," said the Count, "and is at such a distance from the outer door, which is fastened, that to gain admittance to the chambers it will be necessary to force it. Bring an instrument, and follow me."

The servants stood mute and dejected, and it was not till nearly all the household were assembled, that the Count's orders were obeyed. In the mean time, Dorothée was telling of a door, that opened from a gallery, leading from the great stair-case into the last anti-room of the saloon, and, this being much nearer to the bed-chamber, it appeared probable, that Ludovico might be easily awakened by an attempt to open it. Thither, therefore, the Count went, but his voice was as ineffectual at this door as it had proved at the remoter one; and now, seriously interested for Ludovico, he was himself going to strike upon the door with the instrument, when he observed its singular beauty, and with-held the blow. It appeared, on the first glance, to be of ebony, so dark and close was its grain and so high its polish; but it proved to be only of larch wood, of the growth of Provence, then famous for its forests of larch. The beauty of its polished hue and of its delicate carvings determined the Count to spare this door, and he returned to that leading from the back stair-case, which being, at length, forced, he entered the first anti-room, followed by Henri and a few of the most courageous of his servants, the rest awaiting the event of the enquiry on the stairs and landing-place.

All was silent in the chambers, through which the Count passed, and, having reached the saloon, he called loudly upon Ludovico; after which, still receiving no answer, he threw open the door of the bed-room, and entered.

The profound stillness within confirmed his apprehensions for Ludovico, for not even the breathings of a person in sleep were heard; and his uncertainty was not soon terminated, since the shutters being all closed, the chamber was too dark for any object to be distinguished in it.

The Count bade a servant open them, who, as he crossed the room to do so, stumbled over something, and fell to the floor, when his cry occasioned such panic among the few of his fellows, who had ventured thus far, that they instantly fled, and the Count and Henri were left to finish the adventure.

Henri then sprung across the room, and, opening a window-shutter, they perceived, that the man had fallen over a chair near the hearth, in which Ludovico had been sitting;—for he sat there no longer, nor could any where be seen by the imperfect light, that was admitted into the apartment. The Count, seriously alarmed, now opened other shutters, that he might be enabled to examine further, and, Ludovico not yet appearing, he stood for a moment, suspended in astonishment and scarcely trusting his senses, till, his eyes glancing on the bed, he advanced to examine whether he was there asleep. No person, however, was in it, and he proceeded to the oriel, where every thing remained as on the preceding night, but Ludovico was no where to be found.

The Count now checked his amazement, considering, that Ludovico might have left the chambers, during the night, overcome by the terrors, which their lonely desolation and the recollected reports, concerning them, had inspired. Yet, if this had been the fact, the man would naturally have sought society, and his fellow servants had all declared they had not seen him; the door of the outer room also had been found fastened, with the key on the inside; it was impossible, therefore, for him to have passed through that, and all the outer doors of this suite were found, on examination, to be bolted and locked, with the keys also within them. The Count, being then compelled to believe, that the lad had escaped through the casements, next examined them, but such as opened wide enough to admit the body of a man were found to be carefully secured either by iron bars, or by shutters, and no vestige appeared of any person having attempted to pass them; neither was it probable, that Ludovico would have incurred the risque of breaking his neck, by leaping from a window, when he might have walked safely through a door.

The Count's amazement did not admit of words; but he returned once more to examine the bed-room, where was no appearance of disorder, except that occasioned by the late overthrow of the chair, near which had stood a small table, and on this Ludovico's sword, his lamp, the book he had been reading, and the remnant of his flask of wine still remained. At the foot of the table, too, was the basket with some fragments of provision and wood.

Henri and the servant now uttered their astonishment without reserve, and, though the Count said little, there was a seriousness in his manner, that expressed much. It appeared, that Ludovico must have quitted these rooms by some concealed passage, for the Count could not believe, that any supernatural means had occasioned this event, yet, if there was any such passage, it seemed inexplicable why he should retreat through it, and it was equally surprising, that not even the smallest vestige should appear, by which his progress could be traced. In the rooms every thing remained as much in order as if he had just walked out by the common way.

The Count himself assisted in lifting the arras, with which the bed-chamber, saloon and one of the ante-rooms were hung, that he might discover if any door had been concealed behind it; but, after a laborious search, none was found, and he, at length, quitted the apartments, having secured the door of the last ante-chamber, the key of which he took into his own possession. He then gave orders, that strict search should be made for Ludovico not only in the chateau, but in the neighbourhood, and, retiring with Henri to his closet, they remained there in conversation for a considerable time, and whatever was the subject of it, Henri from this hour lost much of his vivacity, and his manners were particularly grave and reserved, whenever the topic, which now agitated the Count's family with wonder and alarm, was introduced.

On the disappearing of Ludovico, Baron St. Foix seemed strengthened in all his former opinions concerning the probability of apparitions, though it was difficult to discover what connection there could possibly be between the two subjects, or to account for this effect otherwise than by supposing, that the mystery attending Ludovico, by exciting awe and curiosity, reduced the mind to a state of sensibility, which rendered it more liable to the influence of superstition in general. It is, however, certain, that from this period the Baron and his adherents became more bigoted to their own systems than before, while the terrors of the Count's servants increased to an excess, that occasioned many of them to quit the mansion immediately, and the rest remained only till others could be procured to supply their places.

The most strenuous search after Ludovico proved unsuccessful, and, after several days of indefatigable enquiry, poor Annette gave herself up to despair, and the other inhabitants of the chateau to amazement.

Emily, whose mind had been deeply affected by the disastrous fate of the late Marchioness and with the mysterious connection, which she fancied had existed between her and St. Aubert, was particularly impressed by the late extraordinary event, and much concerned for the loss of Ludovico, whose integrity and faithful services claimed both her esteem and gratitude. She was now very desirous to return to the quiet retirement of her convent, but every hint of this was received with real sorrow by the Lady Blanche, and affectionately set aside by the Count, for whom she felt much of the respectful love and admiration of a daughter, and to whom, by Dorothée's consent, she, at length, mentioned the appearance, which they had witnessed in the chamber of the deceased Marchioness. At any other period, he would have smiled at such a relation, and have believed, that its object had existed only in the distempered fancy of the relater; but he now attended to Emily with seriousness, and, when she concluded, requested of her a promise, that this occurrence should rest in silence. "Whatever may be the cause and the import of these extraordinary occurrences," added the Count, "time only can explain them. I shall keep a wary eye upon all that passes in the chateau, and shall pursue every possible means of discovering the fate of Ludovico. Meanwhile, we must be prudent and be silent. I will myself watch in the north chambers, but of this we will say nothing, till the night arrives, when I purpose doing so."

The Count then sent for Dorothée, and required of her also a promise of silence, concerning what she had already, or might in future witness of an extraordinary nature; and this ancient servant now related to him the particulars of the Marchioness de Villeroi's death, with some of which he appeared to be already acquainted, while by others he was evidently surprised and agitated. After listening to this narrative, the Count retired to his closet, where he remained alone for several hours; and, when he again appeared, the solemnity of his manner surprised and alarmed Emily, but she gave no utterance to her thoughts.

On the week following the disappearance of Ludovico, all the Count's guests took leave of him, except the Baron, his son Mons. St. Foix, and Emily; the latter of whom was soon after embarrassed and distressed by the arrival of another visitor, Mons. Du Pont, which made her determine upon withdrawing to her convent immediately. The delight, that appeared in his countenance, when he met her, told that he brought back the same ardour of passion, which had formerly banished him from Chateau-le-Blanc. He was received with reserve by Emily, and with pleasure by the Count, who presented him to her with a smile, that seemed intended to plead his cause, and who did not hope the less for his friend, from the embarrassment she betrayed.

But M. Du Pont, with truer sympathy, seemed to understand her manner, and his countenance quickly lost its vivacity, and sunk into the languor of despondency.

On the following day, however, he sought an opportunity of declaring the purport of his visit, and renewed his suit; a declaration, which was received with real concern by Emily, who endeavoured to lessen the pain she might inflict by a second rejection, with assurances of esteem and friendship; yet she left him in a state of mind, that claimed and excited her tenderest compassion; and, being more sensible than ever of the impropriety of remaining longer at the chateau, she immediately sought the Count, and communicated to him her intention of returning to the convent.

"My dear Emily," said he "I observe, with extreme concern, the illusion you are encouraging—an illusion common to young and sensible minds. Your heart has received a severe shock; you believe you can never entirely recover it, and you will encourage this belief, till the habit of indulging sorrow will subdue the strength of your mind, and discolour your future views with melancholy and regret. Let me dissipate this illusion, and awaken you to a sense of your danger."

Emily smiled mournfully, "I know what you would say, my dear sir," said she, "and am prepared to answer you. I feel, that my heart can never know a second affection; and that I must never hope even to recover its tranquillity—if I suffer myself to enter into a second engagement."

"I know, that you feel all this," replied the Count; "and I know, also, that time will overcome these feelings, unless you cherish them in solitude, and, pardon me, with romantic tenderness. Then, indeed, time will only confirm habit. I am particularly empowered to speak on this subject, and to sympathize in your sufferings," added the Count, with an air of solemnity, "for I have known what it is to love, and to lament the object of my love. Yes," continued he, while his eyes filled with tears, "I have suffered!—but those times have passed away—long passed! and I can now look back upon them without emotion."

"My dear sir," said Emily, timidly, "what mean those tears?—they speak, I fear, another language—they plead for me."

"They are weak tears, for they are useless ones," replied the Count, drying them, "I would have you superior to such weakness. These, however, are only faint traces of a grief, which, if it had not been opposed by long continued effort, might have led me to the verge of madness! Judge, then, whether I have not cause to warn you of an indulgence, which may produce so terrible an effect, and which must certainly, if not opposed, overcloud the years, that otherwise might be happy. M. Du Pont is a sensible and amiable man, who has long been tenderly attached to you; his family and fortune are unexceptionable;—after what I have said, it is unnecessary to add, that I should rejoice in your felicity, and that I think M. Du Pont would promote it. Do not weep, Emily," continued the Count, taking her hand, "there *is* happiness reserved for you."

He was silent a moment; and then added, in a firmer voice, "I do not wish, that you should make a violent effort to overcome your feelings; all I, at present, ask, is, that you will check the thoughts, that would lead you to a remembrance of the past; that you will suffer your mind to be engaged by present objects; that you will allow yourself to believe it possible you may yet be happy; and that you will sometimes think with complacency of poor Du Pont, and not condemn him to the state of despondency, from which, my dear Emily, I am endeavouring to withdraw you."

"Ah! my dear sir," said Emily, while her tears still fell, "do not suffer the benevolence of your wishes to mislead Mons. Du Pont with an expectation that I can ever accept his hand. If I understand my own heart, this never can be; your instruction I can obey in almost every other particular, than that of adopting a contrary belief."

"Leave me to understand your heart," replied the Count, with a faint smile. "If you pay me the compliment to be guided by my advice in other instances, I will pardon your incredulity, respecting your future conduct towards Mons. Du Pont. I will not even press you to remain longer at the chateau than your own satisfaction will permit; but though I forbear to oppose your present retirement, I shall urge the claims of friendship for your future visits."

Tears of gratitude mingled with those of tender regret, while Emily thanked the Count for the many instances of friendship she had received from him; promised to be directed by his advice upon every subject but one, and assured him of the pleasure, with which she should, at some future period, accept the invitation of the Countess and himself—If Mons. Du Pont was not at the chateau.

The Count smiled at this condition. "Be it so," said he, "meanwhile the convent is so near the chateau, that my daughter and I shall often visit you; and if, sometimes, we should dare to bring you another visitor—will you forgive us?"

Emily looked distressed, and remained silent.

"Well," rejoined the Count, "I will pursue this subject no further, and must now entreat your forgiveness for having pressed it thus far. You will, however, do me the justice to believe, that I have been urged only by a sincere regard for your happiness, and that of my amiable friend Mons. Du Pont."

Emily, when she left the Count, went to mention her intended departure to the Countess, who opposed it with polite expressions of regret; after which, she sent a note to acquaint the lady abbess, that she should return to the convent; and thither she withdrew on the evening of the following day. M. Du Pont, in extreme regret, saw her depart, while the Count endeavoured to cheer him with a hope, that Emily would sometimes regard him with a more favourable eye.

She was pleased to find herself once more in the tranquil retirement of the convent, where she experienced a renewal of all the maternal kindness of the abbess, and of the sisterly attentions of the nuns. A report of the late extraordinary occurrence at the chateau had already reached them, and, after supper, on the evening of her arrival, it was the subject of conversation in the convent parlour, where she was requested to mention some particulars of that unaccountable event. Emily was guarded in her conversation on this subject, and briefly related a few circumstances concerning Ludovico, whose disappearance, her auditors almost unanimously agreed, had been effected by supernatural means.

"A belief had so long prevailed," said a nun, who was called sister Frances, "that the chateau was haunted, that I was surprised, when I heard the Count had the temerity to inhabit it. Its former possessor, I fear, had some deed of conscience to atone for; let us hope, that the virtues of its present owner will preserve him from the punishment due to the errors of the last, if, indeed, he was a criminal."

"Of what crime, then, was he suspected?" said a Mademoiselle Feydeau, a boarder at the convent.

"Let us pray for his soul!" said a nun, who had till now sat in silent attention. "If he was criminal, his punishment in this world was sufficient."

There was a mixture of wildness and solemnity in her manner of delivering this, which struck Emily exceedingly; but Mademoiselle repeated her question, without noticing the solemn eagerness of the nun.

"I dare not presume to say what was his crime," replied sister Frances; "but I have heard many reports of an extraordinary nature, respecting the late Marquis de Villeroi, and among others, that, soon after the death of his lady, he quitted Chateau-le-Blanc, and never afterwards returned to it. I was not here at the time, so I can only mention it from report, and so many years have passed since the Marchioness died, that few of our sisterhood, I believe, can do more."

"But I can," said the nun, who had before spoke, and whom they called sister Agnes.

"You then," said Mademoiselle Feydeau, "are possibly acquainted with circumstances, that enable you to judge, whether he was criminal or not, and what was the crime imputed to him."

"I am," replied the nun; "but who shall dare to scrutinize my thoughts—who shall dare to pluck out my opinion? God only is his judge, and to that judge he is gone!"

Emily looked with surprise at sister Frances, who returned her a significant glance.

"I only requested your opinion," said Mademoiselle Feydeau, mildly; "if the subject is displeasing to you, I will drop it."

"Displeasing!"—said the nun, with emphasis.—"We are idle talkers; we do not weigh the meaning of the words we use; *displeasing* is a poor word. I will go pray." As she said this she rose from her seat, and with a profound sigh quitted the room.

"What can be the meaning of this?" said Emily, when she was gone.

"It is nothing extraordinary," replied sister Frances, "she is often thus; but she has no meaning in what she says. Her intellects are at times deranged. Did you never see her thus before?"

"Never," said Emily. "I have, indeed, sometimes, thought, that there was the melancholy of madness in her look, but never before perceived it in her speech. Poor soul, I will pray for her!"

"Your prayers then, my daughter, will unite with ours," observed the lady abbess, "she has need of them."

"Dear lady," said Mademoiselle Feydeau, addressing the abbess, "what is your opinion of the late Marquis? The strange circumstances, that have occurred at the chateau, have so much awakened my curiosity, that I shall be pardoned the question. What was his imputed crime, and what the punishment, to which sister Agnes alluded?"

"We must be cautious of advancing our opinion," said the abbess, with an air of reserve, mingled with solemnity, "we must be cautious of advancing our opinion on so delicate a subject. I will not take upon me to pronounce, that the late Marquis was criminal, or to say what was the crime of which he was suspected; but, concerning the punishment our daughter Agnes hinted, I know of none he suffered. She probably alluded to the severe one, which an exasperated conscience can inflict. Beware, my children, of incurring so terrible a punishment—it is the purgatory of this life! The late Marchioness I knew well; she was a pattern to such as live in the world; nay, our sacred order need not have blushed to copy her virtues! Our holy convent received her mortal part; her heavenly spirit, I doubt not, ascended to its sanctuary!"

As the abbess spoke this, the last bell of vespers struck up, and she rose. "Let us go, my children," said she, "and intercede for the wretched; let us go and confess our sins, and endeavour to purify our souls for the heaven, to which *she* is gone!"

Emily was affected by the solemnity of this exhortation, and, remembering her father, "The heaven, to which *he*, too, is gone!" said she, faintly, as she suppressed her sighs, and followed the abbess and the nuns to the chapel.

CHAPTER VIII

Be thou a spirit of health, or goblin damn'd,
Bring with thee airs from heaven, or blasts from hell,
Be thy intents wicked, or charitable,

I will speak to thee.

HAMLET

COUNT de Villefort, at length, received a letter from the advocate at Avignon, encouraging Emily to assert her claim to the estates of the late Madame Montoni; and, about the same time, a messenger arrived from Monsieur Quesnel with intelligence, that made an appeal to the law on this subject unnecessary, since it appeared, that the only person, who could have opposed her claim, was now no more. A friend of Monsieur Quesnel, who resided at Venice, had sent him an account of the death of Montoni who had been brought to trial with Orsino, as his supposed accomplice in the murder of the Venetian nobleman. Orsino was found guilty, condemned and executed upon the wheel, but, nothing being discovered to criminate Montoni, and his colleagues, on this charge, they were all released, except Montoni, who, being considered by the senate as a very dangerous person, was, for other reasons, ordered again into confinement, where, it was said, he had died in a doubtful and mysterious manner, and not without suspicion of having been poisoned. The authority, from which M. Quesnel had received this information, would not allow him to doubt its truth, and he told Emily, that she had now only to lay claim to the estates of her late aunt, to secure them, and added, that he would himself assist in the necessary forms of this business. The term, for which La Vallée had been let being now also nearly expired, he acquainted her with the circumstance, and advised her to take the road thither, through Tholouse, where he promised to meet her, and where it would be proper for her to take possession of the estates of the late Madame Montoni; adding, that he would spare her any difficulties, that might occur on that occasion from the want of knowledge on the subject, and that he believed it would be necessary for her to be at Tholouse, in about three weeks from the present time.

An increase of fortune seemed to have awakened this sudden kindness in M. Quesnel towards his niece, and it appeared, that he entertained more respect for the rich heiress, than he had ever felt compassion for the poor and unfriended orphan.

The pleasure, with which she received this intelligence, was clouded when she considered, that he, for whose sake she had once regretted the want of fortune, was no longer worthy of sharing it with her; but, remembering the friendly admonition of the Count, she checked this melancholy reflection, and endeavoured to feel only gratitude for the unexpected good, that now attended her; while it formed no inconsiderable part of her satisfaction to know, that La Vallée, her native home, which was endeared to her by its having been the residence of her parents, would soon be restored to her possession. There she meant to fix her future residence, for, though it could not be compared with the chateau at Tholouse, either for extent, or magnificence, its pleasant scenes and the tender remembrances, that haunted them, had claims upon her heart, which she was not inclined to sacrifice to ostentation. She wrote immediately to thank M. Quesnel for the active interest he took in her concerns, and to say, that she would meet him at Tholouse at the appointed time.

When Count de Villefort, with Blanche, came to the convent to give Emily the advice of the advocate, he was informed of the contents of M. Quesnel's letter, and gave her his sincere congratulations, on the occasion; but she observed, that, when the first expression of satisfaction had faded from his countenance, an unusual gravity succeeded, and she scarcely hesitated to enquire its cause.

"It has no new occasion," replied the Count; "I am harassed and perplexed by the confusion, into which my family is thrown by their foolish superstition. Idle reports are floating round me, which I can neither admit to be true, or prove to be false; and I am, also, very anxious about the poor fellow, Ludovico, concerning whom I have not been able to obtain information. Every part of the chateau and every part of the neighbourhood, too, has, I believe, been searched, and I know not what further can be done, since I have already offered large rewards for the discovery of him. The keys of the north apartment I have not suffered to be out of my possession, since he disappeared, and I mean to watch in those chambers, myself, this very night."

Emily, seriously alarmed for the Count, united her entreaties with those of the Lady Blanche, to dissuade him from his purpose.

"What should I fear?" said he. "I have no faith in supernatural combats, and for human opposition I shall be prepared; nay, I will even promise not to watch alone."

"But who, dear sir, will have courage enough to watch with you?" said Emily.

"My son," replied the Count. "If I am not carried off in the night," added he, smiling, "you shall hear the result of my adventure, to-morrow."

The Count and Lady Blanche, shortly afterwards, took leave of Emily, and returned to the chateau, where he informed Henri of his intention, who, not without some secret reluctance, consented to be the partner of his watch; and, when the design was mentioned after supper, the Countess was terrified, and the Baron, and M. Du Pont joined with her in entreating, that he would not tempt his fate, as Ludovico had done. "We know not," added the Baron, "the nature, or the power of an evil spirit; and that such a spirit haunts those chambers can now, I think, scarcely be doubted. Beware, my lord, how you provoke its vengeance, since it has already given us one terrible example of its malice. I allow it may be probable, that the spirits of the dead are permitted to return to the earth only on occasions of high import; but the present import may be your destruction."

The Count could not forbear smiling; "Do you think then, Baron," said he, "that my destruction is of sufficient importance to draw back to earth the soul of the departed? Alas! my good friend, there is no occasion for such means to accomplish the destruction of any individual. Wherever the mystery rests, I trust I shall, this night, be able to detect it. You know I am not superstitious."

"I know that you are incredulous," interrupted the Baron.

"Well, call it what you will, I mean to say, that, though you know I am free from superstition—if any thing supernatural has appeared, I doubt not it will appear to me, and if any strange event hangs over my house, or if any extraordinary transaction has formerly been connected with it, I shall probably be made acquainted with it. At all events I will invite discovery; and, that I may be equal to a mortal attack, which in good truth, my friend, is what I most expect, I shall take care to be well armed."

The Count took leave of his family, for the night, with an assumed gaiety, which but ill concealed the anxiety, that depressed his spirits, and retired to the north apartments, accompanied by his son and followed by the Baron, M. Du Pont and some of the domestics, who all bade him good night at the outer door. In these chambers every thing appeared as when he had last been here; even in the bed-room no alteration was visible, where he lighted his own fire, for none of the domestics could be prevailed upon to venture thither. After carefully examining the chamber and the oriel, the Count and Henri drew their chairs upon the hearth, set a bottle of wine and a lamp before them, laid their swords upon the table, and, stirring the wood into a blaze, began to converse on indifferent topics. But Henri was often silent and abstracted, and sometimes threw a glance of mingled awe and curiosity round the gloomy apartment; while the Count gradually ceased to converse, and sat either lost in thought, or reading a volume of Tacitus, which he had brought to beguile the tediousness of the night.

CHAPTER IX

Give thy thoughts no tongue.
SHAKESPEARE

THE Baron St. Foix, whom anxiety for his friend had kept awake, rose early to enquire the event of the night, when, as he passed the Count's closet, hearing steps within, he knocked at the door, and it was opened by his friend himself. Rejoicing to see him in safety, and curious to learn the occurrences of the night, he had not immediately leisure to observe the unusual gravity, that overspread the features of the Count, whose reserved answers first occasioned him to notice it. The Count, then smiling, endeavoured to treat the subject of his curiosity with levity, but the Baron was serious, and pursued his enquiries so closely, that the Count, at length, resuming his gravity, said, "Well, my friend, press the subject no further, I entreat you; and let me request also, that you will hereafter be silent upon any thing you may think extraordinary in my future conduct. I do not scruple to tell you, that I am unhappy, and that the watch of the last night has not assisted me to discover Ludovico; upon every occurrence of the night you must excuse my reserve."

"But where is Henri?" said the Baron, with surprise and disappointment at this denial.

"He is well in his own apartment," replied the Count. "You will not question him on this topic, my friend, since you know my wish."

"Certainly not," said the Baron, somewhat chagrined, "since it would be displeasing to you; but methinks, my friend, you might rely on my discretion, and drop this unusual reserve. However, you must allow me to suspect, that you have seen reason to become a convert to my system, and are no longer the incredulous knight you lately appeared to be."

"Let us talk no more upon this subject," said the Count; "you may be assured, that no ordinary circumstance has imposed this silence upon me towards a friend, whom I have called so for near thirty years; and my present reserve cannot make you question either my esteem, or the sincerity of my friendship."

"I will not doubt either," said the Baron, "though you must allow me to express my surprise, at this silence."

"To me I will allow it," replied the Count, "but I earnestly entreat that you will forbear to notice it to my family, as well as every thing remarkable you may observe in my conduct towards them."

The Baron readily promised this, and, after conversing for some time on general topics, they descended to the breakfast-room, where the

Count met his family with a cheerful countenance, and evaded their enquiries by employing light ridicule, and assuming an air of uncommon gaiety, while he assured them, that they need not apprehend any evil from the north chambers, since Henri and himself had been permitted to return from them in safety.

Henri, however, was less successful in disguising his feelings. From his countenance an expression of terror was not entirely faded; he was often silent and thoughtful, and when he attempted to laugh at the eager enquiries of Mademoiselle Bearn, it was evidently only an attempt.

In the evening, the Count called, as he had promised, at the convent, and Emily was surprised to perceive a mixture of playful ridicule and of reserve in his mention of the north apartment. Of what had occurred there, however, he said nothing, and, when she ventured to remind him of his promise to tell her the result of his enquiries, and to ask if he had received any proof, that those chambers were haunted, his look became solemn, for a moment, then, seeming to recollect himself, he smiled, and said, "My dear Emily, do not suffer my lady abbess to infect your good understanding with these fancies; she will teach you to expect a ghost in every dark room. But believe me," added he, with a profound sigh, "the apparition of the dead comes not on light, or sportive errands, to terrify, or to surprise the timid." He paused, and fell into a momentary thoughtfulness, and then added, "We will say no more on this subject."

Soon after, he took leave, and, when Emily joined some of the nuns, she was surprised to find them acquainted with a circumstance, which she had carefully avoided to mention, and expressing their admiration of his intrepidity in having dared to pass a night in the apartment, whence Ludovico had disappeared; for she had not considered with what rapidity a tale of wonder circulates. The nuns had acquired their information from peasants, who brought fruit to the monastery, and whose whole attention had been fixed, since the disappearance of Ludovico, on what was passing in the castle.

Emily listened in silence to the various opinions of the nuns, concerning the conduct of the Count, most of whom condemned it as rash and presumptuous, affirming, that it was provoking the vengeance of an evil spirit, thus to intrude upon its haunts.

Sister Frances contended, that the Count had acted with the bravery of a virtuous mind. He knew himself guiltless of aught, that should provoke a good spirit, and did not fear the spells of an evil one, since he could claim the protection of an higher Power, of Him, who can command the wicked, and will protect the innocent.

"The guilty cannot claim that protection!" said sister Agnes, "let the

Count look to his conduct, that he do not forfeit his claim! Yet who is he, that shall dare to call himself innocent!—all earthly innocence is but comparative. Yet still how wide asunder are the extremes of guilt, and to what an horrible depth may we fall! Oh!"—

The nun, as she concluded, uttered a shuddering sigh, that startled Emily, who, looking up, perceived the eyes of Agnes fixed on hers, after which the sister rose, took her hand, gazed earnestly upon her countenance, for some moments, in silence, and then said,

"You are young—you are innocent! I mean you are yet innocent of any great crime!—But you have passions in your heart,—scorpions; they sleep now—beware how you awaken them!—they will sting you, even unto death!"

Emily, affected by these words and by the solemnity, with which they were delivered, could not suppress her tears.

"Ah! is it so?" exclaimed Agnes, her countenance softening from its sternness—"so young, and so unfortunate! We are sisters, then indeed. Yet, there is no bond of kindness among the guilty," she added, while her eyes resumed their wild expression, "no gentleness,—no peace, no hope! I knew them all once—my eyes could weep—but now they burn, for now, my soul is fixed, and fearless!—I lament no more!"

"Rather let us repent, and pray," said another nun. "We are taught to hope, that prayer and penitence will work our salvation. There is hope for all who repent!"

"Who repent and turn to the true faith," observed sister Frances.

"For all but me!" replied Agnes solemnly, who paused, and then abruptly added, "My head burns, I believe I am not well. O! could I strike from my memory all former scenes—the figures, that rise up, like furies, to torment me!—I see them, when I sleep, and, when I am awake, they are still before my eyes! I see them now—now!"

She stood in a fixed attitude of horror, her straining eyes moving slowly round the room, as if they followed something. One of the nuns gently took her hand, to lead her from the parlour. Agnes became calm, drew her other hand across her eyes, looked again, and, sighing deeply, said, "They are gone—they are gone! I am feverish, I know not what I say. I am thus, sometimes, but it will go off again, I shall soon be better. Was not that the vesper-bell?"

"No," replied Frances, "the evening service is passed. Let Margaret lead you to your cell."

"You are right," replied sister Agnes, "I shall be better there. Good night, my sisters, remember me in your orisons."

When they had withdrawn, Frances, observing Emily's emotion, said, "Do not be alarmed, our sister is often thus deranged, though I have not lately seen her so frantic; her usual mood is melancholy. This fit has been coming on, for several days; seclusion and the customary treatment will restore her."

"But how rationally she conversed, at first!" observed Emily, "her ideas followed each other in perfect order."

"Yes," replied the nun, "this is nothing new; nay, I have sometimes known her argue not only with method, but with acuteness, and then, in a moment, start off into madness."

"Her conscience seems afflicted," said Emily, "did you ever hear what circumstance reduced her to this deplorable condition?"

"I have," replied the nun, who said no more till Emily repeated the question, when she added in a low voice, and looking significantly towards the other boarders, "I cannot tell you now, but, if you think it worth your while, come to my cell, to-night, when our sisterhood are at rest, and you shall hear more; but remember we rise to midnight prayers, and come either before, or after midnight."

Emily promised to remember, and, the abbess soon after appearing, they spoke no more of the unhappy nun.

The Count meanwhile, on his return home, had found M. Du Pont in one of those fits of despondency, which his attachment to Emily frequently occasioned him, an attachment, that had subsisted too long to be easily subdued, and which had already outlived the opposition of his friends. M. Du Pont had first seen Emily in Gascony, during the lifetime of his parent, who, on discovering his son's partiality for Mademoiselle St. Aubert, his inferior in point of fortune, forbade him to declare it to her family, or to think of her more. During the life of his father, he had observed the first command, but had found it impracticable to obey the second, and had, sometimes, soothed his passion by visiting her favourite haunts, among which was the fishing-house, where, once or twice, he addressed her in verse, concealing his name, in obedience to the promise he had given his father. There too he played the pathetic air, to which she had listened with such surprise and admiration; and there he found the miniature, that had since cherished a passion fatal to his repose. During his expedition into Italy, his father died; but he received his liberty at a moment, when he was the least enabled to profit by it, since the object, that rendered it most valuable, was no longer within the reach of his vows. By what accident he discovered Emily, and assisted to release her from a terrible imprisonment, has already appeared, and also the unavailing hope, with which he then encouraged his love, and the fruitless efforts, that he had since made to overcome it.

The Count still endeavoured, with friendly zeal, to soothe him with a belief, that patience, perseverance and prudence would finally obtain for him happiness and Emily: "Time," said he, "will wear away the melancholy impression, which disappointment has left on her mind, and she will be sensible of your merit. Your services have already awakened her gratitude, and your sufferings her pity; and trust me, my friend, in a heart so sensible as hers, gratitude and pity lead to love. When her imagination is rescued from its present delusion, she will readily accept the homage of a mind like yours."

Du Pont sighed, while he listened to these words; and, endeavouring to hope what his friend believed, he willingly yielded to an invitation to prolong his visit at the chateau, which we now leave for the monastery of St. Claire.

When the nuns had retired to rest, Emily stole to her appointment with sister Frances, whom she found in her cell, engaged in prayer, before a little table, where appeared the image she was addressing, and, above, the dim lamp that gave light to the place. Turning her eyes, as the door opened, she beckoned to Emily to come in, who, having done so, seated herself in silence beside the nun's little mattress of straw, till her orisons should conclude. The latter soon rose from her knees, and, taking down the lamp and placing it on the table, Emily perceived there a human scull and bones, lying beside an hour-glass; but the nun, without observing her emotion, sat down on the mattress by her, saying, "Your curiosity, sister, has made you punctual, but you have nothing remarkable to hear in the history of poor Agnes, of whom I avoided to speak in the presence of my lay-sisters, only because I would not publish her crime to them."

"I shall consider your confidence in me as a favour," said Emily, "and will not misuse it."

"Sister Agnes," resumed the nun, "is of a noble family, as the dignity of her air must already have informed you, but I will not dishonour their name so much as to reveal it. Love was the occasion of her crime and of her madness. She was beloved by a gentleman of inferior fortune, and her father, as I have heard, bestowing her on a nobleman, whom she disliked, an ill-governed passion proved her destruction.— Every obligation of virtue and of duty was forgotten, and she prophaned her marriage vows; but her guilt was soon detected, and she would have fallen a sacrifice to the vengeance of her husband, had not her father contrived to convey her from his power. By what means he did this, I never could learn; but he secreted her in this convent, where he afterwards prevailed with her to take the veil, while a report was circulated in the world, that she was dead, and the father, to save his daughter, assisted the rumour, and employed such means as induced her husband to believe she had become a victim to his jealousy. You look surprised," added the nun, observing Emily's countenance; "I allow the story is uncommon, but not, I believe, without a parallel."

"Pray proceed," said Emily, "I am interested."

"The story is already told," resumed the nun, "I have only to mention, that the long struggle, which Agnes suffered, between love, remorse and a sense of the duties she had taken upon herself in becoming of our order, at length unsettled her reason. At first, she was frantic and melancholy by quick alternatives; then, she sunk into a deep and settled melancholy, which still, however, has, at times, been interrupted by fits of wildness, and, of late, these have again been frequent."

Emily was affected by the history of the sister, some parts of whose story brought to her remembrance that of the Marchioness de Villeroi, who had also been compelled by her father to forsake the object of her affections, for a nobleman of his choice; but, from what Dorothée had related, there appeared no reason to suppose, that she had escaped the vengeance of a jealous husband, or to doubt for a moment the innocence of her conduct. But Emily, while she sighed over the misery of the nun, could not forbear shedding a few tears to the misfortunes of the Marchioness; and, when she returned to the mention of sister Agnes, she asked Frances if she remembered her in her youth, and whether she was then beautiful.

"I was not here at the time, when she took the vows," replied Frances, "which is so long ago, that few of the present sisterhood, I believe, were witnesses of the ceremony; nay, ever our lady mother did not then preside over the convent: but I can remember, when sister Agnes was a very beautiful woman. She retains that air of high rank, which always distinguished her, but her beauty, you must perceive, is fled; I can scarcely discover even a vestige of the loveliness, that once animated her features."

"It is strange," said Emily, "but there are moments, when her countenance has appeared familiar to my memory! You will think me fanciful, and I think myself so, for I certainly never saw sister Agnes, before I came to this convent, and I must, therefore, have seen some person, whom she strongly resembles, though of this I have no recollection."

"You have been interested by the deep melancholy of her countenance," said Frances, "and its impression has probably deluded your imagination; for I might as reasonably think I perceive a likeness between you and Agnes, as you, that you have seen her any where but in this convent, since this has been her place of refuge, for nearly as many years as make your age."

"Indeed!" said Emily.

"Yes," rejoined Frances, "and why does that circumstance excite your surprise?"

Emily did not appear to notice this question, but remained thoughtful, for a few moments, and then said, "It was about that same period that the Marchioness de Villeroi expired."

"That is an odd remark," said Frances.

Emily, recalled from her reverie, smiled, and gave the conversation another turn, but it soon came back to the subject of the unhappy nun, and Emily remained in the cell of sister Frances, till the mid-night bell aroused her; when, apologizing for having interrupted the sister's repose, till this late hour, they quitted the cell together. Emily returned to her chamber, and the nun, bearing a glimmering taper, went to her devotion in the chapel.

Several days followed, during which Emily saw neither the Count, or any of his family; and, when, at length, he appeared, she remarked, with concern, that his air was unusually disturbed.

"My spirits are harassed," said he, in answer to her anxious enquiries, "and I mean to change my residence, for a little while, an experiment, which, I hope, will restore my mind to its usual tranquillity. My daughter and myself will accompany the Baron St. Foix to his chateau. It lies in a valley of the Pyrenées, that opens towards Gascony, and I have been thinking, Emily, that, when you set out for La Vallée, we may go part of the way together; it would be a satisfaction to me to guard you towards your home."

She thanked the Count for his friendly consideration, and lamented, that the necessity for her going first to Tholouse would render this plan impracticable. "But, when you are at the Baron's residence," she added, "you will be only a short journey from La Vallée, and I think, sir, you will not leave the country without visiting me; it is unnecessary to say with what pleasure I should receive you and the Lady Blanche."

"I do not doubt it," replied the Count, "and I will not deny myself and Blanche the pleasure of visiting you, if your affairs should allow you to be at La Vallée, about the time when we can meet you there."

When Emily said that she should hope to see the Countess also, she was not sorry to learn that this lady was going, accompanied by Mademoiselle Bearn, to pay a visit, for a few weeks, to a family in lower Languedoc.

The Count, after some further conversation on his intended journey and on the arrangement of Emily's, took leave; and many days did not succeed this visit, before a second letter from M. Quesnel informed her, that he was then at Tholouse, that La Vallée was at liberty, and that he wished her to set off for the former place, where he awaited her arrival, with all possible dispatch, since his own affairs pressed him to return to Gascony. Emily did not hesitate to obey him, and, having taken an affecting leave of the Count's family, in which M. Du Pont was still included, and of her friends at the convent, she set out for

Tholouse, attended by the unhappy Annette, and guarded by a steady servant of the Count.

CHAPTER X

Lull'd in the countless chambers of the brain,
Our thoughts are link'd by many a hidden chain:
Awake but one, and lo! what myriads rise!
Each stamps its image as the other flies!
                              PLEASURES OF MEMORY

EMILY pursued her journey, without any accident, along the plains of Languedoc towards the north-west; and, on this her return to Tholouse, which she had last left with Madame Montoni, she thought much on the melancholy fate of her aunt, who, but for her own imprudence, might now have been living in happiness there! Montoni, too, often rose to her fancy, such as she had seen him in his days of triumph, bold, spirited and commanding; such also as she had since beheld him in his days of vengeance; and now, only a few short months had passed—and he had no longer the power, or the will to afflict;—he had become a clod of earth, and his life was vanished like a shadow! Emily could have wept at his fate, had she not remembered his crimes; for that of her unfortunate aunt she did weep, and all sense of her errors was overcome by the recollection of her misfortunes.

Other thoughts and other emotions succeeded, as Emily drew near the well-known scenes of her early love, and considered, that Valancourt was lost to her and to himself, for ever. At length, she came to the brow of the hill, whence, on her departure for Italy, she had given a farewell look to this beloved landscape, amongst whose woods and fields she had so often walked with Valancourt, and where he was then to inhabit, when she would be far, far away! She saw, once more, that chain of the Pyrenées, which overlooked La Vallée, rising, like faint clouds, on the horizon. "There, too, is Gascony, extended at their feet!" said she, "O my father,—my mother! And there, too, is the Garonne!" she added, drying the tears, that obscured her sight,—"and Tholouse, and my aunt's mansion—and the groves in her garden!—O my friends! are ye all lost to me—must I never, never see ye more!" Tears rushed again to her eyes, and she continued to weep, till an abrupt turn in the road had nearly occasioned the carriage to overset, when, looking up, she perceived another part of the well-known scene around Tholouse, and all the reflections and anticipations, which she had suffered, at the moment, when she bade it last adieu, came with recollected force to her heart. She remembered how anxiously she had looked forward to the futurity, which was to decide her happiness concerning Valancourt, and what depressing fears had assailed her; the very words she had uttered, as she withdrew her last look from the prospect, came to her memory. "Could I but be certain," she had then said, "that I should ever return, and that Valancourt would still live for me—I should go in peace!"

Now, that futurity, so anxiously anticipated, was arrived, she was returned—but what a dreary blank appeared!—Valancourt no longer lived for her! She had no longer even the melancholy satisfaction of contemplating his image in her heart, for he was no longer the same Valancourt she had cherished there—the solace of many a mournful hour, the animating friend, that had enabled her to bear up against the oppression of Montoni—the distant hope, that had beamed over her gloomy prospect! On perceiving this beloved idea to be an illusion of her own creation, Valancourt seemed to be annihilated, and her soul sickened at the blank, that remained. His marriage with a rival, even his death, she thought she could have endured with more fortitude, than this discovery; for then, amidst all her grief, she could have looked in secret upon the image of goodness, which her fancy had drawn of him, and comfort would have mingled with her suffering!

Drying her tears, she looked, once more, upon the landscape, which had excited them, and perceived, that she was passing the very bank, where she had taken leave of Valancourt, on the morning of her departure from Tholouse, and she now saw him, through her returning tears, such as he had appeared, when she looked from the carriage to give him a last adieu—saw him leaning mournfully against the high trees, and remembered the fixed look of mingled tenderness and anguish, with which he had then regarded her. This recollection was too much for her heart, and she sunk back in the carriage, nor once looked up, till it stopped at the gates of what was now her own mansion.

These being opened, and by the servant, to whose care the chateau had been entrusted, the carriage drove into the court, where, alighting, she hastily passed through the great hall, now silent and solitary, to a large oak parlour, the common sitting room of the late Madame Montoni, where, instead of being received by M. Quesnel, she found a letter from him, informing her that business of consequence had obliged him to leave Tholouse two days before. Emily was, upon the whole, not sorry to be spared his presence, since his abrupt departure appeared to indicate the same indifference, with which he had formerly regarded her. This letter informed her, also, of the progress he had made in the settlement of her affairs, and concluded with directions, concerning the forms of some business, which remained for her to transact. But M. Quesnel's unkindness did not long occupy her thoughts, which returned the remembrance of the persons she had been accustomed to see in this mansion, and chiefly of the ill-guided and unfortunate Madame Montoni. In the room, where she now sat, she had breakfasted with her on the morning of their departure for Italy; and the view of it brought most forcibly to her recollection all she had herself suffered, at that time, and the many gay expectations, which her aunt had formed, respecting the journey before her. While Emily's mind was thus engaged, her eyes wandered unconsciously to a large window, that looked upon the garden, and here new memorials of the past spoke to her heart, for she saw extended before her the very avenue, in which she had parted with Valancourt, on the eve of her journey; and all the anxiety, the tender interest he had shewn, concerning her future happiness, his earnest remonstrances against her committing herself to the power of Montoni, and the truth of his affection, came afresh to her memory. At this moment, it appeared almost impossible, that Valancourt could have become unworthy of her regard, and she doubted all that she had lately heard to his disadvantage, and even his own words, which had confirmed Count De Villefort's report of him. Overcome by the recollections, which the view of this avenue occasioned, she turned abruptly from the window, and sunk into a chair beside it, where she sat, given up to grief, till the entrance of Annette, with coffee, aroused her.

"Dear madam, how melancholy this place looks now," said Annette, "to what it used to do! It is dismal coming home, when there is nobody to welcome one!"

This was not the moment, in which Emily could bear the remark; her tears fell again, and, as soon as she had taken the coffee, she retired to her apartment, where she endeavoured to repose her fatigued spirits. But busy memory would still supply her with the visions of former times: she saw Valancourt interesting and benevolent, as he had been wont to appear in the days of their early love, and, amidst the scenes, where she had believed that they should sometimes pass their years together!—but, at length, sleep closed these afflicting scenes from her view.

On the following morning, serious occupation recovered her from such melancholy reflections; for, being desirous of quitting Tholouse, and of hastening on to La Vallée, she made some enquiries into the condition of the estate, and immediately dispatched a part of the necessary business concerning it, according to the directions of Mons. Quesnel. It required a strong effort to abstract her thoughts from other interests sufficiently to attend to this, but she was rewarded for her exertions by again experiencing, that employment is the surest antidote to sorrow.

This day was devoted entirely to business; and, among other concerns, she employed means to learn the situation of all her poor tenants, that she might relieve their wants, or confirm their comforts.

In the evening, her spirits were so much strengthened, that she thought she could bear to visit the gardens, where she had so often walked with Valancourt; and, knowing, that, if she delayed to do so, their scenes would only affect her the more, whenever they should be viewed, she took advantage of the present state of her mind, and entered them.

Passing hastily the gate leading from the court into the gardens, she hurried up the great avenue, scarcely permitting her memory to dwell for a moment on the circumstance of her having here parted with Valancourt, and soon quitted this for other walks less interesting to her heart. These brought her, at length, to the flight of steps, that led from the lower garden to the terrace, on seeing which, she became agitated, and hesitated whether to ascend, but, her resolution returning, she proceeded.

"Ah!" said Emily, as she ascended, "these are the same high trees, that used to wave over the terrace, and these the same flowery thickets—the liburnum, the wild rose, and the cerinthe—which were wont to grow beneath them! Ah! and there, too, on that bank, are the very plants, which Valancourt so carefully reared!—O, when last I saw them!"—she checked the thought, but could not restrain her tears, and, after walking slowly on for a few moments, her agitation, upon the view of this well-known scene, increased so much, that she was obliged to stop, and lean upon the wall of the terrace. It was a mild, and beautiful evening. The sun was setting over the extensive landscape, to which his beams, sloping from beneath a dark cloud, that overhung the west, gave rich and partial colouring, and touched the tufted summits of the groves, that rose from the garden below, with a yellow gleam. Emily and Valancourt had often admired together this scene, at the same hour; and it was exactly on this spot, that, on the night preceding her departure for Italy, she had listened to his remonstrances against the journey, and to the pleadings of passionate affection. Some observations, which she made on the landscape, brought this to her remembrance, and with it all the minute particulars of that conversation;—the alarming doubts he had expressed concerning Montoni, doubts, which had since been fatally confirmed; the reasons and entreaties he had employed to prevail with her to consent to an immediate marriage; the tenderness of his love, the paroxysms of this grief, and the conviction that he had repeatedly expressed, that they should never meet again in happiness! All these circumstances rose afresh to her mind, and awakened the various emotions she had then suffered. Her tenderness for Valancourt became as powerful as in the moments, when she thought, that she was parting with him and happiness together, and when the strength of her mind had enabled her to triumph over present suffering, rather than to deserve the reproach of her conscience by engaging in a clandestine marriage.—"Alas!" said Emily, as these recollections came to her mind, "and what have I gained by the fortitude I then practised?—am I happy now?—He said, we should meet no more in happiness; but, O! he little thought his own misconduct would separate us, and lead to the very evil he then dreaded!"

Her reflections increased her anguish, while she was compelled to acknowledge, that the fortitude she had formerly exerted, if it had not conducted her to happiness, had saved her from irretrievable misfortune—from Valancourt himself! But in these moments she could not congratulate herself on the prudence, that had saved her; she could only lament, with bitterest anguish, the circumstances, which had conspired to betray Valancourt into a course of life so different from that, which the virtues, the tastes, and the pursuits of his early years had promised; but she still loved him too well to believe, that his heart was even now depraved, though his conduct had been criminal. An observation, which had fallen from M. St. Aubert more than once, now occurred to her. "This young man," said he, speaking of Valancourt, "has never been at Paris;" a remark, that had surprised her at the time it was uttered, but which she now understood, and she exclaimed sorrowfully, "O Valancourt! if such a friend as my father had been with you at Paris—your noble, ingenuous nature would not have fallen!"

The sun was now set, and, recalling her thoughts from their melancholy subject, she continued her walk; for the pensive shade of twilight was pleasing to her, and the nightingales from the surrounding groves began to answer each other in the long-drawn, plaintive note, which always touched her heart; while all the fragrance of the flowery thickets, that bounded the terrace, was awakened by the cool evening air, which floated so lightly among their leaves, that they scarcely trembled as it passed.

Emily came, at length, to the steps of the pavilion, that terminated the terrace, and where her last interview with Valancourt, before her departure from Tholouse, had so unexpectedly taken place. The door was now shut, and she trembled, while she hesitated whether to open it; but her wish to see again a place, which had been the chief scene of her former happiness, at length overcoming her reluctance to encounter the painful regret it would renew, she entered. The room was obscured by a melancholy shade; but through the open lattices, darkened by the hanging foliage of the vines, appeared the dusky land-scape, the Garonne reflecting the evening light, and the west still glow-ing. A chair was placed near one of the balconies, as if some person had been sitting there, but the other furniture of the pavilion remained exactly as usual, and Emily thought it looked as if it had not once been moved since she set out for Italy. The silent and deserted air of the place added solemnity to her emotions, for she heard only the low whis-per of the breeze, as it shook the leaves of the vines, and the very faint murmur of the Garonne.

She seated herself in a chair, near the lattice, and yielded to the sad-ness of her heart, while she recollected the circumstances of her part-ing interview with Valancourt, on this spot. It was here too, that she had passed some of the happiest hours of her life with him, when her aunt favoured the connection, for here she had often sat and worked, while he conversed, or read; and she now well remembered with what dis-criminating judgment, with what tempered energy, he used to repeat some of the sublimest passages of their favourite authors; how often he would pause to admire with her their excellence, and with what tender delight he would listen to her remarks, and correct her taste.

"And is it possible," said Emily, as these recollections returned—"is it possible, that a mind, so susceptible of whatever is grand and beautiful, could stoop to low pursuits, and be subdued by frivolous temptations?"

She remembered how often she had seen the sudden tear start in his eye, and had heard his voice tremble with emotion, while he related any great or benevolent action, or repeated a sentiment of the same character. "And such a mind," said she, "such a heart, were to be sac-rificed to the habits of a great city!"

These recollections becoming too painful to be endured, she abruptly left the pavilion, and, anxious to escape from the memorials of her departed happiness, returned towards the chateau. As she passed along the terrace, she perceived a person, walking, with a slow step, and a dejected air, under the trees, at some distance. The twilight, which was now deep, would not allow her to distinguish who it was, and she imagined it to be one of the servants, till, the sound of her steps seem-ing to reach him, he turned half round, and she thought she saw Valancourt!

Whoever it was, he instantly struck among the thickets on the left, and disappeared, while Emily, her eyes fixed on the place, whence he had vanished, and her frame trembling so excessively, that she could scarcely support herself, remained, for some moments, unable to quit the spot, and scarcely conscious of existence. With her recollection, her strength returned, and she hurried toward the house, where she did not venture to enquire who had been in the gardens, lest she should betray her emotion; and she sat down alone, endeavouring to recollect the figure, air and features of the person she had just seen. Her view of him, however, had been so transient, and the gloom had rendered it so imperfect, that she could remember nothing with exactness; yet the general appearance of his figure, and his abrupt departure, made her still believe, that this person was Valancourt. Sometimes, indeed, she thought, that her fancy, which had been occupied by the idea of him, had suggested his image to her uncertain sight: but this conjecture was fleeting. If it was himself whom she had seen, she wondered much, that he should be at Tholouse, and more, how he had gained admittance into the garden; but as often as her impatience prompted her to enquire whether any stranger had been admitted, she was restrained by an unwillingness to betray her doubts; and the evening was passed in anxious conjecture, and in efforts to dismiss the subject from her thoughts. But, these endeavours were ineffectual, and a thousand inconsistent emotions assailed her, whenever she fancied that Valancourt might be near her; now, she dreaded it to be true, and now she feared it to be false; and, while she constantly tried to persuade herself, that she wished the person, whom she had seen, might not be Valancourt, her heart as constantly contradicted her reason.

The following day was occupied by the visits of several neighbouring families, formerly intimate with Madame Montoni, who came to condole with Emily on her death, to congratulate her upon the acquisition of these estates, and to enquire about Montoni, and concerning the strange reports they had heard of her own situation; all which was done with the utmost decorum, and the visitors departed with as much composure as they had arrived.

Emily was wearied by these formalities, and disgusted by the subservient manners of many persons, who had thought her scarcely worthy of common attention, while she was believed to be a dependant on Madame Montoni.

"Surely," said she, "there is some magic in wealth, which can thus make persons pay their court to it, when it does not even benefit themselves. How strange it is, that a fool or a knave, with riches, should be treated with more respect by the world, than a good man, or a wise man in poverty!"

It was evening, before she was left alone, and she then wished to have refreshed her spirits in the free air of her garden; but she feared to go thither, lest she should meet again the person, whom she had seen on the preceding night, and he should prove to be Valancourt. The suspense and anxiety she suffered, on this subject, she found all her efforts unable to controul, and her secret wish to see Valancourt once more, though unseen by him, powerfully prompted her to go, but prudence and a delicate pride restrained her, and she determined to avoid the possibility of throwing herself in his way, by forbearing to visit the gardens, for several days.

When, after near a week, she again ventured thither, she made Annette her companion, and confined her walk to the lower grounds, but often started as the leaves rustled in the breeze, imagining, that some person was among the thickets; and, at the turn of every alley, she looked forward with apprehensive expectation. She pursued her walk thoughtfully and silently, for her agitation would not suffer her to converse with Annette, to whom, however, thought and silence were so intolerable, that she did not scruple at length to talk to her mistress.

"Dear madam," said she, "why do you start so? one would think you knew what has happened."

"What has happened?" said Emily, in a faltering voice, and trying to command her emotion.

"The night before last, you know, madam"——

"I know nothing, Annette," replied her lady in a more hurried voice.

"The night before last, madam, there was a robber in the garden."

"A robber!" said Emily, in an eager, yet doubting tone.

"I suppose he was a robber, madam. What else could he be?"

"Where did you see him, Annette?" rejoined Emily, looking round her, and turning back towards the chateau.

"It was not I that saw him, madam, it was Jean the gardener. It was twelve o'clock at night, and, as he was coming across the court to go the back way into the house, what should he see—but somebody walking in the avenue, that fronts the garden gate! So, with that, Jean guessed how it was, and he went into the house for his gun."

"His gun!" exclaimed Emily.

"Yes, madam, his gun; and then he came out into the court to watch him. Presently, he sees him come slowly down the avenue, and lean over the garden gate, and look up at the house for a long time; and I warrant he examined it well, and settled what window he should break in at."

"But the gun," said Emily—"the gun!"

"Yes, madam, all in good time. Presently, Jean says, the robber opened the gate, and was coming into the court, and then he thought proper to ask him his business: so he called out again, and bade him say who he was, and what he wanted. But the man would do neither; but turned upon his heel, and passed into the garden again. Jean knew then well enough how it was, and so he fired after him."

"Fired!" exclaimed Emily.

"Yes, madam, fired off his gun; but, Holy Virgin! what makes you look so pale, madam? The man was not killed,—I dare say; but if he was, his comrades carried him off: for, when Jean went in the morning, to look for the body, it was gone, and nothing to be seen but a track of blood on the ground. Jean followed it, that he might find out where the man got into the garden, but it was lost in the grass, and"——

Annette was interrupted: for Emily's spirits died away, and she would have fallen to the ground, if the girl had not caught her, and supported her to a bench, close to them.

When, after a long absence, her senses returned, Emily desired to be led to her apartment; and, though she trembled with anxiety to enquire further on the subject of her alarm, she found herself too ill at present, to dare the intelligence which it was possible she might receive of Valancourt. Having dismissed Annette, that she might weep and think at liberty, she endeavoured to recollect the exact air of the person, whom she had seen on the terrace, and still her fancy gave her the figure of Valancourt. She had, indeed, scarcely a doubt, that it was he whom she had seen, and at whom the gardener had fired: for the manner of the latter person, as described by Annette, was not that of a robber; nor did it appear probable, that a robber would have come alone, to break into a house so spacious as this.

When Emily thought herself sufficiently recovered, to listen to what Jean might have to relate, she sent for him; but he could inform her of no circumstance, that might lead to a knowledge of the person, who had been shot, or of the consequence of the wound; and, after severely reprimanding him, for having fired with bullets, and ordering diligent enquiry to be made in the neighbourhood for the discovery of the wounded person, she dismissed him, and herself remained in the same state of terrible suspense. All the tenderness she had ever felt for Valancourt, was recalled by the sense of his danger; and the more she considered the subject, the more her conviction strengthened, that it was he, who had visited the gardens, for the purpose of soothing the misery of disappointed affection, amidst the scenes of his former happiness.

"Dear madam," said Annette, when she returned, "I never saw you so affected before! I dare say the man is not killed."

Emily shuddered, and lamented bitterly the rashness of the gardener in having fired.

"I knew you would be angry enough about that, madam, or I should have told you before; and he knew so too; for, says he, 'Annette, say nothing about this to my lady. She lies on the other side of the house, so did not hear the gun, perhaps; but she would be angry with me, if she knew, seeing there is blood. But then,' says he, 'how is one to keep the garden clear, if one is afraid to fire at a robber, when one sees him?'"

"No more of this," said Emily, "pray leave me."

Annette obeyed, and Emily returned to the agonizing considerations, that had assailed her before, but which she, at length, endeavoured to soothe by a new remark. If the stranger was Valancourt, it was certain he had come alone, and it appeared, therefore, that he had been able to quit the gardens, without assistance; a circumstance which did not seem probable, had his wound been dangerous. With this consideration, she endeavoured to support herself, during the enquiries, that were making by her servants in the neighbourhood; but day after day came, and still closed in uncertainty, concerning this affair: and Emily, suffering in silence, at length, drooped, and sunk under the pressure of her anxiety. She was attacked by a slow fever, and when she yielded to the persuasion of Annette to send for medical advice, the physicians prescribed little beside air, gentle exercise and amusement: but how was this last to be obtained? She, however, endeavoured to abstract her thoughts from the subject of her anxiety, by employing them in promoting that happiness in others, which she had lost herself; and, when the evening was fine, she usually took an airing, including in her ride the cottages of some of her tenants, on whose condition she made such observations, as often enabled her, unasked, to fulfil their wishes.

Her indisposition, and the business she engaged in, relative to this estate, had already protracted her stay at Tholouse, beyond the period she had formerly fixed for her departure to La Vallée; and now she was unwilling to leave the only place, where it seemed possible, that certainty could be obtained on the subject of her distress. But the time was come, when her presence was necessary at La Vallée, a letter from the Lady Blanche now informing her, that the Count and herself, being then at the chateau of the Baron St. Foix, purposed to visit her at La Vallée, on their way home, as soon as they should be informed of her arrival there. Blanche added, that they made this visit, with the hope of inducing her to return with them to Chateau-le-Blanc.

Emily, having replied to the letter of her friend, and said that she should be at La Vallée in a few days, made hasty preparations for the journey; and, in thus leaving Tholouse, endeavoured to support herself with a belief, that, if any fatal accident had happened to Valancourt, she must in this interval have heard of it.

On the evening before her departure, she went to take leave of the terrace and the pavilion. The day had been sultry, but a light shower, that fell just before sunset, had cooled the air, and given that soft verdure to the woods and pastures, which is so refreshing to the eye; while the rain drops, still trembling on the shrubs, glittered in the last yellow gleam, that lighted up the scene, and the air was filled with fragrance, exhaled by the late shower, from herbs and flowers and from the earth itself. But the lovely prospect, which Emily beheld from the terrace, was no longer viewed by her with delight; she sighed deeply as her eye wandered over it, and her spirits were in a state of such dejection, that she could not think of her approaching return to La Vallée, without tears, and seemed to mourn again the death of her father, as if it had been an event of yesterday. Having reached the pavilion, she seated herself at the open lattice, and, while her eyes settled on the distant mountains, that overlooked Gascony, still gleaming on the horizon, though the sun had now left the plains below, "Alas!" said she, "I return to your long-lost scenes, but shall meet no more the parents, that were wont to render them delightful!—no more shall see the smile of welcome, or hear the well-known voice of fondness:—all will now be cold and silent in what was once my happy home."

Tears stole down her cheek, as the remembrance of what that home had been, returned to her; but, after indulging her sorrow for some time, she checked it, accusing herself of ingratitude in forgetting the friends, that she possessed, while she lamented those that were departed; and she, at length, left the pavilion and the terrace, without having observed a shadow of Valancourt or of any other person.

CHAPTER XI

> Ah happy hills! ah pleasing shade!
> Ah fields belov'd in vain!
> Where once my careless childhood stray'd,
> A stranger yet to pain!
> I feel the gales, that from ye blow,
> A momentary bliss bestow,
> As waving fresh their gladsome wing,
> My weary soul they seem to soothe.
>
> GRAY

ON the following morning, Emily left Tholouse at an early hour, and reached La Vallée about sunset. With the melancholy she experienced on the review of a place which had been the residence of her parents, and the scene of her earliest delight, was mingled, after the first shock had subsided, a tender and undescribable pleasure. For time had so far blunted the acuteness of her grief, that she now courted every scene, that awakened the memory of her friends; in every room, where she had been accustomed to see them, they almost seemed to live again; and she felt that La Vallée was still her happiest home. One of the first apartments she visited, was that, which had been her father's library, and here she seated herself in his arm-chair, and, while she contemplated, with tempered resignation, the picture of past times, which her memory gave, the tears she shed could scarcely be called those of grief.

Soon after her arrival, she was surprised by a visit from the venerable M. Barreaux, who came impatiently to welcome the daughter of his late respected neighbour, to her long-deserted home. Emily was comforted by the presence of an old friend, and they passed an interesting hour in conversing of former times, and in relating some of the circumstances, that had occurred to each, since they parted.

The evening was so far advanced, when M. Barreaux left Emily, that she could not visit the garden that night; but, on the following morning, she traced its long-regretted scenes with fond impatience; and, as she walked beneath the groves, which her father had planted, and where she had so often sauntered in affectionate conversation with him, his countenance, his smile, even the accents of his voice, returned with exactness to her fancy, and her heart melted to the tender recollections.

This, too, was his favourite season of the year, at which they had often together admired the rich and variegated tints of these woods and the magical effect of autumnal lights upon the mountains; and now, the view of these circumstances made memory eloquent. As she wandered pensively on, she fancied the following address

TO AUTUMN

Sweet Autumn! how thy melancholy grace
Steals on my heart, as through these shades I wind!
Sooth'd by thy breathing sigh, I fondly trace
Each lonely image of the pensive mind!
Lov'd scenes, lov'd friends—long lost! around me rise,
And wake the melting thought, the tender tear!
That tear, that thought, which more than mirth I prize—
Sweet as the gradual tint, that paints thy year!
Thy farewel smile, with fond regret, I view,
Thy beaming lights, soft gliding o'er the woods;
Thy distant landscape, touch'd with yellow hue
While falls the lengthen'd gleam; thy winding floods,
Now veil'd in shade, save where the skiff's white sails
Swell to the breeze, and catch thy streaming ray.
But now, e'en now!—the partial vision fails,
And the wave smiles, as sweeps the cloud away!
Emblem of life!—Thus checquer'd is its plan,
Thus joy succeeds to grief—thus smiles the varied man!

One of Emily's earliest enquiries, after her arrival at La Vallée, was concerning Theresa, her father's old servant, whom it may be remembered that M. Quesnel had turned from the house when it was let, without any provision. Understanding that she lived in a cottage at no great distance, Emily walked thither, and, on approaching, was pleased to see, that her habitation was pleasantly situated on a green slope, sheltered by a tuft of oaks, and had an appearance of comfort and extreme neatness. She found the old woman within, picking vine-stalks, who, on perceiving her young mistress, was nearly overcome with joy.

"Ah! my dear young lady!" said she, "I thought I should never see you again in this world, when I heard you was gone to that outlandish country. I have been hardly used, since you went; I little thought they would have turned me out of my old master's family in my old age!"

Emily lamented the circumstance, and then assured her, that she would make her latter days comfortable, and expressed satisfaction, on seeing her in so pleasant an habitation.

Theresa thanked her with tears, adding, "Yes, mademoiselle, it is a very comfortable home, thanks to the kind friend, who took me out of my distress, when you was too far off to help me, and placed me here! I little thought!—but no more of that—"

"And who was this kind friend?" said Emily: "whoever it was, I shall consider him as mine also."

"Ah, mademoiselle! that friend forbad me to blazon the good deed—I must not say, who it was. But how you are altered since I saw you last! You look so pale now, and so thin, too; but then, there is my old master's smile! Yes, that will never leave you, any more than the goodness, that used to make him smile. Alas-a-day! the poor lost a friend indeed, when he died!"

Emily was affected by this mention of her father, which Theresa observing, changed the subject. "I heard, mademoiselle," said she, "that Madame Cheron married a foreign gentleman, after all, and took you abroad; how does she do?"

Emily now mentioned her death. "Alas!" said Theresa, "if she had not been my master's sister, I should never have loved her; she was always so cross. But how does that dear young gentleman do, M. Valancourt? he was an handsome youth, and a good one; is he well, mademoiselle?"

Emily was much agitated.

"A blessing on him!" continued Theresa. "Ah, my dear young lady, you need not look so shy; I know all about it. Do you think I do not know, that he loves you? Why, when you was away, mademoiselle, he used to come to the chateau and walk about it, so disconsolate! He would go into every room in the lower part of the house, and, sometimes, he would sit himself down in a chair, with his arms across, and his eyes on the floor, and there he would sit, and think, and think, for the hour together. He used to be very fond of the south parlour, because I told him it used to be yours; and there he would stay, looking at the pictures, which I said you drew, and playing upon your lute, that hung up by the window, and reading in your books, till sunset, and then he must go back to his brother's chateau. And then——"

"It is enough, Theresa," said Emily.—"How long have you lived in this cottage—and how can I serve you? Will you remain here, or return and live with me?"

"Nay, mademoiselle," said Theresa, "do not be so shy to your poor old servant. I am sure it is no disgrace to like such a good young gentleman."

A deep sigh escaped from Emily.

"Ah! how he did love to talk of you! I loved him for that. Nay, for that matter, he liked to hear me talk, for he did not say much himself. But I soon found out what he came to the chateau about. Then, he would go into the garden, and down to the terrace, and sit under that great tree there, for the day together, with one of your books in his hand; but he did not read much, I fancy; for one day I happened to go that way, and I heard somebody talking. Who can be here? says I: I am sure I let nobody into the garden, but the Chevalier. So I walked softly, to see who it could be; and behold! it was the Chevalier himself, talking to himself about you. And he repeated your name, and sighed so! and said he had lost you for ever, for that you would never return for him. I thought he was out in his reckoning there, but I said nothing, and stole away."

"No more of this trifling," said Emily, awakening from her reverie: "it displeases me."

"But, when M. Quesnel let the chateau, I thought it would have broke the Chevalier's heart."

"Theresa," said Emily seriously, "you must name the Chevalier no more!"

"Not name him, mademoiselle!" cried Theresa: "what times are come up now? Why, I love the Chevalier next to my old master and you, mademoiselle."

"Perhaps your love was not well bestowed, then," replied Emily, trying to conceal her tears; "but, however that might be, we shall meet no more."

"Meet no more!—not well bestowed!" exclaimed Theresa. "What do I hear? No, mademoiselle, my love was well bestowed, for it was the Chevalier Valancourt, who gave me this cottage, and has supported me in my old age, ever since M. Quesnel turned me from my master's house."

"The Chevalier Valancourt!" said Emily, trembling extremely.

"Yes, mademoiselle, he himself, though he made me promise not to tell; but how could one help, when one heard him ill spoken of? Ah! dear young lady, you may well weep, if you have behaved unkindly to him, for a more tender heart than his never young gentleman had. He found me out in my distress, when you was too far off to help me; and M. Quesnel refused to do so, and bade me go to service again—Alas! I was too old for that!—The Chevalier found me, and bought me this cottage, and gave me money to furnish it, and bade me seek out another poor woman to live with me; and he ordered his brother's steward to pay me, every quarter, that which has supported me in comfort. Think then, mademoiselle, whether I have not reason to speak well of the Chevalier. And there are others, who could have afforded it better than he: and I am afraid he has hurt himself by his generosity, for quarter day is gone by long since, and no money for me! But do not weep so, mademoiselle: you are not sorry surely to hear of the poor Chevalier's goodness?"

"Sorry!" said Emily, and wept the more. "But how long is it since you have seen him?"

"Not this many a day, mademoiselle."

"When did you hear of him?" enquired Emily, with increased emotion.

"Alas! never since he went away so suddenly into Languedoc; and he was but just come from Paris then, or I should have seen him, I am sure. Quarter day is gone by long since, and, as I said, no money for me; and I begin to fear some harm has happened to him: and if I was not so far from Estuviere and so lame, I should have gone to enquire before this time; and I have nobody to send so far."

Emily's anxiety, as to the fate of Valancourt, was now scarcely endurable, and, since propriety would not suffer her to send to the chateau of his brother, she requested that Theresa would immediately hire some person to go to his steward from herself, and, when he asked for the quarterage due to her, to make enquiries concerning Valancourt. But she first made Theresa promise never to mention her name in this affair, or ever with that of the Chevalier Valancourt; and her former faithfulness to M. St. Aubert induced Emily to confide in her assurances. Theresa now joyfully undertook to procure a person for this errand, and then Emily, after giving her a sum of money to supply her with present comforts, returned, with spirits heavily oppressed, to her home, lamenting, more than ever, that an heart, possessed of so much benevolence as Valancourt's, should have been contaminated by the vices of the world, but affected by the delicate affection, which his kindness to her old servant expressed for herself.

CHAPTER XII

Light thickens, and the crow
Makes wing to the rooky wood:
Good things of day begin to droop, and drowze;
While night's black agents to their preys do rouze.
MACBETH

MEANWHILE Count De Villefort and Lady Blanche had passed a pleasant fortnight at the chateau de St. Foix, with the Baron and Baroness, during which they made frequent excursions among the mountains, and were delighted with the romantic wildness of Pyrenéan scenery. It was with regret, that the Count bade adieu to his old friends, although with the hope of being soon united with them in one family; for it was settled that M. St. Foix, who now attended them into Gascony, should receive the hand of the Lady Blanche, upon their arrival at Chateau-le-Blanc. As the road, from the Baron's residence to La Vallée, was over some of the wildest tract of the Pyrenées, and where a carriage-wheel had never passed, the Count hired mules for himself and his family, as well as a couple of stout guides, who were well armed, informed of all the passes of the mountains, and who boasted, too, that they were acquainted with every brake and dingle in the way, could tell the names of all the highest points of this chain of Alps, knew every forest, that spread along their narrow vallies, the shallowest part of every torrent they must cross, and the exact distance of every goat-herd's and hunter's cabin they should have occasion to pass,—which last article of learning required no very capacious memory, for even such simple inhabitants were but thinly scattered over these wilds.

The Count left the chateau de St. Foix, early in the morning, with an intention of passing the night at a little inn upon the mountains, about half way to La Vallée, of which his guides had informed him; and, though this was frequented chiefly by Spanish muleteers, on their route into France, and, of course, would afford only sorry accommodation, the Count had no alternative, for it was the only place like an inn, on the road.

After a day of admiration and fatigue, the travellers found themselves, about sunset, in a woody valley, overlooked, on every side, by abrupt heights. They had proceeded for many leagues, without seeing a human habitation, and had only heard, now and then, at a distance, the melancholy tinkling of a sheep-bell; but now they caught the notes of merry music, and presently saw, within a little green recess among the rocks, a group of mountaineers, tripping through a dance. The Count, who could not look upon the happiness, any more than on the misery of others, with indifference, halted to enjoy this scene of simple pleasure. The group before him consisted of French and Spanish peasants, the inhabitants of a neighbouring hamlet, some of whom were performing a sprightly dance, the women with castanets in their hands, to the sounds of a lute and a tamborine, till, from the brisk melody of France, the music softened into a slow movement, to which two female peasants danced a Spanish Pavan.

The Count, comparing this with the scenes of such gaiety as he had witnessed at Paris, where false taste painted the features, and, while it vainly tried to supply the glow of nature, concealed the charms of animation—where affectation so often distorted the air, and vice perverted the manners—sighed to think, that natural graces and innocent pleasures flourished in the wilds of solitude, while they drooped amidst the concourse of polished society. But the lengthening shadows reminded the travellers, that they had no time to lose; and, leaving this joyous group, they pursued their way towards the little inn, which was to shelter them from the night.

The rays of the setting sun now threw a yellow gleam upon the forests of pine and chesnut, that swept down the lower region of the mountains, and gave resplendent tints to the snowy points above. But soon, even this light faded fast, and the scenery assumed a more tremendous appearance, invested with the obscurity of twilight. Where the torrent had been seen, it was now only heard; where the wild cliffs had displayed every variety of form and attitude, a dark mass of mountains now alone appeared; and the vale, which far, far below had opened its dreadful chasm, the eye could no longer fathom. A melancholy gleam still lingered on the summits of the highest Alps, overlooking the deep repose of evening, and seeming to make the stillness of the hour more awful.

Blanche viewed the scene in silence, and listened with enthusiasm to the murmur of the pines, that extended in dark lines along the mountains, and to the faint voice of the izard, among the rocks, that came at intervals on the air. But her enthusiasm sunk into apprehension, when, as the shadows deepened, she looked upon the doubtful precipice, that bordered the road, as well as on the various fantastic forms of danger, that glimmered through the obscurity beyond it; and she asked her father, how far they were from the inn, and whether he did not consider the road to be dangerous at this late hour. The Count repeated the first question to the guides, who returned a doubtful answer, adding, that, when it was darker, it would be safest to rest, till the moon rose. "It is scarcely safe to proceed now," said the Count; but the guides, assuring him that there was no danger, went on. Blanche, revived by this assurance, again indulged a pensive pleasure, as she watched the progress of twilight gradually spreading its tints over the woods and mountains, and stealing from the eye every minuter feature of the scene, till the grand outlines of nature alone remained. Then fell the silent dews, and every wild flower, and aromatic plant, that bloomed among the cliffs, breathed forth its sweetness; then, too, when the mountain-bee had crept into its blossomed bed, and the hum of every little insect, that had floated gaily in the sun-beam, was hushed, the sound of many streams, not heard till now, murmured at a distance.—The bats alone, of all the animals inhabiting this region, seemed awake; and, while they flitted across the silent path, which Blanche was pursuing, she remembered the following lines, which Emily had given her:

TO THE BAT

> From haunt of man, from day's obtrusive glare,
> Thou shroud'st thee in the ruin's ivy'd tow'r.
> Or in some shadowy glen's romantic bow'r,
> Where wizard forms their mystic charms prepare,
> Where Horror lurks, and ever-boding Care!
> But, at the sweet and silent ev'ning hour,
> When clos'd in sleep is ev'ry languid flow'r,
> Thou lov'st to sport upon the twilight air,
> Mocking the eye, that would thy course pursue,
> In many a wanton-round, elastic, gay,
> Thou flit'st athwart the pensive wand'rer's way,
> As his lone footsteps print the mountain-dew.
> From Indian isles thou com'st, with Summer's car,
> Twilight thy love—thy guide her beaming star!

To a warm imagination, the dubious forms, that float, half veiled in darkness, afford a higher delight, than the most distinct scenery, that the sun can shew. While the fancy thus wanders over landscapes partly of its own creation, a sweet complacency steals upon the mind, and

> Refines it all to subtlest feeling,
> Bids the tear of rapture roll.

The distant note of a torrent, the weak trembling of the breeze among the woods, or the far-off sound of a human voice, now lost and heard again, are circumstances, which wonderfully heighten the enthusiastic tone of the mind. The young St. Foix, who saw the presentations of a fervid fancy, and felt whatever enthusiasm could suggest, sometimes interrupted the silence, which the rest of the party seemed by mutual consent to preserve, remarking and pointing out to Blanche the most striking effect of the hour upon the scenery; while Blanche, whose apprehensions were beguiled by the conversation of her lover, yielded to the taste so congenial to his, and they conversed in a low restrained voice, the effect of the pensive tranquillity, which twilight and the scene inspired, rather than of any fear, that they should be heard. But, while the heart was thus soothed to tenderness, St. Foix gradually mingled, with his admiration of the country, a mention of his affection; and he continued to speak, and Blanche to listen, till the mountains, the woods, and the magical illusions of twilight, were remembered no more.

The shadows of evening soon shifted to the gloom of night, which was somewhat anticipated by the vapours, that, gathering fast round the mountains, rolled in dark wreaths along their sides; and the guides proposed to rest, till the moon should rise, adding, that they thought a storm was coming on. As they looked round for a spot, that might afford some kind of shelter, an object was perceived obscurely through the dusk, on a point of rock, a little way down the mountain, which they imagined to be a hunter's or a shepherd's cabin, and the party, with cautious steps, proceeded towards it. Their labour, however, was not rewarded, or their apprehensions soothed; for, on reaching the object of their search, they discovered a monumental cross, which marked the spot to have been polluted by murder.

The darkness would not permit them to read the inscription; but the guides knew this to be a cross, raised to the memory of a Count de Beliard, who had been murdered here by a horde of banditti, that had infested this part of the Pyrénées, a few years before; and the uncommon size of the monument seemed to justify the supposition, that it was erected for a person of some distinction. Blanche shuddered, as she listened to some horrid particulars of the Count's fate, which one of the guides related in a low, restrained tone, as if the sound of his own voice frightened him; but, while they lingered at the cross, attending to his narrative, a flash of lightning glanced upon the rocks, thunder muttered at a distance, and the travellers, now alarmed, quitted this scene of solitary horror, in search of shelter.

Having regained their former track, the guides, as they passed on, endeavoured to interest the Count by various stories of robbery, and even of murder, which had been perpetrated in the very places they must unavoidably pass, with accounts of their own dauntless courage and wonderful escapes. The chief guide, or rather he, who was the most completely armed, drawing forth one of the four pistols, that were tucked into his belt, swore, that it had shot three robbers within the year. He then brandished a clasp-knife of enormous length, and was going to recount the wonderful execution it had done, when St. Foix, perceiving, that Blanche was terrified, interrupted him. The Count, meanwhile, secretly laughing at the terrible histories and extravagant boastings of the man, resolved to humour him, and, telling Blanche in a whisper, his design, began to recount some exploits of his own, which infinitely exceeded any related by the guide.

To these surprising circumstances he so artfully gave the colouring of truth, that the courage of the guides was visibly affected by them, who continued silent, long after the Count had ceased to speak. The loquacity of the chief hero thus laid asleep, the vigilance of his eyes and ears seemed more thoroughly awakened, for he listened, with much appearance of anxiety, to the deep thunder, which murmured at intervals, and often paused, as the breeze, that was now rising, rushed among the pines. But, when he made a sudden halt before a tuft of cork trees, that projected over the road, and drew forth a pistol, before he would venture to brave the banditti which might lurk behind it, the Count could no longer refrain from laughter.

Having now, however, arrived at a level spot, somewhat sheltered from the air, by overhanging cliffs and by a wood of larch, that rose over the precipice on the left, and the guides being yet ignorant how far they were from the inn, the travellers determined to rest, till the moon should rise, or the storm disperse. Blanche, recalled to a sense of the present moment, looked on the surrounding gloom, with terror; but giving her hand to St. Foix, she alighted, and the whole party entered a kind of cave, if such it could be called, which was only a shallow cavity, formed by the curve of impending rocks. A light being struck, a fire was kindled, whose blaze afforded some degree of cheerfulness, and no small comfort, for, though the day had been hot, the night air of this mountainous region was chilling; a fire was partly necessary also to keep off the wolves, with which those wilds were infested.

Provisions being spread upon a projection of the rock, the Count and his family partook of a supper, which, in a scene less rude, would certainly have been thought less excellent. When the repast was finished, St. Foix, impatient for the moon, sauntered along the precipice, to a point, that fronted the east; but all was yet wrapt in gloom, and the silence of night was broken only by the murmuring of woods, that waved far below, or by distant thunder, and, now and then, by the faint voices of the party he had quitted. He viewed, with emotions of awful sublimity, the long volumes of sulphureous clouds, that floated along the upper and middle regions of the air, and the lightnings that flashed from them, sometimes silently, and, at others, followed by sullen peals of thunder, which the mountains feebly prolonged, while the whole horizon, and the abyss, on which he stood, were discovered in the momentary light. Upon the succeeding darkness, the fire, which had been kindled in the cave, threw a partial gleam, illumining some points of the opposite rocks, and the summits of pine-woods, that hung beetling on the cliffs below, while their recesses seemed to frown in deeper shade.

St. Foix stopped to observe the picture, which the party in the cave presented, where the elegant form of Blanche was finely contrasted by the majestic figure of the Count, who was seated by her on a rude stone, and each was rendered more impressive by the grotesque habits and strong features of the guides and other attendants, who were in the back ground of the piece. The effect of the light, too, was interesting; on the surrounding figures it threw a strong, though pale gleam, and glittered on their bright arms; while upon the foliage of a gigantic larch, that impended its shade over the cliff above, appeared a red, dusky tint, deepening almost imperceptibly into the blackness of night.

While St. Foix contemplated the scene, the moon, broad and yellow, rose over the eastern summits, from among embattled clouds, and shewed dimly the grandeur of the heavens, the mass of vapours, that rolled half way down the precipice beneath, and the doubtful mountains.

> What dreadful pleasure! there to stand sublime,
> Like shipwreck'd mariner on desert coast,
> And view th' enormous waste of vapour, tost
> In billows length'ning to th' horizon round!
>
> THE MINSTREL

From this romantic reverie he was awakened by the voices of the guides, repeating his name, which was reverbed from cliff to cliff, till an hundred tongues seemed to call him; when he soon quieted the fears of the Count and the Lady Blanche, by returning to the cave. As the storm, however, seemed approaching, they did not quit their place of shelter; and the Count, seated between his daughter and St. Foix, endeavoured to divert the fears of the former, and conversed on subjects, relating to the natural history of the scene, among which they wandered. He spoke of the mineral and fossile substances, found in the depths of these mountains,—the veins of marble and granite, with which they abounded, the strata of shells, discovered near their summits, many thousand fathom above the level of the sea, and at a vast distance from its present shore;—of the tremendous chasms and caverns of the rocks, the grotesque form of the mountains, and the various phenomena, that seem to stamp upon the world the history of the deluge. From the natural history he descended to the mention of events and circumstances, connected with the civil story of the Pyrenées; named some of the most remarkable fortresses, which France and Spain had erected in the passes of these mountains; and gave a brief account of some celebrated sieges and encounters in early times, when

Ambition first frightened Solitude from these her deep recesses, made her mountains, which before had echoed only to the torrent's roar, tremble with the clang of arms, and, when man's first footsteps in her sacred haunts had left the print of blood!

As Blanche sat, attentive to the narrative, that rendered the scenes doubly interesting, and resigned to solemn emotion, while she considered, that she was on the very ground, once polluted by these events, her reverie was suddenly interrupted by a sound, that came in the wind.—It was the distant bark of a watch-dog. The travellers listened with eager hope, and, as the wind blew stronger, fancied, that the sound came from no great distance; and, the guides having little doubt, that it proceeded from the inn they were in search of, the Count determined to pursue his way. The moon now afforded a stronger, though still an uncertain light, as she moved among broken clouds; and the travellers, led by the sound, recommenced their journey along the brow of the precipice, preceded by a single torch, that now contended with the moon-light; for the guides, believing they should reach the inn soon after sunset, had neglected to provide more. In silent caution they followed the sound, which was heard but at intervals, and which, after some time entirely ceased. The guides endeavoured, however, to point their course to the quarter, whence it had issued, but the deep roaring of a torrent soon seized their attention, and presently they came to a tremendous chasm of the mountain, which seemed to forbid all further progress. Blanche alighted from her mule, as did the Count and St. Foix, while the guides traversed the edge in search of a bridge, which, however rude, might convey them to the opposite side, and they, at length, confessed, what the Count had begun to suspect, that they had been, for some time, doubtful of their way, and were now certain only, that they had lost it.

At a little distance, was discovered a rude and dangerous passage, formed by an enormous pine, which, thrown across the chasm, united the opposite precipices, and which had been felled probably by the hunter, to facilitate his chace of the izard, or the wolf. The whole party, the guides excepted, shuddered at the prospect of crossing this alpine bridge, whose sides afforded no kind of defence, and from which to fall was to die. The guides, however, prepared to lead over the mules, while Blanche stood trembling on the brink, and listening to the roar of the waters, which were seen descending from rocks above, overhung with lofty pines, and thence precipitating themselves into the deep abyss, where their white surges gleamed faintly in the moon-light. The poor animals proceeded over this perilous bridge with instinctive caution, neither frightened by the noise of the cataract, or deceived by the gloom, which the impending foliage threw athwart their way. It was now, that the solitary torch, which had been hitherto of little service, was found to be an inestimable treasure; and Blanche, terrified, shrinking, but endeavouring to re-collect all her firmness and presence of mind, preceded by her lover and supported by her father, followed the red gleam of the torch, in safety, to the opposite cliff.

As they went on, the heights contracted, and formed a narrow pass, at the bottom of which, the torrent they had just crossed, was heard to thunder. But they were again cheered by the bark of a dog, keeping watch, perhaps, over the flocks of the mountains, to protect them from the nightly descent of the wolves. The sound was much nearer than before, and, while they rejoiced in the hope of soon reaching a place of repose, a light was seen to glimmer at a distance. It appeared at a height considerably above the level of their path, and was lost and seen again, as if the waving branches of trees sometimes excluded and then admitted its rays. The guides hallooed with all their strength, but the sound of no human voice was heard in return, and, at length, as a more effectual means of making themselves known, they fired a pistol. But, while they listened in anxious expectation, the noise of the explosion was alone heard, echoing among the rocks, and it gradually sunk into silence, which no friendly hint of man disturbed. The light, however, that had been seen before, now became plainer, and, soon after, voices were heard indistinctly on the wind; but, upon the guides repeating the call, the voices suddenly ceased, and the light disappeared.

The Lady Blanche was now almost sinking beneath the pressure of anxiety, fatigue and apprehension, and the united efforts of the Count and St. Foix could scarcely support her spirits. As they continued to advance, an object was perceived on a point of rock above, which, the strong rays of the moon then falling on it, appeared to be a watch-tower. The Count, from its situation and some other circumstances, had little doubt, that it was such, and believing, that the light had proceeded from thence, he endeavoured to re-animate his daughter's spirits by the near prospect of shelter and repose, which, however rude the accommodation, a ruined watch-tower might afford.

"Numerous watch-towers have been erected among the Pyrenées," said the Count, anxious only to call Blanche's attention from the subject of her fears; "and the method, by which they give intelligence of the approach of the enemy, is, you know, by fires, kindled on the summits of these edifices. Signals have thus, sometimes, been communicated from post to post, along a frontier line of several hundred miles in length. Then, as occasion may require, the lurking armies emerge from their fortresses and the forests, and march forth, to defend, perhaps, the entrance of some grand pass, where, planting themselves on the heights, they assail their astonished enemies, who wind along the glen below, with fragments of the shattered cliff, and pour death and defeat upon them. The ancient forts, and watch-towers, overlooking the grand passes of the Pyrenées, are carefully preserved; but some of those in inferior stations have been suffered to fall into decay, and are now frequently converted into the more peaceful habitation of the hunter, or the shepherd, who, after a day of toil, retires hither, and, with his faithful dogs, forgets, near a cheerful blaze, the labour of the chace, or the anxiety of collecting his wandering flocks, while he is sheltered from the nightly storm."

"But are they always thus peacefully inhabited?" said the Lady Blanche.

"No," replied the Count, "they are sometimes the asylum of French and Spanish smugglers, who cross the mountains with contraband goods from their respective countries, and the latter are particularly numerous, against whom strong parties of the king's troops are some-times sent. But the desperate resolution of these adventurers, who, knowing, that, if they are taken, they must expiate the breach of the law by the most cruel death, travel in large parties, well armed, often daunts the courage of the soldiers. The smugglers, who seek only safety, never engage, when they can possibly avoid it; the military, also, who know, that in these encounters, danger is certain, and glory almost unattain-able, are equally reluctant to fight; an engagement, therefore, very sel-dom happens, but, when it does, it never concludes till after the most desperate and bloody conflict. You are inattentive, Blanche," added the Count: "I have wearied you with a dull subject; but see, yonder, in the moon-light, is the edifice we have been in search of, and we are fortu-nate to be so near it, before the storm bursts."

Blanche, looking up, perceived, that they were at the foot of the cliff, on whose summit the building stood, but no light now issued from it; the barking of the dog too had, for some time, ceased, and the guides began to doubt, whether this was really the object of their search. From the distance, at which they surveyed it, shewn imperfectly by a cloudy moon, it appeared to be of more extent than a single watch-tower; but the difficulty was how to ascend the height, whose abrupt declivities seemed to afford no kind of pathway.

While the guides carried forward the torch to examine the cliff, the Count, remaining with Blanche and St. Foix at its foot, under the shadow of the woods, endeavoured again to beguile the time by con-versation, but again anxiety abstracted the mind of Blanche; and he then consulted, apart with St. Foix, whether it would be advisable, should a path be found, to venture to an edifice, which might possibly harbour banditti. They considered, that their own party was not small, and that several of them were well armed; and, after enumerating the dangers, to be incurred by passing the night in the open wild, exposed, perhaps, to the effects of a thunder-storm, there remained not a doubt, that they ought to endeavour to obtain admittance to the edifice above, at any hazard respecting the inhabitants it might harbour; but the darkness, and the dead silence, that surrounded it, appeared to contradict the probability of its being inhabited at all.

A shout from the guides aroused their attention, after which, in a few minutes, one of the Count's servants returned with intelligence, that a path was found, and they immediately hastened to join the guides, when they all ascended a little winding way cut in the rock among thickets of dwarf wood, and, after much toil and some danger, reached the summit, where several ruined towers, surrounded by a massy wall, rose to their view, partially illumined by the moon-light. The space around the building was silent, and apparently forsaken, but the Count was cautious; "Step softly," said he, in a low voice, "while we reconnoitre the edifice."

Having proceeded silently along for some paces, they stopped at a gate, whose portals were terrible even in ruins, and, after a moment's hesitation, passed on to the court of entrance, but paused again at the head of a terrace, which, branching from it, ran along the brow of a precipice. Over this, rose the main body of the edifice, which was now seen to be, not a watch-tower, but one of those ancient fortresses, that, from age and neglect, had fallen to decay. Many parts of it, however, appeared to be still entire; it was built of grey stone, in the heavy Saxon-gothic style, with enormous round towers, buttresses of proportionable strength, and the arch of the large gate, which seemed to open into the hall of the fabric, was round, as was that of a window above. The air of solemnity, which must so strongly have characterized the pile even in the days of its early strength, was now considerably heightened by its shattered battlements and half-demolished walls, and by the huge masses of ruin, scattered in its wide area, now silent and grass grown. In this court of entrance stood the gigantic remains of an oak, that seemed to have flourished and decayed with the building, which it still appeared frowningly to protect by the few remaining branches, leafless and moss-grown, that crowned its trunk, and whose wide extent told how enormous the tree had been in a former age. This fortress was evidently once of great strength, and, from its situation on a point of rock, impending over a deep glen, had been of great power to annoy, as well as to resist; the Count, therefore, as he stood surveying it, was somewhat surprised, that it had been suffered, ancient as it was, to sink into ruins, and its present lonely and deserted air excited in his breast emotions of melancholy awe. While he indulged, for a moment, these emotions, he thought he heard a sound of remote voices steal upon the stillness,

from within the building, the front of which he again surveyed with
scrutinizing eyes, but yet no light was visible. He now determined to
walk round the fort, to that remote part of it, whence he thought the
voices had arisen, that he might examine whether any light could be
discerned there, before he ventured to knock at the gate; for this purpose, he entered upon the terrace, where the remains of cannon were
yet apparent in the thick walls, but he had not proceeded many paces,
when his steps were suddenly arrested by the loud barking of a dog
within, and which he fancied to be the same, whose voice had been the
means of bringing the travellers thither. It now appeared certain, that
the place was inhabited, and the Count returned to consult again with
St. Foix, whether he should try to obtain admittance, for its wild aspect
had somewhat shaken his former resolution; but, after a second consultation, he submitted to the considerations, which before determined
him, and which were strengthened by the discovery of the dog, that
guarded the fort, as well as by the stillness that pervaded it. He, therefore, ordered one of his servants to knock at the gate, who was advancing to obey him, when a light appeared through the loop-hole of one
of the towers, and the Count called loudly, but, receiving no answer,
he went up to the gate himself, and struck upon it with an iron-pointed
pole, which had assisted him to climb the steep. When the echoes had
ceased, that this blow had awakened, the renewed barking,—and there
were now more than one dog,—was the only sound, that was heard.
The Count stepped back, a few paces, to observe whether the light was
in the tower, and, perceiving, that it was gone, he returned to the portal, and had lifted the pole to strike again, when again he fancied he
heard the murmur of voices within, and paused to listen. He was confirmed in the supposition, but they were too remote, to be heard otherwise than in a murmur, and the Count now let the pole fall heavily
upon the gate; when almost immediately a profound silence followed.
It was apparent, that the people within had heard the sound, and their
caution in admitting strangers gave him a favourable opinion of them.
"They are either hunters or shepherds," said he, "who, like ourselves,
have probably sought shelter from the night within these walls, and are
fearful of admitting strangers, lest they should prove robbers. I will
endeavour to remove their fears." So saying, he called aloud, "We are
friends, who ask shelter from the night." In a few moments, steps were
heard within, which approached, and a voice then enquired—"Who
calls?" "Friends," repeated the Count; "open the gates, and you shall
know more."—Strong bolts were now heard to be undrawn, and a man,
armed with a hunting spear, appeared. "What is it you want at this
hour?" said he. The Count beckoned his attendants, and then
answered, that he wished to enquire the way to the nearest cabin. "Are

you so little acquainted with these mountains," said the man, "as not to know, that there is none, within several leagues? I cannot shew you the way; you must seek it—there's a moon." Saying this, he was closing the gate, and the Count was turning away, half disappointed and half afraid, when another voice was heard from above, and, on looking up, he saw a light, and a man's face, at the grate of the portal. "Stay, friend, you have lost your way?" said the voice. "You are hunters, I suppose, like ourselves: I will be with you presently." The voice ceased, and the light disappeared. Blanche had been alarmed by the appearance of the man, who had opened the gate, and she now entreated her father to quit the place; but the Count had observed the hunter's spear, which he carried; and the words from the tower encouraged him to await the event. The gate was soon opened, and several men in hunters' habits, who had heard above what had passed below, appeared, and, having listened some time to the Count, told him he was welcome to rest there for the night. They then pressed him, with much courtesy, to enter, and to partake of such fare as they were about to sit down to. The Count, who had observed them attentively while they spoke, was cautious, and somewhat suspicious; but he was also weary, fearful of the approaching storm, and of encountering alpine heights in the obscurity of night; being likewise somewhat confident in the strength and number of his attendants, he, after some further consideration, determined to accept the invitation. With this resolution he called his servants, who, advancing round the tower, behind which some of them had silently listened to this conference, followed their Lord, the Lady Blanche, and St. Foix into the fortress. The strangers led them on to a large and rude hall, partially seen by a fire that blazed at its extremity, round which four men, in the hunter's dress, were seated, and on the hearth were several dogs stretched in sleep. In the middle of the hall stood a large table, and over the fire some part of an animal was boiling. As the Count approached, the men arose, and the dogs, half raising themselves, looked fiercely at the strangers, but, on hearing their masters' voices, kept their postures on the hearth.

Blanche looked round this gloomy and spacious hall; then at the men, and to her father, who, smiling cheerfully at her, addressed himself to the hunters. "This is an hospitable hearth," said he, "the blaze of a fire is reviving after having wandered so long in these dreary wilds. Your dogs are tired; what success have you had?" "Such as we usually have," replied one of the men, who had been seated in the hall, "we kill our game with tolerable certainty." "These are fellow hunters,' said one of the men who had brought the Count hither, "that have lost their way, and I have told them there is room enough in the fort for us all." "Very true, very true," replied his companion, "What luck have you had in the chace, brothers? We have killed two izards, and that, you will say, is pretty well." "You mistake, friend," said the Count, "we are not hunters, but travellers; but, if you will admit us to hunters' fare, we shall be well contented, and will repay your kindness." "Sit down then, brother," said one of the men: "Jacques, lay more fuel on the fire, the kid will soon be ready; bring a seat for the lady too. Ma'amselle, will you taste our brandy? it is true Barcelona, and as bright as ever flowed from a keg." Blanche timidly smiled, and was going to refuse, when her father prevented her, by taking, with a good humoured air, the glass offered to his daughter; and Mons. St. Foix, who was seated next her, pressed her hand, and gave her an encouraging look, but her attention was engaged by a man, who sat silently by the fire, observing St. Foix, with a steady and earnest eye.

"You lead a jolly life here," said the Count. "The life of a hunter is a pleasant and a healthy one; and the repose is sweet, which succeeds to your labour."

"Yes," replied one of his hosts, "our life is pleasant enough. We live here only during the summer, and autumnal months; in winter, the place is dreary, and the swoln torrents, that descend from the heights, put a stop to the chace."

"'Tis a life of liberty and enjoyment," said the Count: "I should like to pass a month in your way very well."

"We find employment for our guns too," said a man who stood behind the Count: "here are plenty of birds, of delicious flavour, that feed upon the wild thyme and herbs, that grow in the vallies. Now I think of it, there is a brace of birds hung up in the stone gallery; go fetch them, Jacques, we will have them dressed."

The Count now made enquiry, concerning the method of pursuing the chace among the rocks and precipices of these romantic regions, and was listening to a curious detail, when a horn was sounded at the gate. Blanche looked timidly at her father, who continued to converse on the subject of the chace, but whose countenance was somewhat expressive of anxiety, and who often turned his eyes towards that part of the hall nearest the gate. The horn sounded again, and a loud halloo succeeded. "These are some of our companions, returned from their day's labour," said a man, going lazily from his seat towards the gate; and in a few minutes, two men appeared, each with a gun over his shoulder, and pistols in his belt. "What cheer, my lads? what cheer?" said they, as they approached. "What luck?" returned their companions: "have you brought home your supper? You shall have none else."

"Hah! who the devil have you brought home?" said they in bad Spanish, on perceiving the Count's party, "are they from France, or Spain?—where did you meet with them?"

"They met with us, and a merry meeting too," replied his companion aloud in good French. "This chevalier, and his party, had lost their way, and asked a night's lodging in the fort." The others made no reply, but threw down a kind of knapsack, and drew forth several brace of birds. The bag sounded heavily as it fell to the ground, and the glitter of some bright metal within glanced on the eye of the Count, who now surveyed, with a more enquiring look, the man, that held the knapsack. He was a tall robust figure, of a hard countenance, and had short black hair, curling in his neck. Instead of the hunter's dress, he wore a faded military uniform; sandals were laced on his broad legs, and a kind of short trowsers hung from his waist. On his head he wore a leathern cap, somewhat resembling in shape an ancient Roman helmet; but the brows that scowled beneath it, would have characterized those of the barbarians, who conquered Rome, rather than those of a Roman soldier. The Count, at length, turned away his eyes, and remained silent and thoughtful, till, again raising them, he perceived a figure standing in an obscure part of the hall, fixed in attentive gaze on St. Foix, who was conversing with Blanche, and did not observe this; but the Count, soon after, saw the same man looking over the shoulder of the soldier as attentively at himself. He withdrew his eye, when that of the Count met it, who felt mistrust gathering fast upon his mind, but feared to betray it in his countenance, and, forcing his features to assume a smile, addressed Blanche on some indifferent subject. When he again looked round, he perceived, that the soldier and his companion were gone.

The man, who was called Jacques, now returned from the stone gallery. "A fire is lighted there," said he, "and the birds are dressing; the table too is spread there, for that place is warmer than this."

His companions approved of the removal, and invited their guests to follow to the gallery, of whom Blanche appeared distressed, and remained seated, and St. Foix looked at the Count, who said, he preferred the comfortable blaze of the fire he was then near. The hunters, however, commended the warmth of the other apartment, and pressed his removal with such seeming courtesy, that the Count, half doubting, and half fearful of betraying his doubts, consented to go. The long and ruinous passages, through which they went, somewhat daunted him, but the thunder, which now burst in loud peals above, made it dangerous to quit this place of shelter, and he forbore to provoke his conductors by shewing that he distrusted them. The hunters led the way, with a lamp; the Count and St. Foix, who wished to please their hosts by some instances of familiarity, carried each a seat, and Blanche followed, with faltering steps. As she passed on, part of her dress caught on a nail in the wall, and, while she stopped, somewhat too scrupulously, to disengage it, the Count, who was talking to St. Foix, and neither of whom observed the circumstance, followed their conductor round an abrupt angle of the passage, and Blanche was left behind in darkness. The thunder prevented them from hearing her call but, having disengaged her dress, she quickly followed, as she thought, the way they had taken. A light, that glimmered at a distance, confirmed this belief, and she proceeded towards an open door, whence it issued, conjecturing the room beyond to be the stone gallery the men had spoken of. Hearing voices as she advanced, she paused within a few paces of the chamber, that she might be certain whether she was right, and from thence, by the light of a lamp, that hung from the ceiling, observed four men, seated round a table, over which they leaned in apparent consultation. In one of them she distinguished the features of him, whom she had observed, gazing at St. Foix, with such deep attention; and who was now speaking in an earnest, though restrained voice, till, one of his companions seeming to oppose him, they spoke together in a loud and harsher tone. Blanche, alarmed by perceiving that neither her father, or St. Foix were there, and terrified at the fierce countenances and manners of these men, was turning hastily from the chamber, to pursue her search of the gallery, when she heard one of the men say:

"Let all dispute end here. Who talks of danger? Follow my advice, and there will be none—secure *them*, and the rest are an easy prey." Blanche, struck with these words, paused a moment, to hear more. "There is nothing to be got by the rest," said one of his companions, "I am never for blood when I can help it—dispatch the two others, and our business is done; the rest may go."

"May they so?" exclaimed the first ruffian, with a tremendous oath—"What! to tell how we have disposed of their masters, and to send the king's troops to drag us to the wheel! You was always a choice adviser—I warrant we have not yet forgot St. Thomas's eve last year."

Blanche's heart now sunk with horror. Her first impulse was to retreat from the door, but, when she would have gone, her trembling frame refused to support her, and, having tottered a few paces, to a more obscure part of the passage, she was compelled to listen to the dreadful councils of those, who, she was no longer suffered to doubt, were banditti. In the next moment, she heard the following words, "Why you would not murder the whole *gang*?"

"I warrant our lives are as good as theirs," replied his comrade. "If we don't kill them, they will hang us: better they should die than we be hanged."

"Better, better," cried his comrades.

"To commit murder, is a hopeful way of escaping the gallows!" said the first ruffian—"many an honest fellow has run his head into the noose that way, though." There was a pause of some moments, during which they appeared to be considering.

"Confound those fellows," exclaimed one of the robbers impatiently, "they ought to have been here by this time; they will come back presently with the old story, and no booty: if they were here, our business would be plain and easy. I see we shall not be able to do the business to-night, for our numbers are not equal to the enemy, and in the morning they will be for marching off, and how can we detain them without force?"

"I have been thinking of a scheme, that will do," said one of his comrades: "if we can dispatch the two chevaliers silently, it will be easy to master the rest."

"That's a plausible scheme, in good faith," said another with a smile of scorn—"If I can eat my way through the prison wall, I shall be at liberty!—How can we dispatch them *silently*?"

"By poison," replied his companions.

"Well said! that will do," said the second ruffian, "that will give a lingering death too, and satisfy my revenge. These barons shall take care how they again tempt our vengeance."

"I knew the son, the moment I saw him," said the man, whom Blanche had observed gazing on St. Foix, "though he does not know me; the father I had almost forgotten."

"Well, you may say what you will," said the third ruffian, "but I don't believe he is the Baron, and I am as likely to know as any of you, for I was one of them, that attacked him, with our brave lads, that suffered."

"And was not I another?" said the first ruffian, "I tell you he is the Baron; but what does it signify whether he is or not?—shall we let all this booty go out of our hands? It is not often we have such luck at this. While we run the chance of the wheel for smuggling a few pounds of tobacco, to cheat the king's manufactory, and of breaking our necks down the precipices in the chace of our food; and, now and then, rob a brother smuggler, or a straggling pilgrim, of what scarcely repays us the powder we fire at them, shall we let such a prize as this go? Why they have enough about them to keep us for——"

"I am not for that, I am not for that," replied the third robber, "let us make the most of them: only, if this is the Baron, I should like to have a flash the more at him, for the sake of our brave comrades, that he brought to the gallows."

"Aye, aye, flash as much as you will," rejoined the first man, "but I tell you the Baron is a taller man."

"Confound your quibbling," said the second ruffian, "shall we let them go or not? If we stay here much longer, they will take the hint, and march off without our leave. Let them be who they will, they are rich, or why all those servants? Did you see the ring, he, you call the Baron, had on his finger? — it was a diamond; but he has not got it on now: he saw me looking at it, I warrant, and took it off."

"Aye, and then there is the picture; did you see that? She has not taken that off," observed the first ruffian, "it hangs at her neck; if it had not sparkled so, I should not have found it out, for it was almost hid by her dress; those are diamonds too, and a rare many of them there must be, to go round such a large picture."

"But how are we to manage this business?" said the second ruffian: "let us talk of that, there is no fear of there being booty enough, but how are we to secure it?"

"Aye, aye," said his comrades, "let us talk of that, and remember no time is to be lost."

"I am still for poison," observed the third, "but consider their number; why there are nine or ten of them, and armed too; when I saw so many at the gate, I was not for letting them in, you know, nor you either."

"I thought they might be some of our enemies," replied the second, "I did not so much mind numbers."

"But you must mind them now," rejoined his comrade, "or it will be worse for you. We are not more than six, and how can we master ten by open force? I tell you we must give some of them a dose, and the rest may then be managed."

"I'll tell you a better way," rejoined the other impatiently, "draw closer."

Blanche, who had listened to this conversation, in an agony, which it would be impossible to describe, could no longer distinguish what was said, for the ruffians now spoke in lowered voices; but the hope, that she might save her friends from the plot, if she could find her way quickly to them, suddenly re-animated her spirits, and lent her strength enough to turn her steps in search of the gallery. Terror, however, and darkness conspired against her, and, having moved a few yards, the feeble light, that issued from the chamber, no longer even contended with the gloom, and, her foot stumbling over a step that crossed the passage, she fell to the ground.

The noise startled the banditti, who became suddenly silent, and then all rushed to the passage, to examine whether any person was there, who might have overheard their councils. Blanche saw them approaching, and perceived their fierce and eager looks: but, before she could raise herself, they discovered and seized her, and, as they dragged her towards the chamber they had quitted, her screams drew from them horrible threatenings.

Having reached the room, they began to consult what they should do with her. "Let us first know what she had heard," said the chief robber. "How long have you been in the passage, lady, and what brought you there?"

"Let us first secure that picture," said one of his comrades, approaching the trembling Blanche. "Fair lady, by your leave that picture is mine; come, surrender it, or I shall seize it."

Blanche, entreating their mercy, immediately gave up the miniature, while another of the ruffians fiercely interrogated her, concerning what she had overheard of their conversation, when, her confusion and terror too plainly telling what her tongue feared to confess, the ruffians looked expressively upon one another, and two of them withdrew to a remote part of the room, as if to consult further.

"These are diamonds, by St. Peter!" exclaimed the fellow, who had been examining the miniature, "and here is a very pretty picture too, 'faith; as handsome a young chevalier, as you would wish to see by a summer's sun. Lady, this is your spouse, I warrant, for it is the spark, that was in your company just now."

Blanche, sinking with terror, conjured him to have pity on her, and, delivering him her purse, promised to say nothing of what had passed, if he would suffer her to return to her friends.

He smiled ironically, and was going to reply, when his attention was called off by a distant noise; and, while he listened, he grasped the arm of Blanche more firmly, as if he feared she would escape from him, and she again shrieked for help.

The approaching sounds called the ruffians from the other part of the chamber. "We are betrayed," said they; "but let us listen a moment, perhaps it is only our comrades come in from the mountains, and if so, our work is sure; listen!"

A distant discharge of shot confirmed this supposition for a moment, but, in the next, the former sounds drawing nearer, the clashing of swords, mingled with the voices of loud contention and with heavy groans, were distinguished in the avenue leading to the chamber. While the ruffians prepared their arms, they heard themselves called by some of their comrades afar off, and then a shrill horn was sounded without the fortress, a signal, it appeared, they too well understood; for three of them, leaving the Lady Blanche to the care of the fourth, instantly rushed from the chamber.

While Blanche, trembling, and nearly fainting, was supplicating for release, she heard amid the tumult, that approached, the voice of St. Foix, and she had scarcely renewed her shriek, when the door of the room was thrown open, and he appeared, much disfigured with blood, and pursued by several ruffians. Blanche neither saw, or heard any more; her head swam, her sight failed, and she became senseless in the arms of the robber, who had detained her.

When she recovered, she perceived, by the gloomy light, that trembled round her, that she was in the same chamber, but neither the Count, St. Foix, or any other person appeared, and she continued, for some time, entirely still, and nearly in a state of stupefaction. But, the dreadful images of the past returning, she endeavoured to raise herself, that she might seek her friends, when a sullen groan, at a little distance, reminded her of St. Foix, and of the condition, in which she had seen him enter this room; then, starting from the floor, by a sudden effort of horror, she advanced to the place whence the sound had proceeded, where a body was lying stretched upon the pavement, and where, by the glimmering light of a lamp, she discovered the pale and disfigured countenance of St. Foix. Her horrors, at that moment, may be easily imagined. He was speechless; his eyes were half closed, and, on the hand, which she grasped in the agony of despair, cold damps had settled. While she vainly repeated his name, and called for assistance, steps approached, and a person entered the chamber, who, she soon perceived, was not the Count, her father; but, what was her astonishment, when, supplicating him to give his assistance to St. Foix, she discovered Ludovico! He scarcely paused to recognise her, but immediately bound up the wounds of the Chevalier, and, perceiving, that he had fainted probably from loss of blood, ran for water; but he had been absent only a few moments, when Blanche heard other steps approaching, and, while she was almost frantic with apprehension of the ruffians, the light of a torch flashed upon the walls, and then Count De Villefort appeared, with an affrighted countenance, and breathless with impatience, calling upon his daughter. At the sound of his voice, she rose, and ran to his arms, while he, letting fall the bloody sword he held, pressed her to his bosom in a transport of gratitude and joy, and then hastily enquired for St. Foix, who now gave some signs of life. Ludovico soon after returning with water and brandy, the former was applied to his lips, and the latter to his temples and hands, and Blanche, at length, saw him unclose his eyes, and then heard him enquire for her; but the joy she felt, on this occasion, was interrupted by new alarms, when Ludovico said it would be necessary to remove Mons. St. Foix immediately, and added, "The banditti, that are out, my Lord, were expected home, an hour ago, and they will certainly find us, if we delay. That shrill horn, they know, is never sounded by their comrades but on most desperate occasions, and it echoes among the mountains for many leagues round. I have known them brought home by its sound even from the Pied de Melicant. Is any body standing watch at the great gate, my Lord?"

"Nobody," replied the Count; "the rest of my people are now scattered about, I scarcely know where. Go, Ludovico, collect them together, and look out yourself, and listen if you hear the feet of mules."

Ludovico then hurried away, and the Count consulted as to the means of removing St. Foix, who could not have borne the motion of a mule, even if his strength would have supported him in the saddle.

While the Count was telling, that the banditti, whom they had found in the fort, were secured in the dungeon, Blanche observed that he was himself wounded, and that his left arm was entirely useless; but he smiled at her anxiety, assuring her the wound was trifling.

The Count's servants, except two who kept watch at the gate, now appeared, and, soon after, Ludovico. "I think I hear mules coming along the glen, my Lord," said he, "but the roaring of the torrent below will not let me be certain; however, I have brought what will serve the Chevalier," he added, shewing a bear's skin, fastened to a couple of long poles, which had been adapted for the purpose of bringing home such of the banditti as happened to be wounded in their encounters. Ludovico spread it on the ground, and, placing the skins of several goats upon it, made a kind of bed, into which the Chevalier, who was however now much revived, was gently lifted; and, the poles being raised upon the shoulders of the guides, whose footing among these steeps could best be depended upon, he was borne along with an easy motion. Some of the Count's servants were also wounded—but not materially, and, their wounds being bound up, they now followed to the great gate. As they passed along the hall, a loud tumult was heard at some distance, and Blanche was terrified. "It is only those villains in the dungeon, my Lady," said Ludovico. "They seem to be bursting it open," said the Count. "No, my Lord," replied Ludovico, "it has an iron door; we have nothing to fear from them; but let me go first, and look out from the rampart."

They quickly followed him, and found their mules browsing before the gates, where the party listened anxiously, but heard no sound, except that of the torrent below and of the early breeze, sighing among the branches of the old oak, that grew in the court; and they were now glad to perceive the first tints of dawn over the mountain-tops. When they had mounted their mules, Ludovico, undertaking to be their guide, led them by an easier path, than that by which they had formerly ascended, into the glen. "We must avoid that valley to the east, my Lord," said he, "or we may meet the banditti; they went out that way in the morning."

The travellers, soon after, quitted this glen, and found themselves in a narrow valley that stretched towards the north-west. The morning light upon the mountains now strengthened fast, and gradually discovered the green hillocks, that skirted the winding feet of the cliffs, tufted with cork tree, and ever-green oak. The thunder-clouds being dispersed, had left the sky perfectly serene, and Blanche was revived by the fresh breeze, and by the view of verdure, which the late rain had brightened. Soon after, the sun arose, when the dripping rocks, with the shrubs that fringed their summits, and many a turfy slope below, sparkled in his rays. A wreath of mist was seen, floating along the extremity of the valley, but the gale bore it before the travellers, and the sun-beams gradually drew it up towards the summit of the mountains. They had proceeded about a league, when, St. Foix having complained of extreme faintness, they stopped to give him refreshment, and, that the men, who bore him, might rest. Ludovico had brought from the fort some flasks of rich Spanish wine, which now proved a reviving cordial not only to St. Foix but to the whole party, though to him it gave only temporary relief, for it fed the fever, that burned in his veins, and he could neither disguise in his countenance the anguish he suffered, or suppress the wish, that he was arrived at the inn, where they had designed to pass the preceding night.

While they thus reposed themselves under the shade of the dark green pines, the Count desired Ludovico to explain shortly, by what means he had disappeared from the north apartment, how he came into the hands of the banditti, and how he had contributed so essentially to serve him and his family, for to him he justly attributed their present deliverance. Ludovico was going to obey him, when suddenly they heard the echo of a pistol-shot, from the way they had passed, and they rose in alarm, hastily to pursue their route.

CHAPTER XIII

Ah why did Fate his steps decoy
In stormy paths to roam,
Remote from all congenial joy!
BEATTIE

EMILY, mean while, was still suffering anxiety as to the fate of Valancourt; but Theresa, having, at length, found a person, whom she could entrust on her errand to the steward, informed her, that the messenger would return on the following day; and Emily promised to be at the cottage, Theresa being too lame to attend her.

In the evening, therefore, Emily set out alone for the cottage, with a melancholy foreboding, concerning Valancourt, while, perhaps, the gloom of the hour might contribute to depress her spirits. It was a grey autumnal evening towards the close of the season; heavy mists partially obscured the mountains, and a chilling breeze, that sighed among the beech woods, strewed her path with some of their last yellow leaves. These, circling in the blast and foretelling the death of the year, gave an image of desolation to her mind, and, in her fancy, seemed to announce the death of Valancourt. Of this she had, indeed, more than once so strong a presentiment, that she was on the point of returning home, feeling herself unequal to an encounter with the certainty she anticipated, but, contending with her emotions, she so far commanded them, as to be able to proceed.

While she walked mournfully on, gazing on the long volumes of vapour, that poured upon the sky, and watching the swallows, tossed along the wind, now disappearing among tempestuous clouds, and then emerging, for a moment, in circles upon the calmer air, the afflictions and vicissitudes of her late life seemed pourtrayed in these fleeting images;—thus had she been tossed upon the stormy sea of misfortune for the last year, with but short intervals of peace, if peace that could be called, which was only the delay of evils. And now, when she had escaped from so many dangers, was become independent of the will of those, who had oppressed her, and found herself mistress of a large fortune, now, when she might reasonably have expected happiness, she perceived that she was as distant from it as ever. She would have accused herself of weakness and ingratitude in thus suffering a sense of the various blessings she possessed to be overcome by that of a single misfortune, had this misfortune affected herself alone; but, when she had wept for Valancourt even as living, tears of compassion had mingled with those of regret, and while she lamented a human being degraded to vice, and consequently to misery, reason and humanity claimed these tears, and fortitude had not yet taught her to separate them from those of love; in the present moments, however, it was not the certainty of his guilt, but the apprehension of his death (of a death also, to which she herself, however innocently, appeared to have been in some degree instrumental) that oppressed her. This fear increased, as the means of certainty concerning it approached; and, when she came within view of Theresa's cottage, she was so much disordered, and her resolution failed her so entirely, that, unable to proceed, she rested on a bank, beside her path; where, as she sat, the wind that groaned sullenly among the lofty branches above, seemed to her melancholy imagination to bear the sounds of distant lamentation, and, in the pauses of the gust, she still fancied she heard the feeble and far-off notes of distress. Attention convinced her, that this was no more than fancy; but the increasing gloom, which seemed the sudden close of day, soon warned her to depart, and, with faltering steps, she again moved toward the cottage. Through the casement appeared the cheerful blaze of a wood fire, and Theresa, who had observed Emily approaching, was already at the door to receive her.

"It is a cold evening, madam," said she, "storms are coming on, and I thought you would like a fire. Do take this chair by the hearth."

Emily, thanking her for this consideration, sat down, and then, looking in her face, on which the wood fire threw a gleam, she was struck with its expression, and, unable to speak, sunk back in her chair with a countenance so full of woe, that Theresa instantly comprehended the occasion of it, but she remained silent. "Ah!" said Emily, at length, "it is unnecessary for me to ask the result of your enquiry, your silence, and that look, sufficiently explain it;—he is dead!"

"Alas! my dear young lady," replied Theresa, while tears filled her eyes, "this world is made up of trouble! the rich have their share as well as the poor! But we must all endeavour to bear what Heaven pleases."

"He is dead, then!"—interrupted Emily—"Valancourt is dead!"

"A-well-a-day! I fear he is," replied Theresa.

"You fear!" said Emily, "do you only fear?"

"Alas! yes, madam, I fear he is! neither the steward, or any of the Epourville family, have heard of him since he left Languedoc, and the Count is in great affliction about him, for he says he was always punctual in writing, but that now he has not received a line from him, since he left Languedoc; he appointed to be at home, three weeks ago, but he has neither come, or written, and they fear some accident has befallen him. Alas! that ever I should live to cry for his death! I am old, and might have died without being missed, but he"—— Emily was faint, and asked for some water, and Theresa, alarmed by the voice, in which she spoke, hastened to her assistance, and, while she held the water to Emily's lips, continued, "My dear young mistress, do not take it so to heart; the Chevalier may be alive and well, for all this; let us hope the best!"

"O no! I cannot hope," said Emily, "I am acquainted with circumstances, that will not suffer me to hope. I am somewhat better now, and can hear what you have to say. Tell me, I entreat, the particulars of what you know."

"Stay till you are a little better, mademoiselle, you look sadly!"

"O no, Theresa, tell me all, while I have the power to hear it," said Emily, "tell me all, I conjure you!"

"Well, madam, I will then; but the steward did not say much, for Richard says he seemed shy of talking about Mons. Valancourt, and what he gathered was from Gabriel, one of the servants, who said he had heard it from my lord's gentleman."

"What did he hear?" said Emily.

"Why, madam, Richard has but a bad memory, and could not remember half of it, and, if I had not asked him a great many questions, I should have heard little indeed. But he says that Gabriel said, that he and all the other servants were in great trouble about M. Valancourt, for that he was such a kind young gentleman, they all loved him, as well as if he had been their own brother—and now, to think what was become of him! For he used to be so courteous to them all, and, if any of them had been in fault, M. Valancourt was the first to persuade my lord to forgive them. And then, if any poor family was in distress, M. Valancourt was the first, too, to relieve them, though some folks, not a great way off, could have afforded that much better than he. And then, said Gabriel, he was so gentle to every body, and, for all he had such a noble look with him, he never would command, and call about him, as some of your quality people do, and we never minded him the less for that. Nay, says Gabriel, for that matter, we minded him the more, and would all have run to obey him at a word, sooner than if some folks had told us what to do at full length; aye, and were more afraid of displeasing him, too, than of them, that used rough words to us."

Emily, who no longer considered it to be dangerous to listen to praise, bestowed on Valancourt, did not attempt to interrupt Theresa, but sat, attentive to her words, though almost overwhelmed with grief. "My Lord," continued Theresa, "frets about M. Valancourt sadly, and the more, because, they say, he had been rather harsh against him lately. Gabriel says he had it from my Lord's valet, that M. Valancourt had *comported* himself wildly at Paris, and had spent a great deal of money, more a great deal than my Lord liked, for he loves money better than M. Valancourt, who had been led astray sadly. Nay, for that matter, M. Valancourt had been put into prison at Paris, and my Lord, says Gabriel, refused to take him out, and said he deserved to suffer; and, when old Gregoire, the butler, heard of this, he actually bought a walking-stick to take with him to Paris, to visit his young master; but the next thing we hear is, that M. Valancourt is coming home. O, it was a joyful day when he came; but he was sadly altered, and my Lord looked very cool upon him, and he was very sad, indeed. And, soon after, he went away again into Languedoc, and, since that time, we have never seen him."

Theresa paused, and Emily, sighing deeply, remained with her eyes fixed upon the floor, without speaking. After a long pause, she enquired what further Theresa had heard. "Yet why should I ask?" she added; "what you have already told is too much. O Valancourt! thou art gone—forever gone! and I—I have murdered thee!" These words, and the countenance of despair which accompanied them, alarmed Theresa, who began to fear, that the shock of the intelligence Emily had just received, had affected her senses. "My dear young lady, be composed," said she, "and do not say such frightful words. You murder M. Valancourt,—dear heart!" Emily replied only by a heavy sigh.

"Dear lady, it breaks my heart to see you look so," said Theresa, "do not sit with your eyes upon the ground, and all so pale and melancholy; it frightens me to see you." Emily was still silent, and did not appear to hear any thing that was said to her. "Besides, mademoiselle," continued Theresa, "M. Valancourt may be alive and merry yet, for what we know."

At the mention of his name, Emily raised her eyes, and fixed them, in a wild gaze, upon Theresa, as if she was endeavouring to understand what had been said. "Aye, my dear lady," said Theresa, mistaking the meaning of this considerate air, "M. Valancourt may be alive and merry yet."

On the repetition of these words, Emily comprehended their import, but, instead of producing the effect intended, they seemed only to heighten her distress. She rose hastily from her chair, paced the little room, with quick steps, and, often sighing deeply, clasped her hands, and shuddered.

Meanwhile, Theresa, with simple, but honest affection, endeavoured to comfort her; put more wood on the fire, stirred it up into a brighter blaze, swept the hearth, set the chair, which Emily had left, in a warmer situation, and then drew forth from a cupboard a flask of wine. "It is a stormy night, madam," said she, "and blows cold—do come nearer the fire, and take a glass of this wine; it will comfort you, as it has done me, often and often, for it is not such wine as one gets every day; it is rich Languedoc, and the last of six flasks that M. Valancourt sent me, the night before he left Gascony for Paris. They have served me, ever since, as cordials, and I never drink it, but I think of him, and what kind words he said to me when he gave them. Theresa, says he, you are not young now, and should have a glass of good wine, now and then. I will send you a few flasks, and, when you taste them, you will sometimes remember me your friend. Yes—those were his very words—me your friend!" Emily still paced the room, without seeming to hear what Theresa said, who continued speaking. "And I have remembered him, often enough, poor young gentleman!—for he gave me this roof for a shelter, and that, which has supported me. Ah! he is in heaven, with my blessed master, if ever saint was!"

Theresa's voice faltered; she wept, and set down the flask, unable to pour out the wine. Her grief seemed to recall Emily from her own, who went towards her, but then stopped, and, having gazed on her, for a moment, turned suddenly away, as if overwhelmed by the reflection, that it was Valancourt, whom Theresa lamented.

While she yet paced the room, the still, soft note of an oboe, or flute, was heard mingling with the blast, the sweetness of which affected Emily's spirits; she paused a moment in attention; the tender tones, as they swelled along the wind, till they were lost again in the ruder gust, came with a plaintiveness, that touched her heart, and she melted into tears.

"Aye," said Theresa, drying her eyes, "there is Richard, our neighbour's son, playing on the oboe; it is sad enough, to hear such sweet music now." Emily continued to weep, without replying. "He often plays of an evening," added Theresa, "and, sometimes, the young folks dance to the sound of his oboe. But, dear young lady! do not cry so; and pray take a glass of this wine," continued she, pouring some into a glass, and handing it to Emily, who reluctantly took it.

"Taste it for M. Valancourt's sake," said Theresa, as Emily lifted the glass to her lips, "for he gave it me, you know, madam." Emily's hand trembled, and she spilt the wine as she withdrew it from her lips. "For whose sake!—who gave the wine?" said she in a faltering voice. "M. Valancourt, dear lady. I knew you would be pleased with it. It is the last flask I have left."

Emily set the wine upon the table, and burst into tears, while Theresa, disappointed and alarmed, tried to comfort her; but she only waved her hand, entreated she might be left alone, and wept the more.

A knock at the cottage door prevented Theresa from immediately obeying her mistress, and she was going to open it, when Emily, checking her, requested she would not admit any person; but, afterwards, recollecting, that she had ordered her servant to attend her home, she said it was only Philippe, and endeavoured to restrain her tears, while Theresa opened the door.

A voice, that spoke without, drew Emily's attention. She listened, turned her eyes to the door, when a person now appeared, and immediately a bright gleam, that flashed from the fire, discovered—Valancourt!

Emily, on perceiving him, started from her chair, trembled, and, sinking into it again, became insensible to all around her.

A scream from Theresa now told, that she knew Valancourt, whom her imperfect sight, and the duskiness of the place had prevented her from immediately recollecting; but his attention was immediately called from her to the person, whom he saw, falling from a chair near the fire; and, hastening to her assistance,—he perceived, that he was supporting Emily! The various emotions, that seized him upon thus unexpectedly meeting with her, from whom he had believed he had parted for ever, and on beholding her pale and lifeless in his arms—may, perhaps, be imagined, though they could neither be then expressed, or now described, any more than Emily's sensations, when, at length, she unclosed her eyes, and, looking up, again saw Valancourt. The intense anxiety, with which he regarded her, was instantly changed to an expression of mingled joy and tenderness, as his eye met hers, and he perceived, that she was reviving. But he could only exclaim, "Emily!" as he silently watched her recovery, while she averted her eye, and feebly attempted to withdraw her hand; but, in these the first moments, which succeeded to the pangs his supposed death had occasioned her, she forgot every fault, which had formerly claimed indignation, and beholding Valancourt such as he had appeared, when he won her early affection, she experienced emotions of only tenderness and joy. This, alas! was but the sunshine of a few short moments; recollections rose, like clouds, upon her mind, and, darkening the illusive image, that possessed it, she again beheld Valancourt, degraded—Valancourt unworthy of the esteem and tenderness she had once bestowed upon him; her spirits faltered, and, withdrawing her hand, she turned from him to conceal her grief, while he, yet more embarrassed and agitated, remained silent.

A sense of what she owed to herself restrained her tears, and taught her soon to overcome, in some degree, the emotions of mingled joy and sorrow, that contended at her heart, as she rose, and, having thanked him for the assistance he had given her, bade Theresa good evening. As she was leaving the cottage, Valancourt, who seemed suddenly awakened as from a dream, entreated, in a voice, that pleaded powerfully for compassion, a few moments attention. Emily's heart, perhaps, pleaded as powerfully, but she had resolution enough to resist both, together with the clamorous entreaties of Theresa, that she would not venture home alone in the dark, and had already opened the cottage door, when the pelting storm compelled her to obey their requests.

Silent and embarrassed, she returned to the fire, while Valancourt, with increasing agitation, paced the room, as if he wished, yet feared, to speak, and Theresa expressed without restraint her joy and wonder upon seeing him.

"Dear heart! sir," said she, "I never was so surprised and overjoyed in my life. We were in great tribulation before you came, for we thought you was dead, and were talking, and lamenting about you, just when you knocked at the door. My young mistress there was crying, fit to break her heart——"

Emily looked with much displeasure at Theresa, but, before she could speak, Valancourt, unable to repress the emotion, which Theresa's imprudent discovery occasioned, exclaimed, "O my Emily! am I then still dear to you! Did you, indeed, honour me with a thought—a tear? O heavens! you weep—you weep now!"

"Theresa, sir," said Emily, with a reserved air, and trying to con-quer her tears, "has reason to remember you with gratitude, and she was concerned, because she had not lately heard of you. Allow me to thank you for the kindness you have shewn her, and to say, that, since I am now upon the spot, she must not be further indebted to you."

"Emily," said Valancourt, no longer master of his emotions, "is it thus you meet him, whom once you meant to honour with your hand—thus you meet him, who has loved you—suffered for you?—Yet what do I say? Pardon me, pardon me, mademoiselle St. Aubert, I know not what I utter. I have no longer any claim upon your remembrance—I have forfeited every pretension to your esteem, your love. Yes! let me not forget, that I once possessed your affections, though to know that I have lost them, is my severest affliction. Affliction—do I call it!—that is a term of mildness."

"Dear heart!" said Theresa, preventing Emily from replying, "talk of once having her affections! Why, my dear young lady loves you now, better than she does any body in the whole world, though she pretends to deny it."

"This is insupportable!" said Emily; "Theresa, you know not what you say. Sir, if you respect my tranquillity, you will spare me from the continuance of this distress."

"I do respect your tranquillity too much, voluntarily to interrupt it," replied Valancourt, in whose bosom pride now contended with ten-derness; "and will not be a voluntary intruder. I would have entreated a few moments attention—yet I know not for what purpose. You have ceased to esteem me, and to recount to you my sufferings will degrade me more, without exciting even your pity. Yet I have been, O Emily! I am indeed very wretched!" added Valancourt, in a voice, that softened from solemnity into grief.

"What! is my dear young master going out in all this rain!" said Theresa. "No, he shall not stir a step. Dear! dear! to see how gentlefolks can afford to throw away their happiness! Now, if you were poor peo-ple, there would be none of this. To talk of unworthiness, and not car-ing about one another, when I know there are not such a kind-hearted lady and gentleman in the whole province, nor any that love one another half so well, if the truth was spoken!"

Emily, in extreme vexation, now rose from her chair, "I must be gone," said she, "the storm is over."

"Stay, Emily, stay, mademoiselle St. Aubert!" said Valancourt, sum-moning all his resolution, "I will no longer distress you by my presence. Forgive me, that I did not sooner obey you, and, if you can, sometimes, pity one, who, in losing you—has lost all hope of peace! May you be happy, Emily, however wretched I remain, happy as my fondest wish would have you!"

His voice faltered with the last words, and his countenance changed, while, with a look of ineffable tenderness and grief, he gazed upon her for an instant, and then quitted the cottage.

"Dear heart! dear heart!" cried Theresa, following him to the door, "why, Monsieur Valancourt! how it rains! what a night is this to turn him out in! Why it will give him his death; and it was but now you was crying, mademoiselle, because he was dead. Well! young ladies do change their mind in a minute, as one may say!"

Emily made no reply, for she heard not what was said, while, lost in sorrow and thought, she remained in her chair by the fire, with her eyes fixed, and the image of Valancourt still before them.

"M. Valancourt is sadly altered! madam," said Theresa; "he looks so thin to what he used to do, and so melancholy, and then he wears his arm in a sling."

Emily raised her eyes at these words, for she had not observed this last circumstance, and she now did not doubt, that Valancourt had received the shot of her gardener at Tholouse; with this conviction her pity for him returning, she blamed herself for having occasioned him to leave the cottage, during the storm.

Soon after her servants arrived with the carriage, and Emily, having censured Theresa for her thoughtless conversation to Valancourt, and strictly charging her never to repeat any hints of the same kind to him, withdrew to her home, thoughtful and disconsolate.

Meanwhile, Valancourt had returned to a little inn of the village, whither he had arrived only a few moments before his visit to Theresa's cottage, on the way from Tholouse to the chateau of the Count de Duvarney, where he had not been since he bade adieu to Emily at Chateau-le-Blanc, in the neighbourhood of which he had lingered for a considerable time, unable to summon resolution enough to quit a place, that contained the object most dear to his heart. There were times, indeed, when grief and despair urged him to appear again before Emily, and, regardless of his ruined circumstances, to renew his suit. Pride, however, and the tenderness of his affection, which could not long endure the thought of involving her in his misfortunes, at length, so far triumphed over passion, that he relinquished this desperate design, and quitted Chateau-le-Blanc. But still his fancy wandered among the scenes, which had witnessed his early love, and, on his way to Gascony, he stopped at Tholouse, where he remained when Emily arrived, concealing, yet indulging his melancholy in the gardens, where he had formerly passed with her so many happy hours; often recurring, with vain regret, to the evening before her departure for

Italy, when she had so unexpectedly met him on the terrace, and endeavouring to recall to his memory every word and look, which had then charmed him, the arguments he had employed to dissuade her from the journey, and the tenderness of their last farewel. In such melancholy recollections he had been indulging, when Emily unexpectedly arrived to him on this very terrace, the evening after her arrival at Tholouse. His emotions, on thus seeing her, can scarcely be imagined; but he so far overcame the first promptings of love, that he forbore to discover himself, and abruptly quitted the gardens. Still, however, the vision he had seen haunted his mind; he became more wretched than before, and the only solace of his sorrow was to return in the silence of the night; to follow the paths which he believed her steps had pressed, during the day; and, to watch round the habitation where she reposed. It was in one of these mournful wanderings, that he had received by the fire of the gardener, who mistook him for a robber, a wound in his arm, which had detained him at Tholouse till very lately, under the hands of a surgeon. There, regardless of himself and careless of his friends, whose late unkindness had urged him to believe, that they were indifferent as to his fate, he remained, without informing them of his situation; and now, being sufficiently recovered to bear travelling, he had taken La Vallée in his way to Estuviere, the Count's residence, partly for the purpose of hearing of Emily, and of being again near her, and partly for that of enquiring into the situation of poor old Theresa, who, he had reason to suppose, had been deprived of her stipend, small as it was, and which enquiry had brought him to her cottage, when Emily happened to be there.

This unexpected interview, which had at once shewn him the tenderness of her love and the strength of her resolution, renewed all the acuteness of the despair, that had attended their former separation, and which no effort of reason could teach him, in these moments, to subdue. Her image, her look, the tones of her voice, all dwelt on his fancy, as powerfully as they had late appeared to his senses, and banished from his heart every emotion, except those of love and despair.

Before the evening concluded, he returned to Theresa's cottage, that he might hear her talk of Emily, and be in the place, where she had so lately been. The joy, felt and expressed by that faithful servant, was quickly changed to sorrow, when she observed, at one moment, his wild and phrensied look, and, at another, the dark melancholy, that overhung him.

After he had listened, and for a considerable time, to all she had to relate, concerning Emily, he gave Theresa nearly all the money he had about him, though she repeatedly refused it, declaring, that her mistress had amply supplied her wants; and then, drawing a ring of value from his finger, he delivered it her with a solemn charge to present it to Emily, of whom he entreated, as a last favour, that she would preserve it for his sake, and sometimes, when she looked upon it, remember the unhappy giver.

Theresa wept, as she received the ring, but it was more from sympathy, than from any presentiment of evil; and before she could reply, Valancourt abruptly left the cottage. She followed him to the door, calling upon his name and entreating him to return; but she received no answer, and saw him no more.

CHAPTER XIV

Call up him, that left half told
The story of Cambuscan bold.
MILTON

ON the following morning, as Emily sat in the parlour adjoining the library, reflecting on the scene of the preceding night, Annette rushed wildly into the room, and, without speaking, sunk breathless into a chair. It was some time before she could answer the anxious enquiries of Emily, as to the occasion of her emotion, but, at length, she exclaimed, "I have seen his ghost, madam, I have seen his ghost!"

"Who do you mean?" said Emily, with extreme impatience.

"It came in from the hall, madam," continued Annette, "as I was crossing to the parlour."

"Who are you speaking of?" repeated Emily, "Who came in from the hall?"

"It was dressed just as I have seen him, often and often," added Annette. "Ah! who could have thought——"

Emily's patience was now exhausted, and she was reprimanding her for such idle fancies, when a servant entered the room, and informed her, that a stranger without begged leave to speak with her.

It immediately occurred to Emily, that this stranger was Valancourt, and she told the servant to inform him, that she was engaged, and could not see any person.

The servant, having delivered his message, returned with one from the stranger, urging the first request, and saying, that he had something of consequence to communicate; while Annette, who had hitherto sat silent and amazed, now started up, and crying, "It is Ludovico!—it is Ludovico!" ran out of the room. Emily bade the servant follow her, and, if it really was Ludovico, to shew him into the parlour.

In a few minutes, Ludovico appeared, accompanied by Annette, who, as joy rendered her forgetful of all rules of decorum towards her mistress, would not suffer any person to be heard, for some time, but herself. Emily expressed surprise and satisfaction, on seeing Ludovico in safety, and the first emotions increased, when he delivered letters from Count De Villefort and the Lady Blanche, informing her of their late adventure, and of their present situation at an inn among the Pyrenées, where they had been detained by the illness of Mons. St. Foix, and the indisposition of Blanche, who added, that the Baron St. Foix was just arrived to attend his son to his chateau, where he would remain till the perfect recovery of his wounds, and then return to Languedoc, but that her father and herself purposed to be at La Vallée, on the following day. She added, that Emily's presence would be expected at the approaching nuptials, and begged she would be prepared to proceed, in a few days to Chateau-le-Blanc. For an account of Ludovico's adventure, she referred her to himself; and Emily, though much interested, concerning the means, by which he had disappeared from the north apartments, had the forbearance to suspend the gratification of her curiosity, till he had taken some refreshment, and had conversed with Annette, whose joy, on seeing him in safety, could not have been more extravagant, had he arisen from the grave.

Meanwhile, Emily perused again the letters of her friends, whose expressions of esteem and kindness were very necessary consolations to her heart, awakened as it was by the late interview to emotions of keener sorrow and regret.

The invitation to Chateau-le-Blanc was pressed with so much kindness by the Count and his daughter, who strengthened it by a message from the Countess, and the occasion of it was so important to her friend, that Emily could not refuse to accept it, nor, though she wished to remain in the quiet shades of her native home, could she avoid perceiving the impropriety of remaining there alone, since Valancourt was again in the neighbourhood. Sometimes, too, she thought, that change of scenery and the society of her friends might contribute, more than retirement, to restore her to tranquillity.

When Ludovico again appeared, she desired him to give a detail of his adventure in the north apartments, and to tell by what means he became a companion of the banditti, with whom the Count had found him.

He immediately obeyed, while Annette, who had not yet had leisure to ask him many questions, on the subject, prepared to listen, with a countenance of extreme curiosity, venturing to remind her lady of her incredulity, concerning spirits, in the castle of Udolpho, and of her own sagacity in believing in them; while Emily, blushing at the consciousness of her late credulity, observed, that, if Ludovico's adventure could justify Annette's superstition, he had probably not been here to relate it.

Ludovico smiled at Annette, and bowed to Emily, and then began as follows:

"You may remember, madam, that, on the night, when I sat up in the north chamber, my lord, the Count, and Mons. Henri accompanied me thither, and that, while they remained there, nothing happened to excite any alarm. When they were gone I made a fire in the bed-room, and, not being inclined to sleep, I sat down on the hearth with a book I had brought with me to divert my mind. I confess I did sometimes look round the chamber, with something like apprehension——"

"O very like it, I dare say," interrupted Annette, "and I dare say too, if the truth was known, you shook from head to foot."

"Not quite so bad as that," replied Ludovico, smiling, "but several times, as the wind whistled round the castle, and shook the old casements, I did fancy I heard odd noises, and, once or twice, I got up and looked about me; but nothing was to be seen, except the grim figures in the tapestry, which seemed to frown upon me, as I looked at them. I had sat thus for above an hour," continued Ludovico, "when again I thought I heard a noise, and glanced my eyes round the room, to discover what it came from, but, not perceiving any thing, I began to read again, and, when I had finished the story I was upon, I felt drowsy, and dropped asleep. But presently I was awakened by the noise I had heard before, and it seemed to come from that part of the chamber, where the bed stood; and then, whether it was the story I had been reading that affected my spirits, or the strange reports, that had been spread of these apartments, I don't know, but, when I looked towards the bed again, I fancied I saw a man's face within the dusky curtains."

At the mention of this, Emily trembled, and looked anxiously, remembering the spectacle she had herself witnessed there with Dorothée.

"I confess, madam, my heart did fail me, at that instant," continued Ludovico, "but a return of the noise drew my attention from the bed, and I then distinctly heard a sound, like that of a key, turning in a lock, but what surprised me more was, that I saw no door where the sound seemed to come from. In the next moment, however, the arras near the bed was slowly lifted, and a person appeared behind it, entering from a small door in the wall. He stood for a moment as if half retreating, with his head bending under the arras which concealed the upper part of his face except his eyes scowling beneath the tapestry as he held it; and then, while he raised it higher, I saw the face of another man behind, looking over his shoulder. I know not how it was, but, though my sword was upon the table before me, I had not the power just then to seize it, but sat quite still, watching them, with my eyes half shut as if I was asleep. I suppose they thought me so, and were debating what they should do, for I heard them whisper, and they stood in the same posture for the value of a minute, and then, I thought I perceived other faces in the duskiness beyond the door, and heard louder whispers."

"This door surprises me," said Emily, "because I understood, that the Count had caused the arras to be lifted, and the walls examined, suspecting, that they might have concealed a passage through which you had departed."

"It does not appear so extraordinary to me, madam," replied Ludovico, "that this door should escape notice, because it was formed in a narrow compartment, which appeared to be part of the outward wall, and, if the Count had not passed over it, he might have thought it was useless to search for a door where it seemed as if no passage could communicate with one; but the truth was, that the passage was formed within the wall itself.—But, to return to the men, whom I saw obscurely beyond the door, and who did not suffer me to remain long in suspense, concerning their design. They all rushed into the room, and surrounded me, though not before I had snatched up my sword to defend myself. But what could one man do against four? They soon disarmed me, and, having fastened my arms, and gagged my mouth, forced me through the private door, leaving my sword upon the table, to assist, as they said, those who should come in the morning to look for me, in fighting against the ghosts. They then led me through many narrow passages, cut, as I fancied, in the walls, for I had never seen them before, and down several flights of steps, till we came to the vaults underneath the castle; and then opening a stone door, which I should have taken for the wall itself, we went through a long passage, and down other steps cut in the solid rock, when another door delivered us into a cave. After turning and twining about, for some time, we reached the mouth of it, and I found myself on the sea-beach at the foot of the cliffs, with the chateau above. A boat was in waiting, into which the ruffians got, forcing me along with them, and we soon reached a small vessel, that was at anchor, where other men appeared, when setting me aboard, two of the fellows who had seized me, followed, and the other two rowed back to the shore, while we set sail. I soon found out what all this meant, and what was the business of these men at the chateau. We landed in Rousillon, and, after lingering several days about the shore, some of their comrades came down from the mountains, and carried me with them to the fort, where I remained till my Lord so unexpectedly arrived, for they had taken good care to prevent my running away, having blindfolded me, during the journey, and, if they had not done this, I think I never could have found my road to any town, through the wild country we traversed. After I reached the fort I was watched like a prisoner, and never suffered to go out, without two or three companions, and I became so weary of life, that I often wished to get rid of it."

"Well, but they let you talk," said Annette, "they did not gagg you after they got you away from the chateau, so I don't see what reason there was to be so very weary of living; to say nothing about the chance you had of seeing me again."

Ludovico smiled, and Emily also, who enquired what was the motive of these men for carrying him off.

"I soon found out, madam," resumed Ludovico, "that they were pirates, who had, during many years, secreted their spoil in the vaults of the castle, which, being so near the sea, suited their purpose well. To prevent detection they had tried to have it believed, that the chateau was haunted, and, having discovered the private way to the north apartments, which had been shut up ever since the death of the lady marchioness, they easily succeeded. The housekeeper and her husband, who were the only persons, that had inhabited the castle, for some years, were so terrified by the strange noises they heard in the nights, that they would live there no longer; a report soon went abroad, that it was haunted, and the whole country believed this the more readily, I suppose, because it had been said, that the lady marchioness had died in a strange way, and because my lord never would return to the place afterwards."

"But why," said Emily, "were not these pirates contented with the cave—why did they think it necessary to deposit their spoil in the castle?"

"The cave, madam," replied Ludovico, "was open to any body, and their treasures would not long have remained undiscovered there, but in the vaults they were secure so long as the report prevailed of their being haunted. Thus then, it appears, that they brought at midnight, the spoil they took on the seas, and kept it till they had opportunities of disposing of it to advantage. The pirates were connected with Spanish smugglers and banditti, who live among the wilds of the Pyrenées, and carry on various kinds of traffic, such as nobody would think of; and with this desperate horde of banditti I remained, till my lord arrived. I shall never forget what I felt, when I first discovered him—I almost gave him up for lost! but I knew, that, if I shewed myself, the banditti would discover who he was, and probably murder us all, to prevent their secret in the chateau being detected. I, therefore, kept out of my lord's sight, but had a strict watch upon the ruffians, and determined, if they offered him or his family violence, to discover myself, and fight for our lives. Soon after, I overheard some of them laying a most diabolical plan for the murder and plunder of the whole party, when I contrived to speak to some of my lord's attendants, telling them what was going forward, and we consulted what was best to be done; meanwhile my lord, alarmed at the absence of the Lady Blanche, demanded her, and the ruffians having given some unsatisfactory answer, my lord and Mons. St. Foix became furious, so then we thought it a good time to discover the plot, and rushing into the chamber, I called out, 'Treachery! my lord count, defend yourself!' His lordship and the chevalier drew their swords directly, and a hard battle we had, but we conquered at last, as, madam, you are already informed of by my Lord Count."

"This is an extraordinary adventure," said Emily, "and much praise is due, Ludovico, to your prudence and intrepidity. There are some circumstances, however, concerning the north apartments, which still perplex me; but, perhaps, you may be able to explain them. Did you ever hear the banditti relate any thing extraordinary of these rooms?"

"No, madam," replied Ludovico, "I never heard them speak about the rooms, except to laugh at the credulity of the old housekeeper, who once was very near catching one of the pirates; it was since the Count arrived at the chateau, he said, and he laughed heartily as he related the trick he had played off."

A blush overspread Emily's cheek, and she impatiently desired Ludovico to explain himself.

"Why, my lady," said he, "as this fellow was, one night in the bedroom, he heard somebody approaching through the next apartment, and not having time to lift up the arras, and unfasten the door, he hid himself in the bed just by. There he lay for some time in as great a fright, I suppose——"

"As you was in," interrupted Annette, "when you sat up so boldly to watch by yourself."

"Aye," said Ludovico, "in as great a fright as he ever made any body else suffer; and presently the housekeeper and some other person came up to the bed, when he, thinking they were going to examine it, bethought him, that his only chance of escaping detection, was by terrifying them; so he lifted up the counterpane, but that did not do, till he raised his face above it, and then they both set off, he said, as if they had seen the devil, and he got out of the rooms undiscovered."

Emily could not forbear smiling at this explanation of the deception, which had given her so much superstitious terror, and was surprised, that she could have suffered herself to be thus alarmed, till she considered, that, when the mind has once begun to yield to the weakness of superstition, trifles impress it with the force of conviction. Still, however, she remembered with awe the mysterious music, which had been heard, at midnight, near Chateau-le-Blanc, and she asked Ludovico if he could give any explanation of it; but he could not.

"I only know, madam," he added, "that it did not belong to the pirates, for I have heard them laugh about it, and say, they believed the devil was in league with them there."

"Yes, I will answer for it he was," said Annette, her countenance brightening, "I was sure all along, that he or his spirits had something to do with the north apartments, and now you see, madam, I am right at last."

"It cannot be denied, that his spirits were very busy in that part of the chateau," replied Emily, smiling. "But I am surprised, Ludovico, that these pirates should persevere in their schemes, after the arrival of the Count; what could they expect but certain detection?"

"I have reason to believe, madam," replied Ludovico, "that it was their intention to persevere no longer than was necessary for the removal of the stores, which were deposited in the vaults; and it appeared, that they had been employed in doing so from within a short period after the Count's arrival; but, as they had only a few hours in the night for this business, and were carrying on other schemes at the same time, the vaults were not above half emptied, when they took me away. They gloried exceedingly in this opportunity of confirming the superstitious reports, that had been spread of the north chambers, were careful to leave every thing there as they had found it, the better to promote the deception, and frequently, in their jocose moods, would laugh at the consternation, which they believed the inhabitants of the castle had suffered upon my disappearing, and it was to prevent the possibility of my betraying their secret, that they had removed me to such a distance. From that period they considered the chateau as nearly their own; but I found from the discourse of their comrades, that, though they were cautious, at first, in shewing their power there, they had once very nearly betrayed themselves. Going, one night, as was their custom, to the north chambers to repeat the noises, that had occasioned such alarm among the servants, they heard, as they were about to unfasten the secret door, voices in the bed-room. My lord has since told me, that himself and M. Henri were then in the apartment, and they heard very extraordinary sounds of lamentation, which it seems were made by these fellows, with their usual design of spreading terror; and my lord has owned, he then felt somewhat more, than surprise; but, as it was necessary to the peace of his family, that no notice should be taken, he was silent on the subject, and enjoined silence to his son."

Emily, recollecting the change, that had appeared in the spirits of the Count, after the night, when he had watched in the north room, now perceived the cause of it; and, having made some further enquiries upon this strange affair, she dismissed Ludovico, and went to give orders for the accommodation of her friends, on the following day.

In the evening, Theresa, lame as she was, came to deliver the ring, with which Valancourt had entrusted her, and, when she presented it, Emily was much affected, for she remembered to have seen him wear it often in happier days. She was, however, much displeased, that Theresa had received it, and positively refused to accept it herself, though to have done so would have afforded her a melancholy pleasure. Theresa entreated, expostulated, and then described the distress of Valancourt, when he had given the ring, and repeated the message, with which he had commissioned her to deliver it; and Emily could not conceal the extreme sorrow this recital occasioned her, but wept, and remained lost in thought.

"Alas! my dear young lady!" said Theresa, "why should all this be? I have known you from your infancy, and it may well be supposed I love you, as if you was my own, and wish as much to see you happy. M. Valancourt, to be sure, I have not known so long, but then I have reason to love him, as though he was my own son. I know how well you love one another, or why all this weeping and wailing?" Emily waved her hand for Theresa to be silent, who, disregarding the signal, continued, "And how much you are alike in your tempers and ways, and, that, if you were married, you would be the happiest couple in the whole province—then what is there to prevent your marrying? Dear dear! to see how some people fling away their happiness, and then cry and lament about it, just as if it was not their own doing, and as if there was more pleasure in wailing and weeping, than in being at peace. Learning, to be sure, is a fine thing, but, if it teaches folks no better than that, why I had rather be without it; if it would teach them to be happier, I would say something to it, then it would be learning and wisdom too."

Age and long services had given Theresa a privilege to talk, but Emily now endeavoured to check her loquacity, and, though she felt the justness of some of her remarks, did not choose to explain the circumstances, that had determined her conduct towards Valancourt. She, therefore, only told Theresa, that it would much displease her to hear the subject renewed; that she had reasons for her conduct, which she did not think it proper to mention, and that the ring must be returned, with an assurance, that she could not accept it with propriety; and, at the same time, she forbade Theresa to repeat any future message from Valancourt, as she valued her esteem and kindness. Theresa was afflicted, and made another attempt, though feeble, to interest her for Valancourt, but the unusual displeasure, expressed in Emily's countenance, soon obliged her to desist, and she departed in wonder and lamentation.

To relieve her mind, in some degree, from the painful recollections, that intruded upon it, Emily busied herself in preparations for the journey into Languedoc, and, while Annette, who assisted her, spoke with joy and affection of the safe return of Ludovico, she was considering how she might best promote their happiness, and determined, if it appeared, that his affection was as unchanged as that of the simple and honest Annette, to give her a marriage portion, and settle them on some part of her estate. These considerations led her to the remembrance of her father's paternal domain, which his affairs had formerly compelled him to dispose of to M. Quesnel, and which she frequently wished to regain, because St. Aubert had lamented, that the chief lands of his ancestors had passed into another family, and because they had been his birth-place and the haunt of his early years. To the estate at Tholouse she had no peculiar attachment, and it was her wish to dispose of this, that she might purchase her paternal domains, if M. Quesnel could be prevailed on to part with them, which, as he talked much of living in Italy, did not appear very improbable.

CHAPTER XV

> Sweet is the breath of vernal shower,
> The bees' collected treasures sweet,
> Sweet music's melting fall, but sweeter yet
> The still, small voice of gratitude.
>
> GRAY

ON the following day, the arrival of her friend revived the drooping Emily, and La Vallée became once more the scene of social kindness and of elegant hospitality. Illness and the terror she had suffered had stolen from Blanche much of her sprightliness, but all her affectionate simplicity remained, and, though she appeared less blooming, she was not less engaging than before. The unfortunate adventure on the Pyrenées had made the Count very anxious to reach home, and, after little more than a week's stay at La Vallée, Emily prepared to set out with her friends for Languedoc, assigning the care of her house, during her absence, to Theresa. On the evening, preceding her departure, this old servant brought again the ring of Valancourt, and, with tears, entreated her mistress to receive it, for that she had neither seen, or heard of M. Valancourt, since the night when he delivered it to her. As she said this, her countenance expressed more alarm, than she dared to utter; but Emily, checking her own propensity to fear, considered, that he had probably returned to the residence of his brother, and, again refusing to accept the ring, bade Theresa preserve it, till she saw him, which, with extreme reluctance, she promised to do.

On the following day, Count De Villefort, with Emily and the Lady Blanche, left La Vallée, and, on the ensuing evening, arrived at the Chateau-le-Blanc, where the Countess, Henri, and M. Du Pont, whom Emily was surprised to find there, received them with much joy and congratulation. She was concerned to observe, that the Count still encouraged the hopes of his friend, whose countenance declared, that his affection had suffered no abatement from absence; and was much distressed, when, on the second evening after her arrival, the Count, having withdrawn her from the Lady Blanche, with whom she was walking, renewed the subject of M. Du Pont's hopes. The mildness, with which she listened to his intercessions at first, deceiving him, as to her sentiments, he began to believe, that, her affection for Valancourt being overcome, she was, at length, disposed to think favourably of M. Du Pont; and, when she afterwards convinced him of his mistake, he ventured, in the earnestness of his wish to promote what he considered to be the happiness of two persons, whom he so much esteemed, gently to remonstrate with her, on thus suffering an ill-placed affection to poison the happiness of her most valuable years.

Observing her silence and the deep dejection of her countenance, he concluded with saying, "I will not say more now, but I will still believe, my dear Mademoiselle St. Aubert, that you will not always reject a person, so truly estimable as my friend Du Pont."

He spared her the pain of replying, by leaving her; and she strolled on, somewhat displeased with the Count for having persevered to plead for a suit, which she had repeatedly rejected, and lost amidst the melancholy recollections, which this topic had revived, till she had insensibly reached the borders of the woods, that screened the monastery of St. Clair, when, perceiving how far she had wandered, she determined to extend her walk a little farther, and to enquire about the abbess and some of her friends among the nuns.

Though the evening was now drawing to a close, she accepted the invitation of the friar, who opened the gate, and, anxious to meet some of her old acquaintances, proceeded towards the convent parlour. As she crossed the lawn, that sloped from the front of the monastery towards the sea, she was struck with the picture of repose, exhibited by some monks, sitting in the cloisters, which extended under the brow of the woods, that crowned this eminence; where, as they meditated, at this twilight hour, holy subjects, they sometimes suffered their attention to be relieved by the scene before them, nor thought it profane to look at nature, now that it had exchanged the brilliant colours of day for the sober hue of evening. Before the cloisters, however, spread an ancient chesnut, whose ample branches were designed to screen the full magnificence of a scene, that might tempt the wish to worldly pleasures; but still, beneath the dark and spreading foliage, gleamed a wide extent of ocean, and many a passing sail; while, to the right and left, thick woods were seen stretching along the winding shores. So much as this had been admitted, perhaps, to give to the secluded votary an image of the dangers and vicissitudes of life, and to console him, now that he had renounced its pleasures, by the certainty of having escaped its evils. As Emily walked pensively along, considering how much suffering she might have escaped, had she become a votaress of the order, and remained in this retirement from the time of her father's death, the vesper-bell struck up, and the monks retired slowly toward the chapel, while she, pursuing her way, entered the great hall, where an unusual silence seemed to reign. The parlour too, which opened from it, she found vacant, but, as the evening bell was sounding, she believed the nuns had withdrawn into the chapel, and sat down to rest, for a moment, before she returned to the chateau, where, however, the increasing gloom made her now anxious to be.

Not many minutes had elapsed, before a nun, entering in haste, enquired for the abbess, and was retiring, without recollecting Emily, when she made herself known, and then learned, that a mass was going to be performed for the soul of sister Agnes, who had been declining, for some time, and who was now believed to be dying.

Of her sufferings the sister gave a melancholy account, and of the horrors, into which she had frequently started, but which had now yielded to a dejection so gloomy, that neither the prayers, in which she was joined by the sisterhood, or the assurances of her confessor, had power to recall her from it, or to cheer her mind even with a momentary gleam of comfort.

To this relation Emily listened with extreme concern, and, recollecting the frenzied manners and the expressions of horror, which she had herself witnessed of Agnes, together with the history, that sister Frances had communicated, her compassion was heightened to a very painful degree. As the evening was already far advanced, Emily did not now desire to see her, or to join in the mass, and, after leaving many kind remembrances with the nun, for her old friends, she quitted the monastery, and returned over the cliffs towards the chateau, meditating upon what she had just heard, till, at length she forced her mind upon less interesting subjects.

The wind was high, and as she drew near the chateau, she often paused to listen to its awful sound, as it swept over the billows, that beat below, or groaned along the surrounding woods; and, while she rested on a cliff at a short distance from the chateau, and looked upon the wide waters, seen dimly beneath the last shade of twilight, she thought of the following address:

TO THE WINDS

Viewless, through heaven's vast vault your course ye steer,
Unknown from whence ye come, or whither go!
Mysterious pow'rs! I hear ye murmur low,
Till swells your loud gust on my startled ear,
And, awful! seems to say—some God is near!
I love to list your midnight voices float
In the dread storm, that o'er the ocean rolls,
And, while their charm the angry wave controuls,
Mix with its sullen roar, and sink remote.
Then, rising in the pause, a sweeter note,
The dirge of spirits, who your deeds bewail,
A sweeter note oft swells while sleeps the gale!
But soon, ye sightless pow'rs! your rest is o'er,
Solemn and slow, ye rise upon the air,
Speak in the shrouds, and bid the sea-boy fear,
And the faint-warbled dirge—is heard no more!
  Oh! then I deprecate your awful reign!
The loud lament yet bear not on your breath!
Bear not the crash of bark far on the main,
Bear not the cry of men, who cry in vain,
The crew's dread chorus sinking into death!
Oh! give not these, ye pow'rs! I ask alone,
As rapt I climb these dark romantic steeps,
The elemental war, the billow's moan;
I ask the still, sweet tear, that listening Fancy weeps!

CHAPTER XVI

Unnatural deeds
Do breed unnatural troubles: infected minds
To their deaf pillows will discharge their secrets.
More needs she the divine, than the physician.
                                MACBETH

ON the following evening, the view of the convent towers, rising among the shadowy woods, reminded Emily of the nun, whose condition had so much affected her; and, anxious to know how she was, as well as to see some of her former friends, she and the Lady Blanche extended their walk to the monastery. At the gate stood a carriage, which, from the heat of the horses, appeared to have just arrived; but a more than common stillness pervaded the court and the cloisters, through which Emily and Blanche passed in their way to the great hall, where a nun, who was crossing to the stair-case, replied to the enquiries of the former, that sister Agnes was still living, and sensible, but that it was thought she could not survive the night. In the parlour, they found several of the boarders, who rejoiced to see Emily, and told her many little circumstances that had happened in the convent since her departure, and which were interesting to her only because they related to persons, whom she had regarded with affection. While they thus conversed the abbess entered the room, and expressed much satisfaction at seeing Emily, but her manner was unusually solemn, and her countenance dejected. "Our house," said she, after the first salutations were over, "is truly a house of mourning—a daughter is now paying the debt of nature.—You have heard, perhaps, that our daughter Agnes is dying?"

Emily expressed her sincere concern.

"Her death presents to us a great and awful lesson," continued the abbess; "let us read it, and profit by it; let it teach us to prepare ourselves for the change, that awaits us all! You are young, and have it yet in your power to secure 'the peace that passeth all understanding'—the peace of conscience. Preserve it in your youth, that it may comfort you in age; for vain, alas! and imperfect are the good deeds of our latter years, if those of our early life have been evil!"

Emily would have said, that good deeds, she hoped, were never vain; but she considered that it was the abbess who spoke, and she remained silent.

"The latter days of Agnes," resumed the abbess, "have been exemplary; would they might atone for the errors of her former ones! Her sufferings now, alas! are great; let us believe, that they will make her peace hereafter! I have left her with her confessor, and a gentleman, whom she has long been anxious to see, and who is just arrived from Paris. They, I hope, will be able to administer the repose, which her mind has hitherto wanted."

Emily fervently joined in the wish.

"During her illness, she has sometimes named you," resumed the abbess; "perhaps, it would comfort her to see you; when her present visitors have left her, we will go to her chamber, if the scene will not be too melancholy for your spirits. But, indeed, to such scenes, however painful, we ought to accustom ourselves, for they are salutary to the soul, and prepare us for what we are ourselves to suffer."

Emily became grave and thoughtful; for this conversation brought to her recollection the dying moments of her beloved father, and she wished once more to weep over the spot, where his remains were buried. During the silence, which followed the abbess' speech, many minute circumstances attending his last hours occurred to her—his emotion on perceiving himself to be in the neighbourhood of Chateau-le-Blanc—his request to be interred in a particular spot in the church of this monastery—and the solemn charge he had delivered to her to destroy certain papers, without examining them.—She recollected also the mysterious and horrible words in those manuscripts, upon which her eye had involuntarily glanced; and, though they now, and, indeed, whenever she remembered them, revived an excess of painful curiosity, concerning their full import, and the motives for her father's command, it was ever her chief consolation, that she had strictly obeyed him in this particular.

Little more was said by the abbess, who appeared too much affected by the subject she had lately left, to be willing to converse, and her companions had been for some time silent from the same cause, when this general reverie was interrupted by the entrance of a stranger, Monsieur Bonnac, who had just quitted the chamber of sister Agnes. He appeared much disturbed, but Emily fancied, that his countenance had more the expression of horror, than of grief. Having drawn the abbess to a distant part of the room, he conversed with her for some time, during which she seemed to listen with earnest attention, and he to speak with caution, and a more than common degree of interest. When he had concluded, he bowed silently to the rest of the company, and quitted the room. The abbess, soon after, proposed going to the chamber of sister Agnes, to which Emily consented, though not without some reluctance, and Lady Blanche remained with the boarders below.

At the door of the chamber they met the confessor, whom, as he lifted up his head on their approach, Emily observed to be the same that had attended her dying father; but he passed on, without noticing her, and they entered the apartment, where, on a mattress, was laid sister Agnes, with one nun watching in the chair beside her. Her countenance was so much changed, that Emily would scarcely have recollected her, had she not been prepared to do so: it was ghastly, and overspread with gloomy horror; her dim and hollow eyes were fixed on a crucifix, which she held upon her bosom; and she was so much engaged in thought, as not to perceive the abbess and Emily, till they stood at the bed-side. Then, turning her heavy eyes, she fixed them, in wild horror, upon Emily, and, screaming, exclaimed, "Ah! that vision comes upon me in my dying hours!"

Emily started back in terror, and looked for explanation to the abbess, who made her a signal not to be alarmed, and calmly said to

Agnes, "Daughter, I have brought Mademoiselle St. Aubert to visit you: I thought you would be glad to see her."

Agnes made no reply; but, still gazing wildly upon Emily, exclaimed, "It is her very self! Oh! there is all that fascination in her look, which proved my destruction! What would you have—what is it you came to demand—Retribution?—It will soon be yours—it is yours already. How many years have passed, since last I saw you! My crime is but as yesterday.—Yet I am grown old beneath it; while you are still young and blooming—blooming as when you forced me to commit that most abhorred deed! O! could I once forget it!—yet what would that avail?— the deed is done!"

Emily, extremely shocked, would now have left the room; but the abbess, taking her hand, tried to support her spirits, and begged she would stay a few moments, when Agnes would probably be calm, whom now she tried to soothe. But the latter seemed to disregard her, while she still fixed her eyes on Emily, and added, "What are years of prayers and repentance? they cannot wash out the foulness of mur- der!—Yes, murder! Where is he—where is he?—Look there—look there!—see where he stalks along the room! Why do you come to tor- ment me now?" continued Agnes, while her straining eyes were bent on air, "why was not I punished before?—O! do not frown so sternly! Hah! there again! 'tis she herself! Why do you look so piteously upon me—and smile, too? smile on me! What groan was that?"

Agnes sunk down, apparently lifeless, and Emily, unable to support herself, leaned against the bed, while the abbess and the attendant nun were applying the usual remedies to Agnes. "Peace," said the abbess, when Emily was going to speak, "the delirium is going off, she will soon revive. When was she thus before, daughter?"

"Not of many weeks, madam," replied the nun, "but her spirits have been much agitated by the arrival of the gentleman she wished so much to see."

"Yes," observed the abbess, "that has undoubtedly occasioned this paroxysm of frenzy. When she is better, we will leave her to repose."

Emily very readily consented, but, though she could now give little assistance, she was unwilling to quit the chamber, while any might be necessary.

When Agnes recovered her senses, she again fixed her eyes on Emily, but their wild expression was gone, and a gloomy melancholy had succeeded. It was some moments before she recovered sufficient spirits to speak; she then said feebly—"The likeness is wonderful!— surely it must be something more than fancy. Tell me, I conjure you," she added, addressing Emily, "though your name is St. Aubert, are you not the daughter of the Marchioness?"

"What Marchioness?" said Emily, in extreme surprise; for she had imagined, from the calmness of Agnes's manner, that her intellects were restored. The abbess gave her a significant glance, but she repeated the question.

"What Marchioness?" exclaimed Agnes, "I know but of one—the Marchioness de Villeroi."

Emily, remembering the emotion of her late father, upon the unexpected mention of this lady, and his request to be laid near to the tomb of the Villerois, now felt greatly interested, and she entreated Agnes to explain the reason of her question. The abbess would now have withdrawn Emily from the room, who being, however, detained by a strong interest, repeated her entreaties.

"Bring me that casket, sister," said Agnes; "I will shew her to you; yet you need only look in that mirror, and you will behold her; you surely are her daughter: such striking resemblance is never found but among near relations."

The nun brought the casket, and Agnes, having directed her how to unlock it, she took thence a miniature, in which Emily perceived the exact resemblance of the picture, which she had found among her late father's papers. Agnes held out her hand to receive it; gazed upon it earnestly for some moments in silence; and then, with a countenance of deep despair, threw up her eyes to Heaven, and prayed inwardly. When she had finished, she returned the miniature to Emily. "Keep it," said she, "I bequeath it to you, for I must believe it is your right. I have frequently observed the resemblance between you; but never, till this day, did it strike upon my conscience so powerfully! Stay, sister, do not remove the casket—there is another picture I would shew."

Emily trembled with expectation, and the abbess again would have withdrawn her. "Agnes is still disordered," said she, "you observe how she wanders. In these moods she says any thing, and does not scruple, as you have witnessed, to accuse herself of the most horrible crimes."

Emily, however, thought she perceived something more than madness in the inconsistencies of Agnes, whose mention of the Marchioness, and production of her picture, had interested her so much, that she determined to obtain further information, if possible, respecting the subject of it.

The nun returned with the casket, and, Agnes pointing out to her a secret drawer, she took from it another miniature. "Here," said Agnes, as she offered it to Emily, "learn a lesson for your vanity, at least; look well at this picture, and see if you can discover any resemblance between what I was, and what I am."

Emily impatiently received the miniature, which her eyes had scarcely glanced upon, before her trembling hands had nearly suffered it to fall—it was the resemblance of the portrait of Signora Laurentini, which she had formerly seen in the castle of Udolpho—the lady, who had disappeared in so mysterious a manner, and whom Montoni had been suspected of having caused to be murdered.

In silent astonishment, Emily continued to gaze alternately upon the picture and the dying nun, endeavouring to trace a resemblance between them, which no longer existed.

"Why do you look so sternly on me?" said Agnes, mistaking the nature of Emily's emotion.

"I have seen this face before," said Emily, at length; "was it really your resemblance?"

"You may well ask that question," replied the nun,—"but it was once esteemed a striking likeness of me. Look at me well, and see what guilt has made me. I then was innocent; the evil passions of my nature slept. Sister!" added she solemnly, and stretching forth her cold, damp hand to Emily, who shuddered at its touch—"Sister! beware of the first indulgence of the passions; beware of the first! Their course, if not checked then, is rapid—their force is uncontroulable—they lead us we know not whither—they lead us perhaps to the commission of crimes, for which whole years of prayer and penitence cannot atone!—Such may be the force of even a single passion, that it overcomes every other, and sears up every other approach to the heart. Possessing us like a fiend, it leads us on to the acts of a fiend, making us insensible to pity and to conscience. And, when its purpose is accomplished, like a fiend, it leaves us to the torture of those feelings, which its power had suspended—not annihilated,—to the tortures of compassion, remorse, and conscience. Then, we awaken as from a dream, and perceive a new world around us—we gaze in astonishment, and horror—but the deed is committed; not all the powers of heaven and earth united can undo it—and the spectres of conscience will not fly! What are riches—grandeur—health itself, to the luxury of a pure conscience, the health of the soul;—and what the sufferings of poverty, disappointment, despair—to the anguish of an afflicted one! O! how long is it since I knew that luxury! I believed, that I had suffered the most agonizing pangs of human nature, in love, jealousy, and despair—but these pangs were ease, compared with the stings of conscience, which I have since endured. I tasted too what was called the sweet of revenge—but it was transient, it expired even with the object, that provoked it. Remember, sister, that the passions are the seeds of vices as well as of virtues, from which either may spring, accordingly as they are nurtured. Unhappy they who have never been taught the art to govern them!"

"Alas! unhappy!" said the abbess, "and ill-informed of our holy religion!" Emily listened to Agnes, in silent awe, while she still examined the miniature, and became confirmed in her opinion of its strong resemblance to the portrait at Udolpho. "This face is familiar to me," said she, wishing to lead the nun to an explanation, yet fearing to discover too abruptly her knowledge of Udolpho.

"You are mistaken," replied Agnes, "you certainly never saw that picture before."

"No," replied Emily, "but I have seen one extremely like it." "Impossible," said Agnes, who may now be called the Lady Laurentini.

"It was in the castle of Udolpho," continued Emily, looking stedfastly at her.

"Of Udolpho!" exclaimed Laurentini, "of Udolpho in Italy!" "The same," replied Emily.

"You know me then," said Laurentini, "and you are the daughter of the Marchioness." Emily was somewhat surprised at this abrupt assertion. "I am the daughter of the late Mons. St. Aubert," said she; "and the lady you name is an utter stranger to me."

"At least you believe so," rejoined Laurentini.

Emily asked what reasons there could be to believe otherwise.

"The family likeness, that you bear her," said the nun. "The Marchioness, it is known, was attached to a gentleman of Gascony, at the time when she accepted the hand of the Marquis, by the command of her father. Ill-fated, unhappy woman!"

Emily, remembering the extreme emotion which St. Aubert had betrayed on the mention of the Marchioness, would now have suffered something more than surprise, had her confidence in his integrity been less; as it was, she could not, for a moment, believe what the words of Laurentini insinuated; yet she still felt strongly interested, concerning them, and begged, that she would explain them further.

"Do not urge me on that subject," said the nun, "it is to me a terrible one! Would that I could blot it from my memory!" She sighed deeply, and, after the pause of a moment, asked Emily, by what means she had discovered her name?

"By your portrait in the castle of Udolpho, to which this miniature bears a striking resemblance," replied Emily.

"You have been at Udolpho then!" said the nun, with great emotion. "Alas! what scenes does the mention of it revive in my fancy—scenes of happiness—of suffering—and of horror!"

At this moment, the terrible spectacle, which Emily had witnessed in a chamber of that castle, occurred to her, and she shuddered, while she looked upon the nun—and recollected her late words—that "years of prayer and penitence could not wash out the foulness of murder." She was now compelled to attribute these to another cause, than that of delirium. With a degree of horror, that almost deprived her of sense, she now believed she looked upon a murderer; all the recollected behaviour of Laurentini seemed to confirm the supposition, yet Emily was still lost in a labyrinth of perplexities, and, not knowing how to ask the questions, which might lead to truth, she could only hint them in broken sentences.

"Your sudden departure from Udolpho"—said she.

Laurentini groaned.

"The reports that followed it," continued Emily—"The west chamber—the mournful veil—the object it conceals!—when murders are committed——"

The nun shrieked. "What! there again!" said she, endeavouring to raise herself, while her starting eyes seemed to follow some object round the room—"Come from the grave! What! Blood—blood too!—There was no blood—thou canst not say it!—Nay, do not smile,—do not smile so piteously!"

Laurentini fell into convulsions, as she uttered the last words; and Emily, unable any longer to endure the horror of the scene, hurried from the room, and sent some nuns to the assistance of the abbess.

The Lady Blanche, and the boarders, who were in the parlour, now assembled round Emily, and, alarmed by her manner and affrighted countenance, asked a hundred questions, which she avoided answering further, than by saying, that she believed sister Agnes was dying. They received this as a sufficient explanation of her terror, and had then leisure to offer restoratives, which, at length, somewhat revived Emily, whose mind was, however, so much shocked with the terrible surmises, and perplexed with doubts by some words from the nun, that she was unable to converse, and would have left the convent immediately, had she not wished to know whether Laurentini would survive the late attack. After waiting some time, she was informed, that, the convulsions having ceased, Laurentini seemed to be reviving, and Emily and Blanche were departing, when the abbess appeared, who, drawing the former aside, said she had something of consequence to say to her, but, as it was late, she would not detain her then, and requested to see her on the following day.

Emily promised to visit her, and, having taken leave, returned with the Lady Blanche towards the chateau, on the way to which the deep gloom of the woods made Blanche lament, that the evening was so far advanced; for the surrounding stillness and obscurity rendered her sensible of fear, though there was a servant to protect her; while Emily was too much engaged by the horrors of the scene she had just witnessed, to be affected by the solemnity of the shades, otherwise than as they served to promote her gloomy reverie, from which, however, she was at length recalled by the Lady Blanche, who pointed out, at some distance, in the dusky path they were winding, two persons slowly advancing. It was impossible to avoid them without striking into a still more secluded part of the wood, whither the strangers might easily follow; but all apprehension vanished, when Emily distinguished the voice of Mons. Du Pont, and perceived, that his companion was the gentleman, whom she had seen at the monastery, and who was now conversing with so much earnestness as not immediately to perceive their approach. When Du Pont joined the ladies, the stranger took leave, and they proceeded to the chateau, where the Count, when he heard of Mons. Bonnac, claimed him for an acquaintance, and, on learning the melancholy occasion of his visit to Languedoc, and that he was lodged at a small inn in the village, begged the favour of Mons. Du Pont to invite him to the chateau.

The latter was happy to do so, and the scruples of reserve, which made M. Bonnac hesitate to accept the invitation, being at length overcome, they went to the chateau, where the kindness of the Count and the sprightliness of his son were exerted to dissipate the gloom, that overhung the spirits of the stranger. M. Bonnac was an officer in the French service, and appeared to be about fifty; his figure was tall and commanding, his manners had received the last polish, and there was something in his countenance uncommonly interesting; for over features, which, in youth, must have been remarkably handsome, was spread a melancholy, that seemed the effect of long misfortune, rather than of constitution, or temper.

The conversation he held, during supper, was evidently an effort of politeness, and there were intervals in which, unable to struggle against the feelings, that depressed him, he relapsed into silence and abstraction, from which, however, the Count, sometimes, withdrew him in a manner so delicate and benevolent, that Emily, while she observed him, almost fancied she beheld her late father.

The party separated, at an early hour, and then, in the solitude of her apartment, the scenes, which Emily had lately witnessed, returned to her fancy, with dreadful energy. That in the dying nun she should have discovered Signora Laurentini, who, instead of having been murdered by Montoni, was, as it now seemed, herself guilty of some dreadful crime, excited both horror and surprise in a high degree; nor did the hints, which she had dropped, respecting the marriage of the Marchioness de Villeroi, and the enquiries she had made concerning Emily's birth, occasion her a less degree of interest, though it was of a different nature.

The history, which sister Frances had formerly related, and had said to be that of Agnes, it now appeared, was erroneous; but for what purpose it had been fabricated, unless the more effectually to conceal the true story,

Emily could not even guess. Above all, her interest was excited as to the relation, which the story of the late Marchioness de Villeroi bore to that of her father; for, that some kind of relation existed between them, the grief of St. Aubert, upon hearing her named, his request to be buried near her, and her picture, which had been found among his papers, certainly proved. Sometimes it occurred to Emily, that he might have been the lover, to whom it was said the Marchioness was attached, when she was compelled to marry the Marquis de Villeroi; but that he had afterwards cherished a passion for her, she could not suffer herself to believe, for a moment. The papers, which he had so solemnly enjoined her to destroy, she now fancied had related to this connection, and she wished more earnestly than before to know the reasons, that made him consider the injunction necessary, which, had her faith in his principles been less, would have led to believe, that there was a mystery in her birth dishonourable to her parents, which those manuscripts might have revealed.

Reflections, similar to these, engaged her mind, during the greater part of the night, and when, at length, she fell into a slumber, it was only to behold a vision of the dying nun, and to awaken in horrors, like those she had witnessed.

On the following morning, she was too much indisposed to attend her appointment with the abbess, and, before the day concluded, she heard, that sister Agnes was no more. Mons. Bonnac received this intelligence, with concern; but Emily observed, that he did not appear so much affected now, as on the preceding evening, immediately after quitting the apartment of the nun, whose death was probably less terrible to him, than the confession he had been then called upon to witness. However this might be, he was perhaps consoled, in some degree, by a knowledge of the legacy bequeathed him, since his family was large, and the extravagance of some part of it had lately been the means of involving him in great distress, and even in the horrors of a prison; and it was the grief he had suffered from the wild career of a favourite son, with the pecuniary anxieties and misfortunes consequent upon it, that had given to his countenance the air of dejection, which had so much interested Emily.

To his friend Mons. Du Pont he recited some particulars of his late sufferings, when it appeared, that he had been confined for several months in one of the prisons of Paris, with little hope of release, and without the comfort of seeing his wife, who had been absent in the country, endeavouring, though in vain, to procure assistance from his friends. When, at length, she had obtained an order for admittance, she was so much shocked at the change, which long confinement and sorrow had made in his appearance, that she was seized with fits, which, by their long continuance, threatened her life.

"Our situation affected those, who happened to witness it," continued Mons. Bonnac, "and one generous friend, who was in confinement at the same time, afterwards employed the first moments of his liberty in efforts to obtain mine. He succeeded; the heavy debt, that oppressed me, was discharged; and, when I would have expressed my sense of the obligation I had received, my benefactor was fled from my search. I have reason to believe he was the victim of his own generosity, and that he returned to the state of confinement, from which he had released me; but every enquiry after him was unsuccessful. Amiable and unfortunate Valancourt!"

"Valancourt!" exclaimed Mons. Du Pont. "Of what family?"

"The Valancourts, Counts Duvarney," replied Mons. Bonnac.

The emotion of Mons. Du Pont, when he discovered the generous benefactor of his friend to be the rival of his love, can only be imagined; but, having overcome his first surprise, he dissipated the apprehensions of Mons. Bonnac by acquainting him, that Valancourt was at liberty, and had lately been in Languedoc; after which his affection for Emily prompted him to make some enquiries, respecting the conduct of his rival, during his stay at Paris, of which M. Bonnac appeared to be well informed. The answers he received were such as convinced him, that Valancourt had been much misrepresented, and, painful as was the sacrifice, he formed the just design of relinquishing his pursuit of Emily to a lover, who, it now appeared, was not unworthy of the regard, with which she honoured him.

The conversation of Mons. Bonnac discovered, that Valancourt, some time after his arrival at Paris, had been drawn into the snares, which determined vice had spread for him, and that his hours had been chiefly divided between the parties of the captivating Marchioness and those gaming assemblies, to which the envy, or the avarice, of his brother officers had spared no art to seduce him. In these parties he had lost large sums, in efforts to recover small ones, and to such losses the Count De Villefort and Mons. Henri had been frequent witnesses. His resources were, at length, exhausted; and the Count, his brother, exasperated by his conduct, refused to continue the supplies necessary to his present mode of life, when Valancourt, in consequence of accumulated debts, was thrown into confinement, where his brother suffered him to remain, in the hope, that punishment might effect a reform of conduct, which had not yet been confirmed by long habit.

In the solitude of his prison, Valancourt had leisure for reflection, and cause for repentance; here, too, the image of Emily, which, amidst the dissipation of the city had been obscured, but never obliterated from his heart, revived with all the charms of innocence and beauty, to reproach him for having sacrificed his happiness and debased his talents by pursuits, which his nobler faculties would formerly have taught him to consider were as tasteless as they were degrading. But, though his passions had been seduced, his heart was not depraved, nor had habit riveted the chains, that hung heavily on his conscience; and, as he retained that energy of will, which was necessary to burst them, he, at length, emancipated himself from the bondage of vice, but not till after much effort and severe suffering.

Being released by his brother from the prison, where he had witnessed the affecting meeting between Mons. Bonnac and his wife, with whom he had been for some time acquainted, the first use of his liberty formed a striking instance of his humanity and his rashness; for with nearly all the money, just received from his brother, he went to a gaming-house, and gave it as a last stake for the chance of restoring his friend to freedom, and to his afflicted family. The event was fortunate, and, while he had awaited the issue of this momentous stake, he made a solemn vow never again to yield to the destructive and fascinating vice of gaming.

Having restored the venerable Mons. Bonnac to his rejoicing family, he hurried from Paris to Estuviere; and, in the delight of having made the wretched happy, forgot, for a while, his own misfortunes. Soon, however, he remembered, that he had thrown away the fortune, without which he could never hope to marry Emily; and life, unless passed with her, now scarcely appeared supportable; for her goodness, refinement, and simplicity of heart, rendered her beauty more enchanting, if possible, to his fancy, than it had ever yet appeared. Experience had taught him to understand the full value of the qualities, which he had before admired, but which the contrasted characters he had seen in the world made him now adore; and these reflections, increasing the pangs of remorse and regret, occasioned the deep dejection, that had accompanied him even into the presence of Emily, of whom he considered himself no longer worthy. To the ignominy of having received pecuniary obligations from the Marchioness Chamfort, or any other lady of intrigue, as the Count De Villefort had been informed, or of having been engaged in the depredating schemes of gamesters, Valancourt had never submitted; and these were some of such scandals as often mingle with truth, against the unfortunate. Count De Villefort had received them from authority which he had no reason to doubt, and which the imprudent conduct he had himself witnessed in Valancourt, had certainly induced him the more readily to believe. Being such as Emily could not name to the Chevalier, he had no opportunity of refuting them; and, when he confessed himself to be unworthy of her esteem, he little suspected, that he was confirming to her the most dreadful calumnies. Thus the mistake had been mutual, and had

remained so, when Mons. Bonnac explained the conduct of his generous, but imprudent young friend to Du Pont, who, with severe justice,
determined not only to undeceive the Count on this subject, but to
resign all hope of Emily. Such a sacrifice as his love rendered this, was
deserving of a noble reward, and Mons. Bonnac, if it had been possible
for him to forget the benevolent Valancourt, would have wished that
Emily might accept the just Du Pont.

When the Count was informed of the error he had committed, he
was extremely shocked at the consequence of his credulity, and the
account which Mons. Bonnac gave of his friend's situation, while at
Paris, convinced him, that Valancourt had been entrapped by the
schemes of a set of dissipated young men, with whom his profession
had partly obliged him to associate, rather than by an inclination to
vice; and, charmed by the humanity, and noble, though rash generosity, which his conduct towards Mons. Bonnac exhibited, he forgave
him the transient errors, that had stained his youth, and restored him
to the high degree of esteem, with which he had regarded him, during
their early acquaintance. But, as the least reparation he could now
make Valancourt was to afford him an opportunity of explaining to
Emily his former conduct, he immediately wrote, to request his forgiveness of the unintentional injury he had done him, and to invite
him to Chateau-le-Blanc. Motives of delicacy with-held the Count
from informing Emily of this letter, and of kindness from acquainting
her with the discovery respecting Valancourt, till his arrival should save
her from the possibility of anxiety, as to its event; and this precaution
spared her even severer inquietude, than the Count had foreseen, since
he was ignorant of the symptoms of despair, which Valancourt's late
conduct had betrayed.

CHAPTER XVII

> But in these cases,
> We still have judgment here; that we but teach
> Bloody instructions, which, being taught, return
> To plague the inventor: thus even-handed justice
> Commends the ingredients of our poison'd chalice
> To our own lips.
>
> MACBETH

SOME circumstances of an extraordinary nature now withdrew Emily
from her own sorrows, and excited emotions, which partook of both
surprise and horror.

A few days followed that, on which Signora Laurentini died, her will was opened at the monastery, in the presence of the superiors and Mons. Bonnac, when it was found, that one third of her personal property was bequeathed to the nearest surviving relative of the late Marchioness de Villeroi, and that Emily was the person.

With the secret of Emily's family the abbess had long been acquainted, and it was in observance of the earnest request of St. Aubert, who was known to the friar, that attended him on his deathbed, that his daughter had remained in ignorance of her relationship to the Marchioness. But some hints, which had fallen from Signora Laurentini, during her last interview with Emily, and a confession of a very extraordinary nature, given in her dying hours, had made the abbess think it necessary to converse with her young friend, on the topic she had not before ventured to introduce; and it was for this purpose, that she had requested to see her on the morning that followed her interview with the nun. Emily's indisposition had then prevented the intended conversation; but now, after the will had been examined, she received a summons, which she immediately obeyed, and became informed of circumstances, that powerfully affected her. As the narrative of the abbess was, however, deficient in many particulars, of which the reader may wish to be informed, and the history of the nun is materially connected with the fate of the Marchioness de Villeroi, we shall omit the conversation, that passed in the parlour of the convent, and mingle with our relation a brief history of

LAURENTINI DI UDOLPHO,

who was the only child of her parents, and heiress of the ancient house of Udolpho, in the territory of Venice. It was the first misfortune of her life, and that which led to all her succeeding misery, that the friends, who ought to have restrained her strong passions, and mildly instructed her in the art of governing them, nurtured them by early indulgence. But they cherished their own failings in her; for their conduct was not the result of rational kindness, and, when they either indulged, or opposed the passions of their child, they gratified their own. Thus they indulged her with weakness, and reprehended her with violence; her spirit was exasperated by their vehemence, instead of being corrected by their wisdom; and their oppositions became contests for victory, in which the due tenderness of the parents, and the affectionate duties of the child, were equally forgotten; but, as returning fondness disarmed the parents' resentment soonest, Laurentini was suffered to believe that she had conquered, and her passions became stronger by every effort, that had been employed to subdue them.

The death of her father and mother in the same year left her to her own discretion, under the dangerous circumstances attendant on youth and beauty. She was fond of company, delighted with admiration, yet disdainful of the opinion of the world, when it happened to contradict her inclinations; had a gay and brilliant wit, and was mistress of all the arts of fascination. Her conduct was such as might have been expected, from the weakness of her principles and the strength of her passions.

Among her numerous admirers was the late Marquis de Villeroi, who, on his tour through Italy, saw Laurentini at Venice, where she usually resided, and became her passionate adorer. Equally captivated by the figure and accomplishments of the Marquis, who was at that period one of the most distinguished noblemen of the French court, she had the art so effectually to conceal from him the dangerous traits of her character and the blemishes of her late conduct, that he solicited her hand in marriage.

Before the nuptials were concluded, she retired to the castle of Udolpho, whither the Marquis followed, and, where her conduct, relaxing from the propriety, which she had lately assumed, discovered to him the precipice, on which he stood. A minuter enquiry than he had before thought it necessary to make, convinced him, that he had been deceived in her character, and she, whom he had designed for his wife, afterwards became his mistress.

Having passed some weeks at Udolpho, he was called abruptly to France, whither he returned with extreme reluctance, for his heart was still fascinated by the arts of Laurentini, with whom, however, he had on various pretences delayed his marriage; but, to reconcile her to this separation, he now gave repeated promises of returning to conclude the nuptials, as soon as the affair, which thus suddenly called him to France, should permit.

Soothed, in some degree, by these assurances, she suffered him to depart; and, soon after, her relative, Montoni, arriving at Udolpho, renewed the addresses, which she had before refused, and which she now again rejected. Meanwhile, her thoughts were constantly with the Marquis de Villeroi, for whom she suffered all the delirium of Italian love, cherished by the solitude, to which she confined herself; for she had now lost all taste for the pleasures of society and the gaiety of amusement. Her only indulgences were to sigh and weep over a miniature of the Marquis; to visit the scenes, that had witnessed their happiness, to pour forth her heart to him in writing, and to count the weeks, the days, which must intervene before the period that he had mentioned as probable for his return. But this period passed without bringing him; and week after week followed in heavy and almost intolerable expectation. During this interval, Laurentini's fancy, occupied incessantly by one idea, became disordered; and, her whole heart being devoted to one object, life became hateful to her, when she believed that object lost.

Several months passed, during which she heard nothing from the Marquis de Villeroi, and her days were marked, at intervals, with the phrensy of passion and the sullenness of despair. She secluded herself from all visitors, and, sometimes, remained in her apartment, for weeks together, refusing to speak to every person, except her favourite female attendant, writing scraps of letters, reading, again and again, those she had received from the Marquis, weeping over his picture, and speaking to it, for many hours, upbraiding, reproaching and caressing it alternately.

At length, a report reached her, that the Marquis had married in France, and, after suffering all the extremes of love, jealousy and indignation, she formed the desperate resolution of going secretly to that country, and, if the report proved true, of attempting a deep revenge. To her favourite woman only she confided the plan of her journey, and she engaged her to partake of it. Having collected her jewels, which, descending to her from many branches of her family, were of immense value, and all her cash, to a very large amount, they were packed in a trunk, which was privately conveyed to a neighbouring town, whither Laurentini, with this only servant, followed, and thence proceeded secretly to Leghorn, where they embarked for France.

When, on her arrival in Languedoc, she found, that the Marquis de Villeroi had been married, for some months, her despair almost deprived her of reason, and she alternately projected and abandoned the horrible design of murdering the Marquis, his wife and herself. At length she contrived to throw herself in his way, with an intention of reproaching him, for his conduct, and of stabbing herself in his presence; but, when she again saw him, who so long had been the constant object of her thoughts and affections, resentment yielded to love; her resolution failed; she trembled with the conflict of emotions, that assailed her heart, and fainted away.

The Marquis was not proof against her beauty and sensibility; all the energy, with which he had first loved, returned, for his passion had been resisted by prudence, rather than overcome by indifference; and, since the honour of his family would not permit him to marry her, he had endeavoured to subdue his love, and had so far succeeded, as to select the then Marchioness for his wife, whom he loved at first with a tempered and rational affection. But the mild virtues of that amiable lady did not recompense him for her indifference, which appeared, notwithstanding her efforts to conceal it; and he had, for some time, suspected that her affections were engaged by another person, when Laurentini arrived in Languedoc. This artful Italian soon perceived, that she had regained her influence over him, and, soothed by the discovery, she determined to live, and to employ all her enchantments to win his consent to the diabolical deed, which she believed was necessary to the security of her happiness. She conducted her scheme with deep dissimulation and patient perseverance, and, having completely estranged the affections of the Marquis from his wife, whose gentle goodness and unimpassioned manners had ceased to please, when contrasted with the captivations of the Italian, she proceeded to awaken in his mind the jealousy of pride, for it was no longer that of love, and even pointed out to him the person, to whom she affirmed the Marchioness had sacrificed her honour; but Laurentini had first extorted from him a solemn promise to forbear avenging himself upon his rival. This was an important part of her plan, for she knew, that, if his desire of vengeance was restrained towards one party, it would burn more fiercely towards the other, and he might then, perhaps, be prevailed on to assist in the horrible act, which would release him from the only barrier, that with-held him from making her his wife.

The innocent Marchioness, meanwhile, observed, with extreme grief, the alteration in her husband's manners. He became reserved and thoughtful in her presence; his conduct was austere, and sometimes even rude; and he left her, for many hours together, to weep for his unkindness, and to form plans for the recovery of his affection. His conduct afflicted her the more, because, in obedience to the command of her father, she had accepted his hand, though her affections were engaged to another, whose amiable disposition, she had reason to believe, would have ensured her happiness. This circumstance Laurentini had discovered, soon after her arrival in France, and had made ample use of it in assisting her designs upon the Marquis, to whom she adduced such seeming proof of his wife's infidelity, that, in the frantic rage of wounded honour, he consented to destroy his wife. A slow poison was administered, and she fell a victim to the jealousy and subtlety of Laurentini and to the guilty weakness of her husband.

But the moment of Laurentini's triumph, the moment, to which she had looked forward for the completion of all her wishes, proved only the commencement of a suffering, that never left her to her dying hour.

The passion of revenge, which had in part stimulated her to the commission of this atrocious deed, died, even at the moment when it was gratified, and left her to the horrors of unavailing pity and remorse, which would probably have empoisoned all the years she had promised herself with the Marquis de Villeroi, had her expectations of an alliance with him been realized. But he, too, had found the moment of his revenge to be that of remorse, as to himself, and detestation, as to the partner of his crime; the feeling, which he had mistaken for conviction, was no more; and he stood astonished, and aghast, that no proof remained of his wife's infidelity, now that she had suffered the punishment of guilt. Even when he was informed, that she was dying, he had felt suddenly and unaccountably reassured of her innocence, nor was the solemn assurance she made him in her last hour, capable of affording him a stronger conviction of her blameless conduct.

In the first horrors of remorse and despair, he felt inclined to deliver up himself and the woman, who had plunged him into this abyss of guilt, into the hands of justice; but, when the paroxysm of his suffering was over, his intention changed. Laurentini, however, he saw only once afterwards, and that was, to curse her as the instigator of his crime, and to say, that he spared her life only on condition, that she passed the rest of her days in prayer and penance. Overwhelmed with disappointment, on receiving contempt and abhorrence from the man, for whose sake she had not scrupled to stain her conscience with human blood, and, touched with horror of the unavailing crime she had committed, she renounced the world, and retired to the monastery of St. Claire, a dreadful victim to unresisted passion.

The Marquis, immediately after the death of his wife, quitted Chateau-le-Blanc, to which he never returned, and endeavoured to lose the sense of his crime amidst the tumult of war, or the dissipations of a capital; but his efforts were vain; a deep dejection hung over him ever after, for which his most intimate friend could not account, and he, at length, died, with a degree of horror nearly equal to that, which Laurentini had suffered. The physician, who had observed the singular appearance of the unfortunate Marchioness, after death, had been bribed to silence; and, as the surmises of a few of the servants had proceeded no further than a whisper, the affair had never been investigated. Whether this whisper ever reached the father of the Marchioness, and, if it did, whether the difficulty of obtaining proof deterred him from prosecuting the Marquis de Villeroi, is uncertain; but her death was deeply lamented by some part of her family, and particularly by her brother, M. St. Aubert; for that was the degree of relationship, which had existed between Emily's father and the Marchioness; and there is no doubt, that he suspected the manner of her death. Many letters passed between the Marquis and him, soon after the decease of his beloved sister, the subject of which was not known, but there is reason to believe, that they related to the cause of her death; and these were the papers, together with some letters of the Marchioness, who had confided to her brother the occasion of her unhappiness, which St. Aubert had so solemnly enjoined his daughter to destroy: and anxiety for her peace had probably made him forbid her to enquire into the melancholy story, to which they alluded. Such, indeed, had been his affliction, on the premature death of this his favourite sister, whose unhappy marriage had from the first excited his tenderest pity, that he never could hear her named, or mention her himself after her death, except to Madame St. Aubert. From Emily, whose sensibility he feared to awaken, he had so carefully concealed her history and name, that she was ignorant, till now, that she ever had such a relative as the Marchioness de Villeroi; and from this motive he had enjoined silence to his only surviving sister, Madame Cheron, who had scrupulously observed his request.

It was over some of the last pathetic letters of the Marchioness, that St. Aubert was weeping, when he was observed by Emily, on the eve of her departure from La Vallée, and it was her picture, which he had so tenderly caressed. Her disastrous death may account for the emotion he had betrayed, on hearing her named by La Voisin, and for his request to be interred near the monument of the Villerois, where her remains were deposited, but not those of her husband, who was buried, where he died, in the north of France.

The confessor, who attended St. Aubert in his last moments, recollected him to be the brother of the late Marchioness, when St. Aubert, from tenderness to Emily, had conjured him to conceal the circumstance, and to request that the abbess, to whose care he particularly recommended her, would do the same; a request, which had been exactly observed.

Laurentini, on her arrival in France, had carefully concealed her name and family, and, the better to disguise her real history, had, on entering the convent, caused the story to be circulated, which had imposed on sister Frances, and it is probable, that the abbess, who did not preside in the convent, at the time of her noviciation, was also entirely ignorant of the truth. The deep remorse, that seized on the mind of Laurentini, together with the sufferings of disappointed passion, for she still loved the Marquis, again unsettled her intellects, and, after the first paroxysms of despair were passed, a heavy and silent melancholy had settled upon her spirits, which suffered few interruptions from fits of phrensy, till the time of her death. During many years, it had been her only amusement to walk in the woods near the monastery, in the solitary hours of night, and to play upon a favourite instrument, to which she sometimes joined the delightful melody of her voice, in the most solemn and melancholy airs of her native country, modulated by all the energetic feeling, that dwelt in her heart. The physician, who had attended her, recommended it to the superior to indulge her in this whim, as the only means of soothing her distempered fancy; and she was suffered to walk in the lonely hours of night, attended by the servant, who had accompanied her from Italy; but, as the indulgence transgressed against the rules of the convent, it was kept as secret as possible; and thus the mysterious music of Laurentini had combined with other circumstances, to produce a report, that not only the chateau, but its neighbourhood, was haunted.

Soon after her entrance into this holy community, and before she had shewn any symptoms of insanity there, she made a will, in which, after bequeathing a considerable legacy to the convent, she divided the remainder of her personal property, which her jewels made very valuable, between the wife of Mons. Bonnac, who was an Italian lady and her relation, and the nearest surviving relative of the late Marchioness de Villeroi. As Emily St. Aubert was not only the nearest, but the sole relative, this legacy descended to her, and thus explained to her the whole mystery of her father's conduct.

The resemblance between Emily and her unfortunate aunt had frequently been observed by Laurentini, and had occasioned the singular behaviour, which had formerly alarmed her; but it was in the nun's dying hour, when her conscience gave her perpetually the idea of the Marchioness, that she became more sensible, than ever, of this likeness, and, in her phrensy, deemed it no resemblance of the person she had injured, but the original herself. The bold assertion, that had followed, on the recovery of her senses, that Emily was the daughter of the Marchioness de Villeroi, arose from a suspicion that she was so; for, knowing that her rival, when she married the Marquis, was attached to another lover, she had scarcely scrupled to believe, that her honour had been sacrificed, like her own, to an unresisted passion.

Of a crime, however, to which Emily had suspected, from her phrensied confession of murder, that she had been instrumental in the castle of Udolpho, Laurentini was innocent; and she had herself been deceived, concerning the spectacle, that formerly occasioned her so much terror, and had since compelled her, for a while, to attribute the horrors of the nun to a consciousness of a murder, committed in that castle.

It may be remembered, that, in a chamber of Udolpho, hung a black veil, whose singular situation had excited Emily's curiosity, and which afterwards disclosed an object, that had overwhelmed her with horror; for, on lifting it, there appeared, instead of the picture she had expected, within a recess of the wall, a human figure of ghastly paleness, stretched at its length, and dressed in the habiliments of the grave. What added to the horror of the spectacle, was, that the face appeared partly decayed and disfigured by worms, which were visible on the features and hands. On such an object, it will be readily believed, that no person could endure to look twice. Emily, it may be recollected, had, after the first glance, let the veil drop, and her terror had prevented her from ever after provoking a renewal of such suffering, as she had then experienced. Had she dared to look again, her delusion and her fears would have vanished together, and she would have perceived, that the figure before her was not human, but formed of wax. The history of it is somewhat extraordinary, though not without example in the records of that fierce severity, which monkish superstition has sometimes inflicted on mankind. A member of the house of Udolpho, having committed some offence against the prerogative of the church, had been condemned to the penance of contemplating, during certain hours of the day, a waxen image, made to resemble a human body in the state, to which it is reduced after death. This penance, serving as a memento of the condition at which he must himself arrive, had been designed to reprove the pride of the Marquis of Udolpho, which had formerly so much exasperated that of the Romish church; and he had not only superstitiously observed this penance himself, which, he had believed, was to obtain a pardon for all his sins, but had made it a condition in his will, that his descendants should preserve the image, on pain of forfeiting to the church a certain part of his domain, that they also might profit by the humiliating moral it conveyed. The figure, therefore, had been suffered to retain its station in the wall of the chamber, but his descendants excused themselves from observing the penance, to which he had been enjoined.

This image was so horribly natural, that it is not surprising Emily should have mistaken it for the object it resembled, nor, since she had heard such an extraordinary account, concerning the disappearing of the late lady of the castle, and had such experience of the character of Montoni, that she should have believed this to be the murdered body of the lady Laurentini, and that he had been the contriver of her death.

The situation, in which she had discovered it, occasioned her, at first, much surprise and perplexity; but the vigilance, with which the doors of the chamber, where it was deposited, were afterwards secured, had compelled her to believe, that Montoni, not daring to confide the secret of her death to any person, had suffered her remains to decay in this obscure chamber. The ceremony of the veil, however, and the circumstance of the doors having been left open, even for a moment, had occasioned her much wonder and some doubts; but these were not sufficient to overcome her suspicion of Montoni; and it was the dread of his terrible vengeance, that had sealed her lips in silence, concerning what she had seen in the west chamber.

Emily, in discovering the Marchioness de Villeroi to have been the sister of Mons. St. Aubert, was variously affected; but, amidst the sorrow, which she suffered for her untimely death, she was released from an anxious and painful conjecture, occasioned by the rash assertion of

Signora Laurentini, concerning her birth and the honour of her parents. Her faith in St. Aubert's principles would scarcely allow her to suspect that he had acted dishonourably; and she felt such reluctance to believe herself the daughter of any other, than her, whom she had always considered and loved as a mother, that she would hardly admit such a circumstance to be possible; yet the likeness, which it had frequently been affirmed she bore to the late Marchioness, the former behaviour of Dorothée the old housekeeper, the assertion of Laurentini, and the mysterious attachment, which St. Aubert had discovered, awakened doubts, as to his connection with the Marchioness, which her reason could neither vanquish, or confirm. From these, however, she was now relieved, and all the circumstances of her father's conduct were fully explained: but her heart was oppressed by the melancholy catastrophe of her amiable relative, and by the awful lesson, which the history of the nun exhibited, the indulgence of whose passions had been the means of leading her gradually to the commission of a crime, from the prophecy of which in her early years she would have recoiled in horror, and exclaimed—that it could not be!—a crime, which whole years of repentance and of the severest penance had not been able to obliterate from her conscience.

CHAPTER XVIII

> Then, fresh tears
> Stood on her cheek, as doth the honey-dew
> Upon a gather'd lily almost wither'd
> SHAKESPEARE

AFTER the late discoveries, Emily was distinguished at the chateau by the Count and his family, as a relative of the house of Villeroi, and received, if possible, more friendly attention, than had yet been shewn her.

Count De Villefort's surprise at the delay of an answer to his letter, which had been directed to Valancourt, at Estuviere, was mingled with satisfaction for the prudence, which had saved Emily from a share of the anxiety he now suffered, though, when he saw her still drooping under the effect of his former error, all his resolution was necessary to restrain him from relating the truth, that would afford her a momentary relief. The approaching nuptials of the Lady Blanche now divided his attention with this subject of his anxiety, for the inhabitants of the chateau were already busied in preparations for that event, and the arrival of Mons. St. Foix was daily expected. In the gaiety, which surrounded her, Emily vainly tried to participate, her spirits being depressed by the late discoveries, and by the anxiety concerning the fate of Valancourt, that had been occasioned by the description of his manner, when he had delivered the ring. She seemed to perceive in it the gloomy wildness of despair; and, when she considered to what that despair might have urged him, her heart sunk with terror and grief. The state of suspense, as to his safety, to which she believed herself condemned, till she should return to La Vallée, appeared insupportable, and, in such moments, she could not even struggle to assume the composure, that had left her mind, but would often abruptly quit the company she was with, and endeavour to soothe her spirits in the deep solitudes of the woods, that overbrowed the shore. Here, the faint roar of foaming waves, that beat below, and the sullen murmur of the wind among the branches around, were circumstances in unison with the temper of her mind; and she would sit on a cliff, or on the broken steps of her favourite watch-tower, observing the changing colours of the evening clouds, and the gloom of twilight draw over the sea, till the white tops of billows, riding towards the shore, could scarcely be discerned amidst the darkened waters. The lines, engraved by Valancourt on this tower, she frequently repeated with melancholy enthusiasm, and then would endeavour to check the recollections and the grief they occasioned, and to turn her thoughts to indifferent subjects.

One evening, having wandered with her lute to this her favourite spot, she entered the ruined tower, and ascended a winding staircase, that led to a small chamber, which was less decayed than the rest of the building, and whence she had often gazed, with admiration, on the wide prospect of sea and land, that extended below. The sun was now setting on that tract of the Pyrenées, which divided Languedoc from Rousillon, and, placing herself opposite to a small grated window, which, like the wood-tops beneath, and the waves lower still, gleamed with the red glow of the west, she touched the chords of her lute in solemn symphony, and then accompanied it with her voice, in one of the simple and affecting airs, to which, in happier days, Valancourt had often listened in rapture, and which she now adapted to the following lines.

TO MELANCHOLY

Spirit of love and sorrow—hail!
Thy solemn voice from far I hear,
Mingling with ev'ning's dying gale:
Hail, with this sadly-pleasing tear!

O! at this still, this lonely hour,
Thine own sweet hour of closing day,

Awake thy lute, whose charmful pow'r
Shall call up Fancy to obey:

To paint the wild romantic dream,
That meets the poet's musing eye,
As, on the bank of shadowy stream,
He breathes to her the fervid sigh.

O lonely spirit! let thy song
Lead me through all thy sacred haunt;
The minister's moon-light aisles along,
Where spectres raise the midnight chaunt.

I hear their dirges faintly swell!
Then, sink at once in silence drear,
While, from the pillar'd cloister's cell,
Dimly their gliding forms appear!

Lead where the pine-woods wave on high,
Whose pathless sod is darkly seen,
As the cold moon, with trembling eye,
Darts her long beams the leaves between.

Lead to the mountain's dusky head,
Where, far below, in shade profound,
Wide forests, plains and hamlets spread,
And sad the chimes of vesper sound,

Or guide me, where the dashing oar
Just breaks the stillness of the vale,
As slow it tracks the winding shore,
To meet the ocean's distant sail:

To pebbly banks, that Neptune laves,
With measur'd surges, loud and deep,
Where the dark cliff bends o'er the waves,
And wild the winds of autumn sweep.

There pause at midnight's spectred hour,
And list the long-resounding gale;
And catch the fleeting moon-light's pow'r,
O'er foaming seas and distant sail.

The soft tranquillity of the scene below, where the evening breeze scarcely curled the water, or swelled the passing sail, that caught the last gleam of the sun, and where, now and then, a dipping oar was all that disturbed the trembling radiance, conspired with the tender melody of her lute to lull her mind into a state of gentle sadness, and she sung the mournful songs of past times, till the remembrances they awakened were too powerful for her heart, her tears fell upon the lute, over which she drooped, and her voice trembled, and was unable to proceed.

Though the sun had now sunk behind the mountains, and even his reflected light was fading from their highest points, Emily did not leave the watch-tower, but continued to indulge her melancholy reverie, till a footstep, at a little distance, startled her, and, on looking through the grate, she observed a person walking below, whom, however, soon perceiving to be Mons. Bonnac, she returned to the quiet thoughtfulness his step had interrupted. After some time, she again struck her lute, and sung her favourite air; but again a step disturbed her, and, as she paused to listen, she heard it ascending the stair-case of the tower. The gloom of the hour, perhaps, made her sensible to some degree of fear, which she might not otherwise have felt; for, only a few minutes before, she had seen Mons. Bonnac pass. The steps were quick and bounding, and, in the next moment, the door of the chamber opened, and a person entered, whose features were veiled in the obscurity of twilight; but his voice could not be concealed, for it was the voice of Valancourt! At the sound, never heard by Emily, without emotion, she started, in terror, astonishment and doubtful pleasure, and had scarcely beheld him at her feet, when she sunk into a seat, overcome by the various emotions, that contended at her heart, and almost insensible to that voice, whose earnest and trembling calls seemed as if endeavouring to save her. Valancourt, as he hung over Emily, deplored his own rash impatience, in having thus surprised her: for when he had arrived at the chateau, too anxious to await the return of the Count, who, he understood, was in the grounds, he went himself to seek him, when, as he passed the tower, he was struck by the sound of Emily's voice, and immediately ascended.

It was a considerable time before she revived, but, when her recollection returned, she repulsed his attentions, with an air of reserve, and enquired, with as much displeasure as it was possible she could feel in these first moments of his appearance, the occasion of his visit.

"Ah Emily!" said Valancourt, "that air, those words—alas! I have, then, little to hope—when you ceased to esteem me, you ceased also to love me!"

"Most true, sir," replied Emily, endeavouring to command her trembling voice; "and if you had valued my esteem, you would not have given me this new occasion for uneasiness."

Valancourt's countenance changed suddenly from the anxieties of doubt to an expression of surprise and dismay: he was silent a moment, and then said, "I had been taught to hope for a very different reception! Is it, then, true, Emily, that I have lost your regard forever? am I to believe, that, though your esteem for me may return—your affection

never can? Can the Count have meditated the cruelty, which now tortures me with a second death?"

The voice, in which he spoke this, alarmed Emily as much as his
words surprised her, and, with trembling impatience, she begged that
he would explain them.

"Can any explanation be necessary?" said Valancourt, "do you not
know how cruelly my conduct has been misrepresented? that the
actions of which you once believed me guilty (and, O Emily! how
could you so degrade me in your opinion, even for a moment!) those
actions—I hold in as much contempt and abhorrence as yourself? Are
you, indeed, ignorant, that Count de Villefort has detected the slanders, that have robbed me of all I hold dear on earth, and has invited
me hither to justify to you my former conduct? It is surely impossible
you can be uninformed of these circumstances, and I am again torturing myself with a false hope!"

The silence of Emily confirmed this supposition; for the deep twilight would not allow Valancourt to distinguish the astonishment and
doubting joy, that fixed her features. For a moment, she continued
unable to speak; then a profound sigh seemed to give some relief to her
spirits, and she said,

"Valancourt! I was, till this moment, ignorant of all the circumstances you have mentioned; the emotion I now suffer may assure you
of the truth of this, and, that, though I had ceased to esteem, I had not
taught myself entirely to forget you."

"This moment," said Valancourt, in a low voice, and leaning for support against the window— "this moment brings with it a conviction that
overpowers me!—I am dear to you then—still dear to you, my Emily!"

"Is it necessary that I should tell you so?" she replied, "is it necessary,
that I should say—these are the first moments of joy I have known,
since your departure, and that they repay me for all those of pain I have
suffered in the interval?"

Valancourt sighed deeply, and was unable to reply; but, as he pressed
her hand to his lips, the tears, that fell over it, spoke a language, which
could not be mistaken, and to which words were inadequate.

Emily, somewhat tranquillized, proposed returning to the chateau,
and then, for the first time, recollected that the Count had invited
Valancourt thither to explain his conduct, and that no explanation had
yet been given. But, while she acknowledged this, her heart would not
allow her to dwell, for a moment, on the possibility of his unworthiness;
his look, his voice, his manner, all spoke the noble sincerity, which had
formerly distinguished him; and she again permitted herself to indulge
the emotions of a joy, more surprising and powerful, than she had ever
before experienced.

Neither Emily, or Valancourt, were conscious how they reached the chateau, whither they might have been transferred by the spell of a fairy, for any thing they could remember; and it was not, till they had reached the great hall, that either of them recollected there were other persons in the world besides themselves. The Count then came forth with surprise, and with the joyfulness of pure benevolence, to welcome Valancourt, and to entreat his forgiveness of the injustice he had done him; soon after which, Mons. Bonnac joined this happy group, in which he and Valancourt were mutually rejoiced to meet.

When the first congratulations were over, and the general joy became somewhat more tranquil, the Count withdrew with Valancourt to the library, where a long conversation passed between them, in which the latter so clearly justified himself of the criminal parts of the conduct, imputed to him, and so candidly confessed and so feelingly lamented the follies, which he had committed, that the Count was confirmed in his belief of all he had hoped; and, while he perceived so many noble virtues in Valancourt, and that experience had taught him to detest the follies, which before he had only not admired, he did not scruple to believe, that he would pass through life with the dignity of a wise and good man, or to entrust to his care the future happiness of Emily St. Aubert, for whom he felt the solicitude of a parent. Of this he soon informed her, in a short conversation, when Valancourt had left him. While Emily listened to a relation of the services, that Valancourt had rendered Mons. Bonnac, her eyes overflowed with tears of pleasure, and the further conversation of Count De Villefort perfectly dissipated every doubt, as to the past and future conduct of him, to whom she now restored, without fear, the esteem and affection, with which she had formerly received him.

When they returned to the supper-room, the Countess and Lady Blanche met Valancourt with sincere congratulations; and Blanche, indeed, was so much rejoiced to see Emily returned to happiness, as to forget, for a while, that Mons. St. Foix was not yet arrived at the chateau, though he had been expected for some hours; but her generous sympathy was, soon after, rewarded by his appearance. He was now perfectly recovered from the wounds, received, during his perilous adventure among the Pyrenées, the mention of which served to heighten to the parties, who had been involved in it, the sense of their present happiness. New congratulations passed between them, and round the supper-table appeared a group of faces, smiling with felicity, but with a felicity, which had in each a different character. The smile of Blanche was frank and gay, that of Emily tender and pensive; Valancourt's was rapturous, tender and gay alternately; Mons. St. Foix's was joyous, and that of the Count, as he looked on the surrounding party, expressed the tempered complacency of benevolence; while the features of the Countess, Henri, and Mons. Bonnac, discovered fainter traces of animation. Poor Mons. Du Pont did not, by his presence, throw a shade of regret over the company; for, when he had discovered, that Valancourt was not unworthy of the esteem of Emily, he determined seriously to endeavour at the conquest of his own hopeless affection, and had immediately withdrawn from Chateau-le-Blanc—a conduct, which Emily now understood, and rewarded with her admiration and pity.

The Count and his guests continued together till a late hour, yielding to the delights of social gaiety, and to the sweets of friendship. When Annette heard of the arrival of Valancourt, Ludovico had some difficulty to prevent her going into the supper-room, to express her joy, for she declared, that she had never been so rejoiced at any *accident* as this, since she had found Ludovico himself.

CHAPTER XIX

> Now my task is smoothly done,
> I can fly, or I can run
> Quickly to the green earth's end,
> Where the bow'd welkin low doth bend,
> And, from thence, can soar as soon
> To the corners of the moon.
> MILTON

THE marriages of the Lady Blanche and Emily St. Aubert were celebrated, on the same day, and with the ancient baronial magnificence, at Chateau-le-Blanc. The feasts were held in the great hall of the castle, which, on this occasion, was hung with superb new tapestry, representing the exploits of Charlemagne and his twelve peers; here, were seen the Saracens, with their horrible visors, advancing to battle; and there, were displayed the wild solemnities of incantation, and the necromantic feats, exhibited by the magician *Jarl* before the Emperor. The sumptuous banners of the family of Villeroi, which had long slept in dust, were once more unfurled, to wave over the gothic points of painted casements; and music echoed, in many a lingering close, through every winding gallery and colonnade of that vast edifice.

As Annette looked down from the corridor upon the hall, whose arches and windows were illuminated with brilliant festoons of lamps, and gazed on the splendid dresses of the dancers, the costly liveries of the attendants, the canopies of purple velvet and gold, and listened to the gay strains that floated along the vaulted roof, she almost fancied herself in an enchanted palace, and declared, that she had not met with any place, which charmed her so much, since she read the fairy tales; nay, that the fairies themselves, at their nightly revels in this old hall, could display nothing finer; while old Dorothée, as she surveyed the scene, sighed, and said, the castle looked as it was wont to do in the time of her youth.

After gracing the festivities of Chateau-le-Blanc, for some days, Valancourt and Emily took leave of their kind friends, and returned to La Vallée, where the faithful Theresa received them with unfeigned joy, and the pleasant shades welcomed them with a thousand tender and affecting remembrances; and, while they wandered together over the scenes, so long inhabited by the late Mons. and Madame St. Aubert, and Emily pointed out, with pensive affection, their favourite haunts, her present happiness was heightened, by considering, that it would have been worthy of their approbation, could they have witnessed it.

Valancourt led her to the plane-tree on the terrace, where he had first ventured to declare his love, and where now the remembrance of the anxiety he had then suffered, and the retrospect of all the dangers and misfortunes they had each encountered, since last they sat together beneath its broad branches, exalted the sense of their present felicity, which, on this spot, sacred to the memory of St. Aubert, they solemnly vowed to deserve, as far as possible, by endeavouring to imitate his benevolence, — by remembering, that superior attainments of every sort bring with them duties of superior exertion, — and by affording to their fellow-beings, together with that portion of ordinary comforts, which prosperity always owes to misfortune, the example of lives passed in happy thankfulness to GOD, and, therefore, in careful tenderness to his creatures.

Soon after their return to La Vallée, the brother of Valancourt came to congratulate him on his marriage, and to pay his respects to Emily, with whom he was so much pleased, as well as with the prospect of rational happiness, which these nuptials offered to Valancourt, that he immediately resigned to him a part of the rich domain, the whole of which, as he had no family, would of course descend to his brother, on his decease.

The estates, at Tholouse, were disposed of, and Emily purchased of Mons. Quesnel the ancient domain of her late father, where, having given Annette a marriage portion, she settled her as the housekeeper, and Ludovico as the steward; but, since both Valancourt and herself preferred the pleasant and long-loved shades of La Vallée to the magnificence of Epourville, they continued to reside there, passing, however, a few months in the year at the birth-place of St. Aubert, in tender respect to his memory.

The legacy, which had been bequeathed to Emily by Signora Laurentini, she begged Valancourt would allow her to resign to Mons. Bonnac; and Valancourt, when she made the request, felt all the value of the compliment it conveyed. The castle of Udolpho, also, descended to the wife of Mons. Bonnac, who was the nearest surviving relation of the house of that name, and thus affluence restored his long-oppressed spirits to peace, and his family to comfort.

O! how joyful it is to tell of happiness, such as that of Valancourt and Emily; to relate, that, after suffering under the oppression of the vicious and the disdain of the weak, they were, at length, restored to each other—to the beloved landscapes of their native country,—to the securest felicity of this life, that of aspiring to moral and labouring for intellectual improvement—to the pleasures of enlightened society, and to the exercise of the benevolence, which had always animated their hearts; while the bowers of La Vallée became, once more, the retreat of goodness, wisdom and domestic blessedness!

O! useful may it be to have shewn, that, though the vicious can sometimes pour affliction upon the good, their power is transient and their punishment certain; and that innocence, though oppressed by injustice, shall, supported by patience, finally triumph over misfortune!

And, if the weak hand, that has recorded this tale, has, by its scenes, beguiled the mourner of one hour of sorrow, or, by its moral, taught him to sustain it—the effort, however humble, has not been vain, nor is the writer unrewarded.